THE BERKUT

Also by Joseph Heywood
TAXI DANCER

JOSEPH HEYWOOD

THE
BERKUT

RANDOM HOUSE

New York

To my friends Charlie Mangel and Bob LaRue

The most exotic sort of wolf hunting involves the use of eagles. It has been seen only occasionally in Europe; its real home is Kirghizia, in south-central Russia. The specially bred birds— a subspecies of golden eagles called a berkut—are flown by nomadic tribesmen. The birds weigh only ten or twelve pounds but can slam into a wolf's back and bind its nose with such force that the wolf is almost paralyzed. Often the bird binds the spine with one foot and, as the wolf turns its head to bite, binds its nose with the other foot, suffocating the animal or holding it down until the hunter kills it. The birds are deceptively strong; there is almost a ton of binding force in each foot and the blow of a thirty-six-inch wing can break a man's arm. . . . Kirghizian tribesmen still hunt wolves in Russia with eagles, on horseback, with the aid of dogs.

—BARRY HOLSTUN LOPEZ
Of Wolves and Men

I

THE
ESCAPE

Colonel Günter Brumm strained to slide himself down into the tight cockpit of the toy glider. He was a tall man with a thick body and a large, muscular frame, just the kind of physique that had made him a first-rate officer candidate years before. His fine blond hair, once full and luxurious, was filthy now, and his hairline was beginning to recede, an unacceptable development at thirty-five years of age. His hands were huge, his fingers long, thick tubes that one of his comrades had once dubbed "broomsticks." Most of his height was in his torso, not in his legs, so while the cockpit offered ample leg room, the rest of his body would be wedged in tightly, leaving little room to maneuver.

Finally settling onto the hard seat, Brumm felt around gently with his feet to locate the craft's tiny rudder pedals. When he found them, he wondered if he would be able to feel them in flight through his thick boots. He had piloted a glider only a few times before, and never one this small. It would be a challenge, and the thought excited him.

Satisfied that he was all the way down in the seat, he jammed his kit bag and rucksack onto the floor in front of him. He checked to be sure that the tether from his parachute harness was attached to the gear. His machine pistol, a custom model of the standard weapon used by German troops, was in a special chamois holster tied to his chest that also contained six extra clips.

Checking the control column, Brumm found that his gear jammed the stick so that it could not be pulled all the way back. Like an animal working diligently in its den, he kept moving equipment around until the cockpit was in order. Long ago the colonel had learned that details made the difference in survival; he had become an expert at planning, checking and double-checking every element that pertained to the mission at hand. Finally settled, he exhaled and leaned back against his parachute pack. If this doesn't work, I'm dead, he told himself.

To a professional soldier, facts were facts. He did not fear death; thinking about it did not fill him with dread. It was simply his way of ensuring that his subconscious fully appreciated the situation, and that when he needed it the necessary mental alacrity would be there.

As a special commando, Brumm was one of the few survivors of an elite group that took its orders directly from Adolf Hitler. Among his credentials was a letter from the Führer that provided him with absolute power over any and all Germans, civilian or military. It was a license that enabled him to acquire what he needed when he needed it without the normal red tape. During his time in the special commando unit the colonel had been called upon to perform an endless number of dangerous assignments. But while his physical constitution made him an impressive specimen, it had been his psychological profile that had most impressed the Führer, who demanded final approval of all candidates of the special cadre.

Brumm's body carried numerous scars, which attested not only to the rigors of his profession but also to his durability. Over the years, through France, Czechoslovakia, Russia and countless other locations, he had been wounded so many times that he had lost count. The son of a Prussian officer and grandson of an apothecary, he had grown up with death and corpses. No manner of death bothered him; you were breathing or you were not. It was this comfort with death that made him an efficient soldier.

Brumm checked his watch. If the towplane was on time, the pickup should occur in seven minutes. He hoped that what remained of the short takeoff area would not deteriorate further in the remaining time. The Russians were all around. They had pushed the German armies back from the Oder River in February, then stopped and rested while they resupplied for nearly two months before their final push toward Berlin. On April 16 they had attacked in force, and three days later had pushed parts of the front line twenty-five kilometers west of the Oder River, leaving Brumm's unit behind enemy lines and cut off. Now the Russians were doubling back to clean out isolated pockets of resistance. Although battle maps and reliable intelligence about enemy movements were scant, it was clear to anybody with experience what the Russians intended: Berlin would be razed.

With their tanks having intersected, then opened gaps in the German lines, Soviet infantry had moved up to hit the Germans head-on. A huge artillery duel had developed, and overhead hundreds of tracers now crisscrossed one another in hissing arcs as the two sides sought to annihilate each other. Both sides had stopped aiming; they were simply loading and firing as fast as possible. Eventually one side would be unable to fire back.

That what remained of the German army was pinned down and trapped did not surprise Brumm; the will to fight was gone. What had occurred at Stalingrad told him that the end was only a matter of time. He had been there, had parachuted into the snow to execute a key Russian general, which he had done without the loss of a man, and had gotten out. Hitler had figured that the death of this general would turn the tide, but it had made no difference; the Russians continued to push the Germans back across the thousands of miles they had gained, extracting a horrible toll in the process, both on their enemy and on themselves. The Führer had often expounded on the subhuman nature of Slavs. It was now apparent that it was this primitive nature that made the Russian foot soldier an awesome opponent. Like savages, they were awash in blood and slaughter. He had seen them crawling forward on legless stumps, still firing their weapons. Once he had seen a Russian douse himself with petrol, ignite himself and run into a concentration of German troops. Brumm admired such ferocity.

Every soldier's job was a simple one. Engage the enemy, then kill him. Since Stalingrad, the Russians had taken the objective to heart and had sacrificed millions to accomplish their ends. It was equally clear that they would expend millions more to continue until Germany was razed. At that point they would take everything they could carry and walk back to the Motherland. There would be nothing neat and tidy about the ending of the Third Reich; it would endure an unending blow that killed everything killable.

Sitting in the glider, with the partial canopy open, Brumm felt removed from the battle raging around him. Protected only by a wooden frame and a lacquered canvas hull, he felt aloof, removed from the line of fire. In the flickering artificial light created by fires and exploding rounds, he studied the landscape. It was like most battlefields, only more devastated: craters pocked the earth; trees were shredded into a ground-covering slash; burned-out vehicles on their sides and roofs and abandoned pieces of equipment were scattered around; bodies lay everywhere, mostly frozen in death, but some of the partly living still crawled along searching for help. From time to time he could see soldiers still trying to fight, working their way among the dead, collecting weapons and ammunition. German soldiers, he reminded himself, kept doing what German soldiers were supposed to do.

All this was a collective fact of war. His job was done here; now there was another mission to perform, and upon his ability lay the future of the Third Reich. If anything touched his soul, it was knowing that he had been chosen as the historical instrument. He was eager to begin.

►2   APRIL 28, 1945, 6:35 P.M.

It was rolling forested country interspersed with barren, muddy fields, and the heavy fog hanging over the area made it seem hours later than it was. Berlin had been encircled four days earlier, and now Russian supplies were being pushed forward toward the city as Soviet troops gathered for the final push. Here, east of the city, the heavy fighting had stopped, but the five shadowy men advancing on horseback through the broken forest could hear the thudding of guns ahead of them.

Reaching the edge of the tree line, the horsemen reined in and paused to study the scene before them. To the south was a line of troops twenty abreast that stretched endlessly and silently into the fog. The fields ahead of them were filled with hundreds of riderless horses walking with their heads down, paralleling the route of the Russian army. Nearby a mud-covered red mare was foaling, her head lifted, nostrils flaring as she strained with the final push of new life. Several cows were scattered among the horses, foraging in the brown mud as the soldiers rattled down the nearby road, not talking.

One of the five horsemen left the others and galloped along the trees toward the line of troops, but before he had gone a hundred meters, there was a sharp crack and the horse went down, nose first, sending its rider tumbling wildly head over heels.

Three of the others dismounted immediately. Two of them headed into the forest in the direction of the rifle shot; the third man ran forward in a crouch toward his comrade, diving and rolling the final three meters, stopping beside the man, his pistol drawn, facing toward the trees. The man whose horse had been shot from under him was sitting, legs out, shaking his head. "Hit?" his companion asked. There was no emotion in the voice; long ago they had lost track of the number of close calls they'd had with death; it was always with them and they accepted the fact.

"No, but that was a damn fine animal," the man said, glancing at the dead horse.

"Not important. Here's where we connect with the army. We walk the rest of the way."

Another shot interrupted them, and both of them reacted by crawling quickly forward to take cover behind a fallen tree. Seconds later a form vaulted from the tree line and ran wildly through the mud in front of them. Both men stood, took aim and fired simultaneously. The figure fell heavily and they ran forward. Their two companions emerged breathlessly from the forest at the point where the figure had appeared. "Did he come out?"

"Here," one of the two men said as he reached the corpse and rolled it over with his foot.

When the four men were together, the fifth man, still on horseback, came toward them, his animal snorting and twisting its head under the bit. Reaching the group, he barely looked at the body.

"Only a boy," one of the men on the ground said.

"A German," the man on horseback said sharply; then he kicked his mount lightly and urged it forward into the sea of mud. The others looked at one another, returned to their mounts, gathered their equipment and set off on foot, following the tiny dark form that was now barely visible in the failing light.

▶3 APRIL 28, 1945, 6:40 P.M.

The plan for Colonel Brumm's extraction was as simple as it was dangerous. The nose of the glider was attached to a long elastic cable, which had been developed by a special research team studying new plastics called polymers. One hundred meters ahead of him there was a large loop in the cable, and this was suspended between two poles about sixty meters in height. The plan called for a transport plane to fly low, dragging a trailing hook behind it. The hook would be engaged to the cable loop, which would tighten and pull his glider airborne. Simple and direct—his kind of plan. Those who had designed the system called it "the slingshot."

Over the years, more than two dozen test pilots had been killed trying to perfect this escape method. It had been designed as a way of removing the Führer from the Eagle's Nest in the Obersalzberg, and eventually it had been perfected. More than a hundred pickup sites had been constructed around the country over a period of years and small gliders had been stored at each location. Even though the method now worked, some doubt lingered because most of the testing had taken place on mountaintops. Here in the battered forest the margin for error would be close to zero.

Brumm's main concern, however, was about the ability of the pickup craft to survive. It would have to pass through a heavy artillery barrage in order to get to him; if risk was high for him, it was even higher for the pickup crew. To help, he had ordered German artillery to stand down for three minutes, and now it was only a minute from that pause. The incoming aircraft would have to be on time and make the hookup on its first pass; he doubted it could survive a second try.

He leaned out of the cockpit to listen. Suddenly, the German artillery ceased firing; the Soviet shelling sounded small. Within thirty seconds the Soviets stopped too, their commanders obviously pondering what the German cease-fire meant. Other than sporadic rifle fire and occasional short bursts from automatic weapons, the area was silent for the first time in days, and suddenly he heard the engines of the incoming aircraft.

The plane was near. He couldn't see it, but he could tell from the pitch of its engines that it was banking for its approach. It was low, almost on the treetops. He had no doubt that the pilot would do his job. It was his way to always expect the highest possible level of performance from his subordinates. Those who could not deliver were severely disciplined; those who would not were transferred to other units where requirements and expectations were not so high.

Satisfied that the aircraft was the one he expected, Brumm leaned out of the cockpit, pointed a flare gun into the night sky and squeezed the trigger. A green flare whooshed upward and exploded into a cascade of emerald sparks. He broke open the gun, pulled the spent cartridge and inserted another round. Leaning out again, he aimed the gun along the line created by the glider's fuselage and fired straight ahead toward the tree line. There, hidden under a thin cover of dirt, was a cache of several dozen jerricans containing petrol. The flare drove through the mound into the cans and ignited a huge explosion and fire, which lit the entire area and made the poles holding the cable loop clearly visible. Staring at the device, he was amazed that it was still in place and that both it and the miniature fuel dump had escaped the enemy artillery fire. He took it as a good omen.

The sound of the aircraft died; it was now behind him. He quickly rechecked his harness, put his feet on the rudder pedals and grasped the control column with his gloved hand.

The transport growled slowly overhead, so close that for a moment he thought it would land on top of him. Even with the bright fire ahead, visibility from the cockpit was limited, and he could not see if the hookup had been made. But he could feel it. At first there was a gentle rustling of the glider, then a small slide forward, followed by a firm snap as the cable reached the end of its elasticity. The glider bounced, then lifted. He got control of the rudder, and as he pulled back on the stick the light aircraft shot straight into the sky. As he passed over the trees ground fire leaped up at him, but he ignored the tracers and tried to focus on the towplane.

They climbed quickly, turning slowly but steadily to the south and west.

It had worked! Soon the fighting fell behind him and the dark countryside rolled by underneath. He stabilized the glider directly behind and below the tow craft and reached for his radio.

"Well done," he transmitted calmly. "I'm stable. Turn to heading zero nine zero." The transport turned immediately and the colonel began scanning the terrain below for the landmarks. The crew in the aircraft did not know his final destination; they were to follow his directions. At some point along the way, his plan, which the transport's crew did not have, called for him to drop away.

Brumm felt good. The Russians were behind him for the moment, and once again he was in control of his own destiny. So far all had gone well, and he felt confidence that the operation, which had been painstakingly developed, would succeed.

He had been in a division-level headquarters when the coded message had come through to him. It consisted of only one word. "Wolf," he said out loud.

▶4 APRIL 29, 1945, 1:00 A.M.

The five-man Special Operations Group had worked its way into what remained of Berlin's suburbs from the east, using elements of the Third Shock Army as a protective phalanx. Throughout the fifty-mile push from the Oder River, Vasily Petrov had been careful to protect his small unit; he had no intention of losing any of his handpicked men as the Soviet armies clubbed their way into the Nazi capital. The group was too valuable a resource to be wasted without an appropriate return for such a high investment. It pleased Petrov to think in economic terms; the capitalists might be depraved, but they were also efficient, and he prized efficiency above most attributes. To prevent a premature expenditure of his priceless resource, the small Russian constantly kept his unit behind regular troops, allowing the army to pay the high price for moving ahead. As he and his men trailed a Soviet battalion, he reminded himself that theirs was a mission far more important than laying claim to a few square miles of Nazi rubble.

At 1:00 A.M. the Soviet troops shielding the Special Operations Group emerged from a set of twisting parallel streets to find themselves at the edge of an open *Platz* containing a sunken garden, statuary on pedestals and a radiating pattern of flat stones. Petrov sniffed the scent of lilacs in the spring air with obvious pleasure. But when the Russian infantry began to advance into the garden, he hesitated; something was wrong.

Ezdovo, the Siberian, immediately moved into position beside his leader. An orange glow of fire hovered and flickered over the city, but it was not enough to light the space. Because most of Berlin had lost electricity a long time ago, there was little light except from nearby fires; here, unlike other parts of the city, there were few burning. Ezdovo did not look at his leader, but he squatted next to him, staring into the darkness, shifting his head from side to side to compensate for the blind spot in the eye that limits human vision at night. He had learned the technique as a hunter during the months-long darkness of Arctic winters. "Trouble," he said. It was not a question; in combat his instincts were nearly identical with Petrov's, and when his leader halted, he was already feeling the same wave of suspicion.

Petrov whispered, "You feel it?"

"No resistance," the Siberian said calmly. "Big area, easily defended, a natural bottleneck against anyone coming out of the streets. The Germans wouldn't let us in here if they didn't want us to enter." It was an unexpected development; so far the German resistance they had faced had been fierce, though amateurish. Hitler had ordered a fight to the death, and many citizens were obeying blindly. Now, in a place where a defense action was easy, even natural, there was none. It felt wrong.

"Ambush?" Petrov asked.

Ezdovo rose slowly from his squat to check the progress of the soldiers ahead of them. Some were already nearing the other side of the garden. "No," he said confidently. "An ambush would prevent us from getting this far. It feels like a kill trap."

Petrov needed no further confirmation; he had reached the same conclusion. The area was no doubt mined and set for remote detonation by someone watching from a nearby rooftop. "Move," he ordered suddenly, giving the Siberian a gentle shove. "Idiots," he added in the direction of the soldiers who were now filling the park and taking the respite from fighting as an opportunity to rest and smoke. Petrov saw that the battalion commander was in the middle of his men, his radio operator beside him; they were seating themselves on a low wall of light-colored bricks.

When Petrov and Ezdovo bolted away, the other three men followed. When their leader acted, they did not ask questions; to do so could be fatal. As the five of them ran along the back of the park, several soldiers shouted at them. "Relax, the Nazi bastards are kaput." They raced on, ignoring the cries. Finally they reached the opening of a street that led north and swerved in. As they cut into the opening, Ezdovo stopped, dropped to his knees, lifted his weapon and faced the *Platz* area to cover their backs. When the others were safely past him, he tried to follow, but before he was fully in, a massive flash of light engulfed the park, followed by a shock wave that sent them all sprawling, stunning them and leaving them staring blindly, gasping for oxygen as parts of buildings fell around them.

Gnedin, the greyhoundlike physician and newest member of the group, was the first to recover. Ignoring his comrades, he went directly to Petrov and found the leader of the Special Operations Group kneeling in the middle of the street, covered with a layer of stone dust, bleeding from his ears.

Bailov, the muscular young Ukrainian with long red hair and a close-cropped beard, was next to regain his senses. He was dizzy, his steps unsure, but he clicked the safety off and clutched his weapon close as he went to Gnedin's side.

"Is he all right?"

"Concussion," the doctor said. "Not serious. Check the others."

Because Ezdovo had been last out of the *Platz*, he had taken the brunt of the explosion; the back of his canvas jacket was singed and he was dazed, but he was already on one knee, facing back in the direction they had come, his weapon up. Bailov patted him on the shoulder. "Where's Rivitsky?"

"He was next to Petrov."

Bailov left the Siberian to search for the other man and found him a few moments later. Rivitsky's legs were sticking out of a pile of rocks. At first glance Bailov thought the worst, but a muffled voice barked angrily from under the debris, "Get this shit off me!" The order was punctuated by a long cough. Bailov dug quickly. A wall had collapsed on his comrade, but by luck a support beam had landed first at such an angle that it had shielded the man from the rest of the falling wall. When finally freed, Rivitsky's face was so covered with dust as fine as chalk that he looked like a fat ghost. The sight made Bailov giggle nervously, provoking a poorly aimed swat from the fat man still on his back. "Comrade," Bailov crooned, "is this any way to treat your savior?"

When they had recovered sufficiently, Petrov gathered his men in the shadows. He was still bleeding from the ears, but as always was in command. "Remote detonation," Ezdovo told his leader. Petrov did not hear the Siberian's exact words because his ears were still ringing, but he understood what had happened; over the years he had set the same kind of trap for his enemies, and he knew what the army had blundered into.

Bailov tapped the stock of his rifle nervously, his eyes darting, alert for threats. Gnedin sat quietly, trying to compose himself. It was one thing to see the result of violence and quite another to be a participant. He was still new to all this, and his nerves were frayed by the experience. Rivitsky was still coughing and slapping at his clothes to get rid of the dust; he was the sort of person who, despite his pear shape, took great care in sartorial matters.

The heavy and slow-moving Rivitsky had been born and raised in Leningrad. When the Special Operations Group was afield, he tended to tire easily, becoming short-tempered and complaining constantly. But Petrov did not concern himself with such inconsequential traits; he trusted Rivitsky as much as he allowed himself to trust any human being. It didn't matter that the balding fat man was not cut out for the prolonged exertions of war. He had a steel constitution, an un-bending will and the ability to kill with his hands if anybody got close enough. More important was his mind, his ability to organize, to think logically and to absorb volumes of detail. "What now, comrade?" he asked between coughs.

Petrov was in no mood for explanations. Their mission required getting expeditiously to the Reich Chancellery on the other side of the Spree River. The unit was not to be risked by confronting the ragtag army of German citizens fighting desperately to defend what was already lost. The Special Operations Group was driven by a higher order—much higher—but now their careless infantry escort had stum-bled into a trap. Petrov had no doubt what they would find in the park, but he knew they had to look, if only because they would need a radio in order to link up with another military unit.

The five men moved cautiously through the *Platz* and into the garden, strung out single file with Petrov in the middle, Ezdovo in the lead and Bailov in the rear. When they reached the place where they had last seen the battalion commander, they found only a hand beside the ruin of the wall, some shreds of clothing and a demolished radio, which Petrov kicked, his lips pursed. "When we acquire a new escort, we will secure our own radio," he announced. "We can't afford any more delays and we can't trust the army."

Not wanting to remain in the open, Petrov led his men back in the direction from which they had originally come. Thinking there had been an error, Genedin reminded his leader that the river they sought was to the west and that they were traveling in the opposite direction. As the newest member of the group, he was not yet accus-tomed to Petrov's logic or his uncanny instincts.

"While geometry teaches that the shortest distance between two points is always in a straight line, this seldom holds true in war. In practice, you will find that theory is often different," Petrov said patiently but firmly.

Ezdovo nudged Bailov, and the two men smiled. The doctor would learn as they had—or else.

▶5 APRIL 29, 1945, 4:00 A.M.

.The colonel moved out into the sulfuric haze that clung to the city. He checked the machine pistol slung across his chest. His fingers fondled the selector. Semiautomatic, safety on, he told himself. No accidents tonight. In a gesture of reassurance he touched his jacket pockets where the extra clips were stored.

He had parachuted into the city shortly after eight o'clock the previous night and worked his way south from the suburbs. Choosing a route through the rubble had been difficult, but he found that he could keep a fairly strenuous pace as he jogged along. Every now and then he had to stop and think his way through, around or over a tight space. He had little trouble seeing; Berlin seemed to be baking in a hot orange fire. Russian artillery fell on the city in fifteen-minute storms every thirty minutes. In between barrages, flights of Soviet bombers or solitary fighters dropped bombs or flew low over the debris, strafing randomly. It seemed that everything in Berlin that could burn was already on fire, but he knew better. War of this scale was always beyond a single man's senses or comprehension. From above you might think you had burned everything and killed everyone, but if you flew away, the fires would go out, the sun would rise and people would crawl out of their holes to begin figuring out how to get through the new day. Such was war, and now it had come to Berlin. It looked dead, but he knew that it still teemed with life: Berliners were survivors.

Brumm realized that he was in one of the most sustained and ferocious attacks in military history, but he was not intimidated. He had been on the receiving end before in fighting the Russians. He was a professional. All of his adult life had been spent in situations different from this only in extent. This war, he knew, was lost. It had been lost a long time ago, and with it the Third Reich. All that stood in the way of the Ivans now were a few thousand prepubescent Hitler Youths and their maniacal leaders, some old men, and perhaps a handful of elite army units trying to operate at token strength. Everything he saw told him that the Russians could enter the city now and have it for their own. But he knew they wouldn't; first they would stand outside, inflicting punishment from afar, trying to crush the population. Partly it was a practical decision: Why crawl into the enemy's lair? Partly it was vengeful, a response to what the Nazis had done in their drive across Russia. The Russians always returned what they had received.

As he moved steadily along, Brumm found his mind wandering. *This . . . the Mission of the Great Wolf. I am the anointed one. I alone am the future.* Over and over the words repeated in his mind and took on the cadence of a chant. His heartbeat increased and his pace quickened. *The Mission.* Around him, cringing in hiding, were thousands of Germans, reduced to sets of eyes staring up from the darkness of cellars, waiting for daylight and deliverance. Only he remained above, moving with intent, the hunter, the sole remaining German predator.

He needed to cover a distance of several miles before dawn and, if possible, to cross the River Spree. There were subway tunnels under the river, and even with Russian advance units in the city, the underground tubes would be safe. Herr Goebbels had seen to that very nicely through his Ministry of Propaganda. The ministry's experts had deftly planted the notion that in the event of a Russian invasion the Nazis had a plan to lure the enemy into the tunnels, then flood them with water from the Spree. He knew the Russians would believe this and stay above ground for as long as possible. The Ivans have dark souls, but they don't like the darkness, he told himself. In any case, Brumm was not concerned. There were many potential routes over or under the river, and he had studied them all. Eventually he would get across.

Ahead the rubble ended, opening into the spacious Friedrichstrasse. Looking southward, he fixed his position, using the remains of a steeple. He was not far from the river, he realized, perhaps less than a kilometer. He would move southwesterly to the Schiffbauerdamm and near there descend through one of the monkey holes used by rail inspectors for access to the Berlin tube. Once underground the new battery-powered torch in his pack would light his way and he could move quickly. The immediate task was to get to and under the river without interference. More and more people seemed to be moving around as he got further into the city, and he felt his nerves begin to tighten. Moving to the edge of a small side street, he crouched to make sure his route was clear. There were several vehicles on their sides, gutted by fire, twisted as if dropped and discarded by an angry giant. The road seemed clear of people, though back on the main *Strasse* groups of civilians were moving northward, away from the heart of the city.

He estimated that he had about ninety minutes until the beginning of morning twilight. By the time the sun was up he hoped to be on the other side of the river and safely into his sanctuary. Once across the river, there would be little need to go above ground. He could move all the way to the Chancellery through the mole runs built by bureaucrats.

It took less than fifteen minutes to reach the dam and find the entry hatch, a thick concrete disk with a metal wheel for an opening device. He tested the wheel; it was stuck. He stripped off his pack and tried again, but even with his considerable strength he couldn't coax a response from it. He knew it wasn't locked; Germans were not vandals, so there was no need for locks on such devices. Obviously it had been some time since the tube had been entered for an inspection; now it was probably corroded or jammed by the lack of proper maintenance and lubrication. He needed a lever.

He trotted quickly across the cement walks to a bombed building. Inside, he moved from flat to flat; what he needed was a steel rod from one of the walls, and he knew it was just a matter of looking until he found one. In the back of the building, in a flat with hideous yellow wallpaper covered with dancing satyrs, several rods were bent out of a long gash in the wall. Chunks of rock and mortar were scattered around the floor, but the rods were all still anchored in cement, so he would have to break away the bottom to release one. He moved out of the apartment to search again, this time for a tool. In a front flat on ground level, he found a mallet with half its handle broken away. The head was cast metal and heavy. He could make do with it.

Realizing that the unplanned demolition would take some time, the colonel worked at a brisk pace. He struck the base of the wall to a count, exhaled, inhaled and struck again, over and over, like a machine, never tiring. Mostly the concrete ricocheted away in flakes, but occasionally a more substantial piece would fall heavily to the floor. From time to time he stopped to twist the steel bar with his hands. It was beginning to loosen. Outside it was beginning to grow light, and a new Russian barrage seemed to be under way. Aircraft screamed low along the river, and antiaircraft fire from German batteries was sporadic. They were running out of either ammunition or nerve, he told himself. Perhaps the gunners were afraid to fire for fear of giving away their locations. Whatever their reasons, the wall of flak that once defended Berlin had evaporated.

It took Brumm precisely an hour to free the bar. But the effort was worth it; the bar was stiff, strong and nearly straight, the perfect lever. In no time at all, he congratulated himself, he'd be under the river and the first leg of his journey would be nearly complete. He turned to leave, and found himself staring directly into the muzzle of a machine pistol. The eyes of the young woman holding the weapon were gray, the color of sky just before a snowfall. Where the other Berliners he'd seen were gaunt ghosts, this woman was solid and muscular and had a well-fed, alert look about her. His instincts warned him that he was in extreme danger, and he exhaled to calm himself. "*Guten Morgen*," he said gaily, nodding his head slightly, hoping to take control of the situation.

"SS," she observed. "Your unit number, please."

"Am I a prisoner?" he asked, his voice challenging.

"I haven't decided yet."

"I crossed the river a week ago to reconnoiter Russian positions and movements. Now I can't get back. I tried to go under the river through an access tube, but the hatch is frozen. I need a lever." He held up the steel bar to show her.

"Where are the Russians?" she asked.

"Close. Tanks should be here soon, if they have the courage to come in."

"No hope?" she asked.

"There is always hope, Fräulein," he said gently.

Her grip suddenly tightened on her weapon and it thrust toward his head. "Don't bullshit me, SS man; I'm not your ordinary German *Frau*. I am the new German woman. I no longer lie in my bed waiting to be fucked. I fight like any man to defend my Führer and my Reich."

He saw his opportunity. "Then stand aside and let me pass. I have a mission to complete and you're interfering. Out of my way!"

She smiled. "Herr Colonel, you look and act like a man who is accustomed to giving orders, not taking them. Only, I wonder what such a person would be doing here at this time. There are many SS trying to leave the city, to abandon the Führer."

"Who are you?" he demanded.

She smiled and said nothing. Her eyes sparkled. Her lips were wet. Finally she said slowly, "An avenger of German honor. Our Führer has been betrayed by his generals. The men are deserting their positions. They abandon Germany to the Russians. My dear colonel, we hunt traitors to the Reich. We apply justice in the name of our Führer, Adolf Hitler. I think, Herr Colonel, that you are one of the men we seek."

"We?"

"There are six of us."

"And you believe that I am a deserter?"

"Is it not possible? Where are your orders, your papers? An SS colonel without a weapon, cowering in a bombed building?"

Her words angered him. "Move out of my way, girl. Don't play at the soldier's game. It will cost you your life."

"We play no game," a voice said from behind him. He glanced over his shoulder. There were two more women, both wearing men's clothing and in the same remarkably good physical condition as the first one. One held a machine pistol aimed at him; the other swung a hefty rope at her side. Neither looked friendly.

"Shoot him, Gretchen, and be done with it," the one with the rope said impatiently.

"I'll handle this," the first woman snapped. "The Führer has ordered activation of the Werewolves."

The colonel laughed. "You consider yourselves Werewolves?"

The one called Gretchen looked hard at him. "When the Russians come here, we will go underground. We have safe places. After a while they will relax. Then we will rise from our lairs and strike. There are thousands of us and we are waiting for them."

The colonel thought about what she had said. Hitler had issued an edict to organize the Werewolves, a guerrilla group, and had ordered every city and town to be defended to the death. In some areas, there undoubtedly would be resistance, but if he knew his fellow Germans, most would opt to save their skins. When the Russians arrived, Hitler would no longer exist. As for the Werewolves being a real force, they weren't. Like many of the Führer's final orders, this one had been largely ignored and unimplemented. These women were pathetic, nothing more than ignorant adolescents turned fanatic. Still, they might prove useful.

"Where did you learn about the Werewolves?"

"An officer told us," one of the women behind him said. "A general."

"Who is he?"

"*Was* he, you mean? We hanged the bastard," Gretchen boasted.

"We caught him running away with an Italian whore, so we tried him and executed him as a traitor. He told us a lot before he died."

"There are no Werewolves. It was only a plan, an idea that never took root," Brumm told the women. "There is no massive resistance. There are just you six and whatever stubborn soldiers that are left when the Russians finally arrive in strength. Just us, we few who continue to fight. I don't have time for games," he said. He walked toward the one called Gretchen, moved the machine pistol off-line and brushed by her.

As he passed she struck him across the back of the head with her weapon and sent him sprawling into the hallway. As soon as he hit the floor the barrel of her weapon was pressed tightly against the base of his skull. "On your feet," she said. He did as he was told, rubbing his head as he tried to stand.

They took him out of the building, on a snaking course through piles of building stones into what remained of a thick red brick edifice, then pushed him inside, down a hallway to the head of stairs. "Down, Herr Colonel." At the bottom there was a heavy metal door. "Inside," one of the women said, and he felt a blow across the shoulders and was driven through the door.

He stared, unbelieving. The room was lit by candles—huge ones as thick as arms, probably from local churches. Near the door was another woman, a new one, also armed. In a corner was a young boy, very thin, wearing an immaculate Hitler Youth dress uniform. He was bound hand to foot in a tight bundle and gagged; his body gyrated slowly as he struggled against his restraints. Brumm could see that he was in pain.

"A traitor," Gretchen said from behind him. "We've been hunting them and carrying out the sentence of death."

Psychopaths, the colonel thought. Like Gestapo agents he had known. "What was his crime?" he asked, nodding toward the Hitler Youth.

"His was a crime against the future of the state. He was a homosexual, a weakling. He found him with his lover in his mouth. His lover died fighting. This one fell to the floor and cried for mercy. The Reich cannot tolerate defectives who refuse their duty, especially now. Germany needs children."

"Am I to be tried?" Brumm asked.

"It remains a possibility."

Time was running out. *Erst besinnen, dann beginnen*—first think, then begin, he thought. Brumm lunged at the nearest woman, driving a fist into her solar plexus. As she doubled up, he grasped the short barrel of her machine pistol, twisted it from her grip and spun behind his victim, holding the leader of the women in his sights. It happened so fast that none of the women reacted.

"I have no more time for this," the colonel said angrily, his chest heaving. "I have my duty and you are interfering. In other circumstances, perhaps, I might play with you and see this game to its end, but not now." He aimed the weapon at the leader's face. "Make your decision now, Fräulein. We both die here or you can get out of my way. Either way, there's no more talk. What's it to be?"

She stepped aside and lowered her weapon. "Are you hell-bent on killing Russians and finding traitors?" he asked. She nodded. "Do you want to serve your Führer and the Reich?" All the women nodded. "Good," he pronounced. "Gather your weapons and gear and come with me. If you want to serve the Reich, then God has sent me to you; you will see, my Walküre. Gretchen, is it?" he said to the leader.

"Yes."

"Gretchen, have one of the others get that steel rod from the other building and let's go. We're running out of time." He stalked out of the room and up the stairs.

The women looked at one another for a moment until their leader finally lowered her head. "Move," she said.

He was waiting for them upstairs. "You," he said, pointing to Gretchen. "You are now Obersturmführer; you are my second in command."

"Me?"

"You," he repeated. "Is it too much for you?"

"Waller," she said crisply, "Obersturmführer Waller," and snapped a crisp salute.

"Very good, Waller. Wait here." He went back down the stairs. There was a single shot from below. Then he was back. "That one will feel no more pain," he said. "No more executions; you fight when I tell you to fight. You are now SS."

"There are no women in the SS," Waller said.

"But there have been plenty of the SS in women," one of the others said. They all laughed.

"For the moment," Brumm said, "*I* am the SS, and I say there will be women. I expect total obedience, complete discipline, no different than what I expect from my men. You will swear to it." All six women gathered around him. For the first time he noticed how young they were—late teens, early twenties at the most—and so healthy-looking. He called them to attention and lifted his right arm in the Nazi salute. They followed his lead.

"I swear to thee, Adolf Hitler, as Führer and chancellor of the German Reich, loyalty and bravery. I vow to thee and to the superiors whom thou shalt appoint, obedience unto death, so help me God."

He shook each woman's hand, then kissed each gently on the cheek.

"Waller, are we ready to go?"

"Yes, Herr Colonel."

"Then move."

Ten minutes later they were inside the tube. With the lever the wheel had worked easily. He sent the women down first, then followed, jamming the iron rod into the door's mechanism so that no one would be able to follow them. When he reached the tunnel floor, the girls were huddled together, squatting near a wall. The air was heavy and stale. He flashed his light ahead of them. There were damp spots, but mostly the way ahead was dry. It would be easy going.

"Is there a way out?" Waller asked.

"There is always a way out, Waller, if you keep your wits. Move out."

Phase One of the mission was nearing completion. He'd added some elements not planned on, but the operation hadn't taken into account the possibility of Berlin being awash in lunatics. He needed help; for the time being these girls could provide it.

"Waller," the colonel said softly as they walked, "who taught you to fight?"

"We taught ourselves," she said proudly.

Wer sein eigener Lehrmeister sein will, hat einen Narr zum Schüler, he thought. He that teaches himself has a fool for a master. It had been his grandfather's favorite saying.

►6 APRIL 29, 1945, 9:40 A.M.

Moving his group through Berlin's catacombs, Brumm concentrated on the plan and tasks that lay ahead. In planning this mission they had anticipated mass confusion in the city—indeed, they had counted on it as a key factor—but they hadn't realized how bad it would be. Since parachuting into the city, nothing had gone quite as anticipated. Still, here he was safely across the Spree River and on his way to the rendezvous. This was the critical step. If the rendezvous was a failure or if something had happened to the others, the rest of the plan would be jeopardized; in fact, there wouldn't be any plan, just a desperate attempt at the last moment. But while he understood the implications of failure, he didn't dwell on the probabilities. He had a job to do and would do it to the fullest extent possible, using his abilities and instincts to guide him when necessary. And now he had his Valkyries as extra cards in this gambit.

Having led the girls up from Stadtmitte Station, Brumm felt happy to be above ground again. The shelling from across the river was furious, as was return fire from nearby. Russian aircraft buzzed over the city, dropping bombs and strafing without discrimination. The war had come to Berlin in full fury.

He could easily fix the Russian positions. As tacticians they lacked German finesse and sophistication. The Ivans were very conservative in their approaches to battle. It was not their courage that was suspect but their comprehension of the ways of war. Both he and the Soviets knew that without American matériel the Russians would be under Reich control today. But with Allied equipment and weapons, and their own millions of bodies to throw into the fray, they had pushed relentlessly, until the Wehrmacht was shoved back across the Oder. On the western front, Allied pincers were closing. Vienna had fallen to the Soviets. The Americans, Brumm figured, would now be beyond the Elbe and driving toward Berlin. The British had captured Hamburg and were pushing methodically and cautiously across northern Germany. The massive Reich had shrunk dramatically. Perhaps an East-

West linkup had already taken place; if not, it would happen soon. It had no bearing on his situation one way or another, but, as a soldier, he wondered.

Certainly the Russians were not yet close to the Spree. It was their practice to cover troop advances with artillery fire, dropping a lethal curtain of explosives just ahead of their advancing troops. To Berliners who were noncombatants, this seemed like chaos, but the Ivans were deliberate, and the shells falling in the city told Brumm exactly where they were. Like any other human event, war could be read by those trained in its secrets.

The closer the Ivans got, the heavier the fighting would be and the less willing individual Russian soldiers would be to sacrifice themselves, with the end so obviously near. The Soviet troops, he suspected, would be leery of everything, and because of their caution and the heavy flow of civilians fleeing the city, he calculated that his party could make its escape.

Two blocks from where the Friedrichstrasse intersected the Belle-Alliance Platz, the colonel turned onto a narrow side street. To his surprise, it was relatively free of debris. He sent Waller and two of her companions across the street, and after they were in position he surveyed the area. Unlike most other streets, there were no bodies of German soldiers hanging from the light posts—reminders from fanatics that the city must be defended. Those who tried to escape fighting were being hanged and displayed as a deterrent. This block seemed almost the way it must have been before the Russian assault: neat, quiet and ordinary.

Very few people knew that underneath the tightly packed row of hundred-year-old red brick homes was a system of bunkers built several years before in great secrecy. The construction workers had been slaves and had been eliminated when the work was completed. In all probability, even the residents didn't suspect what they lived on top of.

In the middle of the block, Brumm entered a walkway between two of the brick structures. He opened the back door to a house, using a key that hung from a lanyard around his neck, and went into the flat. Spreading the Valkyries out to cover doors and windows, he left them and went directly to a back bedroom on the ground floor, where he entered a large closet. Closing the door tightly behind him, he loosened a hinged clothes dowel, which was a concealed lever. Pushing it down, he activated a small hydraulic system, and the room began to move downward. After a few feet it stopped and a gruff voice challenged him. "Wolf," Brumm said, and the descent began again, the lift's electric motor humming. At the bottom was a steel door. When the lift settled, the door slid back and he stepped into a well-furnished room whose mahogany paneling and soft yellow lights created a feeling of comfort.

Brumm found himself staring down the barrel of a machine pistol. "Just in case. Damned Russians are all over the place. You're late," the man said good-naturedly. Brumm could tell he had been worried.

Sergeant Major Hans Rau had long blond hair and full reddish facial hair, hence his nickname, "Beard." He was dressed in civilian clothes, but was in fact, like Brumm, a commando. "Everything is fucked up," he complained. "Russian snipers are scampering all over the city, shooting at everything that moves. They're terrible shots! It's pure luck that this street is still standing. At the rate they're throwing in shells, it won't last for long. I've heard a Werwolf transmission from the Elbe: the Americans have stopped their advance."

Brumm froze and stared at his sergeant. "Stopped?"

"Dead in their tracks. Looks like they're going to let the Russians have Berlin."

"Bastards," the colonel swore loudly. "A sellout."

"How does it affect us?"

"We anticipated that the drive to Berlin might spread the Americans out and provide more seams in their lines for our breakout. Now they'll be clustered along the river, covering all the crossing points, which will make it more difficult for us. Where is our Alpha?"

Rau motioned toward a nearby door and winked. "He's in there, filling an accommodating Fräulein with his final seed." He made a curvy line in the air with his gun barrel. "The Alpha is ready and anxious to do his duty for his Reich and Führer—just as soon as he's finished." He laughed loudly and smacked his thigh.

"What about the bunker? Do you know what's going on over there?"

"The listening devices are working. They're beginning to clear out. Several have been dispatched to Admiral Doenitz, with the Führer's final will and testament."

"Who did he send?"

"Johannmeier, Zander and Lorenz left at noon. Boldt, Weiss and Freytag von Loringhoven will go later." These were all aides or assistants of Reich officials; Brumm knew them well. But there was one, more than all the others, he was concerned about. It was Hitler's young Luftwaffe adjutant who concerned Brumm most; they needed him out of the Chancellery area.

"What about von Below?"

"They haven't mentioned him."

"The Führer will see to it that Colonel von Below leaves. He's too dangerous to let linger. Besides, he's Hitler's favorite. Like many of our pilots, that one is a reptile, an iceman. He would see what was going on."

The sergeant major nodded as he pulled an unopened bottle of cognac from a wide drawer in a marble-topped table. They toasted each other silently and held the fiery liquid in their mouths, enjoying its intensity.

"The Americans aren't the only surprises today," Brumm said seriously. "My friend, how do you feel about women in the SS?" A smile crept over his face.

"*Bitte?*" Rau said. It was not like his colonel to make jokes.

▶7 APRIL 30, 1945, 1:45 P.M.

Adolf Hitler sat quietly at the table, picking at a small dish of spaghetti. Now and then he munched a small leaf of wilted lettuce, gnawing it mindlessly like a rabbit.

The Führer's secretaries, Frau Christian and Frau Junge, were relieved that he was in a contemplative mood. The two women, both in their mid-twenties and attractive, had their own worries. Events during recent hours made it increasingly clear that the end of the Third Reich was at hand, and each of them wondered what lay ahead. The Führer's fate was no secret; he'd made his intentions quite clear.

Junge felt abandoned. Her husband was dead, killed by the Russians the previous year. She took pride in his death for the Fatherland, but now she was more concerned about her own survival than anything else. For months the gossip among the bunker's small retinue of women had focused on the brutality of the dreaded Ivans. One night, Frau Goebbels, who was privy to such information—indeed, seemed to relish it—spent the better part of two hours explaining in anatomical detail how the Russians ravaged captive women. She made a point of telling the other women that neither she nor her daughters would be taken by the Russians; she would kill herself and the girls rather than allow the Ivans to use them. Frau Junge had given a great deal of thought to the ordeal ahead and reached a different decision. She would not commit suicide, no matter what happened, but neither would she surrender. She felt trapped between two options, with no alternatives in between. Hitler's uncharacteristically serene mood served only to heighten her own fear.

Christian was a widow too, of sorts. With her soft blond hair and eye-catching looks, she was used to attracting and holding the attention of men. Her husband's cowardice sickened her. There had been no need for him to return to his unit, but he had made clumsy excuses and abandoned the bunker, with fear displayed in his every movement. He was saving his own skin, and hers be damned. Though not a violent woman, she had started having dreams of finding him and killing him. She deserted men; not the other way around. She had made up her mind; when this was over, she would divorce the bastard. Given the mood in the room, she felt no desire for food. But Hitler was attentive to such details and if she didn't make at least a minimal show of eating, he would certainly lecture her on the need for good nutritional habits.

Neither woman spoke. They were unaccustomed to having the burden of conversation on their shoulders. The Führer was renowned as an orator both publicly and privately. As a self-proclaimed expert on every imaginable subject, he used mealtimes to expound at great length, and often inaccurately, on a wide range of subjects. All of those who had to live with him learned early on to leave his rambling pronouncements unchallenged, and to deal with his idiosyncrasies by simply ignoring them. There was no other way to remain sane. What they were not accustomed to was having to cope with a silent Führer, a new role, which he now played by looking up from his food every few moments with a blank smile. Both women wished he'd finish his food and leave, but they knew from experience that he would eat at his own speed. Everything in Germany moved at Hitler's speed.

Behind the three diners, Constanze Manzialy, the Führer's personal cook and expert in his favorite vegetarian preparations, sat on a stool minding her own business. She kept her mouth shut and the others ignored her, which was how she liked it. Manzialy was a tiny woman, and neither smart nor worldly. Most of what she heard inside Hitler's closest circles was meaningless to her. She had only one interest now: to get out of the bunker and return to her mountain home near Innsbruck. She hated being trapped underground in the bunker; she preferred her mountain aeries. While she found it difficult to think, she knew that her ability to understand what was going on now could later save her life, so she concentrated on listening to the others. Some kind of ending was approaching, and there was a lot of talk about leaving. She wanted to know as much as possible about what the others were going to do so that they couldn't ignore her. It galled Manzialy that they treated her like a piece of furniture. If they were leaving, she was leaving with them, even if it meant a confrontation with the Russians. She had heard the stories about what they did to German women, and she had already decided that if captured she'd quickly tell the Ivans that she was Austrian, not German; it never occurred to her that maybe they wouldn't care about the difference. She shuddered at the thought of one of those huge hairy men forcing her to submit to him. She'd tried sex a few times, and it wasn't much even when it was by choice. What would it be like if it was forced? She wanted to cry.

A guard, a corporal, also was in the room, but like the cook, he stayed away from the others and did his best to be inconspicuous.

At about 2:00 P.M., Hitler finally scraped the final bit of food from his plate, burped quietly without covering his mouth, rose and left without a word.

The two secretaries stared at each other. "He ate everything," one of them said incredulously.

"He always eats everything," the other one said sarcastically. Then she added, "I'm surprised he didn't want his cream cakes. He sneaks them, then gobbles them like a pig."

In their private quarters Hitler found Eva Braun sitting on the edge of her bed wearing a shimmering satin slip from Paris. It seemed more silver than white as it moved on the curves of her body.

"Dress well," the Führer said quietly. "We have to show them the proper way. Always we must set the standard." He went off to one of the other rooms.

Eva Hitler felt surprisingly calm. He was right, of course. The others would be watching her, as always. She liked being watched by them. As the Führer's wife, she would show them how a loyal German woman should behave. They would not find her performance wanting.

Standing in front of her wardrobe, she felt small pangs of self-pity. Never again would she be able to wear her fine silk dresses and furs, or the expensive jewelry that had come her way. These are earthly things, she reprimanded herself. She had more important matters to consider. Her final mark in life would be not her high style or soaring spirit but something far more lasting. In the end, it would be she, Eva Braun, the one woman among millions of German women who had captured the ultimate prize. The marriage made it official, and it had come as a complete surprise, the kind of gesture he had made often at the beginning of their relationship. She had taken great pleasure over the years in watching other women claw each other to catch his eye. They looked at her with lethal envy, wondering what it was like to bed the most powerful man on earth. Were the whispers about his sexual habits true? She smiled. With the Führer, everything was true and everything was false; all things were both possible and impossible. It took a special kind of woman to please him. Many had tried and failed. Only she had endured, and now she had her reward. For years he had ignored her, coming in and out of her life only when it suited his convenience. At first she had worried that she would be discarded, but after their first sexual experience she knew he would return. Accepting his unusual desires—or rather, encouraging them—was her ultimate power, the final lock that bound them together. He might experiment with other women, but he would always come back because she performed without question or judgments, and as she came to enjoy their secret life she began to dominate the man who could not be dominated.

She selected his favorite gown, a black dress that fitted snugly, then sat on the edge of the bed and slid her feet into some tiny hand-made Italian shoes, a gift from Mussolini and his woman. She checked the time. She hoped that everything would be over quickly and that nothing would interfere. It wouldn't be fair, she complained to herself. But he had a way of changing his mind suddenly and unalterably; above all else, the thought that he might switch courses now terrified her. She wanted it to be over.

When Eva had finished dressing, she checked herself in the small wall mirror and splashed herself with a heavy perfume. He did not like perfume—or makeup, for that matter—at least not on her. But now she was feeling gay and powerful, and she knew that he would overlook her little transgression. Paradoxically, the Führer had not allowed certain factories making cosmetics and perfumes to manufacture war matériel, maintaining that German women needed these vanities and that the Third Reich could find other ways to produce weapons.

She went past the bathroom into their small living room. In the anteroom between her and the corridor, Hitler was talking to Heinz Linge, his personal valet. On a table in front of the small blue couch two pistols were laid out beside two small black metal tubes, the size of lipstick containers, encasing cyanide ampules. The cylinders had narrow blue bands around them and looked almost elegant.

In the outer room she heard her husband tell Linge, "Wait a full ten minutes after the door is closed for the final time and after all is quiet." Linge acknowledged these instructions in a tone of voice that told her that they would be executed precisely. It was Linge's way.

▶8 APRIL 30, 1945, 2:10 P.M.

Getting into the Chancellery had been relatively simple. Brumm had found a single guard at the entrance; after enticing the man into a nearby room, he had killed him with his knife, then dumped the body outside near a pile of rubble. Once inside they had expected to have an easy time of it, but unexpectedly they had encountered another guard, this one in the subterranean corridor that led to the bunker. Using the Alpha's appearance, they had informed the man that the outer security post was unmanned and sent him up to cover it. The man was reluctant at first, but the Alpha proved to be a powerful inducement and he had gone. If he harbored any doubts about changing posts, Brumm wanted to urge him along, and so he quickly followed the guard. As he approached a turn in the hall, Brumm heard footsteps moving away from him at a fast clip. As he had expected, the man had paused to have another look, but Brumm's approach had sent him scurrying. The colonel knew the sergeant wouldn't turn back again. It would have been better to kill him, but down here there was no place to put the body. Ordering him out of the area would have to suffice.

They had to act quickly, before there were any more intrusions.

This was the critical moment. At intervals along both walls were storage bins behind metal plates, each a meter square. Behind them were fire hoses, gas masks, canisters of emergency water and small portable gas-run generators. Brumm counted six down from the guard station. Using his dagger, he removed the two lower holding screws and pocketed them. The upper part of the plate was hinged, and he pulled it up like a trapdoor, surprised both at the weight and at the easy movement; the fit was excellent. Inside, the compartment was shallow; it held a flat fire hose wrapped around a small metal wheel. At the bottom of the back panel was a small strip of metal with a single flat-head screw. There was no apparent use for the strip; nevertheless, it looked like an integral part of the internal structure. The screw was of a special design; it was spring-loaded, and whether it was loose or tight, it always looked the same. Brumm loosened the screw, gave a hard shove to the back of the compartment with the heel of his hand, and the back swung away, revealing a black crawl space.

The Alpha stood behind Brumm, twitching nervously, looking up and down the hall.

"All right," the colonel said. He formed a step by joining his hands. "Step up." The Alpha stared at the hands, not seeming to comprehend. "Put your foot here and step up there," Brumm said forcefully. "There's a false back. Crawl in far enough to leave room for me. And keep quiet," he added.

The man's foot shook badly. Brumm grabbed it, pulled him forward and boosted him into the opening. Footsteps were coming from the Chancellery as Brumm climbed in, turned himself around and pulled the metal plate down, letting it slip the last little bit. It hit with a soft metallic sound, which he hoped wouldn't be heard. He pulled out his revolver, checked the silencer to be sure it was tight and waited. The footsteps passed without slowing. They were in.

Brumm was sweating heavily; he wiped his brow and crawled into the metal cavern behind the Alpha. He carefully closed the swinging door, making sure it was snug, then sat back to catch his breath. Even if someone noticed that two screws were missing from the outside panel, the inside structure would look perfectly normal. Given the shelling from Russian guns, a few missing screws from a metal door would be perfectly understandable. Now that he was inside, he was feeling much better and far less tense. From here on it would be easier going. He rested his head on his arm and checked his watch. It had taken no more than one minute to remove the screws, load the Alpha and get himself in. Opening his kit bag, he extracted a flashlight.

They were in a metal tunnel, in an area that looked like the junction of a number of tubes. It was part of the illusion. All but one of the tubes that branched off ended a few meters away; only one went deep into the building, and he knew which one it was. He shone the light ahead, catching the Alpha, who squinted in the beam. Crawling by the other man, he tapped him on the foot. "Forward."

"It's dark," the Alpha whined.

"Like hell itself," Brumm told him.

The duct floor was cool, and their crawling made the metal ring loudly. At first the sound bothered Brumm, but when he reminded himself that they were embedded in several feet of concrete, he relaxed and moved forward with confidence.

Twenty meters ahead they found another open area and more tunnels branching off. Brumm left the Alpha at the junction, located his new route and went forward to where the tunnel plunged straight down. He aimed his light downward. Three meters, he estimated, maybe a little less. Shining his light into his kit, he extracted a metal piton, then, using his dagger, wedged it into a seam in the duct's skin. He looped a thin rope through the piton and fastened it quickly and expertly with a series of half hitches. After testing it, he crawled backward to where the Alpha waited.

Brumm explained what they were going to do. "There's a drop just ahead. I'll go first. Let yourself over the edge, stomach down, and hang on to the rope. I'll help you. When your feet hit bottom, turn around one hundred and eighty degrees, then sit. Push yourself forward on your back until you're in the new tunnel. Then roll over on your stomach and keep moving backwards after me." He made the man repeat the instructions twice, until he was sure that he understood. Whether he could do it or not remained to be seen.

Brumm went down first. Lying on his belly, he put his hand up and caught the Alpha's feet, helping to lower him. It was a long crawl to the next wide space. Brumm checked his watch: three o'clock. They were in good shape. There wasn't much time to spare, but they had a practical safety margin. When the Alpha reached the wide spot, Brumm went ahead quickly to investigate the remainder of the route. It wasn't far now; they were almost there.

He found the place easily. It was not quite as wide as the duct, and was cut out of the bottom. A wire from a conduit ran out of the concrete to the right of the section and directly into the top. There were two loops on the sides. Brumm lifted one carefully and peered down through the crack at a bed below. A light was attached to the cut section of the duct, and he knew that from below it looked like all the others in the bunker; it had been designed that way. Satisfied with what he had found, he backed up.

"All right, it's time," he told the Alpha. "Take off your coat and boots." The man did as he was told, and Brumm removed all of his own outer clothing and gear. He'd need only his dagger and the flashlight. "We'll back in," he told the man. "You first, then me."

Within minutes they were in position. He checked his watch again: three-twenty. So far, so good. Soon there should be a shot.

▶9 APRIL 30, 1945, 3:20 P.M.

When his valet had left, Hitler looked at his wife and motioned her to join him. They entered the concrete hall arm in arm. What remained of the inner circle stood there stiffly; they were lined up along the wall, waiting for this historic moment.

Martin Bormann, the secretary of the Nazi party, a virtual nonentity to most Germans, was at the head of the line, smiling his reptilian smile. Eva hated Bormann, and over the years had used every opportunity to undercut his influence. To no effect. He'd risen to stand beside her husband despite her efforts. He was an animal, whose mere presence made her skin crawl.

Goebbels was next. Sweat beaded his high, bony forehead, and his head bobbed back and forth. With his prominent, beaklike nose, he looked like a chicken pecking in the dust. She fought back a smile. How could anybody take the man seriously?

Otto Günsche, Hitler's SS adjutant, stood near Goebbels, looking relaxed and in control of himself, true to form.

Generals Krebs and Burgdorf stood at attention, trying to project proper military bearing, but the fumes emanating from Burgdorf made it clear that he was drunk again. Krebs, a rawboned man whose shaved skull seemed to shine in the artificial light, seemed the steadier of

the two. With his monocle firmly in place, he looked like a carica-
ture of a Prussian officer, an effect he used to the utmost. One of
the more learned and cultured of the group, Krebs was fluent in
Russian, but he was also a schemer like all the rest. No doubt, Eva
thought, at this very moment he's trying to figure out some way
to make a deal with the Ivans after my husband is dead. She had
no illusions about any of these people. She understood them and,
unlike her husband, knew precisely what really motivated each
of them. Such knowledge came naturally, because she was one of
them.

Walter Hewel, the adjutant from the Foreign Office, rubbed his
hands against the cloth of his finely tailored suit. Vice Admiral Voss,
an intense man, looked attentive, but not outwardly concerned about
what was about to happen. This might have been any other conference
with the Führer.

Werner Naumann stood several people away from his boss, Goebbels. This was unusual; normally Naumann was at arm's length, like
an obedient hound. She had suspected for some time that Naumann
had been conducting a discreet affair with Magda Goebbels—though
that Magda could do anything discreet was astonishing. Perhaps his
standing apart now was his way of registering his objection to his
superior's decision to acquiesce to his wife's plan to kill their six
children and themselves, rather than face capture. Of all the people
there, Eva was sure that Naumann would escape unscathed; it was
his nature to survive.

Johann Rattenhuber, the head of the Reich Security Police, stood
rigidly, eyes ahead. He was a hard, fierce man. He would follow the
orders given to him and send those who objected straight to hell.
Hoegl, his aide, stood beside him, trying to emulate his commander,
but he was not cut from the same cloth.

Dr. Werner Haase, the surgeon, leaned against the wall, not from
disrespect but from exhaustion. He held a handkerchief against his
mouth. Droplets of blood showed through, evidence that the tuberculosis which had already claimed one of his lungs was growing
progressively worse. He could no longer stand for more than a few
moments at a time. Even so, Eva knew he was performing surgery
around the clock, under unhealthy conditions in the Chancellery basement. He is out of place among the rest of us, she thought.

Toward the end of the line were four women. Frau Junge and Frau
Christian looked tired, and Else Krüger, Bormann's secretary, who

hated and feared her employer, was visibly nervous. Poor thing, Eva thought, she's like a frightened doe. The fourth woman, Fräulein Manzialy, stood off to the side. At the very end of the line stood Linge, a solid and dependable, though diminutive, anchor.

After a pause, the kind of dramatic hesitation used by the powerful to attract attention, Hitler started down the line, shaking hands with each of them. His expression was cold, each handshake a firm and brief encounter. Eva followed, also offering her hand, but smiling radiantly to everyone except Bormann.

When Hitler reached Frau Junge he said in a soft voice, "Now it has gone so far, it is finished. Good-bye." The woman squeezed his hand tightly.

Eva embraced her. "Give my greetings to Munich, and take my fur coat as a memory," she whispered. "I always liked well-dressed people," she said as an afterthought. Then she added softly, "Tell my parents I love them."

Hitler motioned Günsche aside. "I do not want to become an exhibit in a Russian carnival," he whispered. "When it is done, burn our bodies." Günsche nodded without expression. "We're counting on you, Otto," the Führer added.

The farewells completed, Hitler signaled with a nod of his head for Linge to escort Eva and him back to their rooms. There he motioned Eva inside. She did not look back.

Hitler turned to face Linge. "Old friend, I want you now to join the breakout group."

Linge looked surprised. "Why, my Führer?"

"To serve the man who will come after me." Nobody had any idea what this meant.

The leader of the Third Reich took one final glance at the assemblage and went into the anteroom, closing the fireproof steel door behind him.

Eva had already entered the living room. "Can I have a moment?" she asked in a quiet voice. He dismissed her with a wave of his hand, and she went into the bathroom and turned on the tap.

Suddenly there was a noise at the door and it flew open. The shrewlike Magda Goebbels charged into the room and pleaded with him to change his mind. "You must escape," she shrieked. "Your people need you!"

Hitler looked past her to Günsche, who had tried but failed to keep her out. "I don't want to speak to her anymore," Hitler said softly. Günsche grabbed the woman tightly by the arm and pulled her out of the room, slamming the heavy door behind them.

Hitler went into the living room and sat down stiffly on the blue couch. He picked up the pistols, checking to be sure that each was loaded and ready. Next he carefully opened the metal tubes and extracted thin glass ampules filled with cyanide. He heard the tap water shut off, and Eva entered the room, shaking her head slightly as women do to set their hair. She sat down to his left and pulled her legs up under her, as she did when she sat in front of the fire at the Berghof. She would miss the mountains of Bavaria.

Hitler held out one of the ampules to her and she took it delicately, holding it between polished fingernails. He pointed to the smaller pistol on the table, a Walther 7.35, but she shook her head. He understood; women preferred poison.

At this moment she expected him to step into his private character and say something soothing and endearing. In private he was always like a sensitive child seeking her approval. "Bite down," he said without emotion. "There's no pain."

She felt disappointment, but fought for control. She held the ampule in front of her mouth and watched her husband. He picked up the cyanide ampule with his left hand, manipulating it with ease. Eva's mouth dropped open. In recent months his left arm had become useless, often shaking and twitching beyond his control; now it seemed as healthy as the other. With his right hand he picked up the larger pistol, a Walther 7.65, and cocked the hammer. He held the ampule near his lips and nodded, not looking at her.

She drew a deep breath, said "My Führer" in her soft voice and bit down sharply, crushing the ampule between her teeth. Immediately she pitched forward, her arm flying out to knock a small flower vase from the table in front of the couch.

Hitler stared for a moment, amazed at the speedy effect of the poison, then put down his pistol and the ampule, and pushed Eva back onto the couch. Untying his shoes, he stepped out of them and went quickly into the bedroom, to a spot underneath the ceiling light in the corner. Using his cane, he tapped the unit. A corner of the light lifted and a face stared down through the grillwork. "Hurry," Hitler said nervously to the face above as he moved out of the way.

The light disappeared up into the hole it created. Two thick legs in camouflage leggings swung down through the hole; then a body landed heavily but quietly beside him. Hitler clutched Brumm's arm tightly, but the soldier twisted away and directed his attention back to the ceiling.

"All right," the colonel ordered. Two more legs appeared. Brumm caught them and guided them down to the floor.

Hitler and the Alpha stared at each other. For each it was like standing in front of a full-length mirror. "I am honored, my Führer," the man whispered. Hitler did not reply. He reached for a chair, put it under the hole in the ceiling and began trying to climb out.

The colonel pushed the Alpha into the living room and guided him to the couch.

"Sit," he ordered as he picked up the larger pistol. "Put on the shoes." The man's hands shook too badly to tie the laces, so Brumm knelt and tied them for him. From where he stood, he could see that Hitler was already into the hole, his legs dangling.

The Alpha stared at Eva Braun's lifeless body. "She's beautiful." The colonel did not answer him as he put the cyanide ampule into the man's hand. "Bite down."

The man wavered, his eyes widening with fear. Suddenly the enormity of what was happening struck him and he hesitated. The colonel saw panic flood into the Alpha's eyes, but he had dealt with this sort of fear before. He put the barrel of the pistol against the man's forehead and repeated his order.

Tears formed in the Alpha's eyes, but he put the ampule between his teeth. "Bite, you bastard," the colonel said coldly.

The man closed his eyes tightly and bit down, emitting a high-pitched squeal at the same moment. As he bit into the ampule, the colonel lowered the barrel to the Alpha's mouth and fired. The bullet completely obliterated his front teeth, tore away the back of his head, and splattered the top of the couch and the wall behind with sticky clusters of brain tissue and blood. The body lurched heavily to the right, and the colonel dropped the pistol to the floor, just under the body's right hand. Brumm noticed that a piece of bullet or bone, he wasn't sure which, had exited at the right temple, leaving a small wound that trickled dark blood. Less than four minutes had passed since Magda Goebbels had been removed from the anteroom.

Quickly, Brumm ran back into the bedroom, moved the chair back to its place against the wall and leaped to catch the grille frame above. Stabilizing himself like a gymnast, he swung his legs back and forth to gain momentum, then thrust himself upward, driving himself higher as he gained purchase, finally pulling himself up into the narrow metal ventilation shaft with a single fluid motion. He backed up, reached forward and lowered the light unit into place. Satisfied that it was secure, he put his cheek on the metal and consciously began an effort to slow his breathing, to calm his racing heart and prevent hyperventilation.

For a few minutes it was quiet below; then Brumm could hear the steel door opening. People entered the death room.

He heard Bormann grunt. "Get the doctor."

Moments later: "They are both dead. Get the certificates."

Bormann again: "Get blankets. We need something to cover him."

"Everything's ready in the garden," another voice reported. It sounded like Günsche.

There was no further conversation. In relative quiet the bodies were removed to the Chancellery garden above, to be burned in accordance with the Führer's final instructions.

After there was silence for a while, Brumm looked across at Hitler for the first time. "It is done. Now we wait," he told his leader.

Suddenly Hitler's eyes widened and he began to thrash around, kicking gently at first, but progressively more wildly, making the metal walls of the shaft ring like a huge kettledrum. Brumm reached over and grabbed the Führer by the arm, squeezing with such strength that the pain overrode the cause of the panic.

"Rats," Hitler whispered excitedly, looking behind him.

The colonel tightened his grip. "My Führer," he said coldly, "we have lived the free life of the wolf, but for the moment our brother in arms *is* the rat."

Hitler glared at the colonel, hatred filling his eyes. A pool of clear spittle formed at the corner of his mouth and fell slowly to the sheet-metal floor of the tunnel that hid them from the world.

▶10 APRIL 30, 1945, 3:30 P.M.

There was a single shot, a muted pop that was barely audible through the thick steel doors that separated the cramped private quarters of Adolf Hitler and his new wife from the rest of the subterranean Führerbunker.

The good-byes had been said; it was over. Hitler had given his

Anton Graff portrait of Frederick the Great to his personal pilot, Gruppenführer Hans Baur, with the directive that the flier carry it to safety. Despite many pleas—the final one coming from the over-wrought Magda Goebbels, wife of the minister of propaganda—the Führer had refused to attempt to escape. If Berlin could not hold against the invading Russians, he preferred death to life. He feared capture more than death, though he shared this fear with few. The Russians, he was certain, would display him in a cage, like a common animal. He would not risk it. Berlin was falling. He would go down with it. His decision was irrevocable.

Fifteen meters underground, the bunker's five-meter-thick concrete walls shuddered from the rain of artillery shells above. Less than sixteen square meters of Berlin remained under German control, and even in this final German pocket, Russian snipers were on the rooftops while larger bodies of Soviet infantry smashed relentlessly toward the Chancellery, fighting the battle one building at a time.

Outside the steel door, Sturmbannführer Heinz Linge and Otto Günsche stood guard silently, their faces impassive. They had their orders from their chief and they knew their duty. Nobody was to be admitted for ten minutes—what the Führer had described as a "decent interval." Joseph Goebbels hovered nearby, a deformed gnome who had masterminded the Nazi propaganda machine and helped perpet-uate the Aryan myth, the apotheosis of himself. He smoked nervously, his birdlike head twitching with every inhalation. Martin Bormann, the Reichsleiter who served as secretary of the party, stood steadfast, his arms crossed, a sinister scowl on his face.

Linge checked his watch and nodded to his fellow servant. Günsche opened the steel door, and Goebbels immediately pushed by them into Hitler's anteroom, where he stopped dead in his tracks. Bormann, Linge and Günsche passed by him into the tiny living room beyond. Reichsjugendführer Artur Axmann had arrived too late for the fare-wells, but now he rushed into the scene with the others, his face flushed from having been above ground amid the Russian artillery barrage. His arm stump waved in small circles as he tried to comprehend what had happened.

The two bodies were on the sofa near the back wall. A vase of flowers was on the floor, its water seeping into the carpet. Hitler was at one end of the couch, his body tilted slightly forward, his right hand hanging down over the armrest. His Walther 7.65 was on the floor near his hand. Eva Braun was at the opposite end of the love seat, reclining peacefully, her legs tucked underneath her as she did when-

ever she napped in front of the fireplace at the Berghof. There was
blood streaming from Hitler's mouth, and a smaller wound in the
right temple. The couch was soaking up his blood, and none of the
survivors cared to look too closely. Eva's black dress was wet, her
eyes wide open. There was no apparent wound, but they could smell
the odor of almonds, and there was a slight bluish-gray discoloration
around her lips. Cyanide. Her soft brown leather pumps had been
placed together under the couch.

Bormann and Goebbels gagged from the fumes left by the cyanide
capsules, and covered their faces with handkerchiefs. Günsche stared
at the bodies, then wheeled and strode away. He met Erich Kempka,
Hitler's tiny chauffeur, in the conference area. Earlier Günsche had
ordered Kempka to collect two hundred liters of petrol in jerricans
and bring them to the bunker entrance in the Chancellery garden.
Kempka had argued with him over the phone. He wasn't going to risk
his life trying to get to their fuel cache; it was too dangerous. They'd
have to wait until later in the day, when the Russian gunners paused
to eat or piss or do whatever it was they did in the late afternoon
when the firing stopped. As an alternative, Günsche suggested to Kempka
that he try siphoning what he could from the vehicles in their underground garage. The streets were so clogged that staff cars couldn't get
through any longer, and there was no need for the petrol in them.

"What the hell is going on?" Kempka demanded when he saw the
SS man.

"*Der Führer ist tot*," Günsche said solemnly.

Kempka went immediately to see for himself, but met Linge, who
demanded to know where the petrol was.

"In the garden. One hundred and seventy liters. All we could find."

Brigadeführer Johann Rattenhuber, head of the Reich Security Police detachment for the bunker, arrived after Kempka. Others filtered
in and out of the death room, taking quick looks at the bodies, too
disconcerted or too frightened to look closely or for long. It was the
end.

After some time, Rattenhuber, a practical man with a flair for
decision-making, took over. He instructed the others to take the bodies
up to the garden. Hitler's body was wrapped in a gray army blanket,
leaving the top part of his head visible, but not his face. The Führer's
left arm and legs hung down; his black trousers were the ones he
normally wore with his uniform jacket. One of the bearers wiped
blood from one of his black shoes.

Bormann easily hefted Eva Braun's small body. Her blond hair was in disarray, but she looked more asleep than dead. Linge and Ludwig Stumpfegger, the SS colonel and surgeon, carried Hitler's corpse, with the doctor doing most of the work.

At the foot of the concrete stairs, the tiny Kempka stepped into Bormann's path, blocking his way upward. "I'll take her," he said. Kempka knew that Eva had loathed and feared the Reichsleiter; remembering this, he couldn't stand seeing the man touch her. But she was too heavy for him, and when he stumbled on the stairs, almost dropping her, Günsche and another SS man came to his aid.

The two bodies were taken into the Chancellery garden and placed in a shell hole three meters from the bunker entrance. Günsche folded Eva's arms across her chest and helped douse the bodies with petrol. Kempka moved Hitler's left arm closer to his body. Artillery shells suddenly began to zero in on the area and forced the spectators to withdraw quickly to the protection afforded by the bunker's superstructure. They smoked and fidgeted nervously as they waited for a pause in the shelling. When it came, they continued dumping fuel on the bodies, trying to soak them thoroughly. Eventually the job was completed; the shell hole containing the corpses was afloat in flammable liquid.

They discussed the best way to ignite the funeral pyre. "A grenade," Günsche suggested. But Kempka objected loudly; it would be too brutal and disrespectful of their Führer. As he finished his argument Kempka noticed a rag near an unfolded fire hose. He fetched it for Günsche, who soaked it with petrol. Goebbels, the chain-smoker, produced a book of matches, which he gave to Kempka, who then used them to ignite the rag for Günsche; they all stood back as he lofted it toward the shell hole with a flick of his wrist.

For a moment, time was suspended. They were transfixed by the sight of the burning rag floating slowly up, then fluttering downward. Then the trench ignited with a quiet thump and a plume of black smoke rolled upward like a snake uncoiling.

They watched in silence until Günsche called them to attention. He raised his right arm stiffly and the others followed his lead. "*Heil Hitler*," they said in unison for the final time.

It was done. Adolf Hitler was dead. Ten days after his fifty-sixth birthday, the Führer of the thousand-year Reich smoldered in a makeshift funeral pyre in the war's final battleground.

Well into the evening, Rattenhuber and his men continued to add petrol to the fire. At approximately ten o'clock, the head of the Reich

Security Police told his aide, Captain Schedle, to pick three men he could trust and to bury what remained of the two blackened corpses.

Russian shells were still dropping on the Chancellery area. Schedle and his small detail wrapped the remains in canvas shelter halves and buried them in a nearby shell hole. After they had filled the grave with dirt and mud, the men pounded the earth flat with shovels. Throughout the process they and their officer, like those below in the bunker, had only one thought: escape.

► **11** APRIL 30, 1945, 4:50 P.M.

They stayed in place for a full hour before moving. Brumm wanted to be sure the sounds had ceased in the bunker below them. When he was satisfied that it was safe, he led his charge slowly through the metal tube to where their equipment waited for them. Hitler looked tired.

"From here we have to make a bit of a climb," Brumm said.

"I designed it," Hitler reminded him.

Brumm pushed a pair of scuffed black boots toward the older man. "Put them on." Quickly and succinctly, he explained how they would make the vertical ascent ahead. "I'll lead," he added, and moved into the darkness, his flashlight carving a jiggling path ahead of them.

The climb required a great deal of effort. Though Hitler's condition had been in large part a well-planned act, it had taken a toll. During recent weeks in the bunker he'd had virtually no exercise and his stamina was gone. Brumm was forced to pull him up the vertical wall. When they finally reached the upper level, they settled in at the widened intersection of the blind tunnels. Brumm chewed hard bread as he spread the contents of his kit bag on a small linen towel. Lighting two tallow candles, he held them horizontally to drip wax onto the metal and set them in their drippings. They would give him enough light to work with; he would save the flashlight for more important needs.

The first task was to alter his companion's appearance. The changes had been worked out by Hitler; he reminded Brumm repeatedly that as "Europe's greatest actor" a change in appearance would be an easy matter. He had studied the mysteries and techniques of theatrical makeup and had made numerous sketches to depict how he might look, given different cosmetic modifications. Brumm thought the sketches all looked alike and paid little attention to Hitler's long-winded dissertation on the use of costumes and makeup in Wagnerian opera.

"My hand's still not right," Hitler observed as he held the left arm near a candle. "I've only been off the drugs for a short while. It's getting stronger, but there's been atrophy; in time it will be stronger."

Brumm nodded. "Hold the light," he said. Hitler accepted the flashlight with his right hand and held it under his chin, casting an eerie glow; deep shadows magnified the depressions and wrinkles in his face. Brumm uncapped a small container of concentrated soap, poured a small amount onto the palm of his hand, spit in it, mixed it with his forefinger and rubbed it into Hitler's mustache. When it was properly lathered, he shaved the upper lip clean with a straight razor. Hitler kept his eyes shut while the colonel worked.

The elimination of the mustache produced a surprise. Brumm stared at Hitler's nose; he had never noticed its massive size before. The mustache, a subtle addition that dramatically altered the face, had drawn attention away from it. Perhaps the Führer knew what he was talking about.

Next he rubbed the soap into Hitler's hair. "Trim it back," the Führer instructed.

"No," Brumm said firmly. "We're going to shave it off—all of it." Hitler stared hard at the officer. His shoulders tensed; he seemed to be on the verge of losing his temper, but after a moment he sighed and shrugged, his shoulders relaxing. "You have the razor," he said.

When the job was done, the old Adolf Hitler was nearly gone. Brumm handed him heavy glasses with gray metal frames, the lenses ground to his precise prescription. The new spectacles made the leader of the Third Reich look like some kind of bird.

There remained other changes to be made. Brumm extracted a thick rolled bandage from his kit and unrolled it. "Go ahead," Hitler commanded, accepting the bandage.

Brumm hesitated.

"What has to be done has to be done," the Führer said. "Delay doesn't change the inevitable. Besides, you have the easy part." He turned his back to Brumm and sat back so that his head was in the colonel's lap. Brumm took a deep breath, tensed his hand, lifted it and drove the stiffened heel of his hand down onto the bridge of the man's nose, crushing the cartilage loudly. Hitler grunted under the blow, and tears streamed from his eyes.

Brumm quickly used the bandage to stem the flow of blood, and within minutes Hitler's face began to swell. Both eyes would blacken and eventually shut. The damage to the nose was extensive. At the point between the eyes, the tissue was flat and broken so that the nose now hung downward at an acute angle and seemed to taper to a point. Had he aimed the blow in an upward direction, the Führer would have been dead, and for a moment he pictured a dead Hitler in his lap.

"How's your breathing?"

"Blood inside. Need to sit up. Hurts," Hitler muttered.

Brumm was worried. Pain was not something his companion was used to, and it looked as if he might have some trouble coping. He was accustomed to having drugs for even the slightest discomfort, and in this situation there could be no drugs. Determination would have to serve as his opiate.

"One task remains," Brumm said.

"Don't do anything else," Hitler said, his voice rattling.

"It may help us later." The colonel pushed up his own sleeve to reveal the underside of his forearm. There was a tattoo, a series of numbers.

Hitler shook his head violently. "No. I forbid it. Absolutely not."

Brumm responded softly. "Outside there is chaos. If the need arises, it may be advantageous for us to be Jews from the camps. It could get us through."

"No, not as a Jew."

Brumm ignored him and took Hitler's arm, told him to keep still and began applying the tattoo, using navy blue ink and a thick needle.

▶ **12** MAY 2, 1945, 12:30 A.M.

Several hundred men and women gathered in the darkness under the low ceiling of the garage that served as a coal-storage area beneath the Chancellery complex. They were soldiers and bureaucrats, drivers and bakers, secretaries and sentries, party officials and clerks—all that remained of the once elite Reich Chancellery Group. They had been trickling into position alone and in small groups since early evening. General Wilhelm Mohnke of the Waffen SS, the bunker troop commander, and Otto Günsche, Hitler's SS adjutant, took responsibility for organizing them.

The plan was to divide into small groups, which would jump off at twenty-minute intervals. Each escape group would cross the street through an underground tunnel, then climb up and make a run across open ground from the Wilhelmplatz to Stadtmitte Station. Neither Mohnke nor Günsche had any clear idea of what awaited them. The Russians were all around, mostly on the roofs with rifles, sniping at virtually everything moving below on the streets. Russian artillery was still coming in, but now it exploded in measured salvos, with an interval between barrages. No longer was there a steady, unrelenting rain of explosives, and this offered the Nazis a glimmer of hope. The basic plan was for each group to find its own way across the river Spree, then move northwest through the suburbs, eventually out of the city and northwest to a rendezvous in a forest near Mecklenburg, some hundred and eighty kilometers northwest of Berlin. The hope was not that they could evade capture completely, but that they might avoid being taken by the Russians. Thus, the route they chose would take them quickly through the three Soviet lines that ringed the city and toward the Western Allies, whose hospitality would be far less harsh than what they could expect from the Russians.

For Unterscharführer Gustav Rudolf of the SS, the escape seemed like a hopeless, idiotic effort. The hundred and eighty kilometers to the rendezvous might as well have been eighty thousand or eighty million. There was no way they could get through. He had a premonition of death, which chilled him and made his mouth dry. The thing he had feared most had finally descended upon him and he cursed his bad fortune. He had spent a terrible month cringing in the cellars of the Chancellery, guarding the final stronghold of the Reich. On the thirtieth he'd seen Hitler and had known from that moment that the end was near. The Führer did not look like his old self, and he had been subdued. Later Rudolf had heard that the Führer had killed himself that same afternoon. The whole situation was a nightmare, and the single force that had held together what was left of Germany was gone. Now he was going to be forced to come to grips with an even greater terror. He'd just as soon wait for capture by the Russians. At least he'd be alive; he could cope with whatever came after that. But he kept his opinion to himself, because it was generally believed that capture would bring immediate execution, especially for any German who had served so close to Hitler. Rudolf was not one to go against the grain. He often considered it, but seldom acted.

As the plan for the escape was being formulated, Rudolf tried his best to arrange to stay behind to provide protection for the hundreds of wounded being left in the Chancellery basement, but his officers—fanatics to the end, he told himself—would not hear of it. They praised his courage and zeal for self-sacrifice, but they wanted him with the escape groups to provide cover for the noncombatants, which included a fair number of women. Had they agreed to his plan, he was going to slip onto a litter among the wounded and pretend that he was one of them. Instead, he was being forced out into the city, where people were still killing one another. It irked him that he had to provide protection for women; females never needed protection. Chancellery life was proof of that; they got what they wanted by spreading their legs, and there was no reason to think that the Russian males would be any less receptive than Germans.

As fate would have it, Rudolf was selected to provide combat cover for the first escape group led by Mohnke and Günsche. It included the four women from Hitler's personal staff, a navy vice admiral, some adjutants from a number of organizations and Hilco Poppen, another guard. Rudolf suspected that Poppen, an independent and contrary sort from the Rhineland, would go his own way as soon as the escape group hit the open air. He toyed briefly with the idea of following him, but gave it up, preferring, as always, the security and anonymity afforded by the larger group.

Rudolf made only one hard decision. If any of the big shots fell during the escape, he'd pick their pockets. For months there had been rumors that the Nazi leaders were putting millions of Reichsmarks into Swiss banks. Surely these people would be carrying large quantities of money and valuables, and if they were killed during the escape, they'd have no need for earthly baubles.

The breakout turned out to be more of a nightmare than Rudolf had even imagined. The smell of dead bodies hung in the dust over the city. Berlin was so destroyed that there were few landmarks left to identify. He couldn't understand how they were going to get through such a wasteland. He decided that looking around was too depressing; instead, he concentrated on keeping low, watching only the footsteps of the person ahead of him, as they wound their way along single file in a low crouch.

By 2:00 A.M. the group was reduced to fifteen survivors. They took a short break in the Französische Strasse Station. Mohnke tried to talk two armed guards of the Berlin Municipal Transport Authority into opening a hatch that led into an under-river tunnel, but the two steadfastly refused; opening the hatch was against regulations and contrary to their superior's orders. "Good, stupid Germans to the end!" Rudolf hissed at them after Mohnke stalked away, furiously slapping his Schmeisser against his leg.

Because the guards wouldn't open the passage under the river, they were forced to backtrack to the Friedrichstrasse Station. Emerging above ground, they saw a tank trap on the Weidendammer Bridge and heard German tanks clanking through the rubble behind them. Idiots! Rudolf thought. The tankers were still moving forward to fight. Good evidence of what sort of creatures volunteered to serve in panzer units, he told himself.

Mohnke managed to locate a flimsy catwalk under the main span of the bridge. They cut their way through heavy coils of concertina wire with field pliers and moved onto the swinging two-meter-wide bridge at double time.

Rudolf almost fell several times, but managed to keep running forward, his adrenaline driving him. Below them, the river was red from the glow of fires; bodies that were black dots floated everywhere. As they reached the midpoint on the catwalk, a sniper opened up on them with a small-caliber rifle. Somebody directly in front of Rudolf grunted loudly and toppled over the side into the river, making a loud splash below. All in the group went to their bellies while the leaders tried to identify the sniper's muzzle flashes in order to get a shot at him.

Even though they were prone, they kept crawling forward. Rudolf could feel his uniform shredding, his knees and elbows bruised and cut by the hard surface of the frail bridge. As he got within sight of the other side, he was struck hard in the helmet. There was no pain, just an incredibly stiff jolt. It felt as if he'd run into something, but when he tried to crawl, his limbs wouldn't respond. One of the others wriggled over to him and leaned down.

"Are you hit?" a voice asked.

Rudolf wanted to say that he was all right, but like his lifeless limbs, his voice failed him. He felt his own urine spill down his thighs, both warming and disgusting him. As he lay there unable to move or speak, somebody stripped off his ammunition belt and rifled his pockets, removing his wallet and ripping the watch off his wrist. Others

crawled over him and left him alone on the bridge over the red water.
An officer robbed me, he told himself, struck by the irony of the act.

He was on his belly, unable to see, unable to move, beginning to
feel sleepy. There was no pain, and he was thankful for that. He'd
known all along that he was going to die during the escape, and now
here he was doing just that. "Goddamn officers!" he shouted in his
mind. "Goddamn Hitler. Goddamn . . . goddamn . . ." Then he passed
out.

▶13 MAY 2, 1945, 5:40 A.M.

The two men remained in the tunnel for the next thirty-six hours,
until early on May 2. That morning, shortly before dawn, Brumm led
the way to the hatch. Hitler wore a Wehrmacht officer's coat; both
his eyes were black and swollen and he was still weak, but even with
the pain and discomfort, Brumm could see that he was excited about
moving. They were both eager to get out.

Brumm entered the hall first, then helped Hitler out. The Führer
stood guard as Brumm replaced and tightened the screws in the hatch.
"Where to?" he asked anxiously.

"Toward the Chancellery." They moved as quickly as they could,
but their pace was slow; Hitler dragged his right leg behind him and
stopped often to catch his breath.

They got out of the area without encountering anyone; the Chancellery seemed abandoned. Near a pile of broken beams, Brumm saw
that the body of the guard he had killed earlier was still where he had
placed it. To the west, near the Tiergarten, there were occasional
exchanges of small-arms fire. They're mopping up, Brumm thought.

The two men crossed the Wilhelmstrasse moments before morning
twilight and cut between several badly damaged government buildings.
Bodies, both Russian and German, were strewn everywhere. On a side
street German soldiers had been stripped and hanged by their necks
from light posts. Their eyeballs bulged and their black tongues stuck
out of their mouths like overcooked and swollen sausages. Hitler did
not look up at them as they passed.

On the street ahead there was a brief volley of small arms, but Brumm did not concern himself with it and Hitler was too weak to do anything but follow closely, still breathing heavily. Eventually they crossed another wide avenue where trees were shattered and lying across the brick street. A German Tiger tank was perfectly balanced upside down on its turret, and a black thing, once human, hung from a hatch with its arms extended, frozen in rigor mortis. At the entrance to an alley they found the body of an old woman. Her skirt had been tied around her neck to harness her arms; her legs and thighs were covered with dried blood, and her mouth and eyes were open wide. In the same alley the severed haunches of a gray horse were stacked against a fire ladder that had been pulled from a building. Swarms of flies were everywhere.

When they reached a green building, Brumm pushed Hitler inside and checked to be sure they had not been followed. He assumed that the rooftops were still filled with Russian snipers and that Russian infantry now controlled the area. "Beard!" he shouted up the stairs.

"Up here with the boys," Rau bellowed.

Brumm moved up the stairs and the two soldiers embraced.

"It went well?"

"So far. What's the situation here?"

"Bad case of nerves, but they're doing better than I expected. The Russians came through last night, but they seemed interested only in those buildings that offered resistance."

"Problems?"

"Only one. Two Russians set up camp down below, inside our door. One of the girls enticed them upstairs and they were eliminated. They used *knives* on them!" He leaned close. "Women seem to like cold steel, eh?" He nudged Brumm and winked.

"The girls eliminated them?"

"Clean as a whistle. Zip-zip, two dead Ivans. Not a sound." He looked over Brumm's shoulder. "Where is he? Down there?"

"Go help him," the colonel said. "He's weak. I don't think he'll be able to make the walk. We'll have to carry him out."

"Wonderful," Beard said sarcastically. "More character building." Brumm smiled. The sergeant major had always referred to difficult missions as character builders.

While Beard descended the stairs, Brumm searched for Waller. She was in a doorway to his right. "Get your people into that room," he said, pointing to the door behind her. She gathered the women quickly, their weapons rattling as they filed past him. Brumm signaled for Waller to join them; she did as she was told, but before she closed the door her eyes caught his and held them. Her look had a message, but he was not in the mood to translate it.

Hitler was shaking badly when he reached the second floor. Beard looked at his colonel and shook his head. Brumm took the man's other arm and helped him along the hall to the door.

"Wait," Brumm ordered the sergeant. "Cover." Beard nodded and slid into a shadow. The SS colonel entered the room. The women were on their knees, obviously tired, their eyes red from lack of sleep. In their tattered clothing they looked like waifs, their youth showing through the caked dirt. They smiled at him, happy to see a friendly face; for the moment they could relax their guard. Brumm saw that psychologically they were in poor shape; for the first time, terror showed in their eyes. "I've brought someone I want you to meet," he told them as he swung open the door.

Hitler's back was to the door, and the sound of it opening caused the Führer to turn awkwardly and stare in puzzlement at the girls on the floor. He shuffled inside with small steps and stood stoop-shouldered in front of them, staring down. Only once did he glance at Brumm, but when no explanation was forthcoming, he looked back at the floor.

"Is this another of your men?" one of the girls asked.

Brumm remained silent, watching. It was said that Hitler had a special power over women. They were said to collapse, even to swoon, under the intensity of his eyes. But the eyes now peering out at the girls were nearly swollen shut and radiated nothing. In only a moment the women lost interest in the old man and slipped back into a daze. Only Waller continued to study him.

"I told you that I had a special mission, a mission of the utmost importance to the Reich." The girls looked at Brumm.

He removed Hitler's glasses. The girls still didn't see it; Brumm was satisfied. He took one of his black gloves, pinched off the end of a finger and held it below the tip of Hitler's nose. The Führer slapped the glove away, sneezed and glared angrily at the colonel.

Waller was the first to understand. She gasped loudly, struggled to her feet, bent her head and said in a barely audible whisper, "My Führer." The other girls looked at her as if she were crazy, then at the man, and jumped to their feet. One of them dropped her Schmeisser loudly to the floor, pushed her hands against her ears and began to sob loudly. A smile emerged on Hitler's face, and he held out his right hand in a gracious gesture. The girls moved to him and held themselves against him. Brumm could see the power exerting itself and was amazed by it.

"Waller." She snapped to attention. "Help Herr Wolf." He let the name sink in. "You," he said to three of the girls, touching them on their heads, "resume your watches and tell Beard to come in."

As the girls gathered their weapons and moved out, Hitler found a place by the wall and was helped to sit down by Waller. Immediately he curled into a ball and went to sleep. Waller covered him with a curtain from the flat.

When Beard entered, Brumm sat him down beside Waller. "We have a lot to talk about."

The flames of a large fire snapped loudly as they burned unchecked in a nearby building. A lone rifle cracked somewhere in the streets outside.

▶14 MAY 2, 1945, 11:30 P.M.

Vasily Petrov always began at the beginning. While his patterns of thought were fast, his methods of investigation were not. He took his time and paid attention to details—*all* the details. It was not that he tried to do everything by himself. He knew how to delegate, but he always made sure that his subordinates knew exactly what they were supposed to do and the results he expected. Then he checked periodically to be sure that his orders were being followed. It was a matter of control. Over time he had built his staff to four, all of them different in personality but similar in motivation. Each man was fanatically dedicated to the unit's mission, and each of them was physically robust, with great reserves of stamina and the persistence of a well-trained hunting dog.

The four men felt a distant fondness for their leader. He was hard to know, cold and logical in approach and secretive in nature. But whereas their admiration for Petrov the man was somewhat subdued, their respect for Petrov the leader was strong and genuine. Comrade

Petrov was not a demonstrative man, but all of them knew when he was satisfied with their work. They trusted him and learned from him. Yet with all this, they feared him, too, for Petrov—code name, The Berkut—gave no quarter and countenanced no incompetence. To fail meant death; this was the rule of the Special Operations Group.

It was just before midnight on May 2. Petrov and his men moved slowly through what remained of the darkened halls of the Reich Chancellery. Petrov had intended to reach this destination earlier, but after nearly being caught in the mine ambush, they had been pinned down by stubborn German civilians—old men and adolescents with automatic weapons and stick grenades—and had been forced to wait until an infantry unit arrived to help them eliminate the opposition. Petrov loathed the delay, but he accepted it. His men were fully capable of doing the job, but to have committed them to it might have cost lives, and these were reserved for a higher need.

They entered the Chancellery rubble from the north end, through a shattered window frame. They climbed a pile of stones and jumped into what had once been the lavish interior of the building. They had been told by Soviet intelligence that Berlin was entirely under Russian control, but they had seen for themselves that there remained pockets of resistance, and in making their way into the Chancellery, they were cautious. The Chancellery, they had been told, had been taken by their military comrades during the early hours of May 2. Now Petrov was intent on finding some kind of Soviet military command post. The Special Operations Group was eager to begin its work. Officially they would have no role in the investigation to come—at least not in the work that the Russian SMERSH units would perform. Their mandate was quite different.

On the second floor of the Chancellery, in a large hall the Nazis had called the Blue Room, they found a temporary army control center. Nearly a hundred soldiers were in the room, most of them asleep. A few stood in small groups talking quietly; others were seated on wooden ammunition boxes or working at tables made from doors. Most of the light in the area was supplied by crude pitch torches or flashlights. Three or four large fires were built on smooth spots cleared of debris. Petrov studied the collection of people for a moment, then approached a group of officers near the south end of the hall. "What unit is this?" Petrov inquired.

"Who wants to know?"

"Petrov, Special Operations Group—Moscow." He let the last word sink in.

"Seventy-ninth Rifle Corps, Fifth Shock Army," one of the officers said proudly.

"Where is the number one Nazi war criminal?" Petrov asked stiffly. His men nudged one another and smiled. It had begun: no foreplay, no small talk, right to the target. The Berkut was aloft, searching for its prey.

"Who?"

"Hitler. Where is he?"

"Dead. That's what the Nazis said on the radio," one of the officers said.

"Where is the body?"

The officers shrugged.

"There is a bunker under this building. Have you located the bunker?"

"Anybody know anything about a bunker?" one of the officers called out to the group. Again they all shrugged. A couple of them laughed. Who was this bizarre little stranger?

"I was in the basement," one of them said. "It's filled with wounded, four or five hundred of them. It smells."

"Have you moved the wounded? Have you taken their names yet? What has been done?"

"Nothing," the senior officer, a thick-necked colonel, said incredulously. "We've just fought our way across a thousand miles, and now we're going to take the night off. The basement under here is crisscrossed with tunnels. Seems like all the government buildings are connected underground. No doubt those damned Nazis have left us lots of booby traps. We'll organize ourselves tomorrow when it's light and sweep it clean. As for the wounded Nazi bastards the others left behind, they can wait, too. After all, they're only Nazis. My men are going to sleep tonight. I am Ashiroff. I command here."

"I am Petrov. Come, Colonel, I want to speak to you in private."

As the two walked off to a corner of the darkened hall, Petrov's men grinned expectantly while their leader showed the colonel a document. In seconds the pair was back; the colonel's attitude had changed dramatically. "Georgi," he shouted. "Roust the men. I want a perimeter around this building. I want a man in every possible exit, both above and underground. The prisoners in the basement are to be taken care of immediately. First find out who they are, then get them to an aid station. Records are to be kept of where each of them is taken. Yuri, you see to the prisoners. You're responsible for the list. Alexi, get your men into the basement. All of you listen to me," he shouted nervously to his men and officers. "Be alert, and when Comrade Petrov here asks for help, give it to him. Go!"

The group disbanded with a rush. The officers went among the sleepers, rousing them. In less than five minutes no more than a dozen people were left in the huge room.

"Do you have a scout team that can be assigned?"

The colonel nodded. "Several."

"I want the best one," Petrov said.

"They're all the best," the colonel snapped defensively. "The ineffective ones died along the way."

Petrov pursed his lips. "Then get me the one that had the fewest number of replacements."

When the twelve-man scout team arrived, Petrov briefed them on what he expected. Then the twelve, Petrov and his four men descended into the basement of the Chancellery while the Soviet colonel went off to take care of his duties.

Standing amid the hundreds of wounded who were packed together tightly, Petrov removed his revolver from its holster, cocked the weapon, walked to the center of the room and stood so that all could see him. Silence crept over the Germans; even the critically wounded, sensing danger, stopped moaning. "Where is Hitler?" Petrov said slowly in perfect German.

There was no answer. He repeated the question. Still no answer. He looked around the assemblage and pointed to a tall, gaunt sergeant whose arms were wrapped in soiled bandages. Petrov motioned the man to step forward.

The German stood at attention. "Where is Hitler?" Petrov asked again.

"I don't know," the soldier said defiantly.

Petrov raised the revolver to the man's heart. "Where is Hitler?" he repeated. The German shook his head angrily. Petrov fired a bullet through his heart. The impact sent the body backward onto a litter, and a wounded man shrieked as the body fell on top of him.

Petrov pointed to another soldier, who came forward trembling. "Where is Hitler?" Petrov's voice was still quiet, controlled.

The man tried to respond, but he was too frightened. He began to cry, begging for mercy. Again the revolver came up slowly and exploded, sending the German soldier backward to the floor near the first one.

Petrov selected another soldier, but before he could ask his question, an older man shuffled forward. He wore a surgeon's smock covered with blood, most of it dried.

"I am Haase," the stooped man said wearily. "Doktor Werner Haase. All of these men know that Hitler is dead. The radio said he died in combat. He did not. He killed himself in the Führerbunker. I have been here the whole time and I know this to be the truth. Now, if you're going to shoot me, do it quickly or let me return to my work."

"Show me," Petrov said, ignoring the doctor's bravado.

"Show you what?"

"Hitler."

"You mean Hitler's body?"

"Show me."

"They burned it," Haase answered. "There's nothing left to see. Just ashes, and I don't know where they are. You've come too late to get Hitler."

"Show me," Petrov insisted, his voice still perfectly even. Haase shrugged and limped across the room. Petrov and the other Russians followed.

The doctor walked with great difficulty. He stopped often to cough; he had a deep wet hack. "Tuberculosis," he explained after an extended coughing spell. It took them several minutes to reach their destination. Haase stopped before a thick steel door and stepped aside. "The bunker is in there," he said, pointing.

"How many exits?"

"Counting this?" Petrov nodded. "Four."

The Russians left a scout to guard the door and moved down into the first level of the bunker. Even Haase was surprised to find that the bunker generator was still operating, providing light and stale air. Petrov showed no interest in anything but the exits. At each one he posted a sentry.

In a corner of the lower bunker, Haase showed him a flight of stairs. "This leads to an unfinished tower above; it's not really an exit." Petrov posted a sentry anyway. What you failed to do in a crisis was invariably what you should have done. The Berkut did not make such mistakes.

With the area secured, Petrov ordered a search of the many cubicles on the upper and lower levels of the bunker. While his men deployed, the leader of the Special Operations Group examined a partitioned section of the main corridor in the lower level. The body of a general lay on a worn red carpet runner. The man had a bullet wound in the head; powder burns near the wound told Petrov that it was self-inflicted. Several empty whiskey bottles were on the floor; their necks had been broken off, as if someone had been in a hurry to get at their contents. Glass fragments were scattered around the area. Petrov carefully gathered the debris into small orderly piles with the toe of his boot. The men took thirty minutes to make their search and report back. They had found the bodies of six children: five girls and a boy. Petrov examined them. When he was finished, he had the men put the dead general with the children. Later the doctor called Haase identified the dead man as General Krebs.

After the body had been removed, Petrov sat down with his men. The four extracted small, tattered red notebooks and scribbled and ate field rations as he talked.

"*One*. I want to know the name of every person who was in this area during the past two weeks, with special emphasis on the seventy-two-hour period before the alleged suicide. This includes women. I can smell perfume here, and those children would not have been here without some kind of female escort. Construct the working list from the known. Example: we know the doctor was here. Have him name every person he can remember. As we locate others, repeat the process. Use one witness to corroborate the next witness, and so forth."

Petrov paused while the men made notes. "Focus first on those for whom we have multiple entries," he continued. "Divide your lists into categories. The general can be the first on our list of known dead. Another category will be for those in our custody. Put the doctor's name on that list. Then there will be a group that is missing, but in whom we are interested because they were here at the end and may have information of use to us. We will provide updates of the list of the missing to our military field commanders and security personnel every twelve hours. Instruct them in the proper way to secure, screen and transfer these prisoners. Emphasize that as soon as they find the people we want to interrogate, they are to notify us directly and immediately—anytime, night or day." His dark eyes flashed emphasis. "They are to be isolated from other German prisoners until they are under our control. All records of these transfers and these prisoners' existence are to be given over to us," Petrov said. "No exceptions.

"*Two*. We need facilities. Confiscate a building with two or more floors to house the special prisoners. They are to be isolated. Use our authority to establish internal and external security. There are to be no German-speaking Soviet troops inside this area, only us.

"*Three*. On the ground floor of the facility I want a clerical section established. Use German civilians, females only. No Russian-speaking Germans.

"*Four*. Each prisoner is to be interrogated immediately upon arrival at our security section. A stenographer should be used, and each interrogating officer is to keep his own notes as well." He paused and added, "Write neatly." His men smiled at the admonition. "The transcript and notes are to be put in an individual folder. Each folder is to be placed on my desk, in the order in which the prisoners are interrogated. Each folder should also contain—as the top document—a statement detailing precisely where, how, when and by whom the prisoner was taken. I want the circumstances and the names of those who were with him, along with all the names of those who captured him. Later those soldiers who made the capture will be interrogated, and their statements will be checked against those of the prisoner. Remember, *all* particulars are to be included in these capture reports; nothing is too small to omit, nothing too mundane to ignore. During the initial interviews you are to pay special attention to the names of other Nazis who were in the area at the time of capture.

"*Five*. The prisoners' medical needs should be attended to immediately and they are to be well fed. They are not to be abused physically, although you may use your own creativity and initiative in order to obtain any psychological advantage.

"*Six*. The prisoners are to have no contact with anyone outside our group. If anyone from outside tries to make contact, capture them, keep them and inform me of such developments immediately.

"*Seven*. To repeat what was said earlier: when prisoners are passed to us by other units, there is to be no record of the transfer. These prisoners no longer exist once they are under our control." Petrov paused for effect here.

"*Eight*. During the initial inspection, be especially vigilant for concealed implements of self-destruction. Poison capsules are most likely.

"*Nine*. The prisoners are to be kept in darkness between interrogations. There is to be no light except when they are taking their meals.

"*Ten*. When Tempelhof is normalized for air traffic, I want three transports fueled and ready at all times. Further, whenever we launch an aircraft from this end, I want a replacement launched simultaneously from Moscow."

Petrov looked at his men. He seldom invited questions; if they had them, he expected them to ask. They were supposed to be professionals.

There were no questions. The tiny Russian did not exhort them to do their duty; they knew it well. They also knew the price for failure: death. To be selected for duty in the Special Operations Group was a distinct honor. Such duty brought elevated pay, better living conditions when they weren't in the field and, more important, extraordinary power. Petrov selected his own men. Since its formation nine men had served in the unit. Of the current four, only Rivitsky remained from the original group.

Despite the group's harsh schedules and months in the field, Rivitsky remained fat, with a baby's face, pink flesh and no facial hair. He looked innocent, the kind of man whose appearance disarmed the unknowing, and was fluent in a dozen languages. A forty-year-old widower, he was as ruthless and clever as Petrov. He was a former detective who could philosophize with academics and learned clerics, deal with scientists on the most arcane technical subjects and outdrink the coarsest of Soviet foot soldiers. Rivitsky was Petrov's administrator, a meticulous man who could quickly and efficiently organize any task, no matter how complex.

At twenty-seven, Gnedin, a Muscovite, was the youngest member of the group. Tall and thin, he was the medical expert of the team. He had been trained at the McGill University Medical School in Montreal, and Petrov had recruited him from the staff of a small sanitarium near Moscow that provided medical care to the party's elite. He had a keen mind and exceptional powers of observation.

Ezdovo was the most peculiar member of the Special Operations Group. He was a native Siberian, an outdoorsman with the eyesight of a bird of prey and excellent deductive skills. There was no machine he couldn't fix, and he was an experienced pilot. He had the least formal education of any of them, but in survival instincts he surpassed them all. In the field Ezdovo's skills carried them. He was the quietest of the group, by nature a loner.

The final member was Bailov, the Uke. Like all of them, he spoke several languages. He was muscular, a former athlete who had enjoyed national fame and who, from time to time, was recognized because of his physical accomplishments. What Bailov contributed to the group was unlimited energy. Whatever the task, he would go at it until it was done.

All of them were members of the Communist party and all were devoted to Petrov and his master, Joseph Stalin, to whom they referred irreverently as the Big Boss.

Instructions laid out, Petrov dismissed them, asking only Rivitsky to remain behind. Gnedin, Ezdovo and Bailov left to pursue their assigned tasks. As always when they were alone, Petrov showed no outward signs of intimacy with his cherubic colleague, though Rivitsky felt no discomfort with his superior's formality.

"I can feel him," Petrov said.

"We'll try for the corpse in the morning," Rivitsky said.

"Yes, in the morning at first light," Petrov said distantly. "But he's not here."

▶15 VASILY PETROV

Petrov was born in a small village in the Carpathian Mountains in the extreme southwestern Ukraine. Physically he was an unimposing but distinctive figure. Of slight stature, almost frail, his hair was thick, coal-black and cropped closely, and he had a dark complexion.

Like most men, Petrov was in part a product of his environment. His corner of the Ukraine contains some of the wildest terrain and most savage inhabitants of the USSR. Historically the area has been a melting pot for refugees and extremists from Eastern Europe, Turkey and the Muslim countries to the southeast. In the days of Petrov's youth, the inhabitants of the area were predominantly Roman Catholic, and there were many churches, but despite this Roman influence and considerable efforts of priests to make the inhabitants change their ways, strong beliefs in magic persisted. Pagan rituals were practiced and honored by even the most devout parishioners. It is also a region where feuds between families are measured in generations, where peasant farmers scratch without reward at an unyielding, sterile earth, where hunters and woodsmen live alone in the forests with hermits and bandits. In this land sons are treasured, while daughters are sold for profit. The infant mortality rate remains even today among the highest on earth, a full 33 percent higher than the Soviet Union average.

Petrov was a product of all this, but he was unique in other respects. The term "photographic memory" is one used too generously, but his memory was prodigious; if the phenomenon exists, Petrov was one of its rare possessors.

Physically, only Petrov's eyes were remarkable: like his hair, they were black, intense and menacing, set close together over a thin bridge of nose. His gaze, combined with his soft, almost feminine voice, immediately made people uneasy. Socially he was unvarnished; he talked little and went immediately to the point.

Petrov was a man sensitive to time, driven to accomplish each task as fast as possible, employing every tool at his disposal to that end. During interrogations he gathered information dispassionately, reacting neither positively nor negatively to the testimony of his subjects. He was renowned for his thoroughness, going over and over the same ground, day in and day out, always driving deeper and relentlessly for more information. When necessary, he used drugs on prisoners; he also employed hypnotism with astonishing results. While he never tortured his subjects himself, he consented to the use of outside experts if all else failed.

Petrov was "born" in the party sometime during the 1930s, when he was in his early forties. It was rumored that he had played a role in the assassination of Trotsky in Mexico City in August 1940. Indeed, some sources identified him as the planner of the event; certainly he had both the contacts and the reputation to warrant such speculation. Since he had first surfaced in Moscow, he was always identified with the periphery of the intelligence and security branches of the central Soviet government.

When Hitler launched Operation Barbarossa against the Soviets, Petrov was assigned to a small, elite branch in the NKGB, reporting directly to Stalin and charged with a single mission. For weeks, Soviet intelligence agents and reconnaissance flights had shown Hitler's Wehrmacht massing along Russian borders across an incredibly wide front. There had been more than five hundred overflights by German aircraft, and in the days just before June 22 the overflights had attained massive proportions. There was positive identification of more than a hundred newly built airstrips, all less than a hundred kilometers from the borders. Even though there was convincing evidence of an estimated buildup of more than three million German soldiers, military reports and pleas through channels had gone unheeded by Stalin, who continued to insist that Hitler could be trusted. The Russian leader had been adamant from the first moment he'd been told of the buildup that no Russian soldier was to take any action that might be interpreted by the Germans as provocative. He had a treaty with Hitler; the Austrian had given him his word.

Three days after the invasion began, Petrov was summoned to a meeting in a small room deep in the Kremlin. The walls were lined with shelves of books, all leather-bound and hand-stitched, many of them priceless, most of them never opened by the current tenant. The air was foul with cigarette smoke and there were fresh tea stains on a light-colored throw rug. Maps and charts cluttered the floor in no apparent order. Outside in the corridor, Petrov had found generals with red epaulets and Asian guards with green tunics milling around, getting in one another's way, while they waited for orders. The Germans had charged across the Bug River and established a battle line that stretched more than fifteen hundred miles from the Baltic to the Black Sea. Reports from the front were fragmentary and garbled, but it was clear that three large spearheads of German armor were advancing toward major Russian cities. More than two thousand Soviet aircraft had been destroyed on the ground by the Germans during the first hour of the invasion, and now the Nazis had free rein because of superior air cover. Tens of thousands of Russian soldiers and civilians were already dead or captured; dozens of cities and towns were burning.

Sitting at a small octagonal table of dark wood, Stalin doodled with a goose-feather quill on a sheet of crisp yellow vellum. Petrov was impassive as the Russian leader sketched the head of a wolf, then retraced the outline over and over until it blurred and was obliterated. The only light in the room, which came from a small, hissing kerosene lantern on the desk, reflected off the black onyx inlay in the desk. Finally Stalin turned to face Petrov. He carefully folded the vellum and tucked it into a jacket pocket, buttoning it after the paper was safely stowed. There were dark bags under his bloodshot eyes; his silver-tipped hair looked wet and greasy. His oversize head, sitting on his tiny but muscular body, looked larger than it was and gave him a grotesque appearance.

"The bastard lied," the supreme leader of the Soviets whispered, his voice menacing. "A lie. That fucking Nazi bastard lied to me; he told me he would honor the treaty for a thousand years; he said Germany and Russia were bound inexorably. And I listened to him; I believed him! He even called me *Soso,* and I was touched by his gesture. My family called me that when I was a boy, and I let that Nazi swine call me that! I never want to hear that word again."

"Our army needs orders, comrade," Petrov said.

"Fuck the army!" Stalin roared, his eyes bulging. "Hitler is all I care about. He calls himself the Wolf. The slinking, stinking, lying wolf. I *know* about wolves! The wolf kills sheep. It runs from common dogs and rolls in its own shit." The Russian leader was shaking, trembling, kicking at the maps and papers on the floor, hurling them into dark corners. "So this is how he wants it: Wolf against Bear. Napoleon came and learned the lesson. Now this Nazi wolf comes, this Austrian maniac. I know now, I know. *I understand the game.*"

"Comrade Stalin?"

"The game," Stalin repeated, his voice softening again. "Don't you see? It's me he wants. I've seen his kind before. Here. I have their bones and their fathers' bones, and their sons'; now I'll have his. You want my orders? Find him. Bring him to me. Alive."

Henceforth Petrov's orders came directly from Stalin, with whom he met periodically to discuss his progress. As befitted his mission, the little Ukrainian was given supreme power, authority and autonomy. He pursued his mission with zeal, engaging the entire Nazi Propaganda Ministry of Joseph Goebbels in what is now known in modern intelligence circles as "disinformation."

Hitler feared capture by the Russians more than any other fate. He believed that the Russians would take him to Moscow and put him on display like an animal in a zoological exhibit. The fear was not unfounded. Stalin used Petrov to feed this plan to Hitler through well-placed tips in Berlin itself. This information was disseminated in such a way that it would be sure to reach Hitler's ears from impeccable sources. Petrov and Stalin wanted Hitler to know what was waiting for him; their hope was that it would panic him.

Petrov did not fear that his efforts would drive Hitler to suicide. His psychological profile of the German leader, built in the same way that the Allies constructed theirs, indicated that the leader of the Third Reich, while threatening suicide from time to time because of setbacks during his climb to political power, had never made a genuine attempt. Hitler, the Russian was certain, was all talk, an actor well versed in using his own behavior to create calculated impressions and perceptions. The Russian profile showed that the behavior Hitler had exhibited time and again was that of fleeing from conflicts he could not win. Petrov believed that this was precisely what Hitler would do when the Third Reich collapsed.

In the early 1940s American psychiatric experts interviewed several doctors who had treated Hitler as a patient and arrived at a different conclusion. The OSS shared the profile with the Russians, and Stalin brought the report to the attention of Petrov. It listed several possible outcomes for Hitler, with the most likely being suicide. Petrov rejected the report out of hand. Hitler was first and foremost a coward and therefore a survivor, he believed. The man would try to escape, and it was Petrov's task to intercept or prevent such flight.

Petrov and his unit were with Marshal Zhukov's armies as they battered their way from the Oder River to Berlin in April 1945. The Americans—in fact, all the Western Allies—believed that at this time Hitler was in the mountains of the Obersalzberg in what the Nazis called the Alpine Redoubt. Eisenhower's G-2 was so convinced of this that it was a major factor in the Allied decision to delay a final assault on Berlin; instead they sent their armies across the southern half of Germany to cut off the mountains where Hitler was thought to be.

In December 1944, when the Germans launched their "Watch on the Rhine," the desperate operation the Allies called the Battle of the Bulge, Petrov and his men were in the Obersalzberg area in southeast Germany, investigating the mountainous region for evidence of any buildups. In the absence of such characteristic German preparation, Petrov concluded that the Alpine Redoubt was no more than a red herring, painstakingly and expertly created by Goebbels to divert and divide the resources of the invading armies. Stalin was so informed by his Berkut, and the decision was made to undertake the final drive on Berlin. While Petrov did not know precisely where Hitler was, he knew where he was *not*. The Führer liked to call himself Europe's greatest actor, and this self-image demanded center stage; center stage, Petrov reasoned, was Berlin.

Stalin supported Petrov. In fact, he did much more. He urged the Allies to push into the mountains and gave them false intelligence reports to support their belief that Hitler was in the Obersalzberg. It may have been on the basis of this false evidence that Stalin was able to work out an agreement with Eisenhower that the Allied forces would press no closer to Berlin than the Elbe River, some seventy kilometers to the west of the city. Meanwhile the Russians would advance all the way to the Nazi capital and smash it once and for all. In any event, Stalin wanted Berlin in payment for what the Nazis had wreaked upon the Motherland.

►16 MAY 3, 1945, 7:00 A.M.

The sky was lighter, but the passing of darkness did not cheer Rudolf; he still felt terrible. He moaned and rolled over, wondering if today he would have the courage and the opportunity to move out of his hiding place.

The morning before, he had awakened with his legs hanging off the footbridge. Grabbing desperately at a vertical support, he had clawed his way back to safety. Ahead of him lay his helmet with a dent several centimeters deep. He had been hit, but it had saved him. He'd never curse it again. There had been a haze and he thought it must be dawn. The others were gone. Fires burned as far as he could see. Landmarks were gone; bodies bumped against the shoreline below like beans in a soup bowl. His watch and wallet had disappeared. Behind him he had heard automatic weapon fire, and instinctively he had scrambled forward and fallen down an iron stairwell to the ground below the bridge on the far bank of the river. He had struggled to his knees, trying to recover his mind, but was nearly paralyzed by fear. Another volley had sent him forward into a massive clutter of rubble. He had kept moving until he lost his balance and fell into an opening between overturned slabs of concrete. Rolling under their protective shadow, he had curled up like a fetus and stayed through the day and night.

During the previous afternoon Rudolf had noticed that the artillery shelling had ceased. There remained the muted reports of small-arms fire, but nothing close; there seemed to be some kind of cease-fire, a halt in the fighting. The breakout groups had talked incessantly about Wenck's army coming to relieve Berlin; perhaps he had gotten through and driven the Ivans back!

His head was clearer now. He began to feel hunger, a sure sign that he was on the mend. But it was too soon to leave his hiding place. Even if Wenck had reached the city, the Germans couldn't have cleared out the Russians so fast. Today it was curiously quiet, the silence broken only by the sound of fires and an occasional shot. He peeked out of his hiding place under some concrete slabs from time to time, but there were no people about and this unnerved him. He needed food, but something more powerful inside him kept him where he was, and soon he was asleep again.

He was awakened by voices. They seemed to be some distance away, by the river's edge. He listened. The voices were getting closer. Russians! He began clawing at the soft earth, trying to clear a deeper hiding place under the slabs. Within seconds he heard the voices only a few meters away. He couldn't tell how many were in the group, but there were males and females and their conversation was animated, almost playful. And they were out in the open, not hiding! That goddamned Wenck had *not* arrived; the Soviets had taken the city. That was why the shooting had tapered off; their work was done.

Now Rudolf felt fear and despair as never before. Death now seemed a certain fate. Scuttlebutt said that in East Prussia the Red Army had run over civilian refugees with tanks. Women and their babies had been shot. Several German soldiers had been crucified— an irony that gave birth to the saying that the Ivans not only had Western allies but were trying to recruit God as well.

Rudolf had no knowledge of the Russian language and it was foul to his ear, but he recognized drunks when he heard them. It sounded as if the invaders were settling in; he heard their weapons and gear clatter against the rocks. He looked around desperately for an escape route, but his legs were too weak to lift him. His rock pile was under the Pichelsdorf Bridge, a protected area. No wonder the Russians had decided to pause.

After a while the loud talk subsided and Rudolf heard footsteps. Above him, on a ledge, he could see two sets of calf-high black leather boots. The pairs of boots faced each other for a long time; then they stepped down a level and sat down. Both intruders wore heavy trousers, shirts and soft hats, and for a moment Rudolf was confused when they began to wrestle. They were going to fight! He cringed.

As quickly as the wrestling began, it stopped, and one of the intruders began to undress. Rudolf understood. A woman! The two Russians were going to . . . My God! he thought. They were no more than three meters away, perhaps only a meter above him. If they looked up from their passion, they couldn't miss seeing him. He tried to curl up even smaller and to push back into the shadows of his hiding place.

Obviously the pair was not looking for Germans; they had a more basic diversion in mind. The woman undressed quickly, spread her clothes on a flat rock, lay on her back and beckoned to her partner by lifting her thick legs, as if she were on the verge of delivering a baby. The man, whose upper half Rudolf could not yet see, reached down and handed her a flask. She took a long pull; the fluid ran down her chin. As the man stepped out of his pants she turned over on all fours and spread her legs slightly. He knelt beside her. They both grunted and laughed as he entered her from behind.

Rudolf was as fascinated as he was frightened. He'd seen stag films before, but never had he witnessed the act personally as a spectator. Unbelievably, he felt himself becoming aroused as the man rammed away; the woman kept laughing and urging him on in some sort of guttural cadence, barking at him in their barbaric language. He was amazed at how long they kept going. After what seemed an interminable time, the man withdrew, then jumped down to within arm's reach of Rudolf and scooped up water from the river to pour over himself. As he did so the woman kept talking to him. She was lying on her side, her small breasts hardly moving as she shifted. She had a large tangle of black pubic hair that curled up onto her abdomen. Rudolf stared. It was all a bad dream; it occurred to him that he was dead, and that this was Hell.

The dream ended when a gun barrel was suddenly thrust into Rudolf's hiding place, striking him hard on the forehead. A shaggy head with crooked teeth stared at him with a grin, then shouted happily to the woman.

"Out of your hole," the woman ordered in rough German. She was still undressed, but now there was a huge revolver in her hand and it was pointed at Rudolf. Suddenly he felt cold. He tried to move, but couldn't. A hand jerked him out of his crevice, but he remained curled up tightly, hoping for protection. The two Russians stood over him, their weapons pointed down. He was looking directly up between the woman's legs. Opaque strands of semen glistened in her pubic hair. He stared, unable to look away, disgusted with himself, sick to his stomach.

"Ah," the woman cooed. "Look at it, German. Have yourself a good look. In a moment you'll never care again about a woman's organs." Rudolf began to shake as she squatted slowly beside him.

Suddenly she jumped on him, laughing wildly as she wrapped her legs around him. He could hear her squealing with laughter, pushing down hard, jamming his head against the ground. As quickly as she had jumped on him, she cast him off, and a searing pain shot through his groin; then kicks struck him in the ribs. He was already groggy when the woman stood, lifted her boot and drove it into his face. For the second time in a few hours, he felt himself losing consciousness, but this time he did not go all the way under. The pain seemed to be all through his body, and he felt blood pouring from his nose and upper lip. As they pulled him across the rocks like a dead animal, their voices seemed far away. They tried to stand him up, but he fell over.

In front of him, the woman officer stood buttoning her tunic. "Rank and unit," she demanded in her bad German.

When he told her, she raised her eyebrows and shouted to her companion. Then she leaned close to Rudolf and smiled. "Nazi bastard," she said in German, "you're a lucky man." Then she kicked him in the groin again, and he vomited as they shoved him up an embankment toward the street.

▶17 MAY 3, 1945, 11:15 A.M.

Within twenty-four hours of reaching the Reich Chancellery, the Special Operations Group was comfortably installed in a squat gray building, which Rivitsky had commandeered. It had once served as an auxiliary facility of the Reich Health Ministry, and because of its unique architecture had been relatively undamaged during the Soviet assault. The building had two floors above ground and four below, but unlike other Nazi offices in central Berlin, it was not connected by underground tunnels to anything else. It stood as its own island and had been shunned by the Nazis during their last stand.

Rivitsky liked the layout immediately. The ground floor had once housed what appeared to have been some kind of clerical operation. The top floor contained private offices with ample space, and these Rivitsky staked out for the group's private living quarters. Below ground three floors were subdivided into small offices and rooms that could easily be transformed into holding cells. The fourth and lowest underground level, forty meters below the surface, housed a large kitchen and dining area.

By the time Petrov arrived to inspect their new headquarters, Rivitsky had crews of German women cleaning the floors; others were bricking in doorways and modifying the structure to create an escapeproof maze for the prisoners who would soon be housed there. All office furnishings had been removed from the lower floors and replaced by thin Soviet army bedrolls and mess kits. The holding cells were stark, with no windows, and the external security was being installed. "It's an entry and exit maze," Rivitsky explained to his leader. "To be changed at randomly selected times, without predictability. Concertina wire. Some mines linked to ribbons of *plastit* charges. Automatic weapons on all four corners of the building and on towers outside the fence. The guards will be Asiatics who don't speak German. We'll be secure here."

Petrov moved inside. The internal security checkpoint was a narrow room between two sets of steel doors several inches thick that could be opened only from the inside. When new arrivals were ushered into the room, the second set of doors would open only after the first had closed. It was a system Petrov had taught his people, one favored first by the Cheka and later by the NKVD.

The ground floor of the building had two long rows of wooden desks, and pale German women with their hair tied back in buns worked feverishly over typewriters. Wire baskets were already filling with neat stacks of typed pages.

"Our quarters are upstairs," Rivitsky said. "Papers will come up by pneumatic tube. We'll handle our own paper flow."

"The personnel?"

"Germans, as you instructed. We've taken only those without dependents. They are billeted in tents near here. They come and go under armed escort, and are restricted to the camp when they are not working."

"They accept this?"

"They accept any proposition that ensures they will be fed."

He led Petrov through the corridor and stopped at a bank of elevators. "All the stairwells have been sealed. One elevator goes down to the kitchen in the basement. One goes down one floor to a security entry and processing area. All prisoners will come in this way. The third elevator goes up to our area. It works only by key." He handed a large brass key to Petrov, who pocketed it without examination.

"What about fires?"

"Very little of the building is flammable. We can get people out through the top floor if we have to; there's a steel trap on the roof. There's some risk, but I judged our security need to be greater."

Petrov made no comment.

Rivitsky inserted his own key in the elevator lock; when the door slid open they went down to the second level. There he showed Petrov another double-security setup. His leader saw that some of the mortar along the stairwell was still wet, and questioned its strength. Rivitsky gave him a tour of some of the cells, and when Petrov had seen enough, they ascended to the top floor to survey the furnishings of their quarters. A sophisticated communications center was being installed by Ezdovo, who grunted an obscure song as he worked. Along the walls were several small wooden desks; sheets of cork had been installed on the walls and rows of photographs were already tacked in place.

Rivitsky led Petrov to his room and motioned him to enter. The room was sparsely furnished except for an ornate brass bed with a double thick mattress. "No bedrolls?" Petrov asked.

"A brief chance for creature comfort," Rivitsky replied, smiling. The question was his leader's way of registering his satisfaction.

By midday the rest of the team had arrived, stowed their gear and gone to work.

The first prisoners began to arrive from various internment centers around Berlin and its suburbs later in the afternoon. Professor Werner Haase, the Nazi physician who had showed them the way to Hitler's bunker, was the first to be installed in the new prison. Gnedin gave him a thorough medical examination and reported immediately to Petrov. "Tubercular, advanced, both lungs involved. We'd better get from him what we can now. He's not going to last long."

"How long?"

"With care, in the right setting and with some luck, several months. Here, only weeks or days. Hard to say. He looks malnourished and near exhaustion."

Haase was brought to an interrogation room. It was Petrov's practice never to interrogate a man in the same room in which he was housed. No matter how isolated you kept a prisoner, the place where he spent most of his time was, in his own mind, "home," and therefore potentially a place that might provide him with some psychological comfort. Through long experience Petrov had learned that inmates kept in dark, unfurnished rooms were easier to interrogate. He had also found that naked prisoners talked more readily than those who retained their clothes.

For the interviews of Hitler's Reich Chancellery group, Petrov had decided that further preparations would be unnecessary. Most of the captured Nazis, he was certain, would suffer depression from losing the war and from their capture. In such situations, information often flowed freely; he was determined to take advantage of this by having newly caught prisoners brought immediately under his control.

Dr. Haase glared at Petrov. "You're the one who shot the men."

Petrov spoke slowly. "Tell me what happened during your final time in the bunker with the other war criminals."

Haase stiffened. "I am first a physician and second a soldier. In no case am I a criminal."

"You are all war criminals," Petrov said.

Haase resisted. "I've already made a statement. A stenographer was present. I can add nothing to what I've already said."

Petrov's voice was soft, his tone almost enticing. "Nevertheless, I would like you to repeat it again."

Haase went into a coughing spasm, and Rivitsky gave him a tin filled with cold water. When he regained control, he repeated his story. Petrov made no notes, and after Haase finished, he began his questioning. Haase's story did not satisfy Petrov's expectations; the man seemed to be holding something back.

"Are you sure that Hitler is dead?" Petrov began.

"Yes," Haase said.

"Was it out of character for your Führer to take his own life?"

"I do not wish to reply to that. I was not an intimate of Hitler and therefore could only speculate."

"But you've met with Hitler?"

"Of course."

"You were his physician?"

"Acting. A matter of record, not reality."

"You talked about medical matters?"

"Yes."

"Nothing else?"

"Sometimes," Haase said hesitantly.

"We are told that Hitler is a knowledgeable man, an able and willing conversationalist."

"*Was,*" Haase corrected.

"Did he ever discuss suicide in your presence?"

"Theoretically. He asked me about the—efficiencies of various methods of self-liquidation."

"Efficiencies?"

"Yes. How quickly would death ensue? What kind of pain would there be? What chance would there be for error? Things of this nature."

"He was afraid of pain?"

"He was ill."

"The nature of the illness?"

"I had no opportunity to make a specific diagnosis. It appeared to be a nervous disorder. His face was bloated and swollen. He exhibited some slurring of speech. His left hand shook from some form of palsy. He had to pull his right leg along like a stump. He could hardly walk, certainly not for any distance."

Petrov interrupted: "Left arm and right leg?"

"Correct. That's all I know," Haase said curtly. He was breathing heavily, a cough building from his lungs in small pops.

Petrov had no intention of stopping. Again he circled back. "Hitler asked you about suicide. It was a theoretical discussion, and you advised him theoretically."

"Yes, yes," the doctor said wearily.

"But why you? This still puzzles me."

"I told you that I was his acting personal physician," Haase snapped.

"As a physician—presumably one sworn to preserve life—weren't you alarmed by such an inquiry?"

"The Führer had eclectic interests."

"Has," Petrov corrected. "What was your theoretical recommendation?"

"A simultaneous application of gunshot and poison."

"Simultaneous?"

"Yes."

"Please explain. I don't see how this would be possible—or, more important, what practical value it would offer."

"He wanted to know a method that would ensure death. A cyanide ampule could be placed between the teeth while a pistol rested against the temple. The ampule would be bitten an instant before the trigger was pulled, the effect being instantaneous death by one method or the other. It didn't really matter; by using both, one could be sure that death would occur."

"But this was only theoretical?"

"Yes."

"Has this method been tested in your death camps?"

Haase's mouth dropped open and his face reddened. "I had nothing to do with such things."

"But you knew they existed."

"There were rumors."

"Why would Hitler seek your advice in such matters? I would ask an executioner, not a doctor."

"I was his physician. He considered it a medical subject and wanted an expert opinion."

"You are an expert on suicide?"

"On death," Haase stammered. "A doctor deals with death."

Petrov gave the man a hard look. "In the Soviet Union our doctors deal with life; undertakers deal with death."

Haase struggled to stand. "I've had enough of this."

"Doctor," Petrov said quietly, "if you do not sit down and answer my questions fully, I will have you taken outside and shot immediately." Haase slumped back on his stool, his chin on his chest.

"The Führer feared that poison alone would be ineffective. He asked me to test the poison," the doctor blurted out suddenly after a pause.

"Before or after your consultation on theory?"

"Before. The dog keeper and I took the Führer's favorite bitch and gave her the poison."

"Dog keeper?"

"Sergeant Tarnow. I think he was actually part of the SS detachment in the bunker."

"Together you killed the bitch?"

"Yes."

"Tell me how it was done."

"The sergeant held the dog's head. I held the glass ampule with pliers. When he forced open the dog's mouth, I made the insertion and crushed the poison container. The dog expired within seconds."

"And you reported this to Hitler?"

"Yes."

"Then you had your discussion about theoretical modes of self-destruction?"

The doctor nodded.

"And Hitler, I presume, committed suicide in this precise manner?"

"Undoubtedly. He thought it a sound approach."

"But you did not witness the death or see the body?"

Haase shook his head.

Satisfied that he had everything, Petrov abruptly left the room. Gnedin was waiting in the hall. "I have all he knows. Make arrangements to transport him to Moscow. I want him kept alive. He showed Hitler how to kill himself."

▶**18** MAY 3, 1945, 2:45 P.M.

Rudolf cursed his luck, Germany, Adolf Hitler, Nazi big shots, the Russians and the Russian cunt who had captured and beaten him. Because his testicles were swollen so badly that he still couldn't stand, he was forced to sit on his ass in the rain with his legs apart, hoping the pain would eventually go away.

The German prisoners were in a small courtyard, or what had once been one; now it was no more than a tiny open area surrounded by sloping piles of rubble several meters high. Ivans with submachine guns sat on top of these, staring down at Rudolf and his fellow prisoners. Periodically the guards were brought coffee. He could smell the brew and was tempted to ask for some, but the Russians seemed neither forgiving nor friendly, so he kept his desires to himself.

Nearly two hundred German soldiers were pressed into the makeshift compound. They had no shelter to protect them from the rain, and to keep warm they walked en masse in a circular path, their feet digging a deep muddy track as the hours passed. They stumbled over Rudolf frequently, adding new bruises to his legs and cursing him; Rudolf cursed them back, not caring what their ranks were.

"Get up, you yellow bastard," one of the marchers, an officer, barked at Rudolf.

"Fuck you," Rudolf answered.

The man stood over Rudolf, his fists clenched tightly. He was a major. "That's insubordination. You could be court-martialed and shot."

"With what? Your skin flute? Leave me alone, you maniac."

The major kicked Rudolf in the hip, but the press of the circling marchers pushed him away before he could do any more damage. Rudolf tried to keep track of the man, figuring that he would kick him each time around. He seemed the type.

Rudolf was cold and hungry. Would the Ivans feed the prisoners or shoot them? That bitch had shown just what animals they were; he still had a bad taste in his mouth and an odor on his cheeks that he couldn't wash away even with muddy water. He leaned against the rubble pile and tried to relax.

Near dark a Russian officer entered the prison compound. The marchers stopped when he strode to the center of their area. "Sergeant Gustav Rudolf."

Rudolf heard his name, but remained silent, trying to figure what to do.

"Sergeant Gustav Rudolf, please come forward and identify yourself," the Russian said in an almost pleasant voice.

He tried to think of a way out of his predicament. He was certain they were going to shoot all the German prisoners. That's what they had done on the Eastern front; since then the Germans had been briefed daily on Soviet atrocities. On the other hand, this Russian neither looked nor sounded menacing. Maybe there was a chance. Could he pretend he wasn't in the group? Not likely. They'd recorded his name, rank, serial number and unit when he'd been dragged in. The Ivans *knew* he was in the compound. There wasn't any choice. "Here," Rudolf said feebly.

The Germans in front of him moved away when he answered, not wanting to be identified with anyone who was being singled out by the Russians.

The Soviet major stepped forward and looked down at him. "Sergeant Rudolf?"

"That's me."

"Are you wounded?"

"No. One of your officers kicked me in the balls. I can't stand up." Several of the nearby Germans laughed. The major offered his hand and pulled Rudolf to his feet. Immediately he felt dizzy, but the officer supported him and helped him walk.

"You're a fortunate man, Sergeant. We're moving you to another location," the major said as he escorted him through the security checkpoint to a truck where Bailov waited.

Bailov smiled at the German's approach. This one was weak; he'd spill his guts.

"Rudolf?"

"Yes." Bailov nodded to the major and took Rudolf's arm. Together they helped him onto the tarp-covered bed of a heavy truck. Rudolf crawled forward and lay still, glad to be out of the drizzle.

Bailov signed for the prisoner, accepted the thin file that had been started by the counterintelligence corps and verified the name of the officer who had made the capture and her unit for the Special Operations Group records.

"Thanks," Bailov said, clapping the officer on the back. Then he got into the back of the truck with his new prisoner and yelled to the driver to move out.

"Rudolf of the Reich Security Police?"

Rudolf rolled over and stared at this new man as the truck's motor snorted to life. How many times were they going to verify all this? Bailov helped him onto one of the truck benches and gave him a small flask, but Rudolf hesitated to accept it.

"Vodka," Bailov explained. "It will warm you." He smiled encouragement.

Rudolf held the flask to his lips and took a long pull. The Russian vodka exploded inside him and made him cough, but he drank again immediately.

It was a long ride to their destination and quite dark when they arrived, but the rain had let up and mist had taken its place. Rudolf wondered if he'd be sleeping outside. Bailov led him through a strange maze of triangular metal rods and various kinds of barbed wire. They entered a gray building through a huge metal door, and after it closed behind them, Bailov told him to undress. When the German hesitated, Bailov laughed. "We're going to give you some dry clothes."

Rudolf stripped. The inner steel door opened and admitted an Asian in a white smock. He was fumbling with a rubber glove, trying to put it on, and he gave an order in Russian.

Bailov translated. "He wants to check your mouth to make sure you haven't concealed anything."

"Just my teeth," Rudolf grumbled. The Asian ignored him and thrust a gloved finger into his mouth, gouging along his upper and lower gums, then pressing his tongue down flat in the bottom of his mouth until he gagged. When the man withdrew his hand, he slapped Rudolf lightly across the shoulders.

"Bend over," Bailov said. Rudolf stared incredulously at him, not understanding. "He wants to check your other cavity."

The Russian grabbed him by the head and pushed it down, then signaled him to spread his legs. Hesitatingly, Rudolf did as he was told. The man grabbed his buttocks and spread them wide, then inserted a gloved finger. Rudolf almost fainted from the pain as the man groped around inside him.

With the inspection complete, the inner door opened again and Bailov pushed his prisoner inside. Another armed Asiatic latched the door behind them, sliding a thick steel bar into place. The one in the smock snapped off the glove and threw it into a nearby barrel. Rudolf tried to see how many other gloves were in there, but as he leaned forward to look he saw that they were in an open room filled with clacking typewriters. Suddenly the sounds ceased and Rudolf looked up to see that the offices were filled with women, who were all staring at him. He felt himself flush with embarrassment and anger. Goddamn Russians!

They were almost at the end of the room when a high-pitched voice sang out in German: "Remarkably small gun for a member of the master race." The women roared with laughter, and Rudolf sprinted past Bailov through another set of doors.

"Keep to your work," Bailov warned them good-naturedly, but he was smiling.

Rudolf was taken underground by elevator, cursorily examined by two more Asian armed guards and then shown into a small dark room. "There's a bedroll in there on the floor," Bailov said. "It's not the luxury you Nazis are accustomed to, but at least you will be warm and out of the rain. I suggest you sleep."

"I'm just a soldier," Rudolf said defensively. "I'm hungry."

"I know," Bailov said. "We've yet to find a single Nazi in Germany. It's the most incredible thing. Sleep. Then you'll get a complete physical examination. After that you eat." The door slammed in his face, leaving Rudolf in total darkness. He got down on all fours and crawled around the cell haphazardly until he found the bedding. He dreamed of firing squads composed of smiling women.

When the cell door opened again, Rudolf was already awake. In fact, his nightmares had been so real that he had been unable to sleep for more than a few minutes at a time. Finally he'd lain on his back with his eyes open, fighting off sleep in order to avoid the dreams. The same Russian who had brought him in beckoned him out of the cell.

After a physical exam by a thin doctor aided by a balding fat woman, they made him shower, and afterward doused him with de-lousing powder. The doctor brought him to Bailov again, who bade him sit on a stool in the middle of a small, brightly lit room. The Russian was behind a table, pen and paper in front of him. Gnedin stood in the corner with a pad of paper.

"When do I get to eat?" Rudolf asked weakly.

Gnedin began writing as soon as Rudolf spoke. "When we've finished here," Bailov said. "I want you to tell me everything you did from April twenty-sixth until you were captured."

"Even when I pissed?"

"Everything."

Rudolf thought about the order for a moment, then relaxed and told his story.

Bailov listened without interrupting. The man had a loose tongue, but no focus. More interviews would be needed. Even though he was an insignificant figure, you never knew from whom important information might surface. Bailov had hopes about this one.

When the German finished, Bailov had food brought to him. Rudolf ate like an animal, mopping the last juices from his plate with a large chunk of black bread. "*Gut,*" he said just before he emitted a sustained belch.

Bailov pushed a stack of paper and several pencils across the table to him. "We'd like you to write your autobiography."

"My what?"

"The story of your life."

"From the time I was born?"

"Precisely. When you've done that, we want you to give us a list of all the men in your unit and the names of everyone you remember seeing in the Chancellery in the past two weeks."

"I didn't know everybody in my unit. We had a lot of replacements."

"The names of those you knew will be enough."

"It's going to be a pretty long list. It might take a long time," Rudolf said, seeing a possible bargaining point.

"That you've got plenty of." As Bailov departed the German had already begun scratching away at the paper, quietly mumbling to himself.

▶**19**   MAY 3, 1945, 5:00 P.M.

Brumm led them up and along a steep pine ridge, carefully keeping his small band on the military crest to eliminate silhouettes. Beard had spread them out in a loose box formation with Brumm on the point in front, two wide flankers and himself as the trailer providing a rear guard for the group. The remaining four girls carried the litter bearing Herr Wolf.

Ahead of them the ridge branched off in several directions. They had walked all day with only one stop—more than twenty kilometers, Brumm estimated, a remarkable performance.

They had jumped off in the darkness of the morning of May 3. The plan was bold. They walked out of their hiding place in the green building and pressed westward until they intersected the main flow of civilian refugees near the Tiergarten. In a stroke of good fortune they found an abandoned cart with spoked wooden wheels and metal rims at the end of the street. They loaded Herr Wolf into it and joined the exodus. Two of the girls pushed the cart, their weapons carefully stowed just below their hands. The rest of the group dispersed in the crowd, keeping visual contact but for the most part remaining distant from the cart and its passenger.

Herr Wolf was in terrible shape. His eyes had finally closed from the swelling; he was blind and his skin was an unhealthy gray. A warm drizzle soaked them during the early going, and the girls covered their passenger with a discarded brown canvas picked up along the route. Around noon the rain moved off to the southeast and the sun peeked out, white-hot. At one point—Brumm wasn't sure when—someone had placed three small children on the cart and they rode along quietly, happy to be off their feet. If their mother was nearby, she did not identify herself. With the children, their gear in small bundles and the old man curled up in a fetal position, the wagon's passengers looked like the remnants of three generations of a family.

Russian troops were all along their route, but they seemed to be more interested in the sunshine than in the German civilians. Ivans were perched on their tanks and vehicles, on logs and flat rocks, bare-chested like cold-blooded reptiles warming themselves in the sun.

Parts of the Tiergarten were filled with livestock, and Soviet troops milled around the animals. The horses they rode; the cattle they led away for fresh meat. On a grassy plain Brumm watched several Ivans playing some kind of polo, riding their mounts bareback, holding on to their horses' manes. They rode naturally and wildly, shouting and swearing good-naturedly at one another, seemingly unafraid that they might break their necks now that the war had ended. He lost interest in the equestrian game when he realized that they were using a human head for a ball. The field twinkled with tiny flowers of light as the sun reflected off tens of thousands of brass cartridges.

Near the Havel River, the Russians had gathered a pile of toilets that reached nearly twenty meters in height and twice that in width. Russian soldiers were streaming toward the cache from all directions, toting more of the fixtures. Beard caught his colonel's attention and raised his eyebrows. Brumm smiled.

On an island in the Havel River they saw thousands of German soldiers and men from the Volksturm. The pines on the island had been stripped by artillery fire, and in and among the slash, unprotected from rain or sun, sat the vanquished. Suddenly one of the prisoners dove into the water and began swimming northwest against the current, but a fusillade of bullets bracketed him, then covered him, driving him under the surface in an angry froth. He did not return to the surface. Russian riflemen on the riverbank brandished their weapons in triumph, and one of them did a little dance on a sandy spit of land across from the island as the prisoners watched.

Near the west end of the forest there was a small manicured park with a statue of Frederick the Great, and here several Ivans were setting up camp. The flowers were gone, trampled by horses and vehicles. The head of the statue had been knocked off and was sitting on its neck on the ground. At the wall of a fountain below the statue's pedestal, a young girl—no more than twelve, Brumm guessed—was astride a black-headed Russian, riding him like a horse to the shouts and cheers of his comrades. Two officers watched quietly from a low wall, smoking. Brumm had no doubt about her ultimate fate; the civilians who tramped by for the most part pretended they did not see. The poor creature was no better or worse off than thousands of others, and at this point it was every man and woman for themselves. Still, Brumm felt an urge to spray a clip of live rounds into the Ivans and to bolt into the forest. But his sense of mission intervened, as did his own desire for self-preservation; he kept walking west as the pathetic shrieks of the girl echoed through the forest and finally faded.

Brumm's biggest fear was that he and Beard would be singled out; as far as he could see they were the only able-bodied men in the crowd. But they had gone unnoticed. He had been certain that once the fighting was ended, the Ivans would relax. It was a natural reaction to the end of a battle, especially after one that marked what everyone knew to be the end of the war. In such situations one did not take foolish chances. For all their lack of sophistication, the Ivans were human and as fond of living as any German.

Their destination was a forested area west of Potsdam. Brumm's intent had been to cross the Havel River on a bridge southeast of the town of Werder. Once over the bridge, they could move north into the forest and find cover. The bridge crossing had been his biggest concern, but when they arrived, the Russian detachments guarding it were below on the banks, splashing happily in the shallows with several German women. As they walked across the bridge, Brumm watched as a small baby, left unattended on the bank by its mother, crawled to the edge beyond the group and toppled into the water. He watched the infant struggle and roll in the current as it passed unnoticed under the bridge. It was not a bad ending, he thought; its suffering was over.

After the bridge, the pace of the refugee pack quickened as they tried to put as much distance between them and Berlin as possible. Brumm walked far ahead of his group, helping an old woman hobble along until the road made a severe bend. There he walked off the road into the forest, followed immediately by Waller, and they waited for the others to catch up with them. Beard was the last. After the Werder Bridge he had taken over the cart; Herr Wolf was awake, calm but complaining about the jolting from the metal-rimmed wheels. The children were gone; Brumm did not ask his sergeant what he had done with them. The Valkyries fluttered around Herr Wolf, rubbing his back, trying to comfort him.

Brumm gave them a short break while he and Beard transferred their passenger to a litter. After ten minutes they moved out again, tracking cross-country along the ridges. After the sickening smell of death and sulfur in the city, the fresh air and scent of pines in the countryside were welcome; even Brumm felt better to be in the woods again and off paved roads. But they were not alone. From time to time they saw other individuals and small groups, but none of them seemed anxious to come close.

With several spines of the ridges stretching ahead of them, Brumm led them down to the lowest of them on a hunch. It took them back toward the river, finally ending in a fifty-meter bluff, which dropped straight to a narrow field of rocks at the water's edge. It was exactly what he was looking for. The spot at the end was tree-covered and flat, the ground covered with a deep matting of brown needles, and it connected to the main ridge by a narrow isthmus, which pinched in and suddenly widened again.

He called his group together and gave them their instructions for the night. He placed his sentries along the narrow point; he and Beard would alternate with one of the women to cover the entry from two sides. He trusted the girls' enthusiasm, but they still lacked training and experience. He would not let them build a fire, a decision that brought Herr Wolf's wrath in the form of an angry stare, and they contented themselves with a meal of hard biscuits and thick slices from a cured salami. Herr Wolf did not eat. Angrily he called Brumm over to his litter and pointed out to everyone within earshot that he was a vegetarian; as such, the food provided was inadequate for his needs. Brumm replied that if he did not remain quiet, they might all find themselves with no further need to eat. If their journey took any unexpected twists, they might all end up as vegetarians, scrounging from the land for their food. Herr Wolf hissed an unspoken response, rolled over on his litter and turned his back on the group.

"We'll start before sunrise," Brumm told the group. Then he and Beard went off together for a private huddle.

"Too easy," the sergeant major said. "I don't like it."

"What do you want? To fight every step of the way?"

"I just don't like the feel of it. The Russians are lax; it's not like them. Their discipline has broken down."

"Consider their viewpoint," the colonel said quietly. "They've won; they've had enough. They don't want to find any more trouble, not now. They've come too far to die in some stupid incident during the aftermath. If we can keep to ourselves, the Ivans shouldn't be a problem."

"But you're still worried," Beard said. "I can read you."

Brumm nodded. "You know what it's like after a battle. There'll be looting, troublemakers. We had plenty of our own. They're the real danger. It could be bad until we get into the mountains."

"Maybe we should shoot him and roll his carcass into the river."

Brumm laughed quietly. "To what end? To turn ourselves in? To become civilians? We're not conscripts; we do the impossible. All we have left is this mission and our duty. You and I are professionals, Hans. As long as he lives, we have a purpose; *it's all we have.*"

"He's . . . *insane,*" Beard whispered. He pointed a finger at his temple and made small circles with it. "Did you see his eyes? Like a madman. There were camps for Jews and Gypsies, for Poles, for the old people and the retarded—the whole world will want to get its hands on him. We can't hide from the whole world, Günter, not from all of them."

The colonel patted his sergeant on the arm and smiled. "Can't we? There's a lot more to this than you imagine, my friend. Not everybody in the world wants Adolf Hitler dead."

▶20   SS Oberführer Günter Brumm

An only child, Günter Brumm was born in 1910 in Kaiser's Military Hospital, Berlin. His father had been a career army officer, commissioned as a Leutnant in 1905, who rose to the rank of Oberst and was killed in action while leading an assault on American positions in Belgium on November 11, 1918. It was the final day of the Great War, and he was among the last Germans to be killed in combat during hostilities.

Each August, Elisabeth von Brumm took her son to her family's home in Bad Harzburg, a small rural city of twenty thousand people in the inhospitable Harz Mountains. The boy had barely known his father; as a result, his maternal grandfather, Walther Halter, became a substitute. In Berlin, at the age of six, Günter was enrolled in a prestigious school for the sons of officers. He immediately showed himself to be of high intellect and steely perseverance. At seven he was placed in an accelerated curriculum in the school. After his father was killed in action, his mother moved back to Bad Harzburg, and the boy continued his education in the local school there, again quickly establishing himself as a student of great promise.

Günter's grandfather, an apothecary who compounded medical remedies from natural ingredients but had no formal education, spent a great deal of time with the boy, taking him for numerous outings into the wilds of the Harz, teaching him the ways of wilderness living and survival, camping under the stars, even in the winter months. Under his grandfather's guidance the boy became an accomplished outdoorsman and hunter, a development that his schoolmasters found difficult to equate with his intellectual talents for virtually every subject he encountered. The grandfather, a lifelong resident of the Harz, showed the boy its mysteries: little-known caves and caverns, Teutonic ruins and tight, deep canyons where herds of wild boar dwelt. At eleven Günter was placed in the local *Realschule* for further training preparatory to entering the university. Again his performance was superior; his comprehension of chemistry and mathematics soon threatened to outstrip the knowledge of the local faculty.

His grandfather urged Günter toward a career in medicine, but by the time the boy was fifteen he had already made his own decision: he would follow in the footsteps of the father he had hardly known and pursue a career as a military officer. The grandfather was only slightly disappointed; the boy would be a success at whatever he chose to undertake. With his academic record Günter had no trouble finding a place for himself in a military training academy. This was postwar Germany; under the Treaty of Versailles the German army was limited to a maximum force of one hundred thousand men. The economy was in trouble, unemployment was high, and because of this, the number of men seeking employment in the military was exceptionally high. The boy was enrolled in the military training school in Stuttgart, the same academy that claimed Erwin Rommel as a graduate.

At twenty Brumm became a Leutnant of infantry, and dropped the "von" from his name, not liking the elitism it connoted. He was the top graduate of his class, known both for his brilliance in the classroom and for his cool and flawless decision-making under the harshest conditions in the field. Despite his competence, his rise in the army was anything but spectacular. He advanced to the rank of Hauptmann in 1935, and was given command of a company patrolling the German-Czech border in the Ore Mountains south of Dresden.

New political winds were blowing in Germany and new leadership was emerging to lead the country out of its depression. In 1932 von Hindenburg had been reelected president. A year later he appointed the National Socialist Party leader, Adolf Hitler—an Austrian—to the position of chancellor. Hitler quickly pulled Germany out of the League of Nations. Whatever else he might be, and Brumm had more than a few doubts, he thought this strange Austrian had courage.

Whereas his fellow officers expressed an extreme view of Hitler as either exceptionally bad or exceptionally good for the country, Brumm did not share his opinion publicly; he preferred to observe the man in action first. In 1934 Hitler made military training mandatory for all German males; Brumm supported the action because he thought that the absence of military training tended to make German youth soft, and because most units were undermanned. The new law would ensure that future commands would be at full strength.

In 1936 Brumm's company was among three battalions sent into the Rhineland by Hitler. There they dug in and waited to see what the French response would be. A short distance away the French had more than a hundred divisions they could have sent against the small German force, but as Hitler had hoped, there was no action, only talk. Certain that the crisis had passed and the Rhineland was again safe in German hands, Hitler ordered thousands of engineers and workers into the area to fortify it, building what he called the West Wall.

From 1936 until late 1938 Brumm was posted to Berlin, serving in the Office of Plans and Operations of the OKH (Oberkommando des Heeres, the Army High Command). Once again his keen analytical skills and deep intelligence impressed his superiors, but no further promotions came. In March 1939 he was an acting battalion commander in the takeover of Czechoslovakia. In November 1939 he requested posting to the newly created parachute training program; his request was granted and his skill during training duly noted by his superiors.

In June 1940 Brumm found himself in command of a parachute company. He led his troops in their first combat jumps, into France. One hundred and forty-three German divisions were spread across a four-hundred-mile front as Hitler, with the Netherlands and Belgium already conquered, threw his armies across the Somme. Brumm's unit was the first to reach Paris on June 13, a full day before the main German armies moved into the city. By the end of the month Brumm's company was taken off the line and returned to Germany for additional training. During this time Brumm requested and was granted a month's leave. Part of the leave was spent in Bad Harzburg with his mother and grandfather, part in Berlin with a young woman he'd met during his tour with the Plans and Operations branch.

Christmas, 1940, brought Brumm a new assignment, the command of a special reconnaissance company in the 258th Infantry Division. In late June 1941 he watched in awe as nearly one million German soldiers flooded across the Russian border at the beginning of Operation Barbarossa. Where Napoleon had failed, Hitler was sure he could succeed. Brumm was not so certain; Russia was huge, its people were primitive. They might not be well equipped, but their ferocity was legendary, and, worst of all, the lethal and relentless Russian winter lay ahead. In Brumm's view, the invasion was beginning two months late; unless they were lucky they would be in serious trouble by November. With his planning background and acumen, he noted that no allowance had been made for winter gear; it was a critical oversight and he felt compelled to say something. In a preinvasion planning session Brumm raised the issue, but drew only icy stares from his superiors; the Führer had said it could be done and he had not yet been wrong about anything he'd ordered. Only an SS officer—an Oberleutnant—paid any attention to Brumm's thorough and dispassionate analysis of the situation. This man, a Viennese named Otto Skorzeny, pulled Brumm aside after the meeting and spent more than two hours asking about his views on the invasion plan. Mostly Skorzeny listened—an unusual occurrence, since the few times Brumm had seen him, Skorzeny had made his presence known by the sheer volume of his voice. After asking several pointed questions, Skorzeny told Brumm that he believed the captain had raised valid issues, and that he was impressed with both the captain's sense of organization and his clear analysis. Brumm thought the junior officer impertinent; still, it was satisfying to know that somebody had listened to him, even if it was only a blowhard Austrian.

For the first few weeks after Barbarossa's launch, Brumm began to wonder if he had erred in his assessment. The Russians, who had been crying to the world for months about the possibility of invasion, seemed to be totally surprised by the attack. German combat divisions quickly pushed deep into Soviet territory, often outstripping their lines of supply and forcing them to halt their advance until the rear echelons could catch up with them. Brumm's unit was part of Army Group Center, which had been assigned the responsibility of subduing Moscow. Just as he had been among the first Germans in Prague, and again in Paris, now there was a good chance that Brumm's reconnaissance unit would be among the first in Moscow—quite a triplicate, he congratulated himself.

But he had been right after all; by early October the nightmare was realized. The Russian winter arrived earlier than usual. First came sheets of relentless icy rain that pelted bare flesh and created seas of slime and muck that bogged down man and machine alike. It was the prewinter phenomenon the Russians call *Rasputita*. In October snow fell and the temperature dropped to ten below. The German advance slowed but did not stop, and eventually, with the constant urging of their officers, the Germans fought their way through hordes of undisciplined Russian peasants, armed with century-old shotguns, sabers and shovels with sharpened edges, to reach Moscow.

On December 2, 1941, during a heavy ice storm, Brumm took his unit into the Moscow suburb of Khimki. The fighting was fierce, house to house and hand to hand. Russian women and children heaved grenades at tanks in the streets and sniped wildly from concealment. The temperature was thirty below, and many infantrymen were losing fingers and toes to frostbite. Brumm gave his men a break. They holed up temporarily in an abandoned warehouse and built fires on the dirt floors; for the first time in weeks they were warm.

At daybreak on the morning of December 3, Brumm led a small patrol of volunteers into Moscow proper, seeking to ascertain the enemy's strength. The next morning he pulled his company back closer to the main German salient and reported to his superiors that Moscow seemed to be almost undefended. Given the tenacity with which the Soviets had fought so far, he found this situation difficult to understand, and even more difficult to accept; his instincts told him that something was drastically wrong. He tried to express his concern to his superiors, but they refused to listen. Their explanation was simplistic: there were too few Russians left to fight and nothing left for them to fight with; Germany finally had virtually annihilated its historic enemy. The senior officers encouraged their men to take pride in their accomplishment.

Brumm knew they were wrong. Experience showed that even when the Russians were reduced to fighting with their bare hands, they would charge a solid wall of automatic weapon fire in order to strangle a single German. It was incomprehensible that such defenders would suddenly evaporate, especially in the Russian capital with the German army within artillery range of the Kremlin itself.

Brumm's fear was confirmed on December 6, 1941: the German invaders were stunned by a savage Russian counteroffensive launched across a two-hundred-mile front with one hundred well-armed and fresh divisions. Back in Vinnitsa, in the Ukraine, from where he now directed the war, Hitler refused to acknowledge the urgent communiqués from his field commanders. After reading the reports from his field commanders, the Führer calmly ordered them to continue the drive to Moscow and then went into seclusion to consider matters he considered to be of greater importance to the Reich. It was too late; the Russians had gained both the momentum and the advantage. Within days every German soldier fully understood that a dramatic shift had taken place.

By February 1942 Brumm's small reconnaissance unit had been pushed back nearly sixty-five kilometers; in the process his company had been reduced from a full complement of one hundred to only thirty-five men. Intelligence was reporting that 31 percent of the entire German assault force had been killed or wounded in the Soviet counterattack. The army in Brumm's region had been reduced from 162 divisions to eight; their sixteen armored divisions had only 140 tanks in fighting condition. Seeing the danger and having been separated from his parent infantry battalion, Brumm threw in with a small panzer unit, using his men to perform reconnaissance ahead of the unit's six remaining Tiger tanks. In return, the panzermen transported his people when the path ahead was clear, which it seldom was. Despite the magnitude of the Russian onslaught, the disciplined and well-trained German infantrymen gave ground grudgingly; Hitler had ordered them to fight to the last man and last bullet, and their commanders had no choice but to comply with their Führer's explicit order.

In March, during heavy spring rains, Brumm's adopted tank unit was finally annihilated in a night attack by Soviet armor and rockets. He took his remaining men (now fewer than twenty) on alone, moving southeast toward the Don River and the southern armies of Hitler, which had been assigned the task of taking Stalingrad and the Russian oil fields in the Caucasus. Traveling by night and hiding by day, he led his men slowly through Russian territory for nearly six weeks, finally rejoining the main German units south of a river near the Ukrainian border. Along the way the young company commander took copious detailed notes on Russian units, their strengths and methods of battle. He reached safety with nine haggard survivors; they were received by the Germans with wonder. During a week-long debriefing by intelligence personnel, the young captain described the travels of his unit and their skirmishes as they worked their way back to the German lines. When he showed them his notes, the intelligence experts were stunned; they knew a treasure when they saw one. Brumm had a huge volume of information of exceptional quality, and senior intelligence officials on the Eastern front reasoned that he belonged in Berlin.

So it was that Brumm and his survivors were evacuated to Germany, and upon arrival he was again subjected to an intense debriefing. Later he was reassigned to the Office of Plans and Operations, his experience having elevated him to a new status, that of resident expert on Soviet tactics and strategy. He found himself immersed in all things Russian; his primary duty involved supervising interrogations of selected Soviet prisoners flown to Berlin by intelligence agents on the Eastern front. For particularly difficult prisoners, Gestapo personnel applied their special expertise. It was a brutal and abhorrent job, but Brumm reminded himself of what was occurring in the Ukraine, and this buffered the distaste he might otherwise have felt. A Russian life taken in Berlin might save hundreds of German lives in the east.

In June, German victories in the field began to mount once again. Seeing the need for experienced officers, Brumm requested reassignment to another combat unit. For the first time in his career a request he had made was turned down; he was told bluntly that he was too valuable to be wasted as cannon fodder and could be of more use to the Reich where he was. Brumm felt betrayed; uncharacteristically, he began to spend much of his free time drinking and partaking in the social diversions the city offered.

In the fall the war again shifted against Germany, and Brumm continued his self-destructive ways, falling in with a group of senior Waffen SS officers who had access to a seemingly inexhaustible supply of French champagne and wine and legions of eager young females from the League of German Girls. On several occasions he accompanied his senior comrades to a secluded and well-guarded estate near the city where nearly three hundred young women, many of them in their mid-teens, were barracked. Controlled by the German Labor Front, the establishment was called "recreational," operating under the aegis of an organization called Kraft Durch Freude (Strength through Joy). Brumm was told that his admittance to the establishment was a rarity; normally such places were reserved exclusively for members of the SS, but his fellow officers, who were all SS, said they considered him to be one of them and would ignore the fact that his uniform was the wrong color.

In April 1943 Brumm had a surprise visitor: Otto Skorzeny, the SS Oberleutnant who had so thoroughly quizzed him about his views of Barbarossa. Skorzeny, who was now his equal in rank, swaggered into his office one afternoon, sat down and propped his high leather boots on Brumm's desk. "I have a new job," he told Brumm, "something you might be interested in."

Brumm's interest was piqued; if it would get him out of Berlin and away from his pointless existence, he was interested. It didn't much matter what it was, as long as there would be action. But when he pressed Skorzeny for details, the SS captain smiled wryly and excused himself. "Perhaps you'll hear from me sometime."

A month later Brumm received a wire marked "SECRET" from Skorzeny. If Brumm was interested, the SS major wrote, he might have a job that would challenge his unique talents. Skorzeny did not wait for an answer. Brumm's orders followed within the week.

Brumm was flown to Munich and driven from there to an isolated mountain installation, where he was shown into Skorzeny's office. The beefy Austrian proudly explained that he had been given a special assignment under the Amt VI of the Reich Main Security Office. Skorzeny, who had been sent home from the Eastern front with an ulcer in 1942, now commanded a special commando unit, the Friedenthal. He assured Brumm that they would be undertaking some "very interesting" assignments. He needed a planner, a director of operations planning to whom he could entrust details. Brumm accepted, even after Skorzeny explained that the new posting would entail his joining the SS, a circumstance that would necessitate an investigation of his racial history. Brumm had heard of such procedures but had paid little attention to them; elite military units often had strange traditions and customs.

Two teams of researchers were promptly sent from Berlin to look into Brumm's family background; within several days they were back with their evidence and made their report. There was no trace of either Jewish or Slavic blood in Brumm's maternal and paternal lines going back to the Thirty Years War. The investigators also had sworn statements that there was no mental illness in his family and that his physical characteristics—some twenty different measurements of everything from his sitting height to the distance between his eyes— were within the standards of the elite corps.

In due course Brumm's name was officially entered into the SS pedigree roll—*Das Sippenbuch*—and he took the oath of loyalty sworn by all new officers entering Hitler's Black Order. It was a small concession for his rescue from bureaucracy, and it wouldn't hurt his promotion chances.

▶**21** MAY 5, 1945, 3:00 P.M.

Ezdovo came into the holding facility at midafternoon and made his way up to the group's private quarters. "They have the bodies," he reported to Petrov, who was in the middle of reading an interrogation statement. "Yesterday they found two badly burned bodies—a male and a female—in the Chancellery garden. Apparently they weren't interested, because they put them in blankets and buried them again. But this morning they showed up with a truck, dug them up again, put them in wooden boxes and drove them to SMERSH at the Third Shock Army in Buch. It's on the outskirts of the city."

"You saw them?"

"Only the truck as it pulled away."

"Your source?"

"A lieutenant. She's attached to a SMERSH unit with the Fifth Shock Army." The others smiled as he explained the situation in his own way; as always, there was a woman involved. "I suspect a little territorial jealousy. She claims that while security for the Chancellery area belongs to the Fifth, the Hitler investigation belongs to the Third. She was unhappy, so I shared some of our vodka and consoled her. She told me all about it. She feels much better now."

Ezdovo was short and powerfully built, like a small Himalayan black bear with massive shoulders, a sinewy neck and bulging upper arms. His head was small, out of proportion, and his black curly hair was thinning in back. He had a dark complexion and a face full of scars from a childhood bout with smallpox. By all ordinary standards he was ugly, yet women were drawn to him, much to the envy and amazement of his comrades. It was a mystery the others in the group often talked about.

"Did you share more than your vodka with the poor girl?" Bailov asked with a grin.

Petrov cut the banter short. "What else?"

"They found two dogs with the bodies. Also a bazooka."

Petrov stood up immediately and began putting on his overcoat. "Get transportation."

Bailov reached for the phone. "For all of us?"

Petrov grunted an affirmation.

"Do you think it could be Hitler?" Ezdovo asked anxiously.

"We look, we think, then we decide," Petrov said as he led them to the elevator.

It took two hours to reach the Third Shock Army's headquarters. When they entered, Petrov went directly to the commandant's office, passing through a herd of protesting clerks. In less than two minutes he was back, followed by a corpulent, bald general whose wire-rimmed glasses were askew and who was hopping along, trying to put on his boot as he followed the leader of the Special Operations Group. As soon as he reached the orderly room, the general screamed for his driver. Petrov's group still took pleasure in watching the extraordinary effect their leader had on others.

Petrov rode with the general, and the others followed in their own vehicle. They drove a kilometer or so to a battered string of connected wood-frame buildings that served as a makeshift field hospital.

By the time they arrived the general was dressed, but still lacked control of his emotions. In the hospital he shouted for attention and got it. He demanded to know the whereabouts of Colonel Doctor Shkaravski, chief of forensic medicine with the First Belorussian Front. No one seemed to know, but the group was taken quickly to a small wooden house apart from the rest of the complex. No guards were posted, and Petrov quickly pointed out their absence to the general, who turned pale, then a dark shade of red, and slammed his hands against his fat thighs like a plump bird beating its wings in a mating dance.

Inside the house, eleven bodies were laid out side by side on a scuffed wooden floor. A frail medical orderly was sitting on a wooden chest in a corner, cleaning his fingernails with a small knife. He looked at them when they entered, but did not speak and showed no particular alarm over their presence. It had begun to rain outside; heavy drops pounded loudly on the roof and ran off the gutters in a solid wall. The orderly stopped working on his fingers to watch the rain.

The general jerked the orderly to his feet. "Are you in charge?"

"I'm the only one here," the man mumbled.

"Then you're in charge and have failed to post sentries."

The man smiled weakly. "I'm a medical orderly, Comrade General."

"You're a member of the Third Shock Army, and you are derelict in your military obligation."

"But I arrived here just before you, sir." Sweat was pouring off the man as he shifted his weight nervously.

"You know the penalty," the general screamed.

"*I just got here, Comrade General!*" the man shrieked. "I was told to report to the mortuary, so I came directly over. You can't shoot an orderly for doing what's he's told."

The general unsnapped his holster, removed his revolver, held it with the barrel straight up, like some kind of banner, and pushed the orderly through the back door of the building. The man lost his balance, landed on his back and slid backward in the sparse green shoots of grass and mud.

Petrov and Gnedin ignored the commotion and began to inspect the bodies. The other three watched through a window as the general shoved the man toward a large oak tree. Twice the orderly fell, but the general picked him up each time and kicked him again. When they reached the base of the tree, the general opened the cylinder, closed it, put the barrel to the man's head and fired. There was a puff of smoke, and the orderly twisted and fell on his side. His legs kicked twice, then he was still. Through the rain the sound of the shot was no louder than that made by a child's popgun.

Ezdovo laughed quietly. "Dead soldiers don't repeat their mistakes."

"Shit rolls downhill," Rivitsky observed.

"When the mastodon runs, it's the grass that suffers," Ezdovo chirped.

"All right, let's play sentry until the Comrade General can rally his subordinates," Rivitsky said. "Petrov, we'll secure the area. Do you want privacy?"

"Gnedin will remain with me. A Dr. Chenko was to be sent from Moscow. Bring him to me if he arrives, but our meeting must appear to be purely accidental." Petrov did not want the Russian medical authorities to know that Stalin had installed an observer in their ranks.

Rivitsky, Bailov and Ezdovo went outside and took up positions.

"Observations?" Petrov asked the young surgeon.

Gnedin coughed to clear his throat. "That one we saw in the bunker," he said, pointing to the corpse of General Hans Krebs, chief of the General Staff. "That one is Goebbels. See, they botched burning him, but that profile is unique. And here is the metal prosthesis for his clubfoot. The woman is probably his wife, or one of his whores; he had a propensity for such women and his wife encouraged it. I presume the children we found are theirs, too; there were six."

Petrov poked at one of the bodies with a thin finger and pursed his lips. "Could these be the corpses transported here this morning?"

"They *are* charred, and they're a male and a female. It's possible."

Rivitsky came in and pointed through the windows to a platoon of infantry double-timing into a protective ring. The soldiers took up positions two meters apart, with their backs to the building, their rifles pointing out, bayonets fixed and at the ready. "There are some doctors coming. Chenko is among them," Rivitsky told Petrov.

"Bring him in."

Chenko wore a Red Army uniform devoid of rank or decorations. His black boots were caked with brown mud. He was squarely built, with stunted, bowed legs and long thin arms. His nose was thick and swollen, with blue veins in the tip snaking their way across wide nostrils into wrinkled, leathery cheeks.

"Chenko," Petrov said in simple greeting.

"Comrade Petrov. When our mutual friend asked me to see to your needs, I never imagined it would be so soon. I bring regards from Moscow."

"We learned today that the counterintelligence of the Third Shock Army unearthed two burned corpses, a male and a female. They suspect that these are the bodies of Hitler and his concubine. It is imperative that we view them before the autopsies are done."

"Whatever you wish, comrade, but you should be aware that what is happening here is politically sensitive. Marshal Zhukov is closely monitoring these events. There is considerable pressure on him to identify Hitler, and the good scientists waiting outside in the elements are already favorably predisposed toward tidiness, if you get my meaning."

"I don't give a damn about the politics, Chenko. I seek truth."

"Yes, I understand that. But you must also know that truth is relative to the need of its holder."

Petrov stared at Chenko. "Truth is truth, comrade. What one does with it is relative. Truth gives the full range of options for action, and I intend to have that full range. Are these the new bodies?"

Chenko shook his head. "Below."

The four men went downstairs. In the high-ceilinged cellar, postmortem tables and implements had been set up, and battery-powered

arc lamps stood around two tables like observers. A badly burned and
decomposed corpse was on each table.

"Ripe," Rivitsky muttered.

Gnedin turned on the lights and stood between the tables. "Male
here, female on my right. No easy identification this time; they are in
poor condition."

"What can you tell?" Petrov asked. He found a box in the corner,
turned it on end and sat down, more interested in listening than looking.

"The male has been shot. See the skull fragment missing here. No
telling with the woman, but there appears to be major trauma as well.
The pathologist will have to make a judgment of whether or not the
major injuries were sustained before or after death. If the flesh had
not been burned, the degree of lividity would tell us what we want to
know, but in this condition it will be more a matter of art than science."

Rivitsky stared at the corpses. "How will they make an identification? There's not much left."

"Dental records." Gnedin reached down, hooked the small finger
of his left hand in the male corpse's mouth and lifted it open to reveal
the blackened stump of a tongue and charred teeth. "See, the teeth
are black, but they're still there. Medical histories will also provide
some clues; there are a number of possibilities."

"Still not much to go on," Rivitsky said.

"True. There will be as much guesswork as anything down here."

"Forensics always involves guesswork," Chenko observed.

"Do you want to do the autopsies?" Petrov asked Gnedin.

"I don't think it's necessary. All I need are their reports," Gnedin
said.

"Do you want to observe them?"

"No, I don't want to be swayed by their table talk. If he would,
Comrade Chenko could act as our observer." Gnedin looked at the
older physician to see his reaction. "It's group psychology; as the
autopsy progresses, pretty soon you find yourself thinking like the rest
of the group."

"How long will it take?" Petrov asked Chenko.

"Several hours, I would think. There should be a preliminary report
by morning. I can have it sent to you."

"Bring it yourself," Petrov said. "Ezdovo will remain here. He'll
drive you to us."

When they returned to the ground floor, the general was waiting with five medical officials and several technicians. All of them were huddled just outside the door, trying to avoid the rain.

"Everything is in order?" the general asked eagerly as they approached.

Petrov stopped directly on the stoop above the general and looked down at him. "When the autopsy has been completed, Dr. Chenko is to bring a copy of the preliminary report to me. My man will remain to provide escort."

Ezdovo touched his field cap with his thumb and smiled.

Petrov turned to Chenko. "The report is to be *pure*." Both Chenko and the general nodded.

Not until Petrov and his men were out of sight did the doctors and the general enter the building.

Outside Ezdovo and Chenko stood under the eaves. The Siberian offered his hand and Chenko took it. "I'll be around, Doctor. See that they do a good job." Chenko nodded and returned inside with the others.

Ezdovo felt a chill. He'd seen several nurses inside the hospital, and suddenly he felt the need for a sturdy one with thick hair under her arms. Like home. Somewhere in the complex there had to be at least one who'd warm him up. He turned up his collar to keep the rain off his neck and went off at a trot.

Inside, one of the doctors stopped Chenko and pulled him away from the group. "Who was that man?"

Chenko frowned and leaned close to the doctor's ear. "Comrade," he whispered, *"you don't want to know."*

▶**22**   MAY 13, 1945, 11:30 P.M.

Petrov's men felt they now knew what had happened during the final hours in the bunker. To be sure, there were some minor variations in the stories woven by the various survivors, but the differences were not significant—at least not yet. It was late, nearly midnight, when Petrov called a meeting.

The five men were spread out in their work area, with Petrov in the center, like a professor before his students. The formation for such working conferences was always the same. Rivitsky had procured several freshly baked wheels of coarse black bread. Gnedin contributed a jar of orange marmalade and a full set of black-and-white autopsy photos, which had been enlarged and tacked to the cork walls. Ezdovo brought several bottles of watery German beer, while Bailov produced a full bottle of vodka for each of them along with a yellow crock filled with dill pickles. The last was the gift of an old Jewish woman, who kissed him and thanked him for liberating her from the Nazis. She had lived in the attic of friends since 1941.

Petrov's men were eager for the session to begin. They had worked hard at pulling together all the pieces, and now it was time to attempt assembly. Over time this kind of session had become ritualized. So far they had done the legwork and seen to the collection of a massive number of small details. Now Petrov would work his magic; as with a maestro, all instruments played to his direction.

Bailov opened the vodka and poured a glass for each man. "A toast," Petrov said, raising his glass. They all answered: "To those who have fallen." They drank and chased the liquid with chunks of pickle and dark bread.

Petrov smacked his lips loudly and set down his glass. "We have come a long distance, comrades." He stood up, clasped his hands behind him, lifted his chin and began.

"We have interviewed Baur, Günsche, Haase, Linge, Voss, Mohnke, Rattenhuber, Weidling, Echold and numerous guards from the bunker detachment. We also have the transcript of the Kunz interrogation, and Haase has been corroborated by Schenck, who saw him with Hitler. The guard Mengershausen was interviewed this afternoon; he claims to have witnessed the funeral pyre in the garden. The guard Karnau claims the same, though from a different vantage point. We have the views of Misch and Hentschel, who were the last out, and that of Hoegl, whose health didn't allow him to give us much."

Petrov stopped to look at his men; he often noted their posture to gauge how meetings were developing.

"Still missing are Bormann, Burgdorf, Naumann and the pilot, Beetz. The women Krüger, Junge, Christian and Manzialy remain at large and, given the mood of our soldiers, don't stand much chance of being found alive. Dr. Stumpfegger, who went with Bormann, is still missing, as are Kempka, Hitler's chauffeur, Axmann with his one arm, Schwägermann, Horbeck and some other lesser luminaries. There's still work to do, but we've made progress."

The men smiled.

"Hewel killed himself in the brewery. We have that body," Petrov said. "Who are the other key ones?"

"The women," Ezdovo offered quickly. The others laughed at him. "They were there at the end," he said defensively.

"Agreed," Petrov said. Vindicated, Ezdovo smirked at his comrades.

"Günsche and Linge," Rivitsky offered.

"Yes."

"Rattenhuber. By all accounts he's a cool one, a thorough professional," Gnedin said.

"I concur, Doctor."

"Hoegl, if he could talk; he was Rattenhuber's number two man."

"Yes. When Hitler said his final farewells, Bormann, Goebbels, Krebs, Burgdorf, Hewel, Voss, Rattenhuber, Hoegl, Linge, Günsche, Christian, Junge, Krüger and the cook Manzialy were present. Haase may or may not have been there; in any event, he's in Moscow so we'll have to wait to ask that question. Have we missed anyone?"

Bailov poured more vodka, and Ezdovo opened a bottle of the diluted beer.

"Fourteen people—fifteen if we count Haase—plus Hitler and Eva Braun. Of these, four are dead, five are unaccounted for and we have six in custody. I see Rattenhuber, Günsche and Linge as keys, and we have all three of them. All things considered, it's not an unsatisfactory harvest for such a short growing season. Of those still at large, Bormann should be our number one objective. Linge and Baur think he's dead, but we have no body. Mengershausen swears he was not killed."

"They were in the group with some tanks on the Weidendammer Bridge," Bailov said. "One of the tanks was hit and exploded. He's probably dead."

"Perhaps," cautioned Petrov. "Each of you knows what it's like in battle. Even those things about which you are certain often turn out to be untrue."

"The mirage effect," Dr. Gnedin inserted.

"Like Ezdovo's harem," Rivitsky quipped.

"Taking all the available credible witnesses, here's what happened," Petrov said. He drew a breath before he began. "Before lunch Hitler informed Günsche of his intention to kill himself. Then he had lunch with Junge, Christian and the cook, Manzialy. At this same time Günsche telephoned Kempka and told him to collect petrol. Kempka wanted to know why, and told Günsche that their remaining fuel

supplies were under fire by our artillery. He was told to siphon what
was needed from destroyed vehicles and those in the garage, and to
bring the supplies to the garden. Hitler and the women finished eating
around two-thirty. Afterward he visited briefly with Linge, told him
of his plan and asked him to see to the burning of the corpses, making
sure that the job would be done so thoroughly that the bodies would
be unrecognizable. He also instructed Linge to burn all of his personal
belongings, with the exception of the Frederick the Great portrait; this
he presented to the pilot Baur to take out of the city during the
breakout."

Rivitsky interrupted. "And which now graces our walls." The
portrait had been reunited with its frame, which Baur had left in the
bunker. To hide the painting, he had rolled it around a walking cane
and tied it with string. He'd rubbed the back with mud, but when he
was wounded during his escape attempt, the Russians had quickly
found it and turned it over to Petrov. "Ugly damned thing," Rivitsky
added. "Frederick looks like a fairy."

"Germans never change," Ezdovo added. "They poison six children, then risk their asses for a strip of painted canvas. Who can
understand German logic?"

It was Petrov's way to let them have their little asides, because
often such spontaneous comments led to interesting observations. But
now he led them forward again. "Approximately forty-five minutes
after lunch, the bunker people were summoned to the conference area
outside Hitler's quarters. He wore a gray jacket and black trousers.
Eva Braun was with him; she wore a black dress, brown shoes and a
platinum watch studded with diamonds. They shook hands with the
assembled group. Hitler said little, if anything."

"Out of character?" Gnedin asked.

"Possibly," noted Petrov. "Well taken, but let's come back to that
later. The farewells took no more than five minutes, probably less.
Then Linge opened the door to the apartment. Hitler shook his valet's
hand and told him to leave with the others during the breakout attempt. The door was closed. Günsche went to repost his guards in the
upper bunker, then quickly returned to take up the vigil. Linge also
went upstairs."

"Point of reference," Bailov interrupted. "If Günsche reposted his
men, which ones were reposted and where?"

"Well taken," Petrov said, a hint of excitement creeping into his
voice. "Make a note of that," he instructed Gnedin, who served as

the group's recording secretary. "The door is closed. Suddenly the Goebbels woman rushes down the hall and bursts into Hitler's apartment. He is standing in the anteroom, and she begs him to escape. Günsche, who has returned by now, follows her in. Hitler looks at Günsche and says, 'I don't want to see her.' Günsche removes her. The steel door is closed. An interval of time passes. Those in the corridor hear a shot from within the apartment. It is approximately three-thirty. Still they wait. After a time they enter the room. It is now approximately three-forty."

"They waited ten minutes after the shot," Rivitsky said. "Günsche tells us that he had been specifically instructed by Hitler to wait ten minutes after the shot before entering the rooms. Why ten minutes?"

"To give them time to die?"

"Why only one shot?" Ezdovo asked.

"Valid questions; note them," Petrov said and went on. "There is no agreement on the order in which people entered the apartment. It seems that either Goebbels or Bormann was first, followed by Günsche and a few seconds later by Axmann, who had arrived at the bunker too late for the farewell scene. The bodies were on the couch. Hitler was bent slightly forward, heavy blood flowing from his face. The woman was at the opposite end, resting against the armrest. No blood. Hitler's right arm hung down over the couch. On the floor near his right hand was a 7.65 Walther. Nearby was a 6.35-caliber revolver. Some claim to have seen a hole in his right temple trickling blood, but most of the flow came from his mouth; we have consensus on that point. There were no obvious marks on the woman. The room smelled strongly of bitter almonds—potassium cyanide. Günsche left the corpses and encountered Kempka in the conference area. He told Kempka that Hitler was dead. Bormann didn't say anything, but went to inform generals Burgdorf and Krebs, both of whom were intoxicated. Axmann of the Hitler Youth was left alone with the corpses for a few moments. Linge asked Kempka about the petrol. He was told that one hundred and seventy liters was waiting in jerricans in the Chancellery garden.

"At this juncture Rattenhuber and Dr. Stumpfegger arrive. Linge wraps Hitler's body in a blanket so that only the legs and shoes are visible. Stumpfegger helps Linge carry Hitler's body. Bormann carries the woman, but Kempka blocks his way and takes her away from him. On the stairs to the garden Kempka slips and nearly drops her;

Günsche comes to his aid. As they take the bodies into the garden an SS guard comes around the corner. Günsche screams for him to get out of the way."

"The guard's name?" Rivitsky asks.

"Unknown," Petrov tells them. "Note it. The bodies are put into a shallow depression, an excavation made by an exploded shell. Kempka douses the bodies with petrol. Artillery shells begin to land in the area, interrupting their work. For protection, they are forced to retreat to the doorway of the bunker entrance. When a lull comes, Günsche helps Linge douse the bodies. Günsche suggests that they ignite the fire with a grenade, but Kempka will not allow it. They get the fire started by using a rag ignited with a match provided by Goebbels. The guard Mengershausen is at this time on duty in the Mosaic Room of the Chancellery, an estimated one hundred meters away. He sees the bodies brought out and witnesses the start of the burning process. Another guard, Karnau, sees the fire begin when he walks near the guard tower; he maintains that he was around the corner from the others so that they could not see him. He was close enough to see the faces of the bodies and identified Hitler from his mustache. The rest of the head he describes as 'smashed.' It is now between four and four-thirty P.M. Over the next few hours more fuel is added to the fire. During this period a number of the guards stop by to see what is going on. Reports of these people vary according to the condition of the bodies at the time. Günsche claims that at night the remains of the corpses were tied into canvas shelter halves and buried in a shell hole near where they were cremated; the process was not complete."

"Inadequate heat," Gnedin pointed out.

"The earth was then pounded flat to hide the fact of the burial," Petrov concluded.

"Where they remained until discovered by heroic members of the Seventy-ninth Rifle Corps," Rivitsky said, finishing the story.

"That's all we know now," Petrov said. "What questions do we ask? Where are the holes?"

"The autopsy," Gnedin said. "If the body is Hitler's, then our mission is complete."

"We know what the autopsy says; now we have to analyze it. It bothers me that the Forensics Commission has concluded that none of the bodies autopsied died of a gunshot wound, including that of General Krebs, who was not burned and whose body we saw. If this is a political judgment, I understand it; if it is their considered scientific opinion, then we have serious problems. Either these are the wrong bodies, or all the witnesses are lying."

"Mass hysteria can produce psychosis in a group, but it's unlikely. These are people accustomed to violence and to the bizarre," Gnedin said.

"Krebs was shot," Rivitsky said. "We found the body; there was no mistake about the bullet hole."

"Yes," Petrov said. "For the moment we will assume that our well-meaning forensics experts do not wish to have a war criminal with the courage to shoot himself. Chenko confirms this. His view is that there were clearly gunshot wounds, but he is only an observer to the commission. Its findings are official."

"This is irrelevant," Gnedin said impatiently. "The teeth prove their point. The commission has found the two dental technicians, Heusermann and Echtmann, and complete records. The two of them have been interrogated repeatedly, and they positively identified Hitler and Eva Braun by their dental works, including a prosthesis built for her. This is difficult evidence to refute. It cannot be discarded so easily."

"Objection noted," Petrov said, his voice playful. "Please remember our mission. What the commission believes and reports has no bearing on us. Their findings are of no real interest to us. Again I remind you that we seek the truth, and only the truth."

There was a tone in their leader's voice that surprised the men. He was emotional, but under control; if they didn't know better, it would seem that he was almost teasing them. He was holding something back.

"Ezdovo, share your information with your colleagues."

They all looked expectantly at the Siberian. He made the most of his moment, sipping his vodka and swishing it around in his mouth before he swallowed and spoke. "The SMERSH boys finished with Fräulein Heusermann yesterday. She's a small one—young, blond, bosomy." He demonstrated with his hands. "Chenko told us the commission had asked her to identify the dental work in the jaw taken from Hitler's corpse. I fished her out of SMERSH, told her I was with the commission and that we wished her to make an inspection of the jaw in order to be certain. I told her we understood that she had been under great pressure and that so far she had been very cooperative. She was eager to please me, I can tell you that. I explained to her that she was under arrest, but that we wished to reward her cooperation by allowing her to return to her flat to gather her personal belongings. She was very appreciative."

"I can imagine," Bailov said admiringly.

"Pay attention," Petrov warned.

"I drove her to her flat. At first she was nervous, but then I gave her some vodka and it seemed to calm her."

All the men laughed.

"She relaxed. I asked her to tell me about what it was like to be part of the upper echelon of the Third Reich. She tells me, 'There's lots of parties. They go all night and sometimes for more than a day.' She tells me Bormann is fucking half the women in the Chancellery, then writing letters to his wife about his affairs, giving her all the details. She says Goebbels fucks young ones and insists they can't be any older than his eldest daughter."

"All right," Petrov said with a hint of irritation. "Get to the point."

"We're in her flat. Comfortable. Her Nazi friends have been very generous, and she says she's had lots of boyfriends. I give her some time to pack a valise, and while she packs I take a look around. There are bloodstains in a number of places. She tells me that on the night of the breakout a captain called Helmut Beerman shows up at her flat and begs her for sanctuary. He was one of Mohnke's group, but got separated from them and was scared of crossing the river by himself. Later in the morning, Beetz, Baur's copilot, crawls up to her flat. He's been shot and his skull is cracked open. The girl and Beerman try to help him, but he dies later in the day. They bury him in a rubble pile outside her building. Beerman still wanted to try escaping. He asked the girl to go with him, but when she refused, he took off on his own. It's around noon. She stayed in her flat until a Bulgarian medical student sent by SMERSH came to fetch her for questioning."

"So much for Beetz. We can move him to another category," Rivitsky said. "What happened to Beerman?"

Ezdovo shrugged. "She never saw him again. I finally got down to real business with the girl. I unwrapped a jawbone and laid it on the table. You should have seen the look on her face."

"The jawbone from the corpse in the mortuary?" Gnedin asked.

Ezdovo ignored his comrade's question. "She took a long time. Finally she says, 'It's his.' Whose? I ask. 'The Führer's,' she says. I ask her if she's certain. She's very emphatic, and proceeds to give me a point-by-point match against the Führer's dental records—all from her memory. It was a convincing display. I ask her to confirm that this is the same jawbone she previously examined for the commission. This provokes her anger; 'Absolutely,' she shouts. I then tell her that the jawbone she has just identified was removed from the jaw of an SS sniper killed the day before and charred in a fire."

Gnedin, Rivitsky and Bailov sat with their mouths open, staring at him.

"This news causes her to weep; I let her get it out, then calm her and give her another vodka. I ask her if she had been certain of any of the identifications. She tells me she wasn't. She is afraid of the Ivans, she confides in me; she told the commission what she thought its members wanted to hear. Further, she says that when the SMERSH people took her to Dr. Blaschke's office in the Chancellery, she grabbed a special bridge from a storage box and mixed it in with the other specimens they had. Later, when she was asked to identify the bridge as belonging to Eva Braun, she did so truthfully—a lie of omission. They never asked if it had been installed, which it hadn't."

Petrov stepped in. "Recall that this bridge was the central evidence in the forensics ruling on the identification of the female body as that of Eva Braun."

"But it couldn't be evidence," Ezdovo pointed out. "At the time Hitler's woman died, the bridge was in her dentist's office, not in her mouth. It turns out that Fräulein Heusermann's testimony is entirely worthless."

"I'll be fucked," Bailov said.

"Then who is the dead female?" Gnedin asked.

Petrov paused. "Eva Braun."

Now they were all on the edge of their chairs.

"The body was severely traumatized, probably from artillery rounds landing on the grave in the courtyard, but I'm quite certain it's her."

"Then the male is Hitler after all," Rivitsky said.

"We shall see," Petrov said. "If the number one war criminal was going to stage his own death, what better red herring to offer than the corpse of his new bride?"

Rivitsky jumped in again. "You think he's alive?"

"There's one more factor to consider. Yesterday I visited one of the suburban collection points where they have rounded up various Nazi women," Petrov told them. "They're holding only women in uniform, so it's unlikely that we'll ever see the secretaries again. If they got past our troops—a miracle in itself—they'll go into hiding. They won't be found by us among the refugees; they'll head for the west. But I had another thought that I wanted to pursue. Linge told me that Hitler's cook was an Austrian. It seemed to me that, given our presence, being an Austrian would be preferred over being a German."

"Hitler was an Austrian," Gnedin said, pointing out the obvious.

"True, but irrelevant," Petrov told him. "A large ratio of the SS is Austrian-born. Also irrelevant. What *is* relevant is that Austria was annexed against its will by the Germans."

"That's bullshit," Rivitsky said. "Everyone knows the Austrians welcomed the Germans with open arms."

"The people, yes; the government, no. Technically, Austria has the same status as France or Czechoslovakia or any other country seized by Hitler. Under our agreements with the Western Allies, citizens of these countries must be considered to be liberated by our presence and allowed to return home. Our government has agreed to this."

"A mere cook won't know this."

"She'll be desperate; it's all she's got. I figured out the route Mohnke's group took; she was with him. I walked it myself. There are three hospitals in that area, but only one is handling civilians. I went there and asked to read the patient register. I love the Germans for this; they always keep their records neat and complete. The hospital had seven Austrians in its beds, two of them female. She was one of them."

The men grinned.

"She had been raped and beaten, then shot and left for dead. She had lost a lot of blood, but she was conscious off and on. She told me two things. First, for his final meal Hitler ate a lettuce salad and spaghetti; he ate everything. Second, she said, there was a fifth person present at that final meal, an SS guard, a corporal Schweibel."

"Remarkable," Bailov said, his awe plain. "He eats his entire meal even though he's about to kill himself."

"Interesting," Rivitsky said.

"Once I had his name, I put out an alert for Schweibel. I got a call last night. He was brought here and I questioned him." Petrov picked up a document and waved it. "Not much in here. He went out in the last group and was captured on the other side of the river. But he confirmed the menu of Hitler's last meal and that he ate everything."

Petrov paused. "Next I called on Chenko. The autopsy report does not indicate if the stomach was dissected. They took five cc's of urine from the bladder, but never opened the stomach, according to the report. Chenko confirmed this. The organs had been removed and placed in specimen jars. This morning Chenko and I visited the mortuary. The bodies had already been cremated, but the visceral specimens were intact. Chenko dissected the stomach. He found no evidence of food—none."

"The *lettuce*," Gnedin said in a deep voice.

"The lettuce," Petrov confirmed. "The leaf does not digest easily. If Hitler died only an hour after eating, there would be lettuce in the stomach."

"But they burned the body," Bailov interjected. "That would have destroyed it."

"Only if the fire destroyed the stomach, but the stomach was intact. It was blackened and dried out in places, but the cavity retained its storage integrity and there was no lettuce, as there should have been."

"*If* it was Hitler," Ezdovo said, voicing what they were all thinking.

There was silence in the room.

Petrov sat down, brushed his hair back and picked up his glass. "I'll have another one."

Gnedin walked to the back of the room to be alone. Several minutes passed. Petrov watched as the facts sank into their minds.

"A double," Ezdovo said.

"The German word is *Doppelgänger*," Petrov reminded them. "I have reason to believe that Hitler had three, which he used infrequently—one of them here in Berlin. Undoubtedly there were more. The Seventy-ninth Rifle Corps, in fact, unearthed one of them during its search of the Chancellery garden."

"The body in the water tank."

"Probably arranged by Goebbels before his death, as a final gesture to his master," Petrov said.

"Fascist loyalty."

"It's indisputable," Petrov said. "Do you agree?"

"*Da*," Ezdovo grunted. "The woman's testimony has been unmasked and the empty stomach speaks loudly."

"Yes," said Gnedin. "I think you have something."

Rivitsky nodded. "A strong case."

"Yes," agreed Bailov.

"What's the next step?" Rivitsky asked.

"I report to Stalin. Then we sleep. Tomorrow we begin the follow-up. Consider when a double might have been inserted. My own feeling is that it had to be done at the last possible moment, absolutely the last."

"During the ten-minute delay," Bailov blurted out.

"How?" asked Ezdovo.

"I don't know," Petrov said. "Not yet. But the corpse that is not Hitler's tells us there had to be a way."

Gnedin interrupted. "I still have doubts."

"Explain," Petrov commanded.

"The teeth. Maybe the woman lied to Ezdovo, and even to the commission, but the pathologists still were the ones who actually matched the teeth to the records. I accept the lettuce as a powerful area of doubt—something to be further investigated and considered—but I have to think about this some more. Perhaps we don't want to believe the obvious."

"Let's suppose, for the sake of argument," Petrov countered, "that the double's teeth had been prepared and altered. Not such a difficult matter, and it would not be necessary for the fillings to be identical if you planned to fire a bullet into the teeth. You have to consider the dynamics. Our doctors *want* to identify Hitler—if not alive, then dead. The evidence will be colored by their legitimate desire to be rid of the monster. What we are talking about is making a few small modifications that will enable the investigators to suspend their disbelief.'

"What about the missing testicle?"

"Ah," Petrov said. "A simple matter. First, it has been rumored that Hitler had only a single testicle. It may or may not be true; there's no evidence in the medical records to support it. But consider: if you were Hitler and had an enemy who believed this, what better proof of your death could you provide than a corpse with a single gonad? Surgically removed from the double. I doubt that Hitler lacks one, but he has seen to it that the world has found what it expected, no?"

Gnedin shook his head. "It follows, but this is conjecture, not science."

"In an investigation one always goes from science to conjecture. Science is but a formal way of thinking and classifying what we see, a method of relating what we do know to what we want to know. But this time I feel in my bones and in my mind that the weight of evidence points to our view. The commission is wrong: Adolf Hitler is alive. The question is, where has he gone?"

▸23 MAY 14, 1945, 10:00 A.M.

Petrov, Bailov and Gnedin returned the next day to the bunker below the Reich Chancellery. Bailov located the diesel engine that served as the power generator for the facility, started it and turned on the lighting before the group assembled in Hitler's suite.

"The whole thing is so simple that it's easy to not see the obvious," Petrov said. "Artists spend their entire lives learning how to see. Policemen do the same. Most people go through life looking at the world around them, but never actually seeing what is there. That's our problem. It's all been here right in front of us, so obvious that we simply couldn't accept it. The switch had to have been made at the very last moment, *after* all the witnesses had seen them shut themselves into this area. The clear but invisible fact is that there must be another way out."

"Could he have hidden and waited, then slipped out through the stairs to the unfinished tower?" Bailov wondered.

"No. First, this would mean that the double would have had to be hiding in here for some time before the switch. Secondly, it would be too difficult to hide him from Braun. The double would have to enter through the escape route."

"Unless she knew what he was planning," Gnedin said.

"Yes, that's possible," Petrov allowed. "She was a simple-minded thing, dedicated to her master. But while it's possible that she would agree to a sacrificial suicide to cover his escape, I doubt it. From what we know of her, she was selfish and self-centered. Furs, silk dresses, French underwear, expensive perfumes, jewels—what do these say about Braun? Here they were with the world collapsing above them and she has arranged to keep all of her bourgeois finery with her. It's not likely she would agree to kill herself unless she thought that Hitler would die too. Without him, she was nothing. This has all the signs of a carefully organized operation, planned long before its time. Hitler had plenty of opportunity to flee to his *Alpenfestung* as part of Operation Seraglio, but he chose to remain in Berlin. This in itself is a curious choice that demands further examination. His armies, such as they were, were still fighting in central Austria and in the Munich area. He had some reserves in Italy near the Austro-Swiss border. At the end, despite its losses, the Wehrmacht still managed to control a narrow strip of Germany stretching from the Baltic to Austria. The war was not over, not for an extremist like Hitler. From a military perspective, he retained ample room to maneuver—tactically if not strategically—and enough firepower to continue, if he was careful in selecting where and when his armies fought. His history has always been to flee confrontation in order to scheme again. This is an important biographical fact," Petrov said firmly. "The trend is clear; a man does not change such deep habits. Those who run early run late. It's the nature of the man we're seeking."

The others listened intently.

"It's my opinion that Braun knew nothing of the conspiracy. She killed herself believing they would die together. After she eliminated herself, the switch was made. Weighing all the evidence, this is the only deduction that can be made. It follows that there must be a way in and out of this place that neither the woman nor any of the other Nazis knew of."

"A false wall," Gnedin suggested.

"Or floor," Petrov added quickly. "It's curious that this bunker, which was constructed only recently and built all at once, has two levels. There is no architectural rationale for this level being deeper than the other. If the other level is above, then there may be a route underneath it."

"Wall, floor, ceiling: there are no other choices," Bailov said. "Whichever it is, it has to be in this area, because there is only one obvious way in: through the door to the corridor. If it were I, I'd want direct access to this area to minimize discovery of the double and the plan."

"Precisely," Petrov said. "It's here, near us."

During the ensuing discussion, it was Bailov who suggested that they investigate the light fixtures. Beginning first in Eva Braun's bedroom, they examined the lights mounted in the ceilings. In each, they found only a shallow well that housed the fixture. The wire disappeared from the fixture into a metal conduit, which in turn was embedded in the surrounding concrete itself. The next to the last light they tried was in the corner of Hitler's bedroom. Bailov opened it, but found that he could not extract it from the mounting as he had the others. "This one's different," Bailov reported. "It won't come loose."

Petrov squinted at the ceiling. "Probe it," he directed.

Using a small hammer from an impressive tool bin in the power room, Bailov bashed in one side of the fixture. Bending the metal, he could see concrete. "It's the same. It must be stuck."

"Chip at the concrete," Petrov advised. He was standing directly underneath, watching intently.

"It's several feet thick," Bailov complained.

"Perhaps," Petrov said. Bailov pounded for some time before small flakes began to break loose. After a while he tired and Gnedin took over. It took more than an hour, and Petrov refused to allow them to rest. It was Bailov who finally made the breakthrough. "I'll be damned," he said. "There's a metal plate inside the concrete."

"Leave it," Petrov said. "Let's test some of the other fittings." Working on the others was easier because the lighting units could be removed and more room was available for leverage with the hammer and a sharp chisel. They drove holes in the others to the same depth as the one that contained the metal backing, but they seemed to be all concrete; there were no more plates. After the third one had been tested, Petrov directed them back to the original discovery. Bailov struck the metal several times. "Heavy gauge, but I think we can get through it with a sledge and a chisel."

Gnedin got the tools they needed from a work detail on the grounds of the Chancellery. Using brute force, it took them two hours to pierce the metal backing. With a flashlight, they could see that there was a dark, hollow space above. Satisfied that they were on to something, they used the crowbar to bend the fixture from its mounting and boosted Petrov into the opening. It was large enough to accommodate a man somewhat larger than their diminutive leader.

Shining his light ahead of him, Petrov could see immediately that there was plenty of room up here. This was no secret escape tunnel—just a long, straight duct, probably for maintenance access. Marks in the dust of the shaft's floor told him that someone had been here, though how recently he couldn't tell. Before attempting to explore, he studied the metal support that had held the light fixture. Heavy screws held it in place in the duct. Removal of the fixture, he realized, could be accomplished *only from above*. From below it looked like all of the others, but from above, a confederate could remove the screws, lift out the light, accomplish the transfer, then replace the fixture and screws when the task was accomplished. Given its appearance from below, there would be no reason to suspect that it could be removed and no way to determine the fact without deliberately tearing it apart. This was what they had been looking for. The escape hatch was ingenious, further evidence of how well the flight from the bunker had been planned.

Petrov poked his head down through the opening. He wanted to be sure that this was the only fixture that permitted egress; he had to be certain. "Remove the other fixtures. I want to be sure that this is the only one like this."

"What's up there?" Gnedin asked while Bailov swore at the work ahead of them.

"A large metal duct of some kind. It doesn't seem to serve any purpose. The shaft is large enough to move through. The light was fastened with screws from up here. Whoever designed it had this in mind." Petrov sat back to wait for the work to be done.

"The other lights are all the same," Bailov shouted up after a long interval. "They're all recessed in the concrete."

Petrov grunted acknowledgment. "I'm going to have a look around up here." Crawling forward, he soon reached the first wide area. He studied the metal surface, which looked as if it had been wiped clean. But when he lay flat on his stomach, lowering his face to a centimeter or two above the surface and scanning with his light, he found several small black stains, no wider than pencil points. Moving his face even closer, he guessed what they were and used a small knife to break them loose from the metal. Using a white cloth, he blotted at the dried spots until they stuck to the fabric, then carefully folded the cloth and stored it in an inner pocket of his coat. Continuing the inspection, he located several hairs of different lengths and, as meticulously as before, collected the specimens, wrapped them in another cloth and tucked the evidence away for safekeeping. Satisfied that nothing else remained, he moved on, eventually reaching the point where the shaft turned straight up. He rolled onto his back and slid himself into the vertical shaft, pushing himself up with his legs. Using his flashlight for extra height, he could just tap the top—almost three meters, he guessed. He tried briefly to work up the shaft by bracing his back against one wall and his feet against the other, but it was no use. The metal was too slippery to gain a purchase. He needed help.

Bailov and Gnedin were sitting on the edge of the bed, looking up in anticipation, when Petrov suddenly reappeared.

"What did you find?" Bailov asked eagerly.

"Get rope and bring another light," Petrov said.

Bailov fetched the required items immediately. He wasn't going to miss this opportunity. "Me?" he pleaded.

"No. Send Gnedin; he's thinner. Space is tight up here."

With the help of the disappointed Bailov, Gnedin was boosted into the hole in the ceiling and the two men disappeared. Because of Petrov's size and Gnedin's bony frame, they were able to get into the vertical shaft together. Petrov used the doctor's body as a ladder and climbed to the next level. For the moment, he left Gnedin behind and moved along the chute, his anxiety growing.

Within a few meters there was another wide spot. As he had at the other site, Petrov explored this one methodically, ignoring Gnedin's occasional shouted requests for a report. This time he was disappointed: there was nothing. He sat back to think, and used the light to examine the walls and ceiling. A glint, a different color—he never knew exactly what—at the seam of a wall caught his attention. The metal at the seam was overlapped and near it, high up near the ceiling, was a series of scratch marks. By changing his body position, he could see that the metal had been slightly crimped. After more examination, he decided that something had been wedged under the seam. Why? No answer suggested itself, so he moved on, eventually reaching a dead end. Now the mystery increased; there seemed to be no means of exit and the walls and seams all appeared to be tight. Testing them, he found that the walls resisted pressure; they were quite solid, or seemed so. Yet the tunnel led directly to this dead end. Two views would be helpful. He returned to the vertical shaft to assist Gnedin up to his level.

Gnedin offered up the rope, but Petrov shook his head. "There's nothing to fasten it to up here." The words were out before their meaning hit him. Suddenly he understood the reason for the marks on the wall above: something had been wedged under the overlap, something intended to anchor a rope. "Wait," he told Gnedin, who was reaching up for help.

Petrov turned his light to the lip of the drop-off, but found nothing. "Listen to me," he said quietly. "I want you to get down on your knees carefully, then back into the shaft. Don't touch the floor with any more of your body than you can help."

"Is there a booby trap?" Gnedin asked nervously.

"Tell me when you're in the shaft."

"I'm in the shaft," Gnedin reported with a grunt. "Hit my back on an edge," he complained. "Now what?"

"Use your light. Start at the base of the vertical drop and tell me what you see."

"Nothing."

"Look again," Petrov said from above, adding his light to the bottom.

"There's nothing here," Gnedin said, annoyance in his voice. "Just some dust, like elsewhere."

"Dust, good. What else? What's the dust like? Describe it to me as if you were performing an autopsy. Remember what I said about seeing." He watched Gnedin lean out of his shaft below to look.

"So far as I can tell, it's nothing special. Dirt, some small hairs. Nothing."

Petrov smiled and dropped a cloth to his companion below, its fluttering arrival startling the doctor. "Pick up as many of the hairs as you can find and put them in the cloth, then wrap them carefully." Gnedin did as he was told, muttering over the difficulty in capturing the tiny hairs in the poor light.

"All right, I've got them."

"How many?"

"A dozen, maybe more. Hard to say. They're minute."

"All right, take my hand," Petrov said. "I need your eyes up here."

Back at the dead end, they combed the area on their hands and knees. Like Petrov, Gnedin saw nothing that gave a clue of an opening. Finally, the doctor crossed his legs, leaned against a wall, lit a cigarette and coughed.

"The smoke will interfere," Petrov said.

"I don't care, I need one now. It will give me time to think." Gnedin had set his flashlight down, light first, and as he started to lift it he stopped. "Look," he said, pointing to the metal below his legs.

Petrov leaned over and studied the area under the light. "Almost invisible."

"Scratches," Gnedin announced. Backing off, they discovered small scratches in the pattern of a wide arc, incontrovertible evidence that something had swung inward. The wall before them *opened in, not out.*

"Stay here," Petrov said. "In ten minutes I want you to start striking the wall with the butt of your light at fifteen-second intervals."

"For how long?"

"Until I tell you to stop."

Petrov backtracked, was helped down from the ceiling by Bailov and led him up through the airtight and watertight metal entry hatch into the tunnel that went under the Chancellery. Only then did they notice the metal plates in the walls. They were painted the same color as the smooth wall and blended so well that it was difficult to see them until one looked closely. Stopping at the first one outside the bunker entrance, Petrov used his knife to loosen the screws and lift the panel. Inside was a metal canister marked "Water."

"Storage bins," Petrov said. He began walking slowly down the corridor, pausing often to listen. They were midway down the second long hall when he halted. "Hear it?" he asked Bailov, who didn't.

Continuing on, they finally isolated the sound, which was surprisingly well muffled. Petrov unscrewed the plate and lifted it. A coiled fire hose was inside. The metallic sound was louder now, directly on the other side.

"This is it," Petrov announced. "This is how they did it." Using his hands, he located the single screw in back of the box and loosened it as the pounding continued. "Get back," he shouted to Gnedin, then said to Bailov, "I can't reach it; my arms aren't long enough. Push; it swings in."

Bailov grunted and under his effort the back of the storage compartment gave way, quietly swinging open to reveal Gnedin, who sat calmly smoking a cigarette, a big smile on his face. "Dr. Livingstone, I presume," he said happily to his colleagues.

▶24 MAY 14, 1945, 5:00 P.M.

If the duct indeed was the escape mechanism, then those who used it had to get in it and out of it from the hall. Petrov saw that this had been the flaw in the plan. He ordered reinterrogations of all the captured Chancellery guards, reasoning that because all the Nazis in the bunker seemed to be in general agreement about what had occurred, perhaps someone on the periphery had seen something of interest. He wouldn't rest until interviews were done again, and Bailov and Gnedin were assigned to conduct them.

It was Gnedin who got the break during the second interrogation of Sergeant Gustav Rudolf, and Petrov was summoned immediately.

The leader of the Special Operations Group entered the room and spoke directly to Gnedin in Russian. "What is it?"

"I want you to hear something," the doctor told his leader. He turned to the German. "Tell us again about your final shift on guard in the Chancellery."

Rudolf told his story. Hitler and an SS colonel had come along the hallway where he was posted and told him to move to another location because the guard there had disappeared.

"He forgot to tell us about this during the initial interview," Gnedin told Petrov in Russian.

"Was it unusual to see Hitler outside the bunker?" Petrov asked in his precise German.

"Yes, very unusual at the end. We didn't see him much toward the last."

"And you changed your post because Hitler asked you to?"

"Hitler didn't ask. He told me to change. It was a direct order. Wouldn't you have done what he said?"

Petrov ignored the rhetorical question. "Did you see Hitler often?"

"At the end, no. Before that, yes. Not every day—more like every week, sometimes more often."

"But not at the end?"

"Some at the end, just not as much as before. He used to go back and forth between the bunker and the Chancellery for meetings."

"What was the date of this final encounter?"

"April thirtieth."

"You're certain of that date?"

"Of course."

"What is today's date?"

"I don't know," Rudolf said, astonished. "You keep me locked in the dark. There are no calendars, no clocks. How would I know?"

"But you are certain of the date you met Hitler."

"Sure. We were all aware of the time then. It was running out."

"When did you see Hitler before this last time?"

"A few days before."

"More precisely."

"I can't say; I don't know exactly."

"But you remember the last time."

"Sure, April thirtieth." Rudolf was exasperated. "I'll bet every one of us who was there at the end can remember specific things. We were all frightened. You couldn't help thinking that in a few hours you were going to be dead. I remember April thirtieth because that night my captain told me that Hitler had killed himself in the afternoon. When I heard that, I thought I was going to die too. Only, I didn't."

Gnedin smiled.

"Tell me the story again," Petrov ordered. Rudolf did as he was told, and there were no differences in the details.

Petrov talked in Russian to Gnedin. "I think we need more details from this one. Can you hypnotize him? Is there a drug to help us?"

Gnedin considered. "Hypnotism would be better. What drugs we have are rather crude. I doubt if they'll help. Drugs are more useful for extracting gross information."

"Give it a try."

Gnedin grinned. "Leave me alone with him. Ten minutes, twenty at the outside. If I can't put him under in twenty minutes, I won't be able to do it at all."

Petrov and Bailov waited outside the door; Petrov used the time to think about what the German guard had said. A tightness in his stomach told him that this might be another important break.

In precisely ten minutes Gnedin opened the door and called them inside. Rudolf was still seated on a stool, but his eyes were closed and he looked relaxed.

"Relatively easy," Gnedin explained. "You can ask your questions now. He's expecting them."

"Sergeant, tell us once more about your meeting with Hitler."

Rudolf told the story again, but this time there were more details. Petrov's heart was pounding as he waited for the man to finish. When Rudolf was done, Petrov began. "Hitler handed you your greatcoat?"

"Yes."

"With which hand did he give it to you?"

"I don't understand."

Petrov's eyes narrowed. "His left hand or his right?"

Rudolf's brow creased momentarily. His hands, which had been hanging at his sides, lifted slightly. "Left hand."

"You're certain it was his left hand?"

"Yes, his left."

"How can you be certain?"

"Because as he handed me my coat, he saluted me."

"Show me."

Rudolf lifted his right arm stiffly in the Nazi salute and reached forward with his left arm to Petrov, as if he were handing him something.

"You always salute with your right hand?"

"Always with the right hand," Rudolf said solemnly.

"And he gave you the coat with his left hand?"

"Yes."

"At the same time he was saluting you?"

"Yes."

Petrov's eyes were burning coals. He glanced at Gnedin, who nodded, as if to say, "This is the truth you're hearing."

Petrov returned his attention to Rudolf. "Hitler came from the direction of the Chancellery. Is that correct?"

"Yes, from the Chancellery."

"Did you see him earlier? Did he pass you going the other direction?"

"No, just coming from the Chancellery. That's the only time I saw him."

"Were you asleep at any time in your shift?"

Rudolf shook his head briskly, his eyes still closed. "If the Führer had found me asleep, he would have had me shot. I wouldn't take stupid chances, not this late in the war."

Gnedin smiled, Bailov stifled a giggle and even Petrov offered the hint of a grin.

"What time did you go on duty?"

"Eleven hundred hours."

"And what time were you to be relieved?"

"Fifteen hundred hours."

"A four-hour tour of duty?"

"Yes."

"And after you were off, how long before you were to come on again?"

"Eight hours."

"The entire security force was on a four-on, eight-off cycle?"

"Everyone."

"What time did you see Hitler?"

"At two. I had just looked at the time. There was an hour left in my watch."

"You saw Hitler coming toward you from the Chancellery at precisely two o'clock?"

"First I heard him. You have to learn how to use your ears, and then how to see out of the corner of your eyes. That's how we were trained. They didn't want us staring at the big shots."

"First you heard him coming, then you saw him from the corner of your eye, and then he reached you. And you saw him directly?"

"He stood right in front of me."

"And he told you to change posts?"

"Yes." Rudolf grimaced. "No. The colonel told me first, then the Führer."

"How did Hitler look?"

"I don't understand."

"Was he moving slowly, quickly? Did he have difficulty walking?"

"He looked normal."

"No limp."

"I didn't see one."

"But you knew he had a limp?"

"Everybody knew that."

"And it didn't occur to you that it was odd that he wasn't limping?"

"Sir?"

"You knew his health was bad?"

"Yes."

"And you knew his right leg was impaired."

"Sure. I'd seen it before. It looked painful."

"How do you account for the limp being gone?"

"I don't. Perhaps he was getting better. He had lots of doctors."

"You're sure there was no limp?"

"He walked perfectly, just like me." Rudolf began to stand, but Petrov touched his shoulder as a sign for him to remain seated.

"He stopped and talked to you?"

"Yes."

"How did he seem?"

"Friendly, quiet. Like there was a lot on his mind. But he was always friendly to the enlisted men. He was a corporal before he went into politics."

"His voice was the same? His hair? His eyes?"

"Yes . . . well, sort of. His eyes were different."

"The color of them?"

"No, not the color. It was their intensity. . . ." Rudolf paused. "They weren't bright. He stared right at me and I didn't turn away. *That* was unusual. The Führer made you feel uncomfortable when he looked directly at you."

"But not this time?"

"No," Rudolf whispered, almost as if his subconscious were trying to process the information.

"Was there anything else different?"

"He didn't know my name."

"Why should he?"

"He knew my name before."

"Was there a special reason for this?"

"No, he knew the names of all his people. The Führer's memory for names was fantastic," Rudolf said admiringly. "He was famous for it."

"His memory lapse upset you."

"Just for a moment."

"But you forgave him?"

"I said to myself, 'He's got the whole Third Reich to worry about; why should he remember your name?' "

"Tell me about the SS colonel."

"I can't. He stayed behind the Führer and I didn't dare look too hard. Those SS colonels are tough."

Petrov probed for more information about the colonel, but came up with little. To stand almost directly in front of another human being and not be noticed was a skill, not an accident.

"Are you tired now?"

"Yes. And hungry."

"Just a bit more." Petrov's voice dripped with concern. "I have only a few more questions; then you can rest."

"Thank you."

"When you went to your new post, what time were you relieved?"

"Fifteen hundred hours precisely."

"Did your comrade ever come back?"

"Never."

"Not even later that night?"

"We never saw him again."

"What do you think happened to him?"

"Deserted. His post was by an outside door."

"Why do you think that?"

"We all wanted to get out!"

"Even you?"

"Especially me."

"But you stayed."

"I was afraid to run away."

"I think it was your sense of duty that kept you there, Sergeant," Petrov said magnanimously.

Rudolf shook his head. "I was afraid. I didn't want to die out there."

"But you escaped later?"

"Yes."

"What's the difference?"

"There were a lot of us. I felt safer in a group."

"Yet you were captured anyway."

"Yes, but alive."

"You were captured on the other side of the river on the morning of May—" Gnedin held up three fingers. "May third."

"I'm not sure. It was after they fucked."

Petrov's eyes widened. He looked to Gnedin for an explanation as he spoke to the guard. "I don't understand."

"The Russian officer. I was in some rocks. She and one of her men came back to where I was hiding. They took off their clothes and fucked. It was still morning. They enjoyed it."

"And they saw you?"

"Yes, after they were done. The man took a piss near me, then they found me. She sat on my face."

Petrov looked baffled. Bailov giggled and fought back a laugh.

"A female Russian officer *sat on your face?*" Petrov's eyebrows were standing vertically.

"With her cunt. Then the man kicked me in the balls. They beat me up. I'm still sore." He began to show them, but Petrov again caught his arm.

"Hitler handed your coat to you with his left hand?"

"The left."

"And he walked without a limp."

"He walked normally."

"And you stared him down?"

"It was odd."

"And he couldn't remember your name?"

"I had to tell him what it was, but I didn't mind."

"And the other guard was never seen again?"

"I didn't see him."

"What was his name?"

"Holzmeyer. Ernst. He was a corporal."

"He was a friend of yours?"

"No."

Petrov turned to Gnedin. "Well?"

"We all heard him. It's got to be the truth. The brain retains a lot of information that we can't bring to the conscious mind on demand. Hypnotism opens some kind of door. I don't know exactly how it works, but it does."

"In this state could he lie to us?"

"With training it can be done, but I don't think this one could. We can test him."

The look on Petrov's face told Gnedin to proceed.

"Rudolf, in a moment I'm going to wake you up and you'll feel completely refreshed. Does that sound good to you?"

"Very good."

"When you awake, you won't remember any of this. But first I want you to tell me something. The absolute truth. You understand?"

"Yes, sir."

"Do you like women?"

"Very much."

"Did you have relations with the women in the Chancellery?"

"Yes."

"How often?"

"Every shift I was off."

"Do you masturbate?"

Rudolf paused. "Yes."

"Often?"

His head dipped. "Yes."

"Tell me what you were thinking when the Russian officer and her soldier were making love."

Rudolf mumbled something and Gnedin asked him to repeat it.

"I wanted to take his place."

"What did you want to do to her?"

Petrov stepped forward before the German could answer. "That's enough, Doctor," he said. "I see what you are driving at; if he'd tell us that, the rest has to be the truth. Bring him out of it. I'm going to find Rivitsky."

▶25 MAY 15, 1945, 11:15 A.M.

Logan rode his bicycle as far up the mountain trail as he could, but the trail ended abruptly at the base of a rock field, so he discarded the rusty vehicle and set off on foot through the rocks. It had been humid all night, and now the clouds were rolling overhead in sinister formations. When he reached the middle of the slanting field, the rain descended as if a bucket had been emptied, and in seconds he was drenched. The dust covering the rocks turned slippery, and Logan, trying to hurry, slipped and went down hard, lacerating his knee and skinning both hands.

Finding partial cover under a huge boulder, Logan tore off the bottom of a pants leg and examined the bloody knee. It was a deep cut, down to the bone, and layers of yellow fat showed when he pushed on one side of the wound: it would need stitches, he knew, and lots of them. Of all the rotten times to get hurt. He'd been sent from Zurich to deliver a coded message to Beau Valentine, code name Crawdad. Logan had been uncomfortable from the moment he was given the assignment; he was an office man, an analyst, paid to work with his brain, not his body, and this was the first time since his arrival in Switzerland two years before that he had been asked to do anything outside his normal job. Aside from the discomfort of traipsing around in the mountains, the worst part of this assignment was having to leave the amenities of Zurich; right now the OSS was in high gear trying to find out what the Russians were up to in eastern Germany, and the information was coming in by bits and pieces.

After checking the wound, Logan decided he was wrong; the worst part of this assignment was that he was going to have to deal directly with Beau Valentine, and nobody in his right mind would relish that reality. It was universally agreed that Crawdad was the most unpredictable and unorthodox man in the OSS. When he was given a job to do, he did not care what rules he had to violate in order to finish it.

Now, in the most foreboding terrain Logan had ever seen and in weather conditions that would make the hardiest of men cringe, he would have to find and deliver a message to the legendary Valentine, who openly professed hatred for all OSS office personnel, except his own case officer, who had politely declined the opportunity to visit his charge in his native habitat. It was left to him, and all he had to go on was a crude set of directions and an old photograph of Valentine.

His knee, Logan realized, would need expert medical attention, and if he did not keep moving, the leg would stiffen and cripple him so that he would be unable to move. For now the wound was numb, so he got to his feet, pulled his collar up and moved out into the rain. In the distance, behind a range of mountains, there was the rattle of thunder, like the crackling of snare drums played in an uneven rhythm.

Finally reaching the end of the boulder field, Logan found a muddy area where three trails intersected. His instructions had included the rocks, but not this confluence of trails, and he had no idea which one to follow. As he considered what he knew about the location of the camp where Valentine lived with his Italian and Yugoslavian partisans, a large tan cow came waddling round a bend of the southernmost trail, followed by two young boys whacking at the animal's haunches with long switches. Each of them had a shotgun slung over his back, and when the boys saw him, they quickly unslung their weapons and pointed them at him.

"I'm looking for the American," Logan told them in Italian.

They smiled, reslung their weapons and motioned for him to follow. Falling into step, he hobbled along the trail behind them and their cow, his leg beginning to hurt badly. The thunder was closer now and had increased to bass-drum proportions; with it lightning began to flash, its tentacles seeming to touch distant parts of the landscape.

It took nearly two hours to reach the camp built into the rocks on the side of a steep gorge, a collection of crude canvas and corrugated metal shelters, some as simple as lean-tos. A few pigs waddled around and chickens pecked near the dwellings. As the three got closer, armed men and women began to appear, and soon a crowd formed around Logan. Occasionally someone would poke at him with the barrel of a rifle, but he reminded himself to maintain control of his emotions. He had been briefed about partisans. They had no allegiance save to themselves and one another; if you did something to offend them, they might kill you. This information had chilled him then, but now it helped steady him as they pawed at him.

As they walked deeper into the encampment he counted nearly forty dwellings; there seemed to be a hundred or more people in the knot around him, and no doubt there were more still unseen, a much larger force than he had reckoned. They were dressed in parts of uniforms from several different armies, and some of the men wore brightly colored vests.

At the end of the encampment the group stopped and looked up toward the rocks. A huge man wearing a baseball cap was standing on a rickety porch, staring down with a wide smile. Immediately Logan recognized Valentine, who was holding a white chicken in his right hand. Suddenly, with almost imperceptible rotations of his wrist, he began to spin the chicken like a propeller until it turned into a blur and some feathers flew away from it. After a few seconds Valentine stopped spinning the fowl, popped its head off, and held the bird away from him so that its blood would spurt free. The crowd laughed and the messenger suddenly felt woozy, but before he could collapse, two partisans caught him and carried him up to the dwelling.

Valentine swept a table clean with his arm, and told the men to place Logan on it. When he was in position, Valentine pushed him onto his back, ripped off the bloody pants leg and began poking roughly at the cut, making Logan flinch. "Crawdad?" he asked feebly.

"Call me Beau," Valentine said happily. "Get my kit," he told one of the partisans, who rummaged through a pile of boxes in a corner, eventually fishing out a black leather bag. Valentine placed it on the table, opened it and extracted several instruments and a roll of gauze. Tearing off a section, he draped it over Logan's leg above the wound.

Other partisans were now pushing into the small cabin. "This isn't going to hurt," Valentine announced. "Me," he added after a pause, and the men roared their appreciation of his joke.

"Do you have a doctor?" Logan asked nervously.

"Next best thing," Valentine replied as he continued sorting supplies and instruments. As he unfolded a small kit containing needles and sutures, Logan tried to sit up, but strong hands pushed him down. "Wait," he said. "You're not going to try to stitch me."

Valentine stared at Logan quizzically. "Try? Shoot, no! I'm gonna do it." Logan struggled again, but Valentine sympathetically patted his chest. "Whoa, boy. I've got lots of experience with this sort of thing." He looked around, scanning the crowd. "Where is Umberto?"

"Here," a voice said, and a gaunt man limped to the front.

"Show him," Valentine said.

Umberto stepped up, bent over Logan and revealed a face twisted off center by a scar that began under one eye, descended to the corner of his mouth, climbed back up over the middle of the nose, dropped again to the other corner of his mouth, and finally curled into a whorl of pink flesh just to the right of his chin. The tissue was deep pink, still inflamed, and the scar pulled his facial muscles to the left. Logan tried to move back from the face, but was held in place. "Pretty nice work, eh, Americano?" Umberto asked. His breath was heavy with garlic, and the odor, coupled with the smell of the wet bodies in the room, made Logan queasy.

Valentine held a bottle of whiskey over the wound. "This is probably going to sting some," he said, and the hands on Logan immediately tightened, locking him to the table. Valentine poured the whiskey into the wound and Logan let go with a scream that hung in the room for a long time before finally subsiding into a prolonged whimper. "See?" Valentine asked. "Not too bad," he said. Stripping off his shirt, he gave the bottle to another man and held out his hands. After whiskey had been poured over them, he lifted his wet arms in the air and stared at the knee below him, as if trying to come to a decision.

"All right," he said finally to the crowd, "what's the time?"

"One-fourteen," a voice said.

"Good. Three to one if I don't close it up in ten minutes," he announced.

The group muttered among themselves. "No bet, Valentine," one of the men croaked. "Five minutes, or you got no bets."

Valentine frowned. "Bastards. Okay, five minutes, and because I'm in a generous mood I'll up the odds to six to one." The men immediately crowded around the table, and paper bills and coins scattered around the patient.

Picking up a needle, Valentine stabbed at it with thread but kept missing until a man brought a lantern to help him. Bending, he looked into the wound. "Five minutes will be a bitch, but what's life without a challenge?" He laughed. "But first I need tonic." A man held up a bottle of wine, and Valentine sucked on it without using his hands; the red liquid ran down his chin onto his chest. After several gulps, he pulled his chin in, belched and hunched his shoulders. "Time?"

"One-eighteen," the timekeeper announced.

"On your mark, get set, go," Valentine shouted as he deftly slid the curved needle into Logan's flesh. The patient's head came up, mouth open, then his eyes rolled to white and he fell back, hitting his head on the wooden table with a loud thump.

When Logan came to, he was in a chair on the porch, his leg wrapped tightly in a yellow cloth with grease stains and propped up on a small wooden keg. Instinctively he flexed his leg muscles and pain shot into his thigh from the knee. Finding that staying still eased the pain, he resolved to move no more than he had to. Looking around, he saw that several people were on the porch with him; others were nearby, sitting or standing on rocks, looking downhill. The rain had let up, but it was darker now and the thunder was loud, engulfing them. The darkness was interspersed with lightning that seemed so close that Logan felt the hairs rise on the back of his neck. What were they all looking at?

Leaning forward slightly, he saw half a dozen men below, standing on rocks several yards apart. They were naked except for their boots, and each of them held a ten-foot metal rod above his head. What the hell was going on?

"An experiment," Valentine said from the steps just below Logan. He had a bottle of wine in his hand, and a cigarette dangled from his lower lip. "Krauts," he said. "Stragglers. We tangled with them last night; these six are all that's left. Don't look so almighty with their little peckers shriveled up in the rain, do they?" He laughed.

Another series of lightning bolts suddenly flashed, and the partisans began talking excitedly to one another. Logan tried to analyze the situation. Lightning. Men on rocks. Holding metal rods. Oh, God! "You're using them as lightning rods," he shouted. "You can't do this!"

Valentine turned and looked at him. "Good enough for old Ben Franklin, good enough for Beau. We got bets on which one gets hit first. Course, if it doesn't happen soon, we'll just have to shoot them and be done with it. Much more interesting this way, don't you think?"

"You're crazy," Logan sputtered.

Suddenly a lightning bolt struck at the other end of the camp, and the partisans cheered wildly.

"Now we're cooking," Beau said with obvious pleasure. "By the way," he added, "what brings you up here?"

"Message," Logan said. "Inside pocket in back of my coat. It's encoded."

Valentine grabbed the coat, turned it over, extracted a rubber courier envelope from the pocket and went inside to decode the message.

As he reappeared a few minutes later, another bolt struck, this time even closer than the last, and thunder crashed overhead, making most of the watchers duck. Valentine held a Thompson submachine gun as he walked down the steps. "Shut up!" he called out to the partisans. "You," he shouted to the nearest German. "Are you a scientist?"

The man shook his head wildly. "I'm just a soldier," he whined.

"What about the rest of you?" Valentine shouted to the other Germans, but they all shook their heads.

"Damn," he said, kicking a loose stone down the hill. "I was hoping they were scientists; it would save me a trip to Germany." Turning back to the nearest German, he said, "Go."

The man looked puzzled.

"Go," Valentine repeated, but the Germans stayed where they were. Suddenly he lifted his Thompson and sprayed a burst into the ground in front of the prisoners, who immediately dropped their metal rods and ran wildly down the trail, pushing and shoving one another in an effort to get to the front. Dozens of other guns fired into the air, and there were shouts and laughter as the Germans disappeared.

Valentine turned to Logan. "That really pisses me off," he said angrily. "They didn't even say good-bye."

▶26 MAY 16, 1945, 8:00 A.M.

No matter how often he flew, Petrov was uncomfortable in the air. It was not simple fear; rather, it seemed to be more a question of control. On the ground, even in a train or a speeding automobile, he always had the feeling that he could dismount and go his own way at a time and place of his own choosing. He understood that he could leave an aircraft as well, but it would be a desperate kind of departure, without control. He knew it was irrational; to get out of a moving auto or train was far more dangerous than parachuting. Yet the fear persisted, and he no longer gave it much thought. It irritated him to have to fly, but he accepted it. Orders were orders, and duty required this journey. It amused him to think that the Berkut was afraid to fly.

He had received a typed message addressed to "The Berkut." It had been relayed by Dr. Chenko, who had gotten it from Andrei Vishinsky, the deputy foreign minister sent to Berlin by Stalin. The message, which was unsigned, ordered him to report to Tempelhof for a flight. Petrov knew who it was from: only one man called him the Berkut. Where he might be going was a different matter; he had no idea.

The destination turned out to be Odessa, the Russian port at the northern extreme of the Black Sea. Even with a moderate tail wind, the flight consumed more than six hours, and it was dark when they landed. A black American-built Packard was waiting on the apron with its motor running.

They drove northeast along the coast for nearly an hour. Petrov knew they were nearing their destination by the increasing density of security positions along the route. Finally they pulled off the gravel road onto a dirt lane and crossed through several heavily armed check-points. Ordinarily—in Moscow or at any of Stalin's other normal retreats and haunts—there would have been a search at each post, but this time, whenever they were stopped the driver flashed some papers, the barrier ahead of them snapped open and they drove on.

From his seat in back, Petrov could see a large wooden dacha sitting on a bluff ahead. Far below was a dark sandy beach and the smell of salt was heavy in the air. He noted that hundreds of lights were strung around the perimeter, and guards on foot and bicycles were constantly on the move inside their assigned areas.

Straining to clear the final steep grade up to the structure, the auto chugged onto a grassy knoll and stopped. A guard opened Petrov's door and stepped back. Another guard took his credentials, checking them against duplicates and a set of photographs. Once on the grounds, he had to traverse the usual maze of guards and internal checkpoints, the same system he had installed in Berlin for his own organization. He observed that several antiaircraft batteries were nearby and covered with camouflage netting. He guessed there would be a large radar antenna somewhere in the area, perhaps on the roof of the dacha itself. Reaching the building, he climbed a long flight of wide wooden steps, had his credentials checked a final time and was admitted to the building.

The house seemed empty, something he did not expect. Ordinarily the closer one got to Stalin, the heavier the security became, yet there seemed to be no guards here. Standing at the base of a curved staircase with ornately carved railings, Petrov surveyed his surroundings. He could smell the decadence that had brought on the October Revolution and the civil war that followed. Such an atmosphere required centuries to subside; decades were not enough.

The dacha was richly furnished, and Petrov considered what the capitalists might say if they saw how Russia's leader lived. He understood that appearances were deceiving; every Communist had to work for his keep, and unlike a class born to its wealth, in the Soviet Union nothing was forever. What the party bestowed the party could take away—and frequently did. This was the critical difference that would elude the capitalists. *How* Stalin lived was irrelevant; *that* he lived and ruled were the facts to be reckoned with.

It had been a long time since Petrov had first met Stalin. He had found the Georgian a crude and simple man in some ways, complex and shrewd in others. When it was needed, the man could summon forth an incredibly urbane polish and cultured air. In the years after the Revolution, he had consolidated his power by playing factions against one another. Stalin's style was one of terror, but terror with a purpose: to keep the masses and his enemies off-balance and at bay. He knew that over an extended period of time he could reeducate the masses and force them to accept the circumstances of Communism. Over the years the application of terror, even mass murder, would mold total obedience. Once unquestioning obedience had been achieved, total efficiency would follow. With so many people, no other approach would work. *Then* from each according to his ability, to each according to his need. Once settled, their society could move forward, but Hitler had interrupted the progression. It was a rudimentary formula, but Petrov accepted it.

On the spiral staircase was a red carpet. Gargoyles peered from the walls at him, and mirrors reflected candles and lanterns. There was no electricity. Suddenly Stalin swung into sight in front of him, coming down the stairs. He was buttoning his fly and chewing a black cigar.

Petrov never failed to be affected by the sight of Stalin, not so much because of what he was, but because of what he wasn't. Stalin had leathery skin with deep lines cut into his face. His mustache was thick, the most prominent feature of his leontine head and small body. Only a few inches over five feet, he was shorter than Petrov. Born Iosif Vissarionovich Dzhugashvili, he had come from Russia's poor. Had he been born in Germany, Hitler's policies would have condemned him to death, for his body was deformed. His right hand was considerably smaller than his left, and he often hid it behind his back during public appearances. The second and third toes of his left foot were fused, and even while on holiday at his favorite beaches he waded and swam with his shoes on. His left arm was shorter than his right, the result of an accident in his youth. His teeth were stained yellow and he was bent in posture. All in all, he was living proof of some genetic mishap.

Petrov held no misconceptions about his leader. While Stalin had brought him into the periphery of the inner circle of Soviet power, he knew that his position was tenuous, based solely on his ability to perform. Failure would bring exile to Siberia at best—or more likely, death. Stalin would not tolerate failure or weakness.

Over the years Petrov learned his leader's habits by studying them. Talking in private to him, one on one, was no different from dealing with him in a group or in public. Stalin was always the leader of the USSR, and he let no one forget it. He was a man consistent in his habits, altering them for no person and no circumstance.

His voice, while harsh, had a certain clarity to it, a distinct tone difficult to imitate, and he spoke Russian with a thick Georgian accent. Now, seeing Petrov, he smiled broadly. "Have you found that bastard?" he bellowed from above. Petrov hesitated as Stalin tramped loudly down the remaining steps. "You can talk freely here; it's not like the Kremlin where even the commodes have ears."

He laughed and ushered Petrov into a large living room containing stuffed chairs and a wide table loaded with food. There was hot tea steaming in a silver pot with a serpent's body twisted into a handle; bottles of vodka in hand-tooled leather sleeves; plates heaped with caviar and smoked salmon; wheels of bread with a silver knife embedded in each; great chunks of white cheese in small gold crocks; pickled eggs; mounds of butter heaped like snow in heavy crystal bowls that glittered in the indirect light.

"Eat," Stalin urged. "We'll talk while we eat. I want to hear about Berlin. You know, I've been getting messages from Zhukov. The general fills my office with wires till they drift around in the breeze like autumn leaves. In public he is the great face of stone; in private he never uses one word when a hundred can be substituted. Zhukov maintains that Hitler is dead and that's that—shot himself in the head. I can't believe he'd have the balls to shoot himself like a man."

Petrov filled his plate and poured a cup of dark tea. The two men sat together on a long bench with thick cushions, balancing their plates on their laps.

"Eat," Stalin said enthusiastically. "Try the caviar, taste the fish."

Meals with Stalin were deceiving. Always he seemed the gracious host, urging his guests to sample everything, but Petrov knew it was not hospitality that motivated him. His leader feared poisoning by his enemies, and every meal for him was an exercise in terror and caution. Petrov knew that all of Stalin's food was grown on a special farm tended by political police agents, his own men. The food was shipped directly from the farm to a special laboratory, where it was analyzed in bulk and each item tagged with chemical assay results. The tag also bore the name of the technician who had performed the test. The tea Stalin favored was a special blend, the supply controlled by a woman who traveled in his entourage wherever he went. At meals he would not eat a particular dish until it had been tried by a guest and an adequate amount of time had passed for a possible reaction to show itself. Those who dined regularly with him learned his habits and got fat.

Petrov picked up the smoked salmon and tore off a long sliver with his teeth. He followed it with a chunk of bread dipped in the soft butter, a pickled egg sprinkled with peppercorns and a sip of the hot tea, to which he had added a small portion of honey.

After a time Stalin clapped his hands and began eating. "Try the sturgeon," he urged, his cheeks bulging with salmon. Stalin loved sturgeon. Petrov peeled loose a slice from the bone and tasted it, chewing slowly. When enough time had passed, Stalin tore into the fish, eating what Petrov estimated to be almost a kilo. For a small man who feared poisoning, the premier ate prodigious quantities.

"So," Stalin said, during a series of belches. "What does the Berkut bring me?"

"I believe there is a strong possibility that he is still alive."

Stalin laughed and nearly dropped his plate. "I knew it! That fucking simpleton Zhukov, our avenger in Berlin! He plays to the Western press. He wants power, that one. Hitler is dead, says the great Zhukov. I have his body, bellows Zhukov. Bullshit!"

"It is possible that he does have the body," Petrov said without emotion.

Stalin frowned. "You bastard, Petrov," he hissed. "Don't start with your fucking intellectual equivocations. Don't try to keep all your doors open. The number one war criminal of the Soviets is either dead or alive. I'm not one of your brainy team, you slippery son of a bitch; I know there are only two possibilities—dead or alive. Your job is to tell me which."

Petrov cautioned himself to proceed with care. Stalin was badgering him in a friendly way, but one mistake could send him into a rage, and once he was out of control anything was possible. "Let me explain," Petrov said. He related his story and the facts as the Special Operations Group knew them.

Stalin listened intently, not interrupting. "You base your opinion on the girl's lies, on the stomach with no lettuce and on the fact of the single testicle, is that it?" he said finally.

"And the meeting with the guard on the thirtieth."

"The corpse in Zhukov's hands is a double—that's what you're thinking?"

"Yes."

"You're sure the corpse was both shot and poisoned?"

"That's what our analysis of the forensic evidence demonstrates."

Stalin stared at him, stood up, lit a brown Russian cigarette and looked across the room. "No, you're wrong," he said solemnly.

Petrov tensed.

"The key evidence is the shooting, Comrade Petrov. I've said all along that the coward wouldn't shoot himself. If Zhukov's corpse has a bullet hole, it's not Hitler. That's all I need to know to support your thesis."

"The bullet could have been inflicted after he poisoned himself," Petrov offered.

"Never! None of his cronies would have the balls to shoot him, not even his corpse."

Petrov nodded. One did not argue with such opinions; besides, the conversation was turning in a favorable direction.

"You've interrogated all the Nazi swine. What does it give you? A conspiracy?"

"Undoubtedly, but his confederate had to be someone from outside the inner circle. I'm quite certain that all of those who were in the bunker believe without exception that he committed suicide."

"Where's Skorzeny?" Stalin snapped.

"I don't understand."

"Otto Skorzeny, Hitler's thug."

Recovering from the unexpected introduction of the German commando into the conversation, Petrov said, "We are familiar with the man."

Stalin ignored him and went on. "Skorzeny rescued Mussolini. Skorzeny captured Horthy. Skorzeny assassinated several of our key military people. Whenever Hitler is in trouble, Skorzeny is the man he turns to. Find Skorzeny."

"At this point there's no evidence of Skorzeny's involvement," Petrov said firmly. "There's no mention of him by the prisoners, and he wasn't in the bunker with Hitler after December."

Stalin sat down next to Petrov and put his hand on his shoulder. "Listen to me, Petrov. I haven't gotten to this"—he waved his hand at the room in a sweeping gesture—"without damn good instincts. My guts say Skorzeny. Go back to Germany and find that bastard." He thumped his forefinger roughly on Petrov's chest. "Colonel Otto Skorzeny of the SS. Find him; find Hitler. They stick together like a fart and its stink."

The premier walked across the room, pivoted and returned. His voice grew softer. "You have your orders, my little Berkut. More important, you have my direct *authority*. Do what you need to do." Suddenly he groped in the oversize breast pockets of his jacket and extracted several leather portfolios the size of wallets. "Take these," he said, dropping them into Petrov's lap. They were heavy. "Five in your group, correct?"

"Yes."

Stalin laughed. "One for each of you." He stared hard and his voice dropped lower. "I know you will be successful, comrade. Bring the criminal to me, and you can help me punish him in a way that only he will be able to appreciate." Suddenly his mood changed. Brightening, he grabbed Petrov by the arms. "We'll give the dog the *business*," he said, using the slang from one of his favorite American gangster films.

When Stalin had departed, Petrov continued his meal. The plane would wait. He spread the leather portfolios on the pillow beside him and opened one, unfastening its small black strap. So awesome was the sight before him that he stopped chewing and began to choke. Each portfolio contained a bright red enamel shield. On each was mounted the seal of Stalin's office and the engraved words "Complete Authority." He had heard of such chits before, but he had never seen one. These would open any door for his team; in his hands he held five licenses bestowing absolute power. Such was the phenomenon called the Red Badge. Petrov smiled, closed the leather case and resumed eating.

▶27 MAY 17, 1945, 7:00 P.M.

Petrov slept fitfully during the return flight from Odessa. It was evening when the aircraft bumped onto Tempelhof's pitted runway. By the time he entered the terminal the leader of the Special Operations Group had found a new surge of energy.

The group was waiting for him in their headquarters. Gnedin's feet were up on a table, a thick sheaf of papers in his lap. Bailov was asleep, snoring quietly on a cot, his head buried under a bulky jacket. Rivitsky was writing. Ezdovo had the parts of an automatic pistol spread on a towel in front of him.

Petrov went directly to the table and placed the five leather containers in a row. Ezdovo jogged Bailov with his foot, the latter snorting as he woke up. The four men gathered around their leader.

"Take one," Petrov said. They picked up the containers without speaking and opened them. Petrov watched their reactions.

Gnedin whistled. "The Red Badge. I've heard about it, but I never believed the stories."

"Their weight says they're real enough," Petrov said.

Ezdovo stared at his leather case impassively.

"The ultimate license," Rivitsky said, running his hand over the polished metal. "You've seen the Boss."

"In Odessa."

"A long flight," Rivitsky said with a smile. They all knew how much Petrov hated aircraft.

"Long and uncomfortable," Petrov said sourly. "You understand the meaning of these? Comrade Stalin has been informed of our findings."

"And he agrees with our conclusions," Rivitsky said, brandishing his badge.

"Stalin reminded me of Hitler's penchant for using the services of Skorzeny for special missions," Petrov recounted. "He believes Skorzeny must be involved in this."

"I disagree," Rivitsky said. "Too obvious."

"I've given it some thought," Petrov said. "I share your feeling. Not Skorzeny, but perhaps someone else in that special unit. The premier is correct in assuming that Skorzeny's people would be the most likely accomplices in this kind of conspiracy. I doubt, however, that Hitler would turn to Skorzeny again. He was too well known. However, one of his men . . . that's a possibility we have to examine."

"Skorzeny's name has not come up during the interrogations," Bailov pointed out.

"Understood," Petrov said. "Even so, we need to know where he was and what his mission was at the end. Where was his unit? Who are his people, the key personnel? There are too many unknowns to draw any conclusions now."

"Where do we begin?" Rivitsky asked. "We can be sure there are records; these Germans can't help doing it."

"They record every bowel movement," Ezdovo added with a grunt.

"Might such records have been sent south in April, as part of the move to Berchtesgaden?" Rivitsky asked.

"All of this must be answered in an orderly manner," Petrov said. His men had no doubt that it would be.

The Führerbunker was as they had last seen it. The generator was silent and it was dark. Ezdovo filled the generator's tank with diesel fuel and started it. There was little Soviet security in place. A lone private, a flat-faced Mongolian, sat on the floor of the bunker entrance and looked up at them while he ate dried fish with dirty hands. His rifle leaned against a wall, well beyond his reach. Apparently the higher echelons of the Red Army felt no need to isolate the facility, Petrov thought. They had Hitler's body and the place was no longer important; its status had been reduced to no more than that of a curio, an attraction for those wanting to see where Hitler had killed himself.

Rivitsky and Ezdovo tried to converse with the Oriental, but could find no common tongue. The man grimaced, waved them in and returned to his meal.

In the bunker below, water was standing on the floors. It looked as if the place had seen a large number of visitors in the last three days; furniture was smashed and papers were strewn everywhere. As in all other German buildings, the toilets had been removed.

"We're looking for records, files, official documents. We'll photograph what we find and leave the originals here," Petrov told them.

"Why bother?" Bailov wanted to know. "We can take what we want. Nobody will miss anything in this chaos."

"No," Petrov answered. "Eventually the army will come to its senses, realize what's going on here and claim it for historical purposes. We'll leave what we find."

The team members shrugged. After their leader gave them instructions, they went off individually to begin their search. Petrov waited in the corridor outside Hitler's suite, sitting on a large table that the Führer had used for military conferences.

Ezdovo was the first to report back, carrying several waterlogged volumes on the architecture of opera houses. Petrov's expression told him that the effort was unappreciated. The Siberian dropped the books on the table and retreated quickly to a nearby cubicle.

After three hours of combing the two bunker levels, they were still empty-handed, so Petrov decided to move the search to the Chancellery. They assembled in the same large basement room where they had first found Dr. Haase. Petrov calculated that if any records remained, they would be below ground, away from the artillery.

It was Ezdovo who found them, rows of wooden boxes filled with folders. They were stacked in a hallway in the western part of the building the Nazis called the New Chancellery. There were more than a hundred crates, two-meter cubes stacked four deep. Each crate was neatly stenciled with a listing of its contents; twenty crates were labeled PERSONNEL.

Inside the boxes folders were organized alphabetically. It was all too neat and too easy to be true, and they smiled as they went through the contents. When they found the Skorzeny folder, Petrov decided to keep it. "This is different from the papers in the bunker," he told them. "Anything we find here is undoubtedly duplicated at another site. Redundancy is the key to records' security."

They returned to their headquarters at nightfall, exhilarated. Petrov read the dossier on Skorzeny slowly to himself, then out loud to his men. Like Hitler, Skorzeny was an Austrian, born in Vienna. He had once applied to the Luftwaffe, but had been turned down for flight duty. Subsequently he joined the Liebstandarte Adolf Hitler Regiment in 1940, serving with his unit in several campaigns in France, Holland and Russia, where he suffered a serious bout with gallstones and was returned to Germany for treatment. The medical record was extensive. In Berlin, Skorzeny was assigned initially to an administrative position, but in 1943 he was transferred to a subsection of the Reich Main Security Office and given command of the Friedenthal special operations unit. The unit had been based near Berlin, but had a training facility near Munich. The last entry in the folder indicated that Skorzeny was serving as a division commander in Bach-Zelewski's army corps on the Oder River front.

When Petrov finished reading, the men were unanimous in their opinion: someone would have to go to Munich.

"American territory," Gnedin cautioned them.

"If Skorzeny was on the Oder, he's probably dead," Rivitsky told the others.

"Possibly," Petrov interjected. "But he does not seem the type to let himself perish in a mere battle. He may have been on the Oder at some point, but I'd guess that he wasn't there when we went through. He'll be somewhere else if he's alive."

"So we go to Munich?" Gnedin asked.

"Rivitsky and Ezdovo go to Munich. I'll make the arrangements through Comrade Vishinsky. Right now the Americans are friendly toward us. With English agitation, this won't last, so we have to act quickly."

Petrov told the pair what he wanted. "I don't care about Skorzeny himself; I want his records. I want the names of all the officers of the Friedenthal—the key ones at minimum, the complete roll if possible."

▶**28** MAY 19, 1945, 12:05 P.M.

The Americans were receptive to the request put through official channels by Vishinsky. Their only condition was that the Russians had to be escorted at all times while they were in the American zone. Ezdovo and Rivitsky would be met at the airport by their escort. The flight to Bavaria was rough; a heavy spring front had hit the Alps and hung like gauze over southern Germany.

They found their American escort, an army captain, waiting for them. He was middle-aged, gaunt, with short brown hair and a straight nose that sat flat between high cheekbones. His ears stuck out under a cowboy hat that had once been white but was now a dirty gray, and his sweat-stained uniform hung loosely over a meatless frame. The man wore combat fatigues bleached nearly white by sweat and weather, and the toes of his leather jump boots were scuffed down to the grain. A Browning .45 hung on his hip in a wrinkled black leather holster that was tied to his thigh with a faded shoelace. A bayonet was strapped to the outside of his right calf, and a metal paratrooper badge was pinned above his left breast pocket. The captain's eyes were clear as a cat's, and the overall impression he gave was one of menace. Rivitsky and Ezdovo recognized the signs; he was a frontline officer, an equal, not some rear-echelon mouse.

"Comrades Rivitsky and Ezdovo," the captain said in surprisingly good Russian, "welcome to Munich. I'm Captain Molanaro. Supposed to show you around and take care of you. VIP treatment." Looking directly at Ezdovo, he said, "Neither of you looks like the kind who needs much care." All three men laughed.

"Thank you," Rivitsky said. "We appreciate your speaking our language, but it isn't necessary. We welcome the opportunity to practice our English."

"If you don't mind, comrade, I'd like to practice my Russian. Have to say I'm a bit disappointed, because we thought we were going to meet you people in Berlin, but I guess it just didn't work out that way." Rivitsky thought he detected some bitterness in the officer's comment. "What unit are you with?" the captain asked.

"We're not at liberty to say." Rivitsky smiled.

"No skin off my ass," the captain said in English. The Russians weren't familiar with the slang, but the tone made his meaning clear. "What will it be, Fräuleins or Nazis?"

"We're here to investigate an SS unit that trained nearby. Our mission is to find its personnel records." Rivitsky gave the captain a small piece of paper bearing the unit's name and number.

"War criminals?" Molanaro asked. "Something to do with the death camps?"

"Something like that," Rivitsky said blandly.

"There's a concentration camp near here," the captain said. "Dachau. We liberated it. I never want to go through something like that again as long as I live. It was a sonofabitch. They killed Jews in the camp. Gassed them, then burned the bodies in ovens—men, women, little kids. Never seen anything like it, even in a nightmare. If you're after the people who ran that place or anything like it, we'll help all we can. We want them too."

"We will carve their balls off together," Ezdovo growled. He swished a finger through the air to add emphasis to his words.

"Right," the captain said, patting his knife. "I have a jeep."

They could have walked almost as fast as they drove. Munich was heavily damaged, its downtown reduced to clusters of broken buildings and rubble. German civilians were picking at the debris with shovels and sledgehammers. The rubble was being loaded on horse-drawn flatbed wagons with rubber wheels. The animals in their harnesses stood quietly swishing at flies with their tails.

"You are heavily armed," Rivitsky observed as they drove.

"There's still resistance in the area. Occasional snipers. Some SS units managed to stay together at the end, just over the Austrian border. Every now and then one of them filters its way back to Germany, so we still have some fighting. Fanatical bastards. On the other hand, there isn't a Nazi left in Munich. All the Nazis left or died— just like that," the captain said sarcastically as he threaded the jeep between pedestrians and other Allied vehicles. "A month ago they were the superior race, and now they're kissing our boots as liberators. You can't trust Germans."

"You're learning," Ezdovo responded. "We knew a long time ago not to trust them."

"But your government signed a treaty with them," Molanaro countered.

"True. Our government. We don't control our politicians any more than you do. I'm sure there were good reasons for the treaty, just as I'm sure that Comrade Stalin will never call me to Moscow to explain them," Rivitsky said flatly.

"I know what you mean. Truman doesn't let me in on anything, and neither did Roosevelt." They all laughed.

Near the center of Munich the American stopped at a provost marshal's temporary headquarters, a large oval canvas held aloft by poles from freshly cut pine trees. The captain disappeared inside and returned after a few moments with a smile on his face. "No sweat," he said. "Our MPs always know where everything is. Major inside says the SS had a camp south of town, up in the foothills. I got us a pass to get through our security."

The captain bounced the jeep through a series of bomb craters. When they reached the outskirts of the city, buildings were less damaged and life seemed more normal. Driving higher and deeper into the foothills, they occasionally passed checkpoints manned by small patrols of GIs. Fields were dotted with burned-out vehicles, and twice they saw large contingents of civilians digging in the fields under the supervision of American soldiers. "There was a real nasty fight in this area right at the end," the captain said in English. "They're still burying bodies."

Their destination was a small camp nestled at the end of a narrow valley and surrounded by a pine forest. Lilacs were blooming along the road, and red and white wildflowers were beginning to peek from the high grasses. The aroma was delightful and the sun was high and bright. The weather front seemed to be finally breaking up. To the unpracticed eye the camp was just another small military installation, but both the Russians and the American saw immediately that there was something odd about it.

"Jump towers. Weird place to do jump training," the American captain said, pointing. "Too hilly."

The camp was ringed by several strands of barbed wire more than ten feet high, laid out in three circles. They guessed that the open areas between the fences were mined and soon saw signs in English and German confirming this. An MP in a pea-green undershirt stopped them at the gate, glanced at their passes and waved them in without speaking. The main camp comprised a dozen wooden buildings clustered around a central dirt courtyard. A flagpole stuck out of a loose pile of white rocks in the center. Near the buildings was a large outdoor swimming pool with platforms several meters high at one end. There was a firing range against the hill; the receiving end was battered, its naked earth an ocher scar. Signs in English had been erected on all the buildings.

The men found the headquarters building and parked the jeep in front. The interior resembled the staff bay of any orderly room of any army in the world: wooden desks, chairs and roughly hewn board walls. Someone had removed a painting or photograph from the wall, leaving a dusty outline of the frame; no doubt it had been Hitler's portrait. The metal filing cabinets in the orderly room were empty, but after a brief search they located the contents of the files in boxes in an earthen cellar under the building. The folders themselves were dry and neatly arranged.

The three of them spent the rest of the day going through the folders, the American as eager as the Russians to locate the information. Slowly the list grew from the files, and the unit that had begun as a name and number began to take shape as a living entity, one that amazed them all because of the sheer audacity of the missions the unit had undertaken.

Late in the afternoon the American captain suddenly looked dumbfounded. "Goddamn," he shouted at them, "this is Skorzeny's outfit!" The Russians stared back, not understanding his outburst. They had been reading documents all day that were signed by Skorzeny. That it should register so belatedly with the captain struck them as odd.

"Major General Otto Skorzeny," Rivitsky said.

"Wow!" the captain whistled. "Last we heard he was a lousy colonel. My outfit tangled with that bastard in the Bulge. He infiltrated his units behind our lines in American uniforms. Fuckers spoke English like Americans; they changed signs, blew bridges, really played havoc with us. Lost a lot of my boys because of this guy; we'd like to get even with this s.o.b."

"Skorzeny ran a special commando operation," Ezdovo said.

"You ain't just whistling Dixie, friend," Molanaro said. "Skorzeny sent a special team to kill Ike in Paris during the Bulge. Parachuted his men into France wearing nuns' habits. Can you picture that?"

"Who?" Ezdovo asked.

"General Dee-Wight-Dee-Fucking-Ike-Eisenhower, number one commander of the whole Allied shebang," Molanaro explained.

"Nuns' habits?" Rivitsky asked.

"Roman Catholic sisters—holy women in black dresses with big white bibs," Molanaro said.

"Papal women," Rivitsky said, understanding.

"I forgot," the captain said with a loud laugh. "You people probably don't see too many mackerel snappers, you being atheists and all." He saw that the Russians did not understand. "Roman Catholics eat fish," he added. "Mackerel is a fish."

Ezdovo and Rivitsky nodded. "There are Catholics in Russia," Ezdovo said. "There used to be many before the Revolution. We're not all atheists. People still go to their churches, but the churches and priests can't interfere in matters of the state. I believe your American constitution also separates church and state."

By dusk Rivitsky felt they had what they needed. One gap remained: there was no file or name for the unit's operations and plans officer. All the organization's documents were signed by Skorzeny or a sergeant major named Rau, whose personnel dossier was also conspicuous by its absence. They did manage to find a half-dozen documents where Skorzeny's name was typed, but without a signature; in its place only the initial "B" appeared. Because there were no further records, and because they had photographed all the originals, they decided to return to Munich.

Before leaving, they made a quick tour of the camp. In the armory, the largest of several wood-frame buildings, they found an array of weapons that none of them had ever before seen assembled in one place. There were firearms of all calibers and sizes; grenades, rockets, mortars, mines and gas canisters; scuba and deep-sea diving gear, along with breathing devices used by submariners; skis; several parachutes, including one with a square canopy that resembled an airplane wing; cartons of *plastit* explosives; a lab with dozens of jars marked "Poison" but otherwise unidentified; and a room filled with fuses, many of which they couldn't identify. They also found a water-cooled .50-caliber machine gun of Czech manufacture with a sight that used a beam of light, and a strange-looking flying machine with its propeller mounted on top. "Autogyro," Rivitsky told the American. "It goes straight up and down for takeoffs. There were two prototypes, both destroyed. Perhaps our information was wrong and this is the third."

On the way out, the captain picked up a short-barreled shotgun with a clip shaped like a cake pan, which looked like an oversize Thompson submachine gun. It was an imposing weapon and they guessed it might hold as many as fifty rounds of 12-gauge ammo.

They drove slowly on their way back to Munich, enjoying the warm evening breeze. Near the city the captain stopped the jeep and turned to the Russians. "We can go back to camp—or, if you're a couple of regular guys, we can celebrate."

Ezdovo's eyes lit up.

"I know a spot where we can—fraternize," Molanaro said.

"Fraternize?" Rivitsky asked.

The captain joined the forefinger and thumb of his left hand, then vigorously poked his right forefinger in and out.

"Fraternize!" Ezdovo shouted brightly.

"Technically it's against orders for us to fraternize with Krauts," the captain explained.

"Fraternize," Ezdovo growled happily.

They spent the night drinking warm German beer in a tavern on the ground floor of a small hotel. The three woke up with women in their beds and painful hangovers. When they finally arrived at the American army camp near the airfield at noon, a corporal was waiting nervously for them. "Sir," the corporal said to Molanaro, "CO wants to see you and your Russians PDQ."

The battalion commander was a solidly built lieutenant colonel in his fifties. When Molanaro reported in, he left the Russians to wait outside the commanding officer's office. The look on his CO's face told him that he had a problem.

"You asshole," the colonel hissed. "Are you trying to start another war? These two Russkies are traveling under diplomatic orders, not military papers. If something happens to them, we could have a . . . a goddamn *incident* on our hands!" He ran a hand through his hair. "Let me guess: booze or broads?"

"You're warm," the captain said with a smile.

"I thought you'd bring them back to me yesterday *before* you did anything," the major said. "What do they want?"

Molanaro related what they had found and seen at the SS camp.

"Autogyro, huh? I never heard of such a thing."

"Me neither, but the Russians sure seemed to know all about it."

The colonel stared at the ceiling for a moment, then looked at his officer. "I'm calling a halt to this hands-across-the-sea shit. I don't know exactly what this machine is, but it sounds like something the Russians would want. If they want it, we want it—that's the way it's gonna be from now on. Intelligence says they're stealing everything in Germany that isn't bolted to the ground."

"I don't know," the captain said. "They seemed more interested in records—personnel folders and things like that."

"Smoke," the colonel countered. "They're shittin' you."

Molanaro shrugged.

"Any idea why such a machine would be in a rathole camp like that?"

"It's Skorzeny's camp," Molanaro said.

The colonel jumped to his feet and slapped his desk. "Goddamn! Skorzeny! If that machine was Skorzeny's, you can bet your ass it's top secret. That cinches it, Molanaro. You tell your Russian pals their tour is over—*kaputski*. Stick them on their plane, then take a couple of squads and haul your ass back up to that camp until I can get intelligence up there."

"A couple of squads is overkill," Molanaro said. "There's an MP up there at the gate and the place is mined to the gills. A piss ant couldn't get in there."

The colonel suddenly smiled and sat down, beaming. "Take two squads anyway."

"What's so damn funny?"

"Skorzeny. The Russians are a day late and a dollar short. Our people captured Skorzeny yesterday in Austria." He laughed. "Bring 'em in. I want to see their sorry Cossack faces when I tell them we've got Skorzeny by his short hairs."

Ezdovo and Rivitsky could sense the change in the Americans' attitude. Their escort was suddenly very cool and formal. They showed no emotion when the colonel gleefully informed them of Skorzeny's capture. The major's pleasure in the news was quite obvious. Rivitsky said only, "We would like for you to arrange for us to interview the prisoner."

The colonel turned red and waved his hands in front of his face as if he were warding off some evil spirit. "No way," he said. "I don't have that kind of pull."

"*We* have the pull," Rivitsky told him. After some discussion, the colonel allowed Rivitsky to send a telegram to Petrov through Vishinsky's office in Berlin. It read: ATTN V PETROV STOP HAVE IMPRESSIONS STOP ONE GAP STOP SKORZENY CAPTURED YESTERDAY IN AUSTRIA STOP HELD BY THE AMERICANS STOP CAN YOU ARRANGE INTERROGATION STOP AWAIT YOUR REPLY STOP RIVITSKY.

To the colonel's astonishment, by 6:00 P.M. an order had come from General Eisenhower's chief of staff granting permission for Skorzeny to be interviewed by the two Russians, and an hour later Ezdovo and Rivitsky said good-bye to their American escort at the airport.

"Someday we fraternize again," Ezdovo said with a wink to the captain.

"Can do. Kick Skorzeny in the balls for the Airborne."

"Can do," Ezdovo said in English as he closed the hatch and the plane taxied into the darkness.

When they were airborne, Ezdovo suddenly produced the strange shotgun Molanaro had stolen from the SS camp. "You took it from him?" Rivitsky asked.

"I prefer to think I *liberated* it from the capitalists." They laughed together.

As Molanaro stood watching the Russian aircraft taxi away he was approached by another man. "Evening," the stranger said. "That the Russian aircraft?"

Molanaro turned to look at the man. He was tall, six-five at least, and heavy, two hundred and fifty pounds or more. He wore a tan shirt that hung on him like a tent without pegs. His hands were huge, and his brown eyes were set close together over a thin avian nose that dipped precipitously at the tip. There was a bald spot the size of a silver dollar on top of his skull, but his blond hair was stiff as straw and stood up in the night breeze. He had tiny ears, like small butterflies, and when he walked, his legs seemed to flip forward jerkily as if they were mechanical, their joints in need of lubrication. His size-fourteen feet splayed out at angles.

"Yep," Molanaro said. The man had no insignia.

"Thought so," the stranger said.

Maybe the guy was Red Cross, Molanaro thought, but his suspicions were rising. "Say, pal, what's it to you?"

The stranger smiled and patted the captain's shoulder with one of his massive paws. He understood instinctively that the captain's suspicions had been aroused, and he smiled to defuse a possible confrontation. It was a technique with which he had plenty of practice. Since joining the Office of Strategic Services, he had become adept at deflecting direct confrontations—or creating them; he could do whatever circumstances required. "I'm with the Red Cross," he lied, flashing a false ID. "Just arrived. Haven't seen too many Russians," he added. He was used to the close scrutiny of others; he looked so peculiar that most people meeting him for the first time could not take their eyes off him. Women especially warmed to him, a fact that struck other men as odd. But male or female made no difference when Beau Valentine wanted information; with charm or violence, he usually got what he wanted.

"Me neither," the captain said, relaxing. "Thought we'd link with them in Berlin, but I guess the brass has different ideas about how to run this war." Suddenly he began looking around and, after several glances toward his jeep, went to it and began rummaging through the backseat.

Valentine followed. "Problem?"

"Yeah," Molanaro muttered. He looked up just as the Russian aircraft clattered by, lifted and banked hard to the right, climbing. Then he smiled. "Bastards copped my weapon," he said. There was grudging admiration in his voice.

"What were the Russians doing here?" Valentine pressed. "This isn't their zone."

"Some kind of investigation," the captain said.

"Find what they wanted?"

Molanaro smiled as he slid into the driver's seat. "Not really. I think we've got what they really want." He looked at the Red Cross man. "Need a lift?"

Valentine got into the jeep and grabbed hold of a corner of the windshield for balance. "What is it we have?"

Molanaro depressed the clutch, shifted to neutral and started the motor. "Skorzeny," he said with a chuckle.

Beauregard "Beau" Asherford Valentine stiffened at the name. He had been sent into Germany to "sniff around for scientists." Skorzeny, his mind repeated. This was a scent to be followed. Two Russians searching for Skorzeny. Two Russians being helped by the Americans. He was interested.

"Where can I drop you?" the captain asked.

"Someplace where I can find a beer. Interested?"

"Can't," the captain said. "Duty calls. How about a rain check?"

"You got it," Valentine said. Before he made any moves, he wanted to know what this officer knew about the Russians and their mission. He'd make sure the captain got his beer, and he'd get his information.

▶29 MAY 20, 1945, 12:55 P.M.

Before parting company with the Airborne captain, Valentine got the man's unit number and an invitation to visit. "They'll put you up till I get back," Molanaro said. "Then we can tie one on."

Valentine found the unit and was given a tent to himself. He kicked off his boots, shed his shirt and trousers, lay back on the cot with wooden cross braces that jabbed him in the kidneys and went to sleep.

He woke at noon to find the captain sitting on a nearby cot. He thrust a bottle of beer at him. "Lukewarm, but it's wet." Valentine sat up to clear the sleep from his brain and drained the bottle in one long pull.

Using a shortened bayonet, Molanaro popped the cap off another bottle and handed it to Valentine with a friendly grin. "You OSS?"

Valentine choked on the beer. "What do you mean?"

"First I bump into you just as the Russians are leaving, then I hear from the CO that you're asking a lot of questions about them," he said. "You trying to find them?"

"Not exactly. I'm more interested in information. Can you help me?"

"You bet. There were two of them. Nasty-looking critters with diplomatic IDs. Whole thing was cleared from the top."

"What did they seem to be after?"

The captain laughed. "Not sure. Just like you, they said they were after information."

"I'm more interested in the Russians themselves—everything they did, everything they said."

For two hours Molanaro told his story, first talking, then drinking, backtracking, adding to his recollections. Slowly Valentine began to get a feel about the visit. "Why were they so interested in the records?"

"Beats me," the captain said. "They drew up an organization chart. Near as I could tell they had a complete list, all except for one guy."

"Anything else?"

"Nope. My CO thinks they were after that autogyro gizmo, but I think all they gave a shit about were those folders. After we looked through the records, we had us a quick tour of the camp and headed back to Munich."

"You don't think they were interested in the autogyro device?"

"I don't think so, though they were surprised to find it there. One of them said the Krauts had built two prototypes, which the Russkies thought had been blown away. One of them said kind of matter-of-factly, 'This must be a third one.' That's all they said. You know, like they'd seen a two-headed snake in a jar or something."

"Did you try to pin them down?" Valentine asked.

"Hell, yes. I asked them point-blank if they were after war criminals. They said, 'Something like that.' They were playin' it cute the whole time they were here. Real sneaky bastards. You tangled with any of them?"

Before Valentine could think of an appropriate follow-up, Molanaro continued. "Course, it wasn't all bad. After I got back to camp I told the CO what we'd found and it took him about half an eye blink to figure out that the autogyro was a first-class G-2 goody, so he made me haul ass back up there to hold down the camp till intelligence came in. That's where I've been. Anyways, the way it spilled out, I'm gonna get me a promotion outta the deal; CO just told me a little while ago."

Valentine smiled.

"Can you beat that?" the captain went on. "Dogfooted my way from Normandy to Munich and got diddley squat for what we done. Now I drive a couple of Russians around, luck onto a screwball airplane, and for this I get promoted. Can you figure it? This is one fucked-up war, pal. I show the Russians around, get drunk, get laid and, bingo, I get to put on the gold leaves. CO's gonna make full bull, too."

"Let's get back to the Russians." Valentine didn't want him to stop talking yet.

"Not much to tell. I drove them back after a little recreating with some German broads. I told the CO they were interested in Skorzeny, so he called them in and told them we'd captured Skorzeny in Salzburg. Everybody was looking high and low for Skorzeny because of his connection to Hitler. They may have gotten Berlin, but we got Skorzeny. He really jammed it down their throats, too."

"Austria?"

"That's the place. As soon as the Russians heard that, they got a message off to Berlin, and flew to Austria to see Skorzeny. That's when you walked into the picture."

Valentine was satisfied. Clearly there had been no records in Berlin; otherwise they wouldn't have come to Munich. They had tried to reconstruct Skorzeny's organization, but a key personnel record was missing. They didn't have a name, so they had pulled some long strings to see Skorzeny.

Valentine thanked Molanaro, who took a final beer and departed. As he sat lacing up his boots he thought about what he knew. If the Russians wanted to interrogate Skorzeny, what was their angle?

Valentine headed his jeep out of Munich, but his mind was too active to concentrate on driving. He pulled off the road and sat with his arms crossed. As the hunch came slowly together in his mind, he fought to think it through. The autogyro: it had to be significant. Skorzeny was close to Hitler and had rescued Mussolini on Hitler's orders. Sometimes it seemed that everywhere the Allies turned they'd found themselves head to head with Skorzeny, or in his shadow. Skorzeny liked gadgets and used them. The autogyro was evidence. And where there were gadgets there had to be technicians—engineers and scientists! His orders had been to find scientists; now he had a lead and it smelled like something the Russians were hot for. Valentine slapped his hands on the steering wheel and laughed out loud. "I'm coming to get you!" he shouted happily, not at all sure whom he meant.

▶30 MAY 21, 1945, 4:00 A.M.

The flight from Munich to Salzburg was a short one. The Russian pilots worked their way across the mountains, keeping only a few hundred meters' altitude above the sharp peaks of the Alps. When the plane banked steeply and touched down on a small field south of Salzburg, the two passengers were relieved. Unlike Petrov, they both liked flying, but Ezdovo was a pilot and loathed riding as a passenger. He had learned to trust his fellow members of the Special Operations Group, but putting his life in the hands of a stranger was a different matter. Rivitsky also liked to fly, but he trusted Ezdovo's instincts and was infected by the Siberian's nervousness.

They were met by a full contingent of American military police, heavily armed and not at all friendly, and driven through rolling hills to a house in a small field surrounded by stunted and closely packed pines that whispered in the night wind.

Inside the wooden house was an American general. He had a blond mustache with a hint of red, a pearl-handled revolver and boots polished to the sheen of a mirror. The lobe of his left ear was missing and he wore jump wings on his chest. He was sitting in a high-backed cane chair, inhaling from a small cigar in an ebony holder and blowing crisp smoke rings with the precision of a machine.

The general did not introduce himself, and informed the Russians coldly that Skorzeny would be brought to them forthwith. Guards were posted around the house and out in the ring of pines, and it was clear to Ezdovo and Rivitsky that they were as much prisoners as Skorzeny. Neither of them cared for the feeling, but they masked their emotions and waited patiently for the prisoner.

Near dawn a vehicle rolled up to the front of the house. A door slammed and suddenly Skorzeny came through the front door, handcuffed in heavy irons. The general looked at him contemptuously, and then turned to the Russians: "You have two hours, comrades." He picked up his dented helmet, plopped it on his head and left them.

Skorzeny was huge, nearly six and a half feet tall and heavily muscled. His forearms were as thick as a blacksmith's, and the handcuffs looked exceptionally tight on his wrists. His SS tunic was filthy and unbuttoned; he needed a shave. But despite his unsavory appearance, the commando leader looked at the Russians with a superior air and wrinkled his face, causing the huge scar on the left side of his face to magnify. "Russians," he said with disdain. "I can always smell Russians. And NKVD at that."

"A remarkable feat, considering your own condition," Rivitsky said, sniffing loudly. "We would like to ask you a few questions, General Skorzeny."

"You realize the Americans are listening?"

Rivitsky lifted his palms. "Why not? They are our allies."

"Today perhaps," Skorzeny growled, "but they'll learn soon enough."

"We're interested in the activities of your band of criminals," Ezdovo said gruffly, speaking for the first time.

Skorzeny stiffened. "Criminals! You bastards have your nerve. My men were soldiers, not Gestapo."

"All SS are criminals," Ezdovo said. "We Russians know the SS well."

"It's probable you will be tried as a war criminal." Rivitsky softly applied pressure, testing Skorzeny's response. "Of course, all the Allies will have to agree on that assessment. It will be a political decision, as I'm sure you realize."

"I've nothing to hide and no shame for what I've done. I'm a soldier and a damned good one, Ivan. Both my record and my conscience are clean."

"You're fortunate the Americans have you," Ezdovo said. "If we did, there'd be no need for a trial."

"With such an attitude you intend to assess *my* criminality?"

"If you have nothing to hide, we'd like to ask you some questions about your unit." Rivitsky smiled like a grandfather addressing a child.

Skorzeny thought for a while. "Why not?" he said. "Give me a cigarette." Ezdovo lit one and placed it in the Austrian's mouth. Skorzeny held up the handcuffs. "Makes it difficult to converse."

Rivitsky glanced at Ezdovo, who immediately took a small piece of wire from his pocket, inserted it in the lock and opened the handcuffs with no more than a half-dozen tiny twists. Skorzeny dropped the shackles on the floor, gave them a kick and began to tell his story, embellishing his division's missions, always emphasizing *his* role, *his* decisions and *his* actions. The Russians were amazed and intrigued by what they heard; the range of missions undertaken was difficult to believe. While they already knew some of it, they found themselves wanting to know more, but this was not what they had come for. Rivitsky made notes as the Austrian talked, and from time to time one of them asked detailed questions. Eventually they got to what they were after. "Where were you at the end?"

"The end of what?"

"Please, General. No games."

"It's still colonel. My unit was on the Oder in Bach-Zalewski's sector."

"And you were with your unit?"

"No, I was in Vienna," Skorzeny said with a twinkle in his eye. The two Russians stared at each other. "When?"

"At the end, as you put it. I left the front in early April to join Generalfeldmarschall Schörner. We expected the major Soviet assault to go against Prague. Schörner's headquarters was one hundred and forty kilometers north of the city. On April ninth, when we were informed that Vienna was under siege, I went there by automobile."

"I'm confused," Rivitsky said. "You expected the major assault on Prague, yet you went to Vienna? Can you explain your reasoning?"

"Priorities change as circumstances change. I still had two commando units in Vienna. Also my family."

"What did you find in Vienna?" Rivitsky continued.

"Chaos. The sniveling Communists had led the Ivans into the city and caught the defense off guard."

"What action did you take?"

"At first I tried to rally the defense. In the past, and in other circumstances, I've had some success with this. But it was no use. They were inexperienced young troops, mere boys, who bolted at the sound of someone passing wind. I wired Hitler that the city was lost."

"Hitler?"

"Of course," Skorzeny said incredulously. "Hitler. Who do you think sent me from the Oder to Prague in the first place?"

"Hitler," Rivitsky repeated. "You got this order directly from Hitler?"

Skorzeny laughed. "Ivan, I took *all* my orders from Adolf Hitler.

Directly and only from the Führer. I was Hitler's special weapon, his creation."

"How did he respond to your message?"

"I didn't wait for a reply."

Rivitsky knew he was close. Skorzeny was relaxed and talking freely now.

"What happened to your units in Vienna?"

"I sent them into the mountains to wait for the war to end."

"And your family?"

"Safe."

"You wouldn't care to tell us where?"

Skorzeny smiled again. "No, Ivan."

"I'd like to go back in time a little," Rivitsky said. "Some of your units were in Vienna, some were on the Oder, and I presume you had some with you."

"Only a handful of men."

"Those with you and those in Vienna made it to the mountains safely. What about those on the Oder?"

Skorzeny's lips tightened and his shoulders drooped. "Most of them are dead, I suspect. You didn't take many prisoners on the Oder."

"Who was in command on the Oder? Your executive officer?"

Skorzeny looked at Rivitsky oddly. "No, Radl was with me in Vienna. The Americans have him. Number Three stayed on the Oder."

"Number Three?"

"Brumm. Günter Brumm."

"And you had a sergeant named Rau?"

Skorzeny's eyes flashed with interest. "You have the Beard? He's alive?"

"The Beard?" Rivitsky echoed.

"Sturmscharführer Rau, the best damned noncommissioned officer in the SS. If you had him, you'd understand." Suddenly Skorzeny seemed suspicious.

"Brumm. He would be the Berliner?"

"No, the mountain man. What's going on here?"

Rivitsky checked his watch. "Our two hours are up." He stood and bowed to Skorzeny. "Thank you, General. You've been quite helpful."

Skorzeny leaned back in his chair and inhaled deeply from the stump of another cigarette. "Fuck you, Ivan," he said, exhaling slowly.

Back in the plane, the two Russians had to shout to make themselves heard over the motors.

"What do we have?" Rivitsky asked, playing Petrov's customary role.

"A unit that answers directly to Hitler—was, in fact, his personal creation," Ezdovo yelled. "The records of every officer in Skorzeny's operation except óne. A sergeant major for whom no record exists and who signs papers for the officer who does not exist on paper. It can't be a coincidence that *only* their records have been deleted. I think Brumm's our man. Brumm, the mountain man. A Bavarian, no doubt."

"Petrov will be pleased," Rivitsky said.

▶31 MAY 28, 1945, 9:00 A.M.

In the Office of Strategic Services it was said by none other than Wild Bill Donovan himself that Beauregard Asherford Valentine was a singular specimen in a collection of singular specimens. Born to fourth-generation wealth in a bayou parish near New Orleans, Barry Valentine breezed through Tulane in two years, winning in the process all the academic awards available. By the time he had finished Stanford law school in 1935, "Barry" had become "Beau." A year later he earned an advanced degree in German history at the University of Chicago and took off for Europe to travel and study—to "mess with tongues," as he described it. The trip lasted three years. In 1939 he took a job with the State Department in Washington, D.C., where he labored in obscurity until 1941, when he was recruited by Donovan, who had been reporting directly to President Roosevelt as head of the Office of Coordinator of Information. In June 1942 this unit was split into two new organizations: the Office of Strategic Services and the Office of War Information. Donovan was named to head the OSS, and soon thereafter, Valentine became part of the new group.

Beau Valentine was not cut from typical agent cloth, if only because everyone remembered his appearance. Just as Providence had blessed him with a prodigious intellect, it also consigned him to a life trapped in what he once described as a "corpus colosseus."

Valentine's recruitment into the OSS had been considered odd. Theoretically, said the organization's desk jockeys, he was the worst possible choice as an agent. But the supervising chief for field services argued that it was precisely his appearance that made Valentine a first-rate choice—in effect, because he was such a memorable figure, who would expect him to be an agent? It was the kind of inverse logic beloved in the covert services.

After training and as the war progressed, Valentine successfully completed dozens of assignments everywhere, from Mexico, where he took out a German radio relay station, to Morocco, where he hunted down and choked to death the leader of an extensive Nazi intelligence network monitoring the Strait of Gibraltar.

In the summer of 1943 Valentine and twenty other agents were given parachute training at a base near Cairo, and the event became one of the many insider legends of the OSS. On the day he made his first jump from a static line, OSS people from a wide area came to witness the moment. Nobody was sure that a twenty-two-foot canopy of silk would be able to carry his weight. Those expecting failure were disappointed; his chute popped open normally and Valentine guided himself to the most accurate landing of the whole group by manipulating his risers and slipping the chute in the wind. In the fall of the year he made his first and only operational jump, dropping into Yugoslavia. From there he walked into northern Italy, which was filled with German units and a few partisan groups. Throughout 1944 he was the OSS liaison for an Italian partisan cell operating in the mountains north of Milan. From time to time, frequently against orders, he crossed into Switzerland to visit his superiors and arrange for supply drops for his partisan friends in the Italian Alps.

By the time of his assignment in Italy, Beau Valentine was known throughout the OSS as its top field man. Initially he had been assigned the code name Beefsteak, but as his reputation grew this was changed to Crawdad. He was the kind of man who did things his own way in his own time. He always listened to orders, but in doing so he focused on the desired outcome, not the specified tactics. In his view, *how* a job got done was the prerogative of the person asked to do it.

Now he was at a prison in Wiesbaden, west of Frankfurt. When the war ended in May, he'd been sent into southern Germany to "have a look." Of primary interest were German scientists, especially those who had created the Nazi rocket program. A race was beginning; Allied countries and the Russians were scouring Germany for scientific talent, and Bavaria was the home of many of the scientists and technicians. In Munich he'd stumbled onto the Russian investigating team, and when the American paratrooper captain Molanaro had told him the Russians were interested in Otto Skorzeny, Valentine guessed there might be a connection with his mission. Eventually he'd gotten the whole story from the officer and had gone immediately to Salzburg to try to pick up the Russians' trail, but it had been a fruitless trip. Where the combat soldiers in Munich had been friendly and cooperative, the troops in Austria were tight-lipped. Even so, some well-placed cartons of cigarettes allowed him to confirm that the Russians had been there and that they had met with an important captured Nazi. He was certain it was Skorzeny, but despite a concerted effort to find out, he couldn't nail it down. Using other sources, he learned that Skorzeny had been sent to Augsburg in Germany, and he followed. But by the time he arrived it was too late; Skorzeny had been moved again, this time to Wiesbaden.

Skorzeny was a prize catch for the Americans. Through an OSS colleague, Valentine procured a thick dossier on the prisoner, and some of his colleagues told him that virtually everyone in Army G-2 suspected that Skorzeny might have rescued Hitler at the end of April—or, at the very least, had information about the Führer's demise. For the most part, the American intelligence community was wary of Skorzeny, their fears making him bigger than life. Alluding to a presidential assignment, Valentine persuaded the army to let him interrogate the man, and as sometimes happened with the people he encountered, Skorzeny took a liking to him within a few minutes after the German was brought from his cell. The Americans had installed him with Kaltenbrunner, one of the leaders of the Reich Secret Service. Their cell was wired with hidden microphones, but despite the setup, neither man revealed anything of substance.

The meeting room provided by the army was small, with a single light bulb and a narrow slit window high above them. "Our people believe you were in Berlin when it was under siege by the Russians," Valentine began.

Skorzeny smiled and sent a gust of cigarette smoke toward the ceiling. "So they tell me; they're wrong. I was in the Tauern by then. When you Americans got the bridgehead at Remagen, I was ordered to destroy it. By the time we got our torpedo mines down from the coast, you already had several makeshift bridges across the river. Some of my men were killed in the attempt; others were captured. The failure of that operation pretty much ended the need for a special commando group."

"We know."

Skorzeny tipped back the legs of his wooden chair. "I saw Hitler for the final time on the twenty-seventh of March. The encounter was purely chance. I was in the Chancellery on other business; we met in a long hallway. He looked tired and weak, like an old man. He promised me I would receive Oak Leaves on my Knight's Cross, but I never saw him again. On the last day of April I was ordered to abandon the Oder front and relocate to the Alpine Redoubt, but before I could leave, my orders were amended again and I was told to report to Schörner's HQ in Silesia."

"That first order sending you to the mountains—it was because of a mission?"

Skorzeny shook his head. "All armies in crisis act the same. First they tell you to move; then, if they remember you, they tell you what they want you to do. I assumed I was going there to organize a guerrilla movement."

"But instead you went to Vienna to extract your family," Valentine pointed out.

"That was my first concern. The Russians were already in the city. I tried briefly to mobilize a defense, but it was too late for that sort of thing, so I took my men to the mountains to await the surrender."

Valentine had his own feelings about Skorzeny, but he wanted to put pressure on him. "A tribunal is being established in Nuremberg; they're going to try you on war crime charges."

"To hell with them; they're wasting their time," Skorzeny said contemptuously. "I'm a simple soldier."

"Far from simple," Valentine said with a smile.

Skorzeny took this as a compliment and bowed his head slightly. "Thank you."

"They know that your men infiltrated our lines in American uniforms during the Ardennes offensive," Valentine pointed out.

"*Jawohl,* but we wore our own uniforms underneath. If you prosecute my men, then you must also prosecute Lord Mountbatten. We did nothing the British commandos did not do. They were military actions—irregular, to be sure, but otherwise quite legitimate."

"The critical charge, I believe," said Valentine, "involves the execution of prisoners of war. They believe it was murder—pure and simple homicide."

"I gave no orders to execute American prisoners, and am aware of no such orders from any of my officers. I've heard these allegations before; those atrocities were committed by an SS division, the First

Panzer. We had no relationship with that unit, and the records will prove it without question."

"I believe you," Valentine said. Skorzeny did not strike him as a liar.

Sensing Valentine's trust, Skorzeny seized the opportunity. "I've heard that one of my officers is also here. Can you tell me what the charges are against him?"

Valentine raised a bushy eyebrow. "His name?"

"Radl."

Valentine closed his eyes and watched names and faces tick by in his mind as if he were reading an encyclopedia. When he got to Radl, he stopped and dredged up what he knew about the man.

"It's in the preliminary investigation stage. They'll interrogate him as a way of cross-checking your statements. He was your second in command?"

"Yes. There were only five of us at the end. It was a miserable and inglorious end to the division."

"Five? I understood that you had transferred some of your units to Austria."

"Only companies—the remnants of our division. After the Ardennes disaster we were decommissioned. I reported to Hitler after Christmas in Ziegenhain. I had injured my left eye, and the Führer saw to it that I got first-rate medical attention. At the end of January, Himmler called me; he'd taken over Army Group Vistula and had been given the responsibility of turning back the Russian invaders at the Oder. He sent me to Schwedt to establish a bridgehead there. We made a fight of it for a while, but with what we had it was only a matter of time until we were overrun by the Ivans. In late February I was called back to Berlin and given command of a regular division, with the rank of major general. The English were broadcasting that I was to be put in charge of the defense of Berlin, but that was untrue."

"And then you left the front."

"On February twenty-eighth. It was in the early morning."

"You took some people with you, but left others behind."

"I went alone. Radl was already in Vienna."

"Who commanded in your absence?"

"Colonel Günter Brumm—a good man, my planner." Skorzeny laughed. "The Russians asked me the same thing."

For a moment Valentine was confused. Who was Brumm? He'd seen the Friedenthal file and the division's organization chart, such as it was, but here was a new name. He knew Radl, but Brumm? He lit a cigar and offered one to the SS officer, who refused it. The American's instinct told him to be careful. "Which Russian interrogation was this?"

Skorzeny stared at the wall, obviously tired. "The *only* one . . . in Salzburg."

"But you gave yourself up to American units."

"True, but on that first morning the Americans brought two Russians to talk to me. They didn't wear uniforms—secret police types, I think."

"And they wanted to know about Brumm?"

"They didn't say so in so many words, but that's who they were after. The Russians never say anything directly; you have to interpret what they seem to be saying. Besides, I've conducted a few interrogations in my day and I understand the techniques very well." Suddenly Skorzeny laughed out loud and slapped his leg. "You don't know Günter *either!* I can see it in your face! This is incredible. What's he done to pique so much interest?"

Valentine smiled and made a gesture that acknowledged the truth of the Austrian's perception. "I thought our files were complete, but there is no mention of this Colonel Brumm. An oversight, I presume."

Skorzeny was greatly amused. "First the Russians, now you. Günter would be disturbed to know there was so much interest in him. That one loathed the limelight. I told the Russians he was dead."

They were beginning to connect with each other. "But you don't know that."

"Only a deduction. The Russians overran Schwedt. Günter would have stayed with his men, and they were not trained to run. Therefore he must be dead." Skorzeny gestured with his hands as if to say there was no other possibility.

"You think the Russians were NKVD?"

"Or SMERSH. They wore coveralls; whatever, they certainly were not regular military personnel. I spent two hours with them."

"And you told them what you told me?"

"Some of it. I was in no mood to be congenial. All they seemed to want to know was Günter's name, and I gave them that. Why not? They would have learned it soon enough."

Indeed, Valentine thought. His head began to ache, a sure sign that there was something grinding away in his subconscious. He'd had no concrete directive to follow in coming to Wiesbaden. He was here quite by accident, acting on instinct, and now the feeling he'd gotten at Munich was even stronger.

▶32 JUNE 3, 1945, 8:30 P.M.

The Harz Mountains are like an old man's teeth: worn, cracked, jagged, with gaps and stained by age. By most standards the mountains are not remarkable; from a distance they look inviting, almost soft. Their edges are a cruel deceit: grassy knolls with sparse vegetation, thin trees with new leaves and clouds of starlings darting overhead. From afar it looks like an ideal place for a picnic.

But the interior is quite different. The valleys and canyon walls are thin and deep, strewn with razor-sharp slate and piles of finely edged boulders. Small rivers and streams pop out of cliffsides, gush through trenches worn over centuries and drop without warning back into the earth. Compasses are useless in the Harz; iron deposits keep needles spinning aimlessly, perpetually seeking and never finding magnetic north. The rocks that clutter some valley floors are so sharp that leather boots last no more than a few days. Other valleys are choked with double-canopy forests, assortments of gnarled pines and hundred-year-old hardwoods, with trunks that are scored and flaked. Forest floors are littered with slash, potholes and ferns, and wrist-thick ground vines catch the feet and make the going tough. Underneath the trees it is dark—not the normal, shadowy dusk of a forest but as black and impenetrable as the gate to Hell itself. One does not enter the region innocently. Among the many mountains and forests of Germany those of the Harz are only a wart, but to those who know about such things, the range is considered an earthly version of damnation, a place that gives comfort only to the Devil and his minions.

Even the locals who live in the villages and picturesque small towns that ring the fringes of the mountains seldom venture deep into them. This is the Harz of Goethe's *Faust,* of Mount Brocken and the Witches' Sabbath of the *Walpurgisnacht,* and of the feast of Wotan's marriage to Fricka. There is dark power here, and few care to confront it. While the mountain chain runs roughly from northwest to southeast like a scar, its interior is crosshatched with gorges and box canyons that form a natural maze. Because a compass is useless, one can navigate only by landmarks and memory. Stories abound about foolish city people—usually Berliners—who have ventured innocently into the forests and never returned. From time to time those few who hunt the fringes, or the rare individual who dares penetrate the center, emerge with reports of human skeletons picked clean by scavengers.

For Günter Brumm the Harzwald was home, the one place on earth where he was entirely comfortable, the complete master, as his grandfather had been before him.

For more than three weeks the group had moved steadily west from Berlin, then south in a gentle arc toward the mountains and sanctuary. During the third week, while they were moving through a forest near Horsingen, two of the Valkyries had encountered an American patrol—not a formal expedition under orders, but a motley collection of young, unruly enlisted men exploring without the supervision of officers or noncoms. It was a flanking scout who made the contact, stumbling onto the Americans as they sat in a clearing, taking a smoke break. The girl on point heard the commotion and, as she had been taught by Beard, immediately swung over to investigate. The first girl, Erda, stood her ground, her Schmeisser leveled at a semicircle of armed men. The point, Stefanie, watched from concealment, trying to figure out a way to intervene. Before long she found Brumm beside her. After observing for a few seconds, he understood what had to be done. Stefanie was sixteen, with long blond hair and a Scandinavian appearance; she was intense, anxious to please. Her eyes met Brumm's to seek his direction.

The Americans were beginning to badger Erda. Their intentions were clear; this was no military patrol, only a gang of boys looking for women and loot.

Brumm reached toward Stefanie with his hand. "Your weapons," he whispered softly. She slipped the sling of her Schmeisser and gave it to him, then unsnapped the holster and dagger from her thigh. "Go to Erda. Play along with them. Be cooperative, do you understand?" She nodded. "We'll get in behind them, but you've got to keep their attention." Her pale blue eyes told him that she accepted what had to be done. He patted her arm. "Go."

Stefanie fumbled with her hair, trying to gather it in some kind of order. It had been a long time since she had bathed properly and she stank of sweat. Brumm watched as she moved silently through the underbrush toward the Americans. She had courage, he thought.

As Stefanie reached the opening she saw Erda being jostled roughly by some of the Americans; they were spinning her around and tearing at her clothes. Her weapon was on the ground, beyond reach. Stefanie paused at the opening, drew a deep breath and stepped boldly into the clearing. One of the Americans spotted her immediately, shouted to his comrades and they all turned to look at her. She could see that Erda was frightened. She walked directly to the men, pushed one of them aside and entered their circle. Taking her place beside her friend, she made eye contact with Erda, hoping she would understand that it was important to play along until the colonel and Beard could get into position.

"Can you believe this shit?" one of the soldiers said eagerly.

"They're just kids," another said.

"They'll be women when we're finished with them," a heavyset man with a Thompson said.

Stefanie took Erda by the hand and beckoned to her to sit. As they sat looking up at the men, Erda was puzzled by what was happening. Stefanie began to undress. When she had removed her skirt, she folded it neatly, used it to rest her head on and lay back. Arching her back, she slipped her panties off with a single motion, dropping them on the grass nearby and spreading her legs apart. She motioned encouragement and laughed harshly at the men's hesitation, pumping her hips wildly, egging them on. Erda still didn't understand, but, taking her lead from Stefanie, began to undress. As she lifted her skirt, one of the men pinned her to the ground with his boot and pulled the dagger from the scabbard on her leg. "Friggin' Class A Nazi souvenir," he said, admiring his prize.

"Never mind the lousy knife, Howie. These Kraut broads are hot for it."

"Lookit that crotch hair!" another said with a whistle. "A real blonde."

"I'll be go to hell," the one with the Thompson said as he fumbled with his belt buckle.

"This'll be worth the biggest dose of clap in Europe," another said as he threw his pants aside and dropped heavily onto Stefanie.

Brumm waited until both girls were mounted and well into the act. Beard and Waller were nearby, their daggers drawn and poised.

Brumm stepped out of cover, leveled his weapon and fired as he moved forward, sweeping the Americans without thinking, working automatically and efficiently by habit. Beard and Waller rushed in from the sides, grabbed the two men who were on the girls, rolled them off and rammed their blades home. In less than thirty seconds all eight Americans were dead. The Germans left them where they fell, without their pants. Eventually somebody would find the bodies and report it to the American authorities, who would have no doubt about the circumstances. There would be no search.

The two girls sobbed quietly as they dressed and took up their weapons. "It could have been worse," was Waller's only comment to them. Brumm touched Stefanie gently on the shoulder. "Well done." Herr Wolf stood on the edge of the clearing and stared, his eyes wide, but did not speak.

That had been a week ago and the incident was now only a small memory among the many terrible things they had seen since leaving Berlin.

Now they were on the verge of safety. The canyon was narrow, no more than two hundred meters across, covered with fallen trees, potholes and thick vines, and seemed to curve and twist endlessly. At one switchback Brumm halted the group and walked with Beard into a formation of black boulders at the base of a cliff whose top swung outward above them. All of them had felt the colonel relax when they entered the mountains, and they had relaxed too without knowing it. Surprisingly, Herr Wolf was stronger and leaner, his limp largely gone. Sometimes late in the day, when all of them were tired, he had trouble, but even then he kept to their pace, not they to his. He was also talking more; he'd spent the morning as they struggled up the canyon regaling all within earshot about his boyhood days in Austria and about the trails he loved in Berchtesgaden.

When Brumm returned with Beard, he explained: "There's a cave entrance in the rocks. We'll have to crawl. About fifty meters in, the tunnel opens into a huge vault. Beyond the vault the cave extends for several kilometers. Just before the vault, the tunnel slopes down, and if you look up you'll see a ledge. Climb onto the ledge and follow the branch to the right. It's tight, but we can get through. It will take approximately an hour for each of us to crawl through to the other side."

"What's there?" one of the girls asked.

"Temporary refuge," Brumm said.

"It's safe?"

"I was here a year ago and it hasn't been disturbed since. After we get inside, I'll set traps behind us. Nobody will follow us in, and only I will be able to lead you out."

"Are you sure I'll fit, Colonel?" Beard had a broad smile on his face.

"If not, we'll cut you in half and put you back together on the other side."

"I'll take the bottom half," one of the girls teased. The others laughed.

"I'll be right behind you," Brumm said. "If you get stuck, I'll push you through."

Even Herr Wolf smiled at the prospect of safety and security.

It took much longer than Brumm had estimated for them to get themselves and their equipment through the maze. Beard had terrible problems. In several places the colonel had to use his shoulders to force the big man through. At one point Brumm used his dagger to knock some of the side rocks down, causing a small collapse of the tunnel on Beard and in the process frightening them all.

By the time they were all through the tunnel, the valley into which they emerged was lit only by a nearly full moon. Once in, Brumm tied a trip wire to several fragmentation grenades and set them in a connected series inside the mouth of the entrance. Then he led the group north across the valley, using a game trail that looped several times across a small clear stream with a gravel bottom.

On the far side of the valley they broke out of underbrush to a moonlit sight that took their breath away. Set into a massive cliff face was the façade of a natural stone cottage built under an overhang of cliff that rose more than a hundred meters above. Within a few steps of the cottage was a dam of black logs, the water behind it blocked to form a mirrorlike pool more than twenty meters across. A fish jumped and landed with a loud splash in the pool as they approached the structure.

"Home," Brumm said, the relief thick in his voice. "We're done traveling for a while."

II

THE
SEARCH

Ezdovo was feeling good. The team was together again. It had been hectic and tense during the push to Berlin and the subsequent side journeys to Munich and Salzburg, but now he was beginning to relax. It was time for the others to do their part.

Rivitsky and Gnedin played chess, each arguing about the degree of poor judgment exhibited by the other's moves, chiding his opponent to stop wasting time. Gnedin was the better player, a consistent winner in the highest competitive circles of Moscow, where the game was the closest thing to a religion. He played quickly, sure of his strategy and tactical choices. In contrast, Rivitsky liked to think out loud about his options, talking to his pieces as if they were people, scolding them when an attack failed, wishing them a slow death when they were about to be captured. The two men were very different, and while the surgeon was Rivitsky's superior, the latter often played him to a draw and on rare days even managed to defeat him. While they waged war with intensity, even ferocity, there never seemed to be any residual hard feelings when the games were over. No matter what the outcome, the end invariably stimulated their camaraderie.

When idle, Bailov's interests were difficult to predict. Sometimes he would sleep, snoring loudly or woofing like a bear, making the others throw objects at him in order to get him to turn over. Other times he would lose himself in a book or a magazine. Often he would play his balalaika, strumming soft, haunting chords that impelled Ezdovo to rise to his feet and dance slowly and gracefully by himself, his eyes glazed over as his mind drifted back to the steppes of his homeland.

For his part, Ezdovo liked using their downtime to clean his weapons, a habit ingrained over the years. Often he cleaned the whole group's guns and honed their knives. Mostly he liked to watch and listen to the others and to laugh at their jokes.

Petrov sat alone most of the time, writing, reading, thinking.

The men were comfortable with one another, even Petrov, whom they called Earth Father behind his back, and who was not shy about scolding them when matters did not go as he wished. Outsiders found Petrov aloof and abrasive, but the group accepted his ways, knowing what his powers were and wanting to share in his magic. Petrov was not one who would be picked from the masses as a leader, yet he was the best one Ezdovo had ever served with.

At times, when Petrov was intellectually consumed—which was often—he talked to himself in low tones. This was maddening, because while his voice was audible, it was not loud enough to be understood. He had been in this state now for better than two hours, and Ezdovo guessed that many more hours were ahead.

But he was wrong. The field telephone buzzed. Gnedin reached over from the chessboard and answered it. "What?" He cupped the mouthpiece and called out to Petrov, "Chenko is downstairs. He says you asked him to come."

Petrov snapped out of his state and motioned for Gnedin to have the doctor sent up.

"Chenko brings interesting information," Petrov announced to the group after a brief conversation with the man. His offering an opinion on information before they had heard it was highly unusual.

Since Ezdovo and Rivitsky's return from Munich Petrov had not said a word about their efforts. He had accepted their separate written reports and hummed a melancholy tune while reading them, but offered no evaluation. When the films of the records were developed, he retired to an interrogation room below and remained there a full day and a night; meals were brought to him and left outside the closed door.

While Petrov was in seclusion the four men shared their experiences with one another. Ezdovo's theft of the weapon from the American brought the most laughter. It puzzled them that their leader was moving so slowly; they felt that time was escaping. They accepted that Hitler was alive and were eager to begin the hunt, but Petrov delayed for reasons that he kept to himself, fussing with details, the case files growing larger and larger by the day with no return—at least, no return they could see.

It was Petrov's way to be methodical. "Ours is more work of the mind," he lectured, "than of the body." They had been through it before and knew there was no sense in protesting or trying to accelerate the process; he would not move until he had totally digested what had been gleaned. Once he had explained his method to Ezdovo: "The hunter may take his game in many ways. You can set a trap without bait. Or you can bait the trap in the hope of trapping your quarry. Or you can attempt to drive it, frightening it into going where you want it to. You can also track an animal with persistence and stealth. Or, knowing your quarry's habits, you can determine his destination, then go to the spot and wait for him to come to you." Being a hunter himself, Ezdovo understood these options, but his chief's point was not clear. Petrov continued: "Each method is proven. We know the strengths and weaknesses of each, and we can choose which is most effective for a particular set of circumstances. But none is universally effective; thus the choice of tactics is as important as the hunter's skill in implementing them. True?"

"True," Ezdovo agreed.

Petrov had joined his hands in front of him as if he were praying. "It follows, then, that the most important part of the hunt is the time spent in understanding its circumstances and conditions. If the hunter is committed to his skills rather than to chance, he ponders first."

While one ponders, skittish game often gets away, Ezdovo had thought to himself.

Chenko looked tired. He carried his black medical bag with him, and on entering the room went straight to a cot and sat down heavily, stretching his legs in front of him. "You're going to get me killed, Petrov," he said in a low voice. "Zhukov sought me out this morning. He's in a rage. He accused me of interfering in SMERSH matters, and he's going to order Moscow to have me withdrawn unless I keep him informed of your activities. He's nervous; he wants to know who you are and what your official function is."

"Tell him to consult with Comrade Vishinsky."

"I did that. He's wary of Vishinsky."

Bailov turned to Rivitsky. "And you said the general was stupid." They laughed. Vishinsky was one of Stalin's top conspirators in what all Russians called "wet business"—political murders.

"Zhukov fancies himself a killer," Gnedin said. "Next to Vishinsky, he's a rank amateur and he knows it. No wonder he's wary."

"What did you tell the general?" Petrov asked.

"I told him that you carry the Red Badge."

"His reaction?"

"His flesh illuminated to a patriotic red glow and he departed, huffing like a horse that had just run several kilometers through deep drifts of snow." Regaining his energy, Chenko opened his bag and placed three bundles on the table. In each was a small test tube with a rubber stopper.

The men of the Special Operations Group stared at the specimen bottles. Petrov looked only at Chenko. "You have results?"

"Results, yes, but they are meaningless. I need to know where the samples come from," Chenko complained loudly.

"You will know in good time," Petrov said flatly.

Chenko shrugged like a bear stretching its back muscles. "Zhukov is making noises about telling the Western press of his findings. He wants to bury Hitler and be done with it."

"Zhukov can do as he pleases. He is of no concern to us."

"Yes, well, that's your opinion." Chenko lifted the first test tube. "Sample. Dried fluid. Identification: human blood. Type matches. There are traces of testosterone and strychnine."

He picked up the second container. "Human hair. Pigmented brown. The follicles tell us that these are from two sites: facial hairs and hairs from the scalp, with some of the roots intact."

"Finally," Chenko cooed, turning the third container, "this was the most difficult of all."

"Hemp," Petrov interrupted.

Chenko's face froze in surprise. "How did you know?"

"Simple deduction. Anything else?"

"No."

"You're sure the blood type matches?"

"Yes. Very common, though there was not a lot to work with. A simple analysis to perform, even in the barbaric conditions that present themselves in this place of pestilence."

"It's enough," Petrov said.

Chenko stood silently, waiting for an invitation to remain, but Petrov only stared at him. Finally the corpulent doctor closed his bag, excused himself and departed.

When the elevator had descended, Petrov looked at his men. "This evidence convinces me that Hitler substituted a double and fled."

"But maybe he's been killed by now," Rivitsky offered. It was a thought that had occurred to all of them since they had arrived in Berlin.

"Possibly. We will attempt to make a determination of that. Zhukov has taken his bait. Any new investigations will always come back to the witnesses. Without the guard Rudolf, there is no way they can ever discover the truth. Your thoroughness has tipped the scales in our favor," Petrov told the group.

"There's the damaged light section in the bunker," Gnedin reminded him.

"Temporary. All lights will be repaired and sealed permanently. The same for the entry hatch through the corridor. Eventually the entire structure will be razed; no evidence will exist. Everything we collect during our investigation will be taken to Moscow for storage. Everything else will be eliminated. The Russian people are owed vengeance. We are going to find him. If he is alive, we are going to take him back to Moscow."

"When do we begin?" Ezdovo asked.

"We began the night we arrived," Petrov said. "Now you and Rivitsky have opened an important door for us. This SS Colonel Brumm is the confederate. I feel it. He was Skorzeny's planner. I suspect that Hitler culled him from the group for this particular mission. No doubt the sergeant is involved, too. We are almost ready to go into the field, but first we must know more about Brumm. His records were removed to hide his trail, but their absence in the midst of otherwise perfect order draws attention to him. The colonel has made a serious error; were his records on hand we would have no compelling reason to suspect him."

"We could get more from Skorzeny," Bailov suggested.

"No," Rivitsky replied. "Skorzeny hates us. He won't help us any further."

"It's academic," Petrov interrupted. "The Americans have Skorzeny, and I suspect that's the last we'll see of him. We had our chance, and you did well to get what you did."

Rivitsky and Ezdovo both warmed under the unexpected compliment.

"Our best opportunity will be to use the records we have in order to identify commando personnel among our captives. The units from Vienna are in American or Canadian hands. We will concentrate on the prisoners taken on the Oder."

"Both of them?" Bailov said sarcastically.

Petrov shot a dagger stare at Bailov, who turned away from his gaze.

"There were thousands of prisoners taken," Petrov said sternly. "I've checked. They are in camps. Some are already being moved east."

"First we have to locate the camps," Rivitsky pointed out.

"The trail will grow cold," Ezdovo complained. "The Oder is in the opposite direction. Our quarry will go west."

"Not necessarily. The safest route is not always the fastest. This event has been planned carefully. I suspect they will move to a safe place, a haven already prepared, and lie in. Presumably, Hitler is neither healthy nor strong and will need time to mend. The trail may fade, but it won't disappear." Petrov paused. "We also must consider that in the absence of a hunter the animal often settles into a normal routine and can be more easily taken by surprise later."

"We've done well," Rivitsky said, reaching for a loaf of bread.

"Lucky," Gnedin added.

"Good hunters create their own luck," Ezdovo said.

Their leader smiled. "Ezdovo understands the hunt."

Petrov retreated into his own thoughts. He had heard a rumor, so far unsubstantiated, that a high-ranking Nazi had turned himself in to Soviet authorities with an offer to provide assistance of a special nature. If true, Brumm's past might be revealed more quickly than the others imagined.

▶34 JUNE 3, 1945, 11:50 P.M.

The group stood nervously in the doorway waiting for Brumm to create light inside. The colonel struck a match and fumbled in the blackness to ignite the wick of a kerosene lantern. At first the wick gave off only a tiny red glow; then it turned white and grew, casting a golden glow on all but the deepest corners of the cold stone interior.

When the group saw their surroundings, they gasped in unison. The main room was much larger than the external façade had suggested. Two doors opened off it to dark halls. Despite the building's unusual structure, it seemed to be a normal house inside. The floor was made of hand-hewn but exceptionally smooth and tightly fitted planks, covered with a dark varnish that reflected light. A slightly curving stairwell, which appeared to have been carved from a gnarled tree trunk, climbed up into the darkness from the middle of the room.

One end of the hall was dominated by a cooking fireplace made of stones fitted together solidly without benefit of mortar. At the other end was a smaller fireplace, this one with a narrow opening. The room was furnished with tables and chairs that appeared to have been shaped from arm-thick trees, their natural forms incorporated into their designs. Near the cooking area, fresh water tumbled from a carved wooden trough into a stone basin, and from there down to a narrow pipe set into the wall. It was a simple but ingenious plumbing system.

Brumm went through the room lighting lanterns until the whole area was brightly illuminated. The others moved through the door, dropping their gear just inside the entrance.

"It doesn't seem real," one of the girls said.

"Real enough," Brumm said. "This place is called Stone Cave. What you see here has taken five generations to build. My grandfather's grandfather discovered this valley in the nineteenth century. He hewed out the first rooms; generations since have added their own touches, always expanding it. There are six full rooms on this level and a large loft above. The beds are filled with cured moss—better than feathers. Behind these rooms is a string of caverns. Ancient tribes came here; you'll see their paintings on the walls of the caves."

The colonel noticed that Herr Wolf had cocked his head at an odd angle; he seemed to be mesmerized by some thought that he was keeping to himself. Brumm sat on a chair and lit a cigarette. It was the first time the group had seen him smoke. "More than a century," he said, his voice hinting melancholy. "Five generations. We have everything we need: weapons, ammunition, medical supplies. There's even a small generator waiting to be assembled. It can be operated with water power, and there's plenty of that in this valley. We have a radio, fresh food, roots and plants, small game, fish. As a boy I thought this was paradise."

"Who else knows about this place?" Erda asked.

"Only us. My grandfather is gone. This valley is actually the crater of an old volcano, and so is very fertile. Around us is a maze of valleys and deep gorges, most of which lead nowhere. From above, it looks no different from any other valley in the Harz. To get here you have to know the way."

"What was once found can be twice found," Beard said with skepticism. By nature he preferred open ground and the freedom to move, not a static base, much less one built into a mountain of rock.

"True, but the odds are small. The shelter is invisible from the air;

it can be seen only from the ground, and even then only when you are on this side of the valley."

"Show us the rest of it," one of the girls said eagerly.

Brumm waved his hand. "Explore for yourself." He listened to the girls chatter to one another as they disappeared into the hallways and loft, then shrieking with delight over the beds. When they returned, they were all talking at the same time.

"Come," Brumm said. "There's more." He led them down a corridor and through a thick wooden door into the caverns, where a narrow wooden walkway had been constructed.

They were amazed at the magnitude of supplies stacked on both sides in the darkness. Beyond the storage area Brumm led them down a narrow tunnel cut through solid rock that required them to move single file. As they walked deeper the temperature and humidity steadily increased.

"I know about caverns," Herr Wolf said suddenly. It was the first time he had talked since they had entered the valley. "Further in you can expect the temperature to stabilize at a constant; there will be little variation even if you travel a kilometer into the ground. Such places are ideal for storage. I've given the subject considerable study and have become something of an authority on it." The group did not respond; they had no interest in hearing another long-winded explanation, preferring to make their own discoveries. "Extraordinary," Herr Wolf continued, his voice growing louder and beginning to echo. "It's getting warmer."

Eventually they reached the end, a small open space triangular in shape. The solid rock ceiling above them was at least four meters high. Brumm held his lantern high and stood aside to let them all press into the area. Below them was a pool of water. The room was humid, and steam lifted off the surface. "A natural spa," he explained.

Waller leaned over and dipped her hand in the water. "It's warm! Hot baths!"

"There are minerals in it," Brumm said. "Very soothing for tired muscles. On the far side"—he held the lantern higher and pointed—"there's a ledge under the water, like a bench. The deepest part of the pool is only a little over a meter, so you don't have to be cautious."

As some of the girls began to undress, Herr Wolf blushed and backed into the tunnel. Brumm stopped them. "Later. First there's work to be done." Their disappointment showed. "We work first, then eat, bathe and sleep. Remember your duty, always your duty must come first. Don't let yourselves be fooled by our circumstances. The valley affords us protection, but it doesn't make us invulnerable. We are still in great danger, and everyone must understand this." His voice was cool, deep with authority. "On the other hand," he added, his tone softening, "after your duty is done, your time is your own, and I assure you the warm water will feel wonderful."

While the clean-up detail worked around him, Herr Wolf sat on a wooden bench, his legs crossed and his hands clasped around one knee. For the most part he was quiet, but from time to time he called out for one of the girls to catch a spot of dust she had missed. While they obeyed him without question, Brumm noticed that the girls were beginning to respond to Herr Wolf more as if he were their grandfather than what he had once been. They went about their tasks cheerfully, acting more like the young girls they were than the soldiers Brumm was trying to turn them into.

Satisfied that the housekeeping would be done, Brumm turned his attention to making small doughballs from a loaf of bread. When he had filled a small bowl with them, he beckoned Beard to come outside with him. They walked upstream for almost a kilometer without a light. Beard found himself tripping with nearly every stride, while his colonel walked quickly and smoothly, never stumbling.

"How do you see in this shit?" Beard called out as he stopped to rub a shin.

"I don't." Brumm laughed. "My legs know where they're going. I simply follow them."

When Beard finally caught up, the colonel was sitting by the edge of the fast-moving brook, baiting a hook with a doughball. "Best place in the valley," he told his sergeant. "Three different species of fish. Two in the moving water, usually in the deep pools or at the edges of the riffles. There are also some small, deep ponds of warmer water that contain a species like carp. Bony, but properly filleted and seasoned and cooked long enough, they're quite good. The best fishing is at night. Watch."

Brumm held a light under his arm and pointed it down toward the water. They were directly behind a curve where the water backflowed and formed a dark pool. When he lowered the line until the doughball disappeared just beyond the light, the line immediately snapped taut. A fish broke water and jumped, landing with a loud smack. Brumm jerked it onto the bank with a single snap of his wrist and used his foot to pin it to the ground. Reaching down, he caught it under the gills with his forefinger and hoisted it for Beard's inspection. The thick-sided fish kicked its tail violently and reflected the light.

"White trout," Beard said in amazement. "I thought the only place they existed was in the streams of the Schwarzwald in Bavaria."

"There and in this one valley," Brumm said proudly. "Some kind of evolutionary accident. See how easy it is?" Nearly every drop of the line brought an instant strike. Beard took each fish as Brumm pulled it in and threaded it onto a forked stick. When they had enough, Beard cleaned the fish quickly and expertly with his SS dagger, brushing the offal off the rocks into the fast water, just as he had done as a boy in his own favorite fishing spots.

On the return journey to camp Brumm shared more details about the valley with his sergeant. "There are some small deer and sheep on the south cliffs, domestics gone wild. Many birds in the spring. In the fall, ducks and other waterfowl stop here. One or two people could survive here indefinitely. With the size of our group, we'll use our supplies first and not destroy the natural balance until we have to."

Ever the professional, Beard took this opportunity to tell Brumm that he didn't like leaving the entry cave mined with grenades. "If somebody stumbles onto it and he's not alone, he'll know that the traps are there for a reason. Better, I think, to block off this end naturally and create a barrier that won't arouse curiosity." Brumm agreed; they would take care of it in the morning.

"We're going to be here for some time," the colonel said. "We have to maintain discipline, establish a routine and keep to it. We'll use the time to train the girls. It will keep them fit and active. Those two handled the Americans admirably. I think we can make some progress in turning them into soldiers. That's your primary responsibility."

"How long will we be here?"

"Months," Brumm replied. "At least six."

Suddenly Beard grabbed the colonel's shoulder from behind and stopped him in his tracks.

"The girls . . ." he began. It was difficult finding the right words. Even though they were like brothers, technically Brumm was still his colonel. The sergeant major drew a deep breath and blurted, "*Was sich zweit, das dreit sich gern*—what comes together in two likes to turn into threes."

Brumm laughed. "Why, Sergeant Rau, I think your prudishness is showing."

"Much more," Beard said with a nervous laugh. "They're also
. . . *experienced*. Do we . . . ? I mean, we don't fraternize with our
men. It isn't allowed . . ." He tried to speak with some grace. "We've
always slept with our men, but do we now sleep with our men, if you
get my meaning?"

Brumm smiled. "I've given it some thought. It's a very delicate
balance and a proper question to ask ourselves. It's predictable that
the pressure will build—natural urges and all that. But we can't afford
a pregnancy here, or petty jealousy either. Both could be disastrous.
We have to mold a unit and make sure that all of us pull together."

"It's the togetherness that scares me," Beard said.

"I think it would be unnatural to deny it," the colonel told him.
"But there will have to be some rules—firm ones." Brumm wasn't
sure what they were going to be, but he had ten minutes before they
reached the dwelling to think about it, he told himself.

▶35 JUNE 4, 1945, 1:00 A.M.

For Johann Pescht hate had become the force that sustained him; it
was his deity. He had been a Jew, but no longer. Now he saw himself
as an avenger; he would pay back the Nazis. It was his right; his father
and mother, his wife, Anna, and his five children had all died on the
same day as he was forced to stand aside and watch helplessly while
they marched naked into the gas chamber. Only he had managed to
survive. It had begun in Belsen, a camp in Poland. Then there had
been a long stint in Ravensbrück, north of Berlin, a camp for women
only. He had been sent there to participate in bizarre experiments.
Later he had been sent to Dachau and finally to Buchenwald. It had
been a tour of nightmares.

Pescht was sickened by his own behavior, but he knew he was
powerless to act differently; his desire to live, however despicably,
was stronger than his desire to live morally, and he found himself
doing whatever the pseudomedical technicians and Nazi doctors wanted.
Something inside demanded: Live, whatever the cost. He copulated
before audiences, answering their questions as he labored over his

sometimes frightened, sometimes angry partners. He did his duty before two-way mirrors and for motion-picture cameras, in cold rooms
and hot, in states of disorientation—both depressions and euphorias—
created by drugs, with tight young women and cringing old women,
with women restrained, with some healthy and some first beaten, and
once, the most terrible time of all, with a dead one, a red-haired woman
of thirty who had been starved and whose hipbones protruded like
small wings, the purpose of the experiment being the determination
of the life expectancy of sperm in a cooling corpse.

Toward the end of the war the doctors who had so enthusiastically
pursued their scientific studies began to disappear from the camps.
The medical experiments slowed, then stopped, and there were too
few doctors left even to staff the medical section. Pescht, who had
lived well as a special performer in the research section, found his
security gone, his means of survival taken away; he was shipped to
Buchenwald and there assigned to a burial detachment that did its
work with bent shovels and blunt picks in all kinds of weather, laboring
in shifts of twelve hours or more. During such shifts many of his fellow
workers died, often succumbing in mid-strike against the earth, adding
to their fellow workers' burden.

From the beginning Pescht was determined to survive. He stole
food and clothing from other inmates. He eavesdropped on new arrivals and told the guards everything he heard, sometimes embellishing
his tale-telling with stories of his own creation. There was nothing he
would not do to curry favor with his masters. He knew that survival
at any price—especially at the price of others' lives—was a moral
outrage, yet something stronger inside him overruled his conscience
and impelled him to do what was necessary for himself.

With the ample rations of the medical unit a luxury of the past,
Pescht withered to skeletal proportions. Even after Hitler became chancellor, Pescht had continued to consider himself first a German, a loyal
and patriotic citizen, second a father and husband—and last, by a
good margin, a Jew. Yet his country had declared his kind to be
subhuman, enemies of the state, and shipped the Jews to camps where
the German acumen for organization was translated into mass-
produced death. Worst of all, his God had deserted him. How else
could such nightmares be accounted for? In the early part of his captivity he had prayed long and hard, but eventually he abandoned the
notion that there was a deity; what else could explain such things
being allowed to happen? God was dead; in fact, Pescht reasoned, He

had probably never lived at all. On the other hand, it was clear that the Devil not only lived but thrived.

In late April 1945 Pescht awoke early in his barracks and clumped loudly in his wooden clogs threading his way through the dead and sleeping bodies on the floor. His reputation from Ravensbrück had traveled with him, and after a near-terminal stint with the burial teams he had finally been reassigned to the Lagerschutz, a kind of police force of inmates who willingly cooperated with the Nazis and maintained order inside the compound. As a member of this security unit, his food rations increased but only marginally; still, a gain was a gain. All through Germany there were said to be shortages, and the camps were last on the priority lists.

Pescht was assigned to the camp brothel, where he spent his days and nights running errands. Buchenwald had a large proportion of female guards, many of them Austrians, and most of these coarse peasants used him just as the male guards used the more desirable female Jews in the camp. He didn't mind.

Outside it was still cool and misty. His breath burst into the air and hung above him in small clouds, marking his progress through the muddy campgrounds. He hurried toward the brothel in the hope of finding some morsels of food left over from the previous night's play. But as he walked he began to be aware that something was different. At the brothel he found the girls silently gathered around the fireplace. Usually when he arrived this early they were still in bed. Those not selected for another night's stay were then returned to their barracks; those who had been chosen slept in comfort until the afternoon.

"Pescht," one of the women called out. "They're gone. They left during the night, every one of them. What do you think it means?"

Suddenly he understood what he had felt and not seen. "It means liberation, you simple cunt. The Americans are coming."

Pescht had nurtured a plan. His intent had been to escape, but liberation would make his task easier. Initially there had been fifty inmates brought in on the plot, but disease and punishment had decimated their ranks. For weeks thousands of new prisoners had been arriving, and the original group of conspirators was now spread all over the camp. He had to see the others. He spent the morning contacting them, and when the Americans arrived in the early afternoon, Pescht and his group acted as the camp's official greeting party.

He had planned it well. He took the American commander, a colonel, straightaway to the camp crematorium, told him its purpose, then stood back to wait for the American's predictable response. The colonel stared wide-eyed, paled, stumbled outside and vomited, then went into a violent rage at all Germans and all things German. It was precisely the reaction Pescht had hoped for. Over the next several days he and his unit, which included a few thin females, helped the Americans sort out the mess. Several groups of American generals came and went, their faces taut with anger.

At the end of a week Pescht befriended an American lieutenant colonel from Texas and cornered him. "Some of us want to leave."

"We understand, but it will take some time. You'll need papers, identification. We want to help you locate relatives."

"We have no relatives. Hitler has seen to that." What he wanted, Pescht told the colonel, were sturdy boots, heavy coats and weapons. The colonel balked, but Pescht was persistent and worked on the man's guilt. He told the Texan about his family, of watching his children cling to his wife as they undressed, of seeing them march naked and clinging to one another into the gas chambers, screaming back to him for help. In the end he got what he wanted. The colonel did not ask for an explanation; as a Texan, he understood vengeance in ways that many other Americans might not have.

The group left the camp after midnight with only the colonel to see them off, and moved westward, clinging to the forests and hills. While the group lacked a clear idea of what they would do when they were freed, Pescht had a concrete plan in his mind. They would raid farmhouses and small villages at night. There would be no distinctions made between good and bad Germans. All Germans would be fair game; the avengers would use their years of schooling in the Nazi camps to give the civilians a taste of what had been going on inside the fences.

▶36 JUNE 4, 1945, 3:00 A.M.

By no standard was the meal a feast, but the group had not had a hot meal since leaving Berlin, and the warmth of the food was celebration enough. Brumm cooked the fish, heads on, over an open flame, sprinkling them with liberal pinches of the spices and herbs that hung in small deerskin pouches on the wall near the fireplace. While the trout browned on sticks over the fire, Brumm showed one of the girls some roots in the forest near the dam. When they had an armful, they brought them back and crushed them. Water was added to make a paste. To it he added a sprinkling of brown sugar and slivers of dried apples from a barrel in the storage area. The gluelike concoction was then molded into small flat cakes and toasted in the embers on the edge of the fire. They drank freshly brewed tea made with mountain water and ate in silence, lost in their own thoughts.

After the meal Herr Wolf pulled Brumm aside. "We need to discuss living arrangements," he said mysteriously.

"Such as?"

"I must have complete privacy," Wolf whispered. His statement was half order, half question.

"You can have a room to yourself."

"More than that," Wolf said anxiously. "Nobody is to enter my quarters without my permission. Also, I insist on bathing alone."

"This place affords us many things, but complete privacy is not one of them."

"Nevertheless, I insist on your arranging it."

"I can do only so much."

"You will do whatever is required," Herr Wolf said peremptorily. "Now that the immediate dangers have passed, I intend to play a more active role in governing our affairs. I have always been adept at utilizing the services of specialists. That's what you are; your job was to get us here. Now that we're here, I will assume my rightful authority and the corresponding responsibility."

"If you require privacy, we will do our best to provide it, Führer." The word seemed foreign on Brumm's lips. In Berlin it had been natural, but here in the Harz the title seemed out of place. "It will be up to the others what they do. I'm sure that as our commander in chief, you understand that our first duty is to see to the needs of your subordinates. Often the superior must sacrifice for the greater good."

"Don't lecture me, Brumm. I won't have men and women bathing together publicly, and that's final. There are certain values I will not sacrifice for convenience. You will punish those who disobey."

"No," Brumm said firmly. "Let me remind you that I command here. That was our agreement. I hold you to your word. Of course we could submit it to a vote."

"In the military, orders are given and followed," Herr Wolf argued, his voice beginning to weaken.

"That's in the paper-pushing bureaucracy. In the field there is a more democratic process. Soldiers who have a say in their lives fight better and longer. It's one of the first principles taught in modern military leadership."

"Weak leaders take votes," the older man said harshly. "Strong leaders make decisions and act. Those who do not do as they are told are dealt with forcefully."

"Perhaps," Brumm replied, "but this is an unusual situation that requires us to improvise. We will conduct ourselves accordingly."

"You will follow my orders. I insist."

"I will listen to your suggestions, confer with the others and decide what is best for all of us," Brumm said curtly, shutting off further conversation.

Herr Wolf stepped back and studied Brumm. Suddenly his mood shifted completely, and his frown turned to a smile. "I chose very well," he said smugly.

"You made a choice," Brumm said. "Only the future will tell us how good it was. This is my country. Here we do things my way. When we reach our final destination, we'll think about another arrangement."

"Very well," Herr Wolf said brightly. "I accept the premise. In the Great War I was a common soldier. I knew how to take orders, and by learning to follow them I learned how to give them. I have not changed. My generals couldn't follow orders. That's why we're here— because of my generals. Now I will show you. I order myself to follow your orders." He paused, hoping for a response from the colonel. When none came, he continued, "There. It's done. I have my orders. I'll obey. You'll see."

Brumm could not believe what he was hearing.

"But," whined Herr Wolf, his mood darkening again. "I still demand my privacy. You must honor that."

It was not worth additional discussion. Herr Wolf could have his privacy, but Brumm also guessed that the man's demands were only the first of many they would hear.

When dinner was finished, the group was around a pine table talking, drinking tea, watching and listening to the fire. Herr Wolf had insisted on being the first to bathe and had gone into the cavern. All the girls except Waller seemed giddy.

When Herr Wolf returned and went into the bedroom he'd picked out, Brumm asked, "Who's next? Ladies or gentlemen?"

"Don't you mean officers and enlisted?" Waller challenged.

"Have it your way. Who's to be first?"

"Do soldiers bathe separately from their officers?" Waller continued.

"In barracks, yes."

"What about in the field?"

"Together. They share everything in the field."

"And where are we?"

"In camp," Brumm answered. Beard and the other girls were smiling, enjoying the small contest.

"Agreed. This room is the camp. But the pool? *Not* in the camp." Waller looked at the other girls. "Agreed?" They nodded with animation.

Brumm stood up, covered his mouth and coughed to clear his throat. He had given them a lecture on mixing while Herr Wolf bathed alone. It was important that they understand the rules and abide by them. "You know the rules: no permanent relationships and no jealousy. We must be adult about this or we will have to take up new rules."

"Enough talk," one of the girls squealed.

Brumm bent slowly from the waist, extended his arm in the direction of the hot pool and clicked his heels together. "I bow to the obvious," he said. The Valkyries immediately ran down the hall and into the darkness, howling happily at the prospect of hot baths.

Beard and his colonel lingered at the table. "Are we going to . . . join them?" the sergeant asked.

"Rules of the field," Brumm whispered. "For morale."

"Duty," Beard added, seeing the twinkle in his colonel's eyes.

"A contribution to esprit de corps."

"Tactical instruction." The sergeant major poked Brumm in the ribs. "Let's go, Günter," he whispered. "They're liable to turn to each other if we don't hurry up." He laughed deeply at his own joke, his face turning almost scarlet.

Brumm stopped in the tunnel. "Go ahead," he told Beard. "I'll be there in a moment."

"You won't mind if we start without you?" the big man said over his shoulder.

Brumm went back into the supply area and found what he wanted. Looking around the storehouse reminded him how much had gone into preparing the hideaway. It had taken years and countless journeys to provision the small citadel. First it had been for himself, for he had harbored no illusions about the eventual outcome of the war. Then the project had taken on new dimensions. He had never traveled to Stone Cave empty-handed. Once he'd come on horseback, leading a string of army mules laden with supplies. After unloading he'd released the animals in the outer valley. He wondered what had happened to them.

Waller undressed slowly. The other girls were already in the water splashing quietly, talking nervously, helping one another scrub, thinking about the men who were to join them. Waller liked the feeling of the warm air on her flesh. It seemed natural and nurturing. She tried to remember the last time she had been naked and relaxed, but could not; the past seemed to be another life.

When her clothes were piled at her feet, she stepped to the edge of the pool and tested the water temperature with her foot. It felt warm and inviting. She slid into it, enjoying its caress. It made her skin feel alive and tingly, muddling her ability to think clearly. Since joining the other girls, she had felt compelled to be under control at all times, and it had put a strain on her. Now this self-imposed restraint was losing its purpose. Günter Brumm was in command; she didn't have to worry anymore. Where was he? she wondered as she lathered herself with soap.

Beard turned his arrival into a spectacle, kicking at the water and shouting at the girls. His appearance immediately enlivened the atmosphere. Stefanie, her long blond hair plastered to her face and neck, emerged from the water with an athletic leap and playfully began pushing the giant Beard toward the pool, wrestling with him, each of them sneaking exploratory touches of the other as they fought their mock battle. Soon the other girls came out of the water to join her, and the match intensified. Beard was surprised at the fullness of their small bodies, and by their strength. He had planned to let them push him into the water, but he realized that the five of them were going to do it without his help. He also recognized their hunger because he had it as well. Their hands and what they whispered to him were very direct. Finally he slid into the water like a great fleshy ship. At the last moment he tugged and caught all of them off-balance, so that they all hit with a splash that sent waves lapping over the sides of the pool.

Waller watched Stefanie cling to the sergeant as they floated around the pool. Her friend had always been the most direct of them; she believed in reaching out for what she wanted. The sight gnawed at her. She and her friends were no strangers to sex, but she realized that despite what they had done and been, all of them still harbored dreams of love and of a future binding them to one man. The war had not destroyed that. She did not think about the Führer in this regard, though at times there was something in his eyes that was almost overpowering; he was too old and he was the Führer—unapproachable, forbidden fruit. What concerned her was the other two men. Six women, two men. Had it been the other way around, she would have felt better. How could two of them handle all of them with regularity?

Actually the problem was much worse. Her concern was not for two men, but for one, Günter Brumm. She did not want to share him with anyone else.

None of them noticed Brumm arrive. Suddenly he was just there, sitting by the edge of the pool with two large bottles in his hands. His flesh glowed. Waller gasped. He was muscular, almost beautiful. She had never seen anyone like him.

Brumm walked into the water, holding the bottles high by their thick necks. "Champagne," he said, and the girls turned from Beard to him. He settled into the warmth of the pool and drank from a bottle, feeling the liquid warm him from the inside. Soon they were all seated side by side on the underwater ledge, the two magnums being passed up and down the line.

Gretchen Waller refused to allow herself to join in. She drank quickly and too much, and her head began to spin. Suddenly she pushed her way past the others to Brumm, slid her arms around him and pulled him away toward the deeper water.

"I know I can't keep you for myself," she whispered to him, "but at least I'll always remember that I was the first." Wrapping her legs around him, she kissed him hard on the mouth.

▶**37** JUNE 5, 1945, 9:00 A.M.

When one knows how to go about it, rumors are often easier to confirm than facts. What Petrov had heard was that Heinrich Müller had presented himself boldly to NKVD agents in Poland, claiming that he had in place a vast network of agents that, in return for his life and more mundane considerations, he might "turn" for the Russians. Müller's history was well known; he was among the most wanted of Nazi vermin. Petrov was not surprised by the rumor; on the contrary, it made perfect sense. Müller was a man of considerable accomplishment and undoubtedly able to deliver what he promised. As head of Gestapo Section IV, he had been responsible for the construction and administration of more than seven hundred concentration camps, including those specializing in extermination. Petrov had seen the gas chambers disguised as showers in Polish camps. It had not bothered him in the way that it did others. Millions of his own countrymen were in camps, too—or at least they had been when Hitler had invaded Russia. The difference was only one of style. In Russia the unwanteds and sub-humans were sent north to permanent exile and none returned. The Germans were less patient, perhaps even a bit paranoid. Rather than letting nature and hard labor exact their price in time, the Germans tended to hurry the process with gadgets and methods for mass production. It was a vivid reminder that under fascism the capitalist spark burned on. Petrov admitted to himself that Müller's record would be envied by some Soviets, including some high in the party hierarchy—perhaps even at the pinnacle.

Müller's name had been on the list prepared by the Special Operations Group. He'd last been seen near Hitler on the twenty-eighth of April. Before his disappearance the SS lieutenant general had put out feelers to Russian agents, and Petrov was well aware of these overtures.

The problem now was to locate Müller. With his contacts, he might easily give them a fast way to locate survivors of Skorzeny's units. It was essential that information about the commandos' planning officer be quickly pursued. With his own agents, Müller would be able to get it faster than his own team, Petrov reasoned. He decided to make a few calls around Berlin to see what the Red Badge might kick loose from his comrades.

At Zhukov's headquarters the previous day he had learned nothing, but at Konev's First Ukrainian Front Headquarters in the southern outskirts he found a small lead. Konev's people were living in mildewed tents in a barren field still pitted by artillery. The troops were lounging and cleaning their weapons more from habit than from need. The sun was out, and even Petrov felt a surge of warmth from it.

The main tent could have housed a small circus. Bricks from the nearby rubble supported doors that served as desks and tables. An emaciated sergeant major without boots was rubbing his feet and examining them when Petrov approached him.

"Who maintains the records of prisoners of war?"

"NKVD," the sergeant said, not bothering to look up. "You'd think that after a two-thousand-mile hike my feet would have hardened, but they haven't." He sounded disgusted.

"Central unit or a detachment?" Petrov asked.

The sergeant lifted his eyes to study the visitor. It was not often that someone came around *seeking* the NKVD; usually it worked the other way. "Who knows?" he replied. "The NKVD doesn't make such distinctions."

"You must have records to document the transfer of control."

The sergeant major felt the hair stand on the back of his neck. This one talked too carefully. To survive he had learned to sense trouble, and this little twist of a man smelled like trouble. "I'll have a look at them," he said. Buy time, he cautioned himself. He stood and walked to a nearby table, where he smacked a lower-ranking noncom on the shoulder and ordered him to fetch the files. All the while he kept his gaze glued on Petrov, whose face retained its usual expressionless mask except for the eyes, two black coals on fire. The man didn't move his head to look, but he knew those eyes flickered from object to object. This one was not someone to resist.

"Here they are, comrade," the sergeant major said as the files were deposited on his table. "Let me see," he said, leafing through them in an effort to appear efficient. Powerful men appreciated efficiency. But it was a short-lived display. "I don't know this organization," he said, handing a file to Petrov, who read silently.

"This is the central headquarters group in the eastern part of the city." Petrov returned the folder. "I require transportation."

"The motor pool has vehicles. There are none here."

"There are three lorries outside."

"Reserved for division staff," the sergeant major explained.

"I will also require a driver," Petrov added, as if he had not heard the sergeant's pronouncement.

This was getting difficult. The sergeant major started perspiring. He was not accustomed to such pressure; in his world he made others sweat. "Comrade," he began, trying to think of a way to get himself off the hook, but before he could say more, Petrov produced a small black portfolio, unfolded it and placed it on the table. The sergeant felt himself go faint; his head spun and he felt nauseated. A Red Badge! He had thought it a myth.

"The small lorry will do," Petrov said, adding "comrade" as a friendly afterthought.

The sergeant major made his decision. Long ago he'd learned to trust his instincts. This tiny dark figure was a man of infinite power with, no doubt, little compunction about using it. "I'll drive you myself," he said eagerly, his words out before he realized his commitment.

Petrov nodded and walked outside. The sergeant followed in his stocking feet, carrying his boots and hat under his arms.

It took them two hours to find the NKVD center. The sergeant was instructed to wait, and was relieved when Petrov disappeared inside the three-story building. He thought about driving away, but where would he go? He had no choice but to see this through, whatever it was.

Armed guards moved quickly to block Petrov as he entered, but a quick flash of the Red Badge opened an immediate path through the security men. An inquiry about the identity of the local commander brought the hurried appearance of a short, pudgy man with pale blue eyes and silver hair combed over the top to hide a receding hairline. He stared at the visitor for a moment; then Petrov saw the recognition in the man's eyes and a confirming gulp.

"Petrov," he said, exhaling slowly, trying to force a smile.

"Comrade Shikbava," Petrov responded. "It's a long walk from Moscow."

"Not when it's on the backs of Nazi corpses. Better sore feet than a still heart," the NKVD official responded, repeating a saying born among the troops. He led Petrov to his office on the second floor and told his guards that he and his guest were not to be disturbed. Like virtually everything else in the German capital, the office was covered with thick layers of dust, but the furnishings were first-class and obviously not part of the previous owner's decor. "You like it, eh? It belonged to the Gestapo. Not like our boys. Only a commissar would rate something like this."

"If I remember correctly," Petrov said, "you were securing communications for receipt of Allied messages."

"Your memory is still sound," Shikbava muttered. He opened a cabinet and offered Petrov a brandy.

Petrov observed that his host drank too fast. He was nervous. "Where is Zaya? Wasn't that her name?" Petrov asked.

Shikbava turned pale and waved his arms. "Quiet," he hushed. "You've not changed, you Gypsy bastard!"

"I was told that she lost her features from the beatings, and quite likely her mind as well. She would be better that way, for your special—how did you describe them?—your special appetites." Petrov paused to let his words linger in the air.

Kliment Shikbava had once wielded power inside the Kremlin. He was a man of immense natural talents and perverted tastes, which had been tolerated until he had gone too far. He was an educated man, an electronics genius, the designer of an extensive eavesdropping system that stretched its tentacles across the entire Soviet nation, but he had allowed his perversions to rule him. He had a passion for young girls, preferably covered with layers of soft fat and yet to enter their menstrual cycles. He never slept with the same girl twice, and he used his considerable official channels to purchase and procure them wherever his travels took him. For the most part Russian peasants were still backward and clung to their old ways, because even bad ways, which were well known, were better than the unknown. By such values a daughter was a commodity.

Shikbava's trouble had begun with a trip to Georgia, where he had purchased the services of a young girl named Zaya, a twelve-year-old with long black tresses. Apparently he had been bewitched by the girl, because not only did he keep her with him for nearly a month—a clear breach of his contract with her father—but took her back to Moscow when his trip ended. The girl's father, a boyhood friend of Stalin's, immediately set out by foot for Moscow, and upon his arrival presented himself at the Kremlin. When he was denied entrance, he remained in the city, determined to secure an audience with the premier. Eventually someone in his network of informants told Stalin about the man and his plight. The premier was outraged, and the Berkut was called in to mete out justice.

Locating the girl was a simple matter; Shikbava had installed her in his dacha near the city. She was in pitiful condition. Having been beaten frequently and used sexually by Shikbava's servants when the master was away, she had ceased to exist in the present. When Petrov saw her she had no life left in her. She wore a fine silk gown, and when he entered the room she slipped it off her shoulders and stepped forward to engage him. He held her away, but finally, because she refused to stop clawing at him, had been forced to have her straitjacketed by Rivitsky. She could no longer speak. She had been reduced to the state of an animal with only a single function to perform, and in her twisted subconscious she knew that her performance was the only way to ensure her continued survival.

It was an unnerving experience for Petrov. When he confronted Shikbava, the man had broken down and begged for mercy. He swore that while he was smitten with the girl, he had not stolen her; the abduction had been conceived by one of his subordinates, who had presented her to him as a gift upon their return to the capital. He admitted it was an error in judgment, but he would atone for it.

Shikbava and his domestic and professional staffs were all imprisoned. Stalin had sought Petrov's counsel. He was in a quandary: he felt compelled to avenge the wrong done to his old friend's daughter, but he also did not wish to lose his electronics genius.

Petrov suggested a compromise. The Georgian had in fact made his young daughter available for a price and was not without his own share of guilt. Likewise, the abductors deserved the worst, and the domestics who had abused the girl for their own purposes must be dealt with severely.

Stalin listened to Petrov's words, then issued his decree. The girl's father was beaten severely and submitted to electroshock therapy at the psychiatric institute run by the NKVD for failing to protect his seed as any good Communist father should do. Through a series of interrogations in which Petrov had no part, twenty-two other individuals confessed to having been with the girl or having known about her circumstances without taking action. On Stalin's order, all of them were hanged one morning at Lubyanka Prison. Shikbava was beaten so severely over a period of months that he nearly died, but when Stalin needed him again, he was declared "sanitized" and sent to a hospital for recovery, a process that required nearly a year. Upon his release he was reassigned to an office responsible for establishing and maintaining the complex communications network that would link the Russians with the Americans and the English. This was what he had been doing when Petrov last saw him. It was an important job, but well below Shikbava's full technical capabilities. Petrov knew Stalin intended it to be so; the man would have to work his way back into political favor.

Petrov recalled vividly the girl and her green dress as he sipped his vodka and waited for Shikbava to speak.

"I was reinstated after my"—he groped for a word—"after my rehabilitation. I never saw her again."

Petrov did not respond.

"I've cast off the perversion. I'm celibate now. I'll have to carry that burden forever; now I live only for the party."

"Heinrich Müller," Petrov said, setting down his glass, still half filled. "You have him."

Shikbava tensed. "You haven't changed; you always know everything."

"I need him."

"For what?" Shikbava asked nervously, sweating heavily. "He's mine."

Petrov laid the Red Badge on the other man's desk. The silver-haired Russian stared at it, frightened beyond speech. He had been to the abyss with Petrov before and barely escaped with his life. His scars and broken bones immediately began to throb, reminding him of the power standing before him. He tried to light a cigarette, but his hands were shaking too badly.

"He's here. He's offered his network to us; we're waiting to receive directions from Moscow."

"Get him," Petrov said.

Müller was brought to the office within a few minutes, and Shikbava immediately cleared out. The stout Bavarian had a head shaped like a block. His cheekbones were high, his eyes dark brown, his flesh waxy in appearance; he looked like a well-fed ghost.

"You offer us a network, Müller, but it is unproven. I want to test it. There is a man, Otto Skorzeny."

"Captured in Austria by the Americans," Müller said confidently. "I knew the bastard. Hitler's toy soldier."

"You speak too quickly, Herr Müller. Who was Skorzeny's planning officer?"

"You mean Brumm?" Müller asked arrogantly. "I knew them all."

"His first name?"

"Günter. A cold fish. He was some kind of a hero in Russia. He was the brains behind Skorzeny's hot air."

"He was last seen on the Oder with a division. We want to use your people to scour the camps for survivors of that unit. We need information about him quickly."

Müller was interested. "Why go to so much trouble?"

Petrov stared back.

"The Gestapo has complete records. I can take you to them." He added, "For a price."

"Make your offer."

"A position. Assets. Freedom to operate. My people in your service, but I control."

"Granted," Petrov said. He called Shikbava back into the room and said quietly, "Release him to me."

Müller observed the chemistry between the two Russians. Shikbava had shown a lot of bravado and made promises, but obviously this new man was the one with the power. Shikbava signed the release papers and collapsed in relief when the two left his office. He poured a large brandy and gulped it down. Only as he sat staring at the empty glass did he understand he'd been poisoned. A knot was forming in his stomach. He felt his lungs begin to constrict; his breathing became labored. The harder he inhaled, the more breath he seemed to lose. Trying to stand, he fell to the floor, felt a tremendous weight on his chest and stared up at the ceiling waiting for the end.

The sergeant major was asleep in the lorry. The three squeezed into the cab and Müller gave directions, which Petrov translated for the driver. The way led into the country, down roads still jammed with refugees. Tents and hastily constructed shelters filled the muddy fields and shattered forests.

Their destination was a small outbuilding behind a modest farm. The records were in a steel-lined vault in a cellar. Müller brought up the files, and Petrov recovered those he wanted. He then instructed Müller and the sergeant to move the rest of the contents of the cellar to the lorry.

When the truck was loaded, the sergeant major climbed behind the wheel, started the motor and waited. Müller and Petrov faced each other in the entryway to the cellar. "You've got what you want," the German said. "Now let's discuss my operation."

Petrov suddenly had a revolver in his small hand. He pointed it at Müller's head and cocked the hammer. Müller laughed quietly, unafraid. "Ivan's justice," he said venomously just before Petrov shot him through the forehead, killing him with a single shot. Then Petrov broke a kerosene lamp on the floor and ignited it with a match. It lit with a loud *whoomp,* and he lingered only long enough to assure himself that the fire would destroy everything.

"What was that shot?" the sergeant major asked nervously.

"I heard nothing." As the sergeant moved to put the lorry into gear, Petrov shot him through the side of the head. He pulled the body into the flaming cellar, climbed behind the wheel of the lorry and drove away, not bothering to look back at the heavy black plumes of smoke.

On the drive back to Berlin, Petrov decided it was time to see Stalin again.

▶38 JUNE 8, 1945, MIDNIGHT

They were in Stalin's study. Petrov reported his findings and conclusions with the precision and detachment of an accountant while the premier doodled on sheets of coarse gray paper.

"You're certain of your evidence?"

"Yes. There is no longer any doubt. It's all a circumstantial case, but the conclusion is inescapable."

"You've always been a cautious and meticulous man, Comrade Petrov. I would hate to think that you might make your only mistake at this precise moment in history," Stalin said coldly.

"There's no mistake. My men have been careful and thorough. Adolf Hitler is alive. Or rather, he did not die in the bunker, and General Zhukov, with all due respect, does not have his body."

Stalin smiled, and the dark stains on his teeth caught the dim light. "Zhukov, Liberator of Berlin. He engages in intrigue. Perhaps his eyes face to the east."

Petrov shook his head. "I believe Zhukov to be a competent man. He's a professional soldier with no political ambition. If there is intrigue, he's a victim of overzealous subordinates who wish to please and honor him. Superficially all the evidence points to his assessment being correct; he truly believes that the corpse is Hitler's."

"His subordinates seek to create a cult around the man."

"Yes, that's true. He's a hard man, but his men revere him. He's brought them through the war alive. From a soldier's perspective this is the ultimate gift a commander can bestow."

"Nevertheless, I fear that our general must be taught a lesson—at the appropriate time, of course. I've already recalled him. Did you know that?"

"No."

"Soon we will have a grand parade in Red Square. The Great Victory Parade—a good name, yes?"

"An accurate characterization."

"There will be troops from every unit and front. Zhukov will lead our patriotic fighters from a great white stallion. It will be his finest hour, a tribute. After that I will see to his reeducation. The bastard will learn his lesson or else he'll drill a squad in hell without a pause." Stalin added, "What's your next step?"

"I will spend several days in Moscow. There are some leads to be followed from here. The difficult part now is to find the trail, the right one. Once you know it's there, locating it is only a matter of time. Getting out of Berlin was one thing—and no mean feat—but finding a permanent safe haven will be more demanding. The potential avenues of departure from the Continent are few."

"Spain," Stalin said. "He's with Franco, that greasy little Fascist pig."

"I doubt it."

"Franco was supported by the Germans. He owes them."

"Franco walks alone. He maintained neutrality and did not officially send Spaniards to fight with the Wehrmacht."

"South America, then."

"Possibly, but to reach it requires complex logistics."

"Africa?"

"Unlikely, but conceivable."

"The Near East?"

"Perhaps, but less likely than South America."

"Japan."

Petrov shook his head. "Too far. The Japanese don't like the Germans and they don't tolerate losers. Hitler wouldn't seek protection with what he thought was an inferior race."

"I thrust; you parry. Always you play it close to the vest, comrade."

"Words spoken without forethought are but steps toward the grave."

"A peasant's philosophy."

"A *live* peasant," Petrov said with the hint of a smile.

Stalin roared with laughter and struck his hands against his thighs. "Go then, my Berkut, but see me again before you depart for Berlin."

Petrov walked the halls of the Kremlin, confident that while the leader of the Third Reich was fleeing, he was drawing closer to him. Their paths were converging. Eventually they would collide; the only questions were where and when.

▶39 JUNE 9, 1945, 9:00 A.M.

With Petrov in Moscow for unexplained reasons, the team settled into its own routine. There was plenty to do; they applied themselves to administrative details and the pursuit of minor bits and pieces of information.

By now the unit's walls were covered with lists and photographs as they continued sifting through prisoner records and captured reports in order to find still-missing Chancellery people. For Gnedin the prime target was Martin Bormann, chief administrator and secretary of the National Socialist Party. Interrogations of captured Reich Chancellery Group personnel produced conflicting reports. One young officer reported seeing Bormann on the northwestern outskirts of the city on the night of May 2. But Gnedin did not trust the man; he was a rabbit, frightened and desperate to gain leverage in dealing with his captors. He would sing whatever song they called for.

The story they had heard most frequently was that the Reichsleiter had been killed during an exchange between Soviet and German tanks, and they were inclined to accept this, simply because of the number of these accounts. Yet they were not entirely convinced; doubt persisted because they had no eyewitness accounts of the fate of Ludwig Stumpfegger, the six-foot-six physician who had been Bormann's partner and shadow in the breakout group. Stumpfegger's unusual size made him the sort to attract attention, even in death. The Special Operations Group had seen no unusual specimens other than a four-hundred-pound Gestapo agent who had crawled into a sewer pipe and got stuck. Panicking, the man bit into a vial of cyanide and died on the spot. Bloating caused the body to swell enormously, so that the burial unit had been forced to use cleavers to butcher the corpse like a steer in order to extract it and bury it. This story made the rounds of Russian units, but there were no additional reports of live or dead Germans of unusual physical proportions.

The group did have one report from an escapee that was different from all the others. A corporal, a freckled combat veteran of several campaigns, told Gnedin during his interrogation that while his companions had followed one route, he had broken away from them to go it alone. After crossing the Spree he had looped back in a southeasterly direction.

The man's audacity grabbed Gnedin's attention. "Your comrades took a route that was north by northeast. You swung away from them. Did you give consideration to the danger of being alone?"

It turned out that the corporal hadn't been quite alone. He'd followed Reichsleiter Bormann and the tall doctor.

"When did they leave the group?"

"After the crossing. That wasn't as easy as it sounds. When we got to the bridge, some Russian tanks were on the other span, so Bormann got into one of our own tanks and directed an assault to clear the path for us."

"Where was the doctor during this?"

"Right next to me. We were behind the Reichsleiter's tank, using it as a shield."

"We've had a number of reports saying that Bormann was killed in an explosion during the battle."

"They're wrong. Some of the tanks were destroyed, but the Reichsleiter's made it across safely. There was intense firing. One of the Führer's pilots was killed by one of the Russian tanks, and maybe some of the others as well. I didn't pay much attention."

"Did you see Bormann again after you crossed the river?"

"Yes, he was as close to me as I am to you. Of course he was dead."

The words jolted Gnedin. "I thought you said he was all right."

"I did. But he died later. Really strange. The doctor, too. I saw both their bodies."

"Where?" Gnedin scribbled his own notes to augment the stenographer's transcription.

"On the Invalidenstrasse, near the rail trestle."

"You're certain it was Bormann and Stumpfegger?"

"Of course," the young corporal snapped. "I've seen lots of bodies. I'm not afraid to look at them. It was them, all right."

Gnedin read the transcript again and again. With each reading, the knot in his stomach grew larger. He was sure he had the truth, and he decided to try to confirm it. There must be evidence.

Because Ezdovo was the only one available and because he enjoyed the Siberian's company, Gnedin asked for his help in what he described as "a little outing." They had the German corporal brought from his cell, and took him to the area he'd described in his interrogation. The man walked them through the area, beginning at the place where Bormann had taken command of the tank. On the other side of the bridge they turned east, and he showed them where he'd skirted a Soviet infantry company. For reference Ezdovo had a set of order-of-battle charts in a leather tube. Using these, they were able to identify the battalion that had been responsible for the area; later they would locate the company.

On an elevated track bed the corporal showed them where he'd seen the bodies. There had been no wounds on them, he reiterated, but he was certain that they were dead. Ezdovo and Gnedin fanned out on a methodical search of the area, looking for fresh graves or any sign of digging. When they found a depression twenty meters away, Ezdovo went off to fetch extra manpower, and soon returned with three men with picks and shovels. It was amazing what the Red Badge could do, Gnedin thought.

The grave was larger than they had anticipated; it contained eight badly decomposed corpses. However, by size alone they were sure that one of them was Stumpfegger's. The bodies were taken to a nearby hospital. Ezdovo returned to their headquarters to fetch the two Nazis' medical records, and the next day Gnedin confirmed their identities by autopsy. To make their records complete they took photographs of the two corpses. In accordance with Petrov's standing order, Soviet military authorities were not informed of their findings, but the group knew that Bormann and Stumpfegger were dead. The Germans were reburied in the same hole where they had been found.

That night the Special Operations Group celebrated and the brandy flowed freely. They were eager for Petrov to return so that they could show him how productive they had been during his absence.

▶40 JUNE 9, 1945, 10:15 A.M.

Though rolling banks of yellow clouds threatened rain, Petrov rode his bicycle, preferring the fresh morning air and exercise to riding in an automobile. He had discovered long ago that investigators tended to go to seed in direct proportion to the amount of time spent behind their desks, so he exercised every day, no matter what the weather. His preference was for walking, at a pace most people found painful. It was not a walk, but neither was it a run; it was something strenuous in between that served him well. When he was in a hurry he rode his bicycle, a dilapidated specimen many years old with no fenders and its paint long ago obliterated by tumors of rust.

The Archangel Basilica was a black fortress, a forgotten landmark in a crumbling residential neighborhood near the Moskva River. Pulling into the alley beside the church, Petrov left his bicycle near the door. He liked the church, especially its tall stained-glass windows. Despite the overcast, the centuries-old glass seemed to gather all the available light from without and concentrate it inside the building. Even in winter the interior of the church was bright and alive, a stark contrast to its run-down exterior and the Moscow weather. He made his way to the back of the building, comfortable with its familiarity. He'd been here many times before. Passing through the sacristy, which was lined with books on shelves and withered, discolored cardboard boxes, he walked through a white marble façade onto the raised area that had once served as the altar. Once again it struck him that the difference between churches and palaces was indeed narrow. Both bespoke power; both demanded allegiance under penalty of death or a condemned soul, the difference being only the time frame in which payment would be demanded.

The Archangel, as it had once been known to its parishioners, had ceased its holy mission nearly ten years before. Since the Revolution hundreds of Roman Catholic churches had been confiscated by the Central Committee of the party and reassigned to uses termed "more socially productive." Many of them now housed trade unions or gymnasiums. The Archangel served the state as the headquarters for the clandestine operation known by those inside the Kremlin, with uncharacteristic directness, as Vatican Watch. It was ironic, Petrov thought, that the inhabitants of the church had gone full circle, from listening to Vatican directives in order to carry them out to finding ways to obstruct or deflect them.

The head of Vatican Watch was a sixty-five-year-old former Jesuit known only as Father Grigory. The ex-priest led an elite intelligence network whose sole focus was the Vatican and its officials. Few Russians besides Petrov knew about the operation. Over the years he and the Jesuit had cooperated many times, and a close relationship had developed, first on a professional basis, later on a more personal and amicable level, with the strongest bond being the fact that both had survived various purges. Petrov had always found the priest's information impeccable, as were his analyses; for his part, the hulking priest had come to the same conclusion about the mysterious Petrov, who enjoyed the same kind of shadowy reputation in the Kremlin. They were similar beasts, and to the extent that their secretive and independent natures permitted, they trusted each other.

Father Grigory had been born a White Russian and had served in the Vatican before being reassigned to the Czar's court as part of the Church's state delegation. From his position he saw graphic evidence of the vast gap between the aristocracy and the peasants; the serf class had been liberated in 1861, but with little real effect. Grigory had written many reports on the plight of Russia's poor, but the Vatican had shown little interest. Its power brokers were more concerned with the goings-on at the court, including the maintenance of a list of upper-echelon dalliances among relatives and confidants of Nicholas II, and in finding ways to take advantage of this knowledge, than with the disposition of mere pastoral matters. Lenin had been secretly returned to Petrograd by the provisional government; soon he took control of the Petrograd Soviet, denounced all "imperialist wars" and demanded peace. Nicholas II had already abdicated when, in October 1918, massive strikes ensued. Kerensky bolted from Petrograd, hoping to rally the army behind him, but it was already too late; Lenin had outflanked him and the Bolsheviks had complete control of Russia's principal cities. The Revolution was over; what blood would flow would be spilled in the civil war that followed.

Father Grigory watched as sides were drawn: White—pro-Czar and pro-European intervention—against Red. He chose the latter, disavowing his order and his Church, and declared himself on the side of those who fought to improve temporal conditions. Petrov had discussed the history and events of the Revolution many times with his Jesuit colleague. Both observed that as the revolt dimmed in memory, great gaps still existed between layers of society; even so, it was apparent that a much greater number of Russians were better off under the party than they had been under the monarchy. In the end, this was all that counted. In this the two men were in complete agreement; for both of them the nobler goals of the Revolution still burned.

As always, the priest heard Petrov's approach and turned his head. Even through his thick wire-rimmed glasses, which he called his telescopes, he had to contort his face in a squint to see anything beyond arm's length. "Petrov," he said brightly, "I figured you for dead in one of your own intrigues. What do you need? You never come to Father Grigory until you need him. If I were a young pup, my ego would be bruised by your lack of attention."

The priest's table was in the area of the church where Russian aristocrats had once knelt in reverence for the Holy Trinity. The desk was a cluttered affair, piled with papers, magazine clippings, newspapers and notes of many sizes, most of them torn from larger scraps of paper. Nearby were gray metal filing cabinets with their drawers open. On the periphery were thousands of boxes crammed with papers; throughout the area cartons were stacked more than twice a normal man's height. Father Grigory had no staff or personal bureaucracy; when he needed to write, he scratched his words on paper by hand in largely illegible strokes with broad-tipped pens carved from goose feathers. Despite the absence of worldly trappings, the politically aware in Moscow knew Father Grigory well and were respectful. Through various political purges he had retained his power, and this fact did not escape interested observers; they recognized direct access to the top when they saw it.

"Always the same greeting, priest," Petrov said. "Age is squeezing your arteries closed. It's never 'How are you, Petrov?' or 'Good to see you, Petrov.' You never change."

"I lend stability to ideological curmudgeons such as yourself."

"I need information."

"Ah!" shouted the old man happily. "You see? I rest my case."

"You take pride in small accomplishments."

"Consider me admonished. What's it to be this time?" the Jesuit asked. It was an unusual day when Petrov came calling.

"The Roman Church. It's said that the current Roman pontiff is predisposed toward the Nazis. What can you tell me about this unusual predisposition?"

The priest gestured animatedly toward a packing crate near the table, wiped a soiled porcelain cup with a dirty rag, filled it with hot tea and motioned for Petrov to drink. "*Nazdorovya*, bottoms up," Grigory said before draining his own cup. "Pope Pius the Twelfth, born Eugenio Pacelli, is a hopeless, shameless Germanophile. He speaks German better than you, even inside his personal apartment in Vatican City. It is amazing to think that the highest level of business in the Mother Church is conducted in German. Pacelli was papal nuncio in Munich during the First World War, and from 1920 to 1929 served in Berlin in a similar capacity. His foreign experience enabled him to ascend to the office of secretary of state under his predecessor, Pius the Eleventh, and gave him the recognition he needed to become the most recent manifestation of Saint Peter. His staff is entirely German— virtually all laymen. I sometimes think Pacelli is more German than Bismarck!"

"Hitler is also a Catholic; he was educated in church schools in Austria," Petrov observed.

"Bravo!" the priest croaked. "You don't disappoint me. You've been studying again."

"Only a little reading," Petrov countered, embarrassed because he understood that this was the priest's way of telling him he was a neophyte in such matters.

"Don't think for a moment that the circumstances of Hitler's youth translate into adult Catholicism. They don't. The link is far more temporal and insidious. It reeks of opportunism on both sides of the Alps. I am certain that Pacelli supported Hitler's invasion here."

"The lesser of two evils: Hitler or the Bolshevik atheists."

"That, friend Petrov, is the heart of it. Further, the Germans, in their cultural fastidiousness, have a law that says that if citizens for- mally declare their religious preference—and, as you might expect, they are encouraged to do so—they must be taxed. This tax's specific origins are obscure, but date back to long before Hitler, and you can bet that a Jesuit was involved!" Father Grigory retained great pride in the accomplishments of his former order, if not for its religious mission or fervor. "Imagine this, Petrov. From each good little Ger- man's weekly paycheck the state extracts a tax for the Church. At year's end the government transmits the money—and the accrued interest—in one huge lump to Rome. The tax is called the *Kirchen- steuer,* and it has been paid by the Nazis throughout this current war, as well as by previous political regimes. The most recent payment was forwarded to Rome in December of last year." Father Grigory clasped his hands together. "Here's another curious thing: the German gov- ernment extracts no fee for doing this—undoubtedly an oversight due to the absence of Jewish accountants in the Nazi bureaucracy."

"How much money is involved?"

The priest grinned. "There are an estimated thirty million Catholics in Germany—at least there were before their army ventured across the Bug River. I estimate one billion Reichsmarks annually from the tax. Before the war, America was the largest contributor to Rome, though the funds came in haphazardly because the government there is not involved. But during the war American contributions have fallen off sharply, and for the past five years the Germans have been the primary source of foreign revenue for the Vatican. It will be interesting to see how the Western press reports this story."

"Which you undoubtedly will provide them in a tidy package."

"I do what I can," the priest said with mock humility. "But there's more to it—much more. It's complicated, and even with effective fieldwork and careful analysis, I can only get to the edges of it. The Church was curiously silent as Hitler grabbed the Continent a piece at a time. In return for such considerations, Hitler has made only minimal—it could be characterized as token—interference with Vatican activities. The Church in Germany is much the same as it was before Hitler ascended to power."

Petrov closed his eyes and shifted on his seat.

Father Grigory sipped his tea. "Here we enter the netherworld of behavioral analysis, a new but promising tool for the historian. I can understand the Vatican's position, but why would Hitler be so cooperative? Could it be that he didn't want to risk the anger of thirty million citizens?"

"You think there's more to it?"

"There is much more," Father Grigory told Petrov. "It is clear that early in the war Pacelli had definitive evidence of the death camps and their function. Did the Church and its Pope speak out? Not until the end, when they could avoid it no longer. Did this signify fear of Hitler—or worse, tacit support for his ends? My answer is that the Church under the Pacelli regime had strong historical antecedents for what the Nazis were doing. It was the Church, after all, that first forced Jews to wear the yellow star and forbade them from mixing with Christians. That was in the twelfth century. It's a blemish on the Papists' self-proclaimed humanitarian image."

"And Father Grigory will see to it that this information comes to light."

"Yes, with great relish. At an opportune moment. It will be interesting to see how the Vatican tries to squirm out from under this dark cloud."

"It always seems to manage."

"That's the secret to institutional survival. It will change when it has to; it can be ruthless and forthright when the situation dictates."

"There must be more."

"For centuries the Vatican existed as a vulnerable citadel, a religious enclave, in the heart of Italy, there at the pleasure of the Italians, but only as tenants. They did not have legal right to the geography. It was by some definitions a political entity, though without the political rights or status afforded to others in the family of nations. But it was apart from the Italians, and allowed to survive only through their good graces. Italian politicians always coveted the enclave. Over those centuries there were countless superficial negotiations with the Italian government to cede Vatican property to the Church, and for it to be granted status as an independent state. This finally occurred under Mussolini. He was trying to consolidate his own power and needed the Vatican question resolved in order to get on with his own agenda. In 1929, the year Pacelli returned to Rome, Mussolini and the Church signed the Lateran Treaty. Keep in mind, Petrov, that Hitler was not then in power; he was still struggling for political recognition in Germany, trying to build an organization to finance pursuit of his political ambitions. In the settlement of its dispute with the Italian government, the Vatican received seven hundred and fifty million lire in cash and another billion lire in Italian gold-based bonds with a return of five percent. It's my belief that a great part of th s money—perhaps most of it—was funneled to Hitler's National Socialists in exchange for a number of concessions and promises."

Father Grigory paused to catch his breath, and as he leaned forward his voice dropped by a full octave. "How else can we account for Hitler's sudden and hitherto unexplained overflowing war chest? Contributions from the people? Impossible! They were in the middle of a terrible depression. *The German people had no money, Petrov!* Yet there was Hitler suddenly in possession of an abundance of cash. His people had new uniforms, weapons, everything that money could buy. Money from the Church. If so, we must ask: What did Hitler give in return?"

The Jesuit was in full voice now. "Please understand, my dear comrade, that this is an old man's notion, but there *is* evidence. What if I were to tell you that these promises included repayment of the loan, the elimination of German Freemasonry, pressure against European Jews and, upon taking power, a strong, uncompromising denouncement of Communism—specifically the Russian variety because of our policies on organized religion?"

"What's in your tea?" Petrov asked with a smile. "If all of this is true, the Church will be hard-pressed to defend itself."

"The Church is adept at defending itself. I can't prove all of this—not yet. But I'm convinced that something on this order occurred. It's the only scenario that would explain the known results. A concordat was signed by Hitler and Pacelli a little more than six months after Hitler gained power. The world diplomatic community was stunned by this because, at the same time that Hitler was moving to crush individual freedoms, he was suddenly stepping forward to grant freedom of operation to the German Catholic clergy and to guarantee German citizens that they could continue practicing their religion without interference from the government. Unusual, don't you agree?" Father Grigory did not wait for an answer. "It makes no damn sense, Petrov. After that, the German Freemasons were emasculated, and what happened to the Jews is now a matter of record. As for us, Hitler invaded. That concordat, incidentally, also specifically revalidated the *Kirchensteuer*. There's too much in all of this to be coincidence."

"If there was cooperation at the top, what sorts of interaction existed lower down?"

"The Vatican's agents acted as intermediaries in Germany's behalf in a number of instances, but most of the links were high-level. Right now I'm studying reports that the Vatican is already actively involved in assisting Nazis to flee Germany. Apparently there is a route, a connection of monasteries across the Alps; this pipeline, I'm told, is full of big and little Nazi fish swimming out to sea."

"You have evidence of this?"

"The Italians have loose tongues, and the Vatican employs an unusually low level of vermin to do its dirty work. Our contacts in Switzerland and Rome have learned that over a period of years some top Nazis and many German industrialists have been putting large sums of money, gold and other currencies, into accounts in Switzerland and Argentina. There's no doubt that some of the more forward-looking National Socialists and their sympathizers have been preparing to make a run for it."

"Can you identify who's been behind such transactions?"

"Generally not. That capital has been shifted is unquestioned; the rest is speculative."

"The escape route itself is evidence," Petrov pointed out. "If the Vatican had an arrangement with Hitler, now it is seeking silence by helping Nazis reach safety."

"That's precisely my interpretation," Father Grigory answered.

Standing up to leave, Petrov slowly put on his coat. "I'd like to have more details on the escape network—how it works, the links, as much as you can part with. I'd also like the name of an agent in Italy whom I can trust."

The priest's eyes narrowed; he cocked his head, raised his bushy white eyebrows and peered over his glasses. "So, Petrov, we get to the real purpose of your visit. What are you up to this time?"

"Can you keep a secret?"

Father Grigory nodded solemnly and leaned forward.

"Good."

For a moment the Jesuit registered no reaction. Then, without warning, he fell heavily against the back of his chair and burst into raucous laughter, which thundered through the basilica. As Petrov reached the front portal he could hear the priest still bellowing in the cavernous church.

▶41 JUNE 12, 1945, 2:00 P.M.

Petrov had always liked to sit in the sun by the Moskva River and watch the pigeons and ducks. Most of the pigeons were gone, victims of wartime starvation, but the ducks were migratory, and though some might have been taken, there were always new waves of them. The warmth of the sun's rays relaxed him. Unlike many people, Petrov did not seek solace in one of the parks on the riverbank; he preferred an unpretentious stone bench not far from Red Square. Though he never fed them, the birds came around to beg handouts, and it pleased him to listen to their sounds.

Three days had passed since his meeting with Father Grigory. Yesterday an envelope had been delivered by courier containing details about the Vatican escape network, including maps showing the locations of the mountain lodges and monasteries being used. There was also a hand-scribbled note from the priest, suggesting that Petrov go to his favorite bench at a certain date and time. No reason was given. Sitting now at the appointed time, Petrov smiled. The priest relished the dramatic.

The bench seemed softened by the sun, Petrov thought, like Russia itself. The long harsh winters gave way grudgingly to the change of season. Deposits of blue-green ice often persisted at the base of trees in the forest until June. When it came, spring did not linger. The rains melted the snow and the matted brown grass turned gray, then bright green. Flowers seemed to grow several inches in a single night. Birds returned all at once by the millions, the skies black with soaring flocks and their cries. The trees passed from barren to full bloom as if touched by a magic hand. Petrov loved the spring and hated knowing that it would pass into summer without lingering. He told himself there was not enough spring for his soul, but then what true Russian thought there was? He decided to enjoy the moment and endeavored to put business out of his mind.

Without thinking, Petrov caught himself tracking the progress of an elegant young woman, tall, with black hair. She wore the light brown uniform of the Soviet army with a major's rank on her collar. Several rows of medals were pinned over the left breast of her tunic and jingled like chimes as she walked. Two young boys, close in age, stayed close to her, wrestling with each other, darting around her legs, laughing. One of them carried a toy sailboat.

As the woman stopped directly in front of him the boys scrambled down the bank to play at the water's edge. She warned them to keep their feet out of the river, or else remove their shoes and roll up their pants legs. She was confident both in her authority over them and in their ability to care for themselves. He watched her take a wrinkled pack of cigarettes from a pocket, extract one and light a match by striking it against the leather grain of her boot. She inhaled and held the smoke deep in her lungs. It came out slowly in a narrow stream and hung over her head in the still air. Then she turned to face Petrov and spoke to him. He had expected such a tall woman to possess a deep, masculine voice, but it was so sweet and melodious that it captivated him.

"Comrade Petrov." He was startled by the sound of his name. "I am Talia Pogrebenoi. My former commanding officer gave me a note asking me to meet you. I was told that there might be a position available."

Petrov fought a smile. The priest's tentacles were longer than he thought. He'd already decided that the team needed additional help; Hitler's escape route led to Italy and they'd need someone fluent in the language. Bailov could get by in it, but to gather information of a sensitive nature one needed precision, as well as the ability to blend when it was necessary. Grigory had read his mind. An agent in Italy was one thing; a Russian team member who spoke Italian was even better.

"You have handsome sons, Major Pogrebenoi."

"Talia," she said. "I've been discharged from the army. I haven't had a chance to find other clothing."

"You've been gone a long time?"

"Since the Germans invaded. My boys were two and three then. They're tall now, like their father." Her voice trailed off. "I will have to get to know them again." Her eyes kept contact with his as she talked. She was the kind of woman who made a man think he was the only one alive. It had a powerful effect because she seemed to be able to read one's mind.

"How important is it for you to remain with your sons?" Petrov asked.

She shrugged and flicked her cigarette over the bank. "How important is the work?"

"As important as what you've been doing. Wars don't end when the shooting finishes. There are always new dangers. We've repelled this bunch, but there will be others. It's our heritage." Petrov took out his notebook, wrote something on a piece of paper and offered it to her. She took it and read it. "Tomorrow. If you don't come, I'll look elsewhere."

"I have my records with me. The note said you'd want them." She opened a plain brown purse and passed him a thick, faded file, which he placed on the bench beside him.

"Was it bad?" Petrov asked.

"Were you out there?"

He nodded.

"Then you know the answer."

The boys scrambled up to her when she called them and took their position on either side of her. She smiled at Petrov and headed down the walk with her sons, who were obviously proud of their mother's uniform.

She was tall—six feet or more, Petrov estimated. Muscular buttocks and strong legs. A long tapered neck and broad, thick shoulders. Her hands were wide, but the fingers were narrow and well shaped. His instinct told him that she would fit. When she had gone, the ducks and several geese with misshapen orange bills returned to cluster around Petrov. He leaned back against the bench and let the sun play directly on his face.

▶42 JUNE 12, 1945, 6:30 P.M.

Though it was not that long since the war had ended, the decadence of Berlin had begun to reassert itself. While the very old and very young could not feed themselves and starved, the city's women crawled out of the rubble and resumed their lives. Many were pressed into duty by the Soviets to clear debris and open streets, but others— especially those who preferred easier work—pulled their best clothes from their hope chests, painted their lips with powder made from pulverized brick and went into the streets to ply a very old trade.

Before the surrender, Berlin, like Amsterdam, Hamburg and Marseilles, had been known for its quantity and range of diversions. There was something for every man's need and at every man's price. Even Hitler, who decried prostitution because of its antiprocreational nature, had the good sense not to press the issue. As German soldiers died by the thousands on the Eastern front, Berlin's whores found their business dwindling, until at the end there were no customers at all.

In their interviews with survivors of the Reich Chancellery Group, the Special Operations Group had uncovered testimony dealing with the situation they had come to call the Fegelein Mystery. Petrov himself was not sure it was relevant, but it remained a loose end and therefore something for them to look into while their leader was in Moscow.

Bailov took it upon himself to follow the best lead they had, which wasn't much. What they had learned came from their interrogations of General Rattenhuber, chief of the Reich Security Police. Of all their Chancellery group captives, Rattenhuber had been the most cooperative.

On April 27 Hitler had learned that Himmler had sent emissaries to British agents to explore the possibility of ending the war. When the Führer discovered Himmler's treachery, he went berserk and immediately summoned Fegelein, who since 1944 had been Himmler's personal liaison with Hitler.

General Hermann Fegelein was typical of Hitler's misfits. In the

1920s he had been first a groom and later a jockey. In league with one of Hitler's early supporters from German industry, he was believed to have been involved in fixing the outcome of a number of Bavarian horse races, to the advantage of his benefactor—and indirectly of Hitler, for the money was funneled directly to the party. Always the opportunist, Fegelein had joined the Waffen SS and risen quickly; he also courted and married Eva Braun's lusty younger sister, Gretl. From that point forward he became part of the Führer's inner circle. Even so, he did not abandon his old habits, which included frequent affairs with other women.

When Hitler learned on April 27 that Fegelein had not been seen in the bunker since the previous day, he ordered Rattenhuber to find the general. The security chief gave the assignment to his deputy, Lieutenant Colonel Peter Hoegl, who took a small patrol through the Russian lines to Charlottenburg, where he found Fegelein at home— or, more precisely, in the arms of a beautiful young woman with reddish-blond hair. Hoegl's men recognized the woman, an actress of minor fame, but after cursory questioning released her. Their mission concerned only the general.

Hoegl ordered Fegelein to get dressed, but he begged to be allowed to call his sister-in-law. Hoegl was a fair man; the general had always been friendly enough, and so he allowed him to make the call. Fegelein pleaded with Eva, asking her to intervene in his behalf, but she hung up on him.

Rattenhuber was not present for the interrogation of Fegelein, but he did get the order to carry out the sentence of death, and again it was Hoegl he called upon. A sergeant did the actual shooting, a single round fired through the base of the brain. The body was buried in a shell hole in the Chancellery garden.

Later Hoegl was killed during the breakout attempt. Rattenhuber had no idea whom Hoegl had taken with him to fetch the former jockey, so the only record of the event was based on what Hoegl had reported to him afterward. Did he know the name of the woman who'd been with Fegelein? Of course. She was an actress, quite a talented one, in fact. She was also no stranger to the parties of upper-echelon Nazis. Her name was Lisl Marchant, but she went by the stage name of Honey.

Bailov decided to search for her. Knowing of the resurgence of Berlin's bistros and small clubs, he decided to start there; even if he couldn't locate her, he'd be able to amuse himself. Since Petrov's departure he had gone to the district several times. All the women he met claimed to be actresses and were desperate to make an arrangement with a Russian male who could protect them. Moreover, it wasn't the fun he'd thought it would be; most of them were unattractive and smelled terrible.

Bailov was forced to visit the area during the day because Soviet officials had instituted a strict night curfew; anyone caught on the streets after dark would be shot, and many were. The Red Badge gave him free passage, of course, but at night he might never get the chance to show it. He decided to save the risk of night work until there were reasons to take it.

It was early evening, warmer and more humid than ever. Bailov spent the day fencing with a collection of whores and street women. Their aggressiveness annoyed him. The last form of payment they'd accept was money; cigarettes and canned goods were the preferred currencies. They might look weak and defenseless, but they bargained hard. It was difficult for him to imagine that Russian women would have behaved in the same way had their fates been reversed, but Bailov recognized that the will to survive took precedence over all other human drives. The search for the actress, which had once seemed a promising diversion, was fast becoming a dreary chore.

Bailov was sipping a shot glass filled with bad vodka and wondering what food was being prepared back at the Special Operations Group's headquarters when a scrawny redhead in a tattered black dress slid into a seat next to him and hiked her skirt to display her bony wares. "You don't have a uniform," she cooed. He saw that her neck was filthy and that dirt was caked under her cracked fingernails. "You must be important."

"Are uniforms required?"

"You don't understand. It's said that you're looking for a certain person. I thought you'd have a uniform."

"Are you the one?" he asked. He wasn't in the mood for games.

"No, but I might know something." She touched his arm. "For a price."

"Everything has a price."

She glared at him, and her fingernails clawed at his arm. "Ivan the Terrible," she said contemptuously. "The ruthless Russian master. Your arrogance turns my stomach. Don't judge what you don't know anything about. If you want information, I have it, but you'll have to pay for it. If not, go to hell and stop wasting my time."

Bailov looked her over. She was serious. "What did you hear about my interests?"

"You're trying to locate Lisl Marchant. She was the kind who got roles because of her body, not her talent. She was an ignorant Bavarian slut."

"Was?" Bailov asked.

"Was, is. There's no difference now."

"Bavarian slut," Bailov said. "Not like you?"

"Pig," she cursed. "I wasn't always like this. Even for money I don't have to take your insults. Living is enough."

"Where is she?"

"Alive. My information won't be cheap. I'd rather take it to my grave than give it away."

"That can be arranged," he threatened, sensing a bluff. "How much?"

"Identification papers. A Swiss passport. A ticket to Argentina."

"Who are you?"

"That's not important. What you will help me become interests me more."

He smiled. "You have a problem, Fräulein, and you need my help. You don't really have much to bargain with."

"I know where Lisl Marchant is," she said confidently, "and you want to know, so let's settle on a fair price."

Bailov laughed. "Curfew is coming. You'll crawl back into your hole and I'll walk away, but I won't be back. Where does that leave you? Without a buyer, your information has no value."

"My price is not so high," she said. "Not for your kind."

"My kind?"

"You stink of it. I can tell."

"Of what?"

She was beginning to get nervous. "Gestapo," she blurted.

"I'm Russian," Bailov snorted.

"The name makes no difference. You're the same."

"The price is too high," he said. He signaled a waiter, paid him and pushed his chair back. She turned pale and began sweating heavily. As he walked quickly into the street he heard her high heels click against the cement before she caught up with him.

"Bastard," she whispered. She looked nervously at the people around them.

"It's ten minutes until curfew. I won't pay your price, Fräulein."

She grabbed his arm. "Please!" she entreated.

"You'd better go," he said, enjoying her agony.

"All right," she said, defeated. "Tell me what you will pay."

"That depends."

Her eyes darted around the street, which was now nearly empty of civilians, and then she pulled at his sleeve. "We have to go." She led him down a side street, breaking into an awkward run as soon as they left the main boulevard. "Hurry!" she begged. There was still a lot of rubble, and she stumbled frequently as she made her way through it. Bailov trotted along behind her, amused at her frantic behavior.

Several blocks further along they ran headlong into a Red Army patrol. She was ahead of him and was grabbed by the soldiers. Bailov approached them slowly. They were rear-echelon troops, not experienced, and when he came nearer, they circled him. The woman was being held to one side, a gun against her head.

The group was led by a toothless sergeant, his fingers dark from nicotine. "What's the matter, Nazi? You want some of this pussy?" His German was as crude as his vocabulary.

"No, Sergeant," Bailov said in Russian. "I'm looking for new tenants for the green flats of Lubyanka." The soldiers stiffened. Bailov flashed his Red Badge, and watched with amusement as the men scurried into the shadows to escape.

The woman stared at him. "I was right about you," she said. There was both admiration and fear in her voice.

"If you don't deliver, this will be the worst day of your life," Bailov warned her.

"What's one more?" she answered with a laugh and scampered down the side street ahead of him.

The street where the woman lived looked uninhabitable. All that remained of the old stone tenements were battered façades. She led him into a dark subcellar containing several small rooms crudely built off a central open area. There were people in the cellar, mainly females, most of them old. A woman rocked a baby in a dark corner, squatting, her body weaving slowly to and fro, the scrawny infant at her breast. Nobody looked up when Bailov and the woman entered. Berliners no longer poked their nose into other people's business; one took care of oneself as best one could and ignored everyone else.

The woman lived in one of the small cubicles. It contained a mattress without springs, a chair and a wooden crate on which were stuck several candles. A crucifix hanging on the wall leaned so badly that the Christ figure looked as if it were in the middle of a high dive. Dried palm leaves stuck out from behind the frame. The woman lit one of the candles, and the flame produced a small yellow glow that barely illuminated the area. Bailov observed that her few clothes were hung neatly on wire hangers, and that the tiny room was swept clean. A broom with badly worn bristles stood in a corner.

"Cigarette?" he asked, tossing an unopened pack to her. He watched carefully as she opened it clumsily with her thin fingers. Her coordination was off; disease or nutritional deficiency, he told himself. She sat on the bed with her skirt pulled high up her ghostly white thighs and used the candle to light up, inhaling deeply. "Where's Lisl?" he asked abruptly.

She exhaled loudly and lay back, her arm looped over her face. "Right here," she said wearily.

Bailov grinned. "So you're the ignorant Bavarian slut with the body?"

She nodded. "The same. My ignorance is a matter of record. I said Lisl Marchant got her roles because of her body, not her talent. That's true. You assumed that I meant she had the physique of an actress." She hiked her dress higher. "As you can verify, not true. Very few actresses have what they appear to. The camera can be made to see only what the director wants it to. What counts is the willingness to use your body and, more importantly, the skill to use it. I've been especially gifted, and that's how I got my parts. That's how everyone gets a part."

"An old approach. What of it?"

"I mingled with the wrong people."

"Like SS General Fegelein?"

She sat up, coughing from the smoke, tugged at her dress and swung her legs over the side of the mattress. "Who *are* you?"

"You were with the general when the Reich Security Police came to fetch him on April twenty-seventh."

The woman held the cigarette delicately between thumb and forefinger and swayed from side to side. She stared at Bailov. "No."

"Don't lie to me," he said quietly. "You were in bed with him."

"You *are* Gestapo."

"I am Russian," he answered patiently. "It's said that you were one of his whores."

"An interesting perspective. I've never thought of myself as a whore, though now that I hear it said, it doesn't feel so bad. I didn't know him that well. We were together a few times. I promise you, there were a lot worse people than Hermann. At least *his* tastes were normal. He could get it up like a man, and he helped me."

"You were with him on the twenty-seventh."

She reclined again and sighed. "I'm not ready yet to discuss specifics. Will you guarantee me what I want?" She looked like a child, frail and frightened, but he reminded himself that she was an actress.

"It depends on the nature of the information you have. Tell me about that night."

She looked up at the ceiling. "We had just finished making love. I haven't done it since," she added quickly, glancing at him out of the corner of her eye. "They arrived unannounced—an officer and three enlisted men. The officer told Hermann to get dressed. He was petrified and tried to talk the man into forgetting that he'd found him. The officer's name was Peter. He seemed to be a decent sort."

"But they took him away anyway."

"Not immediately. First they let him make a telephone call."

"Why?"

"To talk to his wife's sister." She looked away.

"Eva Braun," Bailov said. "He was married to Eva Braun's sister, Gretl."

"Yes. His wife was pregnant. He begged Eva to intercede for him."

"What did she tell him?"

"She hung up on him and Hermann began to weep. It was a terrible thing to see. Even the soldiers were embarrassed."

"Then?"

"He got dressed and they took him away. They made him put on his uniform. He was still arguing with the officer when they left."

"What did you do then? Wait for him to come back?"

The woman gave Bailov one of those looks reserved for the truly demented. "Of course not. I helped myself to some things I thought Hermann wouldn't need and left fast. I figured he was . . ." She didn't finish the sentence.

"And you haven't been back?" She shook her head. Bailov let the silence work for him. "Why did you leave so quickly?"

"Because they arrested him."

"They used that word?"

"No, but they didn't have to be explicit. Arrests are something we Germans can understand."

"You feared they might come back and arrest you, too?"

She shrugged. "I believe in being cautious. I liked Hermann a lot, but he was dangerous, you know? Eva Braun's sister was his wife; I didn't relish being so close to all the big Nazis, but it was also exciting, you understand?" She rolled onto her side. "Men don't understand the attraction of power to some women. Physically Hermann was little more than a gnome, but he was on the inside and at the top. He had everything—or, rather, access to everything. It was hard for a girl to pass up. Also, he was very generous to me."

"You never saw him again?"

"No. I swear it," she added quickly.

Bailov sat on the edge of the bed and touched her leg with his hand. "That's not worth the price of a new identity," he said. "You've got to give me more than that."

"That's everything I can tell you." She sighed. "But I can give you everything else I've got," she said in a pathetic attempt to sound alluring.

He stood up. "Inadequate."

Springing across the bed, she grabbed him by the arm. "Please don't leave me," she pleaded. She wrapped her arms around his waist and pressed her head to his stomach. "I need help."

He pushed her away and walked toward the doorway.

"All right." She got out of bed, pulled the curtain across the entrance and pushed him back into the room. "Hermann was planning to leave Berlin. He told me that he could help me leave. I'd have done anything to get out—anyone would have. They were after him. He said he knew Hitler's secret."

Bailov smiled. "You're making this up to keep me here."

"No," she said angrily. "This is the truth. So help me."

"And then he told you his secret?"

She shook her head. "Not exactly. He sort of hinted at it."

He waited.

"He said Hitler was going to be twice the trouble the world expected."

"That's all?"

"He said that if Hitler found out that he knew, he'd have him killed. Do *you* know what he was talking about?"

"No," Bailov said, "but they executed your boyfriend that afternoon."

She sagged visibly.

"Where did he get his information? Eva Braun? His wife?"

"I don't know."

Bailov smiled. "You've told me everything he said?"

"Everything, just the way he said it. My profession requires me to learn lines and remember them. I've told you everything—all of it. I swear. Now will you help me?"

Bailov assessed the situation. It was not the kind of solid evidence Petrov wanted, but combined with everything else they had, it supported their conviction. "Get your things together," he told her.

Her eyes widened. "Not now," she warned. "It's dark. It's too dangerous in the streets. At night they shoot first, then investigate when the sun comes up."

He knew she was right. In the dark a Red Badge wouldn't be a big enough shield. When he told her he'd stay, she fetched a pail of cold water and they bathed in it. He spent the night in her bed, and she used the opportunity to demonstrate to him how a really good actress earned her parts.

In the morning Bailov took Lisl with him to the headquarters of the Special Operations Group and installed her in a cell. After making arrangements for further interrogations by the staff, and for a flight to transport her to the holding center in Moscow, he wired Petrov.

He visited her in her cell that evening. She took her fate calmly, but Bailov felt a strange need to comfort her. "It won't be forever," he said, not knowing if it was the truth or not. "You'll still see Argentina."

"Will I?" she asked. Her eyes filled with tears.

▶43 JUNE 13, 1945, 9:00 A.M.

Pogrebenoi had been an artist, a painter with some potential, and had been well educated. In languages she was fluent in Italian, French, German, Russian and Romany. Her mother was alive and lived in Moscow; her father, an army colonel, had been killed in the invasion of Finland mounted by Stalin. Her brother, a pilot, had been downed and killed on the first day of the German invasion. Her husband, a cavalry officer, perished a few days later. She volunteered for military duty the following month.

Petrov was extremely selective in his recruiting. There were a number of attributes that he required of his subordinates, and the absence of any one of them was enough to eliminate a candidate from further consideration. Above all, he liked people with the quality he called vibrancy. Of intelligence and education, the former was more important, though he preferred a blend. Russian education was less valued than foreign schooling because of the anarchic nature of the Soviet system, which did little to promote either discipline or perspective in the developing mind. He preferred people around him who were driven by curiosity, as he was, and who possessed a certain spark in the way they tackled their assigned tasks. He tried to instill in the members of his team a certain degree of orderly thought tempered with skepticism. They had to be able to absorb and retain a prodigious quantity of details, and to be able to think well enough to tie loose ends together.

Petrov recognized that each individual was unique, with his own peculiar style and sensibility, and he made no effort to mold his subordinates to a theoretical standard. But he wanted people who had an array of practical skills to complement their intellectual capabilities, for often it was the fusion of the practical and the theoretical that drove a wedge through a problem and opened a window to the previously unknown. Further, they had to be physically fit. Their duty was unpredictable, their base of operation changed frequently and often their living conditions were less than optimal. Only hardy people could withstand the stress and constant hardship.

Petrov read Pogrebenoi's file with interest, assimilating its facts. She had left two sons, aged two and three, with her mother, completed six weeks of recruit training in the Urals, and then been sent—on foot—to the front lines in the Ukraine, where Soviet forces were trying desperately to blunt the German advance. In less than four years she rose in rank and responsibility from enlisted recruit to major, with command of a small battalion specializing in forays behind enemy lines. The record showed her to be an excellent marksman skilled in the use of a wide assortment of weapons—perhaps even the equal of Ezdovo, he thought. She had extensive experience in the handling of explosives, she had been wounded four times, and had suffered severe frostbite in her feet, a widespread problem for Soviet troops during the harsh winter of 1942–43.

A quick check with the Office of Defense Records revealed that

Pogrebenoi was politically clean, and was committed to the party. Her efficiency ratings from superior officers were outstanding; had she desired it, a successful career in the military was hers. No reason was given for her request for discharge, and Petrov resolved to pursue the subject during their interview if she showed up. People with success ahead of them seldom changed course, he reminded himself.

When he had finished reading, Petrov smiled to himself. Father Grigory, that meddling Jesuit, had sent him an angel. He'd have to repay the debt. He did not smile about the fact that the priest's choice showed that he might understand what was afoot; Petrov was confident that he'd closed off the inquiry with his offhand remark. Still, the old meddler was crafty; he'd probably thought his way through it, as Petrov would have if the tables had been turned. Or perhaps the priest might have future need of an alliance with Petrov and was simply trying to create a political debt for repayment when the interest rates were right. He wondered if there was a connection between Stalin and Father Grigory. It was a question that he had asked himself before, and he still did not know the answer. Stalin employed many resources and kept them to himself.

Talia Pogrebenoi arrived promptly at nine, the official starting time for the workday of Soviet bureaucrats. In a plain white peasant's shirt with bloused sleeves and a knee-length skirt, she was a handsome specimen. Despite her many war injuries, she walked gracefully and without evidence of a limp. Petrov noted that she wore shoes with heels high enough to satisfy her femininity but low enough to be within the tolerance of the party's views on such matters. Small wire loops dangled from her pierced ears. She wore earth-colored rouge on her lips, muted in such a way to enhance the shape of her mouth, but not marking her as overly concerned with her appearance. All in all, it was a masterly presentation.

"Good morning, Major. Coffee? Tea? Both are fresh."

She smiled and took a seat without being instructed. He liked people who saw the obvious and acted upon it. She sniffed at the fumes wafting from the cup of tea and sighed perceptibly. "It's been a long time since I smelled anything like this." He allowed her to savor her first swallow before beginning his questioning.

"I presume that your presence here this morning indicates your interest."

She did not respond; instead, she fixed a steady gaze on him as she had done the previous afternoon. Once again it was an unsettling experience.

"I've studied your dossier," Petrov said. "Very impressive." She flashed her eyes. "This is a special sort of organization," he explained. "If I offer the position and you accept, you do so for life. If at any time you fail in your responsibilities, you forfeit your life. No trial, no hearings, no appeals. How does that strike you?" He watched her eyes for clues, but there were none.

The woman's chin raised slightly just before she spoke. "The terms are absolute, so I assume that the mission is of critical importance to our country." Her voice was relaxed, but her choice of words was careful. She had complete control of herself. Even the unshakable Ezdovo had blinked and swallowed hard several times when he had heard the terms.

"You don't have to accept," Petrov said. "You can sit here and enjoy your tea, then leave and go on with your life. That's perfectly acceptable; there's no prejudice if you don't take the position."

"Has there ever been a refusal?"

Petrov shook his head and grinned. "Never." It was the first time a candidate had ever asked him the question. She was trying to control the situation, and he liked her aggressiveness. She was subtle and effective, rare qualities in one so young. "Before you decide," Petrov said, "there's a question I would like to ask." He opened her file and tapped his finger on the top sheet. "Your military performance was excellent, your fitness reports impeccable. You had a bright future in the army, yet you asked to be discharged. Why?"

"I joined as an answer to our nation's call in order to do a citizen's duty. Effectiveness and promotions in wartime are a matter of luck. In my battalion most of the officers were killed. They had to be replaced; I was there. In our sister battalion they lost very few. It's all a game of chance. The mission was simple: Kill the enemy. If you're a soldier you go where you're told to go, do what you're told to do, die if it's your time to die. As an officer you send soldiers into battle. It's very basic and uncomplicated."

"You understood your job. Why demean it?"

"I don't," Talia answered, "but neither do I glorify it. The truth is, I am not fit for soldiering. I do not like regimentation."

"Or textbook operations?" Petrov asked. "Let me finish for you. You liked leading your unit behind enemy lines. You liked being in the position of control. You can follow orders when the situation necessitates, but you prefer having responsibility for your own decisions and actions."

"Yes, that's about it."

"Every organization has to have a leader and subordinates."

"I don't disagree," she answered. "But in a dedicated organization qualified subordinates do not have their entire lives planned and supervised in detail. You pick your people for their abilities, then give them freedom to fly. I can sense this in you; you help them when they require it and give them what they need to do their job."

He grinned. "And you would expect that?"

"I would demand it," she said.

"What about your sons?"

"They're in good hands. They're going to be strong. They will accept and support whatever decision I make."

"They're very young. They're not yet at the age where they can grasp the abstractions that affect adult decisions," Petrov said.

Her nostrils flared, her first sign of emotion. "They are Russian boys," she said curtly, but with pride. "They will understand that if their mother must leave them again it is for the sake of their future."

"You're a hard woman, Talia Pogrebenoi."

"Yes, I am," she said proudly.

Petrov sat back in his chair. "How sharp is your Italian?"

"Dim." She laughed. "But it comes back quickly. It takes only a few days."

"Dialects?"

"Four when I was proficient. But now I think I could get by in Milanese or Neapolitan. Everything else is a shade of these."

They studied each other for a while. "Do you want me or not?" Pogrebenoi asked finally.

"That's never been the issue. You understand the terms?"

Her head bobbed once. "They are not complex."

Petrov's mind was made up. "Pour more tea for yourself," he told her. "You have a lot to learn and not much time to do it."

They stayed in the office talking until nearly 11:00 P.M. When they had finished, he gave her a black leather portfolio containing the Red Badge—his own—and instructions on when and where to report to him next.

►44 JUNE 14, 1945, 1:00 A.M.

The Poteshny Palace is a tall stone building, Mediterranean in suggestion but entirely Russian in its character and peculiarities. The roof is oddly shaped and covered with azure terrazzo tile. All of the windows on the ends of the oblong structure have been sealed with cement reinforced by steel rods. It sits on a narrow side street inside the Kremlin's walls, a short walk from the complex of buildings that houses the Senate and Politburo.

Petrov knew that Stalin kept an apartment in the palace, but he had never been inside it. It was after midnight, the peak of the Soviet leader's day. The summons had come after nine, forcing Petrov to hurry his briefing of Pogrebenoi, ending it before he was ready. But it was necessary to finish early; getting through Kremlin security was time-consuming. Inside the palace, guards were stationed every ten paces on the floors, stairs and landings. Every ten paces. This was Stalin's order, and it was done unquestioningly. There were four checkpoints between the palace entrance and the door that ultimately admitted the visitor to Stalin's suite. A guard tapped lightly on the door with the back of his hand while staring straight ahead. An old woman opened the door, waited to take Petrov's hat, received it, stepped to the side and disappeared.

"In here, my Berkut," Stalin bellowed. From what Petrov could see, there were four rooms, furnished with simple, heavy furniture. The office was awash with paper. Documents were piled on a long couch and on three large wooden tables. A single black telephone stood on an end table. The light in the room came from two brass-necked floor lamps and a small light on the main table. Even though the weather had turned warm and the buildings of the Kremlin tended to be stuffy, Stalin still wore a blue tunic of winter weight. He looked tired, but beamed crookedly when Petrov entered, grasped him by the arms and squeezed him in a bear hug, in an uncharacteristic display of affection. "I'm glad you could come."

Petrov laughed. "Who would dare refuse such an invitation? You wished to see me."

The Soviet leader frowned. "So direct, my dear Petrov? You *stinker*," he hissed, using a word he had learned from the American gangster movies he loved to watch late at night when he was on holiday. "Always with the business, always so formal. Relax tonight: we eat, we drink, then we talk."

The dining room was a small box off the office. Its white linen tablecloth was soiled, and for some reason the mildewed canvas curtains covering the windows reminded Petrov of the bunker in Berlin. Once again the table was covered with food. A small pig sat smoky-eyed on a cast-iron platter, baked to a glaze with a reddish-brown hue, tomato and onion slices pinned to its flesh. Loaves of black bread were stacked at one end of the table in a circular arrangement. There was more than any four men could possibly eat. All to be wasted, Petrov thought. Yet it was understandable; given his countrymen's propensity for political intrigue and assassination, Stalin's caution was to be expected. If there was too much to eat, an enemy could not guess which particular dish to poison and would be forced to administer the poison to everything. With Stalin's habits, someone else would always sample before he ate. It had always been so for rulers.

Grasping a bottle of Kakhitian wine by its thin neck, Stalin pushed a badly scratched water glass toward his guest. "My only concession to decadence," he confided. Kakhitian was known throughout the world as the best of Russia's many wines. It was rarely found outside the borders, and what smugglers did manage to bring out fetched an incredible price; even the arrogant French had to admit that the wine was "interesting."

Petrov sipped, enjoying the flavor and bouquet. They drank in silence, and when they had emptied their glasses, Stalin refilled them. "Help yourself," he said, spreading his arms before the food table. Much to his leader's delight, Petrov filled his plate and ate heartily. "Such an appetite for so small a bird," the premier said with admiration.

It was Stalin's style to focus on the physical peculiarities of his visitors, often likening them to the animals he believed they resembled. For Petrov such assaults had always been of minor proportion, but there were stories of real ordeals; the strongest of men were said to walk away wobbly-legged from an audience with the premier, stung by his sharp tongue and hour-long barrages of criticism. It was also

Stalin's practice to invite a man to dinner, feed him lavishly, praise him generously, then have him taken out and shot. There was a saying: A visit to Stalin has three possible endings, and only one of them is good.

After eating, the two men returned to the office. Stalin cleared the couch with a powerful sweep of his hand, sending papers skittering across the room to distant corners. He was in a mood that Petrov had not seen before, and he reminded himself to be careful. Stalin laughed as he surveyed his handiwork and dropped stiffly onto a cushion, bouncing several times until his rump settled in. Then he leered at Petrov as if they were conspirators in some dark secret, and magically produced a bottle of pertsovka, the thick brown vodka that resembled dark vinegar and packed a wallop. To Russian aficionados, pertsovka was the ultimate, to be savored—and above all, to be respected.

There was an apocryphal story that two Georgians—the nationalities depended upon what part of the country you were in—happened upon a half bottle of pertsovka, which they took to their favorite place in a forest outside their village. As they were draining the final drops, a bolt of lightning struck a nearby tree, sending a large limb crashing down on both of them. Their skulls were fractured and they were near death. Villagers found them the next morning and rushed them to a doctor in a nearby city. The doctor lacked the necessary expertise, but miraculously the badly injured men clung to life, though still unconscious. They were loaded onto an aircraft and flown to Moscow, where neurosurgery was performed. Alas, their injuries were so severe that the doctors decided that they would be vegetables even if they ever regained consciousness. The two men were installed in a sanitarium near Red Square, and each day young nurses took them in wheelchairs to the balcony that overlooked Saint Basil's. Years passed. One day the two miraculously regained their faculties at the same moment. They looked at each other, old, their hair and teeth gone, then gazed out on the magnificence of Russian culture, a blurred tapestry of color dazzling their long-idled senses. Finally a great smile filled one man's face and he spoke. "Pertsovka," he whispered to his friend. "The best, yes?"

Stalin drank directly from the bottle and passed it to Petrov, who did the same. It went back and forth until both could feel their senses numbing. Finally Stalin fumbled with his pipe, spilling tobacco from a hefty leather pouch onto his lap. Ignoring the mess, he lit the bowl clumsily.

Petrov had to call on all his concentration to maintain his equilibrium. He could hold his vodka better than most, but this, he warned himself, was vodka only in name. The ember of fire in his belly flowed outward through his limbs, making his fingertips and toes throb. "You wanted to talk," Petrov tried to say but his speech was badly slurred.

Stalin laughed deeply, his body listing heavily. "I want to *drink,* you bastard!" He slapped Petrov so hard on the back that the blow sent him crashing to the floor. Stalin was small, but he had been a wrestler in his youth and was powerful. Petrov's back did not hurt now, but he knew that when he recovered his senses it would ache.

Precisely when it happened Petrov never knew, but he passed out. When he awoke with a violent headache, Stalin was sprawled beside him on the floor, snoring loudly, his mouth wide open. Two empty pertsovka bottles were at their feet.

Petrov struggled to his feet and stumbled in search of his hat. He badly needed sleep and time to recover; his brain, he knew, was still impaired. Not finding the hat, he decided to leave it. As he reached the door he felt a steely grip on his arm. Stalin's face was inches from his; his breath was putrid, but his eyes were clear and focused, his lips wide in a crooked smile. "*That* was a night, eh, Petrov?"

The chief of the Special Operations Group could not respond. His brain searched frantically for language with no success.

The premier's face changed to a hard mask. "Berkut, you bring him back to me," he hissed. "Alive. Here to Moscow." He handed Petrov another wallet, flipping it open to reveal a new Red Badge. "Talia Pogrebenoi," he growled. "An interesting choice by the Berkut," he added just before he closed the door in Petrov's face.

So Grigory *was* connected directly to Stalin. This proved it, but he was in no condition to ponder the implications. He needed sleep. Outside the dawn was breaking.

▶45 JUNE 15, 1945, 6:00 P.M.

While Waller tolerated the harem arrangement and her unremarkable status within it, she relished her time alone with Brumm. Neither of them had spoken of it, but she felt that he shared her feelings. She found him to be physically expressive, a gentle and accommodating lover in their infrequent intimate moments, but they never talked about it and she had to guess at his thoughts.

The night that Brumm told the group he planned to leave the valley on a hunting expedition, they were excited. When Brumm selected Waller to accompany him, the others did not question his choice. His intent was to travel to a nearby area where there was a large population of boars. The meat, he told them, was exceptionally sweet when prepared properly, and he felt they could use the change in fare.

Now they were together outside their valley, and Waller was feeling light-headed, both from the freedom and from Brumm's closeness. The hunt had gone well. He had shot three large animals with an ancient shotgun that had once belonged to his grandfather. She found it curious that only he did the hunting. In the canyon it was a shared activity, the women and men alternating as drivers and shooters, but this time her role was limited to watching at a safe distance.

It was late afternoon when Brumm led her up a narrow draw. He had butchered the game, keeping only the hind quarters of the three animals, which he carried in nets. She assumed that he was taking her to a campsite, so she was puzzled when he dropped his gear at the head of a rock formation. When she questioned him, he only smiled and walked off to a stand of small trees. He returned with a long staff of freshly cut white ash, which he trimmed to a point.

"What are we doing?" she demanded.

"What we came here to do, to hunt." But she could tell by his demeanor that he was up to something more.

"You're going to hunt with a cudgel?"

"No," he said solemnly. "You are—with a spear, in the old way." He refused to explain further; instead, he showed her how to handle the weapon. At first it felt crude and clumsy, but in a short time she managed to achieve a sense of balance and comfort with it. Among the rocks he showed her a place where two large boulders were less than a meter apart. A narrow, well-worn trail led from the underbrush up the draw to the rocks, passing directly underneath where they stood. She still did not understand.

Brumm took a long time to position her correctly. He had her hold the spear with two hands close together but with her arms extended in front of her. "The animal will come up this trail," he said, showing her its path. "When you see it, push the spear out. Like this." He showed her what he expected. "Aim with the bottom of the point. When its nose passes the tip, pull the shaft into your chest and step off the rocks with both feet. Don't jump," he cautioned. "Step. You want to go straight down." He demonstrated for her. "Your body weight and gravity will do the rest."

"This is a joke, right?" But he didn't laugh. Waller was beginning to feel very nervous.

"I'm quite serious," Brumm said.

"Can I get hurt doing this?"

"If you do it wrong, you'll be dead before I can get to you. You must concentrate and do it right. It takes courage."

"Not to mention stupidity," she added disgustedly. "Why don't you just shoot another one and let's be done with it? I'm tired and it's beginning to rain. Why should I do this?"

He grasped her arms, spun her and looked into her eyes. His gaze frightened her. There was a fire in him, yet a coolness that she couldn't describe, something she'd never seen before in any man. It was more like an animal's. "I want you to," he said clumsily. That ended it for her. She could not deny him what he wanted, so she resigned herself to the task and rehearsed what she was supposed to do. Brumm's intensity excited her. She gave no thought to the danger, even though she had yet to see her first live boar. The three he had killed had been shot while he was out of sight, and she'd heard only the reports. But she'd seen pictures of boars, so she was certain she'd make no mistake should one venture up the trail.

The rain began as a mist, but quickly intensified to a barrage of heavy drops that struck hard and stung her flesh even through her flannel shirt, so that soon she was drenched. Even over the rain, she could hear a swarm of flies buzzing around the meat behind her. She wished they were home in the valley. The hot pool beckoned in her mind, but she fought to concentrate.

She heard the animal before she saw it. It was trotting with an awkward gait, its tiny cloven hooves hitting the rocky ground with resounding smacks. Its hair was gray and matted; a hump protruded from the top of its back and accented its tapered head. She'd never seen anything so ugly. Its eyes were wide apart and sinister; yellow tusks curled back from its snout, and it was drooling heavily as it approached. She could hear Günter behind the animal, driving it. He was slapping something against tree trunks, and each time he made the sound the animal accelerated a little, only to slow down again. But it kept coming steadily up the hill toward the rocks on the path directly between her legs.

It was so close now that she could smell it, a foul odor like carrion rotting in the sun that obscured the sweet pine scents of the valley. She felt her adrenaline rise. Her heart pounded; her arms were out, the spear extended. She braced her legs for the step and concentrated on sighting with the point. The boar's nose passed under; she inhaled deeply, pulled the spear's shaft into her chest, gripped it fiercely and stepped off into space wanting to scream in laughter or fear, but instead falling silently with her emotions locked inside. She thought she felt the spear penetrate with a cracking sound, but she had no idea what she had hit and no time to think about it. She landed on the animal's back haunches and glanced off, falling so hard on her back that her wind was knocked out. She felt the animal bump her leg; she couldn't breathe and wondered if she had somehow landed on the spear. She felt intense fear.

Brumm came up the trail at a run. Grabbing her hand, he jerked her to her feet and embraced her, showering her with words with such rapidity that she couldn't understand him. She pushed him away and collapsed; only then did he realize that she was having trouble breathing. When she finally recovered, she cursed him. "What if I had broken my leg?" she said angrily, but before she could continue she felt pain in her calf muscle and sat down heavily. "Look," she shrieked. "The damn thing's gored me."

Brumm examined the leg slowly, a broad smile on his face. It was only superficial, by his standards no more than a scratch. "He was dead when he did it. All that was left was his instinct to kill his enemy. Not enough strength to do any real damage. You're lucky," he said happily.

"Lucky?"

"Take off your shirt," he ordered.

"It's my leg that's hurt!"

"Get the shirt off." His tone told her he was not joking. She did as she was told, the cold rain chilling her as it hit her breasts. She wondered would happen next, but when she questioned him, he grunted, "Be still. Don't talk."

As she watched he rolled the boar onto its back. He used his knees to wedge open the animal's hind legs and felt along its hairy belly to find the point just below where the ribs joined. Poking his dagger into the soft flesh, he slipped his fingers in on either side of the blade, which he worked back toward the animal's tail; the flesh opened easily without bleeding as he avoided penetration of the sack that held its entrails. With the animal opened, he used the palms of his hands to pound the spot where the ribs were joined by cartilage; it gave way with a resounding crack that sounded like the report of his shotgun earlier in the day.

Waller found herself fascinated by what he was doing. He worked with the confidence and dexterity of a surgeon. Using his knife again, he broke through the bone to open the chest cavity, which he spread wide. Steam rose from the organs into the cool air, and she could smell the animal's musk. As she watched he reached inside with the knife, and almost immediately his hand came out holding the animal's heart, a fat, bluish-red muscle not quite as large as his fist.

When he turned to her with the heart, she scooted backward, recoiling from the sight. His hand was covered with thick blood; black liquid oozed between his fingers and fell in syrupy strands.

"Get away from me," she warned weakly as he crawled toward her with an odd look in his eyes. She tried to stand, but he caught her by the belt and pulled her down. "No, Günter, please," she pleaded, knowing it was no use. He pushed her onto her back and placed the boar's heart against her chest. Her mind swam; at first she resisted him, but he was too strong and she was feeling weaker by the moment. She felt disgust and excitement and an incredible warmth as he rubbed the bleeding organ all over her, covering her breasts with warm sticky blood. Suddenly the fright left her, and in its place was something new and entirely different, deep inside her, rising, spreading.

Suddenly he thrust up on his knees, hovering over her. He dangled the heart in front of his face, then bit into it, violently, tearing away a large piece of flesh so that his chin was covered with a grisly red goatee. She was paralyzed, wondering what would come next, but wanting it to happen, whatever it was. The fire inside her was spreading. Then the dead heart was pressed against her lips; she turned her head to the side, trying to escape it.

"Eat," he growled, and forced it into her mouth. She had no choice; she bit into the thing, at first finding it tough and ungiving before her teeth burst through the membrane into softer flesh.

She felt her last contact with reality departing. She was eating uncooked flesh, the heart of an animal that only seconds before had been alive and had tried to kill her. Brumm knelt beside her, blood dripping from his face onto hers, and she knew it was too late to turn back; they had gone too far and there was no stopping. She shuddered with anticipation. His eyes were glazed and he swayed from side to side, almost in a trance. She wished he would hurry; the fire inside her was unbearable. She grabbed at his trousers and pulled them down roughly, reaching for him with her hands. He fell forward on her, rubbing the heart all over her body, into its creases and folds, covering them with blood and a slippery trail. Then he was on her and she arched anxiously to meet him.

Afterward Waller was shaken by the experience. It had touched something primitive inside her, something powerful; she wondered if it was evil.

"Ritual," Brumm explained. "For the first kill. This is our way up here in the mountains." He sat on a rock next to the narrow stream, watching her wash the blood from her flesh. "My grandfather initiated me. His father did the same. It's been the tradition through generations so far back that no one knows when it began. It's always done here in this exact place by my family, and always in the same way. The boar is undisputed king in the mountains. By killing it in the old way, its powers pass to you and you absorb them. You capture its soul by eating its flesh."

Waller contented herself with listening. She was still shaky from the intensity of their lovemaking and the shock of seeing the heart suspended above her face. "Generations? Here? On this spot?"

He smiled.

She thought about it. Why had he done it? The answer came to her without warning. "Günter," she said tenderly, her arms outstretched. He stepped off the bank into her embrace and they stood together for a long time. "I understand," she said. "We're joined now. That's it, isn't it? Your way, the old way."

He held her closer. "It's the closest thing to permanence that I can give you."

She wanted to weep but stopped herself. He was strong, so she would be strong. She felt whole and satisfied—and suddenly and inexplicably playful.

"Günter?"

"Yes."

"The ritual is *always* the same?"

"Always."

"Even the last part?"

He pushed her away and smiled at her. "No. That was my idea."
They fell into the stream together, laughing.

▶46 JUNE 16, 1945, 10:30 A.M.

Pescht and his avengers were renegades. The Americans had brought order, and already Germans who'd had no involvement with Hitler or his thugs were being installed in local governments or helping the Americans with an eye toward taking over later. Groups like Pescht's were a threat to the peace, and the Americans were increasing security measures around towns and villages.

Pescht's Angels, as they called themselves, had traveled a zigzag pattern across the countryside. Initially they had enjoyed freedom of movement, but as the days passed they began encountering heavy resistance. Even isolated farms were not easy targets. The group had been in two firefights with American soldiers and another with a large British contingent.

After their most recent engagement, in which their strength was reduced to fewer than twenty, the group made its way south to the Harz Mountains, where Pescht immediately lost his way. They found refuge in a narrow canyon, where they intended to camp and live off the land while they licked their wounds, regained some strength and determined when it was safe to leave the mountains again.

One of Pescht's men found the opening to a cavern. In the camps they all had become adept at finding places to hide themselves and their possessions in ways and places that men under ordinary circumstances would never consider. Now that they were outside the prison, their habits remained the same.

With a badger's sense of the underground, Pescht's man, a whippetlike Orthodox Jew from Düsseldorf, crawled around in the small cavern, eventually following it through to an opening in another valley, much larger—and much safer, they supposed.

The Angels posted a single sentry in the outer valley and followed Pescht into the new one with optimism and a sense of excitement.

▶47 JUNE 16, 1945, 11:25 A.M.

The previous night, Brumm had cooked boar's meat in the coals of a small fire, and he and Waller ate it with their fingers. Afterward, they made love wrapped in a blanket next to the crackling fire and slept together under a lean-to.

At dawn they ate cold meat, drank from the stream and began the return journey to the valley. Each knew that their relationship had changed, but they did not speak of it; the knowledge alone would have to sustain them.

Between them they had more than a hundred pounds of fresh meat, which Brumm had separated into two equal bundles. The rain persisted, a soaking drizzle that came from clouds hanging close to the valley floors.

When they reached the entrance of the valley late in the morning, Brumm saw immediately that there was trouble. The tracks told him the number of invaders; their pattern told him they were undisciplined. "Intruders," he whispered to Waller. "We'll move up by steps, left-right."

She understood his meaning. It was a two-man trap and reconnoitering formation that they had practiced many times with Beard. They advanced twenty yards apart, maintaining visual contact.

Waller was first to see the sitting sentry. She caught Brumm's attention with a flickering hand signal and pointed. He signaled back for her to cover him and moved forward slowly after shedding his pack.

Brumm stalked the man like an animal. When he got close, he studied him. He was half asleep and filthy. He was still meters away, but the odor was terrible. His boots looked relatively new, and his weapon, an American M-1, was across his lap. Brumm took him from the rear, smashing him behind the ear with the edge of his hand. The guard fell sideways, hit the ground and did not move. Brumm finished him with a quick thrust of his dagger and waited for Waller to join him.

"Cover the cave," he told her as he rifled the guard's clothes. There was no identification. He rolled up the man's sleeve and saw the tattoo. "Jew."

She stared at the body. "What's a Jew doing up here?"

Brumm shook his head. "There are more of them than us and they've gone inside. Come."

In the darkness it was impossible to tell whether the intruders had found the entrance, but when they crawled out of the tunnel into the valley they found a body mangled by an exploded mine, and muddy footprints told him that the intruders were inside. "Damn," he said. "They're here. The tracks are fresh and there's no smoke up the valley near the camp; they haven't found it yet, but they will. We've got to hurry." They stashed the meat in the cave and moved out at double time. His pace was hard, but she kept up with him as they kept low and moved silently. At the stream they paused, still hidden, and looked toward the pond. Within seconds they spotted the intruders hidden in the underbrush on the other side of the dam.

"Beard knows they're here," Brumm whispered with obvious relief. "See how quiet the camp is? He's ready. Look at the bank. The mud has been swept clean."

"What do we do?"

"Get in behind them. Eventually they'll go across to look at the cave. We want to get as many of them as possible into the open. You stay here. When Beard fires, wait till they turn to run, then take them. Keep your shots waist-high; the idea is to knock them down. I'll cover the other end behind them. If you miss any of them, they'll come my way."

Eventually the intruders grew tired of their vigil and began to inch forward. Brumm knew what they were thinking: no tracks, no movement, an empty building. Still, they'd be nervous. They were untrained, but they were wily and armed. With luck, Brumm thought, they would all move at once. No scouts had been posted, and no rear guard; they were rank amateurs.

Within minutes all the intruders were working their way in the open toward the cliff wall. A regular army unit would have sent forward only one man to probe and attempt entry, a minimal expenditure of resources.

Beard's first shots came at exactly the moment Brumm would have chosen. He tensed as there was a blur of movement to his left. He ran to intercept and smashed a man hard in the head as he emerged stumbling from a thick tangle of brush. Brumm wanted at least one of them alive; he had to find out whether this was an isolated group of marauders.

There was more shooting from Gretchen's direction as Brumm jerked the man to his feet and kicked him forward. When they reached the cottage, Beard was already lining up bodies along the bank.

"Who the hell are they?" the sergeant major shouted.

The lone survivor crossed the brook and stood before the dead bodies. Stefanie knocked off the survivor's hat and took a step back. He was a she, with short hair like a man's.

"A Jew?" Beard asked.

Brumm sent Rau and two of the girls to fetch the sentry's body from the outer valley. "Get him in here; I want them all in the ground together. And block the entrance again." It had been a calculated risk to leave the entrance unblocked during their excursion. Now he was sorry he hadn't stuck to procedure. Beard's detail moved out at a fast pace and disappeared into the tree line.

Herr Wolf peeked from the doorway and stepped out tentatively, still clinging to the doorjamb. "What's going on? Who are these people?"

"Jews," one of the girls said.

"Impossible," he corrected her. "There are no more Jews in the Reich. I have that on good authority; you can take my word for it."

"Well, take my word for it," Brumm snapped back. "These are Jews, they are here and they have American weapons."

Herr Wolf lifted his head like an animal trying to see something at a distance and studied the bodies. "Then they are American Jews," he said. "Not German Jews. That explains it."

The survivor suddenly turned to face him. Herr Wolf gasped and backpedaled. "Jewess!" he shrieked, turning to the colonel. "Outrage! How did this happen?" he demanded. "You assured me that our security was adequate, yet here we are the victims of this pack of—" The veins stood out on his neck and his left arm slapped loudly against his side as he spoke.

While Wolf was talking the female survivor watched, studying him. Brumm ignored his leader and kept his eyes on the woman. As he watched, her eyes widened and her mouth opened, but no sound came forth. She pointed toward Herr Wolf, took a partial step forward and pitched onto her face.

Brumm had seen the recognition in her eyes. In that instant the woman's fate was sealed.

▶48 June 16, 1945, 1:00 p.m.

When the woman emerged from her faint a few minutes later, she was given stream water from a tin cup.

"Tea," Brumm ordered. She watched the SS colonel, not knowing who he was, but instantly aware that he was someone with power. The hardness in his eyes clearly frightened her.

She sat up. "Outside, I saw—"

"Your eyes didn't betray you," Brumm said, cutting off her sentence. "You see your situation. I want you to answer some questions. I advise you to be cooperative." His voice was gentle, but she could feel the threat underneath. It wasn't what he said or how he said it; there was something more that made her want to please him and earn his approval. She'd been through this many times and had thought it was behind her, yet here it was again. She had met men like this before, sure of themselves, in control of their situations and willing to do anything to get their way. In the camps she'd learned the art of turning these men aside, being cooperative yet not cooperating. It was a skill honed under the threat of death, and she'd always felt some hope that if she performed well her life would be extended for another twenty-four hours. But this was different; this man would kill her.

"Your name," Brumm said. It was not a question.

"Names are of no use to the dead," she answered.

"You're quite alive, Fräulein, and your tongue is sharp."

"Would that it were a dagger," she said, glaring.

"Your name," he said again. This time the threat had risen closer to the surface. He could be provoked, she noted. It might be something to work with.

"Why not?" she shrugged. "You have everything else. Why not my name, too? Complete your job. You've taken it all, my past, my future, every shred. Nothing remains for Razia Scheel." She stood and hiked her dress to show brown scars crisscrossing her abdomen. Shock was often effective with this type. Do the unexpected, she told herself. "See? All gone. You took my babies from inside, before they were ready."

Brumm drew back. The Valkyries pushed closer to see the woman's belly, but he shoved them back. This was not the kind of person he was used to dealing with. She was either a very clever woman or a crazy one—or both—and she was obviously trying to get the upper hand.

"Look at them. Go ahead. This isn't so bad. You've seen scars before. I had to watch the real horror. They made me pregnant three times, then opened me up, took my babies out and drowned them. There was nothing I could do. I didn't even pray. God wouldn't be there; I knew that. He didn't exist in the camps. Do you understand what I'm telling you?" she asked, pointing at the girls. "You're women. Do you see what's been done to me?"

"Shut her up," one of the girls said.

The woman laughed. "Shut her up. A million times over. Shut them all up. Listen to me, girl, they cut the babies out of me and drowned them. Do you understand what I'm telling you? For so-called science. *German* science. They explained it to me while they did it. Babies live in a liquid environment in the womb. How do they do this, they wanted to know? They used my babies to find out. If we can determine the mechanism of action—that's what they called it— then perhaps we can increase the survival rates for our submariners."

The woman paused and sat back. "Ah, they found nothing. My babies were as stubborn as me. They drowned without giving up their secrets. I was proud of them."

"Razia Scheel," Brumm said. He needed to regain control. Babies cut from the womb? Disgusting, he thought. But her woes were of the past; his mission was the future. He had to have information. He couldn't allow her to ramble on like this.

"Yes, Razia Scheel," the woman said defiantly. "Once a German and a Jew, now a mere subhuman with a number on my arm, an incubator for Nazi science. What will it be this time? The brothel? No, not with all these fine young girls. No need for extra help. Lesbian experiments? That fits, doesn't it? Not enough men to go around now. You're in luck; I have considerable experience in that field as well. You'll find my curriculum vitae quite complete."

"What was the nature of your unit?"

She stared at Brumm. "Listen to yourself. What you want to know is who you killed, isn't it? Can't you ask directly? They were Jews, of course. Who else would have anything to do with a Jewess with a number on her arm?"

"Which one was the leader?"

"That's better," she said. "Much more direct. See how easy it is? Our leader was Pescht. He wasn't much of a leader, but he did the best he could. He led us out of Buchenwald. The Americans liberated us, if this miserable existence can be called liberation. We were avengers. Not very effective, but we were learning as we went."

"Avengers of what?"

The woman opened her mouth wide as if to laugh, but no sound came out. "Isn't it obvious? One could spend a life—or what's left of it—avenging. You'd never run dry."

Beard returned. Entering, he caught Brumm's attention and flicked his eyes toward the dark hall behind them; Herr Wolf was there in the shadows, listening. The woman caught the signal and felt her confidence lag. What lurked in the darkness was far more frightening than an SS colonel.

"When were you liberated?" Brumm asked.

"A while ago. It's hard to remember."

"I assume you had a destination."

"German logic." She laughed bitterly. "There is no destination for Jews here. We're a lost tribe. We talked about Munich last night. Pescht thought there'd be lots of Nazis left in Munich."

"Nazis?"

"Of course. We kill them, just as they killed us. We had years to learn—an extended period of training, you could call it."

Herr Wolf floated silently forward from the shadows, his hands folded in front of his lap in an almost protective posture. "Condemnation rolls easily from your lips," he said. "It's so convenient to measure morality by lives and deaths. You go to the butcher, he slaughters the meat, your rabbi passes on it with a little hocus-pocus and a few magic words, and suddenly there's morality and acceptability. But somebody had to do the dirty work for you."

She avoided the dark eyes that beckoned her. "If only Pescht could have lived a few moments more."

"A perfect prototype of the Jewess," Herr Wolf announced to the others. "Here we see the insidiousness of the race, the most dangerous of the species. Find another to do your bidding. The Jew always needs another instrument." He turned to face them, like a professor before his class. "Now you will understand. I will demonstrate for you. The Jewish race is parasitic, and like all parasites, it carries innumerable diseases. Consider the remora, a small and insignificant fish that attaches itself to the shark. The shark kills, and the remoras in turn feed off it. It provides no benefit to the shark; it only takes for itself. You see?"

His face was bright now, flushed with excitement. "As a young artist of some promise, I was forced to live in poverty in Vienna, and there I saw the Jews up close and how they manipulated and dined off the flesh of German culture. Roosevelt was a Jew; he kept it a secret; he was ashamed of it. Jews often hide the fact of their birth. Roosevelt opposed me; all Jews are against me. With good reason," he added with a demonic laugh. "They knew that I knew, and I let it be known that I, alone in the world, had the intestinal fortitude to act on my insight into their true natures."

He leaned toward the woman, who instinctively recoiled, his voice soft. "Understand, I've never *hated* Jews. That's never been the point. It would be wrong to make war because you hate someone. It was an intellectual decision, a matter of duty, my sacred trust to the German people, present and future. I realized early in my life—during my lonely years in Vienna, and certainly well before the Munich years—that the Jews were given to us as a device from God, a gift, if you will. How else can we explain the pogroms? How is it that in every culture in history the Jew has been a target for destruction? It cannot be coincidence that every civilized culture has identified the same threat. You see? If you study history, finally you have to come back to this, because it occurs over and over again. Pure races—there are very few left— can advance only so far before the impurities from racial mixing create genetic soup. I know this because we've put our best scientists on it. The Jew is no more than a subspecies mechanism for ensuring that periodically we look to the preservation of our own purity. This is fact, not speculation. I had no choice in the matter of eradication; the impurities had to be removed from German society, but I want you all to know that I took the action without rancor."

Herr Wolf touched the woman's face gently and, cupping her chin with his hand, raised her eyes to his. Then, releasing her, he stepped back quickly and beckoned Brumm to approach him. The colonel was not sure what he would say. The monologue had left him wondering if Beard had been right in his earlier assessment of Herr Wolf's mental state. What bothered him most was that this was the first time since they left Berlin that the Führer had asserted himself. What did this mean? More important, what had stimulated it? The woman, yes, but it was too sudden and radical a departure in behavior to be only that. Here, suddenly and without warning, was the Hitler of old, the Führer.

"What do you propose to do with her?" Wolf asked, his tone solicitous.

Brumm did not answer. The question did not require a response. The Führer knew very well what had to be done.

"Yes, well, Brumm, I would like for her to remain with us as my personal guest. Please see to her comfort." With that he grabbed the woman's hand, pressed it to his lips, wheeled and disappeared down the hall. The woman recoiled, holding her hand as if it had been burned.

Brumm immediately gave chase, cornering Herr Wolf outside his room. "She can't stay. She's a threat to security. She could try something foolish, or escape. Where would that leave us? I don't like this."

The old man smiled benignly. "You are a violent man, Colonel Brumm. That's why I chose you. That's why I leave it to you to make sure that there is no problem with my niece."

"Your *niece?*" Brumm blinked hard.

"Of course," Herr Wolf said. "Don't you recognize her?"

Brumm felt a chill. "What are you talking about?"

"Calm yourself, Colonel. That woman is my niece, Geli Rabaul. They say she died in Munich in 1931, but I've always known that couldn't be true. I endeavored to find her, but she had seemingly disappeared. Now I understand what happened: she was taken by Jews as a way of striking at me. But she loved me too much to leave me of her own accord. I've looked forward to seeing her again for a long time. Now, if that's all, I have things to think about." He went into his room and closed the door, leaving Brumm in the hall, his mouth agape.

Rejoining the others in the main room, Brumm put them back to work, then pulled Beard aside. "We've got to talk. After dinner we'll take a walk."

"What's up?"

"I'm beginning to think I should have listened to you that first night on the river," Brumm said.

►49 JUNE 18, 1945, 5:00 P.M.

Pogrebenoi met Petrov at a military airfield outside Moscow. She carried a small canvas duffel and equipment she had drawn at his orders from a special supply unit. Together they sat on the tarmac in a soothing warm wind, waiting for final preparations for their takeoff. When the aircraft was finally ready, a mechanic offered to carry her personal gear.

As Petrov reached the hatch the crew chief tapped his shoulder and pointed to a black Packard that had parked about fifty meters away. The automobile was unmarked and there was no escort, but Petrov sensed who was inside. Leaving Pogrebenoi, he walked over to the vehicle. The rear door was open, a uniformed driver standing beside it. Petrov looked inside. The premier was sitting alone. He wore a gray uniform and heavy overcoat with red strips on the collar; an unadorned officer's cap set evenly on his head. Petrov got in and the door shut behind him.

Stalin stared straight ahead; he was wearing black gloves and his hands were folded in his lap. A partition with a closed curtain separated them from the driver's compartment. "Petrov," Stalin said coldly, "I'm a patient man. I have granted you absolute authority, *my* authority, the authority of the Red Badge. I've been hospitable, shared my pert-sovka with you. Whatever you've needed, I've given, no questions asked. I've given you my trust."

"I'm most grateful, comrade," Petrov said.

"Shut up. I've run out of patience. I expected results from you, but you've brought me nothing." The premier's voice was hard but even. Petrov stiffened. "Your performance is unsatisfactory, comrade. I have ordered you to bring back the monster to me alive. I've no more time for theories, Petrov. Go back to Berlin and do your job. I want results. Do you understand me? Results. You have seven days to give me something substantial. One week or I chop off the Berkut's wings."

The premier reached forward and rapped on the partition. When the door opened, Petrov scrambled out. Stalin turned his head to look at him. "You or him."

The driver closed the door, smiled at the visitor as he got in, and the Packard raced away, its tires squealing on the pavement.

Petrov's legs were weak.

▶50 JUNE 19, 1945, 4:00 A.M.

Ezdovo was waiting in a yellow lorry when the chocks were jammed under the plane's wheels at Tempelhof. He held out his hands to catch Petrov's bag, but dropped it when Pogrebenoi's dark head emerged behind his leader. Without a word she walked confidently across the tarmac, loaded her gear into the back of the vehicle and swung up on the running board.

Petrov offered no explanation for her presence and Ezdovo did not ask. When he could, he sneaked peeks at her as her dark hair flowed in the wind outside the cab. When they reached their head-quarters, the woman followed Petrov inside. Ezdovo could see that she was no ordinary female; she was big, powerful, graceful and very good-looking.

Inside, Petrov observed that the once bustling interrogation center was nearly empty. Desks and tables were stacked one on top of another; files were in heavy cartons, neatly labeled. It pleased him that his men had prepared so well for his return. He had not told them that they would be moving on; they had simply recognized that it was time and had acted accordingly. It was the kind of initiative he expected from them.

The other men did not rise when Petrov entered. This was their way: one respected and obeyed one's leader, but one did not kowtow.

The woman followed Petrov into the room, found a wooden swivel chair, dropped her bag and sat down, the chair squeaking under her weight as she looked around openly.

Petrov immediately began to unpack, then looked at the woman and faced his team. "Major Talia Pogrebenoi, late of the victorious Red Army," he said, with a hand gesture toward the woman. "She is one of us now. I have briefed her thoroughly on our mission."

The men all stood up and looked at her.

Petrov began the introductions. "Comrade Dr. Gnedin," he said. The surgeon bowed stiffly from the waist.

"Comrade Rivitksy." The man came forward and shook her hand firmly, noting the strength in her grip.

"Comrade Bailov."

Bailov smiled awkwardly. "How is it in Moscow?"

"It's becoming summer," she said. Her voice was sweet and soft and somehow didn't fit the rest of her.

Their leader signaled them to sit. They'd been through the routine before and knew his cues.

It was Pogrebenoi's turn to speak. Though women were equal under the law and the tenets of Communism, one could not destroy centuries of cultural prejudice with edicts on paper. She knew they would be skeptical; men always were. She'd been through this sort of rite of passage many times before. "Comrade Petrov has said that I am part of you. I wish to contribute. I hope you will accept me for those things in which we are alike, not because of any—differences." She smiled at them. Her speech done, she was silent. When no one replied, she heaved a silent sigh of relief.

During the awkward pause Ezdovo arrived, carting a wooden crate marked PERISHABLES. "It's heavy," he complained good-naturedly to Petrov. "What's in it?"

Petrov's wide smile put them on the alert. "Have a look," he said.

Ezdovo used a thick-bladed knife to pry loose the top of the crate and whistled loudly when he looked inside. Slowly he raised one of the precious bottles, cupping it in his huge hands as if it were spun glass.

Gnedin jumped forward from his seat. "Pertsovka!" The others crowded around Ezdovo, who chirped at them to be careful; they ignored him and fished their own samples from the straw packing.

Bailov counted the bottles and announced, "Twenty-four."

They all looked at Petrov for an explanation. "Compliments of the Boss," he said. "Please open a bottle," he instructed Ezdovo, who used his knife to pry loose the cork with a simple twist of his wrist. Shots were poured into their mess cups. Petrov noted that the new kit issued to Pogrebenoi had been replaced by another that looked barely serviceable. The soldier in her showed itself; veterans found it hard to discard familiar equipment for new.

No toasts were offered. They sipped the powerful brown liquid, losing themselves in their own thoughts and the inner glow it created.

When enough time had passed for them to savor their drinks, Petrov stood. "Let's hear what you've learned." He looked first to Gnedin.

"Bormann and Stumpfegger killed themselves with cyanide, apparently during the escape attempt. As near as we can tell from the order of battle and where the bodies were located, they thought they were trapped between two of our units."

"Was there artillery at the time?" Pogrebenoi asked.

"Constant. And fires everywhere."

"Trauma-induced panic. They lost their composure and took the first solution they could find."

Gnedin smiled hugely, his reserve gone. "You've had medical training?"

"No. Better than that: infantry. I've seen it happen often."

"Autopsies?" Petrov interrupted, pleased with Pogrebenoi's assertiveness.

Gnedin handed him a folder. "Chenko helped me. There's no doubt about the identities or the cyanide. Stumpfegger's height made it easy."

"Disposition of the corpses?"

"Back in the ground, where we found them."

Petrov grunted acknowledgment and turned to Bailov. "I suspect your duty must have been exceptionally unpleasant." The other men laughed; Pogrebenoi's face showed no emotion.

Bailov blushed. "It wasn't what you think," he said defensively. "It was hard work."

"That's not what they're saying on the Friedrichstrasse," Ezdovo interrupted, before emptying the last of his pertsovka with a loud gulp and smacking his lips.

"You should have seen him," Rivitsky said seriously. "He worked day and night. Terrible duty; it wore him down to nothing."

"Should have sent a veteran," Ezdovo added cheerfully.

"Where did you find her?" Petrov asked.

Bailov looked with annoyance at the others. "She sought me out. She wanted Swiss identity papers and transportation to Argentina. She thinks big."

Petrov's jaw tightened with interest. "Fear. She was afraid."

"Fegelein told her he knew a secret about Hitler. He said that if Hitler found out, he would have him killed."

"Prophetic," Petrov observed. "The question is, are the two premises related?"

"Her fear was real," Bailov said.

"But she is an actress," Petrov countered. "It's her profession to be able to convince an audience."

"She begged for papers. She wants to get out of Germany. We Russians know desperation well enough to recognize it in others. It was no act."

"Did the general share the details of his secret with her?" Petrov probed.

Bailov shook his head. "I don't think she was lying. Fegelein had power, both through Himmler and his marriage. If he was afraid, that was enough to make the woman quake. When the Reich Security Police came and took him away, he telephoned Eva Braun, but she refused to intercede on his behalf."

"If Fegelein knew something, then we must suppose Himmler also knew," Petrov pointed out.

"Dead issue," Rivitsky cut in. "Himmler was captured by the English on May twenty-first. Shaved his mustache, put on an eye patch and wore a private's uniform."

When Petrov paused, Rivitsky continued the Himmler story. "He had perfect papers, absolutely pristine. The English reasoned that a poor slob of an army private would be lucky to have *any* papers, much less a perfect set, and took him into custody. Two days later the bastard killed himself with a Nazi sleeping potion."

"Ah," Petrov sighed, slumping in his seat. "If Herr Himmler knew the secret, he's beyond talking to us. Also Müller, who was next in line. No help there either," he said regretfully. "As it happens, I have preempted any further use of Müller." He paused for a moment to gather his thoughts and explain. "It was necessary. Our colleagues in the NKVD were in the process of bringing Müller over. From our perspective he knew too much about Skorzeny. Our mission requires that we leave no trace along our trail. It's unfortunate. We'll talk no more of it; Herr Müller is dead. It's tempting to dwell on what might have been, but it's what *is* that returns a profit."

They had no idea what he was talking about. "Capitalist philosophy?" Gnedin asked ironically.

"Capitalist insistence upon a return. Don't reject the capitalists out of hand. They look to the future, not the past. Such orientation has value, even to good socialists."

Shifting again, he continued, "We have to assume that Hitler's appearance must also have been drastically altered."

"Surgically?" Gnedin asked.

"No. To change appearance one need only modify certain prominent features. The mustache will be gone, the hair parted and cut differently. A broken nose, perhaps, to thicken it near the bridge. Caricaturists and criminologists learned long ago that small changes in reality can produce immense changes in perception. That's the technique of the makeup artist in the theater."

Petrov gestured with his cup for a modest portion of pertsovka. The leader of the Special Operations Group had no interest in contending with the vodka for control of his brain. The others were less judicious, he noted, but he did not mind; this evening was meant to combine celebration and business. He watched them like an analyst. Over time they had solidified into a truly cooperative and productive unit. They had learned one another's strengths and weaknesses and deferred to another's skill when conditions dictated. Gnedin had lost his intellectual haughtiness, and in so doing seemed to have increased his intellectual capacity. He had learned, as Petrov had hoped, a kind of steely pragmatism from Ezdovo's native cunning and instincts. In turn, the Siberian seemed to be adopting a more cerebral approach to problem solving, learning from the physician. Bailov had brought enthusiasm to them and an excellent blend of special skills. Rivitsky had not changed at all, which was as Petrov expected and wanted. Of all of them, he was more like his leader, and during their years together, Petrov had grown to rely on him in particular. Now he needed his instincts and intelligence as never before. They had six days to locate Brumm.

▶51 JUNE 25, 1945, 7:30 A.M.

For six days Petrov had driven his people to find something that would tell them where Brumm had gone. They had worked relentlessly, sleeping seldom, but the effort had produced nothing, and now they were running out of time. Petrov sat at an empty desk, staring at his tea. In desperation he'd tried to arrange another interrogation of Skorzeny, but though the Red Badge had whipped his own countrymen into a frenzy, and despite repeated initiatives, the Americans had refused; Skorzeny was theirs.

At midnight a few hours earlier Petrov had called the Special Operations Group together. Rivitsky could not be found, but Petrov grilled the others for four hours; when he had finished, they were no further ahead and a sense of dread was beginning to assert itself. He was about to fail. Brumm was gone and they couldn't find him. Now, pushing his cup away, he considered how to tell Stalin, but even the thought made the veins in his neck throb. There was still time, he told himself, and time is life.

Suddenly Rivitsky burst into the room, brandishing an open bottle of vodka, which he banged loudly on Petrov's desk. The other members of the group were right behind him. "Comrade," Rivitsky shouted, "I know that you are not an emotional man, but I would propose a toast. I have uncovered Hitler's secret."

The others watched nervously for a response from their leader, who calmly crossed his arms and said, "You borrow from Conan Doyle." It was a predictable response from their leader.

Rivitsky coughed to clear his throat and took a swig from the bottle.

"Is that necessary?" Petrov asked.

"Yes," Rivitsky said happily, taking another gulp. "The army has collected reams of messages that came from the bunker communications center," he went on. "I read every one of them with the idea that there might be a clue, some hint about where we could begin our search. As I read, I was impressed that Hitler's military decisions were quite sound. The problem was that the various units to which he attempted to give orders at the end simply did not exist. The German General Staff lacked the fortitude to tell him the truth; they chose to let him waste his energies on ghosts. I'm convinced that he believed, to the end, that many of his divisions were still intact and that the failure to relieve Berlin was due to the failure of his field commanders."

"A radical conclusion," Petrov observed.

"Not to my mind," Rivitsky answered. "Had such divisions existed, the outcome might have been delayed considerably, perhaps even reversed. Some of Hitler's attempts were militarily brilliant. Thus, I examined the communications for anything that would fall outside the norm—that is, for an example of shoddy military judgment, a decision that could *not* be supported by military circumstances as Hitler knew them." He paused. "And it was there. Actually," he added, "I looked past it several times before it showed itself."

The group took chairs, sat down and listened attentively. Petrov observed with satisfaction that Pogrebenoi had moved into the arc formed by the men.

Rivitsky unfolded a map and spread it on the floor for all of them to see. "Here are the Harz Mountains," he said, tapping the paper loudly with his finger. "Down here, just below the mountains, is Nordhausen, the provincial capital. Here is the site where the V-2 weapons were being mass-produced underground by slaves."

He showed them the line of the Rhine River. "The Allies were aligned thus." He marked the chart with arrows. "The Americans captured this bridge at Remagen, then their General Patton got his tanks across down here." Again he pointed to the site. "Montgomery and the British crossed up here." He marked the place. "The bunker communications record shows that Hitler and the General Staff organized a controlled withdrawal from the Rhine. Their intent was to slow down the Allied advance from the west so that the German forces could regroup on the Elbe, the next natural barrier they could depend on for a defensive advantage."

"The mountains provide an equally useful advantage," Gnedin interjected.

"Only in an academic sense," Pogrebenoi cut in. Her voice was firm and confident. "If the Germans concentrated their units in higher elevations, they could be bypassed and cut off. We did this to them at Königsberg, at Elbing and at Poznań: it was a standard tactic. By not fighting them, you don't allow *them* to fight. It conserves your resources."

Rivitsky clapped his hands together. "You see," he said happily to the others. "The major sees the tactical situation clearly. Therefore, for Hitler to have chosen to fight in the Harz would have been a stupid decision. I repeat: all of his decisions before and after this decision to make a stand here were basically sound. Hence I conclude: if all decisions before and after this were sound, then he made no mistake in this decision. He had a *reason* for doing it."

"May I interrupt?" Pogrebenoi asked. Rivitsky nodded and smiled. "Can you estimate the size of the blocking force?"

Rivitsky smiled. "Six to ten divisions. Probably not full strength. Sixty to seventy thousand men. With tanks. Beyond that we're guessing. It was not, however, a small force."

"If that's accurate, then you have additional evidence for your thesis," she said.

"Explain," Petrov said to her.

"The contours of your chart show the Harz area to be rugged terrain. Moors, wilderness, a barren wasteland. One would need no more than a fraction of seventy thousand men to block entry to it. It's the kind of terrain best suited to a small mobile force employing unorthodox tactics."

Rivitsky blinked several times as he evaluated her observation. "Of course," he said quietly. "Given the sheer defensibility of the position, the inordinately large commitment seems even more extraordinary."

"What's the point?" Gnedin asked.

"Militarily, absolutely none," Rivitsky concluded. "None whatsoever. At first I think the Americans thought they'd run into Model and his Army Group Eight. But the bunker communications show that the Americans disengaged almost immediately and veered east below the lower Harz."

"Go on," Petrov said. Rivitsky could see that their leader was absorbing the information as fast as it came.

Rivitsky returned to the chart. "Montgomery's group was on top here. Of the Americans, Bradley was in the center, Devers below. The American First Army crossed the Rhine at Remagen. Patton's Third crossed the river south of Mainz. Elements of Patton and Hodges merged near Kassel—here." He tapped the map again, then continued, "Together this spearhead drove northeast to Göttingen. Draw a line here." He did so. "This takes them directly toward the Harz Mountains, on an almost direct line toward Mount Brocken, the area's highest elevation. But when they crossed over the Leine River, they hit German resistance, and with hardly a pause they swerved toward Nordhausen and Halle." Rivitsky took a deep breath. "Meanwhile, the U.S. Ninth Army skirted north of the Harz and drove up to Magdeburg on the Elbe. General Model was surrounded in the Ruhr, and those troops that had been gathered in the Harz Mountains on Hitler's order were left alone with no enemy to fight. Eventually the Americans engaged them, but not until after their strategic goals were secured, and even then it was a token battle. By and large the mountains were left unpenetrated. After all, the Americans were looking toward Berlin, not the Harz Mountains."

"Thus," Petrov said, "the Harz *Festung* remained inviolate. I accept this analysis. If we believe he had control of his faculties—and we, more than anyone else, know that he did—we must accept that this move was made for a nonmilitary reason."

"Even so," Pogrebenoi pointed out, "this does not rule out a simple error, however gross. Every commander makes such mistakes; it's unavoidable."

"I submit," Rivitsky countered, "that there are errors and *errors*. You understand? One miscalculates the enemy's strength, the weather goes bad, one takes a wrong turn or overextends. But look at the map; the mountain range sticks up like a monument. No commander could err in concentrating his forces there. It requires premeditation or monumental stupidity."

Petrov leaned over the map. "A blockade ordered that the enemy can easily outflank. What was the level of resistance along the route in the foothills?"

"Virtually none," Rivitsky said. "Scattered small units. The Americans drove the remaining two hundred and fifty kilometers to the Elbe in less than ten days—an unmolested dash."

Who would notice? Petrov asked himself. Fronts collapsing east and west, orders going out of the bunker, battle reports flooding in. Rivitsky had hit on the key they were searching for.

There was a pause, and then the leader of the SOG spoke slowly, choosing his words with care. "I told you that I was responsible for Müller's death. But my time with him was not without compensation. Before he died, I recovered the Gestapo's records on Skorzeny's personnel—all of them." They waited anxiously. "Colonel Brumm, I learned, was raised in the area once known as the Melicobus."

"That's a new one," Bailov said, making a face.

Petrov stepped on the chart and pointed with his toe. "The area is more commonly known as the Harz Mountains."

There was silence as the implications of this information were digested by the team. Finally Ezdovo raised his cup and grinned at his leader. "Now we hunt for real."

An hour later Petrov called Stalin with the news. The premier listened, then grunted. "Good. Now go get them," and hung up abruptly. Petrov was jubilant; the Special Operations Group and its mission were still alive.

▶52 JULY 5, 1945, 5:10 P.M.

At their elevation the summer was comfortable. It rained infrequently, a sign, Brumm knew, that autumn and snow would come early. Since the incursion of the Jews they had established around-the-clock security and constructed an elaborate minefield near the entrance. It was an intricate maze, an art Beard had learned over many years under a wide range of conditions. To conceal their presence, there were several different routes through the mines, and a different trail was used each day to allow the grasses in the area to replenish themselves. A sentry was stationed in a cuplike rocky outcrop, which provided a full field of fire over the valley's southern end.

With the exception of Herr Wolf's unpredictable ebbs in mood, it was a quiet and pressureless time. A curious bond had formed between the Jewish woman and Herr Wolf, and while most of the time he avoided referring to her as his niece, the relationship made Brumm uncomfortable. The woman was with Herr Wolf at all times; she was the only one of them allowed into his sleeping quarters, she served his meals and she listened to his constant ramblings. If nothing else, she kept him busy and out of the way of the others; from that view her presence was positive. Often the two perched on the rocks near the dam. From time to time Brumm and the others eavesdropped, but Herr Wolf's speeches were not designed for listeners.

Only once had Brumm attempted to talk to him about the future. "We need to discuss the details of what happens next," the colonel told him. It was after midnight, and all the women had retired to their various bedrooms.

Herr Wolf flicked his hand at Brumm. "You take care of it."

"I want to be sure that you understand everything."

"I trust you," Herr Wolf said. He stared at the ground for a while. "Perhaps we should reconsider and remain here," he said finally.

"Neither safe nor practical."

"Discovery by the Jews was an accident, an improbable event."

"For the Jews it was improbable. Not for the Russians. They will come. It will take time, but they'll be here."

Herr Wolf looked at the officer. "A shame. It's so peaceful here. I'd planned to retire, Brumm—did you know that?—to Salzburg. I had no desire for a lifetime of public service. There would have been a new Führer in time. I wanted something like this. A place with privacy, time to read and think, time to plan."

"You will have your refuge eventually, but this isn't it."

"I think I'm too tired to run again."

"You're much stronger now. Your color is back. If the Russians begin to breathe down our necks, you'll have no trouble summoning the adrenaline."

"My mind is tired. And my heart. The Third Reich has crumbled to dust. So much promise, so many years of my life. Nothing remains."

"As long as you live, the Third Reich survives."

Herr Wolf smiled warmly. "Thank you, Colonel. You are considerate to an old man."

"Not old."

"In life's measures, I'm ancient," Herr Wolf said mysteriously.

Brumm didn't reply. He wanted to discuss the plan, not provoke meaningless self-pity. The singular lesson of his own life had been that as long as you could draw breath there was hope. Thus ended the only attempt to discuss the plan before it was implemented. Herr Wolf made it quite clear; it was on Brumm's shoulders.

With the absence of rainfall, the streams in the valley shrank to mere trickles, and Brumm walked up and down the whole area studying the situation. Even if they wanted to remain, the valley wouldn't allow it. Three or four people might find a way to survive without depleting the food supply, but with ten of them it was out of the question. With luck and discipline they'd be able to make it until spring, but no longer.

At this time of day there were few chores to be done. On a bed of fine gravel in the widest part of the largest stream, Beard and the Valkyries practiced hand-to-hand combat. The women seemed leaner, their teenage softness transformed by a Spartan diet and rigorous training into the more mature lines of adult women. With pleasure Brumm watched them exercise as they deftly parried one another's attacks with growing confidence. After a while they broke off training and attacked Beard en masse, wrestling him into one of the last deep pools in the shrinking brook. Never had a sergeant major had such a relationship with his "men," Brumm thought. It was a crazy setup.

Waller came up out of the clear pool, sat beside Brumm and wrung the moisture from her long hair. She was deeply tanned, and the cold water seemed to make her flesh glow. "Someday you'll dunk one of us when we don't want to play," he said.

"That time is already here," she said. The look on her face was peculiar, almost challenging. Beard was standing in the water, waist-deep, his arms crossed, smiling. The other Valkyries were nowhere in sight.

When he understood, Brumm rolled away instinctively, pulling a knee under him for support, but they were on him too quickly. His first instinct was to laugh, but suddenly his arm was locked viselike against his spine, the pain shot through his elbow and his smile evaporated. It took the girls only a few seconds to subdue him and dump him unceremoniously into the creek; when it was done, they stood on the bank and cheered loudly.

Waller remained on the bank with the others. "You see?" she called out briskly.

"Unfair advantage. Ambush."

"One man's disadvantage is another man's advantage," she replied.

"Spoken like a soldier." He laughed.

For a while the group lingered on the bank, enjoying the sun. When they finally drifted away, Waller waded into the water with him and slid her arms around his waist. "Does the SS manual forbid mingling in the daylight?"

"Only when the urge to follow regulations is stronger than another urge."

"I hate rules," she said, pulling him down to her.

Later Beard sat on the stream bank flicking smooth pebbles into the current. How far would the flow carry the pebble before it hit bottom? He picked a target and adjusted each shot, noting that while the strength of the water was constant, the weight and shape of each rock changed the trajectories. Even so, by concentration he found that he could cluster the pebbles near his target.

Night was crawling into the valley, and shadows from the pines near Stone Cave were already climbing the near bank. Close by Brumm talked quietly with two of the girls. When they left, he joined his friend. "I'm too old to be a garrison soldier," Beard said to him forlornly. "I can't get used to all this. I've tried, but it's no good. I don't have the patience."

"You're just feeling sorry for yourself, my friend. How many other men your age have so many sensuous young consorts at their disposal?" Brumm teased. "Besides, our Valkyries still have a lot to learn from you."

"I know," Beard sighed. "I tell myself that every day. They work hard; they learn fast; they follow orders."

"It's important. We'll need them when we leave here."

"Leave?" Beard asked. "I don't believe we'll ever leave here. It's bigger than a tomb, but we can't leave it. It's a goddamned tomb." He thought for a moment, then looked at his colonel. "Besides, where would we go?"

"Is that what's bothering you?"

"Partly," Rau admitted. "Not knowing what's going on out there is also a problem." He motioned toward the rim of the canyon. "We've been beaten again. Will it be like after the last war? No jobs, no army, no money, no food? I want to know what's happening to the German people and to our country."

"It's all finished, my friend. There's nothing left of what you and I knew. The Allies and the Russians are carving her up. If they leave us alone, they fear we'll rise again. The Russians will keep every centimeter of territory they've taken as a buffer against the West. Germany disappears, and in its place there'll be a no-man's-land between the Russians and the West. That's the reality. Perhaps it's better in the long run."

"Better that Germany be destroyed? I can't accept that."

"Nor can I, but then we're not being asked. Our days of choosing are ended." Brumm leaned back and stared up at the first stars of evening twilight. "These mountains have always cleared my head and allowed me to think clearly. Our Germany is not a simple physical and political entity. It's a spiritual condition, a concept; at least that's how I think of it. The German character is one of implicit trust. We trust our leaders, we trust our abilities, we trust in what we think is a God-given destiny for greatness. It's always been so, even when we were tribes in caves. We trust better than any people, I think. But what we lack is confidence. We bemoan every small failure as a large one, and we insist on perfection. That's our weakness. When we lose confidence, we lose control. Our Teutonic blood rises and our emotions overrule our minds. The world sees us as calculating, cold-blooded people—and we are, outwardly. Inside we're a jelly of seething emotions, always on the verge of exposing our Romantic spirits. We can't catch one fish; we must catch them all. It's the German way. If the abolition of the German nation is necessary to protect us from ourselves, then so be it. Losers can't complain or write history books."

Beard went back to tossing pebbles into the water. Birds fluttered overhead, their wings cutting the still air. "Günter?" he asked tentatively at last.

"Umm?"

"You're still full of shit." They both laughed.

From upstream they heard Herr Wolf's voice as he and the Jewish woman emerged from a thicket, walking at a brisk pace as he talked and she listened intently. The time since the bunker had worked a miracle on his health. His arm was regaining strength and mobility, his leg no longer dragged behind him and he acted younger. The elimination of his frequent "vitamin" injections and living close to nature had done wonders. Mentally he also seemed to be more his old self, gaining in confidence and arrogance each day. He had taken to rising at noon and breakfasting with his female companion. In the afternoons they would sit by the radio listening to hourly broadcasts, to which he offered a running commentary while she scratched notes on a pad of paper as if she were his secretary. They ate a light lunch late in the afternoon, after which they always took a long walk. Then they would disappear into their room for a nap, emerging again around midnight for a heavy meal, then sitting around the fire. Herr Wolf could be a superb conversationalist when he chose, but more often than not he preferred to monopolize the conversation, and the woman seemed content to listen.

Brumm had observed that while Herr Wolf had a prodigious recall for facts and seemingly endless tables of obscure statistics, he often strung them together in ways that made no sense. Here was a man with acutely developed intellectual tools, but with no perspective to apply them. But Brumm remained silent in the face of Wolf's preposterous sermons; peace within the group was more important than winning minor verbal skirmishes.

Of all the inhabitants in their small and isolated community, Brumm was most intrigued by Razia Scheel, who remained an enigma. She was never far from Herr Wolf's side and seemed to cater to his every desire, often reacting before he spoke, as if she could read his mind. Brumm considered Skorzeny's theory that after the immediate danger had passed, hostages tended to identify with their captors. Over the course of many missions kidnapping had become almost routine, and in the Friedenthal the psychological profile of hostages was a much discussed topic over beer and schnapps. Every commando unit returning from an operation was thoroughly questioned on the behavior of prisoners, no matter how brief such incarcerations might have been. Radl, Skorzeny's executive officer, acting on his commander's directions, had even commissioned studies by a noted Austrian psychiatrist on various aspects of hostage psychology. Generally their interest in the phenomenon was more practical than scholarly. Each man understood that in certain circumstances a hostage could become an ally, and they were taught to use this knowledge to their practical advantage.

But even knowing this, Brumm still found the woman's behavior remarkable and unexpected. After so many years in a concentration camp, and as a subject of medical experiments, it seemed that she would be demented, a raging maniac waiting for the first opportunity to strike. Yet no such motive was apparent; in a matter of minutes she had been changed from an avenger to a disciple. It was such a fast and complete reversal that it alarmed Brumm, and professionally he did not trust what he couldn't understand. Even more amazing was the fact that she seemed genuinely fond of Herr Wolf and was his gentle but firm protector.

Even in small societies there are pecking orders, and while Razia Scheel had no formal status in theirs, she was in fact the slave of the master, and her proximity to him gave her a certain degree of power and leverage. She flashed her black animallike eyes at all of them but Herr Wolf, who demonstrated no visible affection for her.

The greatest mystery of all was that of Herr Wolf's sex life. At first Brumm had been shocked by the girls' explicit talk about sex; they were as casual about it as soldiers. Early on, Gretchen had told him that the others talked often about the possibility of servicing the Führer's sexual needs—some small wagers were even made—but the object of their speculation showed no inclination to accept their overtures, no matter how overt. Razia Scheel, who was always close by his side, took such advances with seething anger, hissing at the others like an animal defending its territory. Herr Wolf laughed at such displays, and warned the girls that they should be careful of his niece's "protective" ways. Eventually the fantasy had died, and in its place grew a resentment that the leader of the Third Reich would share his bed with a Jew. It was not clear who had a hold on whom, but it was apparent that the bond was a powerful one.

In Berlin it had been well known that Adolf Hitler relished the company of comely young women. Early in his public career he had seldom been seen in public without one of Germany's most beautiful females as his companion. By and large his tastes had been for blond full-busted types with narrow waists and powerful legs. Later there had been Eva Braun, a young, empty-headed Bavarian photographer's assistant about whom sexual legends abounded. Several of Skorzeny's officers claimed to have seen photographs of her in the buff, and occasionally in the intimate embrace of other living creatures, some of them animal. With such a past as Hitler's, the apparent abstinence of Herr Wolf seemed out of character.

The room shared by Herr Wolf and the woman was off limits to all the others, but sometimes passersby caught whiffs of unpleasant odors from the interior and wondered what the two were up to when they were alone.

Now Brumm watched as the unlikely pair approached, arm in arm. Before reaching them, the woman glanced at Brumm, then disappeared into the building, leaving the three men alone.

"Good evening, Sergeant Major Rau," Herr Wolf said pleasantly. He always addressed Beard formally by his rank and name and had said repeatedly that if his generals had been as good as his sergeants, they'd all still be in Berlin. "Would you be so kind as to allow the colonel and me to discuss a private matter?" Beard nodded, rose stiffly, brushed the dust off himself and followed the woman into the dwelling.

Above them a small aircraft droned southeast, flying low over the next valley. At the sound they backed instinctively into the evening shadows. Brumm looked up, trying to identify the plane, while Herr Wolf stared straight ahead, trembling.

▶53 JULY 5, 1945, 9:40 P.M.

After the aircraft had passed, it took several minutes for Herr Wolf to compose himself. When he spoke again the confidence had left his voice, and as he talked he kept staring up at the sky. "I've heard aircraft several times in the past few days," he said nervously. "Are they searching for us?"

"No. Searchers employ a geometric pattern to crisscross an area methodically. There's no cause for alarm when they fly from one horizon to the other."

"I think they are searching for us."

"If they begin a search for us, we'll know it."

"I have instincts for these things," Herr Wolf argued.

Brumm ignored this. "You wanted to see me."

"Yes," Herr Wolf said nervously. He was perspiring heavily even though it was a cool evening. "I'm healthier, but my nerves are not fully recovered," he went on, reading Brumm's face. "I need more time, Colonel, to mend from my ordeal."

"There's plenty of time; I've told you that. When winter comes, it will seal us in here. We'll have until spring to rest and prepare."

"Our supplies are adequate?"

"With discipline they're adequate, but not plentiful. The natural resources of this valley will hold us through fall, but by spring it won't be able to sustain us without irreparable damage. We didn't plan for this many people."

"It was your decision to increase the scope of this operation," Herr Wolf reminded him gruffly.

Again Brumm ignored the comment. "After the snow settles in, I'll go outside to pick up our papers and to try to get a feel for what's going on. Waller will accompany me; the mission will require several days—perhaps as many as fourteen."

"Two weeks?" Herr Wolf's eyes were wide.

"There's no need for concern. Beard will be here. We're safest in winter. The snow will hinder any wanderers. You'll be perfectly secure during my absence."

"You're sure this is necessary?"

"Yes. But it's premature to talk about this, and in any case it isn't what you wanted to see me about."

"Correct. Actually . . . it's about my niece."

"What about her?"

"When we leave, we'll take Geli with us." Herr Wolf stiffened in anticipation of Brumm's reaction.

"Out of the question. We're not prepared for that."

"But you have the others," Wolf whined. "I want my niece to remain with me. It seems fair that we should all have someone."

"No," Brumm said emphatically. "She cannot leave this valley."

Herr Wolf clasped his arms behind his back and looked at the sky, swallowing loudly. "Fine. I understand that. Perhaps then we should give serious consideration to staying here permanently. It's quite adequate for my needs."

"We've just been through that. It's not possible. We are too many, and eventually the Russians will come."

"Then perhaps we should reduce the size of the group. In a war some must be willing to sacrifice."

"We're no longer at war," Brumm answered. It was unnerving; he was negotiating with a child.

"A technicality. We were at war long before the first shot was fired, and we will remain at war as long as I am alive."

"To the world you are dead. You died April thirtieth, and your body was burned. The war is over. We are no longer soldiers, only criminals. Our mission is solely to save our skins."

"But what about Geli?"

"You yourself suggested that we reduce the size of our contingent. We could begin with her."

Herr Wolf backed away, his mouth open. "I reject it, Colonel. Barbaric. You know my views on officers who think and act theoretically. You are only theorizing that the woman will not fit in."

"Theory, hell," Brumm snapped. "I'm here because of pragmatism. That's what this is all about."

"Please control yourself, Colonel. There's no need to profane an intelligent conversation because you lack adequate means of expression."

Brumm felt his frustration rising. "I remind you that she is a Jew."

Herr Wolf stepped forward and wiggled a finger at him. "You are wrong. You have no expertise in such matters. She thinks she is a Jew; that much is true. She even looks like a Jew—to all but the expert eye. But I have tested her thoroughly, and I can assure you that she is Aryan. It is quite possible that the Jews stole her from her Aryan parents when she was a baby; in any case, there is no Jewish blood flowing in her veins. She's the purest of pure. I know my own niece."

"Her parents were Jews. Her husband was a Jew. She admits this."

"She has no parents."

"Because they were eliminated in the camps."

"No proof. And there was no husband. She is a virgin."

Brumm stared at Herr Wolf and shook his head slowly. "She is not going with us."

"But she cannot describe her parents—not a single feature, not a single memory. I remember my mother as if she were standing here now. A child remembers such details, no matter what happens. They are etched in the subconscious. I conclude that she was kidnapped by Jews."

"I will not take her with us," Brumm said slowly, emphasizing every word.

Herr Wolf stepped away as if to leave, then pivoted to face the colonel. His voice changed and the crispness of authority returned. "I see. You will indulge me when it is time and inform me so that I can prepare her." He turned and went inside.

Brumm sank to the ground and stared up at the stars. This was the second time since their arrival that Herr Wolf had pressed an issue with the colonel. Where was all this leading?

▶54 JULY 6, 1945, 3:00 P.M.

Rivitsky complained incessantly from the time they left Berlin, but because his traveling companion was Petrov, he got little sympathy. They were now housed in a small farmhouse near Nordhausen. Two weeks ago they had driven from Berlin to their new headquarters in two lorries, carrying their records, supplies and field gear. Petrov had displayed interest in the sights along the way and made frequent side journeys, which extended their trip by several days when it should have taken less than one.

Russia's victorious army, its mission completed, was lethargic, a lazy giant sprawled across the countryside in a state of relaxation. Few checkpoints were manned; not a single bridge was guarded. Russians make poor garrison troops, Petrov told himself. Near Dessau they passed cavalrymen riding naked, bashing one another with long sticks. Soviet horses grazed near the burned-out wreckage of a dozen Tiger tanks.

It was a cool afternoon, and Rivitsky stoked a fire in the wood stove. "The Americans may be a problem for us," he said.

"I don't think so. Germany will be partitioned according to an agreement reached some time ago. Only Bad Harzburg itself will be in the American zone. Besides, the Americans are still aglow with friendship for their Soviet brothers. If we encounter some who don't share this feeling, we have plenty of vodka to help them change their thinking."

"They will be suspicious of our presence."

"In our own zone? They are the interlopers here. I've also seen to it that Moscow has ordered small units of our comrades to be deployed all around here for a variety of reasons, most of them pointless other than to provide camouflage. One more group won't attract any attention."

"Still," Rivitsky replied. "I'm nervous about it."

"To be expected. We know what we're after; the rest of the world doesn't. You and I have to keep our wits."

"How soon before winter sets in?"

"It will be early up there, as in Russia. The Harz will be under snow before much longer. If they're still in there, they'll have to sit out the winter; in fact, that's probably been their plan from the start. It will give us some time to plan and reconnoiter. If they're in there, the winter is to our advantage, and it will give them a false sense of security."

"We could send Ezdovo into the interior of the upper Harz."

"Then what? I want to take them at the time and under the conditions I dictate; I want him alive."

"Not likely. These Nazis have a penchant for cyanide."

"The littler dogs, yes, but not this monster. He's with Brumm. Right now they're probably safely dug in. It's not like Hitler to dwell on the negative. He'll be feeling invincible; after all, Brumm snatched him from the jaws of death."

"Then they'll fight."

"Only if we force them to. They want to disappear. They'll try to keep a low profile and slip quietly away. Ezdovo and I have discussed this at length. It's an exercise in wolf hunting. There are two approaches: Drive him into the open or trap him. Ezdovo's people use dogs to pick up the scent and push the animal. Or sometimes they butcher a caribou and drag its carcass through the forest. Then the hunter conceals himself and waits. To catch a wolf, one must have patience and nerves. The best hunters attempt to trap a particular beast. They learn his track and trace his movements and habits. Then, when they know him and can predict his pattern, they lay the trap based on what he will do. That is my intent."

"I don't follow you."

"Ezdovo and Pogrebenoi will operate from a small airfield near Magdeburg. We have carefully constructed a search grid overlaying our mountain charts. They will fly as the weather permits and radio their observations to us in code after every flight."

"Aerial reconnaissance?"

"Precisely. It's too big an area to cover on foot. We don't have the manpower and it would not be in our interest to try to mobilize it. Besides, the German colonel has an advantage in there, I suspect. Ezdovo and Pogrebenoi will be our eyes from above."

"When we have their location, we move in."

"No. I simply want to confirm their location." Petrov spread a chart on the table. "See the topography? The Harz is this jut off the central German highlands. If they're in the Harz, they can't stay there; they have to get out of the country. When they move they'll take a route through the most isolated regions of the country. They can't go into France or Czechoslovakia. They have no choice but to move south to Austria or Switzerland, and then on to Italy. I have evidence to support this deduction."

"They might get brazen—grab an automobile and drive south. Or perhaps they have one stashed?"

Petrov considered the idea. "Unlikely. If they were stopped, there'd be no option but to fight. By staying in the wilds they can evade confrontation. Remember, the wolf generally prefers to run away from trouble."

"So the trap will be laid in Italy?"

"Probably," Petrov replied. "I believe they'll wind their way south from the Harz to the Frankenwald, then turn southeast along the spine of the Fränkische Alb, then on to the Alps along the Austrian border. There are four crossing points: the Brenner Pass, south of Innsbruck; the Reschen-Scheideck Pass, near the Austro-Swiss frontier; the Ötztaler Pass between the first and the second; and farther east the Nabfeld Pass." He pointed to each as he spoke.

"All this presupposes that they are in the Harz," Rivitsky reminded him.

"On that count I have confidence that Bailov and the doctor will provide us with a definitive answer. He's in there; they'll confirm it." Petrov folded his map with a snap.

►**55** JULY 9, 1945, 11:00 A.M.

Gnedin entered the town of Bad Harzburg just before noon on July 9. He carried false German identity papers and Russian diplomatic credentials to fall back on if necessary. Bailov arrived the next afternoon.

Within an hour of arriving, Gnedin made contact with the town's two physicians and told them he was a medical corps veteran from the Eastern front. His unit had been routed near Katowice. The Russians had executed the wounded and pressed him and his medical orderlies into a slave unit. He alone had escaped and made his way home to Dortmund, only to discover that his wife and three children had perished in the bombing raids. He had been wandering aimlessly for weeks before finally finding himself in Bad Harzburg. It occurred to him, he told them, that Germany needed his medical training more than ever. The two doctors, both elderly veterans of the Great War, made him welcome and offered him the extra room in their shared surgery.

By Petrov's design, Bailov's insertion was far less precise. His papers showed him to be a Wehrmacht corporal who had been processed by the Americans and released. He was one of thousands of veterans and refugees afoot in the countryside, so it was difficult to get established in a village where they wanted no more people unless they brought some special skills with them. Where Gnedin was accepted almost immediately, Bailov was not. No matter where he tried, or how often, there was no work to be had, at least nothing steady with regular pay, either in cash or food. While he sought a base from which to work he lived in the forests near the village, taking small game for sustenance. Having no luck in the town, he foraged from farm to farm, finally finding a hovel with a woman and her two young girls. She was older than he, perhaps thirty-five, and tired. She told him he could have shelter, but there was no food to share; they had been reduced to eating pine needles. With typical optimism and hard work, Bailov soon changed their fortunes. He produced wild meat, which he'd trapped in the forest. In a matter of days he gave their lives back to them and his presence at the homestead was accepted, with no questions asked about how long he might remain.

The woman was plain, but not unattractive. Underneath her simple veneer Bailov thought he detected an inner toughness, even a hint of danger, to which he was attracted. After the first week she came to his room during the night; she stood at the foot of his bed and stared at him. "My name is Janna," she said, dropping her robe and crawling under the covers with him. Every night thereafter they slept together. The two girls, with encouragement from the woman, began to address Bailov as "Father," and while he was sure it was a trick of his imagination, they seemed to be drawn more to him than to their mother. It was a feeling that made him uneasy.

Gnedin was patient in gathering information. To his surprise, he found both pleasure and challenge in fulfilling the medical needs of the villagers, and in a short time his gentle ways earned him their acceptance.

There was no American occupation force in Bad Harzburg; this honor was saved for the larger communities nearby. But the Harzburgers knew that eventually the Americans would arrive, and a town meeting was called to discuss their political situation. The Bürgermeister, a short man with thick silver hair and a congenital harelip, was nervous as the meeting convened. "Hitler is dead," he stammered. "The war is lost. We no longer control our own destiny."

"We will be occupied?" an elderly man asked from an ancient wheelchair.

"In time."

"Russians or Americans?"

"I think it will be the Americans. The Russians are in all the villages on the other side of the upper Harz. If they were coming, they'd already be here. But if you're afraid, you should leave now and go west. If the Russians come, there'll be no leaving."

"How far west?" the old man asked.

The mayor's anguish was apparent; he did not like the responsibility for such grave decisions. He was a simple man, happy to have the job when it was ceremonial, perplexed when true leadership was demanded.

Gnedin intervened, and the villagers listened attentively. "Perhaps I can help," he said. "I've been out there."

"Herr Doktor," the mayor said, relieved to have somebody else on the spot.

"Go west past Hanover and it should be all right."

"How do you know?" an old woman demanded.

"I don't," Gnedin said quietly. "Not with certainty. But I've seen where the Americans are massed, and I believe there are too many of them west of Hanover for the Ivans to displace them." He knew for certain that Bad Harzburg would be safe, but it helped to have the villagers uneasy; their collective sense of guilt and the fear that stemmed from it could work to his advantage.

"What we need to do," Gnedin went on, "is to prepare by purging the Nazis."

"I'm not a party member," the Bürgermeister said defensively.

"You didn't do anything about them, either," someone shouted from the back of the narrow and drafty hall.

The mayor turned bright red. "Go ahead, blame me. What did *you* do? What would you have done differently if you were in my shoes?" He shook his finger angrily and mopped the sweat from his face. The villagers were silent, and the mayor calmed himself with a gulp of beer from a brown ceramic stein. "You know who they were. The Blockleiters are gone, along with the Zellenleiter and his family. I say look into ourselves for truth. Things happened here. Search your own soul now, before the Russians help you do it."

"His Honor makes good sense," Gnedin added. "I've seen the Ivans close up. They are not monsters—" Several people gasped. "—but they do not share our culture or our ideals. If there is anything to link you to the Nazis, I'd advise you to go west and to do so quickly. The Americans will be more forgiving." He liked seeing the fear in their eyes.

The next day more than half a dozen families and several individuals headed west from Bad Harzburg.

▶**56** JULY 24, 1945, 7:20 P.M.

Surely the Russians had access to duplicate records from the Friedenthal, Valentine thought. If there were no other certainty in life, there was the guarantee that German bureaucracy was committed to redundancy. If the Germans could have reproduced the Rhine so as to have one in reserve for the day when the first dried up, they would have done so. If one was good, two was better; twice two or more was best. It was their way.

The evening air was cool as Valentine drove southeast toward Würzburg and Nuremberg. A sergeant he'd befriended in the Frankfurt noncommissioned officers club, an open-air affair under a circus tent, had stuffed a large satchel with salami sandwiches, cans of Spam, chocolate bars, three cartons of Lucky Strikes, apples, a small bag of walnuts, radishes in waxed paper, a tin of crackers, disposable containers of salt, sugar and pepper, a wheel of white cheese, four bottles of dark red Hungarian wine, several packages of nylon stockings and a large unlabeled bottle of brandy. On the black market Valentine knew that all this represented a small fortune. Carefully bargained with the right people, these items could produce a great deal of information. He would use his hoard wisely; it was in his blood to trade well. The satchel sat on the seat beside him in the jeep.

As he drove, Valentine took measured swigs of brandy to warm himself. By autobahn the trip to Nuremberg was two hundred and forty kilometers; at the jeep's top speed it would take more than three hours. It would be a moonless night and there were no other vehicles on the road. In the back of his mind a voice was urging him to hurry, but he disregarded it and kept a less risky pace.

At a place where the highway crossed over the Main River east of Würzburg, Valentine jumped up onto the retaining wall and urinated into the river below. While he knew Germany well, he still felt chilled by it. He had sensed what was happening in the thirties and his feelings had been borne out. Perhaps it was always there, he thought; something old and evil resided in the land, and the Germans seemed to take nourishment from it. His reason told him that it was wrong to condemn an entire people, but history showed the Germans to be willing followers of every two-bit rabble-rouser who came along each generation. Like their countryside, they seemed to be marked by extremes; there was no center of gravity, no natural social equilibrium. Such thoughts bothered him because, despite their history, Beau Valentine liked Germans.

The meeting between Skorzeny and the Russians was a tough one to figure. If they had Skorzeny's records, why would they have gone to the trouble of flying to Austria to question him? To be sure, Skorzeny had operated on the Russian front, but his missions there had been unsuccessful in comparison with his exploits in the west. Skorzeny's headquarters had been in Friedenthal, only twenty miles north of Berlin. If there were no records there, certainly there would be copies somewhere in the Nazi paper labyrinth. It was only a matter of time until somebody stumbled across them. The officials at Oberursel had been agog with stories of Russian activities. Suddenly the Reds had replaced the Nazis as America's bogeymen; by the hour, new horror stories were traded. From the reports of various intelligence units Valentine had learned that caches of Nazi records were being discovered regularly throughout the country, and that a race was on between the Russians and Americans to see who could find the most. Of course, neither side was telling the other what it had. He could have predicted both the finds and the competition.

After his discussion with Skorzeny, Valentine had used his army contacts to initiate some fast inquiries into the whereabouts of Skorzeny's records. He had the name Günter Brumm, but needed more. He'd spent weeks talking to G-2 types and gleaning the transcripts of the German commando's many interrogations, sifting for information. Precisely what he was interested in he couldn't say. It wasn't something he could verbalize yet. The urge to investigate was more in his guts than in his brains, but he knew that invariably the one was linked with the other. In a sheaf of German notes he found several references to the satellite training center run by Skorzeny's group near Munich. Based on this he'd asked the OSS office in Switzerland to trace the records, and finally they'd reported that the records of Skorzeny's Friedenthal training facility had been shipped to Nuremberg. They also wanted to know what he was doing. Valentine hung up without giving them an answer. In part he didn't know how to answer his superiors, but more important, it was none of their business. They'd sent him into Germany to snoop, and that's what he was going to do, without their interference. Maybe the unit's records wouldn't reveal anything, but he had to see for himself.

He reached Nuremberg at dawn. The city had been flattened by bombs, and in the final assault by the Seventh Army in the middle of April it had taken several days of house-to-house fighting to dislodge the fanatics. In the process the city was almost completely demolished. Valentine knew all this from written reports, but as he drove through the destruction he decided that words didn't adequately relate the reality of what had happened. Some clean-up efforts had begun; even so, few buildings were still standing. Entire blocks had been razed and reconstituted as piles that from afar looked like pointed breasts. Some civilians were already lined up at American food-distribution centers, while others were gathering to begin the day's attack on the rubble.

The Swiss office had directed Valentine to search out a G-2 section charged with beginning the long process of cataloging and reading German documents, a process that he guessed might take decades to complete. The group was barracked in an estate east of the city, and he was not surprised to find them waiting for him. The records he sought were in cartons and had been fetched from a storage area to a room for his own use. As he perused the papers a thin WAC lieutenant with acne scars on her neck and chin brought him a breakfast of dark toast and powdered eggs. He picked at the food while examining the boxes and their contents.

The WAC sat on a nearby table, watching him, working on her nails with a small file as he ate. "None of this has been cataloged, though we've been through the whole batch once already to get a rough feel for what we've got," she said. Her perfume smelled of lilacs, and the scent caused him to look up. "You ever feel an urge to get a rough feel for what you've got?" she asked. Her head was tilted at an angle, and her lips were slightly open. She had stopped filing, anticipating some kind of response to her overture.

"Personnel records or operational stuff?" he asked as he crunched on a mouthful of toast.

She looked disappointed. "Mostly personnel folders, office memos. Nothing terribly exciting." She paused. "This whole place lacks excitement, if you know what I mean. The guys here are all creeps."

She was persistent; he'd give her that. "How much?" he asked.

"Free," she said, sliding down from the table and taking a step toward him.

"I mean how many records?"

Her eyes narrowed. What did she have to do to get through to this guy, stick an asset in his face? "We're not certain. Our notes vary; probably somewhere between two and three thousand folders."

He whistled. "Is there an index?"

"A start on one. Big categories only, but it might help. You're not going to try to go through the whole mess in one sitting?"

"Depends on how long I can last."

She giggled. "I've been wondering the same thing. My name's Angie."

He looked at her. "Sorry, Angie, but this is one of those duty-calls situations."

"Sure," she said. "I've heard that before." She turned to leave the room, her face beginning to turn red, but he stopped her. "I'm going to have to take a break sometime. Where you going to be?" A guy had to cut himself some slack once in a while.

"Third floor. Fourth door on the right. Don't worry about any- thing. We're real informal around here. See you later," she said happily as she closed the door.

It was odd how women were attracted to him, Valentine thought. Homely ones, beautiful ones. The homely ones were so desperate for affection that they'd do anything for it but didn't often get the op- portunity. The beautiful ones put men off and were just as lonely as those at the other end of the scale. It made him sad.

He decided to concentrate on the officers of Skorzeny's organi- zation so that he could develop a sense of the chain of command and of the organization's structure. Before examining the papers, he'd wondered if the chore might take days; he was surprised to find that it required less than four hours. As it turned out, all three cartons with officers' records were together and neatly organized. Of the upper echelon, only Brumm's record was missing, and according to the or- ganization chart that he worked up as he went along, its absence was glaring. In well-organized special units, such holes didn't happen by accident. He also discovered during his research that Radl and Skor- zeny had attended the University of Vienna together, and filed this fact away in his memory for future reference.

Valentine ticked off the options. The Brumm folder was lost; it never existed; it had been stolen; it had been deliberately removed. To know which was correct, he needed a phone. There seemed to be nobody around in the administrative section that G-2 had established in a ballroom off the main entrance. He needed access to some ma- terials but couldn't find them. He'd have to ask for help from the WAC lieutenant.

He walked slowly up the stairs, breathing hard from the exertion. When he knocked, her voice told him to enter. When he saw her on the bed wearing only a flesh-colored slip, he knew what the price of her cooperation was going to be and began undressing. She lay propped up on several fat pillows with her hands behind her head, smiling. "Well, well, it's about time; I thought you were going to pass me up."

"Need your help," he admitted.

It was evening before she finished with him. Afterward, she dressed and took him downstairs to help him get what he needed. She was effervescent in the afterglow; he was tired. While she watched he sent a coded message to the Swiss office over the military teletype. When he finished she tried to induce him to return to her room, but the clatter of the teletype interrupted her and she turned to tend to the machine. The message was not for him, but he was just as glad as if it had been.

Rubbing herself against him, Angie encouraged him to come back soon. "Next time we won't have to screw around with the preliminaries," she shouted after him as he trotted down the stairs toward his jeep.

It occurred to him that this whole thing might be a wild-goose chase and that a wiser man than he would take the WAC back to bed and see to her contentment.

▶57 AUGUST 1, 1945, 3:00 P.M.

The Reverend Cosmo Nefiore inhaled his thin black Portuguese cigar and considered pouring another cup of Cypriot tea for himself. Farraro of the Directorate of Humanitarian Liaison and Earthly Works had sent a note ordering him to an afternoon meeting. Now he found himself alone—"cooling his heels" was the way his American colleagues would put it—in a small building sitting by itself in the Garden of Saint Thomas, one of the many botanical displays inside the Vatican's compact one hundred acres.

Even though he had been in the Vatican for four years, Father Nefiore was still awed by his surroundings. With the diplomatic status of an independent country and more political clout than many nations, the tiny papal state was complete unto itself, a tight maze of narrow streets, gardens and buildings that roughly approximated the shape of an arrow point. The tone of the place was one of power and tradition. He felt both of these at all times, and if he was tempted to forget, someone would soon come along to remind him.

Nefiore had been brought to Rome to teach at the Gregorian University, but before he could even move into his office he had been transferred to the Council of Public Affairs, the Holy See's equivalent of a foreign ministry. The work itself was interesting, if not challenging, and there were many other young men like himself in the department. His job involved the coordination of messages from various agencies in Germany. Some of these came in code that translated into Greek, itself in code, and then into Latin, its final form. It was a complicated system developed long ago by the Vatican. Even when the messages were rendered into Latin, they made little sense; nineteen centuries of experience had made the Church's diplomats supreme masters in the art of circumspection.

From time to time Nefiore was called upon to deliver messages to the Pope's private apartment. The Holy Father's wrenlike housekeeper, Sister Pascaline, a member of the Order of the Sisters of the Holy Cross of Menzingen, had joined the pontiff's staff when he was papal nuncio in Munich and had been with him ever since. She was an able and dedicated gate guard with a sharp tongue and a sandpaper voice. At first Nefiore had found the pontiff aloof and cold but supposed there was an underlying shyness that created the impression. All the Pope's personal business was conducted in German, and his inner circle of advisers—his most trusted counselors—were laymen, not priests. This unusual situation created an enormous number of rumors, as well as jealousy, both inside the Vatican and outside its walls. But once Nefiore had revealed his own fluency in German, he sensed a relaxation in the attitudes of both Sister Pascaline and the pontiff himself.

Only once had Pope Pius XII engaged Nefiore in prolonged discussion. Their talk had centered on Nefiore's perceptions of the Church's position toward Germany. He found the pontiff's questions clear, precise and probing, and he answered them as lucidly and candidly as he could. Nefiore's basic position was that the Church's first obligation was to survive whatever temporal tests might be set before it. He cited Article 24 of the Lateran Treaty, which forbade the Vatican to take sides in disputes between nations. He accepted papal positions that obliged the faithful on opposing sides in the war to commit themselves to their countries and their patriotic duty. As an aside he suggested that Germany's war with the Communists could, if successful, be of immense benefit to the Church in particular, and to the world in general. The Pope probed for clarification of the younger priest's views on a variety of topics, but not once did he offer an opinion or evaluation of the responses he heard. It was a peculiar session and the only one of its kind among Nefiore's contacts with the Holy Father.

Farraro entered the cottage a full half hour late. As director, Farraro, a Venetian and one of the most powerful men in Vatican City, was in charge of liaison with the International Red Cross. The war had created hundreds of thousands of drifting refugees and displaced persons, and it was Farraro's job to see that the Roman Catholics among them were cared for. Nefiore had no idea what the task actually entailed.

"I'll get to the point, Father Nefiore," Farraro said in his raspy voice. He was sweating heavily and mopped himself with a small linen towel, which he kept in a sleeve in his cassock. "Your record is exemplary. You have an excellent mind and you know how to keep your mouth closed." He made a quick twisting gesture with his forefinger and thumb. "You understand the function of my directorate?"

"In broad principle."

"You have been selected to undertake a mission of grave importance to Mother Church."

"I serve willingly in the roles God chooses for me."

"Save your piety for others, Father. God didn't choose you for this mission. Your selection reflects certain . . . let's call them evaluations of your ability. We have to walk in the world as it is, not as we would like it to be."

"But one works for change."

"Or gambles for it. Sometimes gambles fail. In this hour one works for survival. When you see what I see daily, you begin to lose interest in spiritual matters. The starving, the homeless, the diseased don't give a damn about God. Their biology prevents it."

"A rather narrow view," Nefiore said stiffly.

"But a realistic one," Farraro snapped. He studied Nefiore for a moment as if trying to come to a decision. "The job I have for you is quite unglamorous, quite worldly and certainly dirty. It could cost you your life; in fact, I expect it will."

"I'm prepared to martyr myself."

"When you're kneeling at an altar, that's an easy commitment to make," Farraro growled. "You've been too long among the scholars and theoreticians. There will be no martyrdom—not as you think of it—no canonization, no sainthood, no remembrance. I expect you to end up as just another stinking corpse on a pile that already has millions."

The conversation was not what Nefiore had expected; he felt uneasy. "I'm not anxious to die, if that's what you're getting at."

"That's as it should be. But you accept that in certain circumstances one must do his duty, knowing full well that the consequence may be death?"

"I understand that such situations could exist, so I suppose I accept the premise. But this whole discussion seems to have no point. What are we really talking about?"

"The directorate is in the process of arranging the relocation of . . . certain German Catholics. If help is requested, we are committed to providing it."

"Nazis?"

"Catholics first. We are very careful to document the authenticity of baptismal records."

"I understand, but are they Nazis?"

"Their political affiliations and beliefs are not our concern."

"But the Allies intend to try the Nazi leaders as common war criminals. There are many of these people, now that they have lost their hold on Italy and the rest of Europe, who must be brought to justice," Nefiore argued. "We have a moral responsibility to reject such people, Catholic or not."

"Our Church has rendered a decision to provide assistance to German Catholics. This decision involves much that you do not know and will never know. Your duty is before you, Father. How deep is your faith in your Savior and our Church?"

"You are asking if my faith in God and the Church will allow me to perform a task that may be morally unjust?"

"Which *you* believe may be unjust," Farraro said coldly. "You lack the necessary information to make such an assessment."

"I open my hands," Nefiore said. It was an old Italian expression meaning, "I bring no weapons to this conversation; let us speak freely and honestly."

Farraro opened his hands in answer. "We want you to go to Germany to deliver certain documents. In all likelihood you will not return, but if you do, you will spend the rest of your natural life here in the Vatican under a vow of silence."

"Who has chosen me?"

"Suffice it to say that you were selected by an authority at a level you would not care to dispute."

So, Nefiore thought. "An infallible decision?"

"Do not play semantic games, Father. Infallibility is possible only in interpreting God's word. This is purely a temporal matter."

"And if I refuse?"

"If you decline to accept, I can only point out that the pastoral services always need priests."

Banished from Rome. True to form, they understood his motivations. Either way his career was at an end; death lay along both roads. One promised to be fast and with a purpose, however suspect; the other, one of decay and no direction. It was not a difficult choice to make. "It's blackmail," Nefiore said, staring hard at the older man.

"Now you understand."

"I'll go," Nefiore said. "May God have mercy upon me."

"Amen," Farraro said sharply.

▶58 AUGUST 10, 1945, 2:30 P.M.

No matter what he turned up, Beau Valentine's instincts kept pointing him back to Otto Skorzeny. The SS colonel must have some notion of what the Russians were after, and Valentine had a good idea of how to pry the information out of him.

Skorzeny was angry and didn't try to hide it from Valentine. "Now the imbeciles think I tried to kill Eisenhower!" he bellowed as the American entered his cell and sat down. "They're claiming I was a spy. They say I helped rescue Hitler. Next they'll be claiming I'm a leper who fondles little boys! Damned idiots! Where the hell is that American fair play you people are always boasting about?"

Valentine grinned at him. "Who's engaging in hyperbole now, Colonel?"

Skorzeny quieted and leaned back against the wall behind his bunk. "It's garbage," he growled. "The real soldiers always have to fight hardest against the paper pushers. I used Radl to beat them. He's a lawyer, you know. Extremely clever. Whatever they asked for in paperwork, Radl gave it to them, and more. He beat them at their own game and we got what we needed, but it was a hell of a way to operate. Radl had the patience and good humor to handle it efficiently. Me, I lost my temper and ended up putting us further behind than when we started. A good leader knows his weaknesses and delegates such tasks to those who complement him."

"What did you delegate to Brumm?"

Skorzeny looked amused. "Still asking questions about Günter? Interesting."

"How so?"

"In the division, Günter was one of our true professionals, a career soldier. It was purely an accident that I got hold of him, a lucky break. But you know that."

"I know nothing," Valentine said. "There's no trace of Brumm. I've just been to Munich. We have all your records—all but Brumm's; they're gone."

There was a silence. "I see your interest," Skorzeny said at last, "but you can't expect me to provide you with details. I will have nothing to say about Brumm or any of my comrades."

Valentine recognized a quid pro quo when one was presented. "I can see your point, Otto, but consider your position here. There are these charges against you, and they're not made lightly. It's my observation that the adjutant general types are eager to successfully prosecute every German they can find, especially famous ones. Success breeds publicity, and publicity breeds success. American law firms pay big salaries—you understand the process, I'm sure."

Skorzeny crossed his arms and set his jaw. "Let them prosecute. I'm not guilty of any crimes, and they can't prove that I am. They have to prove my guilt, correct?"

"Only in a theoretical sense. These are unusual circumstances, and my hunch is that *you'll* have to prove your innocence. There are prisons filled with Nazi officials, all anxious to save their own skins. Maybe even some of your own men will tell the prosecution what it wants to hear. There's nothing subtle about these court cases; they mean to give the hangman some work."

Valentine paused for effect. He was certain Skorzeny was not as sure of himself as he was trying to appear. "You have your own word, of course. And Radl. Of course you don't know what pressures they'll put on Radl." Again he let the words sink in. "He's probably strong enough to resist, and perhaps you'll be able to depend on some of your other comrades. But they *are* Germans, and that makes them suspect, wouldn't you think?"

"They're honorable men," Skorzeny said quickly.

"I know. But think about this: how much would it help to have some witnesses for the defense from outside your own circle of acquaintances?"

"You, for example?"

Valentine drew back in surprise. "Me? I couldn't help you. What am I? A simple OSS agent."

"I'm beginning to understand what you're leading up to."

"I thought you would. Suppose I told you that there was a certain British agent who had operated in France, and who was eventually captured and interned by the Gestapo in your death camps?"

"I had nothing to do with the Gestapo," Skorzeny said defensively.

"Suppose, through the intervention of Providence, that this certain agent survived; suppose further for the purposes of our discussion that this agent had a special interest in your case—out of professional respect, let's say. Should this man come forward on your behalf, I believe your case would assume a kind of legitimacy that even the prosecutors would find difficult to penetrate."

"I know the man you refer to. I'm glad he's alive. An able soldier, an honorable opponent." Valentine knew that the SS colonel was telling the truth. "But I presume this man needs some . . . encouragement to come forward—is that your meaning?"

"I think you get the point, Colonel. Tit for tat."

"Scratching the other man's back, so to speak."

Valentine smiled. "You've got it. Where does that leave us?"

"And the price is Günter Brumm," Skorzeny said.

"No. The price is *information* about Colonel Brumm. That's all. Just information. Who is he? What is he? What did he do in the Friedenthal Division? Information is all I'm asking for. I would never ask you to betray a comrade."

Both laughed. "Unless you needed to in order to get what you wanted," Skorzeny observed. "What do you need? Günter was an enterprising man. I doubt if anything I can tell you will help you to find him. If he's decided to disappear, there's probably not much you can do about it; he's that kind of man. In any event, it's more likely he's dead, on the Oder front. If you want to find him, ask the Russians to look for his body."

They both knew that the Russians had bulldozed German dead into mass graves. "I doubt they'd be helpful."

Skorzeny retreated into a shell and did not speak for a long time. Finally he said incredulously, "You're thinking that perhaps Günter helped Hitler to escape. That's it, isn't it? You Americans are obsessed with the idea of Hitler's survival."

"Let's say I have some narrow professional interests in the colonel."

"Listen to me, Herr Valentine. Adolf Hitler is dead. He killed himself in Berlin. There's no ghost for you to chase after. *Kaput.* You understand?"

"I agree," Valentine said evenly. "But there are no bodies, no remains."

"Ah," Skorzeny said, letting the syllable drag out. "That's easy. The brotherhood spirits away the remains of their revered leader as a final act of defiance against the invaders. A reasonable supposition, though I'm certain I would have heard something about such an event were it true."

"Are you telling me that Brumm might have removed Hitler's remains?"

"Brumm is capable of anything. It was he who planned the Mussolini rescue. He was a sound thinker, bold and innovative, and he could plan and execute all the details necessary for an operation to succeed."

"What was his relationship to Hitler?"

"None. He was with me once when Hitler decorated us. No more than that. *I* was Hitler's adviser on the subject of special missions. Only me." Valentine could see that the idea of a plot being hatched by Hitler without bringing Skorzeny into it bothered the colonel deeply.

"But there could have been some relationship you were unaware of."

"A mathematical possibility only, not a probability. It would have been impossible to hide such a liaison from me. My contacts were, shall we say, inclusive."

"I would like to know about Brumm."

"Where shall I begin?"

"Wherever you like."

Skorzeny talked nonstop about Brumm for nearly two hours. When Valentine left the cell, he had a better feel for what the Russians were thinking, and a pretty good idea of where to start. He'd baited Skorzeny with the implication that Radl might not corroborate his story. It was a lie; an MP officer had told Valentine the night before that Radl and Skorzeny would be reunited as roommates tomorrow. It did not bother the American to lie; the important thing was to get to the truth and sometimes lies were what got you there the fastest. Usually he followed leads without reporting up the chain of command, but this time something in the back of his mind warned him that he had better make sure that someone higher up knew what he was considering. It would be just like the Nazis to spirit Hitler's remains away in order to deny them to the invaders. It was an interesting possibility, and one he had not considered.

▶59 AUGUST 16, 1945, 9:00 P.M.

Before leaving Rome, Father Nefiore had been required to memorize the personal history of Hauptmann Ernst Pfeiffer, a German army officer from Dortmund. Pfeiffer was dead, but he had not died in combat. He was a deserter who had sought refuge with a priest in northern Italy and had been granted asylum. He died of a coronary only a few days after deserting, and his papers had been preserved for future contingencies.

Nefiore's instructions were to proceed to the village of Wetter as fast as he could get there, but if he was challenged by the Americans along the way, he was to give himself up. His destination was on the Lahn River near Marburg—about eighty kilometers north of Frankfurt. He was assured that if the Americans took him into custody, it would be only for a brief time; Pfeiffer's papers were perfect.

Traveling by bicycle, the priest had made his way into northern Italy, where a guide took him through one of the passes to Switzerland. From there he walked into Germany. At the border the Americans challenged him, but after three days in a massive POW compound near Munich, he was allowed to continue his journey.

His release from captivity was as unceremonious as his surrender. By American reckoning Pfeiffer was squeaky-clean. He was army, not SS, a competent, if ordinary, officer. The Americans provided him with a new uniform and a set of identity papers that gave him the right to go home. They also told him that if he wished to enter the Soviet zone of occupation, he'd have to submit to a separate investigation, and they advised him against it. "Pretty hard ass, them Russians," a corporal told him. "I hear they're loading up German officers and shippin' them off to a jailhouse in Roo-sha. If you got business over thatta way, that's up to you, but I wouldn't go, pal."

Outside the prison compound Nefiore felt truly free. It was a dismal morning, but he'd never felt better or more alive.

He spent the day trying to find a bicycle but by midafternoon gave up and began walking north. Near sundown an Army half-track clattered loudly along behind him. When it drew alongside, two GIs waved at him to climb aboard.

The soldiers had rigged a tripod in the cramped space in back and bolted it to the floor. Suspended from it was a small Sterno stove, and a pot of coffee was brewing, its marvelous odor mixing with diesel fumes, cordite and a thin cloud of dust. They gave him a tin cup and poured it a third full. "When you want more, speak up. This is to keep it from slopping all over you. They just let you out?"

Nefiore nodded.

"They give you a hard time?"

"No, I was well treated."

"Lucky you're not a Nazi."

"You *presume* I am not a Nazi."

The men laughed. "Nothing to presume, friend. If they had the slightest notion you were, you'd still be cooling your heels. How far up the road you traveling?"

"Marburg. My home."

"Me, I'm a Chicago boy," one of the soldiers said. "Sometimes it's hard to remember what it looks like. That way for you, too?"

Nefiore smiled. "Yes. I've been away for a long time."

"Family?"

Nefiore shrugged. "There was a lot of bombing."

One of them unfolded a large map and patted it flat on the vehicle deck. "Show me your town."

The priest pointed to Marburg.

The two soldiers looked at each other as if seeking agreement. Then the redhead said, "I think you're okay, partner. There wasn't much bombing in that area. Old Blood and Guts tore the area up with his tanks, but the flyboys left it alone."

"Old Blood and Guts?"

"You know—General Georgie Hardass Patton Junior. Had two pearl-handled forty-fives, wore riding britches, kept the ugliest dog on earth. The man had balls big enough to roll down an alley and hard enough to get him a strike. *That* George Patton."

"I don't believe I know of him," Nefiore said.

The two soldiers were disappointed. "He led our tanks," one of them said. "Better than Rommel," he added.

"Ah," Nefiore said, recognizing the name as that of a well-known German general, but not knowing much about him. In the future, he reminded himself, he'd have to be careful about conversations, no matter how innocent they seemed at the outset. "I'm tired," he said.

"Grab some shut-eye," the redhead told him. "We're going all the way to Frankfurt, so you got lotsa time."

Nefiore slept lightly until they reached Frankfurt. There the soldiers dropped him off after loading him up with C rations and wishing him luck. It was difficult to understand the generosity of Americans. They had sent millions of men to smash Germany, but now that they had succeeded, there seemed to be no animosity. It was very odd, and one more reminder of why the world should be wary of Americans. The Italians detested the Germans. They had given in to them because of Mussolini, but individually they hated and feared them—and with good reason.

The priest sat in the grass by the side of the road and ate a can of peaches in heavy syrup. The Americans were different: innocent, yet tenacious, fast to anger, fast to forget. The Holy See disliked dealing with Americans because they never played by the rules. American bishops were constantly badgering Rome for explanations of various policies, and openly questioned every request for increased funds. Even so, the money always seemed to come through. The Americans lacked sophistication, said the Italian cardinals; they could never lead the Church until they had more experience with human nature. Nefiore recognized envy when he heard it. The Americans were a remarkable people, and this simple fact irritated a lot who weren't. Their attitude toward Germans was only the latest demonstration of their unique ways.

The road to Frankfurt had been busy, but the road north seemed to have little traffic, and what there was seemed to be almost exclusively military. It was eighty kilometers to Marburg, and after several hours it looked as if Nefiore would have to walk the entire distance. But after only a few kilometers, a motorcycle with a sidecar came along. The driver, a young boy, stopped his machine, dismounted, lit a cigarette, groped at his pants and urinated loudly on the road as Nefiore caught up with him. When he was done, he offered the pack of cigarettes to the priest with the same hand he had used for his personal business. The priest refused politely.

"Not very pleasant weather to be walking," the boy said. "How far are you going?"

"Marburg."

"Kassel for me. I'm a courier for the Americans. I thought I'd hate them—they killed my papa—but they're not bad. Different from the Ivans. What do you think?"

So young, Nefiore thought. A boy playing man. Boys always talked a lot when they were trying to act adult. "An American machine?" he asked earnestly, looking at the motorcycle.

"German," the boy said, astonished that this soldier couldn't tell the difference. "The Americans gave it to me to use. Very efficient with petrol. They give me ration cards for the petrol, but I don't use the whole allowance. I trade for food and other things."

"For your family?"

"My mother went away with our soldiers."

"You are a Jew?"

The boy recoiled with a sour look on his face. "*Me?*" he asked incredulously. He spat. "She went with them because she wanted to. My father was already dead. She liked soldiers. The Führer said that German women should be good to our soldiers. Don't you remember?"

"She never came back?"

The boy dropped his cigarette, mashed it with his boot and then looked hard at Nefiore. "You don't look like a soldier," he said. "I see what remains of the Wehrmacht every day. You're not thin enough. Your eyes sparkle too much. Veterans' eyes are all dull, like there's smoke inside them. I'll have to see your papers if you're going to ride with me. It wouldn't be proper to give you a lift if your papers aren't in order. I work for the Americans, you know."

"Yes, I think you made that clear before." Father Nefiore showed the boy his papers and waited nervously for him to complete his inspection. The boy was a poor reader who mouthed the words silently as he read. "They're A-OK," he finally pronounced in American slang.

It was a tight squeeze in the sidecar, but the boy waited patiently while the priest settled himself. Then he stepped up on the starter, jamming it downward in a violent motion and kicking it into life on the first try. He might be a child, Nefiore noted, but he knew how to handle the machine. He gunned the throttle several times, looked backward to make sure the lane behind them was clear, and shouted, "Hold on tight."

They roared off in a cloud of pebbles and dirt. At first Nefiore was worried, but before long he could feel the boy's mastery over the machine and let himself relax.

When they reached Marburg in the early evening, the boy left Nefiore in front of the massive Gothic edifice of the Church of Saint Elizabeth. Not many people were about. The church was impressive. At the top of its spire was a horseman, a fierce knight of the Teutonic Order. It had been the knights, Nefiore knew, who had built the church seven centuries before. The statue was impressive evidence that even Catholicism could not tame Teutonic ferocity. The structure looked more like a fortress than a house of worship.

Inside, the church was empty. Before him were the nave and an eastern wall filled with magnificent windows of stained glass. To the left of the high altar he found the entrance to the vestry. The floor was covered with dirt, but when he rubbed it with his shoes beautiful patterns of ceramic tiles were revealed. Before him stood the Golden Shrine, a massive work fashioned from copper, an intricate blending of statues in bas-relief, enamel inlays and complicated metal filigree. Precious stones and even tiny sparkling pearls were inlaid in the metal. It lacked the subtlety of Roman artisans, but even to an Italian the shrine possessed a certain raw power.

As he had been instructed to do by Farraro, Father Nefiore found a notch behind the main statue. There was a small box in back; a copper trigger fell easily to his touch and a thin opening in the rooflike structure over the statue appeared. The inside of the opening was lined with cloth. Nefiore's fingertips searched and quickly located a thin package; when he released it from its ledge, it fell down a precut groove into his hand. Slipping the package into his shirt, he pushed the trigger device closed so that it was again flush. He remembered what Farraro had told him: "For seven hundred years the Golden Shrine has been used for the holiest and most secret missions."

He was nervous and perspiring as he turned to leave and found himself face-to-face with another priest, a bald man, short and wide. His eyelids were thick and looked swollen; there was a sparse white stubble of whiskers on his leathery brown cheeks. "It's a pilgrim's church," the stranger said in Latin. "God be with you, pilgrim." As he stepped away, his cassock fluttered momentarily and Nefiore could see that the man had a revolver in his hand.

An armed priest! Things *were* different in Germany. He was shaken. Now he had a package in his shirt that could cost him his life. The last few days had seemed a game, a kind of scavenger hunt. Even in the American prison camp, he had been unafraid, but now his fear was real and powerful.

Nefiore made his way shakily through Marburg, following the Lahn River north to the village of Wetter. It was a tidy place, a sea of white walls and heavy orange-tiled roofs. Here Charlemagne had led his armies across the river. A Roman citadel had once stood here, an outpost at the ford to keep the warlike Huns at bay from the civilized world. He saw the steeple from a hill outside town; using it as a guiding landmark, he went straight to the rectory, a small building behind the simple church. He knocked several times, but there was no response. Inside, he found a chair and sat down to wait. Soon he was dozing.

A hand on his shoulder awakened him with a start, and he found himself staring into the same puffy eyes that had confronted him in Saint Elizabeth's. "I came as fast as I could," the old priest said. "I can't keep up with you young fellows anymore."

Nefiore stared at the man, his mouth open.

The old priest's voice was soft and reassuring. "Here you are safe, Father. Let me take your coat and we'll find you something to eat. Do you like tea?"

▶60 SEPTEMBER 21, 1945, 11:00 A.M.

Valentine was in a quandary. If he called the OSS office in Switzerland and informed his case officer of his suspicions, Arizona might tell him to leave it alone. He was a good man and had some of the instincts of an agent, but Beau thought this was too farfetched even for Arizona to go along with it. Conferring with him was out of the question; there was a better way.

It took him nearly two hours to find an American army unit with the necessary communications equipment, but only a few minutes to bribe a PFC by giving him the names of a couple of local women he could score with. Rather than talking to Arizona, Valentine had decided it would be wiser to call the OSS Control Center.

A male voice answered.

"Crawdad requesting traffic," Beau said. Then he waited for his call to be switched.

Another male voice came on the line. "Crawdad?" Valentine recited a short litany of authenticators and waited for his identity to be confirmed. "Where are you?" the voice asked.

The tone and the question told Valentine to be careful. "Let's just stick to procedure, bub," he said. It was not normal for an agent's location to be asked during a routine check-in. "But for the record you can say I'm out of town with my sick grandmother."

"We haven't had contact with you in quite some time," the voice said with perceptible irritation.

"Granny had amnesia; it was contagious."

"Don't piss me off," the voice said.

"Better'n bein' pissed on," Valentine answered.

"I don't have time for adolescent games with an undisciplined cowboy," the voice snapped. "Cowboy" was the term used by desk jockeys for agents. "Under the authority of a directive issued yesterday, you are hereby informed that all agents are to report immediately to the nearest army intelligence unit and identify themselves."

Something was seriously wrong. "Level with me, pal. What's going on?"

"Follow orders, hotshot," the voice said.

"Why aren't we supposed to report to our case officers?" Valentine demanded. "This is outside procedure."

"Just do it, wise guy," the voice said as the connection broke.

Valentine thanked the PFC and left. It was warm, and banks of puffy white clouds moved across a bright blue background. The news from OSS HQ didn't sound so good, he thought as he lit a cigarette. If his outfit wanted him to report to army intelligence, he'd go back to Switzerland—when he was in the right mood, of course. The OSS desk dicks had always jerked agents around. This time they could wait; he still had work to do. Besides, the idea of returning to Switzerland made him cringe; even the thought turned his stomach. When he needed it, Arizona would give him the dope on what was up.

▶61 SEPTEMBER 26, 1945, 2:15 P.M.

There were times when Rivitsky did not understand his leader and this was one of those times. They had established comfortable if somewhat primitive headquarters in Nordhausen. He had accompanied Petrov to Magdeburg several times to help Ezdovo and Pogrebenoi organize their air-search plan, but it was evident that the two were quite capable in their own right and that Petrov was simply treading water. Ezdovo and Pogrebenoi had begun overflying the Harz Mountains and surrounding areas, covering it foot by foot as they searched for evidence of Brumm. Bailov and Gnedin were in Bad Harzburg looking for leads and had been instructed not to report back unless something solid developed. So far there'd been no word from them.

Three times a day Petrov called the Soviet Air Force's meteorological center in Berlin to receive forecasts for the Harz region; after each call he made notes, which he then tacked to a wooden doorframe, and the stack was now fat and tattered by being brushed against. Two days before, he had received the late afternoon report, written his notes, studied them for a while and proclaimed, "Winter's moving in. It's time to move to Berlin." He offered no explanation.

By noon the next day Rivitsky and he had loaded their truck and begun the drive back. After a morning of visiting various Soviet administrative facilities, Petrov handed Rivitsky written directions to an address in an eastern Berlin suburb called Köpenick. Their destination turned out to be a walled estate on the banks of the Mugglesee, a lake that was technically part of the Spree River in Brandenburg, more than twenty kilometers east of Berlin's center, and before the war a popular stopping area for tourists on the river. A toothless Air Force general met them angrily, disputed their requisitioning of the facility and placed a call to Moscow. Shortly thereafter he abandoned the place to them, tripping over himself with apologies as he departed.

Even after they settled in, Petrov did not explain the reason for their shift in location. Rivitsky had noted that it was Petrov's way to exercise power surgically and with economy, always applying precisely the necessary force. Over time he had come to look on Petrov's judgment with awe; no matter what happened, his leader seemed to know exactly what had to be done and when. But now he sensed something different. Petrov was still cool and reserved, but Rivitsky had the sense of being in the eye of a storm, peering out on a turmoil they themselves had created. Petrov seemed to be turning the entire world upside down. Less than twenty-four hours after reestablishing themselves in the German capital, his authority and machine-gun directives had transformed the once tranquil estate into a massive communications center, fully tended by operators and technicians eager to please.

While Rivitsky saw to the installation of equipment, Petrov went off by himself to think about the remaining loose ends. He had already spent much time trying to obtain additional information about Brumm's sergeant major, but Gestapo records on enlisted men were abbreviated and lacked the detail of officers' dossiers. Doubtless it was a reflection of Hitler's feelings on the relative merits of the two military classes. There was no evidence to indicate involvement by the sergeant major, but neither was there reason to exclude him from consideration. His name was Rau, and there were some indications that he had been born in the southern part of the country, but that was the extent of their information. There were no extant military or civilian records— at least nothing yet. Toward the end, Petrov knew, the Germans had stashed records in every hole and hiding place in the countryside. Reports came in daily of newly discovered caches; eventually something would turn up.

►**62** NOVEMBER 1, 1945, 4:00 P.M.

Bailov's woman turned out to be something more than she appeared. One afternoon she was on an errand with the girls and he was in the bedroom. Later he could not explain to Petrov exactly what had made him search the room. He'd been in the house for nearly four months, and their life had settled into a comfortable, if Spartan, routine. During the day he moved through the countryside, trying to get information about Brumm. Occasionally he met with Gnedin, but the doctor's luck was no better. At night Bailov slept with Janna; it was almost like being married, and his recognition of this made him laugh. Marriage was a condition he had vowed to avoid, yet here he was, and while it was only a charade, it began to get on his nerves.

The woman, he had to admit, was satisfactory for most of his needs. She was physically strong, a tireless worker and a willing partner under the comforter. But it was her intensity that made him uneasy, the fiery gaze from her large green eyes, something fanatical that she kept tightly reined, and because of this he was suspicious. He found himself drawn to the closet in the bedroom. It seemed normal, but his experienced eye discovered a crude but cleverly hidden storage compartment at one end of it, which he opened with a snap to pressure from the heel of his hand.

Inside was a small wicker trunk that contained several interesting items: an automatic pistol with clips, a small riding crop, a black SS tunic with skirt, and two albums of snapshots, all carefully labeled and mounted. The photographs were neatly glued into the black pages of the albums; legible captions had been printed below each one in white ink. There was a group pose: several uniformed women sat on the cowcatcher of a locomotive, their skirts raised almost to their crotches, their legs flung wide apart like gleeful chorus girls. In one photo Janna was surrounded by naked children, boys and girls with flowers in their hair, like small nymphs; another showed her in mock embrace with a swarthy man in a doctor's smock; still another showed a corpse in a wide-striped garment hanging over a roll of barbed wire. Beside the body stood Janna like a big-game hunter, a rifle cradled in her arms, the trophy bleeding beside her.

Janna entered the room while Bailov was sitting on the bed looking through the albums and attacked him instantly. He had expected her to be strong, but he was unprepared for her mastery of hand-to-hand combat. He tried to bind both of her wrists, but she twisted quickly and jerked like an animal, repeatedly kneeing his solar plexus and groin. Finally he ended the struggle by rolling her off the bed and pounding her head against the floor until her resistance ceased.

He sat and stared at her. His own weapons were hidden in the forest, so he put a clip in the pistol he'd found in the trunk and waited for her to come to. She regained consciousness with no fear in her face. Her eyes were hollow, like a cat's at night, and he could feel her hatred. She held her head where he had struck it and stared at the pistol barrel leveled at her chest.

"You have no right," she said evenly. "They are my personal belongings."

"Granted."

"They are private."

" 'Secret' would be a more accurate characterization."

"What will you do?"

"I'm not sure. It depends on you. You know what I am. I am comfortable here," he lied. "But now I'm confused. You gave me the impression that you were a defenseless *Hausfrau* in need of a man's strength—and other male services. Now you flash the talons of a harpy."

"You take yourself too seriously," she said. "It would be better for you not to pursue this."

Bailov smiled. He knew she was hoping for an opening. "Your husband dead on the Eastern front, your children starving." He nodded toward the scattered photographs. "Lies. I want to know who you are and what these mean."

She grinned and relaxed. "May I?" she asked. His look told her it was safe to sit on the bed. "I'm not ashamed," she told him. "I only did my duty for the Führer."

"Death's Head?" He had recognized the insignia.

"Yes, Totenkopfverbande. I was one. You were army. You wouldn't understand such things."

"Try me."

"*Befehl ist Befehl*—an order is an order. You understand the concept of *Befehlsnotstand*—that an order must be obeyed?"

"It is the basis of the military chain of command," Bailov pointed out.

"*Sehr gut*. Germany was poisoned by inferior races. They weakened us and led to the disaster of Versailles. Our leaders determined that if the country was to be purified, the impure elements would have to be eliminated. I served in one of the units dedicated to this end. We were true patriots."

The girls came into the room, sized up the situation immediately and stood close to Bailov.

"Leave us," the woman hissed at them.

"Shoot her," the youngest child said matter-of-factly. Bailov's heart jumped at the words. "She's not our mother. We're not even sisters.

She's a bad woman, Father. Shoot her. Please?" Bailov's senses turned on end.

"You're upset, sweetheart. Come here to me," the woman said with a warm voice and frigid eyes.

The older girl seemed to take strength from the younger one's courage. "We were at the camp, at Dachau. She took us from there. If we'd stayed we would have died. She said she'd let us live if we obeyed her. We are Jews," she said proudly but nervously. The woman sprang from the bed, but Bailov blocked her with a kick to the chest and backed her up with the pistol.

"All right," he warned. "I want the truth. Your name first."

"You have my name. I did not lie about that."

"Why are you here?"

"Bad Harzburg is my home, such as it is. I needed refuge. There was no better place than among these stupid mountain people."

"You are alone?"

"That's why I came."

He decided on a more direct approach. "If you truly are of this place, tell me who Günter Brumm is."

She stared, dumbfounded. "Who are you?"

"Tell me."

"The apothecary's grandson. He was an officer in the SS, a colonel."

"You know him?"

"Who are you?" she repeated. "You're no soldier, at least not a German soldier."

He smiled. "Think of me as an instrument of poetic justice. Tell me about Brumm."

"If I do, will you let me go with my daughters?"

The girls crowded closer to him, clinging to his jacket. "We're not going with you anymore," the younger one shouted.

"Fräulein," Bailov said, "I haven't decided what to do with you, but this I will tell you: unless you tell me what I want to know, and quickly, you'll never leave this room."

She shuddered. "I knew him when he was young. A real loner. He and his grandfather camped in the Harzwald. He was the brightest student in the village, but he went away to military school in Stuttgart. Once we were on leave here at the same time. I tried to—interest him, but he hadn't changed. The SS sometimes attracted that type."

"When was this leave?"

"Summer, 1944. July."

"How long was he here?"

"I don't know. He took off into the mountains, and when I left three weeks later, he still hadn't returned."

"Did he have friends here? Associates?"

She shook her head. "None. He was not the sort of man who needed others."

"You're certain it was Brumm?"

She laughed. "He was not the kind of man a woman forgets easily, especially when you've been with the dregs I have."

After getting the information he wanted, Bailov took the woman into the woods where the girls could not see them and made her dig a shallow hole. When she was finished, she stood, legs apart, and challenged him. "You lack the nerve," she said. He shot her in the eye from five feet away, then dumped her in the hole and filled it in. He felt no remorse: she was a pariah; the world was better off without her. With the woman disposed of, he burned the house, gathered her documents, reclaimed his own weapons and took the girls to Bad Harzburg, an eight-kilometer hike through the first heavy snow of winter. After marching the girls through town and up the stairs to Gnedin's surgery, he entered without knocking.

The surgeon was not happy to see him. "Idiot! You'll ruin everything."

"Shut up, my friend. I had no choice. I've learned that Brumm was here last summer and went off into the mountains, apparently for at least three weeks."

Gnedin stared past Bailov at the children. "Yours?"

"In a manner of speaking."

►63 NOVEMBER 7, 1945, NOON

Bailov and Gnedin arrived at the estate in motorcycles with sidecars during a flurry of wet snow. The girls were bundled in blankets and looked like miniature monks. Petrov and Rivitsky carried them into the villa and set them down by a roaring fire.

Rivitsky observed that the girls called Bailov "Father," and that whenever he left the room they clammed up and looked nervous. It was clear that a bonding had taken place, and it amused Rivitsky to see the unit's avowed bachelor fussing over them like a parent. The question was, where had they come from?

After the girls had been fed and put to bed, the four team members assembled in the drawing room. It took two hours for Bailov and Gnedin to report their experiences to their leader. As they talked, Petrov listened attentively, his hands folded in his lap. He asked few questions. When the two men finished talking, Petrov reflected for a moment, then turned to them.

"Doctor, you are to remain here."

"That's all?" Gnedin asked. After so long in the village, a respite in Berlin, no matter how badly damaged it was, would be a welcome change.

Petrov nodded solemnly and turned to Bailov. "Comrade, the children have formed an attachment to you; there's no future in it for you or them."

Bailov's heart jumped, and his reaction surprised him: he'd been telling himself he'd be glad to be shed of the brats. "We can't just turn them out."

Petrov touched the younger man's arm. "They belong in Palestine," he said, "with their own kind. You and the doctor can make the arrangements, and after they've departed, you will go to Magdeburg to assist Ezdovo and Pogrebenoi."

His instructions delivered, Petrov left the three and went upstairs to the massive library. Rivitsky hugged his comrades. "It's too late to do anything today, so we'll celebrate our reunion," he said with a wink. Moments later a bottle of pertsovka was on the table in front of them.

▶64   DECEMBER 9, 1945, 3:45 P.M.

The snow was wet and heavy under a thin layer of ice, which snapped under their weight and plunged Brumm and Waller up to their knees. They had left the valley two days previously and slogged relentlessly, stopping only to eat cold food and catnap in caves and quickly assembled lean-tos along the way.

At last they reached a small cavern on the southwest face of the upper Harzwald. Waller huddled close to Brumm, hoping for added warmth from his bulk. At least there was no wind in the cave, so it felt warmer. "We'll build a fire when it gets dark," he told her. She understood. Against a light sky the smoke could be spotted, but at night in this kind of weather it would be invisible.

"I think we should stay together," Waller blurted out. She had been thinking about their separating ever since they had crawled out of the valley. It was not the risk she minded; after Berlin she felt that there could never again be comparable danger in her life. The war was over, the armies dispersing; whatever threats lay outside the Harz Mountains, she felt ready to face them. But she was disturbed at the notion of parting from Günter because for the first time in her life she felt whole and happy. In the valley she had to share him, but out here they were free, just the two of them, and she did not want to lose what she held dearest.

"No choice," Brumm answered as he slapped his ice-laden mittens together. "If one of us gets into trouble, the other must return to the valley to tell Beard."

"There won't be any trouble," she argued. "Women can tell these things."

He laughed and caressed her hair. "I put my trust in skill and preparation, not instinct, my sweet." He pulled her to him and nuzzled her neck; it was the first time he had ever done this, and it caught her by surprise. "There are three hotels on the *Strasse* near the church," Brumm went on. "Take a room in the easternmost one and sleep. A real bed will be a novelty."

"Perhaps the hotels have been destroyed."

"It doesn't matter. The principle is to select the easternmost one. If there are none, find the nearest hotel to the east of the church. If there still are none, you try south first, then west, then north. Somewhere there will be an inn. You make objections like a child," he chided her gently.

"I *am* a child, my Colonel."

"Only technically," he said. "Now tell me again what you are going to do."

She frowned. "We've been over this so many times that I won't be able to forget it as long as I live."

"Good. Then it will be easy for you to tell me again."

She sighed and leaned back against the wall of the cave. Her breath exploded from her mouth in small clouds. "I go down to the road and wait for a vehicle to come along. I stop them. I've had a fight with my grandfather and he has thrown me out. If the ride gives me a problem, I don't resist. I let him become—engaged. I eliminate him. Then I drive back here and get you."

"You come back *only* if there's trouble. You must persuade your samaritan to take you to Göttingen."

"When I reach the city I take a room in—Do we have to go through *that* again?"

He nodded.

"In the morning I go to the Catholic church and find the confessional schedule. Then I go to the *Banhof* and get a train schedule. Then I return to the hotel to wait for you in the lobby. When you arrive, I go up to my room and you follow. That's the part I like best," she said mischievously.

"*Gut.*" He smiled.

The next morning Waller shed her heavy clothing and slithered into a tight wool dress and high-heeled shoes that had been smuggled out of Berlin by Stefanie. Before they left, the girls had argued about the extra clothing, but in the end Waller had given in to her friend's vanity, and now she was glad she had. She wrapped her shoes in canvas to keep her feet warm, made her way down to the road below, knocked the snow off her legs and waited. She liked wearing a dress again.

The first vehicle to pass was a large U.S. Army truck. The men in the back shouted and whistled; one threw her a pack of cigarettes, and another grabbed his fly. She picked up the cigarettes and put them in her bag. Other military vehicles came by at intervals, including a long line of mud-covered tanks, which she heard long before she saw. With each passing, soldiers shouted and waved, but no vehicles stopped.

After nearly two hours, and just before she was about to give up her frigid post and climb back up the mountain, a long green sedan approached and slid to a halt nearby. Waller peered inside. A woman driver. She was alone, wearing a U.S. Army fatigue jacket with major's gold leaves.

"Get in," the American woman said. She had a nice voice and small pearl earrings dangling from her ears. Her hair was almost black, pulled back tightly into a bun. There were some small crow's-feet around her eyes, but her skin was clear and she was well made up— all in all, an attractive woman who took pains with her appearance.

Taking in all this with a glance, Waller began to cry, the intensity of her own tears surprising her. The American leaned over, pushed open the door and reached out to help her into the auto.

The woman showed no interest in talking and remained silent while Waller's crying subsided into small sobs. When finally she was quiet, the woman spoke. Her German was good; there was hardly an accent. "What's the problem, dear? You're rather alone way out here, aren't you?"

"My grandfather and I argued. He beat me. I left him. I'm never going back there," Waller said angrily. She was beginning to enjoy her role.

"Never is a long time."

"I've made up my mind," Waller said, setting her jaw. "If I stay with him he'll work me to death." It felt good to pretend. She knew she was convincing. "I'm too young to spend my life on a farm. I want to live in a city, to have a good time."

"There's little gaiety in Germany these days," the major said. "It may be even worse in the cities than back on the farm with your grandfather. People are starving there."

"I'm not worried," Waller said confidently. "I'm a clever girl. I can provide for myself."

"How old are you?"

"Sixteen, but I can pass for much older. I can tell by the way boys and their fathers look at me."

The driver studied her. "Don't you have anything warmer for your feet? You could get frostbite in this snow."

Waller lifted her feet on the dash and untied the canvas bindings; she let her shoes drop and massaged her muscular legs. In the effort to rub the pain from her legs, her skirt and coat gave way to gravity, uncovering the tops of her nylon stockings. The woman whistled softly. "You *are* quite mature, Fräulein," she said. Suddenly her arm knocked Waller's legs to the floor and grabbed at the girl's skirt, tucking it into place over her bare legs.

At first Waller thought it a prudish gesture, that of an older woman trying to teach a younger girl a lesson in propriety, but as the major's hand worked at her skirt, Waller felt her fingers linger inside her thigh and finally withdraw in a long caress. What was this? She wondered how the woman would have reacted if she had reached inside the other leg and touched the hilt of a steel dagger instead of soft white flesh. The thought amused her.

"You will have to be very careful in the city, Fräulein. There are soldiers everywhere—mine, yours, Russians. They are hungry for women, especially beautiful young ones such as yourself."

"I'm not worried. I know how to handle men."

The woman glanced at her. "They are not the same as mountain boys. You must avoid them. I'm sure you're quite self-sufficient, dear, but men have a habit of taking what they want, and if there's more than one of them, you won't be able to stop them. Men are crude, not much more than animals. They're not like women; they don't understand the need for tenderness. Men go right for what they want, and never mind what a woman needs. Stay away from them."

They were passing through a small village. American soldiers seemed to be everywhere. "Not all men are like that," Waller said. "Some are nice."

The major did not reply; she had a decision to make. She had the automobile until midweek. The hunger had been growing inside her for more than a month, and finally she could bear it no more. She asked her CO for leave and a vehicle. He agreed and told her to enjoy herself, but to avoid Soviet territory. To steer clear of trouble, she had borrowed a set of maps detailing the occupation zones and various security checkpoints. She knew the documents were classified, but these were duplicates and she planned to take good care of them. She didn't want to get hung up by security and red tape during her holiday; she had needs to take care of.

"Well, now that you've made your decision, where are you going?" she asked after a pause.

"Göttingen, then south. I'm not really sure where. As far from here and my grandfather as I can get. I visited Göttingen once with my mother. I was just a child; it's probably changed."

The major touched Waller's leg again, finally drawing her hand up to rest just above the knee. Waller did not react. "I hadn't planned to go in that direction, but if you like, I could take you there," the major said. "Would you like that?" Her hand slid upward to bare flesh and her fingers danced on Waller's leg like tiny feathers.

The woman's boldness shocked Waller. Did this sort of situation fit the one described by Günter? It would be easy to kill her with the knife. "You don't have to. I don't want you to go to any trouble for me."

"No trouble," the major said huskily, her hand becoming bolder. Günter had never mentioned trouble with other women. "I'm on holiday and have no plans. I'd like very much to do this for you. Can you give me directions?"

"No," Waller said. "I don't remember. It's south. That's all I know."

"In back there's a map case. Get it up here and we'll find the road."

Waller leaned over the seat, but couldn't reach it. "I'll have to crawl over," she said. Reaching the backseat, she quickly unstrapped her dagger and slipped it into her bag. With those roving hands it was just a matter of time until the woman found the weapon, then where would she be? But since she had a ride all the way to Göttingen, it made sense to stick it out. Obviously it wasn't going to be easy; the woman clearly had designs. She reminded herself that now she was an actress and would have to improvise.

"Coming back," Waller warned. Legs first, she started to slide over the top of the seat, but squealed loudly when the major's hand suddenly shot up between her legs and grabbed her firmly.

As her momentum carried her on over the seat, the American withdrew her hand and laughed. "Very nice," she said with a trilling laugh. Not only was the girl attractive, she had not made the slightest attempt to discourage her advances. She was excited. Hitler had made homosexuality a crime, then sent all the young men out to die. For many German girls there were no males to find satisfaction with, and inevitably they had turned to one another. It had been a marvelous discovery, a rich vein to be mined at every opportunity. Desperation drove people to do things they would never consider in normal circumstances. Were it not for the war, she'd still be Stateside bedding leathery dykes. Here there were real women for the taking, blond, sweet and appreciative. Even those who weren't so disposed could easily be bribed, but apparently this girl would be a willing partner.

Waller was relieved when the remainder of the trip passed without incident. Working as a team, they used the maps to avoid checkpoints. Fresh snow was falling again in huge flakes that made visibility poor and slowed their pace to a crawl. As they entered Göttingen, the major announced that the weather was too bad to continue; she would stay the night. She insisted on buying the country girl a good dinner—one woman helping another—and perhaps a bottle of wine if one could be had.

Günter and Beard had constantly preached about the need for soldiers to be bold in their decision-making. "While you're thinking, the other guy's shooting," Beard would say. Waller was not sure why Günter was coming to Göttingen. She knew he had to meet someone at the church, but that was all. The major had maps, and certainly they would be worth something to Günter. She knew what she had to do to get them and steeled herself for the ordeal. "My name is Gretchen," she said. "What are you called?"

The woman laughed and tossed her head back in a triumphant gesture. "Rosemary. Rosemary Willison," she said.

"Rosemary Villison," Waller repeated.

"Close enough." They laughed.

All three hotels were still standing. Waller made a fuss over the one where she had stayed with her mother, and in the end was able to convince the major to stay in the easternmost one, closest to the church.

"Makes no difference to me," Rosemary said. "None of them are particularly appealing. We can only hope it will be clean and with hot water. I need a bath. Can't wait to get these clothes off." She asked Waller to share a room, but Gretchen refused. "Then the least you can do is let me pay for yours," the major said. "You can save your money for your trip."

Waller agreed. "Two adjoining rooms," she told the clerk, who gave them large threadbare towels and bundles of bedding.

"When you depart, return these," he said. "There is a facility on the floor near you. It will cost extra for hot water if you wish a bath."

"I don't care how much it costs," the major said. "I want one."

They dined at a restaurant in the cellar of a building next to the hotel. It was poorly lit, musty and so damp that they shivered through most of the meal. The fare was carrot soup and a small quantity of pork, mostly fat, shredded into a goulash. The major ordered a bottle of red wine and drank it and most of another before they had finished eating. The more she drank, the bolder she got. Waller drank sparingly.

Rosemary Willison was pleased with herself; this was turning out even better than she had imagined. The German girl was inexperienced but willing. She took her bath in a rush of fantasies of what awaited her a short distance down the hall.

Waller knew the American woman would come to her room in the night and that she had three choices: run; sleep with her; eliminate her. She made her decision.

►65 DECEMBER 11, 1945, 11:50 A.M.

A farmer hauling a load of fresh eggs was Brumm's savior. The truck was ancient, covered with dents and deep rust; it bucked and whined on steep grades but somehow kept going. South of Seesen the ride ended and Brumm began walking south, anxious to catch up with Waller. After a few moments a string of ambulances began to pass by. Toward the end of the line, one pulled over and an arm protruding from a cab window motioned Brumm to get in. The back door swung open and he climbed aboard.

A big man with a blue cap pointed to a seat next to a stack of M-1 rifles. "Going far?" he asked in broken German.

"Göttingen."

"No problem."

Near the outskirts of the city Brumm indicated with sign language that he wanted to get out. His companion hammered the partition behind the driver and the ambulance glided to a halt. No suspicion. No papers checked. Could the entire zone be so lax? It was not what he had expected.

Brumm walked the rest of the way into the city, found the church and took a room in a small boardinghouse. He jammed a chair against his door and slept fitfully with a pistol under his pillow, wondering how Waller had fared.

The next day he found a restaurant adjacent to Waller's hotel and seated himself at a table in front of a window overlooking the street. Near noon he saw her enter her hotel. He paid his bill and followed her. Inside, he found that she had been stopped by the desk clerk. He took up a position nearby and listened to the conversation.

"You and your friend. Will you be leaving today?"

"No," Waller said. "We will stay one more night, perhaps two."

"Baths again?" the man asked with a leer.

"No." As she spoke she saw Brumm. When she reached her room, she left her door slightly ajar and waited. He checked the hallway and stepped inside.

"What's this about a friend?" he asked as she threw herself on him, trembling. "Have you had some trouble?" She pointed to a closet with louvered doors. Inside was a large pile of linens and towels, underneath them a body. He looked to her for an explanation.

Waller held out the map case to him. "I had to do it, Günter. She had these."

He opened the case and spread the maps on the bed. Incredible! Zones, bases, checkpoints, unit numbers—a rich vein of information. It was a windfall he hadn't counted on.

"She wanted to be my lover," Waller said shakily.

He didn't want to hear the details. "Where's the vehicle?"

"On a street behind the building. I have the ignition key."

He held out his arms to her and she clung to him tightly. When she had calmed down a little, he sat her on the bed. "You've done well. We'll have to change our plans. Did you get the train schedules?" She nodded and wiped at an eye with the back of her hand. "Freights, too?"

"It changes all the time. I got what I could."

"Confessions?"

"In the afternoon, every day."

"All right. You remain here. I'll be back."

The confessional was in a dark corner to the side of the altar. Brumm knelt and the door to the screen opened. "I seek entry to the Order of Saint Elizabeth," he whispered.

"How many aspirants in your party?"

"Three."

"Normally we're prepared to deal only with pairs," the voice on the other side said.

"Keep your voice down."

"Remain calm," the voice retorted. "It's safe here. You are all Catholics? All three of you?"

"Yes, all baptized."

"Would you say a prayer for me?"

"Yes," Brumm said. "*Werwolf*. Stop. Wolf."

The voice repeated the words in sequence. "Wait here." The partition closed with a snap and the man's soles clipped the marble floor moving away. Brumm chambered a round, checked his silencer and waited, sweat beading his forehead. In a minute the footsteps returned and the small door between them slid open.

"There is a missal here, my son. When I leave, pull back the screen.

Give me five minutes to leave the church. It's best that we cannot identify each other. You will find the words of Saint Elizabeth quite comforting."

"Thank you, Father." The voice blessed him and left. When it was quiet the colonel slid back the screen, found the missal and stuffed it into his pocket. He waited exactly five minutes then left the church. In an alley behind the hotel he found a back entrance leading up to the guest rooms.

Waller met him at the door with her weapon in hand. He pushed by, opened the missal, extracted an envelope and studied the papers carefully. They were in order. "We'll go back tonight," he said.

Waller walked to the bed, lay down and held her arms out to him. They spent the afternoon making love and catnapping. When dark came, Brumm pulled the car into the alley while Waller went down to the lobby to distract the attention of the clerk. He carried the body down the back stairs, as if the woman were asleep or ill, and put her in the trunk. Then he returned to the American's room and removed her belongings and a half-full bottle of wine.

When Brumm rounded the corner, Waller was waiting by the curb. She got in and they drove slowly out of the town. "Where's the body?" she asked as the auto began to accelerate on a clear country lane.

"In back."

"She was on leave from her unit until midweek. She won't be missed until later. What now?"

"Back to our valley to wait out the winter."

"The automobile?"

"It's going to have an accident."

West of where they would reenter the Harz there was a sheer drop. Together they took the corpse from the trunk and dressed her in her uniform. Then Brumm smashed the wine bottle on the floor and they pushed the vehicle over the side of the cliff. It exploded into flames at the bottom.

"Will anyone see the fire?" Waller asked.

"Perhaps, but it's not important." Changing into their heavy boots, they began their trek back into the mountains.

►66 DECEMBER 24, 1945, 11:00 P.M.

It was Christmas Eve and Beau Valentine had returned to Nuremberg. He had a lot of ideas floating around in his head, but so far none of them had connected. He'd learned long ago that there were times when problems couldn't be solved by sheer willpower; you had to step away, find a diversion and let your subconscious take over. He imagined this part of his mind to be a swamp with a smooth surface. Underneath it was something else, a reservoir filled with every idea he'd ever had, every word he'd ever spoken or heard, every experience. He didn't know why it happened, but if you worked a problem hard and long enough, then let it slide into the subconscious swamp, some sort of biochemical magic took place, and more often than not, the process brought forth new ideas and a fresh perspective.

Parking in front of the building, Valentine walked up the front steps. There was a Christmas tree inside and lights were strung on the walls. He'd always liked Christmas, and now just the sight of the decorations made him glad he'd come.

When he got to the door on the upper floor, he knocked lightly. A sleepy voice called out, "Go away, I'm sleepy."

"It's Santa Claus," he said through the door.

Seconds later Angie stared out at him. "Beau?"

"Ho, ho, ho," he said as he stepped inside.

►67 JANUARY 1, 1946, 9:30 A.M.

For several moments Brumm found himself trapped between sleep and consciousness, caught between a distant memory he couldn't quite grasp and the warm reality beside him. Waller was on her side, pressed tightly against him, her head on his shoulder, one of her legs draped over him. Her head was tilted slightly, her mouth open, and she was breathing deeply and evenly. Sliding gently away from her and out of bed, he stood, stretched and rubbed the back of his neck. It had been a nightlong celebration, with too much wine, and now the stiffness in his muscles told him he was facing a day of misery, the price for loss of self-control. These were rare feelings for him, but sometimes one had to let go and vent the juices that fermented inside a man. For months the group had exercised remarkable discipline; both he and Hans had spent their days training and teaching their Valkyries the skills of soldiers. At night they seldom slept alone, but the pattern was that of a single girl each night; who would be their partner was decided by the girls themselves, and neither the colonel nor his sergeant inquired about the selection process.

Brumm dressed slowly, taking time to think about their situation. Herr Wolf and Razia Scheel took little part in the activities of the group, and while Wolf had made no demands for a long time, Brumm sensed that something dangerous was building inside the man. Herr Wolf and his companion had even stopped eating with the others, and despite repeated attempts by the Valkyries to pull them into their circle, they remained on the outside, aloof and comfortable with each other. Scheel was difficult to understand; she acted like a slave around Wolf, doing his bidding without protest, always beside him, waiting for her next order. It was weird. Brumm supposed that the woman's experiences in the death camps had triggered some kind of survival mechanism, but it was not something he could identify with, and she made him uncomfortable. What did the two talk about when they were alone? What did they do? She was an attractive female, but it seemed unlikely that they were lovers, though some of the odors emanating from their living area made both Brumm and Beard wonder.

Late the previous night the group had gone to the pool in the cave. There they drank and played. Herr Wolf immediately retired with Scheel to their quarters. At midnight there had been a halfhearted celebration of the passing of the old year, and Brumm had been called upon to comment. He was drunk and filled with conflicting emotions. In the end he had simply raised his glass and offered a toast to Germany and Germans, and the others had cheered, then splashed en masse into the pool. Later he had crawled out of the water with the intention of returning to his room to sleep, but one of the girls had jumped on his back and ridden him piggyback style down to her room. They were still in the preliminaries of lovemaking when another Valkyrie threw herself into bed with them and a wrestling match ensued that eventually turned into three-way sex. At one point Brumm looked up and saw Herr Wolf standing in the shadow of the doorway, his arms crossed, the muscles in his face drawn tight. He had fled when one of Brumm's partners began squealing as she reached a climax.

Now, as he dressed, Brumm had a feeling that Herr Wolf was going to cause trouble, and wondered as much about how it would manifest itself as how he would cope with it. There had been heavy snow in the valley for weeks, and it was increasingly difficult to go out. Being trapped inside was dangerous for them all, he knew. Even in small groups that were well adjusted and comfortable with one another, there could be friction when members lacked space to be alone. In this one there were signs of tensions, and Herr Wolf was the main source of them.

Entering the main living area, Brumm found Erda sitting at a table, staring into a cup of coffee. Her hair was tousled and there were bags under her eyes. "Good morning," he said as he poured his own coffee.

"My head hurts," she said simply.

Stefanie was sitting by the fire. She wore an unbuttoned shirt that was too long, and from time to time when she moved, her breasts flashed into view. "It's another part of me that's sore," she said with a giggle.

"Overuse," Brumm teased.

"Not enough," she countered, her tone serious.

The three sat quietly as the others filed in. Gretchen was the last, and after she had made tea for herself, she sat beside Brumm, pressing her leg against his. "I didn't hear you get up."

"You looked too comfortable to wake."

Beard added logs to their fire and poked at them to increase the heat.

Exactly when Herr Wolf entered they weren't sure. One minute he was absent; the next he was there. He was wearing a brown suit, a white shirt and a black tie. His arms were hanging in front of him, his hands joined, and he was glaring at the group. Walking over to Stefanie, he pinched the shoulder of her blouse and said, "Cover yourself." His voice was different and Brumm tensed. "You are a disgrace to German womanhood and to the Reich!" The man's face was turning red, but his voice was still controlled. "If you must carry on like a common whore at night, at least present the illusion of a proper woman during the day when decent people are about."

"Leave her alone," Brumm said.

Herr Wolf turned to face the colonel and slapped his hip. "Stand when you address your Führer!" he screamed. Brumm and Beard simultaneously sprang to their feet in a conditioned response. Wolf's voice was powerful and commanding. "Colonel Brumm, I am disgusted by your behavior. Where is your honor? I would expect the great von Brumm to behave with more decorum. Last night was a disgusting display of human weakness. You were copulating like a common animal."

"You can't—" Beard started to say something, but Hitler turned on him immediately.

"You!" The disgust was heavy in Hitler's voice. "You should be castrated; I expect more from my noncommissioned officers."

Brumm stepped toward the man and tried to take hold of his arm. "Let's discuss this in private."

Hitler pulled away, and suddenly there was a pistol in his hand and his arm was shaking. "Don't touch me!" he screamed. "No one may touch the Führer!"

"Then get control of yourself," Brumm warned.

Hitler laughed a high-pitched squeal. It was the kind of sound one might hear in a mental ward. "Control? You speak to me of control? *You?* You're like all the rest, Brumm. What have you become? I thought I had selected a man with integrity, a man to be relied upon. Instead I find that you are no different. I've let you play at being leader, Colonel, but no longer. You lack vision. I can no longer accept this; from this moment on I command here. I will decide what is to be done by whom, and what is *not* to be done. As always, I must rely only on myself," he added with contempt.

As he talked he used the pistol like a pointer, and each time he aimed it at one of the girls she immediately moved to get out of the line of fire. Brumm and Beard stood their ground, but exchanged a quick glance: something had to be done.

"Crawl back into your hole," Beard said suddenly, and Hitler reacted with a scream. A shot went wide of the sergeant major, struck the stone wall behind him and ricocheted around the room, making them all duck reflexively. "Insubordination," Hitler accused. "I won't have it! You have sworn an oath to me, Sergeant. An *oath!* How dare you question me? Were it not for me, you would still be clawing the ground in poverty. All of Germany is indebted to me; without me there would be no Reich. I alone lifted you out of oblivion, made you something—all of you," he said, waving the gun around the room. "I gave you something; I restored your will and your honor."

"Yes," Rau snapped back. "You gave us the Reich." He swung his long arms in an arc. "This is it. A dark hole dug into the rocks."

Hitler suddenly became calm and his voice dropped. "You do not deserve me. None of you deserve me; you are all unworthy of your Führer. You failed me, and in doing so, you failed Germany and yourselves. As a result, now I am consigned to this icy hell with hormone-driven adolescents and two who masquerade as soldiers." He paused, and his voice dropped even lower. Again the pistol was aimed at Rau, and now the arm was steady. He smiled. "You call yourselves men. All these months and not one of these women is pregnant. Men? I spit on your manhood."

Brumm fought for self-control. Part of him was filled with terror; whatever Hitler had become since the escape, Herr Wolf was gone now, and in his place was the old Führer, in control of himself and filled with rage. In such a state there was no way to predict what he would do. Brumm knew he had to act, but a voice in his head kept whispering, He is your Führer.

Beard could take no more. He started toward Hitler, who tensed and took aim. Brumm used Beard's movement as a diversion and stepped quickly forward, driving Hitler's gun hand upward, then locking it in both of his, twisting backward until the pistol dropped. Using a forearm lock, he tightened his grip and increased the pressure, but despite obvious pain the man did not make a sound. Brumm knew that he had almost reached the point where further pressure would snap the bones in the forearm, but if he relented now, all would be lost. "Herr Wolf," he said calmly. "In a situation such as ours, there is no place for animosity. All here have risked their lives to save yours. All have served willingly, asking nothing in return. You will apologize to them immediately and then we will no longer speak of this." Increasing the pressure a notch, he added, "Now."

"Never," Herr Wolf said. "I am Adolf Hitler."

Brumm tightened his grip again and Hitler collapsed, his knees buckling under the pain. "All right," he said in a hushed voice. There were tears in his eyes.

"Say it," Brumm ordered.

Hitler was on his knees, his eyes down. "I apologize," he whispered, the words barely audible.

Brumm released his hold, jerked the man to his feet by his lapels, and sent him flying across the room with a powerful shove. "Here I am in command," he called to the retreating back as Herr Wolf bolted through the door to his quarters, not looking back.

Beard picked up the pistol and stood beside his colonel. "Our Führer," he said mockingly.

▶68 FEBRUARY 23, 1946, 6:00 A.M.

The weather fronts that slithered down from the North Sea and the Baltic seemed to home in on the Harz automatically and hang there until pushed away by new systems. Good flying days were few, and on those rare occasions when the weather was clear, the Siberian and Pogrebenoi made the most of it.

Ezdovo had selected a cramped Arado 96B, a German trainer modified for artillery-spotting missions. He would have preferred a Soviet aircraft, but none was available and it would have taken too long to have one ferried in. The Arado was easy enough to handle and was fuel-efficient, so light that he could almost glide at stall speed in the air currents above the mountains, thus increasing their time aloft. The only drawback was that the skin of the aircraft was of lacquered canvas, so when they were aloft they had to bury themselves in leather flying suits lined with fleece to keep from freezing.

Pogrebenoi's gender was never a problem. Ezdovo treated her cautiously, as he would have any other new comrade, but his satisfaction with her grew quickly. She'd never flown in a small craft before and she loved it. More important, she was helpful and resourceful; she did anything he asked and had plenty of ideas of her own.

After their initial shakedown flights, they found their charts were inadequate; the scale was far too large for the kind of work ahead of them. Pogrebenoi went to Berlin and returned with a complete set of topographical charts from the Nazi Ministry of the Interior. The new ones were large and bulky, so clumsy to handle in the small cockpit that she reduced them to quadrants, mounted them on fiberboards and enclosed them in clear paper. The result was an easy-to-use segment that fit into the lap and was waterproof. After making two complete sets, she had even taken Petrov's carefully devised search grid and improved it.

"You're at home with maps," Ezdovo observed to her one evening. It was as close to a compliment as he was capable of giving.

"I learned in '42 when we stopped the Germans. Their maps were perfect. I could see that intricate terrain information gave their field commanders an edge on us. We often worked behind the German lines; knowing where we were was critical." She was pleased that he appreciated her work; in turn she liked his quiet and reliable way of doing things. He seemed gentle, a trait she had not seen in a man in a long time.

While Pogrebenoi was efficient and creative with tasks when they were grounded, it was her talents in the air that captured Ezdovo's deepest respect. She had eyes like a bird of prey. Ezdovo would put the Arado into a gentle turn or skid, pull the throttle back to near-idle and ride the wind currents. He had great pride in his own vision, but next to Talia he began to feel like a blind man, and it became a running joke between them. He'd say, "There's an animal down there in that grove of pines." She'd reply, "It's a badger with a torn left forepaw and a tick in his right ear." Then they'd roar with laughter, delighted with each other's company.

It was the middle of February before the fronts cleared away from the mountain range and gave them two solid days in which to work. They flew twice daily, taking off before sunrise in order to arrive over the mountains at daybreak. At midday they'd refuel and have a Spartan lunch, then hop over to their next search grid for the remainder of the day's light.

The Harz was hardly the Alps; it was an aged, eroded range of slate and granite, notable primarily for its contrast to the northern German lowlands. But if the mountains weren't majestic from afar, their interior from above, a confusing maze, was impressive to two old soldiers. It didn't take long for them to understand the extent and complexity of the obstacles below. Even from the air, it was difficult to trace the valleys; they were so narrow and deep that shadows prevented a clear view. Often Ezdovo had no choice but to dip the Arado down to treetop level to survey the terrain. After much trial and error they developed some methods for venturing deep into the valleys. They would make passes until Pogrebenoi was comfortable with the lay of the land; using a broad pencil with soft lead, she would sketch in the landmarks and number each of them. Then Ezdovo would dive down so that they could explore each small area individually and note what they saw on the chart.

Pogrebenoi also used a 35-mm German camera with a telephoto lens to get shots of spots that interested them so that they could study the photos when they were socked in and unable to fly. After each mission she would redo her drawings and sketches in permanent ink, then mount them on a large wall. Their objective was to create a huge, detailed map of the Harz and its environs. When it was complete, they'd have the Red Army cartographic unit in Berlin render it in a smaller, more manageable size.

During their flights they looked hard for smoke plumes, even though they suspected that if Brumm was indeed in the Harz, he would know how to make fire without smoke. Sometimes they did spot smoke, but always on the fringes of the mountains, not in the interior; the only such phenomena within were several pockets of steam plumes from natural hot springs.

On the morning of February 23 the weather closed in again. Ezdovo was awake before Pogrebenoi, and when he looked outside, he knew they were through flying for a while. A fierce wind had created white-out conditions. When Pogrebenoi came out of her bedroom, she found him sitting by the stove with his boots off and a cup of coffee.

"Grounded," he grumbled. She didn't have to look; she could hear the wind. It was the start of the worst snowstorm of the winter. She spent the day refining her renderings by the light of several lanterns.

That evening Ezdovo was shocked to hear the scratchy music of Tchaikovsky coming from a small hand-cranked victrola. Where Pogrebenoi had gotten it he had no idea, but the music was wonderful. He sat in front of a hissing fire studying charts and watching her out of the corner of his eye. She wore a heavy sweater, trousers and wool socks pulled up to her knees over her pants legs, her dark hair free and glistening in the wavering light. At one point she looked up from her drawing and caught the Siberian staring at her. When he turned his eyes away, embarrassed, she smiled at him and went back to her work.

When she had finished her latest drawings, she called him over for a look. He stood close to her, admiring what she had done without comment, her scent overwhelming him. He imagined feeling her through the sweater, and the occasional brushes against her set him burning inside. Before retiring to their sleeping areas, they took a small brandy each and sat cross-legged in front of the fire, not talking.

Ezdovo could not sleep and he knew why. Talia. He loved the sound of her name. She was beautiful and independent, like a mountain woman. They were at ease together, but she gave no indication of any deeper interest. It was frustrating; she was on his mind constantly. He got up from his cot and walked to the door that separated their sleeping areas. He wanted only to look at her, to reassure himself that she was flesh and blood, not a vision that haunted him. Pulling back the curtain, he looked toward her bed but could not see her. Her soft voice startled him. "For a great hunter, you stalk very slowly," she said from the darkness. He heard her bare feet padding across the floor as she came toward him.

▶69 MARCH 24, 1946, NOON

Pogrebenoi had seen the valley twice before, first in late November and then, briefly, during February when the weather had broken for a short time. She was interested in having a closer look at it.

For the most part the aerial reconnaissance team of the Special Operations Group had found itself on the ground during the winter months, and the two Russians had spent their time together double-checking the condition of their aircraft and working on a Packard limousine with a straight twelve-cylinder engine. There seemed to be nothing Talia could not do, and as the months passed their feelings for each other intensified. After their first night together they had discussed the situation at length and decided that it would be improper for it to happen again, at least in current circumstances. In another time and place it would be all right, and both of them wondered if such circumstances would ever present themselves. Their self-imposed discipline hurt each of them. From his years in the party, Ezdovo had formed the rather cloudy opinion that Russian women shared more of their society's work than in other cultures, but he'd never thought much about the implications of this. When he did finally focus on it, he realized that while there had always been Russian women around, they were always on the periphery. Never until Talia had he attended an important meeting in which a woman had participated. It occurred to him that while the Communist party paid homage to equality between the sexes, its practice was much different from its theory. That someone in the party bureaucracy had recognized Pogrebenoi's potential was interesting. If Hitler had accomplished nothing else by his invasion, he had inadvertently fused Soviet society in ways that without the Nazi threat might have required generations.

Such abstract thinking was not typical of Ezdovo, and that Pogrebenoi had served to launch it was further evidence to him of her uniqueness. To reason through what the attraction was did not interest him; it sufficed that the longer he worked beside her, the more he cared about her and the more they trusted each other. Also etched in Ezdovo's mind was the memory of their one night in each other's arms.

Petrov visited them several times during the winter to examine their search grid and the results. Technically Bailov was assigned to them but they saw little of him. Gnedin drove down from time to time to visit, never on business, and they enjoyed his company. During the doctor's most recent visit they'd all become light-headed under the influence of pertsovka, and Bailov, who had returned unexpectedly, took the opportunity to pull Ezdovo aside and grill him about his partner.

"An interesting woman, eh, comrade?"

Ezdovo ignored the remark.

"Have you—?" Bailov joined his thumb and forefinger and used a fountain pen to complete the crude gesture.

Ezdovo flared, partly in embarrassment, but more in anger. Grabbing Bailov, he wrestled him roughly to the floor, then leaned close to his friend's ear. "No, comrade, I haven't. In my part of the country, women look like musk oxen. We prefer nubile young men like you." He buried his tongue in Bailov's ear and sent him scrambling wildly out of the Siberian's hold. He laughed as Bailov kept a fair distance from him while he brushed dust off his clothes.

"The party doesn't like degenerates," Bailov muttered.

"Keep your mouth shut about Pogrebenoi. She's a good soldier."

The weather broke in March, and Petrov's single-craft air force went aloft again. Over a period of several days they flew their grid methodically, photographing unusual landmarks and mapping routes in and out of certain natural formations.

Over the winter Talia had made a note to explore the narrow little valley they had seen, but she did not try to talk Ezdovo into abandoning the overall plan in order to pursue her instinct. The search had to be done the way Petrov wanted it. In time they would get to the valley and would take a close look at it then. She was a patient woman.

The day was sunny and warm, and the two Russians were anxious to be airborne as they inspected the aircraft. Often they had discussed where their adversary might be hiding. Ezdovo was of the opinion that it would turn out to be easily defended from the ground, an isolated spot where there was little chance of accidental discovery, and probably an area with a limited entry. When they saw it, he told her, he would know it for what it was.

They were on their first long pass over the narrow canyon. It was Pogrebenoi who spotted someone sitting on a large boulder just above the valley floor holding something loosely across his legs; it looked like a rifle, but she couldn't be certain. She fired the camera as they passed over and knew she had gotten a good picture.

When they overflew the spot again moments later, there was no sign of any life below. They began to sweep the valley in earnest, flying up and down its length. Ezdovo kept them right at treetop level, always on the verge of a stall to slow them down, so that periodically the struts or propeller cut pine branches from the upper reaches of the mature pines. Pogrebenoi showed no fear; her eyes were riveted on the ground. She trusted Ezdovo as much as he trusted her. As they climbed out of the valley near noon to prepare to make a last pass, she tugged at his arm. "The main tributary of the stream down there widens about a kilometer from where we saw the man this morning. Can you drop below the tree line at that point? I'd like to take some shots with the side camera." During the winter they had mounted a motion-picture camera on a small platform outside Talia's window, and another on the belly. She operated them from inside, using a crude T-handle device to activate the cameras. The devices were spring-loaded, so that when she released the pressure they shut off automatically.

"Show me where," Ezdovo shouted loudly over the clatter of the small motor.

They descended below the valley rim, paralleling the contour of its steep, rough northern wall. As they came up on the location he leaned over to see it. "Not this time," he said, shaking his head. "I'll come around again."

They flew back outside to the other end of the valley. "When we pass that last outcropping I'll cut power, slip to the right and drop the nose for a few seconds," Ezdovo told her. "Then I'll give it full power and pull out over the trees on the other side. No room for an error or a thermal," he warned.

She touched his face with her long hand and held it tenderly.

They were flying along the wall again. He pulled the throttle back to the edge of a stall and the tiny aircraft almost hovered over the trees. If the maneuver worked, they were going to have only feet to spare on the other side, he told himself. The outcropping of rock was almost dead ahead, and they were a good fifty meters below the rim as he eased around it. "Camera ready?"

"Go," she said firmly, but the tiny Arado was already in its turn, nose down. For a fleeting instant she had a feeling of the ground rushing up to meet them, almost as if it were trying to grab them, but even in her moment of fear she activated the cameras and clutched the triggering device tightly. She held her breath as the starboard wing threw a shadow over the water below, but even when Ezdovo rammed the throttle full forward and the plane shuddered wildly, she did not panic.

"We're not climbing," he said calmly.

"Yes, we are."

He checked the needle. The angle was so steep that it only seemed that they were level. They were climbing but still slipping forward on their tail. "We're either going up or into a stall," he told her. Without warning he jammed the stick to the left. The back of the aircraft struck something and the nose pitched forward, but he got it up again and banked right into a level climb. Dead ahead, less than a kilometer away, was the end of the valley, a huge threatening wall of stone that was looming larger. Talia knew they were too low, but there was no room to turn around. "It was a good try," she said calmly. She could see that they were going to die, so she leaned close to Ezdovo and gently held his arm.

"Hold tight," he said tensely. She felt the plane bank hard to the right and then level off again. He had miraculously lengthened the valley with the slight turn, but it still looked to be not enough. Only at the last moment did she realize what he was trying to do. Ahead and slightly above them was a huge rock formation that resembled a shallow dish turned slightly on end. Ezdovo pointed the Arado straight for it and, as it filled the windscreen, guided their wheels onto the granite, keeping the tail up. The aircraft skipped across the formation as if taxiing at high speed. As the downward angle of the rock increased, the aircraft descended into the depression, and, gathering speed, lifted, then dipped; the wheels struck the upslope on the other side hard, but there was enough lift now, and they flew off the top as if launched from a ramp. Suddenly the plane burst off the rock formation over the edge of a neighboring valley, sank, and finally began climbing to a safe altitude.

Pogrebenoi stared straight ahead, gasping for air. It was some time before she realized that their cameras were still rolling. When she released the T-handle and removed her gloves, she found deep red marks on the palms of her hands.

"I didn't think it would be *that* close," Ezdovo said as she threw her arms around him, and the little airplane immediately began to lose altitude again.

▶**70**   MARCH 24, 1946, 12:05 P.M.

Eventually the winter storms stopped coming from the north and spring began to force its way into the mountain valleys. The snow thinned to a delicate crust; vegetation began to fight its way up through the openings. The group's members were all well and strong, and their food supply was still adequate for considerably longer, but Brumm knew it was time to begin preparing for their departure. A particularly warm stretch in late March evaporated the last remnants of snow, and they moved outside again, doing more of their work in the warm sun.

It was some time before Brumm noticed the change that had begun after his conversation with Herr Wolf. The Führer's attitude toward Razia Scheel was shifting. Before, he had treated her like a young daughter, or even a pet; now his attitude seemed different.

Brumm's first inkling of it had come when he found Herr Wolf eating alone in the large living area in the early morning after the girls had gone out to train and do their chores. "She's sleeping," Herr Wolf said quickly, anticipating Brumm's question. "I didn't want to wake her." The SS colonel did not really comprehend until later. Herr Wolf had begun separating himself from her.

On another occasion, after one of Herr Wolf's nightly lectures, he suddenly launched into a long-winded appraisal of the beauty of the girl Stefanie and of her classic Aryan qualities. He also pointed out how well she listened and how intelligent her questions were. It was true that Stefanie asked questions. At first all of them had attempted to do so, but only she had persisted, and for her trouble all she got was scowls from the others, mixed with an occasional angry lecture from Herr Wolf on her lack of decorum. For months Scheel had lorded over the German girls. When she felt it was time for bed, she would tug gently at Herr Wolf's arm and he would immediately rise and end the lecture for the night with the same declaration: "Well, that's enough. Sleep is important to good health. The party demands that we keep our bodies strong, so I shall do my duty." The speech never varied.

On this particular occasion, however, Herr Wolf ignored the woman's signal and told her to go to bed if she was tired. This came after the incident of eating alone and again did not register with Brumm until later.

After the rebuff Razia stormed out of the room, and Herr Wolf continued his glowing appraisal of Stefanie. When eventually he went off to bed, the other girls teased her. "Perhaps you'll win the wager. Maybe you should go to the pool and wait for him to come to you," one of them said.

"Silence," Beard growled. He raised his eyebrows at Brumm, as if to say, Children—there's nothing you can do with them!

Afterward Brumm and Waller went for a walk outside. "What was that all about?" she wanted to know.

He wasn't sure, so he didn't answer.

With the clear weather, air traffic over the mountains resumed. Most of the planes passed high above them, but not long after the warm spell set in, a small craft began making low-level passes over the ridges. It returned several times over a period of days, crisscrossing methodically, circling every now and then over formations that apparently caught the pilot's eye.

Both the colonel and the sergeant knew aerial reconnaissance when they saw it. "It's here for a reason," Beard said matter-of-factly.

"Yes."

"Do you think they've found us yet?"

"No, not yet; they're still searching too carefully. When they stop coming back, that's when we have to worry," Brumm said. "It's time to go."

That night they told their small group that they would soon leave the valley. All the girls except Waller wanted to know where they were going. "Better you don't know," Brumm said. He carefully explained what they were to take and how they were to act. For two nights he rehearsed them for possible encounters with the authorities. They took the exercise as a game and did well. They were bright girls, and most of all they were loyal, a trait that he valued above all others. The pretense of their preparations saddened him.

It was midday, and Brumm and Beard had walked up to the far end of the valley, ostensibly to fish. Beard was caught in the open with his fishing rod across his lap as the plane buzzed down low below the rim, wobbling along just above the trees. For a moment they thought it would crash; the motor was coughing and missing badly and heavy oil smoke poured out of the carburetor vents on the side cowling.

From the shadow of a rock outcropping, they watched as the craft made pass after pass into the valley. It was so low that they could see the two people inside, and the glint from a camera mounted under the struts of one wing told them that their refuge was being photographed.

"It's one of ours," Beard said when the plane had gone.

"No, we no longer have an air force," Brumm reminded him. "Now they know. We can't wait. Tonight we prepare; tomorrow we go at first light."

"I'll get them ready," Beard said.

"Hans, my friend. We can't all go. The flood of refugees has subsided, and we would be too conspicuous and vulnerable in a large group."

The sergeant major swallowed hard.

"Duty," Brumm said quietly.

"My honor is loyalty," Beard answered, repeating the motto of the SS. "All of them?"

Brumm nodded. "All of them."

"Even Gretchen?"

Now Brumm swallowed too. "Her, too."

▶71 MARCH 24, 1946, 1:00 P.M.

Brumm and Rau kept to the shadows on their return to Stone Cave. When they arrived the girls were gathered inside and bombarded them with questions about the airborne intruder.

"Were they looking for us?"

"Have we been discovered?"

"We have to get out," another said, with fear in her voice.

"Calm down," Brumm said. "Don't panic. That's the first rule in battle. They are looking for something, though I doubt if it's us. There was a camera mounted on the aircraft and they got close enough to see what's here. It may or may not cause our discovery, but we cannot assume we're safe; we must presume that their pictures will reveal our camp. Therefore we must leave; it's a matter of prudence. Don't be concerned, my Valkyries; in any event, we are nearly ready for departure, you've been properly trained, we're packed and tonight we'll celebrate. Tomorrow we'll sleep all day, then move out at nightfall."

His speech done, Brumm saw that they were calmer, but Beard had stared at the ground the entire time. Wondering if Rau was up to what had to be done, he patted him reassuringly on the arm and went to help with the preparation of their final meal.

▶72 MARCH 24, 1946, 6:00 P.M.

They did not wait for the film to be developed. When Pogrebenoi telephoned Petrov in Berlin, Rivitsky answered. "It's Talia," she said. "We've found something."

"We're on our way," Rivitsky said and hung up.

Early in the winter Petrov had arranged for a photographic laboratory to be transferred from Poland along with two technicians. Ezdovo and Pogrebenoi were impressed by their arsenal of equipment and the two motion-picture cameras the men helped them mount on the Arado.

The two Russians were still weak-legged when they delivered the exposed film to the lab. It had been a close call and they both knew it. After the pair had had a dinner of black bread and white cheese washed down with local lager, the technicians delivered the film, set up the projector and left. Pogrebenoi hung a sheet on the wall to serve as a screen and they waited patiently for the others.

It was dark when Petrov and Rivitsky arrived in a light aircraft. Without preliminaries, Petrov entered the building and took a seat as Ezdovo switched on the projector. Pogrebenoi narrated as the projector whirred loudly. "Belly camera. First pass down the valley," she said, and cited its grid number. "Near the end I thought I saw someone on the rocks." They all watched the screen. "I didn't see anyone," Gnedin said.

Ezdovo rewound the film. "Play it at slow speed," Talia told him, and the scene flashed again more slowly. She pointed to a speck in the gray rocks. "There," she said. Again the valley rolled before them. The quality of the film was not bad, but neither was it good. "I'm sure I got something," Pogrebenoi said firmly.

"Can we get stills?" Rivitsky asked.

"Already ordered," Ezdovo told him.

"Let me see it again," Petrov said. It was the first time he had spoken.

They watched in silence as the sequence unfolded from the nose camera. When it was over, Bailov hugged Ezdovo. "The Air Force doesn't know what it missed, eh?"

"It wasn't bad," the Siberian said modestly.

"Run the side-camera reel," Petrov said.

Again they were quiet. When it ended Petrov called for lights. "The stills will tell us more," he said.

One of the technicians complained to Ezdovo about the rush order on the prints. "We'll be up all night," he whined.

"Better awake all night than asleep for eternity," the Siberian growled. The two men went to work immediately.

►73 MARCH 24, 1946, 9:30 P.M.

As they prepared the meal there was a sense of excitement, and the girls vented their nervousness with constant chatter. Waller called it their "Last Supper" and soon they all picked up the refrain.

Even Herr Wolf got into the spirit of things. His hair had been freshly cropped, his upper lip shaved. He had regained some weight, but his puffiness was gone and he looked lean and fit. They drank many bottles of wine and ate without concern for conservation. Over their months in hiding they had behaved with propriety, but now the wine and the moment loosened their discipline, and the girls openly made overtures toward the men. Near midnight they all ended up in the hot pool. Brumm began to lose track of what was happening. Some small bottles of clear liqueur made from gentian root were passed around, and its effect further distorted their minds. At one point Herr Wolf called down to the cavern to tell them to extinguish their torches; he was going to join them. Beard dropped his light into the water where it gave off a loud hiss, and then they heard Herr Wolf splash wildly into the water calling for Stefanie. They heard the voice of Razia Scheel as well, but it was dark and they could not tell where she was.

Eventually one of the girls crawled out of the pool and vomited. Her retching lasted for a long time, ending in dry heaves that wracked her body and reverberated off the walls in the cavern. Her nausea infected another girl, who stumbled out of the water, fell, picked herself up and ran for their living quarters.

Brumm drank little, but fell asleep on a rock ledge and awoke a few hours later with a pounding headache and a dry mouth. The torch had been relit. Waller was lying against him in the narrow space on her back. She was in a deep sleep, snoring lightly in little bursts, her blond hair matted to her head. He stared at her for a long time, not wanting to think about what he had to do. Finally he slid her off the ledge into the water. She did not open her eyes as he supported her back with his hand and watched her breasts peek up at him through the steaming water. He looked around quickly. The sick girl was asleep nearby. Waller's head moved; her eyelids fluttered and she smiled up at him. "I love you," she whispered. He kissed her for a long time, then pulled away as she smiled up at him. Grasping her firmly around the neck, he drove her under the water with a powerful thrust of his forearms. At first, thinking it a game, she did not struggle, but her lungs quickly turned to fire and she began to paw at his grip tentatively, then frantically. One of her legs broke the surface and slapped down, raising a small rooster tail. Brumm quickly hooked a heavy leg over her to keep her underwater and held her there, unrelenting.

Gretchen's hands fell away and opened, palms up to him, pleading. He pulled her head closer to the surface to see her face. The whites of her eyes were huge, like eggs, and her mouth was open. As their eyes met, her mouth moved to form words. There was a sudden gulp and a small whirlpool formed near the surface as she expended her final breath and inhaled water into her lungs. He knew it was over, but he kept her under for a while longer to be certain.

Not looking back, he climbed out of the pool and moved quickly to the other girl. As he slid his hand onto her throat, she opened her eyes and smiled, thinking his attention was for another reason. She smelled terrible; vomit was matted in her hair and had dried on her shoulders and breasts. With a quick motion he broke her neck and let her fall back to the rock with a dull smack.

Ahead of him there was a shot. He grabbed a shotgun from a wooden rack and rushed forward into the living area. The door to Herr Wolf's room was open. Stefanie was naked astride Herr Wolf, her arm hanging over the side of the bed, her chin on his face; blood was cascading onto him from a gaping wound in her chest. Brumm took in the scene in an instant, instinctively rolled to one side and backed up into a crouch. Razia Scheel was standing a few feet from the bed with Herr Wolf's revolver in one hand and a small knife in the other; her arm shook wildly as she tried to line up another shot. "It was my place," she shrieked. "Mine!" Brumm fired a single round of buckshot; it cut through her arms into her bare chest, severing one arm and leaving the other connected only by a fleshy ribbon. The knife clattered on the floor and Brumm kicked it aside; then he yanked Stefanie's body off Herr Wolf. With disgust he grabbed up a handful of clothes and threw them at him.

Herr Wolf's shoes were near Scheel, and as he crawled over to reclaim them he whimpered, "The dirty Jew. She tried to kill me. The dirty Jew—"

"Shut up," Brumm ordered angrily.

Beard met his colonel in the hall, his Schmeisser at the ready, as Brumm pushed by him into another bedroom. Two of the girls were in a large bed under a gray quilt, their eyes wide with fear. Beard raised his pistol to fire, but Brumm pushed his arm down. "I'll do it," he said. He broke open the shotgun, ejecting the spent casing to the floor, inserted another round, snapped the weapon shut and swung it toward the bed. One of the girls pulled the covers over her head; the other jumped up and ran to the corner, turning her back on Brumm. He shot the one on the bed first, hitting her just under the throat, almost taking her head off. Then he turned and shot the other one in the middle of her bare back. She fell forward against the wall.

Rau slipped past him and Brumm followed him into the sergeant's room. Before he could act, Beard stepped to the bed, put the barrel of his Schmeisser against the white flesh under Ilse's throat and loosed a short burst. "My . . . honor is . . . loyalty," he stammered.

Brumm tapped him on the shoulder. "Let's go."

Because they had packed the night before, it took less than an hour for the men to prepare for their departure.

Herr Wolf came out of his room and sulked on the hearth while they gave a final check to their packs and weapons. Satisfied that all was in order, Brumm went back into the rooms and cavern alone. Beginning with Gretchen, he used his knife to cut a familiar symbol into the dead girls' foreheads. He was gone for only a few moments; when he returned, his trousers were wet up to his knees.

They left without looking back and moved quickly up the valley to the entrance. Brumm threw three grenades into the minefield, setting off a number of explosions in a chain reaction, and blew the rock used to block their entrance with a quarter pound of explosives and a short fuse. The boulder was blown into several large parts away from the entrance. Inside the tunnel he led the way as they crawled hurriedly through the narrow cavern, scraping themselves as they pushed their packs ahead of them.

Once clear of the valley, they moved at double time through a nearby canyon. At the summit, as they paused for Herr Wolf to catch his breath, Brumm took stock of their situation. Wolf had made the climb relatively easily. His health was better, and it was apparent that now he could handle a moderate physical load. His emotional condition was still questionable, however.

Beard searched the valley below them with his field glasses. "All clear," he reported.

"We have at least a two-day head start. Maybe more," Brumm said.

▶74 MARCH 25, 1946, 6:15 A.M.

The team ate an early breakfast and sat back to wait. Ezdovo, Pogrebenoi and Bailov took Rivitsky with them to the hangar to show him the Arado. Chips had been knocked out of the wooden prop, tree branches had torn a gaping hole in the aft fuselage, and the starboard strut was bent.

When they returned, Gnedin was tacking still-wet photographs to the wall and Petrov was grinning. He tapped one of the photos with the back of his forefinger. "Look at this," he said to Pogrebenoi, handing her a magnifying glass. On the rock where she had seen someone, a small arrow had been drawn. It was not a good shot, but at the very end of the shadow behind the rock, there were two feet cut off at the ankles.

Pogrebenoi beamed.

"Diving into the shadows," Petrov said. "Have this enlarged again," he ordered, "but it will only confirm what we know. Someone's in there and your presence alarmed them. Did you scan the valley before yesterday?"

"No," Ezdovo said. "Only from a distance."

Petrov lit a small cigar. A technician brought in another batch of stills, these from the side camera, then ducked out of the room. He did not know who these strange people were, but they smelled of big trouble.

The near-suicide pass had paid off. In the new stills they saw a man standing in the valley near the stream. "I never saw that one when we flew over," Pogrebenoi said. Other photographs showed the face of a building constructed within the cliff, its front door standing open. They could also see that the wide place in the stream had been created by a dam.

Petrov walked over to the wall chart. "Show me," he said to Talia.

By late afternoon they knew where they were going and how they were going to get there. They would drive west from Nordhausen and go in from the south side of the mountains. They spent the evening preparing charts and assigning duties. All of them could feel their anticipation rising, and welcomed the feeling.

▶75 MARCH 25, 1946, 10:30 A.M.

On a scale of ten Beau Valentine put the Swiss at two: one point for the physical beauty of their country and another for cleanliness. These were the only redeeming qualities he could find in them. That the Swiss had remained neutral throughout the war had been useful to American intelligence operations, but to Valentine's way of thinking, they were no more than antiseptic Krauts. He didn't like them and made no bones about it. Whenever he had felt the need to cross into Swiss territory he had felt depressed about it long after he left. The Swiss drowned themselves in pragmatism. There were no great Swiss philosophers, and in his opinion no painters or composers worth a second look or listen. But the time had come to find out what was going on, and there was no way he was going to report into some ragtag army intelligence unit.

After crossing the border, he caught a train to Zurich. Arriving at the gray office building, he was shown into an office and left alone to leaf through magazines from the States. The office had changed drastically; the original decor had been what Arizona called Early Married, but this was plush, the furniture antique and valuable. There was a handwoven Oriental rug on the floor and mahogany bookcases filled with leather-bound volumes. A silk flag stood in a corner, and the bases of the lamps on the end tables were of thick Irish crystal. Heavy decanters filled with smoke-colored scotch were set out on a bar near the hand-carved desk. What the hell was going on? This was not Arizona's style, but it was his office.

A man came into the office, walked past Valentine without speaking and sat down behind the desk. He opened a drawer, extracted a name plate, put it in front of him and played with its positioning until he had it the way he wanted it. It read: Justin L. R. Creel III. "Where's Arizona?" Valentine demanded. The old field officer had been more than a good supervisor; he had also been a friend. An attorney from Phoenix with a sharp mind and a tongue to match, he had been demanding but reliable. This was no time to be breaking in a new control officer.

"Reassigned."

"Where to?"

The new man scowled at him; to ask such questions was a breach of protocol in the OSS. "You'll spare me a scene if I tell you it's none of your business," he said acerbically. "You've taken a long time to comply with the directive."

"I got busy," Valentine said. The new man's suit was expensive, tailored beautifully; he wore gold cuff links and a fat watch, and his shoes were so shiny they looked wet. When the need arose, Valentine could be the most down-home country boy that ever traipsed through manure; a little voice in his head told him this was one of those times.

"I've had a thorough look at your dossier," the officer said in a precise monotone. "You have had your share of successes and failures. You have a penchant for independent action and a flair for languages. You're also fat, out of shape, dress like a slob and have virtually no future in the American intelligence network. I'm told you like to hear things 'without the frills.' Am I performing up to your expectations?"

"Boy, yewer way outta my league."

The man's eyebrows lifted briefly before he returned his attention to the folder in front of him. "On January twenty-second of this year President Truman signed an executive order establishing the National Intelligence Authority. By this order he created the Central Intelligence Group as the NIA's operating arm."

Valentine contemplated what he'd heard. "You mean the OSS is kaput?"

"Decommissioned by presidential order on October first; it's outlived its usefulness."

"But Donovan's running the new outfit, right?"

"Mr. Donovan and the president do not see eye to eye on matters of national security. The OSS was run with a complete disregard for discipline; Donovan was too free and easy in his management style. He's out, and so are the rest of his kind."

Valentine smiled and leaned forward. "You're shitting me, right?"

"Which brings us to the matter of one Beauregard Valentine. In December of '44 you were provided with forty thousand dollars in gold; our auditors report that there's been no accounting for its subsequent disbursement. We have been unable to ascertain from the Italians that they received this money; my superiors have instructed me to inquire about its whereabouts." The man's tone was that of Nobel laureate to cretin.

"Fuckin' B-17s wasted forty thousand dollars in duds on every mission. Ain't nobody tryin' to account for them, is there?"

The officer pushed his gold wire-rimmed glasses up the bridge of his straight nose and glared at him. "The war's over for you, Mr. Valentine. Men of your ilk are no longer needed; I won't offer my own opinions about whether they were ever needed. So you are finished, Mr. Valentine. But you're not getting away until you have settled all your accounts. The OSS had its own way of doing things; we do things by the book. Our profession is in need of thinning; you, I believe, are what agriculturists would term a weed."

Valentine leaned over the desk and snapped shut the folder in Creel's hands. "All right, asshole, let's get us an understanding." Creel tensed. "I didn't steal anything, and for damn sure not a measly forty thousand bucks." He tapped the closed folder with the heel of his hand. "If you'd bothered to read close enough, you'd have found that I'm what the sociologists call part of that very small and exclusive class, the filthy rich. A regular blue blood, Social Register and all. I don't know who you are and I don't much care, friend. I could buy your wife tomorrow and give her to my Cajun friends for *Bojo* practice. I could blow you away on the street tonight, turn myself in and never spend a day in jail. Friend, you are dealing with the worst trouble you ever dreamed of when you fuck with me, so sit back on your little tin throne and shut your mouth. I came here to talk, and I'm damned well gonna do it."

When Valentine paused, Creel was fully back in his chair, clutching the armrests, still as death, his eyes wide.

"I've got reason to believe that the Russians are still hunting for Hitler's body. I've got one damned good lead—hotter than anything I've ever been around. I need two things from you, Mr. Asshole Case Supervisor Creel. First, I want you write down in your report *exactly* what I'm telling you. Use my words so you don't get it garbled, sonny. Second, I want you to slap a twenty-four-hour surveillance on Hitler's bunker in Berlin."

"That's in the Russian zone," Creel countered, his voice cracking in mid-sentence.

"I know it's Russian territory, idiot! That's why I want surveillance. Around-the-clock with the best people you've got. If anything happens in or around that place, I want to know pronto and not in some cute code. And don't worry about calling me; *I'll* call *you*."

"You are no longer authorized to undertake new initiatives," Creel said defensively. "You are without portfolio."

Valentine leaned forward. "Fuck your portfolio, you upper-case pain in the ass. You call Donovan and tell him the score. Tell him you got it from Valentine. *He'll* tell the new big shots to authorize the goddamned initiative!" He turned away from the desk and sat on a small love seat, his leg draped over one arm. "Pick up your pencil, sonny, and write this down. If I'm going too fast, stop me." He laid out his activities since entering Germany. He had Creel read it back to him, added a sentence or two, and then got up. "One last thing: Italians are like Swiss when it comes to money. I gave the money to my partisans, just like all the other money. If you want to see their bankbooks, ask them. Put that in your report, too."

He opened the door. "Any questions?" Creel shook his head. Valentine smiled, pointed his finger and rotated it slowly. "Then pick up the damn phone, sonny, and get some coverage in Berlin."

The door slammed. Creel read his handwritten notes again, then fumbled with the telephone.

Outside the office Valentine paused to calm himself. The OSS was gone; he was out of a job. Fuck 'em, he decided. This one I'm taking all the way to the end. For Arizona. For Wild Bill. For me.

▶76 MARCH 25, 1946, NOON

They were dressed as farmers. Brumm led them quickly out of the mountains, but as soon as they cleared the wilderness he slowed them to a pace so sluggish that it frightened Herr Wolf. Their route was due south, but winding in its dependence on topography. Their lack of speed was deliberate, the result of a hard lesson well learned. Behind enemy lines you had to convince casual onlookers that you belonged. Haste not only led to errors in judgment, but made you conspicuous. Farmers seldom hurried, so Brumm set a pace that was in keeping with their cover.

With the SS colonel on the point and Beard trailing, Herr Wolf was sandwiched between them. He seldom complained, and did exactly as he was told. The two soldiers each carried a machine pistol tucked into the folds of his overcoat, gunnysacks over their shoulders like sailors, and a cloth satchel containing clothing, medicine and other essentials. From a distance Brumm knew they would pass muster.

The plan was to head south toward the western fringes of the Thuringian Forest, and from there to veer west to an area north of Marburg. This part of the journey was calculated by Brumm to be less than two hundred kilometers, but because they would be traveling with the terrain, the actual distance would be 25 percent greater, he estimated. Figuring an average daily pace of nearly thirty kilometers and, allowing for obstacles and delays, they would reach their destination in nine or ten days.

Brumm had decided that they would travel during the day. It was risky, but Herr Wolf would have too much difficulty in the darkness. Their plan was to sleep from dark to first light, then move out, foraging for their food as they went by stealing from the farms and isolated houses they encountered. Such losses were common to countryfolk, and while the residents might be irritated, it was unlikely that they would make an official complaint.

It had begun raining as they left the Harz and it was still coming down, a soft soaking drizzle that drenched the countryside, activated the soil and christened new flowers. Though they were frequently wet, whenever possible Brumm kept them under the canopies of red-pine forests, their floors covered by a thick matting of aging brown needles. He estimated that it would take seven days to reach the Christianburg area, and he hoped that the charts stolen from the American major would prove accurate.

▶**77** MARCH 26, 1946, 3:00 P.M.

It was a travesty; with the war less than a year into history, the OSS had been mothballed, consigned to the scrap heap. Arizona had been a damn fine case officer, the best Valentine had ever worked with. He'd known how to get the most out of his men in the field without treating them like toy soldiers. He'd understood that "out there" an agent needed freedom to operate, current information to help him make decisions and, above all else, complete support. What it boiled down to was mutual respect. The new man was about as far removed from Arizona as could be imagined. When Ivy Leaguers like Creel started taking control, it was time for old hands to fade away. It was galling to think that Wild Bill could have allowed this to happen.

It had been a long war with a big price tag, and now it was time to move on, Valentine told himself. Back to Louisiana. Maybe a stint in "Nawlins" would clear his mind and help him to decide his future. Birth with wealth was a true burden. To those without, it looked like a cushy life, but it wasn't. The wealth hadn't come to the family in a single stroke of good fortune; it had been accumulated by generations of Valentines, and their riches were not fluid. The lives of hundreds of people depended on the Valentines, and it fell to some selected members to dedicate their lives to increasing the size and scope of the fortune. Every Valentine learned hard economic lessons early in life. The golden principle was that wealth could not remain static; it either grew or diminished, with the former state preferred.

In the existing Valentine clan it was Beau's younger brother Buster who aspired to the stewardship of the fortune, and Beau was more than happy to leave him to it. But if his role was not that of capitalist, this left only one option, for the rich had only two: to increase the fortune or to serve mankind. It was ironic, Valentine often thought, that only the very rich and the very poor—those with everything and those with nothing—had the time or motivation to dedicate their lives to pursuits of a higher order. Serving his country had always been a noble notion, and he knew that what he had done had contributed to the eventual demise of the Nazis. But the job had sapped most of his energy, and now the road ahead was not well defined. In the end he decided that there was one job left to do, the one he had already started, whether Uncle Sam approved or not; he'd see it through, whatever the cost, and when it was finished, he'd pack it in and head for home. There he'd lie low for a while and decide what he wanted to do with the rest of his life.

Following the leads provided by Skorzeny would be a fairly straightforward proposition. Brumm was from Bad Harzburg, and judging from what Valentine had heard from various dogfaces about heavy refugee traffic there, he reasoned it was worth investigating. He drove toward the little mountain town two hundred and ten kilometers north of the cluttered confines of Frankfurt, spending most of the journey trying to figure out what the Russians were up to. It was a frustrating exercise in deductive reasoning. Before leaving Switzerland, he'd done some checking around with his sources: a press attaché at the American embassy, a watchmaker named Hubert, who fenced stolen currencies and other items, and Ermine.

Ermine Malone, who worked in the OSS office in Zurich, had been married three times: to a plumber from Salem, Oregon; to an FBI agent from Philly; and to a drummer from Baltimore, who had been killed in a plane crash during a USO tour in North Africa. She was small but compactly built, shy in public and sexually insatiable when it came to Beau Valentine. He'd never met anybody like her. Like him, she was not what she appeared to be, and he suspected that it was this similarity that bonded them. His sometime lover and friend, she was also his informer inside the agency, his insurance policy.

On leaving the meeting with Creel, Valentine had stopped by her desk, caught her eye and flashed his hand, showing her five fingers. She nodded her understanding and signaled back with three fingers, and added with a whisper, "Tomorrow." They'd meet at three o'clock in her fifth-floor flat.

Her apartment was a cramped studio affair with a large skylight and bare plaster walls. When Valentine entered, the woman fell on him in a fury, kicking him and raining blows at his ribs and forearms with her hard little knuckles. He retreated, trying to fend her off with his huge hands. Eventually her anger gave way to laughter, then to lust; they made love on the floor still wearing most of their clothes.

"You've been off screwing those Eye-tie girls. And not a damn word in all that time," she complained.

"I've been in Germany."

She grimaced. "Worse yet. Blondes with big tits."

"They aren't in much of a mood. I'm sorry," he apologized clumsily. "It was pretty messy at the end; then I got the order to saddle up and hit the road to Krautland. No time to let you know what was going on. Besides, I figured you'd know. You always seem to know where I am."

"Not anymore, Beau; the new bunch is real peculiar. They aren't like the old gang. They're cold-blooded, and all they think about are the Russians. After the president disbanded the OSS they transferred some of our people to army intelligence, some to the State Department, and discharged the rest. Any day now I expect they'll pack me off for the States; only reason I'm still here is that they're short of clerical help, and I know the procedures and filing system."

"I'm really sorry," he said, and when the words were out it surprised him to realize that he meant them. "Look," he went on. "There's no time to rehash ancient history, and whatever comes down the road next, well, we just have to deal with it. I need to know what we have on German refugees. You must have some information. When I was in Italy the partisans used to joke that the Vatican was in cahoots with the Nazis. Is there anything to that?"

Ermine froze. "I can't get that for you. I just can't. Anything else I can try for, but that's really hush-hush stuff and these new people play everything close to the vest."

"You've got to try. If Arizona was here, he'd get it for me, but he's gone and this Creel guy says I'm persona non grata. I've got nobody left to help me."

Ermine didn't answer. Instead, she got up from the floor, straightened her dress and began preparing dinner. When they'd finished eating, she folded her linen napkin, set it beside her plate, crossed her arms and stared at him. "I don't know why I can't say no to you, Beau Valentine."

"I've got a notion," he said, pulling her to him.

▶78 MARCH 27, 1946, 11:00 A.M.

The Special Operations Group used the position of the man in the photograph to approximate the location of the way into the valley. While they were not certain he was a sentry, they guessed a guard wouldn't be far from the entrance. The photographs showed no way in, so they reasoned that the access might be through a cave or tunnel, perhaps natural, possibly man-made. Whichever, they were confident that they had identified its probable location.

Ezdovo led them through the mountains, seldom looking at his compass. He had used Pogrebenoi's drawings to memorize the land-marks along the route; these alone provided him with the directions he needed. The group marched in an extended single file, led by the Siberian, followed by the woman, Bailov, Gnedin, Petrov and, far behind all of them, Rivitsky. Petrov's method was to use the expertise of each member of the unit whenever it was needed and not to worry about hierarchy, but he always insisted on order.

It took them twenty hours to reach the outer valley. They could have moved even faster, but Petrov chose to be careful in order to avoid walking into an ambush. It was one thing to worry about their objective, but there were other factors to consider. There were still plenty of armed German stragglers operating in remote areas: refugee bands—groups of Jews and Gypsies from the death camps—and plain thieves preying on people in Germany's less populated areas. In time such antisocial and counterrevolutionary elements would be cleared away, either by attrition or by Soviet action; in the interim, it was best to err on the side of prudence.

Ezdovo was their best scout, but because of her record with the Red Army, Petrov believed that Pogrebenoi was nearly his equal. Thus it fell on the pair who had found the valley by air to locate its entrance at ground level. On the morning of the twenty-seventh of March the team took up defensive positions in a small valley near the area to be searched, and Petrov sent the two scouts forward into a slate field filled with crevices.

Toward morning's end Talia came trotting back. They had located a natural cavern, apparently the front end of a long series of them. Just before the first large gallery, they had discovered a small tunnel that led off in a promising direction. Ezdovo had remained behind to cover the area.

The team moved into the first gallery. After examining the narrow upper tunnel, Petrov agreed with their assessment. They scouted a bit more, but there seemed no other leads worth following. It was decided that they should explore what they'd discovered and regroup if it didn't bear fruit.

Once again Ezdovo and Pogrebenoi went ahead, and after a short interval she returned to report that the tunnel opened into a valley. "It's a tight squeeze," she warned them as they moved into the shaft behind her.

Reaching daylight, Talia peeked out from the shadows as Ezdovo whistled at her from a rocky outcrop to her right. When he pointed ahead, she understood; the broken ground outside the tunnel showed the unmistakable pattern of a minefield. Pressure detonators, not magnetic. She informed the others in a whisper, then flashed a hand signal to Ezdovo. He signaled back for them to leave the cave one at a time, and with his hand showed her the course to follow. When he waved her out, she moved quickly and expertly, keeping a low profile and darting from side to side along the path until she was past Ezdovo and in position behind a line of granite boulders to provide advanced cover.

The instant Bailov reached her, Pogrebenoi moved on, creeping silently along the base of the steep valley wall to expand their point and defensive field of fire. When they were all in the valley and safely spread out, Ezdovo slid down from his perch, stopped momentarily to confer with Petrov and then joined her. "The mines were deployed in a fan starting near where we entered. Some have been exploded; many remain. They reach into the pines, but not very far. I could see a rough pattern in the ground from above," he told her quietly.

"I don't like being pinned in these rocks," she whispered. "Too flat, too open. Let's get into the trees and see if we can concentrate our formation."

He agreed and signaled those behind to cover them, with special attention on the rocks above, which might conceal an ambush. The two slid their knives from leg sheaths, slung their weapons across their backs, tightened their slings and started across the open ground on their knees, using the knives to probe carefully for buried mines. Within minutes both were certain that the mines were confined to the area near the entrance, but they continued their meticulous probe all the way to the trees, where they searched carefully for the trip wires favored by the Germans.

With a wave of his hand, Ezdovo called the team forward into the pine trees and spread them out in a diamond formation, with Petrov at the center. With the team positioned, they moved out, walking slowly and using all of their senses to assess their new environment. Most of all, they depended on their ears; visibility was limited by dark tangles of low vegetation, and their noses were almost useless.

Eventually they reached a narrow stream, where the valley floor seemed to rise slightly ahead of them. "Hear it?" Pogrebenoi asked Ezdovo.

He grunted quietly. "There's some kind of spillway in the rocks just ahead." They retreated to confer with Petrov as the others remained in position, their attention directed to each side. "We're just below the dam," Ezdovo told his leader. "The structure is in the face of the cliff."

Petrov immediately responded. "Pogrebenoi and Bailov will move upstream to the other side. You will take the middle with Gnedin. Rivitsky and I will move along the rocks; if you encounter trouble before we get into position, all survivors should fall back and regroup here. When you get close, go in alone," he told Ezdovo. "Thirty minutes." They synchronized their watches and Ezdovo motioned for Pogrebenoi to tell the others.

"No shooting," she told them as they set their watches. "We'll set ambushes and wait until Ezdovo calls us in."

The pairs moved out slowly and worked their way into position. From the far side of the dam Ezdovo could see that the door in the façade was open but that several small porticoes in the facing appeared to be closed. There was no sign of movement in or near the structure. At the designated time he stood up and darted quickly across the dam. Bailov remained behind and to his side, watching intently for any sign of life from the stone house.

Reaching the front door, Ezdovo paused, folded into a tight crouch and ducked inside. He was gone for several minutes while the group outside waited tensely, but when he reappeared his weapon was slung on his shoulder as he waved to the others to join him.

As Petrov approached, Ezdovo pursed his lips and nodded toward the building. In the first room they found a girl slumped forward on her face, a Star of David carved into the small of her back. In the other bedrooms were four more corpses, all mutilated in the same way. Swarms of flies and other insects were buzzing around the bodies, and there had been some feeding by vermin and scavengers. The members of the group were not repulsed. All of them had seen worse carnage many times before; they accepted rotting corpses and their disposal by nature's forces as inevitable. A few minutes later they found a girl in the hot spring and another girl nearby. Neither had been shot, but both had been carved.

The group looked at Gnedin for a medical explanation. Petrov followed him around as he examined the bodies, while the others explored the building and surrounding cavern.

The two corpses in the cave were the most troublesome to Gnedin. They laid the girl in the pool beside her dead comrade. "The puncture wound in the heart is a lethal one," the doctor said, "but I would say it was inflicted after she was dead."

Petrov listened attentively, his hands in his pockets.

"See these marks on the throat?" He showed Petrov the bruises and discolorations. Using his knife, Gnedin made a shallow incision just above Waller's pubis and slid the thin blade upward like a zipper to the bottom of the sternum. Working quickly and without hesitation, he made incisions below each set of ribs and another one crosswise, penetrating the lower abdomen. The incisions made, he opened the flaps of skin he had created to reveal the girl's viscera. Her lungs were hard to his touch, and when he opened them they were filled with water.

Gnedin evaluated the evidence for a moment, then looked up at Petrov. "She was drowned. Classic signs. Somebody held her under, producing the marks on the throat. She was mutilated later. The other one's easier; her neck is broken. Judging by the morbidity in the neck area, I'd say she too was also mutilated after death."

"And the others?"

"Shot."

Petrov had all the bodies collected and brought to the cavern. They sat quietly while he walked around the corpses, thinking, reflecting on the stars that had been cut into them. "Ostensibly an act of revenge. Is that what we have here?"

"*Somebody* carved them," Bailov said.

"Yes, the stars. We can't overlook them, can we? One of the

problems that most frequently haunt homicide investigators is their innate need to find what is not really there. All of these dead females and an apparent motive. Less imaginative men might look at them and conclude that it was no more than a brutish act of vengeance. Are we wrong not to accept that? Perhaps that's what we will conclude eventually."

The unit had no doubt that Petrov did not accept this thesis. "Evidence of sexual activity?" Petrov asked the doctor.

"Impossible to tell without a laboratory analysis. For accuracy we need to take specimens and put them under a microscope."

"Evidence of a struggle?"

"I think not, comrade. This one," he said, pointing to the drowned body, "exhibits no evidence of a struggle. No tissue under her fingernails or in her teeth, no marks that might have occurred in kicking or striking at an attacker. If I had to guess, I'd say that she was taken by surprise by someone who was close to her when the attack came. She might have been floating in the water and then suddenly thrust under it and held there until she drowned."

"It couldn't have been done by an intruder," Pogrebenoi said. "They're all unclothed, and they were drinking." She pointed to the nearby empty bottles.

Petrov raised an eyebrow.

"A woman without her clothes feels extremely vulnerable," Pogrebenoi continued. "At such a moment most women tend to be far more alert than men in a similar situation."

"Thank you, Major," Petrov said. "An interesting observation. You think a woman without clothes is likely to be more alert than if she was dressed, and therefore more difficult to intrude upon? Is that it?"

"Even in a group it's true. Women are not as sociable without their clothes. Men will romp together in the nude; it's not as natural for women."

"Not natural," Petrov repeated. "What if a group of women was encouraged over time to behave so? Might this modify instinctual behavior?"

"Yes," Gnedin answered. "Our responses to situations are in large part culturally derived. For example, in the tropics people often go about with no clothing. Such behavior is possible in virtually any society, given the necessary reinforcement. With adequate time you can establish virtually any norm."

"Think about this." Petrov pointed to the drowned body, whose viscera, laid open by the doctor's knife, were now being attacked by flies. "She is in the pool, perhaps with someone else, maybe even a man. A friend? Relative? Her lover? They are floating blissfully when suddenly he grabs her and thrusts her into the water. Having drunk too much, at first she doesn't realize the threat; by the time she does, it's too late."

"It would fit the physical evidence we have," Gnedin said.

"I agree," Pogrebenoi said. "A woman in her lover's arms feels more secure; her guard is down." She glanced briefly at Ezdovo, who looked elsewhere.

Rivitsky jumped into the discussion. "What we see is the aftermath of a slaughter, ostensibly by intruders. The deaths are violent, messy, done quickly. This supports the intruder theory. On the other hand, how could they gain entrance so easily, unless someone was already inside and not considered a threat?"

"An interesting question," Petrov said.

"A boulder was blocking the cave entrance. It was blown from the valley side; the minefield was deliberately detonated," Ezdovo added.

"Your evidence?"

"Explosion patterns, and no bodies in the minefield. It was a hasty attempt to make it appear that the valley had been invaded."

The others nodded in affirmation.

"The rooms show signs of more inhabitants than there are bodies," Pogrebenoi pointed out.

"What bothers me is the dark-haired woman. She doesn't fit. The others are much younger, obviously Nordic. She's older than the others; I believe she is a Jew," said Rivitsky, who had been studying the corpses ever since they'd entered the cliff house. Something else was gnawing at his subconscious, but he was unable to put his finger on it until the others began their discussion.

"There's a tattoo on the inside of her left arm," Gnedin observed. "I also think she's a Jew; regardless, she has at least been a guest in one of Hitler's camps."

"This structure has been here a long time," Talia said. "Some of the furnishings are very old."

"These girls could never have created this kind of hoard on their own. The place is well stocked," Bailov said. "It's like a military outpost. It lacks for nothing, and judging by what's here and how much, a great number of trips would be necessary. In Bad Harzburg we learned that Brumm often came into the mountains with his grandfather for days, sometimes for weeks. They lived off the land. Later, when he was older, he came back on leave and went into the wilderness by himself. I think we have the right place, comrades."

"But where did these girls come from?" Pogrebenoi asked. "They're very young, no more than children."

"For the Nazis there were no children once menstruation began," Petrov said. "That one there"—he pointed to the drowned girl—"despite her age, has borne a child."

Gnedin nodded. Petrov's powers of observation constantly amazed him. "There are faint stretch marks, and other signs."

"I believe that these girls were brought here from Berlin by Brumm. It would not be outlandish to theorize that they were brought along for the sole purpose of providing a ruse, a red herring," Petrov concluded. "How long have they been dead?" he asked Gnedin.

"Three or four days. It's difficult to be precise."

"That would put the time of death within twenty-four hours of the plane's flight through the valley," Petrov said. "Now I'm satisfied. He was here. We'll eat and sleep. We have the trail, I'm certain of it. There's no longer any doubt."

III

THE
PURSUIT

►79 MARCH 28, 1946, 6:30 A.M.

Petrov awoke to the aroma of steaming tea and a whispered conversation between Ezdovo and Pogrebenoi. Though he was wide awake and alert, he remained under his thin bedcover. He'd first seen the signs on the night they'd viewed the aerial footage of the valley. He didn't know for certain that there was a romance between them, but there was no question that a strong bond was developing. He wondered if they were able to separate their physical desires from emotional attachment. It was one thing to sleep with each other because of need and convenience; it was quite another to allow oneself to be trapped by powerful emotions. It had been a gamble to bring the woman on board, he reminded himself. She was handsome, the kind who attracted men naturally and created a wave of lust wherever she went, with no effort—and from what he could tell, no desire—on her part. Because she had commanded a military unit, he had assumed that Pogrebenoi was adept at fending off advances from amorous peers and subordinates, but he also knew that working side by side in a small group was a different situation, especially when the other partner was Ezdovo. It worried him to think of such matters, but it was his job. Even in peace, there would be no room for deep involvements between Special Operations Group personnel, and under present circumstances it was particularly tricky. Even if they had satisfied their carnal needs, there was still time to control the situation, not only for their own sake and because he respected both of them, but for the sake of their mission. He'd been wrestling with a decision. Pogrebenoi had been recruited for her language faculty, but he had been leaning toward sending her with Ezdovo. Now he rejected the idea; Bailov would be paired with the Siberian.

Petrov coughed to let them know he was awake and got up. Within minutes of their commander's rising, the entire team was awake, dressed and ready to move on his orders. Only Rivitsky showed signs of lingering sleep, a normal occurrence. Whatever his appearance, Rivitsky's brain, Petrov knew, was functioning and calculating; it was just that he never looked alert until later in the day.

Pogrebenoi was in charge of the day's meals. Each team member, including their leader, carried a two-day supply of rations for the entire team. By organizing it so, all members could keep their packs loaded and be ready to move out instantly. It was a procedure devised by Ezdovo, who had learned it as a boy on the trail with hunters of his clan.

Talia opened several tins of meat, sliced the contents and laid out raw onion rings. They ate in silence, their attention on Petrov. When the others had finished eating, he was still chewing carefully and delicately sipping his hot tea. Pogrebenoi hefted her pack and checked her weapon, a small-caliber semiautomatic rifle with a long barrel and an empty mount for a telescopic sight, which she carried wrapped in an oilskin in her rucksack. It was an unusual weapon because of its small caliber, but she packed her own cartridges in such a way that the weapon had a long, flat trajectory, making it ideal for accurate shooting at very long distances. It was a sniper's tool.

Gulping down the last of his tea, Petrov cleared his throat and looked at the others. "Last night," he said, "you saw firsthand what we are faced with. When our armies moved into Poland and later into Germany, you saw that many of the enemy laid down their weapons and fled or surrendered, begging for mercy. Now we are faced with different opponents. Those we seek are not common men. One of them is extraordinary—a true soldier, a warrior. I do not know if he subscribes to the old Teutonic legends, but I believe he is as fierce as those legends describe and is committed to completing his mission. He will not be taken easily."

He stood and stretched. "I want you to understand what's at stake. Tens of millions are dead in our country because of Adolf Hitler. To the world the monster is dead. Only we and those with him know that he is alive. This SS colonel took the number one war criminal from under our noses and carried him through our armies to safety here in this valley. If any one of us were to propose such an attempt, he would be sent to an asylum.

"You have always been committed to the party and its goals. Your patriotism is unparalleled in a nation where examples of patriotic sacrifice abound. But we are now to undertake something more important than anything we've ever done before; I remind each of you of your sacred duty. If necessary, you must forfeit your life in seeing this through. From this moment forward you must abandon self and think only about our mission. The pursuit of Adolf Hitler begins; the nearer we get to him, the more careful we must be. Am I right, Comrade Ezdovo?"

"At the time of greatest gain is also the time of greatest risk."

Petrov grunted and assumed a professorial pose. "How can success and failure be equal partners?"

"When the animal has room to flee," Ezdovo said, "its instinct is to do so. It is only when it is trapped and all possibilities of evasion are denied it that it will turn to fight. The craft in hunting safely is to conceal the trap in such a way that at the very moment the animal thinks it has reached safety, it has in reality lost all options. The quarry's illusion of escape must be maintained right up to the precise moment of the kill. It's the subtle hunter who eats fresh meat."

"Push the beast," Petrov interpreted, "but not too hard. Keep it moving; let it know we are hunting, but keep the pressure off. We must hunt with our minds, not our weapons, with our empathy and understanding, not brute force. We must let the animal enter our invisible trap and let him sigh in contentment at his perceived safety, then squeeze the trigger."

There was a pause while Petrov inhaled and held his breath for a long time. "Hitler is to be taken alive."

"That may not be possible," Gnedin said.

"It was not possible for Hitler to get out of Berlin either, but he did." There was no further objection to their leader's command.

Coming out of the mountains, Ezdovo, Pogrebenoi and Bailov scouted ahead, looking for a sign of those who had left the valley. It was Ezdovo who discovered the trail on the far side of the western ridge beyond the outer valley. They gathered around him and waited for him to interpret his findings.

"There are three of them, all men. Two large ones, both of whom are heavy and probably tall. The third is smaller and weaker; he drags his leg slightly." Ezdovo showed them a mark in a muddy place in a rock field and mimicked the limp.

Eventually they followed the trail out of the mountains, down to a road and over it into another forest. They waited just off the road while Ezdovo explored ahead. When he returned, he was grinning. "I have them. They're traveling due south, moving deliberately, and one of them is carrying a postmark."

They stared at him, not understanding the last remark. "Someone has carved a small Star of David into the sole of the shoe of the one who drags his leg," Ezdovo said with a laugh.

Petrov stared in the direction the Germans had gone, then slowly lifted his arm and pointed. "Go after them," he told Ezdovo and Bailov. "Get close, but do not engage them. Pressure them as circumstances allow; I want them to know you're behind them. They will already be nervous and wary; your pressure may force them into telegraphing their plans, even their ultimate destination. Understand?"

Ezdovo acknowledged the orders with a grunt.

"Where are they going?" Bailov asked.

"Italy," Petrov replied.

The four remaining members of the Special Operations Group watched silently as their comrades moved into the forest. Near a line of trees Ezdovo stopped briefly and looked back, then pivoted and disappeared behind Bailov. Pogrebenoi felt her heart beat faster; she knew the Siberian was saying good-bye to her.

▶80 MARCH 28, 1946, 10:30 A.M.

There was a small park a few blocks from the OSS office. It was sunny, but the children sailing boats in the pond were wearing heavy wool coats. Beau Valentine waited near a small fountain and watched the others in the area carefully, telling himself that he was beginning to get paranoid.

Ermine arrived precisely at 10:30 A.M. When she reached him she looked over her shoulder, then furtively thrust a thick manila envelope at him. "I'm scared, Beau."

"Look," he said. "Don't worry about your job. If they fire you, I'll take care of you. My word." He tried to kiss her, but she pulled away and slammed him on the chest with the heel of her hand.

"My job! They'll *kill* me if they find out that I've told you what's going on."

He laughed. "You've been reading too many spy stories."

"Laugh," she said angrily. "You don't know what the hell's going on. The old bunch acted like fraternity boys on a lark. The new ones are something else entirely." Her tone of voice told him he'd better listen. "The Vatican's running some kind of underground railroad for German Catholics. It runs from Bremen to Frankfurt to Stuttgart to Memmingen. Little parishes along the route are used as safe houses and supply points. Priests are feeding and housing people, then passing them down the chain. From Memmingen they're moved to Innsbruck in Austria, and from there into Italy. They call it the Monastery Route. Our people are trying to get people into the system to do some talent scouting."

"For prosecution?"

"You aren't listening," she scolded. "They're looking to turn those people around. There's a big push to get German rocket scientists out before the Russians snatch them. They call that Operation Alsos. The same with intelligence agents, especially those who were on the Eastern front. Us, the Russians, the Brits, the French and even the Canadians— everybody's trying to get a share of the German talent pool. It's all top secret."

He knew about Operation Alsos; he'd been an unofficial part of it. "What else?"

She tapped the envelope. "It's in there, but there's a lot more I don't know. I heard that General Gehlen and his whole espionage network are in the States right now being debriefed. He's not listed as a prisoner, but we have him."

"What about the political types?"

"Too hot, too well known. The focus is on professional cadre— technicians and academics."

Valentine squeezed her knee affectionately, but she pulled away. "What about the other thing?" He'd also asked her to pay attention to any "unusual" events, such as murders or robberies; he wasn't sure how to define it by any other word.

"Several cases, all murders of American personnel by German nationals or presumed German nationals. All but one case has been solved. A WAC from Frankfurt, a major, got herself a pass and took off in a car from the motor pool. She was supposed to be gone for a week. After ten days they put out the bloodhounds. That was in December. They finally found her when the thaw began this month. Ran her car off a mountain road."

"So?"

"It was murder. The car was burned up, but her body had been thrown clear from the wreck and frozen. She'd been stabbed in the heart—a real professional job, according to the postmortem. Somebody went to a lot of work to make it look accidental."

"Hmm," Valentine said. "What else was there on the woman?"

"She was a dyke."

Beau raised his eyebrows and frowned. "She liked girls?"

"Apparently she wasn't long for the army. The provost marshal had been in the process of investigating a complaint from an enlisted WAC who worked in her section at the Frankfurt Medical Depot. It seems the major pulled rank to make the girl cooperate."

"Where'd they find the body?"

"That's the funny part. The car was in a ravine about fifteen miles from a little town called Bad Harzburg, right in the area you wanted to know about. That's a long drive from Frankfurt."

"Yep, and right on the perimeter of the Russian zone. Any signs the Russians were involved in this? Maybe she got lost and some of our Russian comrades had a little sport with her."

"No. She had a whole set of charts with her."

"Charts?"

"Uh-huh. She got a complete set of up-to-date security zone maps from a light colonel in the transportation depot. They showed troop dispositions, checkpoints, the works. Turns out the colonel was a doctor who was holding down the motor pool job until a transportation officer arrived, and he gave her the maps so that she'd have an easier time getting around. They never found them, and the colonel who'd given them to her figured they'd burned up in the wreck and kept his mouth shut. But since then, his maps popped up as missing during some kind of administrative review. So now they know that she had the maps, and though they figure they were burned in the crash, the fact is that nobody really knows."

The maps opened a lot of possibilities.

Ermine stood up. "I've got to get back. I hope this helps." She pulled away before he could kiss her. "Not in public. Maybe we're being watched."

"So what? We were the worst-kept secret in the OSS."

"Call me," Ermine said sadly over her shoulder.

"You bet," Valentine said uneasily. He watched her until she disappeared into a crowd at the edge of the park. He'd been using her for a long time, and only now did it occur to him that he fit the classic description of a heel.

▶**81**   MARCH 30, 1946, 7:15 A.M.

The rest of the team had arrived at the estate early the previous day. Today they had risen early and were waiting for orders from Petrov. He called them into the dark library one at a time.

Rivitsky was first. "You will remain with me, comrade. I need your mind. Stay while I instruct the others. If something happens to me, you will assume command." Rivitsky had always assumed this, but it had never been said before, and his mind swam.

Pogrebenoi was next. She stood before the pair with her feet firmly planted, her legs slightly apart. Again reminded of how striking she was, Petrov now was certain he had made the right decision. "You are going to Italy," he told her. He watched her eyes carefully to see how she took the news. There was a brief flash of surprise, then a perfect blank. To her credit, she did not question the order or the logic behind it, and Petrov felt better because of her response. He outlined her mission for her: she would travel by a roundabout route, by plane from Berlin to Trieste through Budapest; from there she would board a train for Rome. He gave her instructions for contacting an agent in the Italian capital and described the method for doing so. He harbored no misgivings about her ability to perform. "My Italian will be a little rough for a while" was her only comment, and it was accompanied by a broad smile.

Gnedin was dispatched to Switzerland, first to Basel, then depending on developments he would go to Zurich. Petrov explained to him that there was a Vatican effort to help Nazis move out of Germany into Italy. In both Zurich and Basel there were agents of every nationality and plenty of information to be had for a price—or extracted if opportunities presented themselves.

Each member of the Special Operations Group was told how to contact their leader; the final item of business was to select a reassembly site and a date.

That night Pogrebenoi and Gnedin drove to Berlin to catch their flights. Rivitsky watched them go, then went back inside and poured himself a drink. His hand was shaking; Petrov had told him of Stalin's threat after they'd been stymied in Berlin. Now the Special Operations Group was dispersing, each member expected to do his job, and Rivitsky was keenly aware that his life, like theirs, hung in the balance.

▶82 APRIL 1, 1946, 5:00 P.M.

Bad Harzburg was a beautiful, compact village of ancient buildings packed into a steep elbow of the Harz Mountains. Valentine found that its people were at first suspicious of him and nervous in his presence, just as careful as countryfolk in the States tended to be.

Throughout the day he used the cover and credentials of an American journalist for *Life,* and this earned him a certain amount of respect or fear; with Germans it was sometimes hard to tell the difference. "Bad Harzburg has been left to German rule," he told the mayor. "Many cities in Germany don't have freedom. Apparently your village has been found to be relatively free of Nazi sympathies." The conclusion was just what the mayor and the villagers wanted to hear; after his first interview, Valentine found the town leader cooperative, and others in the town soon followed suit.

Of the tools and approaches available, Valentine found the camera the best. It seemed that by merely pointing a camera at a German, you could almost instantly get a fix on what level of support the individual had given the National Socialists; it was a behavioral litmus that seemed effective for both sexes and all ages. Even those who had not belonged to a Nazi organization but who had sympathized with the fascists avoided his camera like the plague. Such responses helped him to frame his questions and to evaluate the information he received.

It was early evening, and he was in the mayor's home. They were sharing a bottle of Riesling before a crackling fire while a starchy meal settled in their bellies.

"There are legions of refugees in Germany, but I don't see any here. Why not?"

"We had them," the mayor replied. "It was unbelievable how many came through here. You know that in the final days of the war there was a huge battle on the edge of the Harz Mountains? Many died, but the Americans pulled away and rolled on to the east, leaving us to ourselves. From the east there were hundreds of thousands trying to escape from the Russians. Many of them came to the mountains for refuge, but thc Harz is an inhospitable place even for those who understand it, so they moved on."

"How did you manage to cope with the influx?"

The mayor laughed. "There was nothing to organize, nothing to share. Mostly we ignored the strangers, and when they saw how poor we were they just kept going."

"None stayed?"

"None permanently. Now and then, here and there, one would remain for a while, but eventually they all moved on. It was no loss to us; it was hard enough to care for our own. We tried to help even though they were strangers—Germans, to be sure, but with different customs, different ways. Like oil and water, it was a bad mix. The only one I regretted losing was the doctor; he stayed for a few weeks. He seemed to fit in and he was an excellent physician, very good with people, though he seemed to be much better educated than we're accustomed to in these parts." The mayor took a long drink of wine.

Valentine leaned forward. "A Nazi? My government is looking for a large number of German doctors who did experiments on Jews in your extermination camps."

The mayor was visibly shaken by the word "your." "They were not *our* camps," he complained. "We didn't know what went on in them. We were told they were work camps for criminals."

"A lot of Germans are saying the same thing."

"It's the truth," the mayor said with anguish, sweat trickling from his temples.

"What about the doctor?"

"He was no Nazi. He seemed to be a Prussian in manner and culture, though he said he was from Dortmund. Poor man—his wife and children had died in the bombings. His papers were in order. He told us he had been with the medical corps when his unit was routed near Katowice, in Poland. He was taken prisoner by the Ivans, but escaped. A very calm and deliberate sort. His language was precise. He seemed more an intellectual than a criminal."

"Sometimes they're the same thing. But he left?"

"It was inevitable, I suppose. Another stranger came one night with two little girls." The mayor stopped and leaned toward his guest. In a hushed voice he asked, "You won't write about this?"

"I can't promise that," Valentine said, wanting to maintain the tension. "I have to write the truth. You know that, don't you?"

"Yes," the mayor lied, not really understanding. In his view the purpose of a magazine or newspaper was to promote the general good and create a sense of community, not to write the truth if it left readers worse off. "The doctor was in his surgery one morning when the stranger came in with the girls. The doctor told his nurse that he had to leave to see to the welfare of two refugees and that he would return. But then he packed his bag and all his other belongings and disappeared."

"Who was the stranger?"

"We don't know," the mayor said, but Valentine could sense that he was hiding something.

"In America reporters have a saying: you can tell us your story or we'll make it up from what we know."

The mayor became more agitated. "I didn't know the stranger. None of us knew him, and only the nurse saw him."

"Reporters learn to sense things, Herr Mayor. I sense now that you are not telling me everything."

The old politician sighed. "I hope our village won't be judged by one person. Most of us are good and simple people. We did not support Hitler, not like those fanatics in the cities. Some of our number voted for him, some even believed him, and most of us were happy to see Germany getting back on her feet. I suppose we'll carry that to our graves."

"Mistakes are not the sole province of Germany," Valentine said, trying to placate the man.

The mayor stared at the fire for a moment, then drew in a deep breath and leaned back in his rocking chair. "There was a young woman from our town. Her name was Janna Friest. Her parents were old, and she was the last of a large family—I can't tell you how many. They lived in the hills near here and kept to themselves. They farmed, but not very well. They were crude people—rough, no grace. During the war the old ones died and all the children left except for the girl, who stayed to finish her schooling. But she was a sour fruit—is that the English phrase?"

"Close enough. You mean a 'rotten apple.' "

The man nodded. "She was a bad girl. She matured quickly and liked boys from a young age. Many of the boys in town, and later many of the men, were with her at one time or another. One of the older men, a man from our town council, got a disease from her and passed it on to his wife. There was a scandal and he enlisted in the army. Fräulein Friest left, too and joined some kind of SS auxiliary for women. But I swear to you we didn't know what she did."

"You had some suspicions, though."

"No more than that. About a month before the war ended she came back here and took up residence in her family farm. She had two young girls with her and claimed they were hers, but we all suspected they were too old; besides, we'd never heard anything about her getting married. She stayed to herself, but when any of us had contact with her she seemed to be a changed woman. Sometimes headstrong young people grow out of it, you know? In any event, the two girls who came to the doctor's surgery with the stranger were the same two that Janna had brought with her. When the doctor left, there was a lot of gossip, so I asked our constable to investigate."

Valentine did not interrupt. The man's story was beginning to take on the proportions of a confession. "We found the house burned and Janna gone—or so we thought. Perhaps she had stolen the children. Or maybe she'd rescued them from some terrible fate. But not far from the house we found signs of digging, and from the hole we uncovered"—he seemed to struggle for a word—"evidence.

"It's an extremely sensitive situation. She was dead, and there were some photographs, as well as other materials . . . from a camp. She appeared to have been a guard in one of those places you mentioned earlier. We were appalled. So then we thought the stranger must have been a relative of the girls, and that he'd somehow tracked her here to reclaim his children. It was logical to think that the stranger had killed her."

"You never saw the doctor again?"

"Never. A great loss to the future of our village."

"And the stranger with the children?"

The mayor shook his head slowly. "Gone."

"Do you think they knew each other?"

"Yes, surely. The nurse heard them talk to each other—in another language, perhaps Russian. I believe they were confederates, but in what scheme only God knows. I hope the children are all right."

Valentine considered the information. Of all the refugees who had passed through the area, only one had remained—two, if one counted the stranger. It could be something, Valentine told himself. "Tell me more about the doctor. Did he have close friends?"

"Only our two physicians, and they were much older than he. They said he was unusually competent and easy to work with. He attended social functions, but had no close acquaintances that we could see. There were no women that we know of. He spent long hours in the surgery and slept very little. He was unobtrusive and dedicated. The only theory I ever heard—and it was from one of the old doctors— was that once he might have worked for a pharmaceutical company. He had great knowledge of and interest in drugs. He was very concerned about the supplies of medicine in the town. He spent some of his time in our chemist's shop, showing him some new methods of compounding."

"Sounds like an American doctor."

"He was a very unusual man."

"What did the chemist think of him?"

"He found him informative and helpful. Our chemist is young, and so not yet set in his ways. Our old chemist would have thrown the doctor out on his ear; he felt no great love for medical men who looked on the healing art as a science."

"Your chemist is new, then?"

"By our standards anyone in the first generation here is new." The mayor smiled, more relaxed now that he was on safer ground. "He came here after Herr Halter passed on in '43. It's not easy to find such people for a small town, but we had enjoyed the advantage of our own chemist for so long that we didn't want to do without."

"Halter?"

The mayor smiled and poured more wine in their glasses. "There could be no other like Herr Halter. I could tell you stories about him for days. He was not easy to get along with even in his prime, and at the end he was impossible, but he was a fine, honest man. He was the most knowledgeable man in our village about the mountains. We always found it difficult to reconcile his interest in the wilds with the cold precision of his profession. He was unique. His grandson and he would camp in there for weeks on end in all weather, even in the winter snows."

"Grandson?"

"Yes. Günter von Brumm." Valentine stiffened as the mayor went on. "A good boy. Quiet, strong. He went to military academy and was a career soldier, but he dropped the 'von' from his name. Not many knew what he was doing, but I did. Old Halter once told me that Günter was part of Skorzeny's commando operation. He didn't come back from the war. He must be dead, or captured by the Russians. It's the same thing, I think."

Valentine let his interest show. "Now, that might be a story for me. One of the villagers who served with the famous Otto Skorzeny, the man who rescued Mussolini. He was SS, right?"

Quickly the mayor became defensive again. "There was SS and there was SS," he explained carefully. "They weren't all monsters. When the Allies hear those words they see red, but the SS was nothing more than an elite military organization, like your own American Rangers and the British commandos. Günter was only a soldier, but a good one. There's no shame for men serving faithfully when national need is declared, even if it was Hitler who issued the call. The village is proud of Günter, though we didn't know him well. He left when he was a young man and seldom returned. When he did come back, he stayed with his grandfather; even when the old man could hardly walk, they went into the mountains together. Halter was proud of his grandson."

"He came back on leave?"

"Yes."

"Recently?"

"No, not since the summer of '44."

"To visit his grandfather?"

"It was a sad scene. He loved that old man. He went to the cemetery; my wife saw him near his grandfather's grave. He left after only one day."

"Leaves were hard to come by then."

"I suppose," the mayor said. "But he went off to camp in the mountains for the last time. Sometimes young people think they know more than their elders. Not Günter; he worshiped his grandfather."

▸83 APRIL 2, 1946, 5:00 P.M.

By boarding early in Trieste, Pogrebenoi had secured a window seat in a cushioned and well-appointed compartment. She immediately stored her suitcase and made herself comfortable.

The train stopped in Venice, Padua, Bologna, Florence, Orvieto and a dozen smaller cities before finally reaching Rome. The Italians called it an express. When Pogrebenoi asked about the long delays, a conductor curled his fist, pointed a finger to mimic a revolver and said, "Mussolini, pow." Having been oversold at every stop along the winding route, the train was overcrowded. In typical fashion, the Italian males pushed their way past women and children to capture seats for themselves—unless, of course, a woman was attractive, in which case the men stopped to boldly pinch and fondle her, or in exceptional instances, to actually give up a seat.

Getting into the country had been an easy matter. She had entered under a French passport and had been careful to dress properly for her Italian assignment. Her dress was of a thin material, cut tight and low in the bodice and high above her knees. She wore open-toed sandals with high narrow heels and found herself enjoying the use of her body and looks to unnerve Italian railway officials. When the Italian security agent examined her passport at the Trieste airport, she had deliberately leaned forward, giving him an unrestricted view of her breasts as she engaged him in hushed conversation. She was careful to give him the name of a hotel in the city, even spelling it out for him. She never said she would be staying at the hotel, but it was clear that this was his understanding. Sweat rolled off his face as he stamped her papers and passed her on with a wink. She watched him slowly scratch down the hotel's name with the nub of a pencil and carefully tuck the slip of paper into the band inside his cap.

She was met outside customs by a Soviet diplomat who drove her to the rail station and bribed a gate official to get her on board early. The other passengers were still sequestered outside the barrier as she strolled lazily down the platform. The men in the crowd whistled loudly and thrust their hands through the fence as she passed by. The noise followed her down the platform like a wave. From her window seat she watched as other women struggled through the narrow aisles nearby. Though they were in the north, it was extremely hot and there was no ventilation. Soon the musk-sweet odor of humanity engulfed her.

As the train was still loading, a thin male entered her compartment, took the seat next to her and without a word grabbed her. She drove her right elbow into his throat, which set him gagging; he stood, trying to get away from her, but she rose and drove her knee sharply between his legs, sending him tumbling into the corridor in a moaning heap. Other men, who had been watching, looked quickly away and left her alone.

The rest of the trip to Rome was uneventful, but by the time she arrived in Rome her early enthusiasm for Italians had begun to wane. They were like children, a constant drain on one's energy. The Termini, like the stations in all the other cities where the train had stopped, was packed with people. Begun before the war by Mussolini, it had never been completed and stood as a national monument to procrastination.

As in Trieste, Pogrebenoi's arrival created a stir among the males in the station. By the time she reached the street and a line of waiting cabs, she had barked a knuckle on one man's front tooth and bruised an ankle kicking another would-be assailant in the knee.

The cabdrivers didn't bother to get out of their vehicles; instead, they simply hung out the windows, each trying to outshout the others for customers. Pogrebenoi got into the first cab she came to and gave the driver a slip of paper with an address near where Via del Corso intersected Via Crescenzio. Her hotel, the Corsair, was four kilometers from Vatican City and only two short blocks from the chocolate glaze of the Tiber. She registered as Sharon Jeune, the identity on her French passport, and was shown to her room, where she bolted the door and soaked herself in a tub. The lukewarm water was colored rust by the pipes.

The next morning she cleaned her handgun and attached the silencer. She carried three clips of nine rounds each and practiced changing them until she could do it quickly by touch. Unlike most women, Pogrebenoi took pleasure in firearms, their weight in her hands giving her added confidence.

As Petrov had instructed, she took lunch at an open-air restaurant whose name translated as House of Exquisite Choices, which it wasn't. She ordered a small bottle of Chianti and some kind of pasta stuffed with some kind of fish that tasted heavily of garlic and iodine. As she began to eat, a hunchbacked priest entered, and after some loud and friendly conversation with the proprietor, he was shown to her table. He looked harmless, even feeble, until she saw his eyes as he looked down at her. "Signorina, I beg your pardon, but the restaurant is crowded today. May I join you?"

Talia glanced around. There were several empty tables. "As you wish, Father."

The old man struggled into a chair and hooked his wooden cane on the edge of the table. "It's hot," he said, wiping the perspiration from his neck with a white linen napkin. For several minutes he was besieged by waiters, all stopping by to make small talk and to seek his blessing, which he mumbled quickly and flashed at them with a wave of his hand.

By the time the priest's food arrived hers was cold. Pogrebenoi watched as he attacked his meal with enthusiasm, scattering bread crumbs on the tablecloth and covering his chin with red sauce. As he was finishing his meal it seemed to dawn on him that she was not eating. "You don't like this food?"

"It's too cold to tell."

He tapped his chest lightly. "*Mea maxima culpa*," he said between belches. "My fault." He blotted his mouth with another napkin. "I was under the impression that you Russians like your food cold." The smile that crossed his face told Talia she had made her contact.

▶84 APRIL 3, 1946, 9:00 P.M.

Ezdovo sat with his weapon across his lap and his back against Bailov, whose breathing told the Siberian that he was already asleep.

They were on a wide bed of slate the color of cold ashes. Below the rock formation a narrow stream cascaded against the bank and raced off in descent. The stream's pressure had eaten into the rock wall and created a place for an egg-shaped vortex of gurgling black water. The two Russians had a full view of the stream and its gorge. No one would be able to get down to their level without considerable care and noise, especially at night. Even in daylight they had found the slate difficult to descend, but it had been worth the effort. Their haven was safe; they would be able to sleep. Their tracking was limited to daylight hours. When darkness came they needed to find a spot whose natural characteristics would alert them to impending trouble so that they both could sleep. They could not afford to sap their energy by staying awake, so the site of each camp was critical.

As Bailov's rhythmic breathing began to affect his own, Ezdovo stared down into the black eddy below and chewed a piece of dried beef. Its only flavor was that of smoke, but it activated his saliva and expanded his stomach to take the edge off his appetite. So far the tracking had been strenuous, but he relished the solitude of the trail and the companionship of Bailov. It was not a matter of conversation; they seldom talked. Rather, it was more the comfortable silence that friends share. Their energies were dedicated to following three Germans. Usually they used hand signals to communicate. Occasionally they made eye contact or grunted. True friendship needed few words.

Ezdovo let his mind turn inward, to the past, to his youth. He was on a grassy bank above the wide, swirling Amur River. Below, on a gravel bar, a large black bear was wading in the shallows pawing for pink salmon. He watched the animal, feeling an urge growing inside him. It was not something he could verbalize, but he felt a kinship with it, its black fur sleek and shiny, a large white diamond on its wide throat. After a while he slung his rifle, stagger-stepped down the steep embankment and waded out toward the finger of gravel. The animal watched him approach, lifted its snout into the wind and caught his scent, then returned to eating the struggling forty-pound salmon pinned under its paw. When he reached the bar, Ezdovo walked toward the bear, which stood at the other end, swaying slightly from side to side. Eventually it forgot its food and tensed at his approach. It dropped its head and blinked repeatedly, trying to focus the man in its myopic vision, sniffing to inhale the scent. Its mouth opened and slammed shut, the sudden snap of its teeth warning the intruder to back off, the sound echoing ominously along the riverbed. Then it backed up until its hindquarters were in the water, dug its thick forepaws into the loose gravel and stood, waiting. Its ears were flat against its skull, the hump on its back quivering as its muscles contracted and released. A deep growl rumbled inside it as Ezdovo stopped no more than a pace away. Suddenly the animal stopped breathing, its sides fully expanded with trapped air. It woofed quietly, then again, and rose to its hind legs.

Ezdovo stepped forward and wrapped his arms around the beast, hugging it tightly. The bear continued to woof quietly, turning as Ezdovo pivoted, saliva streaming from its jaws. After a few seconds Ezdovo released it and stepped back, placed the flat of his hand on the animal's snout and held the touch.

Ezdovo remembered the event as if it had happened only moments before. His father had told him that a Russian of the Siber must come to manhood by embracing a bear. For each man of the wilderness the beast was different and the embracing took different forms. For Ezdovo it had been a dance with a wild bear on a gravel bed in the Amur River, the music provided by salmon leaping and crashing over the rocks.

As a boy in his village near Lake Baikal, Ezdovo had listened to the old men tell their histories. Though he could read, few older people had such skill; instead, they relied on their memories and those of others to pass down history and the lessons of their clan.

The first Ezdovo to see Siberia had been Yatchak Ezdovo, who rode with the Cossack Yermak in 1581. The conquerors of the capital city of Siber had taken Uzbek and Yakut girls and what meager wealth the city had to offer, burned the dwellings and left the heads of Siber's leaders on stripped pine stakes as a warning to others who might consider opposing the Cossack armies of Ivan the Terrible.

In the 1700s, Gelmut Ezdovo was banished, along with other Cossack leaders, to Siberia by Peter the Great. From the loins of Gelmut flowed the seed of generations of Ezdovos. Though he did not know the precise number of generations between Gelmut and himself, Ezdovo felt the warmth of the blood tie. The Ezdovo clan proliferated and spread out across the wastes of Siberia. They were hunters, fishermen, explorers, soldiers, policemen, priests, even scholars. All Ezdovos demonstrated fierce pride in the family name, an independent spirit and integrity marked by a sense of duty and absolute honesty. It was said among them that their blood was the cement of eastern Russia.

Though the family's history was interwoven with Russian politics, in his early years Ezdovo had been apolitical. He was eight when the Great Revolution took place, but it had little effect on his village, for on the eastern frontier even those who claimed royal blood lived hand to mouth. He was still learning his way through life, tending to his traps, sneaking into the beds of wenches and willing wives alike. He preferred the solace of his steep mountains, blue lakes and verdant forests. At the government fur-trading center on the Lena River, his pelts commanded the highest price among traders from Moscow.

Ezdovo's memory was deep and filled with clear images. He'd taken animals in numbers that defied recall, yet he could remember the season's take for every trapline he'd ever run and what he had taken in each trap, including the distinguishing features of each animal.

Several years after the Revolution there was a move to split Siberia from Russia. Legally and politically the area had no status; it was not a state, only a name. But some who saw what had happened in the Soviet west were determined to repeat these events. Factories were built, towns grew, people had work. It was time to fuse east and west, some thought; others disagreed. Though he thought of himself as Siberian, Ezdovo's roots were Russian. To him the two were the same, and he had no patience for those who would make them separate. But for a while the politics of grand scale had little impact in his village beside the lake. His family debated the situation with their neighbors, but no effort was made to become involved. Whatever might happen ultimately would have no effect on them, they felt; they were too small and far way for such things to matter.

They were wrong. Eventually the conflict came to them. Russian soldiers appeared one day in the village asking for Ezdovo. An Uzbek named Muvlovlovich was one of the political leaders of the revolt that had been crushed in the Siber. Most of his followers and confederates had been captured and executed, but Muvlovlovich himself had evaded the authorities and fled north to the Lena River. Ezdovo was barely twenty, but his reputation was widespread, and so when the Russian forces inquired about suitable guides, he had been suggested. They wanted him to help them locate the criminal and he agreed, more out of interest in the chase than from any political conviction.

Ezdovo led the soldiers up the Lena, eventually traveling more than eight hundred kilometers before they caught Muvlovlovich and his pitiful remnant of counterrevolutionaries. During their months together, he came to respect the commitment of the Russian soldiers, so when he returned he sought entry into the party and was accepted. Thereafter it mattered not whether he hunted man or beast. No trail, fresh or ancient, could elude him; when it came to tracking he had no equal.

So it had been that one day Ezdovo found himself before a small man in black with a hawklike countenance and a quiet, almost feminine voice. It was not immediately clear what Petrov's offer entailed, but he recognized something deep and compelling in the little man, and agreed to become part of the Special Operations Group. It was 1942 when he left his beloved mountains and traveled west to Moscow, first on horseback, then by train, and he had not been back since.

Sitting now in the stillness of the Thuringian Forest, Ezdovo thought about his German quarry. No man since Muvlovlovich had moved as much like an animal as this trio they now hunted. Since picking up the trail, the two Russians had double-timed their way south through a maze of ridges and valleys. The Germans had a lead, but even Ezdovo found it difficult to estimate how much. Their objective was to make contact with their quarry and stay with them, but the Germans were crafty, and now it seemed that they were no closer than when they had set out. Brumm knew what he was doing. Repeatedly Ezdovo had found himself ensnared by blind leads and apparent trail ends, each time forcing him into time-consuming backtracking or spirals in order to pick up the trail again. It was both frustrating and invigorating; he loved the hunt. It was clear that the German was an expert at using the terrain to his advantage. He knew how to disguise their passage, and even in areas where this was difficult, he found ways to give them pause. As the days wore on, Ezdovo found his admiration for Brumm growing.

Today had been the most difficult of all. The Germans had gone through a boulder-strewn area, perfect for a directional switch. The two Russians spent the entire afternoon methodically searching in ever-increasing circles, until Bailov finally located a small patch of gray moss marked with a faint heel print. They could not make out the Star of David, but there was a depression in the right place and they knew it was their prey. "It seems they're headed east," he said, hunkering over the sign and looking in that direction, as if he might be able to see them ahead.

"So it appears. But he's not an ordinary man. He's confused us all the way."

"The print is east of where we lost them and it seems to point east, if a single print can point to anything."

"East toward our troops. It doesn't make sense."

"Perhaps they don't know."

Ezdovo growled low. "They know. I don't know how, but their path south has been surgically precise. They have information—a map perhaps. They know where we are and where the Americans are."

"If so, we wouldn't expect them to turn east. It's a surprise. Who would expect it?"

The Siberian smiled. "Brumm understands the psychology of the hunt. They shouldn't go east; therefore they must go east. Yet to go east is to invite capture, and so they can't. See how devious he is, how subtle in his thinking? He gives us only one clue. It's nothing at all, but he knows we will be tempted to fall for it because it's all we have. You see? He gave this to us. The clue says east; we'll go west."

Eventually they located the new trail. It was westward, as Ezdovo had guessed, a swing of nearly ninety degrees off their southern course. Before nightfall they had found the slate outcropping and stopped to rest.

Now Ezdovo felt sleep crawling through his limbs, making them heavy; unconsciousness beckoned him, and he gave in to it. The face of Talia came to him. He saw her black hair, her clear brown eyes, and her scent warmed him as he fell asleep with an aching heart.

▶85   APRIL 3, 1946, 9:30 P.M.

Over the fall and winter Father Nefiore settled comfortably into the routine of the Wetter parish. The old priest, Father Jarvik, had been born in the Bohemian Forest near western Czechoslovakia. Although he was almost seventy, the old man was robust and in possession of a sharp mind, a keen wit and a venomous tongue for his parishioners who strayed out of line. His directives were followed without question, and in return for their loyalty his flock reaped enormous benefits. Father Jarvik seemed to be an inexhaustible source of clothing, food and tools. When a parishioner was in trouble with the authorities, he was there to intercede; when family problems arose, he handled them.

During the several months they were together, Father Nefiore observed that his colleague led a dual life. By day he was the incarnation of the Good Shepherd; by night he was something entirely different. The small parish church bore the name of the Sorrow of the Redeemer, a name whose significance grew for Nefiore as he watched the old priest single-handedly manage what he concluded could be nothing else than an escape network. Two or three times a week shabbily dressed strangers of both sexes and all ages would come to the church. Often they arrived in family units; usually it was the woman who came to the door to talk with Father Jarvik. Not once was Nefiore privy to the substance of these hushed conversations, but he could see from the windows of the small rectory that others often hung back in the shadows while the conferences took place. At times, especially when the weather was bitter, strangers were taken to the rectory cellar for the night, fed and given cots and blankets. They were always gone before the sun's first rays appeared.

On many nights Nefiore found himself alone while Father Jarvik traveled to undisclosed destinations for unexplained purposes. The old man would simply say just before leaving that he had to be "out" for the night or for several days, but he always returned when he said he would. As time passed, Father Nefiore assumed more and more parish duties, saying masses, conducting catechism classes for the village's young, officiating at confirmations and weddings, attending the sick, troubled and dying. Early on, he had resumed the use of his own name, and Father Jarvik explained during a Sunday sermon that the new priest was an Italian of German descent sent by the bishop temporarily to help him. The villagers accepted Nefiore quickly; his penances were firm enough to convey the severity of given sins, but not excessive, and he was a good listener, though not afraid to say what he thought. The women, especially the older ones who doted on all priests, liked him immensely.

If Nefiore had any weakness, it was a certain nervousness that people found in him, a kind of posture that made him appear to be guilty of something, though God knows what sin a priest could have on his conscience. It was not a major issue for the congregation, merely a trait they attributed to his foreign birth.

It was evening. Nefiore was in the kitchen cooking blood sausages in a large skillet when Father Jarvik came up from the cellar. The old man stretched when he entered, ladled himself a mug of hot coffee from the pan that stayed heated on the wood stove all day and sat down. Nefiore put a plate in front of him, then speared the sausages with a fork and dropped them on their plates. Jarvik ignored the food and stared at the younger priest. "You came here for a purpose," the old priest said after a silence. "It's time for you to go."

"Where?" Nefiore asked nervously.

Jarvik did not answer, but pulled on a wool overcoat and hat and went outside. Nefiore grabbed a heavy cape with a hood and followed, running to catch up.

They took Father Jarvik's horse, a huge black mare with a shaggy coat still thick from winter, and hitched her to a small buggy. Nefiore noticed that she seemed unsteady, almost off-balance as she stood waiting to be harnessed, and thought it must be old age. They loaded the boot of the carriage with several parcels and two baskets filled with bread wheels, then drove quietly out of Wetter past a ruined *Schloss* on a nearby hillock. Among the ruins dozens of small fires flickered like fireflies. "Catholics?" Nefiore asked.

"Who knows?" Jarvik answered. "The forest has become a melting pot, an ethnic stew." He laughed at his own joke. "They're displaced— refugees from eastern Germany and Poland, Ukes, Czechs, Latvians, Croats and a dozen more nationalities."

Passing through a dense forest of red pines, the road narrowed to no more than a trail. Branches whipped at them and wet clods of mud clung to them as they raced headlong through the funnel at high speed. "Father Jarvik!" Nefiore cried as he tried to dodge the branches. "Slow down—before you blind the horse!" It was all he could think to say, though it was his own well-being that he feared for.

The old priest only laughed and snapped his whip again. "She's already blind! That's why she steers so well! Don't worry, Father, you won't die an accidental death."

After a long gallop at high speed, Father Jarvik slowed the horse to a walk and Nefiore began to relax. The animal's flanks were lathered with white foam; its breath, coming in gasps, exploded into the cold night air in small bursts. In the forest around them, the Italian once again began to see small fires on both sides of the trail and far into the trees. When the buggy stopped, the old man handed him the reins. "I have an errand here. Let her graze—just give her her head, she knows what to do—and don't leave the buggy." He darted into the shadows.

Sitting alone in the cool night air, Nefiore felt a chill. He pulled his overcoat up to his chin and hunched down in it. At first he thought his discomfort was from the temperature, but soon it became apparent that he was being watched from the darkness. He could not see them, but he knew they were there and that there were many of them.

"You're not German," a tiny voice said accusingly from the darkness.

"Who says this who can see in the dark like a bat?" he countered.

"It's not so dark. We have our fires. When they go out, *then* it's dark." There was awe and fear in the young voice.

"What makes you think I'm not German? Perhaps I'm Russian."

"No," an older voice said hoarsely. "The Ivans smell like horse piss on cold soil. You're not Russian."

"I *am* German."

"You try to be," another voice chimed in. "But you have an accent. Only slight, but it's an accent."

A feminine voice interrupted. "Are you with the old priest?" There was no affection in the question.

"No, he's with the priest's horse," someone said, and laughter echoed all around him.

"That horse keeps dangerous company," a voice said menacingly.

Before Nefiore could think of a reply, Jarvik returned and climbed up into the buggy. "I see you've been entertaining my sheep." He laughed.

"Who are they?"

"I don't know their names. I think of them as part of my flock. It's enough."

After leaving the forests, they drove for some time along a dirt road, passing through several small villages. Eventually the ground began to rise and the old priest guided the buggy onto a small side lane that climbed a winding route up a long line of steep ridges. They were in the forest again, but now the trees were mature and spread their canopy over them like an umbrella blocking the stars. For nearly an hour they traversed the hilly road, switching back on the face of each ridge, climbing higher.

"This doesn't appear so steep from below," Nefiore said.

"It is a deceiving place," the old man said simply.

Eventually the road straightened in a long, difficult climb. The mare coughed as she slipped in the mud; her sides heaved mightily, but she kept a steady pace. It was dark, but at the very top Nefiore could see an opening and the outline of a small church. Drawing closer, he saw that the walls were white, and that there was a low iron fence around it. Another building of stone and an even larger building— probably a barn, Nefiore thought—sat astride the trail. "What is this place?" he asked.

"For you, my young friend, this is destiny." Jarvik's voice was low but hard.

Nefiore felt a chill.

The priest halted the buggy. "Get down, Father." Nefiore did as he was told. A cloth-covered parcel dropped heavily at his feet. "I don't know what your precise mission is, Father, but this is where it begins. You have certain instructions to pass on, is that correct?"

"Yes."

"*Sehr gut.* And you know your code word?"

"Yes, it's—"

"Don't tell me! It's none of my affair. My job is to bring you here. They told you of the importance of your mission?"

"Yes."

"You fully understand what is required?" The old man's meaning was clear. "Inside the church you will find supplies to sustain you. There is enough. I urge you to stay inside the church; don't venture out here. You are to pass on the package at all costs."

"What about the other inhabitants?"

Jarvik chuckled. "There are no others. You are alone, Father. This church is built on the oldest evidence of man in northern Europe. This is antiquity, older than Rome. A Celtic fortress once sat here, a citadel of ancient civilization keeping the barbarians at bay. Primitive man hunted wolves with white-ash spears in this forest, and it hasn't changed since then. There is a volcano here; it holds the ghosts of centuries. Stay in the church, for your own safety and that of your mission."

So this was it. A tiny stone church in a dark German forest. He'd known all along that there was indeed a mission, but now it had leaped out at him with no time to think about it; he had become so absorbed in the parish that it had begun to fade from his mind. He was afraid. "Father Jarvik, will you hear my confession?"

The old man grunted, and Nefiore knelt in the mud beside the buggy. When he had finished, Father Jarvik granted absolution and turned the buggy back down the mountain. "What is this place?" Nefiore called as the distance between them widened.

"Christianburg. This is Christianburg."

"Go with God," Nefiore said to himself.

"Do your duty," Jarvik shouted back as the blind mare began to race wildly down the steep grade.

Nefiore checked his watch. It was a half hour before midnight.

▶86 APRIL 4, 1946, 2:00 A.M.

The three men moved into the Christianburg wilderness during a driving storm that blew up suddenly and splattered the leafless trees with huge drops. The forest muffled the noise, making it sound like a distant firefight.

Herr Wolf surprised his traveling companions by guessing their location. "I know this place," he said. "That shithead Göring used to bore us with long-winded tales of his exploits in this forest; he brought me here twice. Did you know that the traitorous swine was the Chief Forester for the Reich? It was his avocation, and he whined until I granted him the title. Given his failure with the Luftwaffe, he should have concentrated on hunting small animals that couldn't shoot back." The disgust in Herr Wolf's voice was clear. "Shithead" was his favorite epithet for those not in favor.

"There's a church here," Brumm said.

"I am more familiar with the plan than you," Herr Wolf snapped. "It has historic value. An old church built on the site of an ancient Celtic fort. A dramatic touch for our little adventure, don't you think, Sergeant?"

Herr Wolf constantly played up to Sergeant Major Rau, who for the most part ignored the older man's attention. It was one thing to serve the Führer as a national symbol; it was quite another to serve the man who had held the title. Beard had long since shed his awe; he continued to do his duty only from allegiance to his colonel and the SS. The killing of the girls still sickened him; had he and Günter been alone, they would still be alive. In his mind Herr Wolf was responsible for their death. That he and his colonel had actually done the killings was immaterial; Herr Wolf was the cause. As German soldiers and professionals they had been obligated to do their duty, but at night when it was cold and he was alone on the damp ground, duty was not a consolation for the loss he felt. He missed his Valkyries. Never had a man had such good fortune. Over time, Günter had spent more and more time with Waller, which left the other five to his good keeping. And how he had kept them! What bothered him most was the loss of their company and their youthful exuberance. Now, after only twelve days on the trail, he found the need for a woman over-whelming him. It bothered him; during his long career he'd never before been prey to such powerful feelings. Women were morsels consumed during furloughs, never during duty. The loss of the girls had weakened him in ways he'd not dreamed possible.

Brumm decided to use Herr Wolf's sudden interest in geography to good purpose. He made a small shelter from a tent half and spread out his map. Using his flashlight, he asked Herr Wolf for his opinion. "I make us to be about here; do you agree?"

Herr Wolf took the light from him and studied the map for several minutes, then announced that they were a little farther from their objective than Brumm's estimate. It never failed; no matter what po-sition Brumm thought them to be in, Herr Wolf disagreed by just enough to bring home the point that *he* was the expert.

Discounting Herr Wolf's opinion, Brumm estimated they would reach the end of this leg of the journey in less than an hour, but he did not share his opinion with his companions.

He turned out to be right. Climbing along the rim of a long ridge, they entered a break in the forest and found a wide field of knee-deep grass. The colonel called his sergeant forward with a soft whistle. The rain was still lashing them and visibility was poor, but with their practiced eyes they could make out the shape of a small building at the end of the meadow.

"It's the church," Brumm said. "There are two entrances, one from the cemetery on this side, the other at the opposite end of the building. You take him and cover the back." He leaned close to his sergeant. "This is where we pick up our papers. We have to get what we need from this place, Hans, or we're lost. If something happens to me, you must get them at any cost." The tall sergeant major grunted his un-derstanding.

Herr Wolf followed them closely as they began their low zigzag approach along the edge of the field. The nearer they approached, the better they could see the church. It was an eerie white, and even in the absence of moonlight, it seemed to glow. A pointed black steel fence, chest-high, marked the churchyard perimeter. Inside, grave-stones were pitched at drunken angles, many of them toppled flat. Brumm boosted Herr Wolf over the fence, then watched as his sergeant slid into position behind a small mound only a few meters away from the back door.

Brumm left the other two and moved in a crouch around the

church, hugging the wall closely. In front he stopped to listen, but the night was filled only with the sounds of the rain drumming loudly. Although he was wet and cold, he was glad for the weather, which allowed him to move in complete security. Pausing in a dark shadow near the door, he screwed the silencer tightly onto his pistol, then tried the door handle. It turned with little sound; when he heard the catch release, he pushed the door open just enough to squeeze through.

Inside, candles were burning on the small altar. He tucked his cap into a jacket pocket, pushed his wet hair back from his forehead and walked ahead quietly, trying to keep the sound of his wet boots to a minimum. The church seemed empty, but at a small open door to one side of the altar he could hear rhythmic breathing, the regular drone of a heavy sleeper. Peeking inside, he saw that the man was against the wall away from the door. Checking behind him, he studied the church one more time to be certain there were no doors other than the one covered by Beard. Then, gripping his pistol tightly, he took a deep breath and leaped across the room in a swift charge, knocking the sleeping man onto his back with a firm kick. Dropping to his knees, he held the barrel of his pistol hard against the man's head.

"Not a word," he growled. The man looked up at him, confused, blinking wildly to clear the sleep from his head.

"*Werwolf*," Brumm said.

"A beast of myth," the man stuttered. "There are none for you to fear in this place." The words let Brumm breathe easier.

"You have something for me?"

The man nodded and pointed toward a parcel on a small circular table in a corner of the sacristy.

"Get it," Brumm ordered, sending him forward with a shove. The man caught his balance and grabbed clumsily at the package.

"Open it," Brumm said. The man tore wildly at it until the contents spilled on the table. The colonel pushed the man to his knees, bent his head forward and rested the pistol barrel on the nape of his neck. "Don't think too loudly, my friend." Using his flashlight, he quickly inspected the contents of the package. It contained exactly what had been promised. He lifted the man to his feet by an arm and pushed him toward the door. At the back entrance to the church he whistled and Beard answered. The nearby candles wiggled in the air current from outside.

Father Nefiore trembled as two dark forms rushed into the alcove.

"There's a room behind the altar," Brumm said. "There's a package on the table in the corner."

The smaller of the two men pushed past the priest and darted into the room, then reappeared shortly. "Put it in your bag," Brumm ordered. Nefiore watched in fascination as the man knelt and opened a duffel. When he stood, the light revealed his features clearly, and Nefiore, recognizing him, sucked in his breath so violently that the sound startled Brumm, who wheeled to see the priest and Herr Wolf eye to eye.

The priest's eyes were wide, his mouth agape. In his mind countless images flashed and he heard Farraro's words: *We don't care about their politics. They are all Catholics.*

Brumm led Nefiore out into the night and rain. They moved quickly through the graveyard, stopping once to pick up the priest when he stumbled over a broken headstone. At a corner of the cemetery the colonel told the others to wait. Vaulting the iron fence, he disappeared into the darkness. When he returned, he helped the priest over the fence. They moved as one into the field and stopped at a circular pile of rocks. "Move them," Brumm told the priest, who immediately dropped to his knees and began pawing wildly at the pile.

Nefiore bloodied his knuckles on the rocks, and by the time he had removed one section, revealing heavy planking, he was so weak that Brumm shoved him back into the grass. Beard took his place, hoisting the planks and pushing them back to reveal the blackness of an old well. Brumm tested its depth with a rock the size of his fist and grunted with satisfaction when the sound of it striking bottom was nearly inaudible. "If you have prayers to make, now's the time," he told the priest.

"Have mercy," Nefiore pleaded.

"I do," Brumm answered. Nefiore's rosary rattled as he slipped it from a pocket, and the three waited impatiently as he muttered on his knees. "Hurry up," Brumm whispered angrily. "We can't wait all night." As soon as Nefiore had finished his prayer, blessed himself and joined his hands, Brumm shot him once through the head. Beard slid the body headfirst into the well, and while Herr Wolf stood nearby with his arms crossed over his chest the two soldiers re-covered the opening.

Satisfied that the body was beyond easy discovery, they moved across the field at a brisk trot and kept up the pace for nearly an hour. Finally they took shelter under an overhang of flat rocks in an alder swale. It was not deep, but it was dry in back and out of the wind, which seemed to be decreasing, a sign that the storm might be abating. Opening Herr Wolf's duffel, Brumm held up three diplomatic passports bearing the official seal of the Vatican. The two soldiers smiled at each other while Herr Wolf tucked himself into a ball and went to sleep with a frown on his face.

▶87 APRIL 4, 1946, 8:00 A.M.

It was raining hard when Bailov and Ezdovo crossed the field that harbored the Christianburg church. They crouched in the grass, their weapons at the ready. The trail had petered out some hours before, but Ezdovo was confident that their prey was on a straight course, so they had kept pushing hard in order to catch up. If the rain continued, the Siberian knew they might lose the Germans entirely; it was imperative that they establish contact soon. When they had started in the morning, he'd had a feeling that the German lead was no more than a few hours. When the trail vaporized in the rain, he simply stayed on the course heading, gambling that sooner or later they'd either pick up new signs or overrun their quarry.

Now, as they looked at the tiny church in the distance, Bailov raised his eyebrows as if to say, What do you think?

"Territory's different here. No dwellings in two days. No people. Their heading led us this way; now we know why. They must have been heading for this place," Ezdovo said.

"Do we go in?"

Ezdovo answered by tightening the straps of his pack and checking his weapon. "Our Germans won't be in there," Ezdovo said, "but somebody else may be." They moved out, splitting up, keeping communication to quick hand signals.

Bailov stayed on one side of the church while Ezdovo circled and returned. They decided to go in from the two ends simultaneously. Having learned long ago the value of direct assault, they checked their watches, got into position, flung themselves through the doors at nearly the same instant, rolled across the stone floor and came to their feet fluidly in a crouch.

They seemed to be alone. They searched the church quickly but thoroughly, and in the sacristy found signs that someone had been there recently. A table contained bread wheels, American canned goods with Red Cross markings and slices of cooked meat. Bailov sniffed at the food, then stuffed it into his pack. In the transept they salvaged small candles from their holders, and Ezdovo found an unopened bottle of red wine in the sacristy.

"A meeting place," Ezdovo said as they hunkered in the cemetery.

"They added someone to the party?"

Ezdovo shook his head emphatically. They fanned out to begin searching for evidence. Soon the Siberian found prints in the mud near a corner of the fence around the ancient graveyard. Putting a hand on the rail, he vaulted over and landed on the other side without a sound. Bailov watched in fascination. Sometimes his friend seemed to think and act more like an animal than a man.

The trail led Ezdovo to a pile of rocks. He squatted and read the signs. "Four came, three left," he told Bailov as they began unstacking the stones. When they had uncovered the planks, Ezdovo stepped out of his pack, uncoiled a long rope and looped it around his waist, under each leg and up under his armpits, creating a harness with a series of half hitches. "Let me down," he said. Bailov looped the other end of the rope around his waist, cinched it tight and braced his feet against the rocks to give himself a purchase as Ezdovo disappeared down into the hole.

After several minutes the rope went slack, then Bailov heard a short whistle from below and began the hard job of pulling. In a minute the Siberian popped out as if he had run up the vertical wall. "A priest," he said as he began to free himself of his harness. "Shot once through the back of the head. There must have been a drop. Papers, perhaps, passports—something of that nature. But he was waiting here for them, and he wasn't a local. The food inside shows that."

"How long ago?"

"Six hours, maybe less. We're close now. If we're lucky, tomorrow will be the day we connect," Ezdovo said.

▶88   APRIL 4, 1946, 9:30 P.M.

Beau Valentine was on his back, gasping for air, darts of pain leaping from his tailbone to his upper back. With enormous effort he rolled over and saw his jeep on its side; it was covered with mud, and clumps of scrub brush were caught in the twisted metal. Instinctively he started to crawl toward it, but instantly the odor of gasoline sent him quickly in the other direction. When he reached an uprooted tree, he slid into the hole under the roots, expecting an explosion at any moment. When none came, he turned his attention to examining his condition; there seemed to be no broken bones, but the pain in his tailbone persisted and his left shoulder was sore.

Climbing back up to the road above, Valentine tried to figure out what had happened to him. It had been raining for almost an hour and the visibility had gotten progressively worse. He'd considered stopping to put the canvas top up on the vehicle, but by then he was so wet that it didn't matter. The road was washboarded and slippery. These conditions, coupled with the play in the steering mechanism had forced him into a prolonged, semicontrolled skid along the mountain road. Then he was in the ravine, his wind knocked out. There was a small hump in the road and his tire marks showed that he'd fishtailed, though he didn't remember it. Maybe he'd fallen asleep.

His destination had been Berchtesgaden, a town in the mountainous area called the Obersalzberg about thirty-five kilometers south of Salzburg, Austria. It had been Hitler's favorite place, and here he'd had both an estate and a mountain headquarters, which he called the Eagle's Nest. At about the time the American army reached the Elbe River, Ike's intelligence people were advising him that Hitler was in the Berchtesgaden area, getting ready to conduct a final stand from the mountains that he had dubbed the Alpine Redoubt.

There was some indication that this information had been planted by Nazi agents and that Eisenhower and his staff had taken the bait, resulting in Berlin being abandoned to the Russians. This turn of events did not sit well with a lot of Americans, and it was now being whispered in many circles that Eisenhower had not been as effective a leader as he should have been. In fact, a few Nazi stragglers had found their way into the mountains and made a halfhearted try at resistance, but the effort petered out as winter came and food became scarce. To Valentine all of this was irrelevant; what mattered was that Hitler had spent a great deal of time at Berchtesgaden and had made many of his decisions there. Now he was hoping to find people who had been involved with Hitler or his operations in peripheral ways. In trying to develop leads, he had learned early on that "little people," those in menial jobs and with minor responsibilities, often offered insights that full-blown insiders couldn't. Precisely what he was looking for here was not fully formulated. The decision to go to Berchtesgaden was not one derived from reason; rather, it was instinctive, based on directions provided by his inner compass that always took control when there was no clear course to steer.

The extent of his plan had been to go to Berchtesgaden; the rest he'd play by ear. But now even this first step was screwed up; he was still about fifteen kilometers from the town and the rain was getting worse. The investigation would have to wait; for the moment he needed shelter and sleep. A kilometer or two back he'd seen several small houses near the road. He decided to backtrack and seek help.

Valentine had walked only a short distance when he heard a muffled sound behind him. Turning, he saw a horse-drawn cart hurtling toward him out of the darkness; a whip was cracking as the horse thundered on. Valentine stepped to the middle of the road so that the driver could see him, but when the horse was only a few meters away, its nostrils flaring and foam flying from its mouth, he knew he had not been seen, and threw himself to the side. As the cart passed, the horse stumbled, the whip cracked several times, the vehicle slid sideways to a halt and a gruff voice cursed.

The driver wore a flying coat and a leather helmet with flaps that stuck out like wings. His face was round and covered with light-colored stubble. "Your jeep?" he asked in perfect English.

"Slid off the road," Valentine said.

The man motioned with his whip for him to climb aboard, but it was a long step up, and Valentine's legs were weak. He slipped, but a hand caught him and hauled him aboard. The man had incredible strength. "Behind," the man said. Then the whip cracked and they were off.

Valentine tried to shove his duffel bag into a space behind the seat, but something was already there and the bag wouldn't fit. Reaching back, he got hold of the object, pulled it out and stared, not understanding.

"One of my legs." The man laughed. Valentine saw then that he was held in his seat by a strap across his lap. He had no legs below the knees, but a small wooden T had been built across the front of the cart and pads had been fitted to both sides of it. The man's stumps were jammed into the pads, which acted as holsters and, combined with the strap, helped give him stability in the seat. "My own invention," he explained.

As the cart shot over a small rise and down a steep incline, Valentine grabbed at the seat and held tightly to avoid being thrown out as they raced downhill. They never reached the cluster of houses he had seen. Instead, the driver turned off the road and aimed the horse along a narrow, bumpy trail that wound around the contour of a mountain. Eventually they reached a clearing and the man reined in the horse, which stood with its sides heaving. He strapped on his wooden legs, then slid over the side and made his way to the back of the cart, where he took down crutches that had been tied to the backboard. Valentine saw a hut built among huge pine trees, but before the man made any move to go inside, he unharnessed the horse, then slapped it on the haunch. It whinneyed and trotted off into the tree line. "You're getting old, horse," he shouted in German at the animal. "At least you have all your legs!"

As soon as they were inside, the man lit a lantern and started to build a fire. When the interior was illuminated and the fire going, he took off his coat and hat, sat down and extended his hand. "My name is Gottfried. I'm a ghost," he said with a broad smile.

▶89 APRIL 5, 1946, 10:10 A.M.

Ezdovo had been right. The new trail led south along the calm Lahn River. They found the Germans' overnight stop; buoyant, they followed at a brisk run. Contact finally came at midmorning, when the Russians topped a small ridge near the river and saw the three Germans a kilometer away, moving due south across a grassy plain, strung out in single file.

Bailov laughed and broke into a little dance, kicking his legs out in front of him and slapping the heels of his boots. "We did it, eh?" Ezdovo was quiet and relieved. Bailov would never know how many doubts he'd had along the way, how often he'd been forced to guess. The German colonel was someone to be admired. But though Brumm had made no major errors, Ezdovo had been able to follow him, thanks in part to somebody who had carved the symbol into one of the Germans' boots.

"What now?" Bailov asked.

"We stay up here on the ridge, keeping pace with them. I want them to see us."

Ezdovo got his wish. As he expected, Brumm did not react immediately. The Germans stopped to rest and eat in plain sight at midday, but when they resumed their march they veered suddenly away from the river into a heavy forest. The Siberian watched as the three men ducked into a steep hillside of hardwoods. "We go down," he told his companion.

"They've seen us?"

"The leader knows. I figure they're in the woods right now trying to get their field glasses on us. We'll stay here for a moment to give them a good look, then fade away. Later today we'll let them see us again."

The game was on. Ezdovo felt alive as he stood wide-legged on the ridge. Look at me, Colonel, he thought; I'm up here.

▶90 APRIL 5, 1946, 11:00 A.M.

Brumm had a premonition of trouble long before he caught a glimpse of the two men on the ridge behind them. Beard felt it, too; he had begun swiveling his head and stopping every few paces, as if approaching a possible ambush. Only Herr Wolf seemed unaware. Maybe it was nothing, Brumm thought. Probably just a couple of locals, or perhaps more of the dispossessed; there were still plenty afoot in small groups. Most of Germany seemed to be adrift and wandering the hills and back roads. But by the time they halted to eat and rest, Brumm knew the threat was real. Criminals, perhaps, or once-honest men turned desperate by circumstance. Whatever they were, he was determined to be cautious.

They were in an open field that smelled of wild onions. Herr Wolf was curled up by a fallen log, his eyes closed, his hands folded under his head. Beard sat on a nearby stump, pawing at the ground with a boot. "They're still up there, Günter."

"I know. They're looking us over."

"Troublemakers?"

"Maybe. We'll have to test their interest."

After their break, they began angling away from the river. When they reached the forest, Herr Wolf complained loudly. "I prefer the fields. Better footing. My leg's aching. Explain why we're going in here." The two soldiers ignored him.

Neither Brumm nor Beard looked back. The sergeant major entered the trees first and immediately swung around in a short arc to provide cover for his companions. As Herr Wolf prepared to enter he caught a brief glimpse of the sergeant's movement, stopped in his tracks and shouted, "What's going on, Sergeant?" Brumm caught up with the older man, planted the palm of his hand in his back and drove him forward into the foliage, causing Herr Wolf to catch his feet in the tangled ferns and tumble forward, scraping his face as he hit. Beard moved quickly to cover Herr Wolf's mouth with his hand and indicated by the look in his eyes that he must remain silent. Herr Wolf obeyed without further objection, his eyes darting around to locate the source of danger.

When Brumm scanned the ridge above the river, the two men were still there, standing in the open. They were armed. When he had seen enough, he helped Herr Wolf to his feet. "We may have ourselves some trouble. We're going to have to push hard for a while. You're going to have to keep up."

"Go!" Herr Wolf said anxiously. He stared at the place where they had entered the forest, as if expecting someone to come crashing in after them at any moment. It wasn't clear what had alarmed them, but his companions were on edge. Herr Wolf felt an ache begin in his belly. His pulse accelerated and his mouth became dry and sticky.

►91　APRIL 6, 1946, 2:00 P.M.

Valentine's host was strange in appearance and abrupt in his behavior. His hair was blond and thinning, almost translucent, his skin that of an albino, but his eyes were normal, a shade of green. He had a flat nose, no chin, thin lips and a head with indentations that made it look like a partly deflated ball. Though he was short, the wooden legs he'd made for himself made him taller than his torso suggested.

Valentine had been with Gottfried for two days. On several occasions he had decided to leave for Berchtesgaden, but each time he'd stopped himself and stayed on. The man, who said he was twenty-nine years old, looked sixty and sickly, but he was robust, seldom still, climbing around his hut or the nearby forest, talking incessantly to himself and everything around him. It occurred to Valentine that he was dealing with a nut case, one of those inexplicable casualties of life, but he sensed there was more to the man than met the eye. Several times he had asked him to drive him into Berchtesgaden, but Gottfried always replied in the same way: "I deal in probabilities, not possibilities." Valentine had no idea what he meant.

Now it was afternoon. The sun was bright, but a slight breeze put a cool edge on the mountain air. Since morning the man had been splitting wood while Valentine stacked the pieces in neat lines three feet high. Gottfried had not asked for help, but when his guest pitched in, he had not refused it. At last, having finished the exhausting task without a break, he sat down heavily, stripped off his prostheses and began rubbing his stumps.

"Who are you?" Valentine asked. Gottfried had already told him that he was the son of a diplomat, raised in England, and that he was a graduate of Sandhurst.

His host laughed happily. "You mean *what* am I?" He immediately put his legs on again, strapped them into place, stood, tested them, took up his crutches and headed into the pines. "Come," he called out and Valentine followed. The trail was nearly vertical, and while the American had trouble negotiating the grade, the other made steady progress. During one of his many pauses, Valentine noticed that there were holes in the ground, and that the man used them for his legs and crutches; it was a subtle and ingenious ladder, but the holes seemed to have been worn into the ground rather than put there intentionally. At the top of the ridge he caught up with Gottfried; he was waiting outside another hut, this one larger than the one he lived in, but of similar construction. The doors were like a barn's and were padlocked. The man opened the lock and clicked it into place on the crossbar of a crutch. "Always losing things," he said as he flung open the doors.

Inside there was the camouflaged fuselage of a small aircraft, its nose facing out. "I was a captain in the Luftwaffe, a test pilot," Gottfried said. "I was scheduled to be part of the ME-262 project. Do you know of it?"

"Jet propulsion," Valentine said. "They flew late in the war. Not enough to have any effect, but they were said to be excellent craft. Entirely new technology, a new era of aircraft." Some of the scientists being sought by the United States had been part of this project.

Gottfried acknowledged the information with a solemn nod. "One day my commander called me to his office. 'An order has come from the Führer,' he said. 'The Führer requires our best man; the Führer needs you.' I wanted to know what for. My commander says, 'We serve the Führer. Trust him.' They sent me to Berchtesgaden, and while there was no flying, no mission that I could discern, it was wonderful duty. They had comfortable accommodations for me, the best food, endless champagne, the best beer and willing women. It was a pilot's dream. But then they introduced me to the project and the good times ended."

"What sort of project would require the services of a pilot here in the mountains?"

"Hitler was afraid of being captured. His engineers devised a scheme to snatch him from the jaws of trouble. They would place a glider on top of the Eagle's Nest, and if the fortress was in danger of being taken, the Führer would be placed in the craft along with a pilot. A power-driven aircraft would swoop in and snatch the glider from the ground, carrying it to safety. Once aloft, the pilot would cut loose from the tow craft and use the thermals in the mountains to make his way to a secret landing field, where people would be waiting to take the Führer to safety."

Valentine felt chills. "Sounds crazy."

"Of course," Gottfried said happily. "It was Hitler's idea; what would you expect from that one? Nevertheless," he continued, "the engineers were committed to making the project work, and they did so. By the time of my arrival, three test pilots had been killed in the effort. Three tries, three dead. I was the fourth. It was no wonder I was so well treated. I took one look at the contraption and told them to fly it themselves. I was a test pilot, not a circus stuntman. In the end, however, I had no choice. It was late afternoon when the test took place."

The man moved to the fuselage and lifted the canopy, propping it open with a stick. When Valentine touched the plane lightly with his hand, the entire fuselage shuddered. "Wood and canvas," Gottfried said. "The wood is special, from some tree in Tanganyika. The craftsmen sliced the wood into slivers, then glued them together with a special compound. In this way they made pieces that were exceptionally strong, but light and flexible. In the air the plane could withstand powerful forces and hold together, and it could be broken down into components and taken with the Führer wherever he went.

"On the day of the test I was not nervous—don't ask me why. There were few witnesses. The mother ship connected with me on the first pass and we came off the ground in good order. I tested the steering and it was fine, though I could feel pressure on the nose, a downward trim, but there was nothing I could do about it. Lateral control was excellent and required very little pressure. When we reached altitude, I used a lever to cut myself loose, but when I tried to level off and float, the nose pushed down. I tried everything I could, even dipping the nose down to build speed, but no matter what I did, I was set in a downward path. I knew there was no way to get out of it, so I picked the most open place I could find and aimed for it. Unfortunately the construction that makes the craft so strong in the air makes it like tissue when it strikes something solid. Even if it had been a controlled landing, I believe it would have come apart; in this case it simply disintegrated.

"I never lost consciousness. I lost one of my legs in the crash, and the other was shattered and bleeding badly. I used some cord to make tourniquets and waited for help to come. When it did, it was a hunter from those houses on the road. He carried me back, and it was he who cauterized the stump and removed the other leg, which couldn't be saved. It was a miracle that I survived the crash, and an even bigger one that I didn't die from infection."

"If Hitler's headquarters had everything, then they surely had the best medical services."

Gottfried laughed. "Life is neither logical nor orderly. The hunter was evading military service. The army searched for me and the craft, but they never found us. By the time I was well enough to travel on my own several months later, I couldn't see any reason to go back. Officially I was dead, and that seemed to me to be as good a finish as I could hope for. Some of the local people knew about me, but they left me alone and referred to me as the ghost. Now none of this matters. Hitler is dead, the rest of his Nazi lunatics are gone, and Germany is the better for it." For emphasis, he stomped one of his wooden legs on the floor.

Valentine turned to the fuselage. "But you said your craft was destroyed. What's this?"

"It is the one I flew," Gottfried said proudly. "I rebuilt it. Climbed back up there and brought it down here, a piece at a time. Took me months."

"I don't understand."

The man shrugged. "Don't try. When some people go to the hospital to have their gallstones taken out by the surgeon, they put them in a jar and display them in the parlor. I don't understand it either. You do what you are compelled to do."

That night Gottfried described the workings of the escape system in detail, drawing diagrams and demonstrating with his hands, as all pilots do when they talk about their craft. For Valentine the whole thing was an unlikely, almost nonsensical discovery: Hitler had created a plan to allow for escape. This was important information. It didn't matter that it was a harebrained idea; it was the intent that mattered. That the Führer had thought seriously enough about escape to entertain this bizarre scheme was beyond anything Valentine had previously considered. "What happened after your crash?"

"I heard that more died," Gottfried said, "but that eventually they perfected the system. Apparently the engineers discovered the design error that doomed me and corrected it."

"And then?"

"There were pilots on duty around the clock at the Eagle's Nest to await the Führer's call."

"What good was the plan if he was in Berlin or elsewhere?"

The man laughed. "Don't underestimate these people. They may have been psychopaths, but they were Germans. They were wed to the principle of redundancy. I heard rumors that several stations were built around the country so that a pickup could be made virtually anywhere. It didn't require much space, and all that was needed was a couple of poles, and some cable for the plane to pick up the glider. Who would notice?"

The next morning after an early breakfast, Gottfried hitched his horse to the cart and drove Valentine to Mount Kehlstein; after reaching the base of the mountain, it was a twisting, nearly vertical sixteen-kilometer climb of hairpin curves to the place where an entrance to an elevator had been blasted into solid granite by slave laborers. When they finally reached the Eagle's Nest, it was midafternoon. The ghost led his American friend up to a small ridge line and showed him the two poles that served as the launching pad for the glider. "I'll be go-to-hell," Valentine said.

▶92 APRIL 6, 1946, 6:30 P.M.

Shadows cast by the setting sun gathered over the Tiber. Small ripples running under a gentle breeze caught the rays and reflected them in a thousand winks as Pogrebenoi ambled along a broad walk overlooking the water. It was still hot and humid; the panorama of the city beyond wavered as rising heat deflected light waves and gave the scene a surreal quality.

It had been four days since she'd had lunch with the old priest, and while undoubtedly he was her contact, he had shown no inclination to discuss the mission or anything else she thought important. Still, he had proven to be an able and willing talker. He regaled her with stories about the Romans and their peculiar ways, and she had found herself laughing until her eyes filled with tears and her stomach ached. Nevertheless, she was irritated by his obvious avoidance of more substantive issues. At the end of lunch he had told her that evening strolls along the Tiber were often "enlightening" for visitors; then he had limped from the restaurant and melted into the crowded streets.

Now, as she walked along, she wondered what progress was being made in Germany. She felt a knot in her stomach whenever she thought of the team, especially of Ezdovo. In combat she had known the camaraderie forged by deprivation and shared danger, and what she

felt for the members of the Special Operations Group was similar—
and yet different, too. These were men unlike one another—indeed,
unlike any she had ever known before. It was as if God had reached
down through the instrument of Petrov to anoint his finest creations,
so that on this holiest of missions He would be assured of success. To
think that Petrov had selected her left her short of breath; she was
proud—as a Russian, as a woman, as a soldier. It did not strike her
as ironic that God might choose to work through the party, which
recognized the existence of no supernatural being. What the party said
for official consumption was one thing; what Russians believed was
yet another. Like millions of her countrymen, Talia believed in God
and in life after death. To her the Devil was real. What struck her as
ironic was that the Roman Catholic Church might be shielding Adolf
Hitler, the cause of twenty million Russian deaths. If the blabbering
priest could help her to do her part, she was determined to work with
him, whatever it might require. But as she walked she found herself
wishing she was with Ezdovo. The notion embarrassed her; she hated
moments in her life when her frailty was naked, and this was one of
those times.

As the end of twilight approached and there still was no sign of
the priest, Pogrebenoi resolved to return to her hotel and try again
the next night. It was a long walk, but she covered the route at a brisk
pace. After so many years in sturdy boots, the paper-thin soles of her
pumps made her feet hurt, and several small blisters were forming.
Being a soldier, she paid careful attention to her feet. In Russian winters
even one day of carelessness in such matters cost toes, even an entire
foot. She was proud that in her unit the cases of trench foot and
amputations from frostbite had been the lowest in the division. Such
losses couldn't be eliminated entirely, but good hygiene could minimize
them, and she had become a fanatic on foot care.

It was dark when she decided to shed her shoes. She carried them
by their straps and enjoyed the freedom as her feet slapped loudly
against the Roman pavement; she didn't care that the cement was
shredding her nylon stockings.

She was within sight of the hotel when a dark form stepped from
a doorway and blocked her path. Sensing a threat, she braced herself
and picked up her pace to give herself added momentum. Closing in
on the stranger, she gauged the remaining distance and weighed her
tactical choices. If attacked, she decided, she would take him below
the knees with a kick, then try to use a hand or elbow on his Adam's

apple. She had been hand-to-hand against men before and knew that their weight advantage could be used against them with the proper leverage. It was almost amusing, she thought, to think about the shock to this Italian in the fleeting second before she maimed him.

No attack came; instead, a vaguely familiar voice offered a loud and friendly "*Ciao.*" The greeting stopped her in her tracks as surely as if she'd been struck, but she managed to respond in turn. The form took on shape. He was straighter now, less hunched than at their luncheon; she was face-to-face with her priest once again. Or was she? The clerical garb was gone; in its place he wore a tiny brown fedora and the coarse clothing of a workingman, complete with dust that seemed to rise from various parts of his body when he shifted his weight.

"I found no edification along the river," Talia said.

"Perhaps not, but it was beautiful, was it not?" the priest asked. "I never visit Rome without taking the time to watch the sun set on the river."

"One such experience would have been adequate."

"I'm sorry about that," he said apologetically. "I never intended for us to meet there. I wanted only to be sure that you weren't being followed. I was near you last night and again this evening. Now I'm satisfied that there's no special interest in you."

His words triggered alarm in her; it had never occurred to her that anyone might follow her. "I crossed the border without incident," she said.

He laughed and took her arm. "Rome is a dead end. Our business is in the north. In Genoa," he said, as if he'd made the decision in the same instant he spoke.

When they reached the hotel, she tried to pull away from his grasp, but he maintained his grip on her arm and kept walking. "My things are in the hotel," she said.

"Already taken care of. I've paid for the room. You're free and clear."

A dark sedan was parked at the curb ahead of them. He opened the street-side door and held it while she slid into the passenger seat. It was a tight fit. Her bag was on the floor in back, and while the priest walked around to the driver's side she checked its contents quickly. She was examining the clip in her automatic when he got behind the wheel and started the motor.

Roman traffic is legendary, with good reason. Its inhabitants drive where they please at speeds they choose. Miraculously, most accidents are minor: bent fenders, crushed bumpers, broken glass and scraped paint. Somehow they avoid turning the streets into a circus of carnage. The priest weaved through the streets like a bird through a thick forest, his hands and feet a blur as he shifted up and down, swerving in and out of tight spaces between other equally erratic vehicles.

"Odd," he said to her as he maneuvered the auto out of the center city. "The streets are the final habitat of Italian courage. These people love their machines—more than their women, I suspect. The first time I drove an automobile here, I thought I would succumb to nervous collapse, but now I derive a peculiar pleasure from it, a sense of trying to out-Roman the Romans. A deep-seated antisocial drive, no doubt," he added as he took the machine around a narrow corner on its two outside wheels.

Traffic thinned as they sped north across the Apennine foothills. Eventually other automobiles disappeared entirely, and with the road clear ahead of them, they accelerated. She had to admit that he was adroit behind the wheel, guiding them deftly through severe ascending and descending turns, often with their tires screaming in opposition to the centrifugal force.

After a long time the priest spoke again. They had dropped from the mountains to a coastal plain. "Italians love intrigue," he said. "They're consumed by the nearness of danger, though they seldom go all the way to face it. Down south, of course, the Sicilians are an exception, but that's because of their ancient Arab blood. The Arabs take their danger seriously." He patted her thigh; she reacted by pulling away. "An apology," he said sincerely. "I've been too long among my Italian brothers; I have their habits. I'm an old man, comrade; you have nothing to fear from me. I've dedicated my life to higher pursuits—though I have *known* life, biblically speaking." He laughed infectiously.

He was a strange man, but Talia's instincts told her to trust him. "How far to go?" she wanted to know.

"Sleep," he urged her. "It's all right."

Pogrebenoi dozed with her head against the window and her small handbag for a pillow. The pistol was on the floor, just below her fingertips.

▶**93** APRIL 8, 1946, 8:15 P.M.

Beau Valentine was back in Nuremberg. No matter what he found or theorized, his mind always turned back to Skorzeny. It was hard to know where to look—or even what to look for. When faced with a puzzle, it was Valentine's way to make a list of the knowns in order to focus his thoughts, and so far the only real known was the scar-faced German commando. He made his notes on a stack of loose onionskin paper with a pencil he sharpened with his pocketknife. Throughout his life he had used this method, and now as he turned it to the case at hand he felt sharp.

Fact: Hitler was in Berlin when it fell; correction—just before it fell. This was verified by witnesses who saw him and also by radio broadcasts he made to the nation.

Fact: First the Russian commander of the Berlin garrison announced publicly that his troops had found Hitler's body. Twenty-four hours later the same commander reversed himself to Western reporters in a formal statement. He'd made a mistake; they didn't have Hitler's body.

Fact: Stalin told several people at the Potsdam conference that the Russians had not found Hitler's body. He is said to have told President Truman that Hitler was still alive and at large.

Fact: Ike was on record to the American press that he thought Hitler was still alive.

Fact: Otto Skorzeny was Germany's leading commando and reported directly to Adolf Hitler. He was selected by Hitler to rescue Mussolini and given other sensitive assignments.

Fact: Skorzeny met alone with Hitler on many occasions.

Fact: Skorzeny's units had a record of remarkable successes in unusual military undertakings.

Fact: American interrogators worked hard on Skorzeny to get him to admit that he was on the Oder front in late April '45."
(Here Valentine jotted an aside that it was unlikely that such ques-

tioning was the result of creative thinking or individual initiative on the part of the interrogators. In all likelihood there had been a directive from above instructing the interrogators to pursue the subject. If it *did* come from above, then there must be reasonable doubt at higher levels about Hitler's fate.)

Fact: Skorzeny was not on the Oder front in late April; he was in Austria on Hitler's orders. This has been corroborated by Radl, his number two, and by several other witnesses. No matter what magic or mischief he was capable of, Skorzeny couldn't be in two places at once. If Hitler's body was spirited away, Skorzeny was not the culprit.

Fact: The Russians sent two men to Munich to search the records of Skorzeny's unit at its special training annex. Their probable intent was to construct an organization chart of Skorzeny's unit. I saw for myself that the records of the SS unit were complete, with the exception of two missing personnel folders.

Fact: The Russians sent the same two men to Austria to interview Skorzeny immediately after he surrendered to the American army.

Fact: Skorzeny confirms the interview by the two Russians. He believes that they wanted to find out more about his number three, Günter Brumm.

Fact: One of the two missing folders is that of Günter Brumm.

Fact: Unlike Skorzeny and Radl, Brumm is a professional soldier, a career man.

Fact: Brumm was on the Oder front at the end. He was close to Berlin. This provided opportunity. His ability provided means. (Here it occurred to Valentine that he was beginning to see a direction in the facts.)

Fact: Brumm is still missing. Possibilities: he is dead, his body missing; he is alive and actively evading capture; he is alive and being held by the Russians." (Valentine stopped himself here; he must stick to facts and not speculate or draw conclusions.)

Fact: Brumm's home was in Bad Harzburg.

Fact: Brumm was last seen in his hometown in the summer of '44, when he went camping after visiting his grandfather's grave. Strange behavior given the war situation and Brumm's unique level of responsibility. Highly unusual to take a leave at such a time, stranger yet for one to be granted." (He made a note to himself: "Ask Skorzeny about Brumm/leave/summer '44? Who authorized?)

Fact: Hitler ordered development of a last-gasp escape system. (Another note: Possibly operational. He placed a question mark behind the note and bracketed it.)

Fact: If anyone has found Hitler or his body, they aren't saying.

Valentine scratched his ear and sipped cold coffee. Those were the facts. He could see three common threads: Hitler, Brumm, and a Russian effort to identify Brumm. While it wasn't verifiable fact, he was also sure that Russian agents had been operating in Brumm's hometown after the war ended, and there could be no other reason for their presence than to seek information about the colonel. He had three strong threads, and he underlined them in his notes. Now it was time to begin a little creative weaving.

On a new piece of paper Valentine wrote "Hitler," and under the name listed the possibilities:

1. Dead, body still buried in the rubble near the Chancellery.
2. Dead, body found by Russians, but being kept secret. (If so, why?)
3. Dead, body taken away by his followers and buried where it couldn't be found by the invaders. (In Berlin? Near Berlin? Bavaria? Elsewhere?)
4. Hitler is alive, a captive of the Russians and they're keeping it a secret. (But why keep secret the greatest coup of the war?)
5. Hitler is alive, but hiding. (Where could he go? Where *would* he go?)

He suddenly thought of another alternative.

6. Hitler alive but suffering from amnesia. (Valentine wrote this down, but then scratched it out; it was too unlikely. Stick with facts and the obvious possibilities. Analysis is based on discipline, he reminded himself.)

He studied the entries under Hitler's name, which seemed to cover all the possibilities. It was time to thin out the list. He eliminated both possibilities involving the Russians. While they might keep the information secret from the Allies, it was clear by their actions that they were still searching hard. There was no point to a search if they had either the man or the corpse. They were also saying publicly that they didn't have him, and for once Valentine decided to believe them. The Russian options were out. He also crossed out the possibility of the body still being buried in the rubble. G-2 said that the Russians had dug in the Chancellery garden like moles, even after claiming they had found the bodies of Hitler and Braun. If they really had the bodies, why more digging? This was further evidence that the Russian options weren't viable. For a moment he considered the chance that the body had been obliterated by Russian artillery. Very small, he decided. The Russians had found lots of bodies in the area, or at least so they had told the Allies.

This left only two alternatives: Hitler was dead, his body spirited away by his fanatical followers, or he was alive and hiding. Valentine felt sweat building under his arms. Could he be crazy? He was just one man, and he didn't have all the information available to G-2 or the higher levels of the OSS. Yet here were two seemingly inescapable conclusions that seemed solid enough to pursue. Could it be that the Allied intelligence services simply hadn't come to grips with these possibilities? Could he have erred in his reasoning? No, dammit. His facts, while few in number, were substantial. In his entire life he'd never made a mistake in this kind of reasoning exercise; he knew he was right.

The prospects excited him. Hitler dead or alive? The Russians reported that he had committed suicide. Both the Americans and the Brits had captured people who had been in the bunker at the end, and the Russians had their own witnesses. Our bad guys against your bad guys. But was it true? Would Hitler kill himself? No matter what the Krauts claimed, he wasn't sure.

The OSS had developed a psychological profile of Hitler, the result of a project begun in '41, before Pearl Harbor. At the time Wild Bill Donovan was head of an obscure agency from which the OSS was spawned. By '43, OSS lived and Donovan was at the helm; he ordered the completion of the profile of Hitler, one that ideally would have some predictive value; otherwise it would be a waste of time and resources. Psychoanalysts were assembled in teams. People were located in Allied countries who had known Hitler personally at some point during his life, and were interviewed over and over until every nuance of their impressions of the Nazi leader was captured. Libraries and other sources were plumbed by teams of researchers. By the fall of '43, the OSS had a detailed picture of their adversary. They knew how he talked, how he thought, the location of every wart. The report was shared with Allied leaders and intelligence services.

Valentine had gotten wind of the report from Ermine and she had pilfered a copy for him, which he had devoured. It had concluded with a projection of eight possible ends for Hitler, with a probability analysis for each. On one end of the spectrum, under "least probable," the report cited endings of a natural death for the German leader or capture by the Allies. Possibilities of higher probability included assassination, flight to another country and insanity. Further up the scale, the report listed his being toppled in a revolt, followed by death in battle. While the report wasn't explicit, there was an inference in this evaluation about the strength of the German underground. In July of '44, it had warmed Valentine to know that some German generals had tried to assassinate Hitler in France. The report had been off base on that count, so it certainly wasn't infallible. It concluded finally that a Hitler suicide was the "most plausible outcome." To support its contention, the experts offered a bunch of shrink jargon, which boiled down to Hitler's being a true psychopath, and of his having made so many threats of suicide.

Valentine couldn't refute the report's conclusion. "Hitler dead, body stolen," he wrote. He circled Brumm's name again. "Why?" One of Hitler's own bizarre ideas, a final touch of theatrics? His final denial of what the world wanted most? If not alive, the world needed the corpse to see for itself that the monster was finally dead. Only the forensics people could officially proclaim an end to the nightmare. Without the body, the Germans would say he'd gotten away and the fantasy of the Third Reich would persist. This had to be it, Valentine decided. Brumm had to have been in cahoots with the Führer. But where would he take the body?

Valentine reviewed his notes. *Fact:* Brumm's home was in Bad Harzburg. *Fact:* Brumm was on leave in the summer of '44, was seen in the village and he went camping. Holy shit! It hit him like a fist in the stomach. The Harz Mountains! That's where Brumm would go. That's what he knew best, them thar hills!

The initial elation soon passed. It wouldn't make sense to hide the body in Germany permanently, mountains or no mountains; Brumm would want to get it out of the country. So he was right back where he'd been. The question was not so much where he would go as how he'd get there. He tried to speculate, but didn't get far. He took a final drag on his cigar and stamped it out on the floor. A cloud of acrid smoke curled up from his feet.

Okay, Brumm's running some kind of zany gambit. Call it fact. Where to? But no matter what he speculated, there just wasn't any evidence to hang it on. And despite what the evidence pointed to, there was still the matter of the ghost and his glider. Hitler did not want to die; of that Beau was certain.

It was no good. There was not enough information to make even a wild-ass guess about a destination. Valentine crawled onto his cot, covered his head with a pillow and tried to will himself into deep sleep. Instead, his mind remained active. He saw the coffin of Addie Bundren on the back of a wagon, bumping across the red clay of Mississippi. If Faulkner could conjure up such a strange obsession, why not Brumm? The thought stayed with him throughout the night.

▶94 APRIL 9, 1946, 6:00 A.M.

It was early morning when Brumm's group reached the steep banks of the river. By his reckoning, they were several kilometers downstream of Worms on an isolated stretch of the Rhine.

Four days and nights had passed since the two strangers first appeared in their wake and began stalking them; there was no other way to describe it. There was no more pretending about drifters or petty criminals; not only were they following them, but they knew what they were doing. No matter what Brumm did, the two pursuers had managed to stay with them, keeping their distance. The Germans had tried forced marches and radical changes in direction, but to no avail. Sometimes the pair was behind them, sometimes on their flanks, but they were always pressing, almost taunting them. The two were unpredictable; they weren't amateurs, of that he was certain. It was their constant distance that bothered him the most. Had they closed for a fight he would have felt better, but no attack came. The two men simply stayed with them, pushing gently. He could sense a trap, but he kept his feelings to himself.

At Bad König Brumm had decided to try something new. He turned his party west and made directly for the Rhine, going two days and a night without resting for more than a few minutes at a time. The pace had reduced Herr Wolf to a state of near physical collapse; he was deteriorating fast and his whining turned to gasping pleas. "You're killing me, Colonel," he whispered angrily during the long night run. "We're going west. It's not part of the plan. We have to get to Memmingen."

Brumm stopped him in his tracks and held him by the shoulders. Herr Wolf's chest was heaving, and he sucked air in loud gulps. "Circumstances have changed," the colonel told him. "We're under active surveillance. We have to do something to lose them. We're going to get a boat and take it up the Rhine."

Herr Wolf complained no more thereafter.

There was a low mist on the river at sunrise. Until it cleared, Brumm could only hope that their sudden spurt had given them a little distance and time.

Soon after dawn the fog lifted like a slow curtain. Brumm found a spot along the riverbank where the water curled in a wide turn. Several craft passed, either too small or too large for their purposes, but after an hour a wooden boat with high gunwales chugged into view, headed upriver. Raw lumber was stacked on its decks, and it rode low in the water. Brumm positioned Beard in a cluster of brush and high grass and made Herr Wolf lie down on his back. As the boat neared, the colonel shouted and waved his arms to attract the crew's attention. Two men amidships waved back and the boat turned a few degrees closer to shore.

"Ahoy," one of the boatmen called out. "What's the trouble?"

"My father's fallen into the water and is unconscious. Please help me," Brumm shouted back.

Instantly the vessel veered directly toward the bank. The blunt bow struck with a jolt, and a man with a ragged black coat jumped off with a line, holding the bow in place while another crewman came ashore with a medical bag. No words were exchanged as the second man reached Herr Wolf and bent down to examine him.

Beard shot the man holding the line and picked it up. Brumm fired a bullet through the head of the one bending over Herr Wolf, then swung up on the deck before the dead man had stopped twitching. He ran directly aft; the helmsman was picking up a dented oilcan with a long handle when Brumm killed him with a single round to the throat. Quickly he checked the boat for other inhabitants. There was a cramped cabin aft with no head room, four short wooden bunks and a small galley that stank of rancid grease. The engine was underneath, its hatch covers open. Aforeships, there was another cabin belowdecks filled with more lumber.

Brumm dragged the helmsman's body forward and dropped it on the bank near the other two. "Bury them?" Beard asked.

"No time. Just get them out of sight. We've got to get out of here before we attract attention."

Herr Wolf stood staring at the bodies as Beard stripped them and threw their clothes onto the deck. He stuffed the bodies under a web of exposed tree roots near a small inlet and broke off a large bough to add additional cover. Then he helped Herr Wolf to board and guided him aft along the narrow walkway. Brumm stood on the bank, tossed the line onto the bow and pushed the nose of the boat off the shore, jumping aboard as it came free.

Beard peeked down into the hatch to look at the engine. It was a simple device, more reliable than powerful, so they would not be racing upriver.

Brumm took the helm and steered a course into the middle of the current. As they wallowed forward, he slipped into the coat of one of the dead men, then put his feet on a keg of nails and studied the other boats on the river to see if anyone was showing any interest in them.

Beard came out of the cabin with two mugs of hot coffee and sat beside his colonel. "How is he?" Brumm inquired.

"Curled up under a quilt on a bunk. He'll soon be snoring. I don't think he could have lasted much longer. Neither could I," he added.

Neither man spoke for a long while.

"I used to dream of being a captain on this river," Beard finally said wistfully.

"You're not a Rhinelander."

"No, but it's only fifty kilometers. I'd hike over to below Freiburg and camp on its banks. Those were the days," he said nostalgically. "At night the excursion boats would come along, all lit up in the darkness. I could hear their music and the voices of their passengers singing. I imagined myself a captain in a tight blue uniform with golden braid, beautiful women around me, my crew jumping to my orders."

Fifty kilometers? There were still some options, Brumm realized. "Where was your home?"

"Bleckheim, a village near Schluchsee. Mountain country."

Brumm gave the helm to his sergeant and spread his charts on the deck. With luck and a little gamble, they might even get back on schedule and on course. Let them try to follow us now, he thought.

▶**95** APRIL 9, 1946, 4:00 P.M.

Ezdovo spewed a long stream of Yakut curses when he discovered that the Germans had not stopped for the night. "Ten hours!" he bellowed at Bailov. The care with which the trail had been concealed was gone. The signs were obvious; the Germans were in full flight and headed due west. Ezdovo glared at his map and clenched his teeth. "The river," he muttered as he began to trot forward.

They reached the river late in the afternoon when the sun was low, casting a golden glow on the water. In minutes they found the three bodies and read the signs. "They've got a boat," Ezdovo told his comrade. He struck himself in the chest angrily and rocked on his heels as he stared out over the water. How could he have not sensed that they were going to bolt? Brumm's thinking was sound. They must be tired, and on the river they could keep moving and rest at the same time. Now the question was, where were they headed? The river kept no tracks. The two of them had no option; they had to get a boat too. But the idea of killing innocents didn't sit well. Not all Germans were animals or enemies. The war was over, and there was no reason to spill blood needlessly if it could be avoided.

"We have to get a boat," Bailov said. He was kneeling on the edge of the river, watching the late-afternoon traffic flow by. "They must have lured one in, then killed the crew."

"We're not going to do what they did," Ezdovo said. "Besides, there's too much traffic now, too many witnesses. We'll keep moving upriver and see what develops." He was sure their quarry had gone upriver; they hadn't come cross-country so far to switch directions now.

After dark the two Russians found themselves looking down on a village built on the lip of a steep hill above the wide river. A long wooden stairwell wound downward to a cluster of boats tethered to buoys in a small sheltered bay. They watched from hiding until activity around the boats ceased, then slipped downhill, selected a sturdy craft with a small cabin and cut all the other vessels adrift. Bailov poled them away from shore, letting the current catch them and carry them downriver. When the lights from the village had faded, Ezdovo started the motor, crossed to the far side of the Rhine and reversed course to head upstream against a small ripple and a quartering head wind. By morning the boats from the village would be scattered downriver. It would be a long time before it was discovered that one was gone permanently.

The Siberian let Bailov steer; he had to think. It was at least two hundred kilometers upriver to the Swiss border. Surely the Germans wouldn't try to cross into Switzerland; they'd have to leave the river before then. Was this their original plan, or had they been spooked into a desperate move? The bodies on the shore suggested panic.

After coming so far, Ezdovo found the thought of failure frightening to contemplate. It was a feeling he was unaccustomed to and uncomfortable with. To continue upriver hoping to reestablish contact was tempting, because the only realistic alternative was to contact Petrov. In the end he concluded that it must be done; Petrov had to know. It was a matter of honor, and to continue with no more than hope would be irresponsible. More important, he knew, he needed help; the Germans were slipping away. The decision made, he felt his composure returning, and he began to consider what he was going to tell his leader in Berlin.

It was nearly midnight by the time Ezdovo got through to Berlin. Rivitsky answered, and soon Petrov was on the line.

"Trouble," Ezdovo said. He outlined their predicament and how it had happened. The critical point was that Brumm had disappeared, and the Siberian had no idea where he had gone.

"You're certain you forced this action?" Petrov asked.

"Without question," Ezdovo confessed. "I was too aggressive, and they're more skittish than I anticipated."

"There are no leads?"

"None," Ezdovo said. "They're gone."

Petrov touched the back of his hand to his cheek and reached for a pencil. This was a disaster in the making. "How can I reach you?"

"Not possible," Ezdovo said. "Communications are bad. I'll have to call you."

"Very well. Every day. Call at eight, noon and six without fail."

"Do you have any ideas?" Ezdovo asked. It was a question he dreaded asking because it was their last hope.

"No," Petrov said quietly. Then he hung up and sat heavily in his chair, staring at the telephone. Stalin would have to be told.

▶**96** APRIL 10, 1946, 12:15 A.M.

Petrov called Stalin and found him at the Kremlin. There was a delay while one of the premier's aides fetched him, and when he finally picked up the phone it was immediately apparent that the premier was irritable. "What do you want?" he demanded.

"Petrov."

"I *know* who I'm talking to! Do you have him?"

"No."

There was a moment of silence. "When will you have him?"

Petrov's stomach was churning. "We've lost him."

There was another pause, and when Stalin spoke again, his voice had changed pitch and was low and growling. "Comrade Petrov," the voice on the phone said, "you were selected for this mission because you have always been a man who produced results. But in Berlin you lost that bastard's trail, and I explained then the price of failure. Did I not?" Stalin did not wait for an answer. "Petrov, neither I nor the party will tolerate failure. Your past successes do not entitle you to fail now. I do not want to know the details, Petrov. Your job remains the same: Find him and bring him to me. If you deny me my revenge, then you will take his place." Suddenly he screamed: "I *want* him, Petrov! Now! Here! Stop fucking around out there and do what you were sent to do!"

Petrov was shaking. "Comrade—"

"Shut up!" Stalin snapped. "I want results, not one of your professorial analyses. If you can't do the job, I will send someone who can, and when I do, I will have him fetch the Berkut as well. But only one of you will make the return trip alive. Do I make myself clear?"

"Perfectly," Petrov said softly.

"Then there is no further need for conversation. Do what you were sent to do. You have one purpose in life, Petrov, and therefore only one reason for living. If I have not heard within five days that you have found the monster's trail again . . ." He did not finish, but hung up gently.

▶97 APRIL 11, 1946, 9:40 A.M.

The priest said his name was Giacomo, but Pogrebenoi knew it was a lie. He was no Italian; beneath his easygoing exterior there was steel. He kept up an incessant chatter, talking in such a way that he might be taken for a fool. After their departure from Rome, they had driven to Genoa, arriving on April 8 and installing themselves in separate rooms in a small hotel near the waterfront. With the war ended, the Italian port was packed with freighters carrying supplies from the West for much of southern Europe.

Now they sat in a small café and talked over glasses of tea. Petrov had given her four precise instructions. First, examine the shipping, particularly outgoing vessels, cargo and passenger. Second, get a feel for the traffic of German refugees and DPs. Were they moving out of Italian ports? If so, where, in what numbers, and what was the nationality of the carriers? Third, is there any evidence that the Church is shielding Germans? If so, what is their route of travel and what is the level of traffic? All this she shared with her companion, who shed his simple manner for the moment and listened carefully.

The fourth area of inquiry Pogrebenoi kept to herself. Petrov wanted her to find out how many of the ships in port had Vatican connections. The information would be difficult to discover, for besides direct ownership the connection might be no more than a contract for cargo or a certain number of passengers. "Refugees are the key," Petrov told her. He had mentioned his own far-reaching inquiries and told her that when she found what they were looking for, she would know it.

She would begin her search tomorrow.

▶98   APRIL 12, 1946, 5:00 A.M.

For two days Petrov buried himself in his notes and stacks of captured German records. Somewhere, he knew, there had to be a clue, but whereas in normal circumstances he would have been confident of finding the answer through careful investigation and deliberation, he was now filled with doubt, and found his powers of concentration faltering. Initially he had considered going back to Müller's records, but realized that it was a waste of time; while the folder for Brumm had given his birthplace and scholastic record, evidently enlisted men were considered too unimportant for any background information, and Rau's file had only his birthday, medical records and citations. Petrov found himself unable to organize his thoughts, and because of this he began to skip haphazardly through everything, concentrating on nothing. Finally, he understood what he was doing: he was simply shuffling papers from one stack to the next, accomplishing nothing. He had not slept since Stalin's threat, and when Ezdovo had checked in the night before, he had left it to Rivitsky to tell the Siberian there had been no breakthrough. His eyes were sore and his shoulders ached. He needed a shave and a bath, fresh clothes, hot tea. Somehow he had to trick his body into giving him another surge of energy. Descending from the library, where he had assembled his records, he went into the kitchen and found Rivitsky asleep at a small table, his head on crossed arms, loose notes scattered around him.

Petrov left him alone. After bathing and shaving, he dressed himself in fresh clothes and went back to the kitchen to boil water for his tea. With a small teapot in hand, he returned to the library again, but instead of attacking the problem, he sat in a soft-cushioned chair, crossed his legs, poured a cup of tea and sipped it slowly, enjoying both the aroma and the flavor. While bathing he'd carefully considered his predicament and decided that intensifying his efforts would not produce a commensurate return. There was still time; having hammered away at the problem for two days, now he should back away and allow his subconscious to take over. All the information they had was already internalized; he could recite entire documents from memory. Now it was up to his brain to do the rest—or else luck; he didn't care which. Time was of the essence; there were three days left until Stalin's deadline, but even more important was that with each passing day Brumm was gaining time and distance.

The original owner of the estate the Special Operations Group had commandeered had been a German industrialist who had helped arm the Nazis. After the war he had tried to flee the country but had been caught by the English in Flensburg. Now a prisoner in Nuremberg awaiting trial, the businessman, who claimed aristocratic lineage and the title of Graf, stubbornly denied having had anything to do with the Nazi regime. The man had been a collector. His house, a sprawling structure with black marble floors and white marble baths equipped with gold-plated fixtures, was filled with paintings and bronze statues of nubile young women and men engaged "athletically"—as Rivitsky put it—in various sexual pursuits.

Of all the riches, it was the library that interested Petrov most, and so he had established himself among its high, deep shelves, housing hundreds of leather-bound books of all sizes and shapes. Apparently the count fancied himself a mountaineer. An entire shelf was filled with geological texts, explications of rock- and ice-climbing techniques and biographies of famous climbers. Now, looking for something to entertain himself, a small volume entitled *Guides of Germany* caught Petrov's interest. It was an ill-written, turgid account of the lives and exploits of ten German guides of the German and Austrian Alps. The author described them as being "without peers" and was careful to note that he had climbed with all of them. It was his contention that the conquest of various Asian mountains, while popularized by the press and pursued by British climbers, was less a measure of the true climber's expertise than of his financial backing. The Germans whom he extolled had never stood on the oxygen-deprived peaks of Tibet; rather, they had taken a less glorious but more difficult approach, choosing to conquer the mountains in their own backyard with little more than brains, courage, a sturdy pair of climbing boots and an occasional rope.

One of the German masters described in the book was a Herr Rau of the village of Bleckheim. The connection did not dawn right away. Petrov returned the book to its place and went downstairs to join Rivitsky for a meal. They began eating, and Petrov's mouth was full when his subconscious fired its message, causing him to cough, then choke. Wasting no time, he called Gnedin in Basel and instructed him to proceed immediately to Bleckheim to glean what he could about the Rau clan.

"Where?" the surgeon asked.

Petrov gave him instructions and told him to get there as quickly as he could, using his diplomatic credentials to cross the border.

"Why?" Gnedin asked.

"Two of our old friends may soon be there. They were hiking and got separated from a larger group. One of the larger group, we have reason to believe, hails from the village. His father was a climber."

"Am I to greet the larger group?"

"No. Seek information and call me immediately."

"I understand."

At eight o'clock Ezdovo reported in and Petrov snatched the telephone from Rivitsky's grasp. "Petrov here," he began. "Listen carefully. East of Mühlheim there is a village called Bleckheim; it's the home of one of the travelers. Ask for the doctor there. You'll know him, I believe. Be expeditious."

Ezdovo considered what his leader was saying. Brumm was from Bad Harzburg; Bleckheim must be the sergeant's home. If they'd left the river, it would make sense to head for familiar terrain. It was speculative, the Siberian knew, but it was more than he'd had moments before. "And after that?"

"Confer with the doctor. He may have the prescription," Petrov said, hanging up.

Next Petrov called Stalin, who sounded groggy when he got through to him.

"The enlisted man is from a village called Bleckheim," Petrov explained quickly, not wanting the premier to have a chance to interrupt. "It's a short distance from the Rhine to the village; I'm certain that's where they've gone."

"And after that?"

"Italy. We pushed them off their planned route, but given where they are now and what we know about the Church's involvement in moving German refugees, their destination must be Italy."

"A ship?"

"Undoubtedly."

There was a pause at the other end as Stalin considered what he'd heard; then he coughed several times and said in a deep voice, "No more chances, comrade. Let me remind you that you are not a cat."

▶99 APRIL 14, 1946, 2:45 P.M.

The doctor had spent nearly two days in Bleckheim, using his easy style to coax information from the wary villagers. Nestled in the low Alps south of the deep lake called Schluchsee, it was a collection of small stone cottages, dirt streets and a wooden Lutheran church with a high, thin steeple. Its inhabitants were mountain people, fair of skin and suspicious. Many of them worked as guides for the "flatlanders" who visited the area to tackle the great peaks south of the lake. Thick-coated dogs with blunt noses roamed the village seeking handouts, and children played quietly in small groups beside herds of black and white goats.

For the most part the Bleckheimers were courteous and proper; behavior, Gnedin guessed, was the norm for their encounters with all strangers. Unlike other parts of Germany where food was in short supply, these people seemed to have plenty.

For a cover, the Muscovite surgeon employed the same story he'd used in Bad Harzburg. He told them he wanted to find a place to resume his medical practice, but not just anyplace; he wanted a place not too large, where his expertise would be needed, a place where he could become an integral part of a community, where every life counted. It was not an unusual story, and the Bleckheimers accepted it at face value. They'd seen so many refugees since the latter stages of the war and heard about so many tragedies that they were no longer moved by such tales, and saw all newcomers as potentially disruptive elements in the long-established social harmony of their village. But a doctor was a different matter. Having its own doctor gave a village a certain status. The nearest hospital was forty kilometers distant, and the village midwife, Frau Halle, was frail and getting on in years. For no other reason than to assist with difficult births, a doctor would be a godsend. However, they were much too stoic and reserved to invite him to stay; deep down they needed assurance that his ways would not be too different from their own. As a result, they watched him closely and discussed among themselves what they observed. He was being tested.

His effect on them was just what Gnedin had hoped for, and he played it for all it was worth, hinting here, teasing there, leading them on. It might be a good place to settle; to be sure, it was satisfactory in summer, but what were the winters like? Before long, villagers were seeking him out to extol Bleckheim's virtues. They thrust food at him in huge portions, gauging his intentions by the magnitude of his appetite. When he was not hungry and did not eat with his customary enthusiasm, a black mood descended on them. He was not going to stay, they told one another, and blamed those who had fed him previously for their bad luck. Their mood began to vary almost by the hour. At breakfast—hard buns, white cheese and salami—they were jolly, but by midday and the first bowl of *Leberknödelsuppe* they were morose. By the time they offered him chopped onion and apple sandwiches for the evening meal, their mood would have again turned bright. To Gnedin they were typical countryfolk: aloof, secretive, set in their ways, superstitious. But just as he had expected, the more they pressed him for a favorable decision, the more information they began to give him.

It was the Lutheran parson who told him about the Rau family. Before the war the Raus apparently had been among the most sought-after mountain guides, and had specialized in leading expeditions of experts on difficult climbs. Alas, they were gone. The elder Rau had died in an avalanche in '43 with several army officers who had hired him. On the day one decided to make a life of climbing, one put one's own name on a death certificate, said the red-faced cleric. The time would be decided by God. Besides, he explained, the mountains did not kill people. Nature was neutral; its laws applied equally in all instances. On the rocks it is the climber who kills himself, or so went a mountaineer's proverb. So it had been for Herr Rau.

The elder Rau's wife had died a few weeks later in her sleep. It was often thus with men and women who committed to marriage early and for life. Eventually they fused into a single entity, so that when one died there was no force to sustain the other. There had been a son, a huge man with flaming red hair. The village had assumed that he would become a mountaineer like his father and continue the family tradition, but he'd surprised them all by joining the SS and going away with the damned Nazis. Gnedin noted that this adjective-noun combination had become permanent among the townspeople. The younger

Rau, concluded the preacher, looked like a Teutonic chieftain, and he hoped he'd gotten his gotten his just reward, along with the rest of Hitler's thugs.

"What happened to their residence?" Gnedin asked. The minister shot him a suspicious look. "In the event I decide to settle here, I'll need a place of my own," the doctor explained.

"It would be no good. Too far away. It's four kilometers up a steep grade. You couldn't have sick people walking uphill such a distance. A doctor, like a shepherd of God, belongs near his people."

"Eventually I'll build in the village," Gnedin lied. "But this could do to begin with. Is it still there?"

"It's empty," the minister told him. "Too far away for most people." Seeing an opening, he added, "If you were to make such a commitment, I believe the village might build a place for you. In fact we could begin right away," the hope apparent in his voice.

"Still thinking about it," Gnedin said in order to terminate the conversation.

▶100 APRIL 14, 1946, 10:00 A.M.

On April 12 Talia had sent Giacomo on to Milan. If necessary, he was to continue into the mountains. In Rome, he told her—verifying what Petrov had gleaned—it was said openly that the Church was moving refugees across the mountains, giving them refuge in its remote monasteries. "Rumor is fine for the Italians," Pogrebenoi told the priest, "but I need evidence and facts." The purpose of his trip was to get them for her.

As soon as Giacomo departed, Pogrebenoi took a bus into the heart of Genoa and bought herself several new dresses, paying sinfully high prices to the capitalists. Still, the fine silk felt wonderful against her flesh; she salved her guilt by reminding herself that her work was for the party, and that she should not let her personal feelings get in the way.

All major ports are controlled by central offices that provide pilots for incoming and outgoing ships and coordinate the thousands of tasks necessary to keep shipping moving smoothly, Petrov had explained to her. A port was run by its harbor master, and he would have the information she needed. Petrov did not suggest how she might obtain it; he expected her to use her ingenuity and do whatever was necessary.

Pogrebenoi dressed in her new clothes and set out for the Genoan Port Authority in a huge building on a pier. It had a marble façade pocked by bullet scars and a fountain inside its atrium. The interior was typically Italian: loud, filled with fast-moving men in tight suits trying to look important, and young secretaries in tight skirts and too much makeup attempting to look busy, but not too busy to flirt with the steady stream of passing males. From experience, Talia knew that their apparent efficiency was no more than an illusion; these were people who liked the appearance of work, not the work itself.

The harbor master's office was different. It was quiet, the women in the office were older, dressed conservatively, and there was an immediate sense of order. She asked a lot of questions of an old woman with gray hair, working her way toward the only one that counted. The name of the key official in the Port Authority was Guglielmo Luci. She watched him in his office behind a glass wall. Sixtyish, balding, with gray eyes, frown lines permanently etched at the corners of his mouth. No good; he smelled of integrity.

Signor Luci had three assistants, and one, a short, dark-haired man with brown eyes, had the look of corruptibility. She hung around the building for the remainder of the day and watched him. He left his office several times to visit other parts of the building, and during his excursions always managed to flirt with younger females along the way. His name was Paolo Bettini, she discovered after asking questions of the women in the area, married, three young children, of a good family, with no connections to the Fascists. His future was solid.

For three days Pogrebenoi followed Bettini to observe his routine and habits. He came late to the office and took long lunches at a restaurant near the water called Scali. It was quiet and elegantly appointed; male waiters with black bow ties scuttled between tables. From a distance she saw Bettini's roving eye, but he was subtle about it; he preferred to induce his women to come to him. He was just what she was looking for.

Today had clinched it. Having finished a dinner of cheese, hard bread and wine in her room, Talia planned what she would do next.

▶**101** APRIL 15, 1946, 9:30 A.M.

Gnedin called Petrov. "I've found the child's birthplace," he said. "Empty, of course, but quite suitable for a new tenant. It has a marvelous view."

Petrov understood. This was the Rau they sought. Gnedin had scouted the family residence, and both the location and the way it was built provided an excellent defensive position. "A wonderful place for a child, you say? Plenty of space for one to play, I trust."

"A great deal," Gnedin answered. "Bolovichovic would find it to his liking."

Pyotr Bolovichovic was a Belorussian who had led Russian partisans behind German lines during the early stages of the invasion. His code name was Hermit. Despite his patriotism, he was a loner who hated people, and it had been a standing joke among Russian intelligence officials that when the war was over, they'd have to keep importing Germans for the Hermit to fight; otherwise, the antisocial bastard would turn on them. Bolovichovic hated all men and fought only because he was a sociopath. Eventually the Germans, through an informer, had caught him in the southern Ukraine and used horses to pull him apart while Russian prisoners were forced to watch. Bolovichovic had always chosen campsites that could be easily defended and abandoned.

Petrov made a decision as he talked to the surgeon. "I understand that firewood is difficult to find in that region. Natural fires are rare at high elevations. Do you understand?"

"Yes."

"Having made such an observation, one might find it useful to confer with a nearby expert in Genoa." Petrov spoke slowly, carefully choosing his words. Gnedin understood that this meant that Talia was in Genoa; it was necessary to be vague in case the phones were being monitored.

Gnedin paused. "Yes, I know that professor. He's reputed to have an excellent staff," he added mischievously.

"Good," Petrov said. "From my limited knowledge, I would guess that a few days would be an adequate period of observation. If the wolf hasn't shown itself by then, you can assume it's taken another route of migration."

"Thank you," Gnedin said, and hung up.

Petrov shouted for Rivitsky, who came running. "We're leaving," he told his lieutenant.

"Italy?"

"Genoa."

▶ 102 APRIL 15, 1946, 10:30 A.M.

Valentine was lost. Damn Faulkner! Where did you look for a corpse? He'd drawn up a hundred scenarios, only to crumple the pages and throw them against the wall. It was a wasted effort. His senses of logic and instinct both seemed useless, and this left him feeling empty and angry. He had followed every lead and hit a wall each time. The whole thing was preposterous. A crazy Nazi colonel lugging Hitler's decaying corpse around the countryside. Who would believe it? He admitted to himself that he was still not sure that *he* believed it.

In desperation, he called the Zurich office from a filthy hotel lobby. After several rings a female voice answered.

"Ermine?"

"Beau," the voice answered in a frightened whisper. "I've been waiting for you to check in. Everything's gone crazy here."

"Are you secure?"

"No. Listen to me, Beau." Her voice was filled with urgency. "This is an open line; you know that task you asked Creel for? Well, I've got information."

Immediately he was frightened for her; information was power to bureaucrats like Creel and they guarded it carefully.

"Beau, honey, they're running with it on their own now, even flying people in from the States. You wouldn't believe what's happening—here, Berlin, everywhere. If you come back here, they're going to give you an escort home."

Bastards. "Hang up, Ermine."

"Not yet," she said anxiously. "I can help you."

"No."

"Please," she begged. "Meet me at the Flower. Forty-eight hours?"

The Flower was their name, a bedroom joke, for a small hotel near the southern shore of Lake Constance.

"They'll miss you."

"No. All the old personnel are being rotated. I'm being sent home. I'll just fade away."

"All right, at the Flower. I'll follow you in."

"I understand." She hung up.

The Ivy Leaguers were swooping in sooner than he'd expected. Now the whole American intelligence community would be on edge, snooping around *his* case. Obviously they didn't know anything yet, but the tempo would soon increase.

Back in the jeep, Valentine checked his maps to find the quickest route to St. Gallen. As he pulled onto the road, his mind turned to Ermine. He could almost smell her, and the thought excited him. Brumm could suck eggs for a few hours, he told himself. He shifted all the way into high gear with a quick double clutch and pointed the jeep into the night.

▶**103** APRIL 16, 1946, 1:45 P.M.

Before her quarry arrived at the restaurant, Pogrebenoi slipped a large bribe to the maître d', who immediately seated her at the table next to Bettini's regular one. She sat in a chair that placed her in profile and hiked her skirt high to give him a good view. When Bettini entered he was accompanied by several other men from the Port Authority, but luckily none were from the harbor master's section. She made sure that he spotted her, then spent the rest of the meal making eye contact with him. He was hardly able to contain himself, and when his companions left, he lingered. Walking by his table, she feigned a stumble and he leaped to catch her.

"Signor Bettini?"

"Yes," he said arrogantly, not surprised that she knew his name. Bettini considered himself a very important man.

"Monica," she said quietly. "I find you a fascinating man; you have an important position. You must find it difficult to find"—she paused—"diversions." As she let the word roll off her lips she showed him her hotel key. "You know the place?"

He nodded.

"In an hour," she said, dropping the key into his jacket pocket.

Bettini arrived precisely on the minute, and after admitting him she handed him a glass of wine. His promptness told her he was eager, but he looked both nervous and cautious. "Do we know each other?" he asked suspiciously.

"No, but we're going to change that in a few moments." She began to undress. His Adam's apple bobbed as he gulped his wine. "I've watched you, Bettini. I've seen you with those young girls. Do they give you pleasure?" She laughed. "Of course they do," she said, answering her own question. "You are a handsome man. Doesn't your wife give you what a man needs?" She was down to her undergarments. "I can see that a man like you needs a woman, not inexperienced young girls, not a mere obedient wife." She removed the remainder of her clothing and sprawled on the bed.

"How much?" he asked boldly. "Bettini does not pay for a woman."

She smiled softly. "No, Bettini. You're not listening to me: *I want you.* Monica *gives;* Monica does not sell. Do you understand?" His expression was blank, his mouth partly open. She shifted her hips suggestively and propped herself on the pillow. "It's hot," she whispered. "Don't you think it's hot, Bettini?"

"Paolo," he said as he began to undress.

▶104 APRIL 16, 1946, 2:00 P.M.

They had not seen their pursuers for eight days, but Brumm assumed they were still behind them. He'd worked his way up the river carefully, hiding out along the shore during daylight and covering only short distances at night. He was trapped between the need to get off the river in order to head for their rendezvous in Italy and ensuring that they lost their pursuers.

Now the boat was sunk in the river. He had weighed many possibilities, considering alternate routes back to their original course, but they were behind schedule and time was important; the ship would leave with or without them. It would be more dangerous now to improvise, but there was no choice; they had to get to Genoa.

Beard had told him that once in Bleckheim he could make them disappear in the mountains. "Nobody will find us among those rocks," the sergeant major said.

After a final look at the river, Brumm and his companions headed east.

▶105 APRIL 16, 1946, 5:00 P.M.

Despite Petrov's training, Gnedin still found it difficult to destroy in the absence of a clear threat. His profession had taught him to save at all costs. It was only a farmhouse, he told himself, and a German one at that. They had shown no scruples about the villages and cities of the Soviet Union. Yet the idea of simply burning it to the ground made him uncomfortable. It was a well-built place, a product of care and hard work, and these were qualities to be respected.

He had doused the building with kerosene, and now stood, torch in hand, trying to summon up the will to finish what he had started. It was the house of an enemy, he reminded himself. He recited his sacred duty to the Motherland. But he saw that the timbers had been laid straight with the skill of a master craftsman, and that the stones had been trimmed and carefully sized to fit tightly with no mortar. There was history here—not the kind in books but that of families, shared around the hearth in the snowy months. Here were the ghosts of generations he could never know. He felt bile rising in his throat.

But there was also Petrov. "Fires are rare." His leader's meaning was easily understood. So be it, Gnedin decided; he lit a rag with the small torch and dropped it through the door. The kerosene ignited with a sudden thump, and the heat drove him back from the dwelling.

Moving to the barn, he repeated his act. For several minutes he was not sure if the fires were adequate; there was a lot of stone inside. But when dark smoke began pouring from the upper floors and the roof shingles began to change color, he knew it was done. He had no desire to watch. The Bleckheimers had told him that two steep trails led down to the Rau house. They were hidden from view on the flat area and could be located only by landmarks. He climbed upward, found the trails and soon located a point between them where he could see portions of both. After building a small shelter between two boulders, he settled in to watch and wait as the smoke billowed into the sky.

The fire burned all night. He let it cool during the next day, and at dusk went down to the ruins to investigate. The heat had caused some of the stone walls to buckle, but enough of them still stood to serve another purpose. Back in the village he'd gotten a notion, something completely out of character for him; it had come to him as he brooded over what had to be done. From his pack he extracted a brush and a small can of red paint, which he'd bought in the village. If the fire did not make his point, he would leave something else for the Germans. His first effort at arson, he reasoned, demanded an extra flourish.

▶106 APRIL 17, 1946, 6:30 P.M.

As villages went, Romanshorn wasn't much: a tidy little square, always clean; three small white churches, all Protestant. The houses were white, too, of stucco and natural wood with orange-tile roofs, built close to one another on stone stilts because of the heavy snows that swept across from the German side during the long winters. There were flower boxes everywhere, but all the blossoms were the same color. Antiseptic living, courtesy of the Swiss.

Valentine had first discovered the village during his wanderings in Europe before the war. In summer the small bay far below was filled with powerboats that rooster-tailed their way in and out of the harbor with little regard for the yachts wallowing under canvas.

The hotel was low and flat, with only two floors, and was run by an old couple. In true Swiss fashion they left their guests alone. The building itself had undergone a number of reconstructions, resulting in a dozen comfortable suites and skin-shriveling hot water. No meals were served on the premises, but every morning pots of hot water, tea bags and Italian coffee were left outside the guests' doors. It was a place where people did not mix; those who patronized the Romanshorn Inn came to be with each other.

During the war Valentine had brought Ermine to the place for their first time together. They had left the suite only once, to grab a quick meal in the village café. Ermine, who never seemed to get enough to eat, declared at the end of their three-day holiday that her idea of paradise would be to recline on the soft featherbed all day waiting for Beau to "pleasure her." Valentine found it ironic that Ermine, who could not bring herself to discuss sex even in the most abstract terms, had virtually no inhibitions once her clothes and the lights were off and they were on a bed. There was nothing she would not attempt with enthusiasm, and nothing they tried that failed to please her. Sometime during that first visit he had referred to her most private part as her "flower," a description that set her to giggling nervously. From that moment, the hotel became the Flower.

Judging by what Ermine had said on the phone, Valentine reasoned that an official border crossing would provide a fix on his position for the OSS. Swiss border officials were quite receptive to performing as "spotters" for various intelligence agencies—for an appropriate stipend, of course. It did not bother him to make an illegal crossing; he'd been doing it for years and knew all the tricks and various routes. To Valentine, borders were tools designed to keep the simple-minded at bay. If countries wished their borders to be real, they should imitate the Chinese and build a wall. There being no such barrier, he felt free to come and go as he pleased.

To reach Romanshorn and its hotel, two illegal border crossings were required. First he crossed from Germany into Austria by following an isolated track through a mountain saddle east of Lindau. He left the jeep in the hills near the village of Hohenems and crossed the Swiss frontier on foot southeast of St. Gallen. A farmer gave him a lift into the small Swiss city, where he caught a bus to his final destination. It was an easy trip with no complications.

It was dark when he reached Romanshorn. The proprietors recognized him, and while their eyes suggested a certain satisfaction in his return, nothing in their demeanor would reveal to even the most astute observer that they had ever laid eyes on him before. He was certain that Ermine had already arrived, but he was also sure that although she had given them no indication that she was waiting for a visitor, they would know. Those who came to the Flower came in pairs; nobody came alone with the thought of remaining so.

Standing at the registration desk, Valentine turned the book around and read. She had signed in as Sally Asherford. The name amused him; she'd been among agents for so long that her habits and thoughts were affected by the company she'd kept. He did not sign in; instead, he made a tiny check mark next to her name and turned the book around, passing the fountain pen back to the woman behind the desk. She snapped a polite little bow, the formal acknowledgment of his acceptance, and he went upstairs.

Having locked the door behind him, Ermine stood and looked at him. She wore a sheer peignoir held up by two thin straps that dipped low across her breasts, revealing a deep cleavage. The massive areolas of her breasts were dark shadows peeking through. A long double strand of pearls was draped around her neck and small golden tears dangled from her earlobes, catching the light and twinkling like early stars. She wore white satin slippers with platform heels, their height accenting her well-formed legs. He whistled his admiration. In all the time he had known her, she had never dressed this way before. She always wanted intimacy to be in darkness, and was uncomfortable when he attempted sex play away from the bed. Now she did not let him speak, but stepped forward, pressed her finger to his lips and led him to bed.

Afterward they held each other and did not move. Finally she got up and fetched her makeup case. "I have a friend in the photo section who gave me these." Valentine immediately wondered if her friend was male or female; was he jealous after all this time? The thought was disturbing. The photographs were black-and-white, eight-by-ten glossies, blowups of the originals, and each was labeled on the back with the subject's name, rank and position in the Nazi hierarchy. Valentine sifted through them slowly. Some he recognized; most he didn't. "Reports from Berlin indicate that all these are survivors of Hitler's entourage. They were all in or near the Chancellery at the end. As far as we knew, all these people were dead or in Soviet prisons. Now we think we know which ones are alive. Apparently the Russians have been keeping a lot to themselves and not sharing information with their beloved Allies. Uncle Harry is not very happy with Uncle Joe. Creel and the others are now wondering how many other things the Russians haven't told us."

"All of these people were with Hitler at the end?" he asked.

"So it seems. They all tried to escape on May second. These are the more important ones."

"Amazing," he said softly, spreading the photos on the bed in rows. "So many survivors." The Russians had pounded hell out of Berlin at the end, yet all of these people had lived through it. The significance of this weighed heavily on him. With so many alive, it was not unreasonable to assume that virtually anybody who was there at the end could have survived. The information proved it was possible to get out of Berlin—maybe even with a corpse in tow. "What else?"

"Not much. Creel has established a team to look for war criminals. Apparently the Nazis organized some sort of escape system before the war ended. Like an underground railroad, with safe houses, the whole ball of wax."

Valentine stared at the ceiling. "Can't blame the bastards; if they stay, they hang."

"The strange part is that this escape route is run by Catholic priests and monks."

Valentine looked at her. "You mean by Germans masquerading as priests?"

She shook her head. "No, by real priests."

If Brumm was on his way out of Europe, perhaps he was relying on the Church. It wasn't much to go on, but it was all he had, and he had a friend who would know more about it.

Ermine rolled onto her side and hooked a leg over his. "Let's forget all this, Beau. Leave it to somebody else. We've had enough of Europe and of war. We can disappear."

Valentine considered the proposition. It occurred to him that he really was seeing her for the first time. As an agent it was his job to use people for whatever mission he was running at the moment, and he had used her as he did all the others he'd met. He'd never really thought about any of them in the framework of a relationship; it had always been more of a business arrangement, a matter of convenience. He'd thought about Ermine from time to time when he was with his partisans, but even then it was more of a physical longing, a remembrance of the passion and safety they had enjoyed in Switzerland. That part of her was so all-fired powerful that it tended to obscure thinking about her in any other way. But here they were in the Flower again, and this time it had been *her* idea. She had taken risks for him— extreme risks. He glanced again at the photographs. She had guts and principles. He felt a surge of shame for how he had treated her; she deserved a lot better.

"Penny for your thoughts," she said gently.

He ran his hand up her leg. "All right," he said, grinning.

She sat up. "You mean it?"

"Sure," he said. "After a bit."

She fell back and moaned. "After a bit. You mean after we follow one last goose."

"After *I* follow it," he corrected her.

Ermine's face hardened. "If you go, I go. Two damn fools are better than one."

"You want to go to Italy?" he asked.

She had risked herself for him. To hell with Hitler, he thought. He swept the photographs to the floor and pulled her to him.

▶**107**   APRIL 18, 1946, 5:46 A.M.

Never, as a child, as a medical student or as a surgeon, had Gnedin ever imagined that he would be a soldier, much less sitting hidden with a rifle across his lap.

Mother had raved about his long fingers; he would be a concert pianist. She saw to it that he had the lessons and that he practiced, but in the end there was something else inside him. Unlike other medical students who had found their calling early by taking care of brothers and sisters or fetching home injured creatures for salvation, it was the process of diagnosis that first captured his fancy. Given the millions of unseen microbes that inhabited both man and the earth, how could one find the guilty one in order to know what to do? It fascinated him to stare into microscopes and see the world hidden from human eyes, to watch monstrosities mate, grow and die. Later he had discovered the magic and exhilaration of entering a living human body to take pulsating organs in his hands and mend them.

As a student he had relished his time with blackened and shriveled cadavers that stank of formaldehyde. He disassembled bodies like a master mechanic, exploring the flesh, bones, muscles, cartilage and tendons like an engineer. Gnedin loved autopsies. Bodies came to him whole and unmarked or in boxes and gunnysacks filled with broken and charred bits and pieces. It was a challenge to solve the mystery of death, though he knew that the *real* mystery was that of life. His job was to discover how a man died, not why; reasons were for detectives and philosophers. Above all, he valued the aloof objectivity of the pathologist, the attitude of seeing all, missing nothing. In the end, however, he ruled out forensics as his lifework. He liked live patients and the satisfaction of empty beds instead of full drawers in the morgue. He was a skilled surgeon, an innovator and risk taker, who rose at a very young age to the Soviet Academy, and his life ahead seemed promising and filled with challenge. Then Petrov had entered his life.

Gnedin had been in the morgue working on the body of a nine-year-old girl who had died during an appendectomy. She had been his patient, a beautiful child with fair skin, a ready smile and spindly legs, and her death had hit him hard. There had been no evidence of a heart problem during the workup or operation—not until it was there, and then it was too late. The inexplicable death was a surgeon's nightmare. Now he had her chest cavity open and was examining the heart prior to removing it. Her arteries were clear and healthy; there was no apparent reason for her to die, and he was determined to solve the mystery.

He never knew how long Petrov had watched him. Only when he spoke did Gnedin realize he was not alone. The strange little man's voice was soft but crisp, and filled with quiet authority. He was slightly bent—an obvious spinal defect, possibly correctable—with long black hair and dark eyes. A large beaver hat made his head look miniature, and his woven coat reached almost to the floor. "Perplexing," he said in a strangely appealing voice. "The child dies; you cannot accept it."

Gnedin stared at him. "A doctor learns to accept death."

The stranger held up a long bony finger. "Only when you reassure yourself that it was not you who beckoned the reaper." He was smiling.

"Death is a biological phenomenon. There is always a reason if one looks close enough and has been trained to see." Who was this creature?

The man's finger danced like a tiny wand, carving the air with tiny curls. "You confuse philosophy with biology, my young doctor. One finds the biological signs of death and life, but one never knows the reason for either. In that child's chest is a shattered heart. That is biology. Perhaps you will discover a defect in it, but have you answered the question of what killed her? The real question you avoid. Why should *this* child have the defect? Why at *this moment* and on *your* surgical table? These things you will never know, even if you spend the remainder of your life searching for the answers."

The truth of the stranger's words penetrated. Gnedin's legs felt weak; he had to sit down.

The man stepped closer to him. "Don't despair, Doctor. To not know the reason is not important. We can't know; therefore it's of no significance. What you do has value; someone must manage our biology. We all do our best to ruin this innately weak flesh. The question that thinking men must ask is, Of what magnitude shall my impact be? Most men have limited visions for themselves and for everything else. Life is harsh and cruel; it encourages short sight. How far can you see, Dr. Gnedin?"

The surgeon studied the strange man, who held out a small piece of paper to him. "Opportunities are few, young man. You can go back into the chest of that child, but it's a dark, narrow world." He turned to leave, then hesitated at the door. "You can reach me at that number tomorrow. *Only tomorrow.*" Then he was gone.

Gnedin worked the remainder of the night. In the end the result was always the same. There had been a bad valve in her heart. It had stuck and she had died, just like that. He knew how her heart had failed, and when. Professionally the bits of information added up to *why*, but Gnedin knew they didn't. The stranger's words haunted him. Probably he was a mental case; hospitals seemed to attract such types. He drank hot coffee and stared at the piece of paper; after a while he dialed the number.

Thus the young surgeon had come to join the Special Operations Group. Since then he had seen a lot of life and death, and in the process had realized the meaning of the larger impact promised by Petrov that night in the morgue. He did not regret his decision.

At dawn a flock of small birds scrambled loudly from their rocky nests below him and performed aerial acrobatics nearby. He rubbed his eyes to remove the sleep and stared out, trying to focus on the shadows where the birds had been. Animals, he had learned from Ezdovo, did not move like this without reason.

At first there was only one of them: a large man, dressed simply. But he moved too gracefully to be a farmer or a mere wanderer. He materialized out of the shadows, stood dead still and turned slowly, carefully examining the rocks above and below him.

Instinctively, Gnedin crouched, checked his watch and reached for his field glasses, but stopped himself. A lens against the rising or setting sun was dangerous; it could pinpoint his location. He'd have to rely on his eyes.

Another figure emerged from the same shadowy location as the first. This man was different; he walked with a slight hitch and without the caution of the first.

The third man was more like the first, tall and sure of himself, powerfully built.

Gnedin felt a surge of adrenaline. The three men moved along the trail and over a hummock, temporarily out of view. When they re-emerged he could see that the lead man and the trailer were armed. "My God!" he whispered, the word sounding strange on his lips.

▶108 APRIL 18, 1946, 5:50 A.M.

Sergeant Major Rau felt his heart pound with anticipation. It had been a long time since he'd been home. He would caress every board and stone and brew hot coffee for the others.

But when he got to less than a hundred meters from the farmhouse, he stumbled and caught himself. The odor was unmistakable. Little was left, and by the look of it, this was no natural fire; only arson could be responsible for such complete devastation.

Beard moved down to the homestead with his Schmeisser at the ready, circled the ruins once slowly, then walked through the middle of the charred timbers and broken walls. Without looking around, he jogged quickly back to the rocks to rejoin his companions. "We've got to move," he told Brumm. "Right now."

"I'm tired," Herr Wolf complained. "We walked all night again. My leg hurts."

Beard ignored him and looked into his commander's eyes. "It's

been burned. Deliberately." The look in his eyes said there was more
to it and that the colonel should see for himself.

Brumm darted down the hill and returned immediately.

"I think I'll have a look," Herr Wolf said. The other two had
suddenly taken to acting peculiar again, and whenever this happened
it usually meant trouble. As he tried to stand, one of Brumm's massive
hands pressed down on his shoulder and forced him to sit again.

"It's your territory," Brumm said to his sergeant major. "What
are our options?"

"We came in on the north trail. Another runs west. They're the
main routes up here."

"Nothing else?"

"There's a southern route to the Swiss border. Very difficult going—
a lot of climbing."

"Traffic?"

"None. It was a route used only by my family. You have to know
it; you can't see it."

"Where is it?"

"Up the west fork and then down over the side. It's a vertical
descent. There are some pitons—or there were. We have enough line
to do it in short stages."

Brumm lifted Herr Wolf by the coat. "Is this really necessary?"
the older man complained.

"Is breathing?" Brumm snapped.

The two soldiers squatted by the cliff's edge and the sergeant major
showed his colonel the route they would follow. "It's hard until we
get over there," he said, pointing to a distant ridge line. "But it should
be secure."

"Will it be hard for him?" Brumm asked, nodding toward Herr
Wolf.

"It will be hard for all of us," Rau said. He leaned closer to his
colonel and whispered, "What does it mean?"

Brumm remembered the red Stars of David that had been painted
on the stone walls of the burned farmhouse. "The funnel is narrow-
ing."

"How did they know?" Beard whispered back, but his colonel did
not respond. He was getting rope from his pack and uncoiling it.

▶109 APRIL 18, 1946, 9:20 A.M.

Gnedin still sat against the rocks. The three men had disappeared over a cliff nearly three hours before, but it hardly seemed to matter. Petrov had been right: every man *could* have an impact.

Only two of the men had gone down to the ruins, and each had stayed for only a short moment. Afterward they had hunkered down on the trail together for a few minutes and then moved upward, showing none of the caution that had marked their arrival.

Gnedin had watched them closely and realized that their new route was swinging them away from the sun. Soon they would be in perfect position for him to have a safe peek through the binoculars. He waited until they were in place and lifted the glasses, focusing as he found them in the eyepieces.

It was the figure in the middle who took his breath away. He fingered the focus, twisting it with his forefinger, his hand shaking, and stared unbelieving as the man looked almost directly up at him.

Sitting back against the rocks, Gnedin fought for control of his emotions. The hair was shorter and lighter, his mustache was gone and his nose not so straight, but there was no mistaking the identity. The monster was alive!

▶110 APRIL 18, 1946, 6:00 P.M.

For two days Bettini had been coming to Talia's room—before work, at lunchtime, after work. After they'd made love this time, she begged him to take her outside. They went down to the bay and walked hand in hand. He was nervous about being so public, but she clung to him like a young lover and kissed him frequently, and his lust pushed away his anxiety. Near a stone wall she grabbed him roughly and shoved his hand up her skirt. Suddenly a photographer appeared and snapped them when they were deep in an embrace, his arm under the folds of her skirt. Bettini shoved her away and stared at the man, his eyes wide with fear, his teeth clenched tightly.

Pogrebenoi spoke to the photographer. "You got everything?"

"*Si, signora,* all of it."

"The bedroom, too?"

He nodded. "Some of my best work."

"Go," she commanded. "If you do not hear from me by the appointed time, you will send them to his wife, to Signor Luci and to the newspapers."

"*Capito,*" the man said. He tipped his hat, snapped the lens cover on his camera and trotted away.

As Bettini stared at her with loathing she said teasingly, "Monica gives, but a girl has to make a living, eh, Bettini?"

"Blackmail," he hissed. "Whore!"

"Adulterer," she replied calmly. "Call this a little game of *morra.* You've had your sport; now I'll have mine. I want you to take me to your office. No delays; if you try any tricks, those photographs will be sent and you'll be ruined. It's one thing to take a lover; it's quite another to be so indiscreet as to be caught flagrantly. You're very enthusiastic, and I'm sure the camera will be true to you."

His head dropped and tears filled his eyes as she slipped her arm inside his and led him down the wide walk toward the Port Authority. She had no doubt that she'd get everything she wanted, but it made her sick to her stomach when she thought of Ezdovo.

Bettini was shaken to the core. If the woman let the photographs be published, he was ruined. He cursed his stupidity; no woman came on like that without reason. They used themselves as traps; like their sex organs, they were clams waiting to ingest what they needed. What an idiot he had been! All of her groaning and moaning, the shrieks and the screams—all lies! He remembered her astride him, riding him, her skin coated with sweat, her upper lip curled back in a leer. All fake. There was no more real fire than with Cella. But at least Cella was an honest wife; when he needed it, she delivered without fail, whereas this one lied and was an evil whore.

They walked side by side up the stairs that curled around the central courtyard of the massive Port Authority building. All the while she made small talk, touching him, flashing her eyes at passersby, throwing her head back like a lioness gloating over a fresh kill.

Bettini used his key to open the harbor master's office complex, then quickly locked the doors behind them. Was a photographer watching them this time? He stood in the door to his office, his arms folded in defiance, while she looked around, picking up various objects on the leather desktop.

"Elegant," she observed. "You must be well paid for such responsibility."

Here it comes, Bettini thought: blackmail. "My salary is only that of a public official. Quite modest."

Not by Russian standards, Talia thought to herself. "I see."

Whatever it was that she wanted, Bettini wished she'd get on with it.

"I understand there is a master schedule for traffic through the port."

He stared at her; why didn't she just name her price? "Six weeks forward, updated daily."

"Fetch it," she ordered. It was only the first demand in what turned out to be a long evening. After compiling a list of all of the ships scheduled to arrive in port, she used another set of records to find the port of call before and after Genoa for each vessel. Petrov had ventured no concrete speculations on a final destination, but he had offered likely itineraries. "First, the ship we're seeking will have few stops— no more than three or four, and perhaps as few as two. The ports of call will be unusual, not places where ships normally visit. The ship will travel off regular sea-lanes, so the ports it calls at may suggest unusual routes. One works from one piece of information to another, do you see? The ultimate destination will have an indigenous German population. Rule out Brazil and Argentina; they're too obvious. Consider countries with a strong connection to the Church. Look for an itinerary combining all this and you will find our answer."

It had seemed so simple when Petrov explained it, but now with all the paper spread out and her eyes tiring, it was hard to keep everything straight. Eventually she identified a dozen possibilities that, for one reason or several, fit the profile. The list of routes completed, she had Bettini fetch shipping manifests. What he produced was a cardboard box filled with rumpled sheets of thin paper. Four of the ships were scheduled to take on passengers in Genoa. The first of them would dock April 24 and depart four days later; the other three were slated to lay over, one of them for as long as ten days.

"What about passenger lists?" Pogrebenoi asked. It was hot inside the building. She unbuttoned the front of her dress and saw Bettini lean forward. Even now the fool had no control over himself.

Bettini was angry. Why did she tease? He was in his swivel chair with his feet on a long credenza. "The owners have them. We get only the finals, just before departure or immediately after arrival. Our job is limited to counting heads."

"And if the ship sinks?"

"That's the owner's problem, not Italy's or Genoa's. He sells the berths." He wished she would button herself up again.

Talia considered other angles. "The owners must post security in case of damage in order to use the port facilities?"

"Yes, a small fee gets them a temporary 'time in port' insurance bond. Our profit is small. The Maritime Authority gets a portion, and so does the transportation agency. Then there are the damned unions to contend with as well. The damned Reds are behind the unions. The workers demand this, demand that. Who the hell do they think they are? In ten years, the blood-sucking Communists and their union puppets will cripple the country. Say what you will, Il Duce kept the Reds in their place."

"Yes," Pogrebenoi answered sarcastically, "especially the partisans."

"Filth."

"Bettini, you have one more task. I need the papers of these ships." She handed him the list.

He folded his arms, refusing to accept it. "No more. I've done all I can," he said stubbornly. "You've gotten what you want; now leave me alone." His voice was trembling.

Pogrebenoi was certain Bettini had the connections necessary to obtain the information. She had bested him, and now his male ego was beginning to feel its bruises. At first he'd been frightened beyond speech, but over the course of the evening he'd begun to recover his balance. It was time to assert her control once again. She began to undress.

Bettini sat up. "What are you doing?"

She unbuttoned her dress quickly and let it fall to the floor. In seconds she was standing before him in her underwear. She lifted a thin letter opener from his desk, slipped it inside the top of one of her hose and slit it with a flick of her wrist. Hooking her silk briefs with her thumb, she tore them loudly from her hips. Then, with Bettini blinking wildly, she drove her fist into the inside of her thigh. A large welt raised immediately and began to redden before his eyes. He stared up at her as she bruised the other thigh. Then she kicked her leg against the corner of the desk, producing a small cut on the shin; a thin trickle of blood dribbled down her foot spreading into a dark blotch. Turning to face him, she offered her hand, but he cowered like a frightened child. Her arm snaked out and captured his wrist, yanking him to his feet; in the same motion, she drove a thumb into the underside of his wrist, causing him to yelp with pain and open his hand like a claw, which she pulled down the side of her face. His nails burned as they tore open her flesh, and quickly she felt a wetness on her cheek. Shoving him into his chair, she picked up the telephone. "Operator, give me the police. Emergency. Please help me!" With each word her voice was more shrill.

Bettini jumped up and grabbed at the phone, but she kept him at bay with one arm. Tears flowed from her eyes and her voice took on the shrillness of fear. "I'm being raped," she sobbed into the phone.

In desperation Bettini dove to the floor and ripped the telephone cord from the wall. "Are you insane?" he screamed, shaking his fists at her.

Talia's demeanor became calm, almost serene. The tears had left narrow black rivers of mascara on her prominent cheekbones. There was the hint of a smile on her lips. "I want the names of the owners."

"No!"

She slapped him hard and he tried to retaliate, missing her at first, but following up immediately, punching and slapping wildly at her. His assault caught her off-balance and she fell backward to the floor under his weight, her mouth filling with blood from a lip split by his fist. Through instinct and training, she drove her foot stiffly upward, the long heel catching him solidly in the groin and spinning him away clutching at himself. By the time he'd recovered, her revolver was pointed at his head. He froze; the pistol had a silencer.

Her voice was hard. "You'll get the registries or I'll go down to the street and get help." She stepped back so that he could have a full view. "Who wouldn't believe there'd been an attempted rape? It's one thing to seduce a woman, but rape?"

Bettini hung his head and sobbed quietly. Picking up her clothes, she led him to an outer office and dressed while he made a call. She felt sick.

▶111   APRIL 18, 1946, 11:00 P.M.

By nature Pogrebenoi was a cautious woman. Bettini seemed to be a broken man, but she reminded herself of the danger from a wounded animal. He had made the call to an official in the Maritime Authority, and within an hour a messenger arrived and was admitted while Talia stayed out of sight. When the man left she took from Bettini the envelope that had been delivered and tapped him gently on the cheek with it.

"You've got what you want; now get away from me, whore," he said, not looking at her.

She smiled. "Yes, you did pay for it, didn't you?" Opening the envelope, she read the information, which proved to be well organized and complete. It was a small comfort to know that someplace in Genoa there was at least one Italian bureaucrat who was competent.

"What about the photographs?" Bettini asked sulkily.

"I'll retain them as insurance," she said as she brushed by him into the sticky night air. Her first concern was security. She doubted that Bettini himself would be a threat; with Italian males, personal retribution was seldom the problem. He might try to call in outside help, but as long as he thought the photos might be published, she was certain he'd leave her alone. Still, she decided to take no chances.

It was before midnight when she got back to her room, and the first order of business was a bath. The bruises on her thighs were already turning purple, her muscles ached and she felt dirty and violated. What would Ezdovo think if he knew what she'd done? Men could be funny about such things. What they took for granted in themselves, they rejected as weakness or, worse yet, depravity in women.

After the bath she packed her clothes, dropped a summer dress over her head and slipped into sandals with paper-thin soles and low heels. Before Giacomo went off to the north, he had given her directions to another hotel near the Piazza Dante, which he described as "safe and sturdy." He would meet her there as soon as he could. "Once you've checked in," he cautioned, "stay put."

It was after midnight when she left her hotel. A night fog was eddying in the narrow streets, causing the streetlamps to dim to an eerie yellow. She carried her purse over her right shoulder and her suitcase in her left hand. A small pistol in a hard leather holster was strapped to the inside of her left thigh, the grip facing forward; if necessary, she could smoothly cross her right hand over, snatch the pistol from her left leg and drop to shoot. She had practiced the maneuver in her room.

Because of the fog she considered hailing a cab, but none were about and she was in no mood to wait around; a stationary target was too vulnerable. Besides, she told herself as she began to walk, the fog and the absence of a moon would give her more freedom. After so long in the field, she was still unaccustomed to being closeted in rooms or vehicles. She was used to being alone at night; her unit had engaged in far more night actions than in the light of day. At first she had been troubled by the darkness, but in time she had come to welcome it as an ally, and now she wore it like a warm coat.

She had walked several blocks before she realized that she was being followed. The city felt unfamiliar, and for a moment she almost let herself be pushed ahead by fear before she checked herself and considered the situation. Pursuers seldom were the actual threat. An old Cossack proverb said, "Fear not the enemy you see."

Talia walked on at a steady pace, leading her tail into a dark side street, an alley with many potholes. As she neared its end, an intersection with another thoroughfare, she saw her opportunity and edged toward the middle of the alley so that the lights ahead would give her pursuer a clear silhouette. Just before she reached the end, she dropped to her side and rolled like a parachutist, jolting herself against the wall, releasing her bags and drawing her pistol. If she had executed the move correctly, the follower would think that she had made a run for it at the end of the lane; in bad light, sudden movements in place often look like extended motion. She also knew from experience that the human eye was inadequate in the dark. One could not look directly at an object; the eye had to keep moving in order to have any vision. She hoped her follower was careless.

Seconds went by before she heard the sound of feet running down the alley. Her follower had taken the bait and was hurrying to catch up. Pogrebenoi raised herself to a squat and braced to attack. As the figure drew abreast, she stood and aimed a kick at his heels. He fell hard on his shoulder and she was on him immediately, one hand grabbing a shock of greasy hair, the other jamming the pistol barrel firmly against his temple. He reeked of garlic and sour body odor.

"Don't shoot!" he cried. "Mistake."

"If so, the mistake is yours. You were following me. Now that you have me, what is it you want?"

"Not following you," he whimpered. "On my way home. I have a wife and children."

She jerked his head back almost to his spine and pushed the gun harder into his flesh. He began to gag. "Your wife is soon to be a widow," she told him.

"They said to rough you up," the man cried through pain. "That's all."

"Who?" she asked, tightening the pressure.

"You're breaking my neck," he squealed. "I don't know. It's God's truth." As she tightened her grip even more she heard him gurgle. If she pushed any further, his neck would snap. She reduced the pressure to give him the wind to speak.

"It's business. A job, you understand? Not personal."

"You would beat me for money?"

"I told you, I have children to feed. It's not easy. I'm a veteran with no pension. They said I could find you at your hotel. You have some photographs and papers. 'Teach the whore a lesson,' they said."

She thrust his head against the stones to stun him, then quickly frisked him. He had a knife in his coat pocket and a large revolver in his belt, which she threw into the darkness. Bettini, she thought. She had been right to be cautious. The bastard had no balls to do it himself; he had to pay for it.

Her assailant was recovering. "Where are your confederates?" she demanded.

"*Cosa?* I don't understand," he said weakly.

She knew he was lying. "I know you have help ahead." She applied more pressure and thrust the barrel of the pistol between his legs. He jumped when the weapon touched him. "Feel that? There's a silencer. Tell me where your confederates are or you will be a poorer excuse for a man than you are now."

"My brothers," he sobbed. "We didn't expect you to leave the street. They've gone around to get ahead of you." She looked up the alley. There was no sign of them yet, but they must be getting close; time was running out. She leaned close to his ear. "Tell your employer that Monica sends this to him." She rolled the man over on his back, stood and drove her foot down hard between his legs. A scream ripped through the fog as he doubled up and groped frantically at his groin.

Pogrebenoi moved to the wall and waited while the man's long shrieks continued to pierce the night. In a few seconds two figures arrived at the head of the alley and moved toward him. "The whore crushed my balls," he cried as his legs kicked reflexively.

"Jesus, you let a miserable whore do this to you?" one of them chided angrily as they lifted him and helped him into the street. Pogrebenoi followed almost in their footsteps, using the moans of the injured man to mask her movement. When they reached the sidewalk, they turned left and she ducked right, throwing herself into the doorway of a building. When she was sure they were gone, she took a few moments to breathe deeply. If Bettini was true to form, he'd bolt when the news got back to him. It was amusing to think of him trying to dream up some excuse to leave Genoa. She was relieved; this should take him out of her hair and let her get on with her work.

The hotel was just as Giacomo had described it: old but sturdy, with a small lobby and only one entrance. The exit door on her floor was boarded shut.

By the time she opened the envelope again in her room she realized what bad shape she was in; the day had taken its toll. She needed sleep, but first she had to go through the information carefully. Switching on the small lamp by the brass bed, she read slowly. Petrov's words echoed in her mind. "When you find what you're looking for, you'll know it."

He was right. She smiled and lay back on the thin pillow. The ship was called *Il Pesce Bianco*. It would arrive in six days, and it was unmistakably what they were looking for. Folding the paper, she tucked it into the waistband of her underwear and fell asleep with the pistol in her hand, the safety off.

▶112 APRIL 18, 1946, MIDNIGHT

Farraro sat in a century-old wrought-iron chair. Like the Church, the strength in the metal had not been sapped by time. With a slight shift in weight, he rocked in the chair, the motion drawing him deeper into himself. When something was well constructed, it could endure; that was the lesson to remember.

Nefiore was dead, as expected. One made decisions—some good, some bad, most without consequence. Church, government, family: a few in each institution decided the fate of others. It was the way, and it was not for weaklings.

The old priest stood up and adjusted his cassock. These were momentous times. God's work needed doing. He was glad to be at the center and proud to have the responsibility on his shoulders.

There was much to do. On the twenty-fourth of April a ship would dock in Genoa to pick up European "missionaries." Farraro did not know who they were or who they had been, and he did not want to know. It was irrelevant. It was his decision alone as to who they would be and where they would go. He had the power. The halls of Vatican City were filled with intelligent and ambitious men; he would rise above them all, he told himself.

For the moment, however, the problem was not so grand. Through a series of circumstances he did not yet fully understand, the records of the ship had passed today into the hands of a harlot. Undoubtedly she had no comprehension of the importance of the information she held, but that did not matter. Farraro sighed. It would have been easier if she had kept to her customer's wallets and carnal needs. But greed, he knew, had no limits in some people. She had stumbled into something over her head, a possession she would soon lose. She had to be removed immediately. He had already issued the order.

▶113 APRIL 19, 1946, 5:10 A.M.

As a soldier Pogrebenoi knew firsthand the value of sleep. In the field one took it when and where one could. She had slept in small caves scooped from snowdrifts, in swamps filled with mosquito swarms, on the side of steep ravines with her arms hooked around saplings to prevent her sliding, in trees while German infantry camped below her, in barns among livestock, and in rainstorms so heavy that she'd almost drowned. Sometimes sleep lasted a few moments, sometimes two or three hours. You took it when it came, and soldiered on when it was no longer possible.

Now sleep came almost instantly, but it was the tense kind that left her muscles in tight knots. It served the body rather than the mind, giving her only the physical strength to endure and to think, but no more. Soldiers did not dream; always it was a matter of preparing for the next ordeal, and always there was another one ahead, often worse than what they had imagined.

To the men and women in her command, their major's ability to sleep for a few minutes and appear refreshed and in control when she awoke was remarkable. In her army, company-level officers were not appointed from above but from below, by their comrades in the ranks, and it was her stoicism and reliability that had brought her an officer's rank so early. At first she feared the responsibility, later she warmed to it, and by the end she was dulled by it; behind her was a trail of bodies that her orders had killed. When peace came, there were visits from generals, even a famous field marshal, an official state hero. She was in line for promotion and a career; her war record would serve her well. She barely listened to them and had no interest in their propositions. She would serve her country—of that she was certain—but no more in charge of other lives. She would work in her own way, depending almost entirely upon herself, and Petrov had delivered this to her.

It was done, she thought as she reclined on the bed. Fortunately the beds of the Dante were hard. After years in the field, it was difficult to get accustomed to anything soft, and she was determined not to fall victim to creature comfort now that the army was behind her. To sleep on a hard surface helped keep one fit.

But this night, sleep remained just beyond reach. Her mind drew up memories, some forgotten, others repressed because there had been no time or place for them. The boys came to her mind, and she watched them playing along the river. They were good sons, loving but independent, with qualities of both sensitivity and ferocity. So be it; as Russians, they must grow up understanding that they alone carried the weight of the future on their backs. For Russians there were only other Russians; no others could be trusted.

At some point she drifted into sleep, on her back, arms and legs spread, and snoring lightly. A familiar voice woke her, a hoarse one with a suppressed laugh behind it. "Don't move," it said, and while there was tension in it to induce alertness, it spoke in such a way as to give her confidence. "I've come back with some interesting news," the voice said, "but I can see your time must have been equally fruitful."

"Giacomo?"

"Returned from the high country. You've had some trouble."

"It's taken care of."

"Apparently not." Now she could see him, peering from the side of the window that overlooked the street in front of the hotel's entrance. "There are men down there covering the street and lobby, and I believe there's one on this floor as well. I've been watching them for some time. They're waiting for you."

She was thoroughly awake now, sitting on the side of the bed, fastening the silencer on her weapon by touch, as she filled him in on what had happened.

He laughed. "*Bellissimo.* You tampered with the psyche of the delicate Italian male. That he wanted only to see you beaten and humiliated is a measure of both his ardor and his fear of you. Had he been truly vindictive and sure of himself, he would have paid for your murder." Again he chuckled to himself. "His face must have been something to see when that photographer appeared."

"Yes, there was stark terror on it," she said.

"This group is not from your scorned lover," Giacomo said. "These are professionals, not workers trying to earn a few lire to keep their families alive. We'll have to be careful with them. You are ready?" He laid out a plan for her, one in which she was the centerpiece. She changed clothes while he talked. "We have to take one of them alive, at least for a few moments. Since he's the closest, we'll take the one on this floor." She was to take the papers and nothing else. If they had trouble, they would split up and meet later. He explained what she should do and how to cover herself during evasion. The principles were remarkably similar to those used by soldiers in the same situation.

Near the lift on Talia's floor was a small lobby with two armchairs. One of them was occupied by a thin man with dark hair pasted into place with oil, reading a newspaper. As she approached she noticed that it was an old paper, obviously something he had picked up in a hurry for a prop. Giacomo had been astute in seeing the trouble; she wondered how he had gotten by the man.

She pushed the button for the lift and waited, placing herself so as to draw the guard's attention away from the hall. "You," she said loudly. "How much will you pay?" A waxen face peered around the corner of the paper. "Yes, *imbecille,* I'm talking to you. How much will you part with? I have some time now and I can see that you're interested."

The man blinked furiously. His lips moved, but no words came out.

"The shy type," she said with a leer. "I'll give you a special rate. I don't have time to waste. Either you want it or you don't. What will it be? I have business to tend to." She stepped toward him and twirled, making sure that the skirt floated high. "See? Have a peek at the goods. Pretty nice, eh? Never had an unsatisfied customer. Maybe you'll become a regular."

"I'm only visiting," the man said weakly.

"Better yet!" she exclaimed. "Your wife will never know, and you'll always carry a memory of your time with Monica. I know my business—and yours too, if you get my meaning."

As she poked at him with one of her sandals, he pulled his legs to the side, trying to avoid her touch. "I'm not married," he said brusquely.

"Perfect. A randy bachelor with horns. That makes me the lucky one. Come," she said, extending her hand to him. "Let's go have a ride together. I have a nice soft bed just down the hall." She grabbed at him and caught his arm. He resisted, but she managed to get him off the seat and partially on his feet before Giacomo sprang suddenly from behind to catch him by the neck. The man gagged and resisted, but Talia could see that the hold was tight. Giacomo danced him down the hall quickly and bounced him into her room. She closed the door behind them, then returned to take the man's seat near the lift. Holding her pistol in her small handbag, she positioned it in her lap so that the gun was pointed directly at the elevator doors.

Giacomo returned in a few minutes. "I had to be a bit more direct than I'd hoped for, but we have what we need. We have to leave here now together. This is more serious than I thought. Once we go, do what I say. If I fall, don't let yourself be taken alive. Can you do that?"

Their roles had reversed. Now he was giving the orders and she was listening. His voice told her that she had no choice, though she wondered what could be so threatening. "I understand," she told him.

Instead of descending, they climbed up the stairs to the roof of the hotel and made their way to the nearest building with a short jump across the gap. They moved at a brisk pace over the rooftops for a long time, so far that it seemed they might never come down, but eventually, after looking over the side, he grunted and led her down a long series of stairwells through darkened halls. At the entry they paused while he went out to sit on the stoop, looking up and down the street like an old man with too much wine in his belly. He spoke to her without turning around. "Walk quickly across the street, then up to the corner. Walk fast. Women are always frightened of being alone. When you get there, go left and duck into the second entrance you come to. Remove the silencer. If you have trouble, I want to know where you are."

Talia brushed by him and crossed the street at a trot without looking back, the heels of her shoes clipping the pavement like shots from a small-caliber pistol. Reaching the other side, she hurried to the corner, turned left and ducked into an entry, then looked back in the direction she had come from.

Several minutes went by before she heard anything. When she did, it was a cheery voice singing a low melody, the words slurred to indicate that the owner of the voice was tipsy. The drunk came slowly, weaving across the expanse of sidewalk, stopping now and then to survey the path ahead. At one point he stopped and stood teetering on the curb as he urinated into the street. As he got closer he said, "Move out ahead of me. Go fast. Wait at the end of the block." She did as she was told, and moments later Giacomo joined her. When he was sure that they had eluded pursuit, he led her north to another part of Genoa.

By noon the priest had installed them in a small house in the northern fringe of the city. The place was owned by an old woman who seemed genuinely pleased to see him and gave only a perfunctory glance at Talia. While the old woman worked on a breakfast in the kitchen, the two drank espresso and chewed on pickled green peppers.

"They wanted you," Giacomo said. "They had instructions to eliminate you quietly and to recover certain information."

"Only Bettini knew about the information."

"In Italy no secret is known by only one person. If the information was important to you, it is important to someone else. There's always a balance, an equilibrium, in these matters. From what you told me, your friend Bettini is not the kind to trade in information. He told them, but his motive was personal vengeance; theirs is state security."

"State security?"

"Thou art Peter, and upon this rock . . ."

It was hard to consider the Vatican a state, but it was that in fact and practice. "They sent assassins?"

"Surprised? They are not strangers to violence. Propagation of the faith requires pragmatic men. Those who conduct the affairs of their state may speak a dead language and look different from their secular counterparts, but the power brokers in all states are cut from the same cloth. They do what they must, and pray for forgiveness on the grounds that it's for the greatest good of the greatest number."

"There is a ship coming to Genoa to pick up refugees—missionaries, they're called. The ship is owned by the Vatican, but it sails under a Greek pennant," Talia said.

"A relationship of long standing. What do you want to do next?"

Quickly she tried to calculate the date and her instructions. "We wait."

Giacomo leaned toward her. "Petrov is coming soon, I trust?"

Talia could not hide her surprise. At no time had she mentioned her leader's name. "Who are you?" she blurted out.

"Espresso?" he asked, the pot poised above her cup.

▶**114** APRIL 19, 1946, 4:00 P.M.

Following Petrov's orders, Ezdovo and Bailov made their way to Bleckheim on a forced march. They were tired, but were determined to
reach their destination and find Gnedin.

When they reached the village, Bailov did the talking for them,
buttonholing an old man in the square. Almost immediately other
Bleckheimers gathered around. They were veterans of a medical unit,
the Russian said, and were seeking a comrade, a surgeon. The villagers
were immediately suspicious. There was a doctor, but how had the
two of them known to look for him in Bleckheim? Bailov asked the
old man if he had served in the war. No? Well, then, the methods
used by soldiers to keep track of one another would be outside his
ability to comprehend. Military men knew how to find one another;
it had always been so. The villagers thought about it. The stranger
seemed short-tempered and had a mean look about him. Besides,
veterans, for whatever reason, did seem to stick together. What did
their doctor friend look like?

Bailov described Gnedin and the old man nodded. It sounded like
their doctor. He had moved to a farmhouse higher in the mountains;
they could wait here for him if they liked. Bailov asked for directions;
they'd rather go to him.

Outside the village, the two Russians checked their weapons and
started the long climb at double time.

► **115** APRIL 19, 1946, 5:30 P.M.

Bolzano looked the same as it did the last time Valentine passed through, only more crowded. It was a place that always made him nervous. Its people were more German than Italian, and many of them made no bones about their allegiance. The town looked German, spoke German, cooked German, thought German, and now it was packed with refugees who undoubtedly were German. If there was a network for a pipeline of Nazis from the north, there would be information about it in Bolzano, and he knew who would have it or would be able to get it.

At a café on the western slope of the city Valentine left Ermine sleeping on the front seat of her blue sedan and entered through the rear entrance directly into the kitchen. It was evening and the cooks were busy; the slightly rancid odor of olive oil mingled with the other aromas of seafood from the Venetian gulf, cheeses, sausages and fruit. Passing through the kitchen, he made his way to a small office hidden in a wall beside a large meat locker.

The proprietor's name was Bela, a stooped old curmudgeon with a few tufts of hair left sticking out of his multicolored scalp, his head covered with flakes of dried skin. The desk was littered with slips of paper, dirty plates stacked one on top of another, a fat green bottle of Chianti and a can filled with cigarette butts. Bela looked up and squinted to focus on the intruder, a growl beginning in his throat. "Valentine?"

When the American sat down, the Italian did not move. "I thought you'd be back in the States by now," he said in English, his Brooklyn accent strong. He smiled crookedly and extended a leathery hand. "So you can't turn loose of Italia, eh? Me, I'd leave tomorrow, but I'm broke." He rubbed his hands together. "Fuckin' Germans are fuckin' tight, *capisce?*"

It was a familiar tune. Bela had been born in America, but as a young man had fallen in love with tales of the old country, and had returned to the land of his parents and taken citizenship. He was always threatening to chuck it all and return to the States, but Valentine knew it was only a pose. Bela, who looked like a doddering old man who couldn't remember names and spilled half of what he ate, was deceptive. The German troops, who had eaten at his restaurant and garrisoned in the area until the end of the war, were genuinely fond of the old man, never suspecting that from his small establishment he commanded four regiments of partisans who obeyed him unquestioningly. He was Valentine's last hope.

"You're not here to see Bela for old times."

"I've heard that the Krauts are coming over the mountains in big bunches."

"Like a shad run up the Hudson. But it's slowing down. Them with a reason to git have got, if you get my meaning."

"There's supposed to be an organized route, some kind of system."

Bela laughed. "Like the Oregon trail." He took a swig of wine, made a face and offered the bottle to Valentine. "Too warm, but better'n a kick in the ass."

"I need information."

"Sure. You're tailing some Krauts, right?"

"I've heard the Church was involved in this."

The old man's eyes turned hard and he touched a finger to his lips as he got up and pushed the door closed. "You gotta be careful with that kind of talk. Rome's got more ears than we had during the war. This ain't like New York, with Mick priests brown-nosing the politicians. Here they run things. The only difference between the Church and Cosa Nostra is their uniforms."

"Word has it that the Nazis are being hidden in monasteries."

"For a while they were, but it got too hot. This area's been crawling with Jews packing pieces. They've got the routes busted up now; they're using camps and cabins up in the hills." To Bela all mountains were hills. "Nothing special, same kind of things we did. Back up there you can stash people pretty easy."

"I need to know about a particular party."

"Forget it," the old man said. "If you're looking for a name, you'll never get it. It's too complicated, and they got layers of security set up. Even they don't know who they've got in their pipeline. You're wasting your time."

Valentine's mind raced. "What's the end of the route?"

"Genoa, usually. Maybe a few pickups along the coast from time to time, but that's pretty risky. Most of them are taken to Genoa, then shipped out to the Middle East or South America. Lots of Krauts have moved through the system."

"They go out a few at a time?"

"Usually, and most of them have first-class papers. Once they get on a ship and leave Italian waters, they've got it made. At that point they're who their papers say they are."

"And at the other end?"

Bela shrugged. "No questions asked. Customs officials probably don't even shake them down. I hear some of them have big assets in Swiss and Argentine banks. The South Americans aren't going to turn them away if they bring capital in. Economies are going to be built on some of these Krauts."

"What I really need—"

"Is to have your old friend Bela check on some outbound shipments, right?" Bela interrupted. "I can have someone take a look. Probably there's not much we can find out, but for my old pal Beau Valentine I can spend a little sweat."

"I don't want to be ungrateful, but how fast?"

"A day, a week—it depends on how lucky we get." He held up a card that he took from the drawer in his desk. "My grandson runs this joint near Genoa. Good chow, no bugs, clean hookers, everything a man could want. You got wheels?"

Valentine nodded.

"What's your specific interest?" Bela made a mark on the left edge of the card with a paring knife.

"An SS colonel named Günter Brumm. And a corpse." Valentine described Brumm.

Bela screwed his face into a wrinkled mask. "A stiff and a big bastard, eh? Not much to go on."

Valentine nodded.

The old man stood, put his arm around his friend and grinned. "An SS colonel and a stiff? You still have weird ways, my friend." He gave the card to Valentine. "Drive to Genoa and give this to my grandson. He'll take care of you. I'll make a few inquiries and let you know, okay?"

At the back door they shook hands. "I can't walk out with you. Lousy ticker." Bela said, pointing to his heart. "Besides, I don't want anybody making a connection. In here I know who's on my side; out in the street, I have no control. It's a lousy world, Valentine." The American rubbed his friend's shoulder affectionately. "Hey," the old man said brightly. "For you? Anything. We got mutual history. In Italy that's all that counts. Long as I'm stuck here, I try to live with it."

Valentine laughed. Bela would never leave.

"Don't take no wooden nickels," the old man shouted after him as Valentine carefully picked his way through the crowded kitchen for the last time.

▶**116** APRIL 19, 1946, 5:45 P.M.

Ezdovo poked at the blackened timbers with the toe of his boot while Bailov knelt outside covering him. The light was poor and a cold wind was beginning to blow across the ridge. The pattern was clear; somebody had started the fire. But who?

Bailov's whistle interrupted his thoughts and he went outside. The younger man was standing by a stone wall that had once been part of the barn, his arms crossed, his weapon cradled across his chest. "Take a look," he said, nodding to the wall.

There was a red star painted on the light-colored stone, a job done in a rush because the paint had run, leaving long thin streaks. They circled the structure, and on all four sides found similar stars. Ezdovo looked up the mountainside. "Signal," he told Bailov, who squeezed off two quick shots, paused and fired a final single.

The answer came back immediately: a single, a pause, two fast rounds, another pause, a final single. The two men smiled to each other and moved to the base of the rocks to wait.

Gnedin announced his arrival with a long whistle, followed by a familiar shriek that was supposed to be a rendition of a Siberian greeting yell, but which he had never mastered and came out as a sound his comrades described as "halfgoat, halfcat and all pain." He bounded down the rocks behind them, landing in a cloud of dust. The three men embraced with delight.

To be safe they spent the night at the doctor's lookout above the farm, building a small fire and enjoying warm food for the first time in days. Gnedin told them what he had seen, and in the morning showed them the lip of rock where the Germans had disappeared.

"You have the stomach for climbing, Doctor?" Bailov asked.

Gnedin peered over the edge, shaking his head. "Even a fly would fall off that."

"Do you see any German bodies down there?" Ezdovo asked.

"No," the doctor said, giving a brief glance to the rocks far below.

"Then it can be done. They chose this place. There had to be a reason."

After a short preparation Bailov was lowered over the side and eased his way down the cliff, using his feet like shock absorbers and for balance. Eventually the face dipped in sharply, leaving him dangling in space several hundred meters above a boulder field. With a yell he asked to be lowered more; as he dropped he could see that farther down there was a ledge, and that pitons were hammered in place alongside it. Clearly the route had been chosen by an expert rock climber.

Back on top, he told the others what he had found. "It's a trail . . . more or less."

"We follow," Ezdovo said, anxious to get going. "We'll get down behind them, reestablish contact and keep pushing them. They've already acted desperately. When they find we're still following, they'll do it again."

"I'll never make it," Gnedin said weakly as he looked over the side.

"Consider it another chapter in your education," Ezdovo said.

Bailov grabbed the doctor by the shoulders. "If you don't make it, can I have your boots?" They all laughed as they began preparations for the precarious descent.

▶117 APRIL 19, 1946, 6:00 P.M.

Petrov and Rivitsky were taken by Soviet air courier to Copenhagen, where they used Swiss passports and new identities to purchase tickets on a British commercial flight to Brussels. From there they flew to Geneva, where they passed through customs without inquiry. Taking separate cabs, they went into the city, where Rivitsky picked up an automobile left for them near a yacht club on the shore of the lake. They drove south into France and raced along the hot coast, crossing into Italy via Monaco and Menton. At the Italian border they were waved through and continued on to Genoa. It was early evening when they reached the grimy seaport.

For Rivitsky it was exhilarating to be shed of Berlin and the destruction. Even in summer the German capital remained a gray waste filled with a powdery dust that covered everything and got into the lungs. It was not healthy there, he told Petrov. It was good to see green forests again and people who were well dressed and normal. It made him wonder what the weather was like in Russia; what scars would they find when they returned home?

Genoa was bustling as its inhabitants hurried home. Rivitsky drove carefully, cursing the Italians and their erratic driving habits. Bicycles scraped the car, and police argued with motorists and pedestrians alike at crowded intersections, causing mass confusion. Their destination was a warehouse on the waterfront east of the city center. It was buried in an area with dozens of other storage facilities, all with unpainted walls and tin roofs rusted from salt spray; they found it only because it had no identifying number—all the other buildings were marked.

Rivitsky drove the automobile up to a side door and leaned against the front fender to smoke while Petrov reconnoitered. Gray gulls floated over the buildings, squawking obnoxiously. Like the city, the birds seemed dirty, not like the majestic gulls on the Black Sea, which were white and pure. The sea breeze was strong, a familiar scent of decaying fish and petrol. Ports always smelled the same, Rivitsky thought.

Behind him, Petrov whistled and signaled him to swing the vehicle around the corner. By the time he reached the front a large door was swinging upward to admit him. Inside, the building was nothing more than a thin shell of metal, like an aircraft hangar. Petrov had him move the machine to a walled area housing several small office cubicles, where it was well hidden.

They entered the area of the cubicles with Petrov leading the way. The place was musty and still and gave Rivitsky an uneasy feeling. Their route twisted through offices, eventually taking them to a small cubicle stacked high with topless wooden crates and a long narrow rack containing fifty or more black oars with green blades standing like emaciated sentinels. When a panel in the wall suddenly swung open, Rivitsky was not surprised to see a long stone stairwell leading down. After a long walk another stairwell led them up to a landing and a steel door, which Petrov struggled to open. Rivitsky did not move to help; if his chief wanted assistance he would ask for it. Once inside, Petrov dropped a thin steel bar in place and led Rivitsky down yet another hallway, this one damp and moist. Stone stairs led them up into a large room. Light poured down on them from above, and for the first time since entering the warehouse, Rivitsky felt more like a man than a mole. Below them there was a slip and a long wooden boat with housing over its large inboard engine.

Petrov shed his overcoat and opened his bag while Rivitsky waited for an explanation. But his leader said only, "We'll settle here," then trudged slowly up the stairs to a higher level. Rivitsky followed, to discover a slit window looking out on the port of Genoa. They must be in the same building they'd driven into, but in a part reachable only through the passageway. It would be easy to defend, but difficult to escape from if the need arose.

Petrov stood silently for a long time, staring out at the darkening harbor. "It won't be long now," he said finally.

►118 APRIL 21, 1946, 3:15 P.M.

They had been on Beard's vertical trail for almost three full days. It would have been rough going even for the two veterans alone, but with Herr Wolf between them, always on the verge of falling or actually hanging like a dead weight, they were nearly exhausted. The cloth was gone from the knees of their trousers, and their shins and hands were covered with abrasions and open cuts. Worst of all, they were dehydrated, urinating brown dribbles as their bodies consumed their final reserves of fluid.

Brumm gave grudging credit to Herr Wolf. Where formerly he had simply gone along like a puppet with broken strings, he now threw himself into the descents and climbs with true zeal. Unfortunately he was neither strong nor robust, so despite his willingness, Brumm and Beard found themselves carrying him. They appreciated his efforts, but he remained a burden.

Because of his greater experience as a climber, Beard led for the first time. This meant that he made the difficult ascents and descents first, and often twice, in order to brief and instruct his comrades on the tactics and tricks to be employed on the next stage. It was slow going, but they kept at it as steadily as their strength would allow, resting only between particularly difficult stretches.

It was during one such interlude near the crest of a high ridge that Brumm turned his field glasses on the walls they had already conquered. Beard was tied to Herr Wolf and they were below the colonel, trying to work down the smooth side of a vertical structure that Beard called the Baton. It required a circular descending route like a ribbon wrapped around a Maypole.

Far off, Brumm spotted movement on one of the rock faces behind them. At first he thought he was seeing wild sheep because they had noticed several of the timid mountain creatures in the last few days, but after focusing on the moving figures, he knew that the specks were human and that they were following the same route Beard had taken. Though they were difficult to see, Brumm could tell that the three men moved efficiently and well on the steep wall.

Brumm knew they were in trouble. These must be the same ones who had pushed them off course to the Rhine, and now they had help, perhaps a mountain guide. There was no other explanation; the appearance of climbers in this hellish place couldn't be sheer chance. They were being pursued again.

Even before he had changed their plans and darted for the river, Brumm had felt that their pursuers were not simple adventurers. They moved too deliberately and with too much discipline to be mere amateurs looking for easy pickings. No, these were professional hunters, the kind who made their living tracking men. He also had no doubt that they were Russians.

Along their route over the last four weeks, they had skirted many military camps, but there had been no evidence of a general alert in the Soviet, French or American zones, no patrols crisscrossing their path, as there would have been if a full-scale manhunt was under way.

Beard called up from below, telling Brumm to descend. The colonel slid his field glasses back into their leather case and secured the remainder of his gear. Taking hold of the rope, he looked out over the edge, saw Beard signal a direction for him to swing toward, and started down.

It followed that the men behind them were independent of the occupying armies. He quickly examined the possibilities. Only two seemed to hold water. They might be agents from Rome. But Rome had no way of knowing who they were or that Herr Wolf was not what he appeared to be. All arrangements with the Church envoys had been made in ways that guaranteed secrecy for individual identities. Many people had come out of Germany under the aegis of the Vatican, and there would be still more, but there was no way for the Papists to know exactly who was in their pipeline. It had been so designed in order to protect both the hunted from being tracked down and their rescuers from embarrassment.

So it came down to a single possibility, one that Brumm preferred not to think about: Russians, probably a special team. He cursed quietly as he swung slowly down toward the ledge .where the other two waited. There had been only a single error: the guard in the Chancellery. There had been no way to get rid of him; he had been there where they had expected no one to be, a shaking coward hiding underground from danger, an empty model for the recruiting posters. He'd figured the man had little chance of surviving the final Soviet assault; even if he did, the chances were that the Soviets would be so disorganized that to find one key man among thousands of German prisoners was virtually impossible. Yet it was the only explanation that fit, the only way it could have happened. It had to be a special unit, like the team of assassins once sent by Stalin to execute Skorzeny.

The pursuers' strategy seemed obvious, an old hunting trick. Push the quarry and force him to break his pattern in order to disrupt his escape plan. And it had worked; already Brumm had been forced to break away. From this point forward, he decided, they must head for the monastery as quickly as possible, whatever the cost. Even so, a team such as this could be an immediate threat. No doubt they were part of a larger effort, controlled from a distance. One of them had been at the farm in anticipation of their arrival. The red paint had been meant as a message. That no ambush was waiting for them at the farm meant either that the Russians were not yet ready to fight or that they wanted the Germans to continue their journey. The trap would be ahead; he'd have to think about that.

For the moment they needed to get out of this wasteland and onto terrain where they could make better time. But first they needed to delay their pursuers. Brumm considered backtracking to create an ambush. The Russians would not expect direct confrontation from the pursued. But if these men were of the kind he believed them to be, they would adjust quickly to a firefight and then he and Beard would be outnumbered by one; Herr Wolf would have no value in such a situation. Booby traps were a possibility, but their materials were limited and it would take considerable time to set them properly. Their best hope was to divert their followers, Brumm decided, to deflect them long enough to gain time. It was the only way out. He turned his mind to the problem as he landed on the ledge beside the other two. It would require a bold act, and soon.

▶119 APRIL 21, 1946, 5:00 P.M.

It was eerie and unsettling. On the one hand, Valentine felt like a kept pet waiting for food; on the other he felt calmer than he ever had before. Ermine, her hunger for sex temporarily sated, was sprawled on the bed, a pillow across her stomach, fast asleep. He considered getting into bed beside her, but decided against it; she might wake up and want to be pleasured again.

Bela's grandson had barely acknowledged them when they showed up two days before, but had appeared later at their door, gushing with friendship and advice. Genoa was drowning in agents and vagabonds—*scugnizzi*—who would kill for a used pair of shoes, but his American friends needn't worry. He had armed companions in the rooms on their flanks and across the hall; they were safe.

The young man knew nothing about what Valentine sought, but was reassuring: "Grandfather always provides." He suggested they take their meals in the room until they had their information. As soon as he left, Ermine wrestled Valentine to the bed, but his heart wasn't in it and wouldn't be until he'd gotten what he'd come for. The problem was, he still wasn't sure what that was.

▶120 APRIL 21, 1946, 6:20 P.M.

By nightfall the going was much easier. They were just below the crest of a tree-covered escarpment, resting among small shrubs. Where a small rivulet formed a pool in the rocks, they stopped to drink and fill their water bags.

Brumm had made his decision; command necessitated facing reality objectively. There was no room for emotions.

He took Beard off to the side while Herr Wolf lay with his face in the water, slurping loudly. "We have company again." Reflexively the sergeant glanced back in the direction they had come. "They're not close yet," Brumm explained. "I saw them briefly this afternoon, three of them now. We have a full day, maybe more, depending on how well they can climb."

"The farm," Beard said.

"To frighten us. They had two behind us, a third ahead. He may have seen us when we passed through. We have to assume they know the truth and that there are more ahead of us, but that they're not ready to make a move yet."

"We're almost out," Beard said. "We'll soon be able to cover a lot of ground."

"We have to divert them," Brumm said. "We need time to hide our route." They were walking together along the edge of the precipice. "What's west of us?"

"More of this. Very difficult."

"Is there a place where we could get down? An especially difficult line would be best."

"There's a place near here. You can get down, but not back up. My father called it the Devil's Arrow."

They explored the edge, with Beard explaining in detail what the descent required. It was exactly what Brumm wanted.

"You have pitons?"

"A few," Beard said. "There's nothing permanent on this face. We'll have to do it on our own."

"I have no intention of climbing down," Brumm answered. "I only want them to think we did and to follow. It has to be convincing. We have to leave them something to entice them over the edge, something they'll have to investigate." He did not look at his friend.

Beard considered the problem. He thought he could use four or five pitons to reach a ledge below. He outlined their placement for his commander; they had to be placed exactly right in order to provide an unexpected discovery and temptation for the men behind them.

Brumm agreed. They were losing light fast. With his colonel's help, Beard drove the first piton into place, connected his rope and went over the side, grunting with effort. Lying on his belly to serve as an anchor, Brumm watched his friend work his way carefully down the steep face. It required four pitons a few meters apart for him to reach the ledge below. A wind was rising.

"All set," Beard called up. It was getting cold and his arms were tired.

"Climb up."

Rau began the ascent, glad to be done for the day. His shoulders ached and he was thirsty again. When he reached the next-to-last piton, he looped his arm in his rope and rested, to gather strength for the most difficult part of the ascent.

"Hans," Brumm said from above. "From that ledge—are more pitons needed?"

"No," Rau called back. "The descent below is steep, but there are handholds. This is the bad part up here, especially if you're coming up blind or without pitons. You can get down without them, but up? Impossible." He drove his toe against the wall and shifted weight to pull himself up.

"Hans," Brumm said again. Beard leaned his head back to make eye contact and stared into the black hole at the end of his colonel's pistol. "I'm sorry, Hans, but they have to believe us. It must be."

Beard looked down at the rocks hundreds of meters below. He had always been afraid of falling. He looked back at his colonel, his voice even. "Shoot straight, Günter."

The pistol coughed once, and the sergeant major fell backward, flat on his back, spinning clockwise. He struck two outcroppings, finally landing at the base of the wall in shadow, so that Brumm could see only his feet in the poor light. He holstered his pistol, recovered the rope and, with the handle of his dagger, struck a rock hard, leaving a small white nick. It would be enough.

Herr Wolf was propped near the small pool a hundred yards back of the cliff, his belly full, a contented look on his face. "We camp here tonight?"

"No," Brumm said. "We push on." He gathered Beard's pack and weapon and studied the terrain. Herr Wolf struggled into his pack and rose clumsily. "Where's the sergeant major?" he asked, trying to look past the colonel into the darkness.

"Doing his duty," Brumm said quietly. He moved up the mountainside with Herr Wolf close behind, puffing in the thin atmosphere, looking backward, wondering when the sergeant was going to catch up with them.

►121 APRIL 22, 1946, 6:30 A.M.

Ezdovo moved back and forth along the rim like an anxious cat, always returning to the rock with the white nick. "I don't like it," he told the others. "They stopped here to do something. They took water at the spring, then came down here." He turned around and pointed upward. "Their route should continue that way. Easier ground, better speed. They can't cross the Swiss border. They have to head east for Austria."

"We'll have to go down to see," Bailov said.

Ezdovo considered the remark. He was measuring how long it would take to explore this lead against the time they would lose if it was a false one. The scar on the rock was just subtle enough to be real; if it had been any more obvious he would have ignored it. In the end he agreed with Bailov; they had to take the time to see what was below.

Rigging a harness for Bailov, they lowered him. In seconds he reported back: "Pitons down here. Let me down some more." They played out more rope, feeling Bailov's weight at the end. "Up," he shouted from below after a few more minutes, and they strained to get him back to the top.

"There's a body down there," Bailov reported calmly. "The pitons lead to a ledge thirty meters down. From there it looks as if we can descend, but it's a long way; it will take us all day." He poked an elbow at the doctor. "You think you've had some bad climbs? Wait till you get over the side of this one. It even made me dizzy for a moment."

Ezdovo leaned over the lip with his field glasses. He could see the feet of a body. He considered following his instincts, but duty required that they descend; Petrov did not like loose ends. "We'll go down," he said grudgingly. The others could tell it was not what he wanted to do.

Bailov had been right; it took them most of the day to reach the bottom. At one point on the descent, they found a splotch of dried blood on an outcropping. "He must have hit here," Gnedin observed.

They squatted around the corpse like hunters examining a dead stag. There was a small hole in its forehead just over the right eye, and the back of the head had been blown away.

Bailov spoke first. "Bullet. No gear." There was no need for debate or discussion. They all understood what the body meant; the SS colonel had murdered his sergeant to delay them, and they had fallen for it.

They tried climbing back up and reached the ledge the next morning, but they could not get up the last thirty meters. "A blind spot," Bailov said. "You can get down, but not up unless somebody's on top with a line. The bastards."

"He must have seen us from one of the ridges," Ezdovo said. "This wasn't panic; it was artfully done. By the time we get back up there by another route, they'll have days on us. They're gone." His voice sounded tired. "He knows what we are now; he'll be looking for a place to fight. We have to back off."

Gnedin interrupted. "Petrov told me to report to Genoa if they didn't show up at the farm."

"Italy it is," Bailov said. "Petrov will need us."

After an uncomfortable night on the ledge they descended again, then traveled east before they found a crossing near where the Rhine narrowed on the Swiss border. There they presented diplomatic credentials to the border guards and were waved through; two hours later they caught a train south.

▶122 APRIL 23, 1946, 3:00 P.M.

They did not leave the house for five days. For Pogrebenoi it was a difficult time. Whereas earlier Giacomo—if that was really his name—had been a source of comfort, now he was an object of intense suspicion. He had an easy, disarming manner about him, but there was also a darker side, a deep, hidden intensity that made him as alert as an animal. Why and how did he know Petrov's name? It was a question she asked herself over and over. Even though her leader had made the arrangements that had put her under Giacomo's protection, it would have been unusual for him to have used his own name. She didn't like it, and her soldier's instinct kept reminding her not to let down her guard. At night she kept a chair jammed under the door, and she slept in a corner with her pistol in her lap. So far the man had not hindered her mission. She considered eliminating him, but that would mean killing the old woman, too. It was not a matter of conscience or squeamishness but a practical concern: two bodies would be more difficult to dispose of than one. Besides, she told herself, this Giacomo—whatever his game—might still be of use to them.

Above all, it was imperative that she get her information to Petrov. Without it, all might be lost. The ship would arrive tomorrow and depart on the twenty-eighth. He had given her instructions for the rendezvous. When the signal came, she was to go to a certain piazza at 4:00 P.M. and wait five minutes, no more. If the pickup failed, she was to leave and try again the next day, an hour earlier than the first attempt. She was to repeat the cycle seven times; then, if no contact had been made, she was to make her way as quickly as possible to Trieste and get in touch with Soviet officials there. Petrov had explained to her how to do this.

The main newspaper in Genoa was published in the early afternoon—when the printers weren't on strike, as they had been all week in a dispute over union status. Every day the old woman from the house went out to get a paper, coming back each time empty-handed, complaining that the *Comunisti* were godless troublemakers who didn't know how to do anything else. Today she was gone longer than usual, and when she returned, she stopped at the end of the walk and talked animatedly with a younger woman and a child, who danced around the adults, trying to amuse herself.

Eventually the old woman hobbled inside with her shopping net bulging with hard rolls and shiny brown packages of uncooked noodles. Pogrebenoi stood anxiously beside the counter waiting for her to unpack; the newspaper was the last item to be dropped on the table and she pounced on it immediately, bringing a sour look to the old woman's craggy face.

The single-column advertisement ran several inches deep and dealt with political turmoil in the Italian Communist party; a splinter group calling itself the Red Left was attempting to dislodge the established party leadership. The ad listed several political goals, the foremost being the elimination of Fascist remnants still serving in the Genoan city government. In each corner of the display ad there was a line drawing of a clenched fist. Beside the symbol on the bottom right there were three small stars, Petrov's signal to her.

She had to act fast. Talia immediately phoned the newspaper. At first nobody seemed to be able to help her, but eventually, using a combination of charm and persistence, she got a man on the line who claimed to have some modest knowledge of the paper's advertising. The ad, she learned, originally had been scheduled to run on the twenty-first of the week, so it was the fourth day of the sequence. The next attempt would be at 1:00 P.M. on the twenty-fourth. She felt a sense of relief until it occurred to her that she couldn't let Giacomo out of her sight. This meant that he would have to come with her to the rendezvous. This was against Petrov's instructions, but it was important that he learn that Giacomo somehow knew his name and decide for himself what was to be done about the man.

▶123 APRIL 23, 1946, 9:15 P.M.

After arriving in Genoa the three Russians proceeded to the wharf.
Stopping at a café, Gnedin made a telephone call. Half an hour later
an automobile pulled up outside. Rivitsky looked at his comrades and
gave them a big smile. Bailov and the doctor got into the backseat,
Ezdovo in front.

"Good news?" Rivitsky asked.

"I saw them," Gnedin announced.

"We lost them in the mountains," Ezdovo added glumly. He was
wondering where Talia was, and if she was safe.

▶124 APRIL 24, 1946, 1:02 P.M.

This morning she had gotten up early, dressed and found Giacomo in
the kitchen nursing a small glass of Chianti. He whistled when she
entered and flashed his teeth. "We're going out?" he asked, reading
her mind.

"Yes," she said coldly.

They walked several blocks side by side before she flagged down
a cab into the city. It dropped them near the piazza and they strolled
through a small garden with a dry fountain. Pigeons were gathered
around a collection of old men on benches. At the far end of the block
she paused at the curb and checked her watch.

"Pickup?" Giacomo asked.

"Stay close."

Two minutes after the hour a black sedan veered out of traffic
from the far side of the boulevard and squealed its tires on the hot
pavement as it lurched to a stop at the curb in front of them. Pogrebenoi

opened the back door and got in, Giacomo following closely with a smile on his face.

The automobile surged forward before the door was closed. Rivitsky looked back at her, his expression letting her know that her companion's presence was not according to the plan.

"Perhaps I should make other arrangements for myself," Giacomo said quickly, again showing an uncanny sense of knowing what others were thinking.

"Stay," Talia said. "I'll take care of it."

Giacomo sat back, amused. "The Italians call Genoa the city of surprises—a reputation with historical antecedents," he chirped happily. "It's said that the Genovese made Pisa's tower lean more precariously."

"Be quiet," Pogrebenoi commanded with a scowl.

Rivitsky inspected his passengers through the rearview mirror. The change in the woman was profound. She was tanned and her dark brown hair had bleached in the sun, so that it seemed to radiate light. Her fingernails were painted, her lips looked full and red, and there was a soft hue of gray on her eyelids. Standing on the curb she had looked stunning, elegant in silk, with an aristocratic air about her. As a rule, Rivitsky preferred his women thick of waist and leg, with large breasts to fill a man's hand and give him something to grab on to, but Pogrebenoi's appearance gave him pause. Originally he had assessed the woman as a peasant; now he felt he had been wrong.

Her companion was another matter. His mindless banter was only a thin mask. This man with dark eyes like polished onyx was dangerous. Pogrebenoi had better have a good reason for bringing him along. Petrov loathed surprises when they were at his expense. It wasn't clear what she intended, but Rivitsky resolved to take no risks; if the man made the slightest move, he would kill him. He drove with his left hand on the steering column, leaving his right hand free; if he had to shoot, it would be over his left shoulder. Just as he repositioned his body to gain some leverage, Giacomo said, "I won't be any trouble." He held his hands high for Rivitsky to see, and they made eye contact in the mirror. There was an instant and mutual understanding, one professional to another.

In the maze of soot-covered warehouses, Rivitsky drove a winding route, doubling back occasionally to be sure that they were not being followed. At their destination he jerked to a halt before a bank of green garage doors. The one before them opened and he drove in, then parked the automobile out of sight.

Bailov came out of the shadows and greeted them, walking past Rivitsky and the stranger to hug Pogrebenoi, who hugged back, and then led them underground through a series of damp, narrow tunnels, lighting their way with a single flashlight.

The place was empty. Pogrebenoi sat down, carefully crossed her long legs and tugged at her skirt to keep it down. Rivitsky had gone to fetch Petrov. She was disappointed that she had not yet seen Ezdovo, and immediately began to worry about him. Their night together had been a momentary lapse, but a bond so powerful had formed that it made her as nervous as a maiden, and she was sure that he felt it, too. Ezdovo was a self-contained man. She admired this in him, but there was also in his quiet a sense that he had endured great pain, and she felt a stirring to soothe him. At first her feeling had been more fascination than anything else—that and lust; it had been a long while since she'd found a man she had wanted to bed. Eventually, after she realized that she was thinking about him more and more, she knew that her feelings had gone far beyond simple fascination. When she had been in bed with Bettini, it had been Ezdovo she fantasized about, and while the Italian sweated over her, she had come to realize that she loved the Siberian. More important, she had reached a decision; she would tell him how she felt. Where was he?

Petrov came down the stairs slowly, stopping partway down to look at Pogrebenoi, and she felt a chill under his gaze. The penalty for failure in this mission was well understood. They had gone their separate ways and done their jobs; now it remained for them to be reunited and for their leader to process the information and decide how successful they had been.

When Petrov's eyes fell on Giacomo, he stiffened visibly on the stairs and gripped the iron railing so tightly that his knuckles turned white.

"Petrov!" Giacomo boomed. "I hoped you would be glad to see your fellow conspirator."

"Grigory," Petrov said. A smile worked its way across his face.

The two men embraced at the bottom of the stairs while Rivitsky and Pogrebenoi looked on, baffled.

"When you came to the Archangel, I thought it was odd. Your interest in the Church was—well, let's say it was unusual. Your parting line gave me great amusement; I haven't laughed as hard in years. But after you left, I couldn't get you out of my mind. What is the old warbird up to this time, I wondered. I had my own ideas, but no way to confirm them. What the hell, I needed to get out of Moscow."

"Stalin told you," Petrov said.

The priest grinned.

"Pogrebenoi," Petrov said, his meaning clear to Father Grigory.

"Unrelated. An act of friendship. Even the great Petrov has a friend or two. The major's name came to my attention through an intersection of coincidences. I offered her to you because I thought she was what you needed for your group. I never saw her before we met in Rome." He turned to look at her. "See, she has no idea who I am, Petrov; you must enlighten her. Know this, however: though you don't heap praise on your colleagues, Petrov, you carry the fire of pride in your heart. Talia has done great work here for the Motherland. Great and dangerous."

Petrov turned to Talia. "This is Father Grigory of Operation Vatican Watch. His organization is in many ways—more than I thought—like our own."

"You're a crafty little bastard," the priest said happily. "Did you think that our Georgian bully would put all his potatoes in the same sack?"

"Then you *are* a priest?" Pogrebenoi interrupted, no longer able to restrain her curiosity.

"Not as you would understand it," Grigory said. "You're a tempting morsel," he added, causing her to blush.

Petrov was glad to have his suspicions confirmed. The priest was right; he should have known. Fleas upon fleas. It was Stalin's way to build redundancy, and therein controls, into everything. There were many questions he wanted to ask Grigory, but they would have to wait; this was not the time.

"Talia?" Petrov asked. It startled the woman to hear herself addressed by her leader by anything other than a surname.

Self-consciously Pogrebenoi patted her dress to cover her legs. "A ship arrived today and will depart the twenty-eighth. It will carry three hundred missionaries to Santiago, Chile. The ship flies a Greek flag, but it is owned by the Church."

"Missionaries new to the cloth?" Petrov asked.

She nodded.

"You're certain about the ship's registration?"

Father Grigory stepped in. "This information cost her dearly. It's sound, Petrov. I've known for some time that there were Vatican-owned vessels, but until her work I was unable to verify specifics."

Petrov grunted.

Grigory continued. "Germans and Austrians have been filtering into the northern part of Italy since the war ended. For some time now, concentrations of these people have been increasing in monasteries. As arrangements are made, small groups are moved to Genoa and placed on ships for transport to other locations. This group is the largest ever; it has been accumulating for weeks at the Benedictine abbey near Mount Poli. Saint Benedict's children are now concentrated there. These are practical men, Petrov; what Rome wills they provide. Benedictine houses have served as the Church's fortresses in the pagan world for centuries. It is fitting that the Nazis are there."

Petrov assessed the situation. Brumm must be moving east from the Rau farm. Obviously he had a clear destination in mind; otherwise the pressure of the team in Germany would have driven him into France or Switzerland. He had to be moving to Italy; there was no other possibility. Further, Genoa was the only port large enough to provide anonymity and some assurance of efficiency. Naples was crawling with Americans and a fleet of Allied warships; besides, it was too far south, adding too much risk. The Vatican-owned ship and the unusually large group of "missionaries" were the keys. Brumm had already demonstrated his propensity for boldness; he had left Berlin openly, hidden only by the crowd, then had holed up close to Berlin rather than running for deeper cover. Now, at the critical moment, it was reasonable to assume that he would repeat the pattern. There would be no secret U-boat; they would simply blend into the crowd of missionaries and leave Europe with new identities, two among many. Petrov's stomach told him that this was the moment, and that they had little time for final preparations.

▶125 APRIL 25, 1946, 8:00 A.M.

The dog was lying at his master's feet, his head resting tentatively on his forelegs. Their sheep were grazing in a small pasture above them. The old man was tired, and it felt good to sit down. Fifty yards below them, screened by bushes, was a small saddleback, the highest point of the pass that led into Italy. Bela had sent word to all of his eyes in the mountains to be on the alert for a big man. He might be alone or in the company of others. The question was, how big was big? Since receiving the message five days before, the old man had pondered this, often seeking the dog's counsel. But the animal was used to his rantings and simply wagged its tail in support. The shepherd supposed, finally, that if he saw such a specimen of manhood, he would know. One relied on experience. He'd seen big men before; he'd judge from them, and meanwhile there was little sense in brooding about it. His job was to guard his flock and to watch. After so many fights with the Germans, this was the sort of simple task he welcomed.

As often happened when they were in the mountains, it was the dog who alerted him by tensing and growling menacingly. When the old man looked down, he saw two figures on the trail below. One was larger than the other, but was he the "big man" sought by Bela? Lifting his binoculars, he watched the pair pass directly below him. The large one had the other by the arm, dragging him along at a brisk pace. The scene made him laugh; they were comical. The smaller man was older, and clearly didn't like being dragged along; it was just like old people to resent orders from younger people.

"Well, dog, is that the big man Bela seeks?" the shepherd whispered. The animal growled softly again, then wagged its stumpy tail.

When the two strangers were gone, the shepherd took a pigeon from a small wooden cage that he always carried with him, scribbled a message on a scrap of paper, secured it in a tube attached to the bird's leg, rubbed the back of the pigeon's head and pitched it aloft.

"Soon Bela will know what we've seen," the old man told the dog.

►124   APRIL 27, 1946, 4:20 P.M.

Bela's grandson let himself into Valentine's room with a passkey and found the couple in bed. Valentine was half asleep, wearing undershorts, an arm curled over his face. The woman was under the covers beside him, one of her breasts peeking over the sheet, and the boy's gaze immediately locked onto her anatomy. "My grandfather sends his regards," he stammered. Valentine lifted his arm; Ermine stirred, but did not wake up. When she moved, her other breast fell into view, and the boy stepped closer to the bed. "He says to tell his friend Valentine that there's a ship in port to pick up passengers from beyond the mountains. You understand what he means?"

As Valentine rubbed his eyes, Ermine shifted to her side and the sheet fell further down, leaving her uncovered to the waist. "Grandfather says to tell you that the big man has been seen in the mountains, but that there's no stiff." The boy stumbled over the word. "The big man has a traveling companion, a live one, but older and smaller. Grandfather says to remind you that swine always travel in pairs."

Valentine sat bolt upright, pushing the sheet off the end of the bed and uncovering Ermine completely, causing the boy to exhale loudly. "Beau," she complained, reaching blindly for the sheet.

Valentine tried to digest the information. "You have the ship's name?" he asked. Brumm had a *live* companion! The boy handed the American a slip of paper with the vessel's name and location written on it.

"How do I get on board?"

"I don't know," the boy said. He was still staring at Ermine, who had rolled onto her back. "Grandfather says you should remember that a guinea is a guinea in Genoa or Hell's Kitchen. He says you'll know what to do." His message delivered, he took a final glance at Ermine, briefly touched the front of his pants and let himself out.

Valentine stared at the piece of paper and concentrated on what the boy had told him. He understood Bela's meaning: he was to employ Ermine as a diversion. She'd get the attention of any man, but especially a Genoan dockworker.

He got up, stepped into his trousers, and thought about what he had to do. Brumm was headed for Genoa. Probably, he cautioned himself. With a live companion. It didn't make sense. Where was the damned body? Then it hit him. What were Skorzeny's exact words? "You think perhaps Günter helped Hitler to escape?"

"Holy shit!" Valentine yelled.

Ermine sat up. "Beau, honey! You look like you've seen a ghost."

He stared at her and smiled. "My second one," he said, remembering his trip to the Eagle's Nest. Could Brumm have gotten Hitler out of Berlin alive?

▶**127** APRIL 27, 1946, 10:00 P.M.

Though there was no longer any sign of pursuit, Brumm found it difficult to relax. It had been six days since Beard's death, and Herr Wolf sought conversation at every opportunity. The colonel had no stomach for it. His sergeant major had understood that the mission was paramount; their eyes had met only momentarily, but he knew. Still, Brumm did not like thinking about it. First Gretchen, now Hans. It was a high price to pay for principle: his lover and his friend—his only friend, he thought, in recognition of what the relationship had become.

Perhaps Beard had been right from the beginning: it might have been better to be shed of the burden. Yet in his mind he knew that one could not twist fact and fate. What was, was. One could not selectively ignore some facts and conjure up alternatives; that was the work of artists, not soldiers. Waller was dead. She had served her purpose willingly. So had Beard. Tears would not change what was.

Danger loomed ahead. That they were no longer being pursued was not a comfort. The previous chase had shown too much deliberation and intent to assume that it had now been abandoned. Still, for the moment they were alone.

The monastery sat high on the side of the mountain, a gray specter that seemed to hang precariously, cheating gravity. Brumm was nervous. The road up to it—it was more a widened trail—seemed to be an endless serpent of switchbacks, with plenty of blind turns and overhangs that were ideal for ambush. From the very beginning, this had been the part of the plan that made him most uneasy. Until now they had depended primarily on themselves for their own security. But at their secret meetings Hitler had not shared his colonel's concerns. "Next to the Church, the Third Reich is an amateur in matters of security and intrigue. These monks are hermits. They delude themselves into believing that their asceticism in some way sanctifies their lives. They march to their abbot's drum and the abbot to Rome's. It is their tradition to provide sanctuary to outsiders. It will be perfect; you will see."

They waited until dark to make their ascent to the Benedictine abbey. If there was a trap along the way, darkness would help them. But they made the climb without incident. While they waited, Brumm bandaged the lower half of Herr Wolf's face. It was too late in the game to risk having him recognized now.

A monk in a filthy robe met them at the gate. He was lame, one foot twisted inward a full ninety degrees from his leg, which was shorter than the other. After examining their papers, he admitted them to a large open courtyard. From there they were taken to a damp storeroom, where baths were drawn for them in huge copper tubs. Herr Wolf refused to disrobe while the monks were present, so Brumm ushered them out politely and stood guard while his companion bathed himself. When he'd finished, Brumm crawled into the lukewarm water and cleansed himself as best he could. Afterward he put Herr Wolf's bandage in place again.

After their baths the men were taken to a cell and left alone. Herr Wolf talked nervously, in overlapping sentences. "Brilliant to arrange it through the Benedictines. They opposed us, you know, the only order in Germany that did. Who would believe that they would be the key to my salvation? In Lambach as a boy I attended a monastery school—did you know that, Colonel? I sang in the boys' choir. I believe I could have made a living as a singer. I was impressed with ecclesiastical pomp and circumstance; I adapted many of their costumes and symbols for our own purposes. People are always impressed by ceremony and the trappings of power. The Church has given a great deal of attention to detail. Had I not chosen differently, I might have risen to the throne of the Church. An interesting twist, eh?"

Brumm ignored these ramblings. Later they were brought a meal of fresh bread and thick, savory mutton stew. A bottle of the abbey's own fruity red wine came with the food, but both men left it alone; they would need their heads clear from here on. They ate at a small wood-block table using crude implements, their only light a small candle in a black metal sconce on a nearby wall.

When Herr Wolf finished eating, he crossed his legs, folded his arms ceremoniously and stared at Brumm. "Admit it, Colonel. It has gone exactly as we planned. The priests have given us a bath and a meal. Next they'll clothe us. I always wondered what it would be like to wear the cloth. Now we shall both have the opportunity to know."

Brumm did not answer. Very little had gone as they'd planned and he was still worried about pursuit.

"Only one element in all this is unsatisfactory," Herr Wolf continued. "Your timing in getting us here was not what it should have been. I expected to have a week to rest, perhaps more, but now it seems I'll hardly have time for a good night's sleep. I believe you overreacted when you took us up the river. It was unnecessary. Professional soldiers, I have observed, tend to be too conservative in estimating degrees of danger."

The SS colonel listened because he had no choice; he was trapped. All politicians were cut from the same cloth: successes were theirs; failures were the fault of others.

"Had I been consulted," Herr Wolf went on, "and let me remind you, I was *not*—I would have recommended that we lay a trap for our pursuers and surprise them." His eyes were glazed and his hands punctuated his words, one hand chopping at the other in short, violent strokes.

Brumm sighed. The man was entirely self-absorbed; whatever the subject, he was the center around which all else revolved. There was never room for doubt, never a second guess. Brumm looked at him; how had someone so obviously demented come to be Germany's leader?

When their plates had been cleared, an older monk with a jagged scar that began under one eye and stretched down to his upper lip appeared. "Welcome," he said. "Your credentials are in order. I must ask each of you one question." He turned to Brumm. "Are you Catholic?"

"Yes."

"And you?"

"Yes, of course," Herr Wolf mumbled through the bandage. "I was educated a Catholic. I even considered the seminary."

"Very well," the priest said without emotion. "Our faith recognizes no political borders. It is the history of the one true Church to provide sanctuary to all Catholics, no matter their national origins."

"We are grateful, Father," Brumm said, marveling at the theater of the moment. Surely the man must know the truth.

"I shall not ask who you are or who you have been. You have reached out to your Church in your time of need and it has extended its benevolent hand. We are all children in the eyes of God. Praise be to God. Tomorrow you will be taken to Genoa by bus to board a ship. If there is nothing further I can do for you, I bid you safe journey.

May God go with you." The old priest lifted himself slowly and raised his hand. "In the name of the Father and of the Son and of the Holy Spirit. Amen."

It was still dark when they were awakened. They were given badly worn robes and sandals, then fed in their cells. Later they joined in a queue and wound their way down to the base of Mount Poli, where several old buses were parked. Brumm picked one with an empty front seat behind the driver, pushed Wolf in ahead of him and told him to keep his head down. The colonel watched nervously as more people, some in robes, some without, came down the mountain and filled the vehicles. He wished they would hurry. To reassure himself he patted the weapon concealed under his robe.

▶128 APRIL 28, 1946, 7:10 A.M.

It was early morning when they arrived at the dock. The embarkation area was fenced off and several *carabinieri* with sidearms were strutting around. Near the ship's stern, several bare-chested men were slowly moving supply bales with burlap covers up a narrow ramp with dollies.

Valentine's plan was simple. "Put your arms around me," he said to Ermine.

She stared at him. "Are you crazy?"

"Do it!" There was no humor in his voice.

They embraced for a long time, then walked arm in arm closer to the longshoremen. Valentine swept Ermine into his arms again, making sure the men could see them. As they kissed he ran his hand over her body, and the workmen responded as he'd hoped they would, with catcalls and whistles of admiration. He picked her up and placed her on a stack of wooden pallets, then took out a pack of cigarettes and gave her one. "Show them your legs," he whispered. "Beautiful morning," he called over to the nearest of the men.

"For you," the man shouted back. "We have only this cargo to make love to." He snapped his hand in a signal of male fellowship.

"She's only my sister," Valentine joked.

"A very affectionate sister," another man called back. "You're fortunate; my sisters look like dogs and kiss me on the cheeks."

"With your pants down?" another teased.

The higher Ermine's dress rose, the closer the men came. Eventually they were in a small knot close to the Americans. Ermine felt both embarrassed and excited by their attention. What the hell was Beau doing?

"It's a big ship," Valentine said admiringly.

"We load bigger ones," one of the longshoremen said. "Two or three times bigger than this stunted little fish."

Valentine noticed that a tall man with thick forearms and a knee-length leather apron had an air of authority, and said to him, "You're in charge?"

"No. The foreman is forward, seeing to stowing the load. With a tub like this, you have to be careful or a high sea will knock it over."

"What's the cargo?"

"Mostly émigrés."

"We've never seen the inside of a ship before," Valentine said.

"Nothing special to see."

"Do you think we might have a look around?" He winked at the man.

"The foreman would have our jobs. Work isn't easy to come by these days."

Valentine motioned to the man to come closer and slipped a thick roll of lire through the wire mesh. "For your trouble," he said. "She's married," he whispered. "We won't be long, and we'll keep out of the way."

The man did not look at the money, but folded his hand over it and slid it into a pocket under his apron. "If you get caught inside, I never saw you before." He leaned closer to Valentine, licking his lips as he spoke. "The boys," he said with a nod, "they'd like to watch."

Valentine smiled. "She's new at this. Give me some time to get her warmed up, okay?"

"There's a hatch and a ladder straight ahead," the Italian said. "It takes you up to the first deck. There are some staterooms in there; use the one marked 'B.' " He winked and stepped away to open the gate for them. As Ermine walked through, one of the men grabbed at her and she dodged him with a playful smile.

When they reached the stateroom, Valentine locked the door and loosened his shirt. It was sweltering. "What now?" Ermine asked nervously.

"First we perform, then we try to look like we belong." He turned her around, unzipped her dress and pushed her gently onto the narrow bunk. As they embraced he could hear a porthole opening above them.

▶**129** APRIL 28, 1946, 1:30 P.M.

Ezdovo and Pogrebenoi were dressed as priest and nun and mixed in with the crowd, awaiting their turn at the gangplank. Father Grigory had accompanied them to the gathering point and scouted for them. The area from which the émigrés would board had been cordoned off by locked wooden gates, the kind used in cattle pens. There was no security beyond this area; once inside, the travelers seemed to be left to manage their own boarding, including carrying their personal luggage. There was no priority; they went up the gangplank as they reached the head of the line. Outside the enclosed area a handful of *carabinieri* stood, making a minimal display of trying to keep the massive influx in order. Among the travelers, many languages could be heard, but few spoke Italian. Those charged with controlling access to the embarkation area gave little attention to those in clerical garb, so the two Russians went through the wooden gates without a challenge. While they waited to board they ignored each other and kept their eyes on the mass of people boiling around them.

Petrov had been explicit in his instructions: Find the pair, but once found, take no action until the ship is at sea.

Once aboard, they moved immediately to the fantail. Their plan was to meet every hour in the same location; between each rendezvous they would circulate. Their first task was to reconnoiter the ship thoroughly in order to learn its layout.

First Ezdovo went down into the bowels of the vessel to scout the engine room. There were only two hatches leading in and out, which encouraged him; when the time came for action, it would not be difficult.

Talia began her search in the cabins above the main deck. Passengers were crammed into each small cubicle, and she noticed that they seemed sullen; there was none of the joy that generally went with ship departures, and each traveler watched his cabin mates cautiously. The tension on board was palpable.

When they had completed their initial circuit, the two Russians met again at the fantail and talked as they looked out over the rail at the crush still wending single file up the gangplank. "It's impossible," Talia said. "There's no manifest, no cabin assignments. They'll be invisible in this mob. We're not going to have enough time."

"Brumm will stand out," Ezdovo said quietly. "He's tall. Remember, you're looking for a commando. He won't blend in; you know the look." She felt a surge of relief; even in clerical garb there was little chance the colonel could be mistaken for anything other than what he was. As they moved apart they let their hands touch briefly.

▶130   APRIL 28, 1946, 2:15 P.M.

When the passengers began to board, Valentine and Ermine went topside and mingled. There seemed to be few crewmen around, and those they encountered ignored them. Ship departures were always confusing, and the sailors were used to them. Despite the unusual nature of the human cargo, Valentine hoped the unstructured atmosphere that normally attended such leave-takings would give them freedom and anonymity.

Valentine had always been acute in making quick and accurate assessments of people. From childhood he had been able to walk into large groups and size up individuals, almost as if they radiated some kind of energy that only he could detect. The feeling he got from these passengers was not good. It was unnerving; he received nothing but an overwhelming sense of evil and fear. Never in his life had he felt anything like it, and it made him nervous. Of all the passengers he encountered during the embarkation, it was a tall nun with Slavic features and a feminine air who riveted his attention. She moved smoothly, like an athlete, and he decided that at some time in her life this was what she must have been. He also felt a deadly intensity emanating from her, but not evil. She passed by him several times, and it occurred to him that she was searching carefully and methodically for someone.

Ermine found a wooden deck chair, and Valentine told her to be on the lookout for a tall, heavyset man ("he'll look like a football player") while he roamed around. He had only Skorzeny's description of Brumm to go by.

"What am I supposed to do if I see him?"

"Follow him."

When he returned after circling the upper deck, Ermine was on her feet, gesturing to him with a wild look on her face. "I saw him."

"Brumm?"

"I think so. He came up the walkway right after you left."

"But was it Brumm?"

"I don't know, but he was really big. Shoulders like yours." She demonstrated with her hands.

"Alone?"

"I couldn't tell. He stuck up above the rest; that's how I saw him. He went through there," she said, pointing to an open double doorway that funneled passengers into a large salon. Leading him into the room, she pointed to a spiral metal staircase. "And then down there."

Valentine took her by the arm and pulled her aside. "You remember how we got on board?"

"Sure."

"Good. Get off the same way—right now."

Her face hardened. "No way. I'm staying with you." But Valentine's eyes told her she was fighting a losing battle. She slipped her arms around his neck and kissed his cheek. "You win," she said. "This time . . ." When she reached the dock, she turned and saw Beau leaning on a railing. He pursed his lips, nodded slightly, winked and disappeared. Ermine felt dizzy.

▶131   APRIL 28, 1946, 2:20 P.M.

Brumm and Herr Wolf ascended the gangplank and pushed their way into the crowd of passengers already on board. Brumm led, while his companion followed, holding on to the larger man's robe. It took them twenty minutes to find a cabin. The room already had several occupants: two men, a woman and a young girl. Brumm stepped inside, looked them over and said, "Out."

"You have no authority here," one of the men protested.

Brumm grabbed the man by the hair, pulled him off his seat and rammed the barrel of his automatic against the man's cheek. "This is all the authority I need, and I'm not accustomed to reissuing orders." He pushed the man toward the door; the other three inhabitants of the room were already gone. Throughout, Herr Wolf stayed behind Brumm; his face was still bandaged and he kept his gaze downward.

Brumm immediately locked the door, closed the curtain over the porthole, took out his automatic pistol, checked to be certain a round was in the chamber, and placed it beside him on a small couch. Herr Wolf retreated to the darkest corner and sat on a bunk, knees together, hands clasped in his lap. He looks like a frightened child, Brumm thought. Within minutes the man was asleep. The colonel looked at his watch; they should be raising the anchor soon.

▶132   APRIL 28, 1946, 3:45 P.M.

The boat in the slip was painted black and had no markings. During the war it had belonged to the Italian navy, who used it as part of their coastal defense setup and raced it up and down the coast. It was capable of forty knots and had been fitted with extra fuel drums to give it extended range. If all went well, it would enable them to reach Algiers, where an aircraft was waiting.

For crew, Petrov had Bailov at the helm, Rivitsky, Gnedin and Father Grigory, who had returned to report that Ezdovo and Pogrebenoi were safely aboard. The priest, for the moment an integral part of the Special Operations Group, was in high spirits.

They had no route to concern themselves with. They would follow the ship out of port, keeping at a distance, and would board only after Ezdovo and Pogrebenoi had done their jobs.

When the ship passed by the warehouse on the afternoon tide, the small boat backed loudly out into the harbor. Bailov set the throttles at a speed just above idle and listened to the screws burble in the water beneath them. They turned in a gentle arc and followed the ship out to sea, heaving slowly among crosswind swells as they entered open water.

▶133 APRIL 28, 1946, 8:00 P.M.

When Pogrebenoi could not locate Brumm, she became angry. Wherever she went, there were few men as tall as she, and none of Brumm's stature. After a while everyone began to look alike. In the corridors the odor of vomit was beginning to settle in. The sea was relatively calm, but the ship vibrated violently under the gentle swells and those with weak stomachs reacted naturally, creating a chain reaction. Everywhere she went she saw crowds of people on the decks using suitcases for pillows. It was chaos, a ship loaded dangerously beyond its capacity. On deck she counted enough lifeboats for only two hundred people, and the lockers marked for life preservers were packed with luggage. The ship was a disaster in the making.

After one of her hourly meetings with Ezdovo, she went down to a lower deck and walked slowly through the tangle of legs and bodies. There was nothing unusual, except that now the only language in evidence was German—different dialects, but German nonetheless. They were at sea, in international waters, under diplomatic credentials. Whatever fear the Nazis had suffered during the embarkation process had disappeared; the open arrogance of some of them now shocked her and made her want to scream out the truth to them and watch them panic.

On each deck, Pogrebenoi strained to peek into cabin portholes. In one she saw a tall man, but before she could study him, he saw her and closed the curtain. All the passengers are spooked, she thought—with good reason.

The ship wallowed through the water, riding low under the weight of its cargo. Standing at the port rail, she felt the engines throbbing through the poorly fitted metal deck plates. She wondered where Petrov and the others were and looked aft, but saw only darkness. She had never felt so alone.

Ezdovo was at the starboard rail, smoking. "Any luck?" she asked anxiously as she slid to the deck and patted it as a signal for him to join her. Their legs touched and she moved closer, not caring what others might see.

Ezdovo raised an eyebrow. "Conduct unbecoming a holy sister," he chided.

"I don't condone celibacy even for the party."

"In the cloth or not, it seems to be our fate."

"Nothing is forever," Talia said.

"Nothing except this infernal ship. I've been from one end to the other and top to bottom. I can't believe we haven't found Brumm. He has to be here."

"Perhaps they're not."

"The hairs on my neck are standing up," he answered. "They're here; it makes sense."

"Petrov's conclusion."

"And mine. Petrov's reasoning is sound."

"Perhaps you grasp at straws."

Ezdovo stared hard at her. "I don't compound one error with another," he said coolly.

She knew he was still bothered by losing the trail in the mountains. "What happens if we don't find them?"

"We go all the way to Santiago and wait for Petrov's instructions there. It's our only option."

"An ocean voyage wouldn't be so bad," Talia said. "It might even be enjoyable. A holiday." She pressed her leg against his and he responded.

"On the floor?" They laughed.

"The problem is," she went on, "they're all beginning to look alike to me. What are we going to do, make a cabin-by-cabin search?"

"If we have to, we will."

"I'm tired," she said, moving closer to him.

"I want to tell you something," he said gently. "When we're finished here, I want you to come back to my Russia with me. It's far away from Moscow, a world away, a country of great mountains, deep snows and lakes—many lakes." She squeezed his arm and for a moment they huddled together, dreaming of the future.

But it was no time for such thoughts, and soon they separated to renew their search. Talia had taken only a few steps when it hit her, the sudden clarity of it causing her to grasp the rail and inhale deeply to regain control. Catching up to Ezdovo, she grabbed his arm fiercely, spinning him around. "I saw him," she said. Her eyes were gleaming as they had on the day they narrowly missed crashing in the Harz Mountains.

"Brumm?"

She nodded animatedly.

When they reached the porthole it was still covered. "He's in there," she said.

"Alone?"

"I saw only him. There wasn't time to see any more."

Counting portholes, they went around the corner and entered the corridor. A little black-haired girl in a navy blue jumper, her thumb in her mouth, was huddled against an older woman directly across from the cabin. "May I talk to you?" Talia whispered to the woman.

"My niece," the woman said. "Her mother—my sister—is dead. Her father, too. We're all that's left."

"What's your name?" Pogrebenoi asked the child.

"Franziska," the woman answered for her.

"You have a pretty little smock."

"It's new, Sister," the child said brightly in a tiny voice.

"Who is in that cabin?" she asked the woman softly, pointing at the door.

▶134   APRIL 28, 1946, 8:20 P.M.

The cargo hold was dark and Valentine had taken his time getting into it. If Ermine had really seen Brumm, he had to be on board somewhere. He began his search in the hold; there, to his amazement, were six wooden coffins, side by side in the aft area. Doubling back to see what the crewmen were doing, he saw that they were busy eating; he had time to investigate.

Moving back to the boxes, he tore one of them open, not worrying about the sound. The engines were nearby and the cargo hold was engulfed in an earsplitting din. Prying the lid of the first coffin lose, Valentine lifted the cover and stared. It was filled with guns wrapped in rags and heavily greased. He moved on to the other boxes and, sweating heavily, opened each of them. Four of them contained weapons, one of them paperwork, the last small boxes of jewelry and some paintings that had been carefully rolled up.

Having finished his search, Valentine went topside. He needed a smoke and some fresh air. Now he was certain that his theory about Hitler's corpse was a mistake; what he was looking for was the Führer himself. Could it be true?

▶135   APRIL 28, 1946, 10:20 P.M.

The two Russians took up positions at either end of the short companionway outside Brumm's cabin. It was important to know if the SS colonel would venture out of his lair or sit tight. In the nearly two and a half hours since they'd found him, all had been quiet.

Ezdovo made his way past the sleeping bodies in the corridor and joined Talia. He checked his watch. "It's time. They're sitting tight. It's the first night out; they're still wary."

"What if they change locations when we stop the ship?" she asked.

"It's a risk, but we both have work to do. An old tub like this developing an engine problem may worry Brumm, but it's not likely to make him do anything. He's got a good hideaway right now, and he's not going to give it up quickly. In any event, after you've done your part, you must hurry back here and cover the door in case they try to move. If they try to come out, use your gun to force them back; you'll have to keep them pinned down until the rest of the team boards to help us. There's only one way out of there; that's our advantage."

"And only one way in; that's their advantage," she said grimly. She had been in frontal assaults before.

Their hands touched briefly and she kissed him lightly, her tongue lingering in his mouth. "I love you," she said. His answer was increased pressure on her hand.

When they separated, Ezdovo descended into the ship while Talia's mission took her upward. Finding a seaman who spoke Italian, she asked if she could visit the bridge. He was Catholic, he announced; how could he refuse a nun, and a beautiful one at that?

At first the captain seemed annoyed at her presence, but Pogrebenoi soon charmed him and found herself in his chair with a fresh cup of Persian tea. She asked many questions about the ship's operation, but hardly heard the answers because she was evaluating the situation.

With her in the control room was a sailor, the captain and the first officer. A steward in a soiled white tunic was in a far corner, reading a newspaper. As she watched them she planned her attack.

▶136 APRIL 28, 1946, 10:30 P.M.

While waiting to board the ship, Ezdovo had watched earlier arrivals embark by gangplank directly up to the ship's deck, but he also saw that some cargo was being loaded through a large hatch above the waterline. Outside the hatch was a small permanent platform attached to the ship. Before Grigory left, Ezdovo had told him to guide the boarding party there; he would help them aboard.

Now, in a locker in the tunnel outside one of the hatches leading to the engine room, the Siberian found a metal rod and a roll of heavy-gauge wire. Using them, he secured the aft hatch so that it could not be opened from the inside, then entered through the forward hatch. In his pockets were four small canisters containing lethal gas.

A seaman, stripped to the waist and dripping sweat, accosted the Russian near the hatch. His mustache curved below his chin, and a gold ring was hooked through his right earlobe. He was sitting near a series of valves smoking a Turkish cigarette, and when Ezdovo entered, he stood up. "You can't come in here," the sailor said. "Off limits. You go," he shouted over the scream of the engines.

"I don't understand," Ezdovo said in German.

"*Kein Deutsch,*" the man said. "English?"

"A little," Ezdovo said. He made a sign with his fingers.

"Go up," the man said in a heavy accent.

The Siberian ignored the order. "This makes the ship go?" He pointed to the gauges.

"Yes. Makes go," the man said. He was getting annoyed.

Ezdovo stepped toward him. "Down, stop ship? Up, ship go?"

The man nodded in exasperation. Nosy Germans. He'd give this one a quick explanation and get rid of him before the first engineer came after him.

"Like this," the Greek showed Ezdovo. "Up, go. Down, stop."

Ezdovo smiled like a retard. "Down, stop," he repeated, then shot the man once in the throat and turned to the edge of the landing. Several sailors were below, all absorbed in their work. He pulled a gas mask over his head, tightened the straps and heaved the canisters into the engine room below. Only one crewman heard the canisters clatter; as he looked up, Ezdovo shot him, the silencer issuing a quiet grunt and causing the automatic to recoil in his hand. The man fell backward into a shadow, and as Ezdovo watched, spasms shook his legs.

He stayed in position until no men were left standing in the engine room; it had taken only two minutes for the gas to work. He let the second hand on his wristwatch make another full circuit before reaching for the controls to stop the ship. When he pulled the lever down, the engines shuddered and the vessel lurched and slowed to a drift in the sea as its screws stopped.

▶**137** APRIL 28, 1946, 10:35 P.M.

As the captain called to the steward to freshen Talia's cup the vibrations that rattled the decks suddenly stopped.

The captain, with white hair and a thick nose with protruding veins, immediately shouted angrily into a tube that looked like a funnel. "Is there a problem?" Talia asked innocently.

"Nothing serious, Sister. A small problem in the engine room—nothing to be alarmed about. It's an old ship and sometimes she's temperamental. Like a good Greek woman," he said with a forced smile. Sweat was building under his arms, and she could sense that he was shaken.

"Would it be better if I left?"

"Yes. That would be good. You can come back later."

Bidding them farewell, she paused at the entryway and assessed the situation again, then stepped outside and withdrew her revolver. Checking the silencer to be sure it was snug, she pointed the barrel up, slid her left hand under the handle and her grip hand and drew in a deep breath, letting it out slowly.

Having decided on the order of attack, Pogrebenoi stepped inside the control room and aimed at the steward. Because he was off to one side, she killed him first. Then she swiveled slightly and shot the rest of them from right to left, from no more than a few paces away, holding the weapon in both hands, squeezing off each round with double action, her eyes wide open. All but the first officer fell when they were hit; he tried to pull himself to a side hatch, but she finished him with a second shot, this one in the back of his head, then quickly reloaded. She found the signal blinker, which was covered with a tight-fitting tarpaulin, just off the bridge. Passengers looked up at her from the deck below as she stripped off the canvas cover and turned the switch. The light hissed loudly as it came on; she flicked the control lever open and closed several times and waited; aft and to port came the distant answer. Returning to the bridge, she pulled a pin from a smoke grenade, dropped it on the deck, and then ran down the stairs until she met a crewman.

"There's smoke up there," she said. The sailor looked at her, not understanding, so she led him partway up the stairs and pointed. As he bolted past her she raced down to the second deck; she had to get to Brumm's stateroom and wait until Ezdovo arrived with the others. She removed her costume as she ran. Her heart was pounding as she reached the deck and peered down the companionway. People were still sleeping on the floor, and nobody had seemed to notice that the ship was no longer moving.

▶**138**   APRIL 28, 1946, 10:38 P.M.

With Bailov expertly controlling their speed and direction, Petrov kept the low-slung boat in position 45 degrees off the wake of the ship, a kilometer back, all lights out, following the larger vessel like a shark waiting for its next meal.

"Your people may have a difficult time," Father Grigory said as they sat in the cramped cabin drinking tea. He was wearing faded coveralls with wide stripes, a yellow Star of David on the breast. The grip of a small pistol peeked from a leather holster under his right arm.

The sea remained smooth, and because the ship had turned east and accelerated to a cruising speed of eight knots, their ride was easier. Ahead of them lightning flashed in a cloud formation low over the horizon. "Above us," Bailov shouted down through the open hatch, anticipating his leader's concern. "A little squall. No problem."

"If we don't get the signal?" the priest asked.

"We break off and head for Algiers. When they arrive in Santiago, we'll be waiting," Petrov said quietly. He had been over the plan in his mind a thousand times, and he had no doubt that the signal would come.

"Assuming that Greek rust bucket doesn't sink along the way," Grigory said cheerfully, adding a dollop of brandy to his tea.

Gnedin and Rivitsky were working with small mounds of *plastit*, attaching remote fuses and detonators. The priest looked at them and made a face. "This is as close to eternity as I want to get for a while."

Calling them together, Petrov reviewed the plan once again. They would wait for the signal from the ship. Ezdovo would stop the engines by gassing the engine room, and when the vessel was dead in the water, they would board and take their man. Petrov, Grigory and Rivitsky would board. Gnedin would remain at the helm and stay close, maintaining power. While the boarding was taking place, Bailov, who was dressed in a dark blue wet suit, would set the charges on the hull under the waterline. When they were safely away, they would do what had to be done. Few would survive, and those who did would report that Jews had boarded the ship to remove a passenger.

"Comrade Petrov," Grigory said, interrupting. He was pointing forward. "Isn't that what we're waiting for?" A light was blinking in the darkness ahead of them.

▶139 APRIL 28, 1946, 10:40 P.M.

As soon as he noticed that the deck had stopped vibrating, Brumm tensed and reached immediately for his pistol. Standing up, he pulled the curtain back. It was dark, but people were gathered outside on the deck. Opening the porthole, he asked, "What's going on?"

"The engines seem to have stopped," a voice said in German. "It's to be expected. This is an old derelict run by Greeks."

Brumm closed the porthole and sat down. Herr Wolf stirred in his sleep, made a smacking sound with his lips, and rolled over.

▶140   April 28, 1946, 11:00 P.M.

Ezdovo had already picked out the fastest route to the boarding platform. The engines were stopped; the engine-room crew was dead, and
anyone else entering would die quickly. The gas was German: odorless,
colorless and lethal, producing death from respiratory collapse in less
than two minutes, Gnedin had said. They had found it in a Nazi death
camp in eastern Poland. The Russian troops who captured the camp
tested it on some of the SS guards who had been wounded and were
unable to escape. Ever practical, the Russians tried various masks on
the guards, and found two different filters that protected against the
deadly substance. Word of the gas moved through SMERSH to Moscow and back into the field to Petrov, who sent Bailov to fetch a
supply for the Special Operations Group's future use.

Ezdovo went quickly to the cargo hold, where he opened the side
cargo hatch and swung it open. Standing on the platform, he held
tight to an iron rail for balance and watched the dark shape of Petrov's
craft riding high as it raced toward him. He shone his flashlight out
into the darkness, using the group's established signal to verify his
location. The ship was wallowing in the ocean's swell, but he had no
trouble dropping the boarding ladder attached to the underside of the
platform.

The cutter, low in the water, spewed a gray rooster tail of foam
behind it as it veered sharply toward the ship and slid in smoothly
with its engines grinding into reverse. Petrov was first up the ladder,
an automatic rifle at the ready. He was wearing faded clothes of vertical
gray and purple stripes, the uniform of prisoners of Nazi concentration
camps. Ezdovo had seen them before, but never on anyone who was
alive.

When Grigory and Rivitsky joined Petrov on the platform, the four
of them moved through the cargo hold, climbing a series of ladders
up to the decks. Petrov had decided on a direct frontal assault, using
surprise as the critical element. As they ran past dazed, half-sleeping
passengers, there were some shouts. Their weapons were in plain view,

but they moved so fast that those they stepped over reacted almost as if they had seen apparitions.

Pogrebenoi was at the end of the corridor on the second deck, and as soon as she saw Petrov, she drew her pistol. "Third door on the right," she said.

For a moment Petrov paused. Father Grigory took a position against one bulkhead and watched along the companionway for possible interference. Rivitsky, puffing from the sudden exertion, stood with Pogrebenoi, both of them behind Ezdovo and slightly to each side of him, with Petrov behind all of them. They waited for their leader's order. "Alive," he reminded them.

Ezdovo fired a single shot into the door lock, then smashed it open with his shoulder, and the three burst into the room with their weapons extended at waist level. Brumm got off a single shot, which hit Rivitsky in the thigh and sent him sprawling.

Ezdovo and Pogrebenoi fired simultaneously, their bullets striking Brumm in each shoulder and knocking him down.

"Enough," Petrov said firmly.

Petrov recognized Hitler immediately. He was apart from Brumm, trying to keep his eyes down and his face hidden, but there could be no mistake. The mustache was gone, the hair was lighter and combed differently, but it was he.

Brumm was on the floor, his arms useless at his sides; using his legs to turn onto his back, he looked up at the intruders. The leader of the Special Operations Group stared down at the SS colonel. "I congratulate you, Colonel. You are an elusive man. I commend your resourcefulness." Günter Brumm exhaled slowly and grimaced.

Petrov turned to the other man, his eyes burning. "Adolf Hitler, I arrest you in the name of the Russian people, on the authority of Joseph Stalin, supreme leader of the Union of Soviet Socialist Republics. You will come with me." He might have been a village constable arresting a petty thief. There was no emotion in his voice, no exhilaration; there was only duty.

Herr Wolf looked at Brumm. "This is a mistake," he cried. He pulled back his sleeve to show the tattoo on his forearm. "See, I'm a Jew," he said, waving the arm at Petrov. "You can't do this to me. I've suffered as much as any of you. You must help me."

"Take him," Petrov ordered crisply to Ezdovo, who grabbed the man roughly by the arm and yanked him toward the stateroom door. As they moved, Herr Wolf balked suddenly, letting his legs go limp and dropping to the deck.

"Colonel Brumm!" he screamed. "Don't let them do this! Stop them. I order you!"

Reaching into his pocket, Petrov handed a syringe to Pogrebenoi. She unwrapped it, spurted a small stream of fluid into the air and told Ezdovo to hold the prisoner still. Before she could inject him, Herr Wolf gave a long, high-pitched shriek of terror and voided himself. The odor immediately filled the closed room as Ezdovo held him against the deck until the drug took effect.

Günter Brumm watched without emotion; he felt no pain. The foulness of his leader assaulted his ears and nose. He remembered Beard hanging over the edge, accepting with equanimity his oath to the SS and his Führer. He remembered the warmth of Gretchen in his arms; in age she had been barely a woman, but she had loved him, even as he held her under the waters of the hot pool in the cave and watched the last bubbles of air rise from her lungs to the surface. Fidelity, he thought, the cement of Teutonic culture, its first virtue. No more! He had done his duty. It was ended forever. The thousand-year Reich was finished, adrift in a Greek ship on the sea that had given rise to civilization. It was fitting that it end here, he thought. He felt at peace with himself. At Herr Wolf's pathetic appeal he could only smile.

In the passageway people were awake when the group emerged. "Jews," a voice hissed from the crowd. But they shrank from Petrov's presence, the Star of David on his breast pushing them back like a crucifix before the Devil, and made no attempt to interfere. Whatever they might be as a group, these Germans had cast off their political affiliations and common ties; now they were alone, each committed only to his own survival. "One among you ran the camps that took my people," Petrov said in his rehearsed speech. "For Jews everywhere we have come to claim our vengeance. Remember this forever. From this day forward, the Jews of the world will be united. And we will be armed. For now, we take only one of you, but soon we will come for you, too. Run while you can—*if* you can," he added menacingly.

As Father Grigory helped Pogrebenoi lift Hitler, Beau Valentine rounded the corner and saw a man with a gun. It was Rivitsky. "What's the commotion here?" he called out.

"None of your business," the armed man said angrily, brandishing a pistol at him. Valentine retreated immediately, but stopped around the corner and peeked. Another armed man and a woman were dragging a limp body down the companionway. A smaller man followed. The man he'd seen first limped along last, dragging his leg and leaving a trail of blood as he went. As the procession passed, Beau tried to see whom the man and woman were dragging, but the prisoner's head was down and he couldn't see the face. "Finish up," the small man called back to another, who was standing in the stateroom doorway.

Brumm and Ezdovo were left alone. "We have great admiration for you, Colonel Brumm," Ezdovo said. "It was I who followed you. Comrade Petrov believes you to be a professional and a man of principle. I am to inform you that we have set explosive charges below the waterline, and that when we are safely away we will detonate them. Comrade Petrov gives you your life as a professional courtesy. You have only a few minutes. We suggest you move quickly if you wish to save yourself."

"What if I survive? You're not afraid that I'll tell the world that Adolf Hitler is alive and in your hands?"

"Who would believe you?" Ezdovo replied with a smile. "And if they did, would you be strong enough to keep *yourself* alive? There would be many who would want to take vengeance on the man who denied them Hitler. We have no reason to fear you, Colonel."

The German smiled; the Russian was right. When they had gone, he considered his options. Only one made sense. Günter Brumm lay back on the deck and waited for the end. He was free at last.

▶141   APRIL 28, 1946, 11:25 P.M.

Valentine was shaking. What the hell were Jews doing on the ship? Who were they hauling away? He had not seen the face. Could it have been—? How the hell did they get on board? When the procession had passed, he cautiously approached the cabin across the hall and looked inside. There was a man lying on his back on the floor. Brumm! Valentine drew his automatic and stepped inside.

The German lifted his head, a puzzled look on his face. "Who are you?"

It was time to take a chance. Valentine flashed his credentials. "OSS."

Brumm smiled, then began to laugh. "The Americans, too?" he said. His laughter grew louder until tears ran down his cheeks. "Too late, my American friend. Hitler is gone and your Russian allies have mined the ship. We're going to die here. All of us." His laughter was still echoing in the companionway as Valentine ran down the stairs, four at a leap, to the crew area. People were everywhere, nervous like cattle before a storm, milling and moody, but not yet out of control. In the crew's quarters he opened a locker and found a single kapok life jacket. Putting it on, he tightened the straps as he ran up to the main deck.

A sailor blocked his way. "What's going on?" he challenged. "What are you doing in this area?" Valentine struck the man in the nose with the heel of his hand, and felt the cartilage drive upward into his brain. As he slumped to the deck Valentine stepped over the body, tucked his pistol in his belt, climbed the railing and hovered for a moment to get his balance in order to push off hard.

Several passengers on the deck near him grabbed at his trousers. "Don't worry," a woman's voice said soothingly. "They'll get the engines started. It will be all right; you'll see." The voice was one of certainty.

Valentine cupped his hands over his crotch, inhaled deeply and jumped out as far as he could. He struck hard and went deep. When he bobbed to the surface he began to swim, fighting his way up long salty swells into the wind, taking a breath only every ten or twelve strokes. The explosions came before he expected them. They were unspectacular dull thuds, but the sound and shock carried easily through the sea, and he knew the ship would sink. Keep swimming, he told himself. The big bang would occur when the sea spilled into the white-hot boilers. When it did come, it was a huge blast that lifted a red-and-white fireball into the sky and rained debris on him for nearly a minute. When he could see again, the ship was gone; all that could be heard were a few pitiful voices screaming for help. Valentine scanned the surface for flotsam and finally spied a large object not far away. It was a flat cork-filled raft, low in the water but stable, and he managed to pull himself onto it before collapsing. He could hear voices in the dark, but could see no survivors. Once a child's voice shrieked that there was "something" in the water. Sharks, he realized, instinctively drawing up his legs and somehow getting all of his body onto the raft. Soon there would be a feeding frenzy. Knowing it was useless to look for others, he lay back, riding the waves before the wind, alone with the terrible knowledge that would stay with him the rest of his life.

EPILOGUE

The train in the Odessa freight yard consisted of a black diesel, four Pullman cars with a flatbed on each end and a rust-colored caboose. The flatbeds had low walls of armor plating and firing ports. At the center of each, a small Czech ack-ack gun was mounted on a large steel tripod. Each antiaircraft weapon was surrounded by air-cooled, American 50-caliber machine guns. For an attack from above, each car's gun placement was designed to provide a deadly field of fire, though in its several years the train had never been attacked, and now that the war was long over, it seemed unlikely that it would ever be. Still, Stalin liked his personal train secure; above all else, he took comfort in weapons, the more the better.

The soldiers who served in Stalin's personal guard were handpicked men who would follow any order immediately and die in defense of their leader. Those who failed just once to execute even the smallest directive from their superiors were shot without trial or comment. Each understood that his duty must be performed perfectly every time. Now these men were posted in a defensive circle around the train, as alert and ready as a combat division on the verge of battle.

The special passenger in the train was still drugged. Dr. Gnedin had watched over him personally since they snatched him from the ship, seldom leaving him for more than a moment. The compartment in which the prisoner was kept had been stripped bare. The windows were covered by steel plates, and there were no carpets or furnishings, so there was nothing he could do to kill himself. Having brought him this far, Petrov was determined to see the mission through. He and the remaining members of the Special Operations Group were gathered in a small mud-brick building by the rail siding. It was a bright blue morning with a gentle swirling breeze that created small dust devils and lifted them into the sky. The assault of the ship had taken their final reserves of energy and strength. The journey to the coast of Africa had been rough, but the transfer to the aircraft was smooth and quick, and Ezdovo had flown them to Odessa with Pogrebenoi in the copilot's seat. Now Petrov had summoned them for one more briefing. It was to be their final time together, for only he, Gnedin and the priest had orders to proceed to Moscow. On a white cloth on the floor the five Red Badges were lined up side by side, and the team sat patiently against the walls in the dim light.

"I remind each of you," Petrov began without preamble, "that what you have accomplished must remain a secret of the state. To violate your oath of confidence will bring immediate retribution to all of us." He paused to look at his people. "We have done what we were asked to do. I do not know if we will ever meet again." His voice cracked slightly and he coughed to regain control. "I know that if needed, you will always be ready to do your duty." He looked at each of them, his little black eyes penetrating deeply, then picked up the badges and rolled them into a small package. The four of them smiled as one when their leader carefully tucked in the corners of the cloth at the end, attentive to the smallest detail.

Petrov paused in the doorway to look at each of them a final time. His eyelids narrowed until they were nearly closed and he pushed his fingers through his black hair. "Major Pogrebenoi and Ezdovo, please remain here. The rest of you . . . may go." His voice cracked again and brought forth a gasp. "My . . . friends," he said with difficulty, and then fled through the doorway.

The individuals of the team stared at one another. It was over. All the years together were finished. They embraced, clinging to one another. It was Bailov who finally broke the silence. "Who has the damned pertsovka?"

"There's one bottle left," Rivitsky replied, rubbing at his eyes. Brumm's bullet had passed through his thigh, leaving no permanent damage, but his leg was still stiff, causing him to use a cane. "It's in my pack." The two of them started out the door. "You'll join us?" Rivitsky asked Talia and Ezdovo over his shoulder.

"In a moment," Ezdovo said.

After a few minutes Father Grigory pulled back the canvas flap that served as a door and peered in at them, a wide grin on his face. "Comrade Petrov asks me to tell you that if you two have not grasped by now the fact that you are in love, he orders you to confront the issue immediately." The priest laughed loudly as the couple blushed bright red. "Ezdovo, Petrov suggests that you take this woman to your mountains and make yourselves a family. Comrade Stalin has issued an order that there be more Ezdovos, and desires that this occur within a biologically acceptable time. To you, Pogrebenoi, Petrov says thank you and wishes me to express his personal affection and gratitude. He also asks me to offer you a gift—from him, from us, from your country— to both of you."

Two small boys stumbled clumsily into the dark room, wide-eyed with fear. When they saw their mother, they threw themselves at her and, clinging, sobbed in her arms.

When the train began to pull away, Ezdovo, Talia and her sons walked out of the mud-brick building. Petrov was standing in the door of the last Pullman car. The four waved to him, but he did not respond. He was staring out across the countryside, his arms folded across his chest, chin up, his black eyes intense.

They watched silently until the train had disappeared. Then Ezdovo turned to Talia and scooped the boys into his arms. "I'll show you my home in the mountains," he said.

"Is it bigger than Moscow?" the youngest asked.

"And better." Ezdovo smiled.

▶143 JULY 1, 1946, 2:40 P.M.

It was afternoon, cool and windy. The silver-brown James River stirred under a gust, and chocolate eddies spiraled toward the grassy banks. Beau Valentine sat with his back against a spindly silver maple tree. He chucked a small rock into the river and observed for the hundredth time how completely it was assimilated, how no evidence remained when it sank. Ermine was nearby, her head on a fallen log, watching him with the kind of attention reserved only for the special of heart.

It was not so much a nightmare as a peculiar dream. It had happened; of that Beau was certain. He had been on the ship with Adolf Hitler. The ship had sunk. When the sun came up the next morning there was nothing left—no debris, no bodies, not even an oil slick, just him, clinging to the raft. He had floated for two days until the current carried him close to a small rocky island near Corsica. He swam ashore and walked up a bluff to a small house with a dirt floor, where they fed him.

He had talked his host, a fisherman, into sailing him back to Genoa. The Corsicans did not ask him how he came to be on the beach, or what boat he had fallen from. It was not an unusual event; over centuries many men had washed up on their beaches. Sometimes they were dead, sometimes alive. Ships went down. Such events were God's will.

In Genoa Valentine used an old agent's trick and wired his Swiss bank for money. Ermine, he was certain, had already left for the States. He paid an exorbitant price to a Genoese cabdriver to take him to the Swiss border, and once again crossed the border illegally. In Geneva he purchased a new identity for himself and caught a train to Paris. From there he flew to London, from London to Idlewild in New York, from New York to Washington, D.C., by train.

Valentine reported to the old OSS headquarters in the capital, and was debriefed by personnel in the new National Intelligency Agency. He told them everything up to the war's end and about his early searches for German scientists, but refused to divulge the details of most of his final months in Europe, describing the period only as "personal business."

"Had yourself a final fling with some European bimbo?" the case officer probed.

"Something like that."

With his identity restored, he bought a new car, a black Ford with a powerful engine and a white top. It cost him twice what it was worth, but he didn't care. What good was money if you felt guilty about spending it? It pleased him to have a new car, and that alone justified it.

Ermine had resigned by letter before he returned. From Geneva he had wired her: SAILED STOP SANK STOP SWAM STOP OK STOP SEE YOU SOON STOP LOVE ME? DON'T STOP YR. FLOWERMATE. When he picked Ermine up at her mother's house in Virginia, she had a strange look in her eyes, a look that he couldn't identify, but she didn't say anything.

Jamestown beckoned him; he was not sure why. He had been there once before, years ago. Something inside told him to go again. It was afternoon.

Ermine did not say she was disappointed with the place, but he knew she was. It was no more than a few old stones piled on a low island that had once been a peninsula. "Not much to it," she said.

"I know. That's what I remembered from the first time. I guess I had to know it hadn't changed."

"Can we go now?"

"Not yet," he said, hugging her tenderly. He still had some knocking around to do, he said, and she respected his mood. For the last four days, sunrise to sundown, he had spent his time walking and sitting in the ruins. Now, with another rock under the surface of the river, he felt like talking. Ermine was ready to listen.

"The Brits left a nice little community here and came back to nothing," Valentine said. "Nobody knows what happened. All dead. A few broken stones, some yellow bones—that's all they found. Probably looked a lot like it does now. It's the mystery that lives; it's the one thing people can't come to grips with. They can't stand not knowing."

Ermine came over to him and hooked her arm through his.

"They weren't Jews," Valentine said. "They were Russians."

She had no idea what he was talking about.

"Our senses don't always tell us the whole story. Airplane pilots learn the hard way. Their bodies say one thing, their instruments another. If they go with their senses, they're dead. I saw Jews, I heard Jews, but they were Russians—some kind of special unit with one mission."

"NKVD?"

"Nope. Something special. Very small. Dedicated people. They had that look."

"He's alive, isn't he?" she asked quietly.

Valentine looked at her. "Yes. The Russians have Hitler. Alive."

"And you?"

He laughed a cruel laugh. "What would I do with him? They can have the bastard. Poetic justice. Of all of us, they had the best reasons for wanting him. For us it's more a matter of principle, an academic need for justice or completion. Americans are big on finishing things. For the Russians it's necessity; they want their vengeance."

Ermine snuggled against his massive arm. "You finished it, Beau."

"Yessum, I finished it."

"What will they do with him?"

Valentine leaned his head back against the trunk of the tree and smiled. "That's a hell of a question," he said, as he slipped his arm around her and pulled her close. "A hell of a question."

"Do you think they'll try him?"

Valentine grinned and traced her mouth with his forefinger. "Not a chance."

▶144 JULY 18, 1947, 11:00 A.M.

In the summer of 1947 Berlin was still cluttered with the debris of war, but the streets were finally clear and Berliners had returned to their independent and self-indulgent ways, learning to cope in their divided city and making the political differences wrought by the Allies work for them instead of against them. At night the cafés and clubs along the Friedrichstrasse were filled with soldiers in uniforms speaking many languages, and once again the whores were prosperous.

Vasily Petrov stood across the street from the ruins of the Reich Chancellery. It was hot, and a Russian demolition crew nearby was raising clouds of dust.

He had placed the charges himself. The bunker had been closed and padlocked for nearly a year by order of Joseph Stalin. It was dark inside and cool, full of mold that constricted Petrov's breathing. Even so, he had worked slowly and meticulously, selecting each site and connecting each firing wire as if it were the only one.

Several workers, waiting, stood along the street behind him. Petrov wiped his forehead with a handkerchief, folded it and tucked it into the back pocket of his trousers. Taking a final look at the squat concrete structure across the street, he depressed the lever with a smooth, unhurried stroke.

The ground rumbled underfoot as a huge plume of dirt and smoke burst upward into the swirling currents overhead. Satisfied that the destruction was complete, Petrov walked slowly up the street to the waiting construction superintendent. When he nodded, the man began barking out orders, and instantly the motors of bulldozers coughed into life.

"What the hell was that?" a voice said near Petrov.

"One of those Nazi buildings," someone replied.

►145 MARCH 5, 1953, 2:00 P.M.

Petrov was feeding a family of Russian geese when he was approached by a brevet colonel, resplendent in winter dress uniform. "Comrade Petrov?" The little Russian, stooped by arthritis that seemed to grow worse by the day, looked up without speaking. "You must come to Kuntsevo; the end is near."

"How long?" Petrov asked quietly.

"Not long," the officer told him. "He's unconscious now."

So it had happened. On February twenty-eighth Stalin had suffered a cerebral hemorrhage, and had been lingering near death since. It had been almost seven years since he had stood with the team along the railroad siding outside Odessa. Seven years.

"Tell them I will be there," Petrov said. As he shuffled slowly toward his automobile his driver scrambled to open the rear door for him. "The Kremlin."

The guard at the door of the Poteshny Palace snapped to a position of readiness as Petrov approached. The soldier's sergeant challenged him while the guard held his Kalashnikov at the ready. When Petrov showed them the Red Badge, the men melted away.

There was a chill in the basement. It had always been a problem in the great halls and monuments built by Russian royalty. At the end of the corridor he passed through another security station and descended in a small elevator far down into the earth. At the bottom another security unit checked his credentials before admitting him through a square steel door. Inside was another door, which he opened with a key that he kept around his neck at all times. For seven years he had followed this procedure twice a day, missing only once for a period of less than forty-eight hours when he had flown to Berlin. The room was painted with thick white enamel, like that in a surgery; the floors were of tightly fitted ivory tiles. But despite the sterility and cleanliness of its surfaces, the odor from the room always brought Petrov to the brink of nausea.

In the middle of the room, suspended from the ceiling, was a cage of stainless steel bars, and in it, a living thing that looked vaguely human squatted. There was not enough room for it either to stand or to lie down. Stalin had designed the cage and personally overseen its construction by captured German engineers. Over the years it had become increasingly difficult to keep the beast alive. Sores had formed on its legs and induced gangrene, causing an amputation first of the left leg above the knee, and later of the right leg just above the ankle. Dr. Gnedin had performed the operations, with Petrov assisting. Technically the beast lived, but it was no longer a man. To be sure, there was a body in the cage and its heart beat, but its mind and soul had long ago evaporated and it had not spoken in five years.

When they arrived from Odessa, they had been met by a special panel truck, and the prisoner had been taken directly to the palace and to the room where Petrov now stood. The monster had been stripped of his clothes and locked into the cage, and Petrov had watched alone as the man struggled violently, screaming first for vengeance, later for mercy.

Thereafter the beast was fed only enough to sustain life. It lived in the wastes of its own body and was not allowed to wash. The structure in which it was suspended prevented normal sleep and rest, and so it began a cycle of short naps, always interrupted by pain from its body's extremities.

It was amazing to him that a living creature could deteriorate so far and still be alive. Watching the creature now it seemed that it had happened fast, the increments of change suddenly collected in a single moment. But it was not true; the present always deceived. The process had been slow and agonizing and Stalin had relished every moment.

Normally Stalin came on Sundays, usually in the early afternoon, and he never skipped a Sunday unless he was away from Moscow. But there were other visits too, and each time the premier wished to visit, Petrov was fetched from wherever he was to escort his leader. Sometimes during these unscheduled visits Stalin would be seething, the blue veins in his temples sticking out. Other times he would be brooding, and while to Petrov the mood resembled sadness, he knew that Stalin was incapable of this emotion. On rare occasions Stalin would be joyous and ebullient, and as the years passed Petrov came to understand that the beast was a secret reality from which the premier drew his resolve, as if its existence was living proof that whatever he wanted done could and would be done.

Stalin's routine never varied, even when the visits were unscheduled. Petrov would walk two steps ahead. When they entered the room the eyes of the two adversaries immediately locked. In the early years the eyes of the beast in the cage flashed hatred; it screamed, howled and threw itself against the bars until the room flooded with sound and Petrov's ears ached for hours afterward. But no matter what the beast said or did, Stalin never reacted. He stood with his hands clasped in front of him and watched. After no more than a few minutes, he would smile, nod slowly once, walk out of the room, board the elevator and return to his world outside. As the years passed, the beast's out-bursts faded to incoherence, then to the whine of an injured animal: finally it lapsed into silence and its eyes went blank.

Now the legless beast in the cage shifted its weight on its stumps as Petrov approached. The man dressed in black always meant food, and it had learned over the years to behave itself in Petrov's presence lest the food be withheld. Time no longer had meaning. In the white room it was always bright. The beast slept with its arm curled over its eyes, jamming itself against the bars in peculiar positions in an effort to find the darkness that would bring sleep. Its eyes were swollen red and protruded from the skull. Its hair was caked and matted and stuck out from its head and face at odd angles. It hissed as Petrov drew nearer, anticipating, yet dully apprehensive and wary. This was not the normal feeding time; yet the man was here. Danger. Different. The beast pulled back its arm and held it across its face like a narrow shield.

Petrov pulled his revolver from his holster and put it on the floor just out of reach of the cage. He spoke softly to the beast, in the same tone of voice that he used to speak to his geese. "I am instructed to inform you that Iosif Vissarionovich Dzhugashvili is dying." The beast scratched at its crotch violently, suddenly tortured by the burrowing of the vermin that lived on its flesh. It cocked its head to the side and studied Petrov, blinking slowly. For a moment the eyes flashed brightly, and the Russian saw recognition in the dark pools. "Stalin," it said slowly, trying to remember. It was the first word it had said in five years.

Suddenly the beast voided itself, spraying the cage with feces. It looked at Petrov and a ghastly smile began to form on its face. Its lips were dry, cracked and covered with sores. The mouth opened to reveal blackened stumps of broken teeth, and it gripped the bars tightly, pulling itself toward Petrov, pressing its face to the bars. It opened its mouth wide like an attacking predator, turned its head to the left, raised its eyebrow and hissed with an intensity that sent a chill down

Petrov's spine. "I . . . still . . . live," it said hoarsely, its eyes gleaming.

Suddenly it thrust its arms through the bars at Petrov, and from deep inside it came a ringing scream of defiance. Petrov felt the hairs on the nape of his neck stand straight up, but he stepped forward, reached into the cage and caught the beast by the throat with both hands. Its eyes widened at the strength in Petrov's grip and it tried to pull away. Its head began to roll slowly from side to side. "I still live," it croaked again, pounding its chest, pushing feebly at Petrov's arms, trying to loosen the crushing grip, saliva spilling in long strands from its mouth.

Petrov concentrated on touching the fingertips of his two hands together at the back of the beast's neck. As the moment drew closer, all strength left it and it slumped against the cage bars, beginning to convulse in the throes of death. But even then, it kept repeating, softer and softer, "I live, I live, I live." Finally Petrov's fingers touched and he twisted his hands upward so that the beast's spine cracked loudly. The beast was dead.

The guards were nervous when Petrov rejoined them. Over the years they had become familiar with the strange, limping little man who came twice a day. Only Petrov, Gnedin and Stalin had ever been inside the room. Over the years the guards had learned not to think about what might be kept inside. Their entry was forbidden, and though some of them were consumed by curiosity, it was a subject they never discussed even with each other, and none would have dared to go inside even if he could. When one lived in the heart of the Supreme Soviet, one learned to be deaf, dumb and blind.

When Petrov told them to leave their posts, they hesitated, but seeing a look in his eyes that frightened them, they cleared out; he was the one with the Red Badge. When they were gone, Petrov went to a small storage room and fetched supplies that had been cached long ago. Working alone, he constructed a wall threebricks deep over the steel doors and then ascended in the elevator. When he reached the ground floor, he directed the security detachment to move to the other end of the building. Then, with another key, which he had also carried for seven years, he opened a small wall safe and pulled the lever inside, detonating a charge that brought down the elevator and its shaft, closing the hole for eternity.

▶146 MARCH 5, 1953, 9:50 P.M.

Petrov had driven to Kuntsevo and was taken directly through a phalanx of security men to Stalin's bedroom. The premier looked small and insignificant in his canopied bed. Candles flickered on nearby tables, and a huge Chinese tapestry of a dragon hung over the headboard, the light making it seem alive. "Comatose," someone said as Petrov entered; when he showed them his Red Badge, they cleared the room. Standing at the end of the bed, he waited. On the floor there was a sheet of paper covered with simple drawings of a wolf's head in red ink.

Stalin stirred and his head lifted slightly. His eyes flickered and opened. "My Berkut," he said, his voice clear but weak. "I'm dying."

Petrov nodded, picked up the paper and a pen, drew an X through one of the heads, and held it up. "It's done."

Stalin's eyes widened; his nostrils flared and a wide smile swept across his face. "When?"

"A few hours ago."

The Russian leader eased his head back to his pillow and exhaled, his face freezing into a mask, the mouth wide open. Petrov touched the premier's throat to check for a pulse; there was nothing. He checked his watch: it was 9:50 P.M. and Joseph Stalin was dead. He set his Red Badge on the end of the bed, put on his hat, took a last look and left. Finally it had ended.

AUTHOR'S NOTE

The Berkut is fiction, a creature of imagination spawned in the cracks
and uncertainties of history. We know a lot about the final days of
Hitler and his Third Reich, but despite everything at our disposal, we
do not know what happened to Hitler at the end. We suspect, we
theorize, we speculate, but we don't *know*.

My intent was to take what is known and weave these facts in an
alternative pattern, another possibility. It's speculative, to be sure, but
much of what is here is real.

Many of Hitler's senior advisers were with him in the Führerbunker
under the Reich Chancellery at the end, and after Hitler's suicide these
people attempted a mass escape through the Russian lines. Many of
them were captured by the Russians and imprisoned for ten years, but
others escaped successfully and only a small number were killed in
the attempt. The sequence of events immediately before and after
Hitler's suicide presented here is faithful to official reports and primary
sources, and where differences of opinion exist, I have used those facts
on which there seems to be some agreement.

The Russians alternately reported having Hitler, or his body, and
having no idea where he was. This is *fact*. It is also fact that in the
summer of 1946 the Russians flew all of the major players in the
bunker drama back to Berlin, where a film was made in the bunker
using the Nazis themselves rather than actors to act out the final drama.
Why? This has never been explained, and the film, to my knowledge,
has never been seen by anyone from the West, though two American
journalists saw the filming in progress one night. Why such a reen-
actment if the Russians had found Hitler's body a year before? And
why no autopsy report until twenty-three years later? The Russians
finally published an official autopsy report in 1968, but its intent seems
more political than scientific, and there are some serious flaws in the
scientific methods employed during the autopsies.

The role of the Catholic Church in aiding German refugees after the war is well documented, and there have been numerous works published on the failings of the Church and Pope Pius XII during the war.

Otto Skorzeny was real, of course, and after the war he was suspected by the Allies of having helped Hitler to escape, though he denied it.

The Office of Special Services (OSS) did commission a psychological profile of Hitler that predicted possible outcomes for the German leader; while suicide was selected as the probable outcome, there were many others as well.

There is also the matter of an odd battle staged by the Germans in the area of the Harz Mountains after the Allies crossed the Rhine; this battle, both then and in retrospect, makes no strategic sense.

There is much more, but what we know, it seems to me, is not nearly as important or interesting as what we don't know.

Stalin wanted Hitler; he felt that the German leader had betrayed him, and the cost to the Russians was an estimated twenty million dead, about twice the number of people who died in Nazi death camps. It is ironic that Stalin, America's amiable ally Uncle Joe, probably surpassed Hitler's body counts in what the crude Georgian called "wet business."

Did Hitler die in Berlin's ruins in 1945? History suggests that perhaps only one man on earth knew the truth about Hitler's fate, and he died in 1953. His name was Stalin.

All things are possible, for better or for worse. Keeping the monster alive so that we might have the accounting we were denied in 1945 has social value for all of us—even in fiction.

J.H.